A Prisoner's Welcome

A Prisoner's Welcome

Book One
of
The Abyss Walker Series

Shane Moore

VANTAGE PRESS
New York

This is a work of fiction. Any similarity between the names and
characters in this book and any real persons, living or dead, is
purely coincidental.

Published by Vantage Press, Inc.
419 Park Ave. South, New York, NY 10016

Manufactured in the United States of America
ISBN: 0-533-15301-8

Library of Congress Catalog Card No.: 2005906888

0 9 8 7 6 5 4 3 2 1

For Christopher Wayne Nix, may he find all he seeks no matter how elusive it becomes

Fools! The beginning and end shall be with the suspicion of an innocent child. Her actions alone will set the great wheel in motion that will bring about an eminent change in the existence of reality. This change will echo off of the halls of Merioulus and cascade down into the depths of the abyss!

—Warning from the lips of the wicked
great red dragon, Renagargus,
just as he was set about his prison—

Introduction

In the beginning, there were only the gods. In their wisdom they created all forms of man. Man rose to oppose, worship, love, and curse them. Since the beginning of their creation, men did in kind to themselves that in which they did to the gods. Some men were born to be kings, some rose to be leaders, and a few were thrust upon the throne, but most merely tried to live their simple lives in peace. This is a story of such a man. He would strive to achieve all the things he could, and some he could not. He is no hero, nor is he a villain, though he crossed many of each in his lifetime. This story is of a man that was seemingly cursed by the gods that created him and men that he walked among. This is the story of Ecnal.

And so it begins . . .

A Prisoner's Welcome

Prologue

Azure clouds floated slowly on the heavens of a perpetual twilight. Magnificent birds of all species soared with angelic grace high above a floating city. The conurbation rested on the wisp of a fog that progressively lumbered among the great cumuli. The myriad of breathtaking colors danced in an atmosphere that, in itself, is more spectacular than can be imagined. Shades of light from every spectrum glimmered on the heavenly rivers and sparkled from the jewel-encrusted buildings of this fantastic city.

High above the planes of the clouds, far beyond the imagination of mortal men, dwelled Merioulus, the inconceivably beautiful city of the gods. It was a magnificent metropolis, constructed of sparkling marble buildings of the purest sallow, that would tower over the largest man-made structures. Fertile green gardens, riddled with amazing flowers and plant life, littered the incredible city, as did wonderfully crafted fountains and statues depicting gods and goddesses in their glory. Water of the purest blue trickled from these statues and filled great shimmering pools that were constructed under them. The largest and grandest of these buildings was home to the most powerful of gods, known as Dicermadon.

Dicermadon, the god of gods, sat in his mighty golden throne of jewels. The jewels were so finely cut that light danced from their facets like a shimmering rainbow cowl that enveloped the god king. His mighty bronze hand, bearing rings of every known metal, held up his weary head as he frowned deeply. His creased face looked down upon the world and gazed at beautiful Panoleen. She had once been the goddess of mercy. She had once been his love, if ever a god king could have one. In anger he slapped away a golden chalice that held his wine. The cup clanged as it bounced and skipped across the marbled floor, spilling all of its contents before it came to rest near the beautiful sandaled feet of Leska. She stood in a pale green dress that shined like an infinite sea of glimmering lights,

1

flickering with each tiny ripple on an amazing surface. Her russet hair was long and straight with flowers that seemed to sprout up around her as she passed by. The angelic goddess picked up the chalice with her delicate fingers as she casually walked to the jeweled throne. She slowly and deliberately placed the goblet just within the god king's reach. The chalice slowly began to fill itself, and within a few seconds, it was completely full. Leska turned and faced Dicermadon, tilting her head with an alluring gaze. Her sparkling olive eyes gazed up with admiration and respect.

"What troubles you, my great lord of lords?" Leska asked in a comforting tone, as her soft hand rubbed the knee of the god king. "Surely you are not troubled by Panoleen's new love?" Leska asked, though in truth, she was jealous of the fallen goddess, Panoleen. Though she now held the god king's favor, his heart would always belong to the banished harlot. By the scowl on his face, Leska knew that he was indeed troubled by Panoleen's love, and in truth, so was she. Panoleen had been the goddess of mercy before the council banished her from the heavens for frequenting with a mortal man. The gods had tried and sentenced her to live a mortal's life on the realms. Now, Panoleen was a mortal and dwelled among them—a fitting punishment, the council had thought. She would age as they did, and die, thus ending any threat to the pantheon she may have become. And since Panoleen was one of the Breedikai, or original gods, she had no soul. Once she died, she would cease to exist. What troubled Dicermadon, as well as Leska and all the other gods, is that she had met a lover and was soon to be wed. Her lover had no way to fathom the depths of power that dwelled within his bride to be. He was a simple warrior of the church that worshipped Dicermadon himself. Beyond the insult of choosing one of the god king's followers, the entire pantheon of gods feared what would happen if the pair conceived a child. For despite all the power of the gods in Merioulus, not one could prophesize about the birth of her loins.

"She must be stopped!" bellowed Dicermadon, smashing his chalice flat with his ring-encrusted fist. Wine shot out in all directions splashing himself and Leska.

She calmly wiped the wine away, and placed her soft comforting hand on his massive arm. "We cannot, my mighty lord. It wouldn't be right. We do not interfere with . . ."

Dicermadon cut her off with his booming voice as he jerked his powerful arm from her grasp. "Do not begin to tell me what I can and can't do, Leska! Let me remind you of your station! I am Dicermadon! Lord of lords! King of kings! God of gods!" he growled as his powerful visage glared at her while the arms of his throne cracked and splintered under his prodigious grasp.

Leska was knocked to the floor by the sheer power of the god king's voice. Every tapestry, painting, and decoration rattled and shook as his words echoed down the halls of Merioulus. All the gods stopped what they were doing and looked toward the god king's chamber, for they knew he was angry. Leska trembled from the presence of her king and the power of his voice. She raised her head, placing her hair over her ear with her delicate finger. "But, my lord, it is by your own decree that none of us that call ourselves good may intervene in the happenings of the mortal realm."

Dicermadon's expression softened and he smiled at Leska's bravery. "You are correct, my loyal servant. You often remind me of why you are the Earth Mother. Your wisdom of the realms is unchallenged by all. But I am Dicermadon, and my acumen is unmatched by even you. You are correct. I dare not interfere with the earth, but the evil gods hold no such decree. They would be pleased to learn of the identity of our fallen goddess, many enemies she has. It would seem the wench has lost her right to be shielded from their scrying eyes."

The other gods in the chamber mumbled amongst themselves at such a notion. The room was quiet for a moment, before another god burst into the chamber. The air cackled at the intense heat wafting from his being. He wore a robe of molten lava that dripped and singed the floor as he walked, and large flickers of fire danced around his eyes and his hands, while his hair was aflame like the bowels of hell. Ripples of heat distorted the air around him and Leska could feel the searing flame of his power as the god neared. He bowed deeply in a genuine show of respect and admiration before the god king. "My great king of gods, in Panoleen's behalf, I urge you to reconsider. I remember a time not so long ago, that your greatness held her in high favor. Certainly the approval of our lord of lords is not so fickle," the god said, rising after speaking. His molten cape seemed to flow in an ethereal breeze while his defiant eyes of flame raised and stared into the deep blue eyes of Dicermadon.

3

"Great Flunt, . . ." Dicermadon began as he sat back in his throne and crossed his mighty bronze arms over his thick chest. "You are the last one I would have thought to speak in the behalf of our fallen harlot."

Many other gods had gathered at the entrance to Dicermadon's great chamber to witness the spectacle. They all gasped aloud as the god king proclaimed Panoleen as a harlot, and many began to whisper and talk softly amongst themselves.

Dicermadon waited for the whispers to silence and he began again. "I do not need the council's approval of this matter. Panoleen is no longer one of us. The goddess of mercy no longer exists! All that remains is a filthy wench that wishes to wed another mere mortal. Such a union cannot exist between a Breedikai and man, and that fact alone is why the shield *will* be lifted."

Silence fell among the crowd; some shook their heads in disbelief. Dicermadon began again. "I am Dicermadon, god of gods! I care nothing for two pitiful mortals, nor the happenings under their sun. Now leave me, all of you! I have no desire to discuss the matter further."

All the gods left the chamber, including the fiery-eyed Flunt, and the satisfied, smiling Leska.

One

The Journey

The cold rain fell from a dark sky and pounded hard against the sides of the small wooden house. Large spouts of rainwater poured off the roof and drained into huge puddles around the base of the small building. The sizeable globules pounded like a thousand tiny drums of war driving an army into battle. Inside the home, the smell of smoke and ash filled the small room from the roaring fireplace. Crackling and popping, the fire matched the tune of the dreary evening. Davohn Ecnal sat in his old oaken chair and stared angrily at the fire. It had been many evenings that he sat and waited for his son. Davohn was a simple man from the southern reaches of Beykla that had been orphaned at a young age. He had been taken in by a fur trader, learning the ways of trading hides and cutting wood. Though woodcutting kept him on the cusps of poverty, it was honest work and he enjoyed it. He had married his childhood friend Sonya and had a son, Elijah, who helped around his small farm. About eleven years ago both became inexplicably ill and died. Davohn was crushed and withdrew from his friends and family, spending most of his time working or trying to stay busy. He later moved north from the small town of Portia, and settled in Bureland. There he had found and adopted an orphaned boy, named Lancalion. Davohn called him Lance for short.

Davohn smiled as he recalled the many fond memories that he had of himself and Lance over the last few years. Though they had good times, he and Lance disagreed on more than a few beliefs. Davohn despised the use of magic, save for the divine powers of the priests or clerics. He felt magic was a tool only to be wielded by the godly, not by mere men, while Lance seemed to be more open-minded about such topics. It was a sign of the times, Davohn thought. The woodcutter had always known there was something unique about Lance from the day he found him wandering in the woods. Strange happenings always seemed to follow the boy. Davohn just figured that the gods pitied and looked after the lad.

A flash of lightning followed by a thunderclap roused the old woodcutter from his doldrums. He focused on the front door to catch even the slightest glimpse of movement. His old eyes narrowed as they studied the door's every contour. Smiling warmly at the small nicks in the soft wooden door, he drifted back into the past. He fondly recalled the time he caught Lance tossing daggers into the wood and how he scolded the boy of barely seven years for making the nicks in the door. Lance had argued that he needed to throw the daggers at the door, because he didn't want to hurt the trees. Davohn tried repeatedly to explain to Lance that trees didn't have feelings. Lance argued that if a seed felt the sun, and it was able to grow upwards instead of downwards, then it was evident that trees had feelings. His poor son always had an innocent love for all things. That is why his parents' murder must have affected him in the way it had. Davohn had surmised through talk from the few traveling merchants that Lance was born from a wealthy and politically powerful family far south of Beykla. The family, for whatever reason, had been mercilessly slaughtered. Though some tales said it was militia, and others said it was by orcs, the fact they were cut down didn't seem to ever be refuted. So Davohn never disclosed where he found Lance. He would hint the boy rode in on a merchant wagon from the south, but no one ever really questioned him about it. An orphan boy was not uncommon. It was a few years later that all the orphans, or Ecnals—the surname for all orphans, were being killed throughout the kingdom. Davohn always feared those killers would come after him and Lance, but they lived unnoticed in their small town. Eventually the murders subsided and the woodcutter forgot about them. But Davohn noticed as Lance aged, the boy secluded himself from people and from the world. He spent countless hours in the city with who knows who, doing who knows what. Those city men weren't men of honor, much less men of goodness. They spent much more time drinking and partaking in escapades with women than they did helping the community.

A large knot of anger slowly rose in Davohn's throat. That boy had lived with him since he was six, when they happened to cross on the trail. Just because his parents had been those of a high station in some city or country, south of where Davohn became a woodcutter, did not mean he could fraternize with such ruffians. Soon Davohn's anger subsided and he drifted back to his adopted son's childhood. As Lance aged, he seldom, if ever, helped with the work and chores around the farm, let along took the wood into the city. Lance always said that woodcutting was work of a simpleton, and that he wouldn't subject himself to such peasant tasks. Davohn's heart pounded as he relived the ungrateful words of the boy. How dare he speak about honest work as if he was above it! It was at that moment he mustered his resolve. That boy was going to learn some lessons tonight. Whether he was a season away from reaching his manhood mattered little. It wasn't age that made a man. It was how he carried himself in the world.

*   *   *

Lance pulled his thin sable cloak tighter around his face to keep out the driving rain. The long black robe that had many silver runes along the cuffs and collar clung to his cold skin. Relentless drops of rain poured over his body and managed to creep into small crevices of his cloak, soaking the precious robe. He shuddered as an ice-cold drop of rain ran down the small of his back. Lance regretted having to wear the robe in the rain, but he needed to look noble, and being a woodcutter's son, he owned nothing else that even remotely resembled nobility. He carefully checked his leather pack that hung down from his waist to ensure the rain was only penetrating his cloak. He couldn't afford for his books to get wet. Lance wasn't exactly sure of all the magic in the four books in his pack. He knew they were called the Necromidus and that many believed them to be evil. The young man couldn't understand why someone would think magic was evil. An evil man might use it, but that did not make it inherently evil. No one ever claimed the knife that a murderer used as evil, only the man that wielded it. So Lance surmised that if he wielded that magic in the four books, that wouldn't make him evil either. Lance had found the books on a dead looted body in the woods miles from his home a few years past. He kept it hidden until he learned to read well enough to understand its contents. Lance knew Davohn didn't know of his studies or the degree of his talents. He didn't dare take the chance drying out his pages at home because Davohn might find them. Lance was well aware of how his adoptive father viewed magic, especially any magic from the Necromidus.

"It is the way of a lazy man to find strange energies to do honest work," Davohn had told Lance. The words had offended the boy profoundly. His mother had given him a sleek black robe as a gift. She said it would save him one day when he was in a time of need. Somehow using it in the middle of the driving rain in Bureland wasn't his idea of what she meant. Since he had always had an unexplained talent in magic, and his mother was quite an accomplished wielder of the arcane arts, Lance inferred he would one day do the same. The young mage drifted back from the rain storm and remembered how his mother would give him a "sparkly kiss," as she called it, whenever she put him to bed. He smiled fondly recalling how she would blow him a kiss, and the small gold glittering powder would dance across the room until it hit him on the cheek, bringing the feel of her warm lips to his tender face. She would then turn and close the door, leaving him in a beautiful dark bliss. Lance's memory unconsciously shifted to a darker time. He recalled the day the men in polished bronze-colored armor and bright red silk capes barged into his home and spoke to his mother. He was afraid of the armored men and cowered in the corner in the other room. He heard his mother scream, then cry, as she thudded limp to the floor. Lance heard a man speaking softly trying to console her, and then he heard more men thunder into the house, their armored boots softening as they walked on the large red silk rug that depicted a sword through a bright yellow crown. His father had been given the carpet by a duke for his meritorious service in some trial. There were angry words and then enraged spell casting. The smell of burnt energies and scorched flesh overpowered the house just before the deadly silence.

Soon after, Lance heard another voice—an angry voice. The voice commanded soldiers to search every inch of the house until something was found. He heard the nice man that helped his mother arguing with the loud angry man. Lance clutched the small backpack that contained his robe and a few books from the library and gracefully moved his finger in a waving motion and chanted a few simple words. When he finished, hundreds of thin, bright red weaves of magical energy shimmered around him. When Lance finished with the small shining net, he faded from view into the corner of the dark room. He had never tested his magic on people before, only vicious animals in the forest. He hoped against hope that it would work against the scary men. After a short time, the scary men and his father left the house. He heard banging against the doors and windows of his home, and the muffled voices of the soldiers laughing and joking outside. He dismissed his spell and made his way through the house. There was a burnt smell hanging in the air and he could hear the crackle and pop of a fire that seemed to roar louder and louder outside. Lance rushed into the living room where he found his mother dead on the floor. Her face was badly burned from what appeared to be magical fire. There were several pages of strange writing scattered around her crumpled form. Lance never bothered to see what those papers were before he snuck out the narrow passage in the basement, which his mother had told him about in the event that a day like this would come. Lance made his way through the tunnel and into the forest. He glanced back only once, and he cried himself to sleep for the next few weeks from the images of his father hanging dead from his rope swing in the front yard, and of the raging inferno he once called home.

Lance wandered through the forest as he traveled to the north, and managed to find refuge in an orphan house. There he was given the orphan surname of Ecnal, though he seldom felt at home and often ran away, moving from house to house, maybe to six in all, until he ended up with Davohn. Davohn also had been an orphan child and currently was a woodcutter. Lance remembered how he was forced to work outside, hauling manure and doing other despicable jobs. Yet, for some reason, he took a liking to the gruff simple man. Lance soon grew to appreciate Davohn for all he gave him, but he didn't like the disgusting way the woodcutter chose to live his life. Lance laughed as he recalled how he would use some of his magic, unbeknownst to Davohn, to tease him. He once caused Davohn's axe to be repelled from his grasp as he chopped wood. As Davohn would raise the axe over his head, Lance would cast one of his many self-made dweamors. This one in particular caused whatever item Lance chose to be repelled from a certain target. So when Davohn raised the axe, it would fly from his grasp, sometimes thirty feet.

The weaves were simple to Lance, sometimes consisting of a few scores of magical strands.

Davohn would look surprised, and study his hands, as if the answer were sweaty palms. Unsure of why the axe flew from his hands, but noticing Lance's amusement, Davohn would repeat the axe tossing as if it were a game he intended to play just to make the orphan smile.

When Lance was eleven, Davohn took him to Bureland, a tiny hamlet north of their farm. The woodcutter was delivering some wood to the Inn of Aldon. There was a common room there where many men gathered to eat, drink, and rent rooms. While they were inside, a drunken man tried to incite a fight with Davohn. Lance noticed that his adoptive father wasn't sticking up for himself, and the man was saying awful things.

Lance focused on the man's skull, sending out a fine, tightly woven net of magical strands that enveloped the drunken ruffian's head, and soon thereafter, nothing but belches were coming from his mouth. The more the man tried to speak, the more he became embarrassed, and soon everyone was laughing heartily while the man ran from the bar. Davohn, like a few other patrons, was afraid of what happened. For a long time many thought the woodcutter to be some kind of wicked warlock.

Lance was awakened from his daydream by a soft, raspy voice. The cold windy rain and the black of night were soon around him again.

"Here ya go man; these were not easy to come by. There isn't much here. I hope they're enough," a man said with a twitching upper lip.

Lance eyed the dark man. He was probably thirty years old and was missing one of his front teeth, and it seemed he had not shaved in a few days. He had small scars across his nose and next to his eye, which both continued to twitch uneasily as Lance viewed the leather pouch in the pouring rain.

"About my money . . ."

Lance looked up and held his hands palm up, gesturing to the rain. "Well I can't very well pull them out and look here in this rain now can I?"

The scarred man shifted uneasily as rain dripped from the hood of his thick dark cloak, and his one tooth jutted out from his nervous twitching lips as he spoke. "I'm not going anywhere without my money or these papers."

Lance held the brown leather case in his hand. He sent hundreds of tiny white strands of energy around the leather case and then into it. He felt the magic pour from his fingers and stretch deep into the case, changing the papers from detailed reports to ink portraits of himself. Lance held the leather case without speaking until he felt the invisible energy leave from his hand. The man grabbed the leather case, oblivious to the spell Lance had cast, and pulled lightly.

"Look, just open it a little. I'll shield it with my cloak. If they look like the ones you want, you give me my money!" the man said quickly as he looked around them nervously. He was growing uneasy and impatient.

"Forget it," Lance replied. "You have stolen nothing to help me. Take this gold for your silence, these worthless papers, and be gone," Lance said angrily as he turned and began to walk away.

The man took a few steps after Lance walked down the wet muddy road. "You are going to pay me for nothing?" he asked hesitantly as he dangled the fat leather coin purse in the air.

Lance turned and looked at him. "I didn't specify what exact papers I wanted. It isn't your fault you have no talent for recognizing anything of value."

The man began to argue about the insult, but the gold in his hand held his tongue fast. "What do you want me to do with these?" he asked as he waved the brown leather pouch in the pouring rain, his wet arm glistening in the light from one of the many covered lanterns that lighted the muddy streets of Bureland.

Lance shrugged as he walked further down the dark road, and shouted, "I wouldn't get caught disposing of them around here."

The man watched Lance walk down the muddy street into the darkness before he hurried away into the night. Lance ducked behind a building and watched the thief run down the muddy street toward the Inn of Aldon. Sludge splashed up on his breeches as his feet landed in the many puddles formed from the cold autumn shower. As the thief ran, he held his cloak tight around him as if it were possible for him to get any wetter. Lance watched the thief look around nervously in all directions as he neared the two-story

11

inn. Smiling with the gold and the leather case in hand, the thief went inside. The inn wasn't the largest establishment, but was the most prevalent in about two day's ride. Many adventurers, merchants, and other traveling people stayed there. It had a reputation for being adequate for the well-to-do, but the common room was rough enough to attract a few unsavory characters. Gambling was expected there, and if you were lucky a few serving wenches might give you more than a smile.

Lance plopped in the mud next to the tree where he had spoken to the thief, spreading a small amount of the wet earth on the bottom of his cloak and a small amount on his robe. Lance stood and surveyed himself, making sure even the tiniest amount of muck was in place. When he was satisfied, Lance strolled toward the inn.

Two men stalked forward in the wet stormy night. They made no attempts to get out of the rain, or to keep the cold autumn shower from soaking through them.

The pair eyed the streets and alleys suspiciously as if they were going to jump up and attack them. The men wore russet leather armor with small, rounded off metal studs that protruded on their chests and backs. The rain beaded up and ran off their well-oiled leather. Lance guessed they took great pride and care in their equipment. Their swords hung loosely but confidently at their sides. Lance had grown up in this small town, and immediately recognized the two as city militia. The city militia were as feared as they were respected in Bureland. They often fought brigands and stray orcs that happened near or into the city limits. They were certainly not ones to cross swords with if you were a commoner.

Lance ran to the men, pretending to hold his robe and his cloak to avert them from becoming any more wet or muddy in the downpour. He approached slowly, as if distraught, and spoke to the larger of the two men. The huge man hadn't shaved in a few days and wore a snug-fitting leather cap that hugged his head tightly. The coif, or leather cap, was worn by all city militia across Beykla, not just in Bureland.

The coif moved and bulged as the large militiaman's jaw muscles flexed while he spoke. "What brings you out here in this nasty weather, noble sir?" the militiaman asked as he eyed Lance suspiciously.

Lance tried to appear scared and shaken as if he just endured a

12

terrible ordeal. "I was accosted by a vile ruffian, good sir! What else would bring a man of my stature out in this driving rain!" Lance said wiping away drops of water from his face and flinging them at the ground as if he was disgusted.

The militiamen's faces were cold and unyielding, and Lance was having a hard time gauging if they believed the charade. "And what did this . . . vile ruffian look like?" the larger man chided, his voice riddled with doubt.

Lance continued with his story undaunted. "He was a disgusting creature with a scar from his nose to his eye. He had one tooth, and oh, his breath! It was more revolting than his ragged appearance," Lance said as he pointed to the inn. "He ran in there, the vermin! He took a pouch from me, a leather pouch. It had portraits that I paid an artist to render of myself. He also took my coin purse of one gold and twenty-six silver."

The large guard whistled between his teeth as rain dripped from his chin, and he leaned forward to look Lance in the eye. "That is a lot of silver to be carrying around."

As Lance looked into the eyes of the big man, he grew angry and more impatient. This guard was simply trying to be difficult. Lance started again and spoke with spite and authority. "I am aware of that, sir. I should have had more gold and less silver as to keep my purse from bulging, this is irrelevant. I demand that you do your civic duty, go into that inn, and retrieve my belongings!" Lance demanded with fear and hope behind his guise of nobility.

Lance hoped the anger ruse would make the man think he was truly a noble. Lance didn't have any social standing, but he had studied how the nobles that occasionally visited Bureland had acted, and the young mage hoped he was arrogant and whiny enough to fool this militia guard.

The guard frowned and raised his voice as to match Lance's. "And how are we to know the gold is yours, sir? Are you going to say you will recognize it?" the man said with an increasing sarcastic tone while rain and spit sprayed from his mouth. "Wait, I know. Your gold is yellow and will look like a small round sun!"

Lance thought the ruse must be failing. He must at least salvage the package. Lance had waited too long to find out this information to be thwarted by a simple militia guard's inferiority complex. So Lance began again. "I'm sorry, sir. This whole ordeal

13

has been very traumatizing for me. I understand if you can't return my money, but please get my portraits! They are worth more than any amount of gold," Lance said submissively, trying to appeal to the militiaman's need for superiority.

"Well it serves you . . ."

The smaller guard cut him off. "We will return your money and your leather case. Please excuse Harold's rudeness, this is his first night on the job," the shorter guard said, raising a single eyebrow as he looked at the bigger man. ". . . And he isn't performing as well as I had hoped."

The larger militiaman frowned in embarrassment and contempt at his superior's chastising comments, but accepted the criticism for fear of further reprimand later.

Lance followed the two militia guards as they stormed toward the inn. Lance had to make large strides to keep up with the two militiamen. The large one had a scowl of determined anger across his face. Lance was glad he was following the big man, instead of the big man following him. By the size of him, Lance doubted that anyone would want to be against him.

The streets of Bureland were a wet soppy mess. The cold autumn rain had eased for the moment, yet water still poured from the guttering and trickled down into the swollen ditches. Though the rain poured off of the two-story inn, the majority of the buildings of Bureland were mostly one story, their angled roofs were made of either wood or clay, and layered as they pitched downward to prevent the heavy Beyklan rains from seeping in. The buildings themselves were primarily wood; though occasionally there were some of stone. The structures that were two stories were most likely those of businesses or some other importance. The Inn of Aldon was two stories and made of stone.

As they neared, Lance fidgeted his hand in his pocket nervously. If this scheme didn't work, not only would he have lost those papers, and his coins, but he could find himself in prison for hiring the rogue. However, Lance hoped the rogue would be as interested in staying out of prison as he was.

As the trio walked into the common room of the inn, the smell of ale, smoke, and body odor wafted into them as if the stench itself was repulsed and trying to escape. The common room was large, holding about ten or twelve tables that were mainly used for gambling and eating. The bar was at the south side of the room near the door they came in. There were many dull rusted lanterns hanging from the low rafters in the ceiling which illuminated the room quite well. Serving wenches hustled about the room, filling and refilling drinks, ensuring each patron had as much ale as their coin purses would allow. Across the room, Lance could see the rogue he hired, playing cards with some other rough looking men. There were eight other men seated at the thick wooden table, yet the oaken slab looked as if a few more could sit comfortably. The men ranged from large and tall, to short and fat, but all carried weapons of some kind and looked as if they could arm a small garrison. A large wooden staircase on the north wall erupted from the busy room and went up into a long black hall.

Lance swallowed nervously and pulled his hands from his pockets. He hung his wet cloak on the brass hook next to the door and ran his cold wet hands through his coarse black hair. The warmth of the inn, despite its pungency, felt splendid compared to the cold autumn shower outside.

The innkeeper was an average-sized balding man with a pot-belly, who shouted angrily at the two militia soldiers. "What's the idea, you two? Hang your cloaks up. I don't pay my wenches so they can follow you around just to mop up the water you string about!" the innkeeper said as he advanced from behind the counter toward Lance and the two guards.

The smaller guard drew his sword, and the sound of steel being drawn halted the conversation of the entire room. Regardless of the activity that was being conducted before them, whether for business or pleasure, all men turned and looked at Lance and the two militiamen. When the thief's eyes met those of the city militia, he jumped up, knocking his chair over behind him as he ran between tables making his way across the east wall. Chairs and serving wenches were knocked over as he rushed toward the stairs. The larger militiaman dashed after him, cutting him off in an angle through the center of the room. The smaller guard slid his sword back into its scabbard as he hurried along the west wall.

The thief paused as he reached the north wall, drawing his short sword as he stood waiting while the big guard came toward him. With sweat beading up on his face, the thief had reached his resolve. Whether he'd escape or die, getting arrested was not an op-

15

tion. As the large guard approached, he drew his mammoth sword. The blade was twice as long as the thief's and was polished, reflecting the light from the room like a mirror.

The large militiaman's face tightened and his knuckles turned white as he approached the thief. A foot shot out from a chair next to the big man, causing him to trip and fall. The room erupted in laughter.

The thief darted for the stairs again with his sword in hand. The smaller guard turned to cut him off, avoiding a second foot that shot out as he ran past. He had closed the distance to the thief and now only a single table stood between him and the stairs. The thief didn't slow as he leaped from the floor onto the table with his sword held high. Flagons of ale and plates of food scattered across the table, spilling as the thief ran across it. Patrons that were amused before as the militiaman fell, now shouted angry curses and raised fists as their evening meal was spoiled by the fleet-footed outlaw.

Lance focused his mind on the power that seemed to swirl within him. He never really could describe the feeling of the power that dwelled inside of him. He often linked it with the feeling of one's hand when it is not in use. He knew it was there, just waiting for him to command. Lance called on the inner force and sent out scores of small snake-like wisps of energy that only he could see, creating a weave that seemed to fall on the thief's hand. As soon as the magical weave hit the thief's sword, it shot from his grasp, just as it was brought down in a killing thrust toward the guard. The militiaman waved his sword in a defensive motion to deflect a strike that didn't come.

The thief didn't miss a stride after losing his blade. He leaped from the table, over the small guard, and landed on the stairs. The outlaw took the stairs two at a time as he bounded up them effortlessly. The small guard hurried up the stairs after the thief, snatching the coin purse and leather case and tossing them at Lance's feet. All eyes of the common room turned and looked at Lance as he casually picked up his leather pouch and his coin purse. He reached over to the hook and removed his cloak before turning and walking out of the inn. Sounds from the common room resumed as Lance strolled into the night.

The wet muddy street smelled like fresh rain, washing away the usual smell of the local cattle that seemed to hang in the air.

Though the rain had stopped, and the stars were trying to peek between the breaks in the clouds, buildings and trees still dripped steady amounts of rainwater. Lance was wet and a little shook up, but no worse for wear. He had managed to get the leather pouch and his coins back, and none too soon he thought—the spell that turned the papers into portraits wouldn't have lasted much longer.

Remembering the dweamor he had cast on the leather case, Lance peered into it, making sure the papers were still there, then he checked his coin purse. The small leather bag seemed heavier than before and Lance grinned when he peered inside. It seemed his rogue friend not only had scored a few extra coins while playing cards, but must have added his own coins in as well. Smiling at his good fortune, Lance made his way east, to the end of town. He had managed to get these mysterious papers for free, managed to make the thief an outlaw, and prevented the thief from being linked to him in case the documents were noticed stolen. Lance would have preferred to have the thief arrested, but all in all he considered it a successful endeavor.

The young mage hurried to the edge of town. He didn't want the thief catching him if the rogue had managed to elude the guards. Lance had exhausted most of his energy and didn't have the focus to control anymore magical weaves, and another altercation could have proven deadly.

Lance glanced around the village as he ran past a group of small wooden houses. He studied each one carefully, trying to recognize the house of Jude, his only friend. Jude wasn't skilled in magic. In fact, Jude wasn't skilled in anything, save for cleaving a man in two with a sword or axe. Jude was nearly a foot taller than Lance, and twice as wide. Lance smiled as he recalled how he managed to save the big man from a group of smaller men that were angry at him for taking their money in a game of cards. By hurling a few spells to spook them, Lance defused the hostile encounter. Jude always claimed that Lance had in fact saved the group of men, and it wasn't until Lance saw him fight later that he believed it so.

He hurried past other small wooden houses that littered the edge of town in a disarray of streets and alleys, coming to the shack Jude lived in. It was quite small, the old wooden walls were eroded away, and a soft glow of candle light beamed from under the bottom of them. Soft drops of rain dripped down from the edges of his roof into Lance's dark hair. He ducked under the small roof in an attempt to keep the tiny drops of cold water from seeping between his cloak and his neck. Lance never understood why his friend lived in such indigent conditions. The large swordsman made more than enough money to afford a better home, or at least one with guttering and sturdy walls.

Lance rapped his delicate knuckles across the hard wet door. He looked at them, not so much as calluses, or scars, yet he knew they were deadly. The door swung open quickly as light and the smell of biscuits wafted from inside. Lance turned and met the silhouette of the large man mid-chest.

"Are you going to come in, my friend, or just stand staring wide-eyed at your pretty little hands as if you wish to bed them?" the looming figure asked with a deep and powerful voice.

Lance extended his diminutive hand. The big man took it firmly in a warm greeting.

"Perhaps I have already had my wicked way with my *pretty* hands," Lance said with a nefarious smile.

Jude recoiled with an angry glare as Lance piously wiped his huge hand on his trousers and shook his head. "Come in out of the rain before it washes the guile from you. It would be difficult for me to recognize you then."

Lance ignored Jude's remark and stepped into his friend's home. There were many leaks in the ceiling that dripped steadily into pans and buckets. There was an old crumbling fireplace on the far wall with barely burning embers. Frail rafters held up the leaky ceiling and a lantern sat on a small stump that was brought in to act as a table. A large wooden chair streaked with dark stains and splintered at its base sat next to the thick stump that was in the center of the room acting as a small table. Jude led Lance to the makeshift table near the fireplace and bid him to sit as he pulled a rickety chair out for himself. Lance sat down after carefully examining the chair to ensure he wouldn't soil or tear his cloak.

"So what, may I guess, is the reason for the visit of my humble castle?" Jude asked with a tentative smile, gesturing wide with his thick muscular arms.

Lance smiled in turn and pulled the leather case from inside of his cloak, tossing it on the table in front of Jude. Jude pulled the case close and examined it carefully before he opened its heavy decorated flaps. Lance was always careful with Jude. Though he appeared to be just a big man whose talents lay with his sword, Lance learned that Jude was able to read. That alone was a rare talent that would get him a much better job than digging trenches. That fact made Lance decide he was a valuable friend, and one not to underestimate.

Jude opened the case with his thick fingers and looked at the three sheets of strange writing. "When did you get this?" Jude asked without looking up.

Lance paused for a moment before he answered. "I have known you a long time, my friend. If I were to guess I would say that you not only know when I got it, but whether I have looked at it or not."

Jude smiled warmly, took a sip from his flagon, and swallowed slowly. He wiped his mouth with his sleeve before he responded. "Well . . . I'd say because the outside of the case is wet, and seemingly valuable to you, you got it tonight while you were outdoors. Since your hands are wet, and these pages are not, I would also guess you haven't looked at them either," Jude said as he studied Lance's face. "Have I passed your test, friend?" Jude asked.

Lance shifted uneasily. "What makes you think I am testing you?"

"You have been testing me for almost a year, I would say. Are we finished with these games or are you ever going to tell me what you have up your sleeve?" Jude asked, folding his massive arms under his thick-barreled chest.

"Why, my arms of course . . . and a small adventure," Lance said, smiling ruthlessly. His sinister grin even made Jude swallow hard.

"Lance, I know we are friends, but I have since learned that your so-called adventures usually involve trouble, a lot of trouble," Jude said trying to appear uninterested.

Lance pressed further. "So what you are saying, my gargantuan friend, is that you are afraid of a little adventure?"

"No, what I'm saying, Lance, is that whenever you are involved, there is no such thing as a 'little' adventure. A lot of trouble would be the correct term," Jude said, strengthening his resolve as he pushed away the leather case. "Lance, I have a lot going for me here. It may not seem like a lot to you, but it is all I have. Furthermore I . . ."

Lance interrupted in a soft, solemn voice. "I think the people who murdered my parents were looking for me instead."

Jude looked at Lance with an astonished gaze. "What do you mean? I thought your parents died in a sickness, and gave you up to protect you from getting the sickness they suffered from?"

This was what Lance had always wanted to believe, that his parents weren't slain at the hands of the magistrate; that they loved him so much they gave him up to protect him from a plague sweeping across the earth like a scourge. As Lance aged, the lie was easier to tell, as if the more he spoke it, the more it came to be true. Oh, how Lance wished it were true. He wished for anything but the truth, so that he didn't have to hear the screams of his mother, so that the guilt of hiding as she was slain was washed away, as the truth might be. Instead it always reared its ugly head, to snap at him. Lance sighed deeply, letting his shoulders slump, as he looked up with tired eyes. "Jude, my parents . . . my parents were murdered when I was six. My father hung from my swinging tree outside of my home and my mother was burned by the very magical fire that she so often commanded. The guards were looking for me, but I hid by using my own magic until they were gone. Then I ran as fast as I could."

Jude growled at the mention of Lance's foul magic. He knew his friend used it, though he did not know the extent of his ability. Jude hated magic. It was something mysterious and dangerous that was best left to the gods. He had heard stories of how the strongest of warriors were defeated by an old man in a robe because of magic. The old man had no armor, no sword, no way of defending himself save for that which was unseen. Men were burned to a crisp without any fire nearby, and others were turned to solid stone. Jude wanted to speak up, to tell his friend of how magic was trouble, but he felt the pain in Lance's voice and let him finish.

". . . The goddess of mercy must have been watching out for me that day, because I wandered through the woods, surviving on what little I could find. I bounced from orphanage to orphanage until one day I met a man in a wagon. He was a woodcutter and was taking some small trees he had felled into town. He said I could ride with him as long as I didn't fly away. I had always dreamed of cre-

20

ating a magical weave thick enough to allow someone to ride with the clouds. I learned later, much to my disappointment, that Davohn didn't have any idea about magic, so I kept my secret. I told him my parents were killed in a sickness and that I ran away to keep from my aunt Nancy. I told him she was awfully mean to small children, and that I wasn't even sure where she lived since I had traveled for many months. But after a while I believed he figured out that there was no sickness."

Jude studied Lance's face. He had rarely seen his friend so open and honest. Yet Lance was known for his flair at storytelling. Jude had seen him tell a man a bold-faced lie at a bar. Somehow the man believed it—not only believed it, Jude thought, but had gone to the grave believing it. It was Lance meddling with that damnable dark power. How he wished his friend didn't meddle with such things, but Jude realized that was who Lance was, and if he were to accept Lance as a friend, he would have to accept his magic also. But he didn't have to like it, he recounted to himself. "Lance, you know we are friends, but I thought you had a better grasp on religion . . ." Jude knew Lance had great knowledge about various religions and spirits. ". . . But there is no goddess of mercy . . . Is there?" Jude asked deep with uncertainty.

Lance smiled at his friend's query. He loved to talk, and to teach. "Well Jude, my mother taught me that some of the gods were forgotten by men, that they were cast from the heavens. She said the goddess of mercy was one of those gods."

Jude shook his head and sat back in his chair. He raised his large fingers to the bridge of his nose and grimaced. "So what do you wish of me, Lance?" His question seemed to linger in the air as he waited for Lance to respond.

"Well my friend, I need a swordsman. I was hoping you could be that for me. As I swing the blade of energies and knowledge, you swing the blade of steel. Of that blade, I know nothing," Lance said with an uneasy grin, hoping that a small admittance of inferiority would spur Jude into agreement.

"Lance, I have known you most of my life. You cannot afford my sword, and I cannot afford to go without income."

Lance glanced down and forced a forlorn look upon his face. "What is the minimum amount per week you would charge for your sword?" Lance asked as though he was asking the executioner if his blade was sharp.

"One gold a week," Jude replied as he swallowed. He hated to disappoint his friend, but he needed to keep him from going on some foolhardy journey. This was the best way, he thought. Jude reasoned that he would appear as if he wanted to go but was unable to. This in turn would keep Lance from going and saving the friendship at the same time. Jude knew that once Lance had it in his head to do something, he was more than determined to get it done. He was resourceful too . . . then Jude realized it was too late, he had been tricked. A small leather bag overloaded with coins landed at his chest on the thick wooden stump in front of him.

"Well then swordsman, I'll pay you two gold a week, double the amount you asked for, and you will find ten weeks worth of pay in the purse. I'll see you in the morning," Lance said as he left the home of his friend with a smile on his face.

As Lance made his way out of the small, one-room shack, Jude sat blankly staring at the glittering gold coins. This was more money than he had ever seen in his life. He just hoped he would live long enough to spend it.

* * *

Hector De Scoran, the king of Nalir, sat rigidly against his golden throne. The tips of his armored hands clicked impatiently against the arm rail as he studied the text of the ancient book.

A day shall come to pass when the mother of mercy shall bear child. This child will be like no other, for gods and men alike will seek to vanquish him. The hate from the hells dwells within his mind, as compassion for the meek guides his heart. If allowed to live, this child will bear the false testimony of the gods, as he ascends the throne of righteousness, while working the magic of evil. The evils of the realms will oppose him, but they will be crushed asunder as the scorpion under an anvil or fire, for he shall command evil and good alike unto his ascension . . .

The king's deep scowl was all that echoed in the elaborately furnished study chambers. His scholars had studied years on this tome of prophecies, yet only at minor success. Hector slammed the dusty text shut as he angrily gazed about the chambers. The room was magnificent and lined with beautiful tapestries depicting great battles and places of beauty, yet it provided no solace for his frustration.

Light flickered from the candles as shadows danced across the floor. On the far end of the room, two gigantic marble pillars lined an ornately carved door. The thick wooden door was made out of polished oak, the hinges were made of cultured brass, and the door's supports were encrusted in a plethora of jewels. As Hector rose from his throne, the leather under his heavy, sable metal plates of armor creaked and popped. The armored king stood erect and stretched his weary arms before sweeping back the long blue silk cape that hung from his shoulder. The faint torchlight revealed his armored shoulder with an intricate design in the shape of a silver scorpion. For centuries the arachnid had been a symbol of the kingdom's power and strength. As Hector glanced down and at the design, he ran his fingers across the raised symbol. Remembering words of his father and his father's father, Hector would not allow any enemy of his crown to defeat his long lineage, regardless of what measures or sacrifices would be required.

The opening of his chamber door interrupted his moment of vanity. A man in clad leather armor hurried to the base of the throne and bowed to one knee, lowering his head, never daring to look up. "My lord, I bear message from the scouts," the man said, never looking up, nor in any way expressing the extreme fear that swirled inside him.

"Speak!" Hector commanded as he glared down at the messenger, as if he intended to strike him dead at any moment.

"My lord, the scouts report that two men are traveling north from Bureland toward Central City. One is a large man, armored in chain, and the other appears to be without armor or sword. He wears the house symbol of Ecnal," the messenger said, his voice dripping with fear.

Ecnal, Hector thought. Ecnal was no house of nobility. In fact, Ecnal was, or at least very nearly was wiped out by his own hand. The only surviving members that Hector was aware of were a woodcutter and some old women, and no woman of Ecnal would be of mercy or virtue. The house of Ecnal was an orphanage that took in children from rapes, deaths, and prostitutes. He had originally feared the prophesied child was a Ecnal, but after many years of having them slain, Hector decided that it could not be.

The dark king lowered his voice as he spoke. "And why, messenger, is this information valuable to me? We wiped out all the Ecnals years ago. I doubt this man is one."

"In my lord's infinite wisdom, I will never know its true value, but I was told the cloaked one does carry a Necromidus," the man said as he cowered under the imposing glare of his king.

Hector's face tightened as he pondered the information. The Necromidus is a rare collection of four books containing the basic incantations of necromancy. All four books are essential at progressing in that particular school of magic.

"You have done well, my messenger. What is your name?" Hector asked with an arched eyebrow.

The man, dwarfed by the power of Hector, shifted nervously on the floor, never looking up. "Optis . . . Optis Midigan, my lord."

"You have done well, Optis. Continue to serve me competently, and you shall be rewarded," Hector responded piously.

Optis grinned as he continued to bow on the floor. His palms, wet with perspiration, were pressed firmly to the cold marble. He dared not lift his head. He was a little worried when Soran had picked him to deliver the message to the king, but it was turning out to be a blessing in disguise.

Optis tried to hide his pleasure, though his widening grin betrayed his glee. "Yes, my lord. How may I serve you on this day?" Optis asked quietly without raising his head.

Hector arched his thick dark eyebrows as he regarded the cowering man before him.

"You shall return to Soran with my orders. However, if the seal of this letter is broken . . ." Hector said as he held an ivory scroll case aloft and presented it to the cowering messenger. The case was immersed in ornate carvings and symbols, and was about a foot long. Hector gave pause before he finished, as Optis studied the case with wide eyes. ". . . I will be very displeased."

Optis nearly fainted in panic as his mind raced at what might happen to him if something might befall the letter. "Only in my death shall another disturb the letter," Optis proclaimed as he puffed out his chest proudly.

24

The king's eyes narrowed. The messenger quickly withdrew, sensing Hector was not pleased.

"Optis, I urge you to ensure the letter is not disturbed, even in your death. For the icy fingers of my vengeance extend far beyond the realms of the living," Hector warned dangerously.

Fear gripped Optis; scarcely able to speak, he let out a meek voice. He had no idea how the king could hurt him after he died, but he was aware the king had arcane power far greater than most who walked Terrigan.

"Yes, my lord," was all the timid, cowering Optis could say through a large lump in his throat.

Hector reached down and opened a long ivory tube. His thick fingers stretched in and pulled several parchments, and placed them on the tall wooden podium that was before him. Dabbing the large exotic quill into the inkwell, he wrote:

Soran,

Once again you prove your worth. Even though you haven't identified the child the prophecies speak of, you have found someone, and the very least, something, that interests me. The council of seven still work to un-ravel the prophecies. Sometimes I am forced to motivate them. Sometimes I motivate them for sheer enjoyment. I await your loyal service to my crown.
Hector

Hector dabbed his wax seal on the message and stepped down toward Optis. The messenger still shook from the king's proclamation of punishment after death, and cowered as Hector placed the letter in his knapsack. "Your task has been set, messenger. Do your duty," the king said.

Optis quietly stood, turned, and strode toward the door, strain-ing to keep from breaking his hurried walk into a full run. When the sound of the chamber door clicking shut echoed across the room, Hector returned to his golden throne and re-opened the ancient text. "... *When the mother of mercy shall bear child* ..." Hector frowned as he read. Who is the mother of mercy? Did she already give birth? Why was she called the mother of mercy? All of these questions confounded the dark king.

Hector gently closed the tome and stepped down from his throne. He glided across the smooth marble floor to a small wooden door against the north wall. The old wood creaked as he opened the heavy gate, revealing a large stone balcony with many green potted trees and beautiful oaken tables and chairs. Great tapestries depicting the black scorpion with an azure background hung from the balcony walls. Large vines of ivy reached out over the edge of the balcony and hung down the side of the castle walls. Moonlight and a soft breeze poured in the throne room. The sound of the night breeze blowing through the leaves of many trees resonated on the stone balcony from below. Blue silk curtains, which hung from the railing, were casually blowing in the wind.

Hector sat down at one of the oaken tables and carefully opened the ancient text again. He read awhile and in frustration slammed the tome shut. This prophecy confounded him. The sages were certain his kingdom was the one named within as the scorpion, though they admitted they had no idea who or what the anvil of fire was. He glanced out over his kingdom. He could see lush green trees for about six miles, then after that, he knew, was hundreds of miles of deadly swamps. He felt trapped for the first time in his life. Before, the swamp isolated him from invaders and served as a perfect defense, keeping his kingdom from being conquered. But now . . . he took a deep breath. Now it seemed to serve as a cage holding him until the anvil of fire arrived, whatever that may turn out to be. Hector stood up from the table and scooted the large oaken chair back under it. He picked up the heavy tome and tucked it under his arm as he made his way back through his throne room to his bedchamber. He closed the large door, locked it, and sat on the corner of his giant bed. He placed the book on the stand next to it and removed his heavy armor. He was so exhausted he left the thick steel armored plates laying where they fell, and climbed into bed. As the dark king plopped down on the soft mattress, the many silk pillows seemed to envelop him, and he struggled to keep awake. ". . . At least I know it is a male child that is born," he thought to himself before drifting off into a deep sleep.

*   *   *

Davohn sat in his soft wooden chair—how he loved the green, supple, velvety fabric that lined the sitting area. He remembered how Lance worked most of a summer doing extra jobs at the library

26

to buy him something nice for his birthday. The fond reflection of his adoptive son was washed away by the distant rumble of thunder and the rising breeze that seemed to whisper through the thick leaves of the large trees that enveloped the old woodcutter's house. Davohn quickly forgot about the approaching rain and ran his fingers down the smooth contour of the armrest while his heavy woodcutting axe leaned against it. The dark polished oak had served him on many a day as he thought of work, play, or just anything that demanded more than passing reflection. The brief shower had let up an hour ago, though it seemed a heavier rain was soon to arrive. Lance would have no excuse for not coming home. The rain would have provided an explanation, but he should have been home before it started. Yet, now there was a brief dry spell and the fool boy still wasn't home. Anger tore through Davohn as he recalled how many times in the past Lance had not come home on time, and the night he didn't come home at all.

Though Davohn was angry, he reflected back to when Lance was a small child. The boy was always independent. Even at age six, when Davohn had found him, Lance had been alone in the wilderness for more than a month. The boy clutched a small leather backpack that he refused to let out of his sight. Davohn had always wondered what was in the pack, but respected Lance's right to keep it secret. The woodcutter thought it had something to do with Lance's ability to survive as long as he did in the wilderness. Any other small child would have been eaten by a wild animal or by something far worse. The deep woods of Beykla were known to hold many creatures that were not quite man and not quite beast. They would have made short work of a child, yet the boy confidently strolled up that day. He was hungry and dirty, but no worse for wear. Davohn pondered if the gods were keeping a watchful eye on him.

The aging woodcutter rose from his seat, slowly stretched his tired old muscles, and walked into the kitchen of his home. It wasn't a large home by any means, but it was more than adequate for him and Lance. Davohn took on the surname Ecnal because it was the name given to the orphans of Beykla. Since Davohn himself was an orphan, he felt the name would serve him well. There were many other Ecnals, or orphans, so no matter where he went in the world, he might find a brother or sister. Since he presumed Lance was an orphan, Davohn hoped the name Ecnal might give him a sense of family other than his immediate family.

Davohn retrieved a wooden flagon from the cupboard, and poured himself a drink of water from a plain clay pitcher. No sooner did the water touch his lips than he heard the front door blow open. Placing the cup down on the wooden counter, he walked into the living room and stared at the front door that was standing wide open. A soft cool breeze flooded the room. The smell of the wet grass and mud wafted into the small house from the outdoors. To Davohn's confusion, the trees outside weren't blowing hard enough to force open the door, making the aging woodcutter wonder how the door blew open if there was no wind. In fact, it was relatively calm outside. As Davohn closed the door, he began to feel a twinge of panic. If the trees were not swaying, then there was no way the wind could have blown the door open.

Davohn saw a slim shadow shift from his right from inside of the room. Before the woodcutter could react it was too late. Shooting pain tore through the back of his right leg, forcing him to the ground. A second strike hit him in the right side of his head, knocking him prone. Fighting for consciousness as he lay on the floor, Davohn wasn't quite sure what had exactly happened. Warm blood ran down the side of his face and pooled around him. Davohn felt stinging pain in his scalp as his hair jerked his head up and a grown man sat on his back, pressing a cold razor-sharp piece of steel against his neck.

"Where is the mage?" the figure said with a raspy voice from atop him. Davohn could hardly understand the thick voice. "What mage? Only . . ."

The blade was abruptly taken away from his throat, and the pommel of it was pounded into the side of his head a second time. Davohn fought for consciousness while he felt the cold steel of the blade as it came to rest under his chin again.

"Answer me, woodcutter. I know he lives here," the raspy voice said again.

Davohn screamed inside. Another blow to his head would knock him out. He must not die, not like this. He felt the blade move from under his chin. It was now or never. Before the blow could land, Davohn turned his weight and hunched forward. He felt the man flail as he toppled over his right shoulder. Davohn stood and his weak legs shuddered under him. He ran to his chair and reached down to grab his axe, but to his horror it was gone. Davohn dropped to the floor and frantically searched the darkness while the intruder laughed.

"You didn't think I would just leave that crude weapon there so you could try to stick it in my chest, did you?" the raspy voice taunted.

Without pause Davohn turned and ran for the window. He lowered his head and outstretched his arms. He heard the sweet sound of breaking glass and the rush of the cold night air as he toppled head over feet, landing in the soft mud on his back and sliding a few yards. Scrambling up, the old woodcutter ran into the night and the dark forest quickly swallowed him. Warm sticky blood dripped from his head and into his eyes. He tore away a sleeve and tightly wrapped his forehead. He could feel small pieces of glass and wood protruding from his arms and shoulders. After a quick inspection to see if he had any serious injuries, Davohn's mind raced. Who was that man, and why was he at his house? Who was the mage he was looking for, and who in their right mind would hunt one? Davohn didn't know a mage, much less why someone would dare to try and kill one.

What if Lance came home? That murderer would kill and torture the poor boy when he arrived. With new resolve, Davohn turned and headed back to the house. As he neared, he could see a thin haze of smoke as it filled the forest. Davohn ran through the trees as fast as his weak legs would carry him. He could see his house was completely engulfed in flames, lighting the area like a noon sun. Davohn was forced to raise his hand against his face to shield it from the intense heat that poured off of the fiery blaze. Just as he cleared the tree line, Davohn saw something move from his right. He screamed out in pain as the flat head of his axe rammed into his right leg. His shin shattered, sending the old woodcutter toppling face first into the mud while numbing pain shot up his leg, making him weak. Davohn turned over and stared at the face of the killer. The assassin raised the axe over his head, and plunged it deep into Davohn's chest. The dying woodcutter gasped weakly, trying to claim a breath that would not come.

"Your boy should not have crossed, Grascon the Nimble," the

29

assassin said as he stared over the mortally wounded woodcutter with his scarred face twitching violently.

As Davohn's vision began to fail, he stared at the face of his killer. He stared at the one-toothed smile and the ugly scar that went from his nose to the corner of his eye. Then he stared at nothing.

*   *   *

Lance shifted uncomfortably in his saddle as the hot autumn sun beat down on his pale brow, making him sweat uncontrollably. His back and legs ached and his head hurt terribly from the long, arduous ride. He was hungry, and worst of all, he didn't like the smell of his horse. The damned filthy animal reeked. This trip was turning out to be more than he bargained for. Lance turned his weary head around and looked at Jude. The swordsman was sitting on his horse sporting a wry smile across his face. Jude's heavy hips rolled with the sway of the animal in a strange melodic dance. He showed no sign of discomfort; in fact he seemed to be enjoying himself. He wore a new suit of chain armor that glistened in the light, and his large great sword hung across his back, the huge leather strap that held the sword in place crossing his massive chest from his left shoulder to right hip. Jude's long brown hair dangled and bounced about his shoulders as he slowly plodded down the trail.

Lance wondered how his large friend was so accustomed to riding, but quickly became resigned to the fact that any proficiency on a horse took time to become skilled at. Just as he studied long and hard to be a skilled mage, Jude must have studied equally as hard at learning to ride. Lance wiped his sweaty brow with his sleeve as the hot sun baked him in his dark sable robe. The trees alongside the trail loomed over them, but seldom blocked the bright autumn sun, providing only small breaks from the searing heat. The trail the pair rode on was overgrown with grass, save for two parallel marks torn by occasional wagon wheels, and was home to hundreds of tiny chirping bugs and small birds.

"So . . . uh . . . where are we going?" Jude asked as he picked his teeth with a twig while looking at Lance, awaiting a reply.

"I thought you were a hired sword," Lance said with a smirk.

He knew Jude hated being the last to know about anything, especially something he was involved in.

"Well I am, but if I am to use that sword you hired, I might need to know who to use it against," Jude said, now smirking more than Lance.

"You are to use it against anyone who might harm us," Lance said sarcastically. "It's a good thing I'm doing the thinking on this journey."

Jude looked forward and frowned. It was bad enough his friend trapped him in this journey, and was treating him like any other sell sword, but for two gold a week . . . He would just about endure anything. "When an enemy attacks, dear friend, be sure to remind me which hand to swing my sword with. I wouldn't want to be accused of thinking," Jude fired back.

"If these armored men coming down the road attack us, start with your right hand. I'll advise later if you need to switch," Lance said as the smile began to slowly fade from his face.

Jude quickly glanced forward, straining his eyes to see ahead through the haze. About a hundred yards up the trail he could see three men riding toward them. They were clad in brass-colored scale armor with bright red silk capes that hung down behind them. The light breeze flowed over the horsemen, lifting the capes up over the horse's rump. The barrel-chested war horses wore brass-colored barding over their heads and chests. The two rear men rode side-by-side while the center man rode a few feet ahead of the others. He had a wooden standard affixed to the left side of his saddle that rose a few feet above his head. The red and white flag depicted a tilted crown with a sword through the center of it. On the left side of the crown the flag was red. On the right side of the crown the flag was white.

"Beyklan high guards," Jude said flatly. "They shouldn't be this far south without a purpose."

Lance sat transposed as the men in the bright brass-colored armor burned into his memory. He unconsciously recalled how the man in polished bronze armor and a red silk cape, much like these, came to his home that horrific day. Lance recalled the men stomping across his father's red silk rug, and a tilted crown and a polished long sword piercing the middle of it. He remembered his childhood

31

terror as he hid from the armored men. His childhood terror now transformed into anger as the men approached.

"The uniforms these men wear today are the uniforms that the men wore when my parents were murdered," Lance said with a murderous tone.

"Don't get any bright ideas, Lance. Not even ten gold a week would be enough for me to become an outlaw from the crown of Beykla."

Lance turned to Jude and spoke in a deep quiet voice. "My soul screams for vengeance, my friend."

Jude swallowed hard and moved his horse closer to Lance. "These men would have been but babes when your parents were murdered. Do not hold them accountable for crimes of the throne," Jude whispered.

The soldiers' finely trained animals stood still with their ears backward toward them as they halted in front of Lance and Jude. "Good afternoon, citizens. I am Sergeant Oswald Thorrin," the lead man that held the standard proclaimed in a loud voice.

Lance and Jude did not respond and the sergeant shifted uneasily in his saddle, looking them over. When the sergeant did not receive a reply from the strange pair, he decided to explain his intentions better. "We are looking for a man. He is wanted for stealing wares from one of the stores in Central City. The man is about ten hands high, brown hair, and is missing the index finger on his left hand. He is almost . . ." the sergeant scowled as he was rudely interrupted by Lance.

"What did he steal?" Lance asked.

The sergeant paused as an annoyed expression crept on his face. "What he stole isn't important. What is important . . ."

Lance urged his horse forward, ignoring what the sergeant was saying, and pushing his way between the soldier's horses.

Jude followed Lance and also pushed his mount past the soldiers. The guard's horses stumbled to get out of the way of the thick-chested war horse Jude rode.

The brass-plate clad sergeant jerked his horse's head around roughly, and shouted, "You dare ignore a sergeant of the Royal Beyklan Army?"

Lance continued to ride on, not turning his head back, as he shouted over his shoulder.

"If you are unsure if I dare, sergeant, wait until I and my swordsman round this bend and are out of sight, then ask yourself the question a second time. If you are too daft to come to a conclusion at that point, I am sure one of your lackeys will enlighten you," Lance said sarcastically while Jude chuckled under his breath.

The sergeant's square-jawed face flushed red with anger and he turned his horse and trotted ahead of Lance and Jude. "You dare insult the king!?" the sergeant growled.

The dry leather of Lance's saddle creaked as he looked around the sergeant in a haughty fashion. "I don't see any king, only a corpse if he continues to pester a wizard and his swordsman. But if I did see the king, and he asked such preposterous questions, I needn't insult him, for if he spoke as you do, his own stupidity would do it for me," Lance taunted.

The sergeant drew his sword and leveled it at arms' length at Lance. The finely crafted blade shined in the bright afternoon sun.

Jude nervously looked at Lance, waiting for the command to cleave the men with his great sword.

"You will bow down to me and beg forgiveness from the crown!" the sergeant commanded as spittle sprayed from his clenched teeth and he growled.

The other two soldiers slowly drew their long swords. It was obvious they were intimidated by Lance and Jude more than the sergeant was.

Lance calmly cleared his throat and spoke to the flushed sergeant. "Sergeant, you cannot make demands when you are asleep on your horse."

As Lance finished speaking, he channeled the magical energies that naturally existed and swirled around all things. Only men trained in the arcane arts had the ability to see the magical weaves, and fewer yet had the ability to bend and weave them into spells. Lance had always been able to easily see the strands and bend them easier yet. Lance quickly and quietly wove a thin net of green energy and let it gently fall over the sergeant's head.

The sergeant suddenly dropped his long sword and slumped forward over his horse. The shiny razor-sharp sword fell harmlessly from his grasp and clanged against the ground. His horse sidestepped under the shifted weight of the sergeant as he fell forward onto the horse's neck. The two other soldiers looked at each

33

other and nervously urged their horses forward. It was clear they were afraid of the young wizard and his large swordsman.

"Your sergeant is fortunate that he only sleeps," Lance said calmly. "When he wakes, tell him he is alive only because I didn't wish to kill him today. If he returns and I see him before the moon cycles again, I will strike him dead with a word," Lance said, pausing to ensure he had the men's attention. "Do you understand?"

The soldiers nodded nervously and grabbed the reins of the sergeant's horse, pulling the dun along the trail as the sergeant's body lay slumped over the saddle.

As their horses' hoofbeats faded into the distance, Jude turned to Lance. "One of these days, my friend, you are going to tell me all the tricks you can do, so I don't swing my sword prematurely."

Lance turned and smiled at Jude. He had never seen his friend so disturbed. Lance knew it had something to do with the encounter because Jude didn't like the use of magic, but Lance didn't believe anything he would do could spook his long-time friend.

"Did I alarm you, Jude?" Lance asked, studying Jude's face as he answered.

"I just don't like things you can't see or feel," Jude whispered solemnly.

Lance frowned and looked over at his friend. The young mage raised his hands in the air while he shrugged his shoulders. "Well I'm sure the sergeant felt it."

Jude didn't respond immediately, he just turned and faced the road while his face flushed, his thick jaw muscles flexed, and he grinded his teeth. "You hired me for my sword, yet you make me feel as if I was hired for company, rather than protection."

Lance shifted uncomfortably in his saddle and chuckled, dismissing his friend's concern. "Jude, believe me, when we encounter someone worthy of your blade, I shall be the first to scream your name in my defense. I just felt those guards were undeserving to die at the hands of someone such as yourself."

Jude turned to level a stern gaze at Lance. The swordsman loathed not knowing where the journey was taking him. He decided to concede the point, even if Lance thought he had played into his hand. Jude despised battles of wit and just wanted to be an equal. Lance was the only real friend the large swordsman ever had. "Look, I'm sorry. I just am not taking too well to being your hired help. How about I return your gold and we spend the rest of the journey, regardless of where it leads us, as the friends we have always been," Jude suggested with a half smile because he thought it came out better than it sounded when he said it to himself.

Lance grinned wide, exposing his perfect teeth. "As you wish my friend, but we do need someone to watch the money. And since I have a flair for the extravagant and you, my friend, are known to be quite frugal at times, you can manage our adventure fund," Lance suggested, pausing as he waited for Jude's response.

"Well, I could but—" Jude started to say before Lance cut him off.

"Good, then it is settled."

Jude just smiled and shook his big head from side to side. "Lance, you could talk a dragon right out of his scales."

Lance reached over and jovially slapped his hand on the back of Jude's thick, armored shoulder. "I hope you are right, my hulking friend, that might be useful someday." Both men had a hearty laugh.

The two traveled on through the vast deciduous countryside. Lance gazed in wide-eyed wonder at the expansiveness of the Beyklan land. Beykla was a beautiful kingdom that had forests as vast as oceans. As far as the young mage could see, there were rolling hills and large trees that were speckled in an autumn coat of deep red yellows and browns. He surmised it would take an incredible army to defend such a country as this. An enemy army would be able to hide throughout the countryside for years without being detected. Though the many wandering patrols like the one they encountered often reported findings they saw, if they employed assassins the dark professionals could pick off such patrols long before they got close to the main force. Lance knew, from speaking with wandering adventurers in Bureland, that Beykla was having difficulty with the dwarves from the Pyberian Mountains in the northwest near the kingdom of Adoria. When Adoria began the civil war with Andoria, Beykla angered the dwarves by outlawing trade with Andoria. Most of the dwarves' incomes came from trading with the feuding nations. The dwarven High Council met with the King Thortan Theobold, and the Beyklan king refused to hear the dwarves' pleas for the end of the sanctions because of a dispute regarding the dwarves' taxation on their mined goods. When the king refused to lift sanctions, the dwarves returned to the mountains, and they haven't paid any taxes since. That was almost two years ago. The civil war lasted less than eight months before Andoria was conquered. Lance knew little of warfare, but he knew that eight months was a short war. There were rumors that the Ka-Harkians, a kind of mountain people, aided Adoria in the war to gain a piece of land from what was left of Andoria. Lance had never met a Ka-Harkian either, but he knew them to be expert swordsmen as a people. Even the women were quite skilled with blades. Ka-Harkia had never been at war, much less conquered, because all of the plants that grew on the mountains were highly toxic from minerals having been eroded from rainwater, and mighty melting glaciers that slowly roamed deep in their country. So in turn, all the animals were toxic to outsiders. As a result, the Ka-Harkians, as a people, were immune to most poisons by simply living off of the land.

Lance wasn't sure what lay beyond Adoria. He knew there was a great swamp, but other than that it was a mystery. Though he had seen little of the kingdom he lived in, Lance felt as if the world was at his feet. He was finally on his own, to do as he wanted.

Lance placed his hands on the rear of his hips and stretched his back. The sun had nearly set as they rode through the evening. As the bugs began to chirp and the air started to turn cool, Lance wondered if Davohn was angry with him for leaving without saying good-bye in person. Lance hoped the letter he left was good enough for the difficult but loving man. Lance sighed and inhaled the cool fresh air and then exhaled deeply before turning to Jude. "So when are we going to camp, my friend? I am more than ready," Lance asked as he struggled to conceal a grin.

"Whenever you wish, but I was hoping to ride at least until it is dark," Jude said with pure seriousness.

"Till dark? That is at least an hour away," Lance said miserably. His feet and toes were tingling, his inner legs were sore and felt a few inches longer, while his back felt like he had chopped enough wood for Davohn to burn in a lifetime.

Jude seemed to enjoy Lance's torment, and as Lance grimaced, his grin steadily grew. "Well, if I knew where we were heading, I would have a better time gauging how long to ride or how early we could camp."

Lance let out a groan of defeat. "Okay Jude, we are heading to Central City."

Jude's expression turned from curious to excited. "Central City! Why would we go there?" Jude asked. He was beginning to get worried. Central City was a great city—the greatest city in months of riding in any direction. Jude had only been there once as a child and even then it was a frightful place. The buildings were all made of stone and towered over the streets. Some were so high only the noon light of the sun would shine on the street. He knew of the great coliseum that existed there. There were many celebrated swordsmen there, and great thieves. In fact, Jude guessed just about everybody that lived in the city was someone great. Jude was comfortable in his proficiency around Bureland because he was one of the most skilled fighters there. He was both feared and respected. But Jude knew that no one in Central City would have heard of him, and worse, that he may have to prove his skill as a swordsman, and that could bring trouble from the magistrate.

"Do you read Nalirian?" Lance asked from nowhere, acting as if the mere question alone would solve all of Jude's fears.

"What does Central City have to do with Nalir?" Jude asked. The large swordsman had heard of Nalir. It was an evil kingdom to the far south on the west coast of the continent. He feared the answer Lance might give would be as dubious as the answer to where they were going.

"Well, my friend, I do not speak nor read Nalirian, therefore I am forced to seek console in Central City at the city's library," Lance said.

Jude fingered his thick leather saddle horn. "Well if we must go there, then we must, but I have been there before. It is a dangerous place," Jude warned.

Lance smiled and waved his hand to dismiss his friend's fears. "Jude, you have grown large and strong by eating the food you cook yourself, and I can think of nothing more dangerous than placing those toxic substances you concoct into your mouth. If you can survive that three times a day, I assume the realms hold no terror you could not surpass," Lance said with a wry smile.

Jude gave out a small chuckle, but his face did not relax. Lance was frustrated at his friend's strange superstitions. Jude was a mighty swordsman. Lance had seen him wield a sword in such a way as to make the skilled look less than novices, yet the large swordsman was terrified at this place. Lance decided he needed to find a way to get Jude to loosen his grip on the fear of the unknown.

*   *   *

Tharxton Stoneheart stood erect in the deep underground tunnel. His long braided red beard hung from his chin with two large golden rings woven into the bottom tip. He wore large metal plate armor affixed by thick leather straps to his chain mail tunic. Ancient dwarven runes danced up and down the thick massive plates that covered his well-armored arms. His large hand rested atop the hilt of his mighty hammer that hung upside down on his side. The hammer was made of a dark black ore that had been heated then shaped countless times until it was forged into the spectacle of the weapon it was today. The head was over fifty pounds and bore intricate dwarven runes of his clan and his lineage. At the center of the hammer's head was a bright crimson ruby that danced and glittered in the flickering torchlight of the passage. The hammer had been his father's, and his father's father, and so on. Over twenty generations of Stoneheart dwarves had wielded the fantastic weapon.

Tharxton surveyed his clan as they worked on shaping and clearing the deep passage they had been excavating for over ten years. The bearded folk relentlessly carved the tunnel through the thick rock that laid under the surface of the forest that was east of their home, the Pyberian Mountains. Steadily working the stone and hauling it away, the dwarves made the colossal eastern shaft. Tharxton ran his thick callused finger over the gigantic passage that was sculpted by expert craftsmanship. Huge oaken timbers that were saturated with oil and tar were fastened together by thick iron plates. Long rail tracks erupted from the darkness and brought huge carts spilling ore and debris. Occasionally the dwarves might find a vein of some precious metal or gem that they would quickly mine, but for the most part they worked diligently at lengthening and widening the subterranean passage.

Tharxton eagerly rubbed his hands through his coarse red beard. How he longed for the day he could lead his mighty armies down the passage and smite the Beyklans for their treachery. He was pleased that the dwarven council had approved his request for

38

war. Tharxton's own family had suffered countless tragedies at the hands of the Beyklans' selfish sanctions, as did his clan. When the Beyklans outlawed trade with the Andorians during the war, his family, as well as most dwarven families, lost everything they had saved. Without the trade, the dwarves could not get many of the foodstuffs and medicines they needed to survive. Unlike most clans, the Stonehearts dwelled in the Pyberian Mountains. The mountains were rich were precious metals, gems, and ores, but held little natural caves that contained the many mushrooms and foods that other dwarven clans lived off of. Clan Stoneheart relied on trade from Andoria and Beykla to supply the goods they could not find naturally. But since the demise of Andoria and the sanctions from Beykla, the dwarves were beginning to have to rely on a barter system for commodities. The Beyklans maintained they were trying to ensure no one interfered in the civil war between the Adorias, but the dwarves believed the Beyklans were trying to cripple them and keep their clan submissive by paying their outrageous taxes. Though Tharxton was king, he also had to obey the clan's council, so his attack against the keep that the humans erected some twenty years earlier to monitor their taxation was delayed. This lengthy delay was a blessing in disguise. The dwarves had a passage under the mountain over thirty miles long. It had taken over twenty years to build, and just as the dwarves feared, the humans grew jealous of the dwarf prosperity. Though Tharxton was sure his ancestors could not foresee that the Beyklans would attack by attrition, the attack was less efficient. Tharxton had ordered his army to resume digging the tunnel directly under the Torrent Manor. The Torrent Manor was located between the Beyklan capitol of Dawson, and Central City. In fact, the keep was erected solely to oversee the taxation of the dwarves. Tharxton and his people viewed the keep as a symbol of their slavery. How he longed to destroy this monument to their captivity. The young dwarf king smiled wide with anticipation as he imagined destroying the keep and the Western Beyklan Army while he tugged at his large, red beard. He wasn't old for a dwarf. In fact, he wasn't even very old for a king. He didn't dress like a king and he seldom wore silk or fine garments. He kept his long beard braided and was seldom seen without his weapons or armor. Tharxton had been an expert armorer and weapon smith. He forged his own armor complete with ancient family runes, and a reddish tint to the metal that made him gleam like a warm ember when he was in the sun, though he often wore an heirloom other than his own. Tharxton wore a great helm with a red plume that hung down his back to his rump. He had worked most of his life forging weapons, trying to make them superior in weight, shape and style. In time, he learned to wield the weapons with great mastery that enabled him to rise through the ranks of the army until he made general. The former dwarven king, Dalton Thornfist, had gotten sick and named Tharxton king before he died. Tharxton was afraid at first, and begged the king not to make him accept the crown. Tharxton complained that he knew nothing of being a king, that he still wasn't quite learned at being a general. But his pleas fell on deaf ears and Tharxton became an unlikely king. The dwarven nation of Stoneheart didn't mourn the loss of their old king long. They embraced Tharxton with open arms and made him proud to lead them. *And lead them he would,* he thought. His men had nearly completed the tunnel and it would soon be time to set the anvil in motion.

*   *   *

It was nearly noon on the sixth day of travel when Lance and Jude arrived at the first farmhouses near Central City. Lance gazed wide-eyed at the rolling fields that surrounded the dirt path. The wind blew the browning wheat, causing a long ripple that floated on the tops of the plants as a swift wave would roll on the open sea. Lance often found people in the fields, working and tilling the land. They seldom raised a hand in acknowledgement to him, though Lance frequently raised his. Lance glanced over at his friend. Jude was riding quietly as if he were less than impressed with the vastness of these farms, or their infinite rolling fields.

"Jude, do you not gaze on such farms with wonderment?" Lance asked. "Surely these farms are the greatest that you have ever seen!"

Jude chewed on his bottom lip as he thought for a moment before answering. "Lance, Central City is full of many wondrous things, but it is important that we do not become enthralled by them. That is when the cutpurses will hit us!"

40

Lance frowned. "In the daylight? Surly they wouldn't be so callous as to try something in the middle of the day!"

Jude chuckled and shook his head slowly from side to side. "Lance, the thieves here are very skilled, many could easily steal from you during the day."

"What about the local magistrate?" Lance asked worriedly. "Don't they arrest these thieves?"

Jude was becoming frustrated with his friend's ignorance to the ways of the city. "Trust me Lance, they wouldn't do it if they couldn't get away with it."

Lance frowned deeply. He didn't come all this way just to get robbed by some second rate thief. He would study some spells to foil those who would be so foolish as to stick their fingers into his pockets. "Let us find a farmer that would put us up for the night."

Jude slowed his horse, half-confused. "Lance, dusk is about seven or eight hours away, why would we want to stop now?"

Lance continued on, ignoring his friend's confused stare. "Well, my fine swordsman, we both could use a good night's sleep, and I would like to learn as much about this town as possible."

Jude hurried his dun back up to Lance's. "What makes you think a farmer would put us up for the night?" Jude asked.

Lance shrugged his shoulders. "If they are anything like the farmers back in Bureland, they will welcome some silver."

Jude nodded his head. In truth he could use a nice sleep, even if it was in a barn, and the thought of some soft hay to lay in made him yawn. He decided that Lance had a good idea, though he doubted his assumption that a few silver coins would sway the farmers into letting them stay.

Lance and Jude rode slowly down a long dirt trail. Tall brown grass grew along the sides of the dirt-strewn route, and the bright autumn branches of large trees silently drifted over the top, enclosing the path with a cave of vegetation. A cool breeze drifted by, lightly blowing on the ever browning autumn leaves. As they approached the end of the small dirt trail, it opened up, revealing a large two-story house. The dwelling was made of wood and stone and had bright green shutters with a porch that extended all the way around from the front to the side. Two thick wooden columns that were ornately carved depicting flowers and vines winding their way around each other supported the porch. Behind the house were three larger buildings and a smaller one-story structure similar to the house, but without the winding porch. There was a large silo on the south part of the farm that was made of smooth sandstone-type bricks and was about twenty-five feet tall. The conical top was made out of thin wooden slates, layered much like the roofs in Bureland. Many large cows and other livestock gathered around the base of the silo in a fenced area. Men were working all over the farm. Few paid more than a glance to Lance and Jude.

"Maybe we should leave, my friend. This is one of the largest farms that I have seen. I'm sure the owner will not enjoy any visitors," Jude said nervously. He had never seen a farm so vast. Using his experience as a warrior, Jude glanced around the farm. He had witnessed many tactical advantages that normal farms did not possess nor even concern themselves with. Jude's biggest concern was the narrow slits in the roof of the silo. Jude, in his experiences, knew expert marksmen often lurked behind those narrow transoms to rain down arrows of death on unsuspecting enemies.

"Nonsense!" Lance said as he grinned wide. "This is the grandest farm I have ever seen. I wish to speak to the owner and congratulate him on his beautiful home!"

Jude began to disagree with his young friend when a middle-aged man approached. He was dressed in a plain leather tunic and breeches and had long brown hair that bounced on his shoulders as he walked.

The man bowed courtly and smiled. "Greetings to you from Master Hentridge."

Lance smiled. "Greetings to you, my name is Lance, and this is my friend Jude. We have traveled many days and are seeking refuge from the elements."

The man gestured back toward the farm. "We are simply farmers, good sirs. I'm afraid that we have not the accommodations you might be accustomed to, but if you please, I shall take you to see Master Hentridge," he said, gesturing behind himself again.

Lance smiled as he nodded his head. "It would please us greatly sir, for we surely seek shelter, but good company would please us even more."

The worker turned and led them toward the house as Jude nervously glanced around the farm. Many people toiled about, but in contrast to Jude's suspicions, no one he saw carried any visible weapon. Jude carefully watched the many farm hands caring for the livestock, tending to a large garden behind the house, and loading grain from the wagon to begin planting in one of the many fields as they were led into the vast farm.

The middle-aged man took them around the rear of the house near the garden. There was a large open-topped wagon parked alongside the vegetable patch. The wagon was made of thick wood and had many arrow scars inside. It appeared as if it would take several horses to move the huge farm cart. The wagon listed to the right front side where Lance and Jude witnessed a pair of legs jutting from underneath.

"Master Hentridge, travelers here to see you, sir," the middle-aged man that led them back said.

"Eh? What was that?" an average-sized man mumbled as he crawled out from under the wagon. He had thick, short brown hair that made his ears seem to stick out, his face was covered in grease and tar, and he was covered from head to toe with wood shavings.

Lance and Jude handed the reins of their horses to the servant and waited for an introduction. Master Hentridge stood up, wiped his hands on his pants and shirt, and extended his hand toward Lance. Lance looked at his dirty, greasy hand hesitantly while Jude instantly took the dirty hand, shooting Lance a sidelong glance.

"A pleasure to meet someone of your standing, good sir. I am Jude and this is my traveling companion, Lance," Jude said as he gestured to Lance, who seemed to still be repulsed at the offer of the filthy hand.

Lance recovered and interrupted before Jude could go on. "Yes, it is a pleasure to meet you, good sir. We have been traveling for most of the week and would like to stay the night at your grand establishment and partake of any stories or advice you may feel in your heart to give us in regards to—"

Lance was cut off by Master Hentridge. "Does your friend always talk so much?" he asked, looking at Jude. "A simple `we will pay you for a night's rest' would have done fine," Master Hentridge said, turning to Lance. "When a man talks too much he makes me think he is hiding something; I don't like men who hide things."

Jude began to speak, but he too was cut off by the greasy man. "I need a silver piece from the likes of you two to stay at my farm. All meals are served at the ringing of the bell. You have but a few

43

minutes to get served and eat before my men all start back to their chores, so I suggest you don't lollygag. You will stay in the servants' quarters by the silo . . ." he said, gesturing to the small building that was built just under the silo. "I have a few empty beds there you can have, any questions?"

Jude and Lance looked at each other and then shook their heads.

"Good, don't get in my men's ways. Also, everything on this here farm, including a dead rat if you find it, is mine, got it? So no getting your grubby mitts on my stuff or I'll have them whacked-off," Master Hentridge said flatly. The greasy man called for a stable hand to tend to their horses, and no sooner finished his speech when he turned, picked up his sack of tools from under the wagon, and walked away.

"This way please," said the middle-aged man that met them when they first arrived. He motioned them along past the garden to the south part of the farm, as the stable hand led the horses to the stables. They passed a large fenced-in area that was home to over a score of cows and oxen. The fence was made of stone at the base and the upper part of the fence was made of wooden rails. It was over six feet in height and was connected to a large barn-type building in which the animals were housed. The silo was connected to an auger system that ran into the same fenced area to feed the livestock. The auger was made of iron and was housed in a stone trough that was sixty feet long. A wooden side panel covered the auger's blades and protected the livestock from getting their noses too close. The auger appeared to be cranked by a large-wheeled capstan that was powered by several workers.

A few farmhands took a moment to glance at Lance and Jude as they were led along toward the servants' quarters. Jude glanced up at the silo's roof to the murder holes, half expecting arrows to fly down from them. Lance seemed more interested in the workers, often looking them up and down while testing his theories as he watched them carry out their duties. Satisfied at his estimation of leaders and workers, Lance focused on where he was being led.

The servants' quarters was about forty yards from the base of the silo. Jude tried to estimate whether they were in bow range from the tall thin silo, while Lance was busy admiring the building's simple architecture. Inside the servants' quarters almost twenty bunk racks were crammed into narrow rows to strategically allow each one equal space. Every bunk had a folded sheet and blanket on a canvass mattress. Jude and Lance found a rack at the far end of the room and placed their gear on it.

Lance climbed onto the bottom rack and lay down, placing his hands behind his head as he sighed. "Just think, Jude. You thought this was a bad idea. We have a good bed and a dry place to sleep tonight with little worries of the beasts of the forest."

Jude grunted as he climbed up on the top rack. "I'd rather face the beasts of the wild. At least you can see their fangs as they lust for your blood. I bet the likes of these hounds would be more inclined to stab at our backs instead of our bellies," Jude said as he climbed onto the top bunk. The bunk sagged deeply and groaned under the weight of the great man. Lance gasped, jumped from his rack, and ran to the wall.

Jude gave him a puzzled look. "What is the matter with you Lance? Find a mite in your bunk?" Jude chuckled as he looked below at the surprise on Lance's face.

"I bet an oxen would be better supported by the top bunk than you! Perhaps I should rethink our sleeping arrangement," Lance retorted with a frown.

Jude shrugged his shoulders and plopped down onto the floor. He grabbed his dirty leather pack and tossed it on the bottom rack. He took his coin purse and placed it on his belt, and neatly slid his sword under the sheet and the mattress and practiced drawing it until he did so with a short swift movement. Satisfied, he placed his hands behind his head and quickly drifted into sleep.

Lance placed his pack next to Jude's, removed the Necromidus and began to read. The cover of the ancient book was made of some kind of animal hide. Lance wasn't sure of the book's exact origin, but he thought it to be elven. The pages were made from a papyrus type of sheet, yet the letters were all made into strange symbols and scratches. Lance rubbed his sleek chin as he tried to imagine how anyone made any sense of the arcane writing. He knew some mages cast encryption spells on their books, but he wasn't sure if this one was encrypted or not. The pages seemed to be normal, not enchanted, yet he couldn't make hide-nor-hair of the writing. If they were enchanted Lance could relax his vision, and if the item he was looking at had any magical dweamors about it, he could slowly begin to see the weave. But as he stared at the Necromidus, he saw nothing save for the twisted symbols of the arcane instructions. Lance thumbed through the pages looking for some pictures or sketches that might shed some light on how to begin the incantations. Toward the end of the first book, Lance saw some sketches of hand movements, but he didn't dare try them, not knowing the correct invocations. He had heard many horror stories depicting wizards and such, trying to cast spells without having all of the components, and the story always ended in disaster. Lance strained his eyes on the ancient script of the Necromidus, and suddenly the deep symbols and sketches began to swirl in a myriad of directions, forming small codes and meanings. Lance blinked in astonishment and the script returned to the way it was before. He rubbed his eyes and refocused on the page. As he stared at the ancient script it began to swirl again before him. Just as he was about to make something out of the text, he would blink and the new symbols would be lost to the original nondescript signs. Lance slammed the book closed in frustration. He would be a patient man. His mother had told him many times as a youth to beware the fury of a patient man—that a patient man's vengeance would be untimely, ever burning, and inescapable.

Laying back on the lumpy mattress, Lance opened the leather pouch he had received from the rouge in Bureland. As he had done many times throughout his journey, he tried to decipher some of the text. Yet again, Lance only became more frustrated. He shoved the hard-covered manuals and the text back into his pack, plopped down from his bunk and looked back at Jude who was sound asleep. It was in the middle of the afternoon, so Lance decided to take a walk around the farm. The room was dark and congested anyway and he desired more of a sociable setting.

The door to the small servants' quarters groaned as Lance pushed it open. The bright sun of the afternoon shined down from behind thick white billowing clouds. Glancing around the farm, Lance saw few workers moving about. He walked through the farm on a northern dirt trail and approached a heavy man wearing a thick leather apron. He was covered in soot and wore heavy leather gloves that were stained and burned in many places. In one hand was a pair of sturdy metal tongs that were grasping a red hot horseshoe and the other hand grasped a scarred hammer. The man placed the horseshoe on a durable metal anvil that was about three feet tall. The anvil was so large that Lance wondered how it was ever moved from where it was created. He doubted even Jude could budge it, let alone lift it.

The man ignored Lance and began to pound the shoe with his hammer over and over again, shaping the red hot shoe. The ringing was intense, but Lance ignored the shrill sound and walked up to the burly smith. He was middle aged and was showing signs of balding. He was somewhat plump, but still looked quite capable of doing his job. As Lance neared, the man stopped hammering, looked at the horseshoe he had just created, and tossed it into a bucket of water that was sitting next to the anvil. The horseshoe sizzled for a moment, then became silent in the bottom of the wooden pail.

The man looked up at Lance and wiped the sweat and grime from his brow. "Eh, what'cha want from me? Make it quick, I have work to do," the large man said through a yellow-toothed grin.

Lance stroked his chin as he gestured around the farm. "Where did everybody go?"

The smith used the tongs and reached into the water and grabbed the cooled horseshoe, studying it as he spoke. "They went to work. The field hands are in the fields and the others are in Master Hentridge's house preparing supper," the smith said as he quickly turned and walked back to the small shack and closed the door. He could hear the ring of metal on metal as the smith pounded another shoe.

Lance turned and walked toward the large barn at the northern part of the farm. The barn was as large as it was old, and it was the largest barn Lance had ever seen. Its wood was aged and somewhat warped. There was a large door about ten feet off of the ground, revealing an expansive hayloft that was almost empty, save for a few rouge bails that were tossed about. Lance could see many horses through the open foyer in the bottom floor of the barn. The two huge foyer doors were gaping wide open, exposing the vast stables inside. Lance walked up to the open doors and peered within. He could see a young boy, maybe thirteen years old, that was tending to the animals within. The boy smiled when his eyes met Lance, and he hastily closed the stall in which he was working and trotted over.

Lance wasn't a large man by any standards but he towered over the boy.

Lance smiled and extended his hand for the boy to shake. "My name is Lance, good sir."

The boy's face reddened at being called sir. He shyly shifted in the dirt floor of the stall and reluctantly took Lance's hand and shook it. "Hi, my name is Korrin, I'm the stable master."

"Good afternoon, Korrin. How are you today?" Lance asked even though he thought his smile scared the boy. Korrin was generally timid, and was frequently troubled by things of little or no consequence.

Lance realized that the boy was apprehensive and broke the uneasy silence. "I hear you are doing a fine job as stable master," Lance said, hoping that his compliment would smooth things over with the boy.

Korrin turned from Lance and gestured to the stables. "Over thirty head of horses, well, thirty-two counting your pair, and I am in charge of them all," Korrin stated proudly.

Lance smiled at the stable boy's newfound bravery. He guessed the boy hadn't reached his thirteenth season of life, but that if the boy did indeed run the stables, by the look of things, he was doing quite a fair job. The stables were large and encompassed the entire ground floor. It even looked as if they could easily house another ten horses without difficulty. The stalls were made of solid wooden bulwark that had large bars at the top to allow feeding. The feed and hay were neatly stacked in bins near the far end of the barn and the tack and saddles were oiled and in good order.

"So what is it I can help you with?" Korrin asked.

Lance fished around in his pockets for a moment, thumbing a gold coin over and over in his nimble fingers. "Well, Master Korrin. My friend and I had two horses brought in here. I was hoping to exchange them for some better ones," Lance said as he pulled out the gold coin and allowed it to dance across the boy's gleaming eyes. The boy followed the coin wherever Lance moved it.

"This coin could be yours, Master Korrin . . ." Lance said, leaving the rest completely up to the boy's imagination. Lance could see the dreams of wealth gleaming from the boy's face as he hungered for the coin. But just as he was reeling him in, the boy stopped, turned, and began to walk toward the feed bins, stealing an occasional glance to the stalls. In truth, this was a grand farm, yet the need for so many horses weighed on Lance's mind. He had counted maybe a two score of oxen, which was more than adequate to run this enormous farm. Yet Lance struggled to find the need for so many horses. He was no businessman, yet Lance guessed the cost of feeding and housing so many horses would be high, very high.

Lance stepped around the stable boy to one of the stalls. The wood was too thick to hold merely plow horses. The animal inside was surely no normal plow horse. Lance could see the animal's corded muscles rippling under thin hide. The horse was large, even if it was a war horse. It had patches of missing hair near its mouth and the side of its nose and Lance recognized these scars were not customary to plow horses. Plow horses were reined from the side of their heads, pulling away from their muzzle, not across them. Lance noted this fact with a visible scrutiny. The thick walls of the stall were wider than normal and the extra wood was another high cost, an additional oddity Lance noted in his head. This farm was a mystery to be solved, Lance thought to himself.

The stable boy saw Lance's scowl as he studied the stalls and decided his new visitor had seen more than enough. "It is time to go, sir. Your horse is not in that stall," the boy chided.

Lance gave him a glare, but said nothing. He was more angry at himself for allowing his own suspicions to be noticed by the stable hand. Lance wrestled with how he might diffuse the boy's idea that he had discovered something. The last thing Lance wanted was to uncover some thieves guild or some kind of hidden outlaw sect. All he wanted to do was get to the library and have the Nalirian text translated. He didn't have time for petty distractions that really didn't concern him.

As soon as Lance had concocted some way of diffusing the stable hand's suspicions, the boy shrugged and motioned Lance down the aisle deeper into the stable. "Your horse is down here sir, I didn't mean no disrespect. I was just worried you might try to hurt the master's warhorse."

Lance beamed. He was right. The animal was no plow horse. Lance wanted to get to Jude and share these revelations with him. He still suspected this was no ordinary farm. The boy motioned him to follow deeper into the barn.

Lance stopped. "Never mind, good sir, if Master Hentridge has

49

a mighty war horse, then I am well assured my beasts are in the finest care," Lance said as he turned to walk away.

The stable boy, still eager to earn the gold coin that was promised, followed closely on Lance's heels. "Good sir, you said I might be able to earn that gold coin," the boy said as he eagerly rubbed his hands together, staring at the pocket where Lance had placed it.

Lance slowed and tossed the boy a silver coin. "If you do not spend this coin and my horses are in good order when I return to claim them, I shall give you that gold penny," Lance said boastfully, patting his pocket.

The stable boy smiled and nodded. "Yes sir, I will, sir," he said as he turned and picked up a pitchfork and began his daily duties. "I'll hold you to our deal. I'll be sure to tend your horses right nice and I'll be expecting my coin when you return," he said dutifully.

Lance smiled and waved as he walked from the stables and hurried toward the barracks. He must tell Jude about what he discovered and see what the mighty swordsman had to offer on this subject.

As Lance walked out of the stable into the early evening sun he inhaled the deep rich smell of the autumn forest that surrounded him. Lance smiled at the excitement of being on his first real journey as a man.

"You pestering my brother, outlander?" came a soft but deadly voice, from behind Lance.

He turned to see a young woman with long straight red hair. She was wearing a dark blue outfit that hugged her hips and her breasts, showing her elegant and beautiful body. She had a sable cloak that hung over her shoulders and flowed in the slight evening breeze. The cloak was bunched at the top by a ruby pendant, and the hood was dangling over her back. Her beautiful green eyes seemed to bore into him.

Lance smiled awkwardly as he fidgeted with his hands. He resigned in placing them behind himself, and clasped his fingers together. "Oh heavens no, I was just asking him to show me the stables," Lance retorted.

The woman's tone softened after seeing Lance offered no threat. She eyed him up and down, measuring his every feature from his thick square jaw to his soft manicured hands. She looked for rings, but found none. She looked for any sign of a weapon protruding from under the folds of his fancy black and silver traveling cloak, but she could not see one. He stood flat-footed to her, and his finely groomed air told who he was. "A filthy mage," she whispered under her breath, too soft for Lance to hear.

Lance felt her scrutinizing eyes falling over him, though he was too taken aback by her beauty to notice her comment. He held his gaze transfixed on her visage as if he were entrapped in the bowels of some kind of a spell.

The woman noticed his blatant staring and after a few moments she realized that he was maybe a full four years younger than she. It was unlikely that he was a mage. She had come across a few mages in her day—few that had any talent or were older than she. Yet this boy had all the markings of a mage, even down to his flat-foot stance that would spell certain doom for someone trying to yield a blade. Perplexed, she offered her name.

"I am Tamra, who might you be?" she asked, relaxing somewhat but keeping her muscles tight, ready to spring to her defense if needed.

Lance smiled eagerly and extended his hand. "I am Lance from Bureland, traveler to Central City. I am pleased to meet you," Lance said. He kept his deep green eyes fixed on hers.

Tamra was mystified. Rarely had she met a man that was disciplined enough to keep his eyes where they belonged, though in truth she enjoyed his handsome visage. *A pity*, she thought to herself. He was but a boy, and the dogs of Central City would surely mark him for easy prey. "What takes you to Central City, boy?" Tamra asked condescendingly.

The insult bounced away unnoticed as did the fact she didn't take his hand in greeting, but the mention of his trip ripped him back from the bowels of his infatuation. Lance didn't want to be rude to Tamra. In truth he found himself eagerly wanting to impress her in some way, yet he was not at this farm to impress some pretty face. He was on a desperate mission to learn about his past. He didn't fear Tamra would harm him, though he considered himself above her talents. Lance knew he may have been followed, either by the betrayed thief, or by the magistrate itself. He didn't want this beauty to have any knowledge that might bring her harm. "Well my lady, my motives are my own, though I admit they are purely honorable," Lance said, beaming as though he might have impressed her in some minor way.

"So be it, Lance from Bureland," she said as she flashed a wry smile. "But take heed, the dogs of that cursed city will give you many fleas if you dally in your departure," Tamra said, giving him a wave of farewell as she headed toward the main house.

Lance turned and ran to Jude. He smiled the whole way.

I remember my chance meeting with beautiful Tamra. She was a radiant beauty, whose inner light shined more brightly than most. Surely, she underestimated the power that dwelled deep within me. But how could she have known? Even mighty Jude could not fathom the inner strength in which I possessed. Perhaps that is what my giant friend feared. Not my power, but the measure of it. He was unable to discern the power of a wielder in the arcane arts. Poor Jude. Smart as he may have seemed, he was merely a swordsman. He lacked the intelligence and wisdom he needed to truly understand the secrets of magic—but just as a swordsman studies the pommel of an enemy's sword and gazes upon the nicks and scratches that told the tale of countless battles, just as he sees the confident way a sword hangs from the wielder's hip and the measure of stride that a swordsman uses with the constant shuffle of weight to always give the flow of balance, ready to enter combat at a single moment.

A mage displays similar attributes, as does a thief or any with a skilled trace. A true master will learn to appreciate these subtle but powerful tools. I did. Though in truth had it not been for my friends through my journeys as a young mage, death would have long ago claimed my soul. But now, even death himself fears my name.

—Lancalion Levendis Lampara—

Two

Dwarven Blood

The rapidly waning sun fell silently on the large farm. Bright rays of red and orange fell through the autumn trees, giving the bustling farm a celestial glow. Hundreds of small flying insects were illuminated by the evening rays as they danced and floated about, occasionally being eaten by songbirds that were taking breaks in their evening ballads.

Lance rushed to the small bunk house near the long shadow of the stone and burst into the room, pausing to find his friend and their bunk. Lance could only see a few silhouettes of servants and workers as he scanned the room. Some were laying on their racks, others were up playing a game of stones in the waning light of the far window. A few men could be heard snoring, but most were speaking softly or struggling to finish a game of cards before the light vanished completely. As Lance closed the door, many of the workers grumbled angrily at being disturbed. Lance paid them no mind as he rushed to Jude, who had now awakened from the commotion.

Jude sat up, strummed his hands through his hair, and shook his head from side to side as he watched all the eyes of the room glaring at Lance. His friend was skilled at many things, that much be sure, but the amount of wisdom he possessed was lacking, to say the least. Jude was glad he was able to be on this journey for his friend.

Lance rushed to Jude's side. He whispered softly to Jude more to avoid eavesdropping than to keep from disturbing others. "My friend, we must go somewhere and chat. I have discovered a few things I want you to know about. You are skilled in these ways," Lance whispered.

Jude pressed closer to Lance. "Is it dangerous, my friend? We attract much attention to ourselves by speaking in this manner," Jude responded, though he really wanted to lay back down and sleep. He was sure they were safe for the time being in this place. A few of the men even spoke to him and offered a sip from a coveted flask. Though the company was less than pleasant, Jude was more comfortable here than on the trail.

Lance nodded slowly. "Perhaps you are right—in the morning then," Lance said as he crawled into his rack.

*　　*　　*

"My king, my king! We have nearly broken through!" the proud dwarf proclaimed as he ran.

"Steady, me good miner. Ye must piper down," Tharxton said with a soft voice as he clasped the sooty dwarf by the shoulder. "How much farther do we need to tunnel, first miner?"

The dirty dwarf blushed under the thick layer of sweat and soot. The title "first miner" is one of great admiration and respect. "Me guess is just a few dozen yards of soft clay, then we break through the dungeon wall and into the pigs' soft underbelly!" the dwarf whispered excitedly as he rubbed his hands together.

Tharxton smiled and stroked his thick, braided red beard while the miner wiped soot and sweat from his eyes and smeared it on his trousers. The dirty messenger looked eagerly back down the passage and then back toward his king, who was already deep in thought. He bowed low at Tharxton's feet. "My lord . . ." The dwarf swallowed hard in great anticipation. ". . . shall I fetch the watch and give the word to assemble the army?"

Tharxton nodded slowly. "Aye . . . fetch the watch, my brother dwarf. For on the morrow's night, we shall avenge the wrongs our people have suffered under the greedy hand of Beyklan tyranny. They shall feel the power of my wrath, and then they will fear the day they wronged Clan Stoneheart!" Tharxton said, as he watched the backside of a dirty dwarf running eagerly down the corridor.

Tharxton said a silent prayer for his people. He felt a deep sadness for them. The dwarf king knew many of his kin would die in the battle. He feared the attack on the Torrent Manor would just be the beginning. The Beyklan were a proud people. They would not accept defeat so easily.

The dwarf king moved back toward the entrance of the deep tunnel. He gazed at the giant wooden beams used to support the ceiling and the intricately carved arches that spanned the large rooms at the entrance of the mine. He marveled at his people's wonderful artwork that had been carved into every inch of the polished stone. Tharxton lowered his head in defeat. Even if his people were successful at the battle of the Torrent Manor, they would suffer great losses. Members of Clan Stoneheart were not warriors by nature; they were great artisans and craftsmen. The dwarf king knew they would lose more than their lives in this excursion, though they had few other choices. Tharxton slowly walked from the tunnel and into the west valley. He squinted into the bright afternoon sun and raised his hand to his brow to shade them from the light. He sighed as a scruff old dwarf approached. He recognized the tall dwarf as General Amerix. General Amerix was over four hundred years old and one of the oldest dwarves in Clan Stoneheart. He had seen countless battles, and was a seasoned general and soldier. Tharxton knew of no one that was better in combat. He was cruel, ruthless, and cunning, the perfect warrior. He was almost five feet tall, exceptionally tall for a dwarf, and had seen more battles than Tharxton had seen days. His dull plate-mail armor bore a thousand nicks and scratches, and his shield a thousand more. His great silver-streaked black beard hung to his knees and shook as he walked. All the dwarves jumped to get out of the way of this dwarven giant as he strode confidently toward Tharxton.

" 'Tis a rumor that has reached me ears, that we a'be fightin them human dogs soon," Amerix said with an evil grin.

Tharxton stared deep into his steel blue eyes. How many horrors danced in Amerix's mind? How many battles did it take to turn a once good dwarf into a cold killer like Amerix? "Aye, it's true," Tharxton replied solemnly. "We will march at the morrow's dusk. It will be a bloody affair and many a dwarf will die."

Amerix smiled and ignored Tharxton's fears. "Aye, but many more humans will bleed the ground red with their stinking blood!" Amerix proclaimed proudly as he pounded his chest with his fist.

Tharxton felt himself getting angry at the general's callousness. "Are you so eager to spill our kin's blood, general? If you need another nightmare to have, I can send you alone against the humans!" Tharxton stated flatly as his face began to redden.

Amerix, sensing the king's increasing anger, spoke to match his tone. "Aye, you could do that, my king. And 'twould be a grand pleasure to be alone, spilling our enemies' blood, than to be standing next to me own kin that was more suited for kitchen duty of the women folk than glories in battle!" Amerix retorted with an evil grin as he looked at Tharxton's hand that now grasped the pommel of his war hammer. Amerix longed for a battle with the young king. He knew that most of the men were loyal to him, and the ones who were not were at least loyal to their clan.

Tharxton realized he was gripping the weapon and calmed himself. A small crowd was forming around the two dwarves, and Tharxton needed to end this quickly. "You may have seen many a battle, general, but I am king. If I deem kitchen duty is to be had by simpleton or *general*, it will come to pass," Tharxton growled quietly with his teeth clenched.

Amerix leaned forward to whisper in the king's ear. " 'Tis true, you are king, and I am general. But at anytime you wish it, you may draw your hammer and we shall see who remains in what authority."

There was eerie silence as both men stood still with their eyes locked in a deadly gaze. Amerix's steel blue eyes bore into Tharxton's dark brown ones. Neither dwarf so much as blinked for many minutes.

Finally Tharxton broke the silence, but not his stare. "General, your men await. Are you going to continue this childish game or are you going to prepare the war you lust so much for?"

Amerix remained silent for a moment. He desperately wanted to put this boy king in his place, but he had many things to accomplish before he set out with his men. "Aye, you win this round king, but beware. General Amerix Stormhammer is your ally only in war. In politics, he is your bitter enemy," Amerix said as he turned and walked toward the crowd, barking orders.

Tharxton let out a sigh and hung his head. He was deeply saddened by Amerix, but a wry smile crept upon his face when he thought of the men of Torrent Manor when they faced such a foe.

Amerix stormed off from the confrontation. Intense anger ripped through his old muscles. He forced his way into the crowd and began to shout out commands at the dwarves to prepare for the upcoming battle. They all raised their arms high and shouted out in cheers when they were told they would be going to war. While Amerix relished the shouts to the upcoming battle, Tharxton hung his head in sadness at the sound of the cheers. How he hated to spill the blood of any race, let alone spilling the blood from a foe as powerful as Beykla.

"Why does our king hang his head?" asked a young dwarf standing next to general Amerix. "We are about to have our greatest victory!"

Amerix was silent for a moment, then turned toward the dwarf. His stern visage held a disapproving gaze. "A crown is a heavy mantle indeed. If ye wore it, me doubts you would hold your head as high for any period of time," Amerix said, roughly poking the much younger and smaller dwarf in the chest. The young dwarf didn't miss the opportunity to hurry off and aid in the battle preparations. A disapproving look from Amerix was more than required to send any dwarf running, let alone a painful poke in the chest. Amerix glanced out of the corner of his eye.

Everywhere he looked he could see dwarven soldiers, maybe six thousand in all, readying weapons in the valley before the great mine. Sounds of song and praise to Leska, the earth mother goddess, echoed throughout the valley. The morrow would be a great day, a great day indeed.

For the rest of the evening Amerix prepared his men for the approaching battle. Tharxton had marched them several miles down the newly dug shaft toward the dungeons of the Torrent Manor and they camped a few miles from the entry site. Tharxton and the others were nervous about the morrow's eve, but Amerix relished it. It had been over fifty years since his last major battle. Approaching the end of his life, the grizzled old general feared he might die withered in a bed, rather than on the field of battle. Now, with the upcoming conflict, he had a chance to die like a true warrior.

Amerix laid out his sleeping roll and went into the rituals of his god. He didn't worship Leska, the earth mother goddess. He followed Durion, the god of the mountain. When Amerix came into Clan Stoneheart he was forced by Leska to take an oath, though secretly he continued to worship the god of his old clan, Clan Stormhammer. Clan Stormhammer worshipped the mountain god because he was warlike, just like his kin. After the attack from an army of dark dwarves and a white dragon, Amerix joined Tharxton's clan.

The old general cleaned and oiled his ancient plate armor and sharpened his wicked battle axe. When he finished caring for his equipment, he lay flat on his back, closing his old weary eyes. He dreamed of a thousand screams from the humans as they fled the cut of his deadly blade.

Amerix was awakened by his aide. The young dwarf became enamored by Amerix's tales of battle and by the power of his god, Durion. Amerix trusted his aide and a few hundred other dwarfs with his life. Though he served under Tharxton, Amerix longed for the day to take the crown, either by force or political ascension, though he preferred by force.

The old general rose slowly and glanced down at his muscular, scarred arms. There were scars on top of scars, yet somehow the resilient dwarf had managed to survive each one. He rubbed his thick, callused hands over his old muscles. They were once strong and harder than steel. Now they weakly hung from his bones. He was still stronger than most of the clan, but two hundred years ago there wasn't a dwarf around that could beat him in any feat of strength. He was the largest dwarf in clan history, and arguably the strongest anyone had ever seen. He was a legend among his people, and was honored more than the king himself. The dwarves followed Tharxton's orders because he was king. They followed Amerix's orders because he was a hero to them.

Amerix rubbed the sleep from his eyes and sat up. "Watch," Amerix called out quietly.

"Yes, general," came a gruff voice from the outside of his tent.

"Watch, ye will stay behind with King Tharxton. He won't be marching with us. Meself and most of our brethren will set out and attack the Torrent at dusk. The king, in his distaste for battle, will remain behind and arrive after we have secured victory and his presence at the Manor will be a safe one," Amerix said as he stood up and began to remove his sleeping robe.

The watch stood in the doorway, shocked at what Amerix had told him. "Our king won't be joining us in battle?" asked the stunned dwarf, his jaw hanging low in disbelief.

"Aye, 'tis true, watch. But I value ye as a faithful aide, or I would not have told ye our king's true motives. 'Tis better this way, watch. Our king is wise to leave the fighting to the true warriors. He doesn't have the stomach for it."

The watch fumbled with his hammer. "General, I have seen King Tharxton fight. He is second to no dwarf, save but yourself," the watch said, upset and nervous at this new development.

Amerix didn't miss a stride. "Aye, I agree the king's battle prowess rivals even me own honed blade, but the king hasn't just ordered us to defeat Torrent Manor. He has ordered us to slaughter all of its inhabitants."

The watch gasped and grabbed at his chest in horror as he slumped back away from Amerix. "Even the human women folk?" the watch stuttered as he asked the question he feared the answer to.

"Aye, even them. The king wants to strike fear into the hearts of the Beyklan dogs. He wants the survivors to return to their beloved Torrent Manor and see their families killed, their women raped, and their children slaughtered. Only then will our enemies fear Clan Stoneheart! Tell the men the king said any who lack the courage to do what needs to be done to preserve our own families' safety can stay behind with the women folk! Let the glory be for the brave on this fateful night! Now go, watch. Wake our brothers and spread the word. I'll be marching from the end of the tunnel in thirty minutes. Have them and the miners ready," Amerix said.

The watch stood in disbelief and stared at General Amerix.

"Now!" the general shouted.

The watch turned and scurried into the camp to awaken the dwarven soldiers. Amerix reached for his armor as he had done thousands of times. He ran his stubby fingers over the many nicks and scratches. Would this be his last battle? He doubted it. He was beginning to think the goddess protected him in his battles, for he was never killed. Durion wouldn't protect him, just give him strength. Yet he had been in countless situations where he should have perished, but somehow he always survived. His was a sight to inspire fear, with his thick arms placed on his chest plate. The old general forcefully snapped and strapped the leather supports with a dark grimace. Amerix picked up his mammoth axe and slid it into place over his back. Then he gave a silent blessing to Durion for all the mountain ranges in the world, and slowly placed his great helm over his head. His armor had magnificent dwarven runes from top

60

to bottom and his helm bore hundreds of small dents. It had a miniature row of iron spikes that erupted from the center nose guard and splayed back over his head, and two horns of a ram that spiraled around on each side.

As Amerix stepped from his tent, the cool stagnant air of the mine washed over him. He longed to smell the stale scent of blood rather than the stale air of this cave. The soldiers that were nearby were awestruck at the spectacle of the ancient general fully garbed in his metallic robe of war. Amerix strode purposefully to his men who had gathered at the end of the tunnel. His large battle-scarred shield swayed as he walked.

Amerix reached back and drew his giant axe, raising it high into the air. "Let us show them Beyklan dogs how a true arm fights a war!" Amerix proclaimed.

Silent cheers erupted from the men as they jabbed armored fists toward the cavern ceiling.

Amerix led his army down the passage toward the end of the mine, where the miners were hard at work burrowing deeper toward the dungeons of the Torrent Manor. The passage they had carved was about thirty-five feet long and about six feet high. The ceiling was rough and had a few small wooden timbers. Amerix noticed the passage had been rigged to collapse. He ignored the fact. It was a strategy for many dwarven clans to collapse their tunnels on their withdraw, sometimes to bury opponents, other times to seal off any way to follow as they withdrew.

Amerix looked behind at the wave of dwarven soldiers marching with him. His grim visage cracked an evil smirk. There were probably a little over five thousand soldiers that had gathered to follow him into battle. He imagined King Tharxton awakening to find he only had about eight or nine hundred soldiers in his once six-thousand-man army. Another smile, much larger than before, crossed his face while he marched on a few minutes longer, then he gave the order for the men to begin the drums of war. The dwarves eagerly complied and began to pound their swords, hammers, axes, and any weapon they had, against their shields, causing a thunderous booming that echoed down the corridor and rattled small rocks and debris.

*   *   *

"What was that?" the prisoner asked the guard.

The sentry clad in red stained leather armor rose to his feet from his rickety wooden chair. "You mean that vibrating from the floor?" the guard asked back.

The prisoner shrugged his dirty shoulders and slumped back against the cold stone wall. His cell was plain, except for his wooden dish where food and water were commonly mixed together in some strange soupy concoction. The prisoner nervously glanced around the dungeon. The bare cells were a twenty-foot square. The stone ceiling was over ten feet high, and large wooden rafters loomed in the darkness. There were probably a hundred prisoners in the cells for some reason or another. Most were underfed and starving and all but one were male. The prisoner didn't know the female's name, or anything other than that she was brought in last night. The guards shackled her to a large iron ring that was mounted to an iron plate on the floor. He wondered how she might reach her food bowl since she was shackled to the far end of the room. The guards had been rough with her, but he didn't think she had been raped or anything. He guessed she was a thief or something like that. He waved at her last night after she was brought in, but she ignored him. He didn't mind. He was used to getting such receptions from the guards and new prisoners alike.

The sentry in the red leather armor walked over near the far wall and bent low to the ground. He pushed his ear as close to the cold stone floor as he could.

"What do you hear?" asked one prisoner as he pressed his dirty face into the crease of two iron bars.

The guard ignored him and raised to his knees. He reached over for a food plate, dumped out the food, much to the prisoner's complaints, and placed the empty dish on the floor. He opened his water skin and poured some water into the platter. The guard and a few prisoners watched as the water in the plate rippled with steady vibrations.

"What is that all about?" called one prisoner.

The guard ignored him and hurried down the hundred-foot corridor to the stone stairs at the far end of the dungeon. He fumbled with his keys in urgency at the large iron door. The sentry's hands trembled as he hastily turned the key. Straining, he managed to slowly open the heavy door and scooted to the other side, closing the exit behind him. The rumble of the thick iron door echoed down the hollow dungeon corridors as it boomed shut.

The prisoners began to talk amongst themselves nervously. The vibrations were now an audible sound and came from behind the far corridor wall. It sounded as if someone, or something, was pounding or scraping the wall from the other side. Their eyes trained on the wall as a tiny hole formed about four feet from the ground. A small amount of rock and debris fell from the hole and made a tiny pile of rocks and dust at the base of the wall. The prisoners were so transfixed on the hole that they didn't notice the lone female prisoner pull a tiny piece of metal from her mouth. She took her finger and placed her long brown hair behind her ear as she diligently worked the lock. She labored meticulously for over a minute while the other prisoners stared at the wall. Turning and twisting, she worked the small, thin metal rod into the heavy lock that bore her shackles to the floor. Within moments, the lock made a quiet click and fell to the floor with a loud clang. The other prisoners looked back over to where the woman had been but they saw only darkness and the rusted chain that once held her in place. One prisoner began to protest and point out that the woman was missing, but the guards burst into the room from the staircase before he could speak. The four guards, wearing bright red and gold leather armor, entered the room, followed by a man that wore polished brass-colored banded mail. His red, silk, flowing cape trailed softly behind him as he strode purposefully down the hall. His heavy boots thudded as he marched down the corridor past the cells toward the far wall, oblivious to the empty cell that once held the woman. Every prisoner hurried to the far end of their cells. Many a prisoner had been stabbed or beaten because he got too close to the Duke's son as he patrolled the dungeon.

"It was here, my lord . . ." the guard protested, pointing to the base of the wall at the end of the hall. "I heard it plain as day, some kind of thumping or something like that," the guard stated nervously.

The Duke's son looked down at the base of the wall and stuck his finger into the tiny pile of rock dust that had gathered there. He trailed up the wall and found the small hole there. He turned to the guards and wiped the dust from his hands. "It seems something has been burrowing behind this wall, probably for some time now. It shows how well you observe your surroundings."

The guard stepped back and looked at the wall as he spoke. "But my lord . . ." he protested. "You could feel it from this side of the wall. It sounded like a thumping sound."

The Duke's son removed his polished helm and held it in his left hand. He wiped his long blonde hair from his face and placed his ear to the side of the wall just above the hole. "I don't hear anything at . . ." A hollow thud from the other side of the wall interrupted the Duke's son. He stopped speaking, though his mouth stayed wide open and his lower jaw and lip began to quiver. His eyes were wide in shock and a tiny gasp of air escaped his mouth. To the other sentries' horror, a small trickle of blood began to flow from under his chin and dripped onto the stone floor. Then came a barrage of dwarven voices from the other side of the wall. The wall trembled and shook, and then it collapsed!

*   *   *

Amerix stepped to the wall and peered through the tiny hole they had made. He could see a stone corridor that was a hundred feet long. It wasn't too wide, but large enough for the dwarves to march down, three abreast. They needed to charge through quickly though, in case the humans tried to barricade them in the dungeons. It would be a bloody affair when they fought their way out of the dark stone basement.

Amerix studied the many cells walled off with solid iron bars. In the rooms were mostly underfed and dirty men. A horrid odor wafted from the hole, making the old general scrunch his large nose in disgust. Amerix ignored the putrid smell while he gazed into the room with his miners still standing nearby. Amerix ran his fingers across the thin remaining wall. His miners had done an excellent job fragmenting it down to a mere inch in thickness. His troops drumming their weapons on their shields had caused enough sound and vibrations that the scraping was difficult to hear.

Movement on the other side of the barricade caught Amerix's eye. He watched in curiosity as four men walked hurriedly down the hall in confident strides. The lead man wore a Beyklan royal guard uniform, complete with a helm and flowing silk cape.

The four approached the hole but did nothing else. He could hear them speaking, but Amerix didn't understand the human tongue. The old general watched the armored figure, who he assumed to be some kind of a leader, bend down and look at something at the base of the wall, then remove his helm and place his ear against the partition, then speak a little more. Amerix debated on fetching an interpreter, but he decided to speak his language. It was a mutual kind of language with all races, the language of war. Amerix paused and studied the height of the man. He motioned for one of the miners to give him a pickax. Amerix rubbed some dirt into his hands for grip, took the sharp tool, and steadied it in his massive hands. With a mighty swing he drove the pickax into and through the thin stone wall. He felt the pickax pierce the stone and lodge into something much softer. Amerix watched through the tiny hole in the wall as the armored man quivered in the troughs of death. Smiling a sadistic smile, Amerix ordered his men to charge the wall. Hundreds of dwarven soldiers, led by Amerix himself, rammed through with their shields outstretched. The thin stone collapsed under the force of the wave of dwarven might. Dust and debris fell for a moment, clouding the air of the dungeon. Amerix burst through the dust to see four humans in red leather armor standing wide-eyed in disbelief. Amerix took advantage of their surprise and hurled the pickax with so much force that when it struck the first man, the tool embedded itself all the way to the wooden shaft, lifting the man from his feet. Before the first man landed on the stone floor, Amerix drew his axe from his belt, and in a sweeping motion, cut into the second man. The guard cried out in disbelief as he tried to keep his entrails from spilling out.

As the other two guards turned to flee, the first two were finished off by the merciless swarm of dwarven demons. Amerix sliced at the rear of the closest fleeing man. His axe tore a deep gouge into the back of the guard's leg and the force of the blow nearly tore it off. He toppled to the floor, grabbed at his wounded leg and screamed, but his screams were cut short as the dwarves behind Amerix's charge finished him. The last guard managed to reach the heavy door. He fumbled with the latch and pulled on the iron ring. The door creaked in protest and the iron hinges squeaked from the door's weight. Amerix took another step and hurled his axe down the corridor at the fleeing human sentry. The axe tumbled end-over-end through the air with great precision. A sickening cracking sound was heard as the axe slammed home into the man's back. It hit his spine just above his rump. He crumpled to the floor and began to drag his useless legs up the stairs. Amerix ran to him, ripped his axe from the dying man's back. As the old grizzled general started up the dark stone stairs, the hollow thud from the man's skull being crushed brought another sick smile onto his demented face.

Amerix and his men burst from the dungeon into the small room beyond the stairs. Its walls were made of wood and it had a few inexpensive tapestries hanging from them. Amerix kicked over the trivial wooden table, spilling the drinks and the leg of mutton that were on it, and barred the door. He turned and faced his men who were able to squeeze into the small room.

"Okay me men, now the fightin' begins!" Amerix bellowed. "First wave will head for the portcullis. I want its controls smashed and it down. Second wave I want to pour into battlements and take down their cursed arches. The remaining troops will focus on the survivors that will be in the south quarter, shacking up in the main building structures. Cut every living human down. I want the horror of today's battle to forever ring in the hearts of these human scum. Let the vultures feast today me men, for today is the day of Stoneheart, the day of our liberation!" Amerix shouted as he turned and unbarred the door. He waited for a few minutes for the word to pass down the corridor to the leaders still down below. Sweat began to drip from his face and run into his silver-streaked beard. He wiped it away as his eagle-like eyes prepared for battle.

*   *   *

The evening sun had set an hour ago and darkness had completely fallen on the Torrent Manor. Dark silhouettes patrolled around the edges of the battlements and around the small pyres mounted on wooden poles to light up the dark walkways of the keep. Most of the local farmers and merchants had closed their shops up for the night and had either left the keep or had gone back to their residence among the heavy stone towers and buildings that littered the interior. Many families of soldiers resided in the keep, as did unlucky peasants or drunkards, though they spent more time in

66

the dungeons than they did roaming the fairways. Atop the west battlement that overlooked the west road into the Torrent Manor were the night officer and several watches. Security had been increased after talks with the dwarven clan of the Pyberian Mountains had broken down into both sides threatening war. Though it was unlikely that the dwarves had the resources to create siege engines, or feed and arm an army to march against the sturdy walls of the Torrent Manor, the king had ordered a second detachment of soldiers to remain within the walls and had sent a hundred tons of grain and several scores of cattle.

"Sir, the watch reports that he heard some kind of commotion from the magistrate's office."

The large man looked out across the vast forest from atop battlement one, out to the western night sky, with his hands firmly grasped behind his back as he enjoyed the cool night breeze. "Never mind the sounds, watch. You know, as well as I, how the Duke's son enjoys the interrogation of the criminals. I'm sure he is having a time with that farm girl who claimed he raped her," the watch commander said, shaking his head incredulously. "I mean the absurdity of someone of his stature being with a farm girl, and then raping her no less. She probably threw herself at him, and he rejected her, so she tried to get even," the watch commander stated flatly. "Besides the whooping and hollering were probably the male prisoners showing her what a rape really is."

The watch glanced back nervously toward the magistrate's house, then toward the west. He was afraid to tell the watch commander there had been reports of dwarven voices coming from inside. He realized how absurd it would be—there was no way dwarves could have gotten in the keep unnoticed. The watch knew dwarves were not good thieves or assassins. The only thing dwarves were known for were making carvings, weapons, armor, and mining. He thought about mining for a moment. "Sir, there were reports of dwarven voices coming from the magistrate's office," the watch said as he looked at the ground and shuffled his feet. "I . . ."

He was cut off by the watch commander. "Dwarven voices? Come now, our concern was duly noted. No one will claim you did not report what you were told was heard. But how do you suppose they got inside of our keep? Hmmm? By tunneling, perhaps?" the watch commander asked condescendingly. "I tell you this, no dwarves are going to tunnel some three hundred miles underground to attack a keep with an army inside that could easily destroy them. I know you have heard rumors that the dwarven king threatened war, but he has no backbone. He is a child in dwarven eyes, and his council fears us militantly. They would never be so bold as to attack. And if the fools did, we would cut them down like the short bearded dogs they are. Our scouts have made no reports of dwarven activity within a hundred miles of here. And if a dwarven army did march, we would crush them when they arrived. This keep's walls are impenetrable from the outside," the watch commander said, gesturing around the courtyard below them.

Suddenly an alarm was sounded from within the keep. The watch commander and the sentries turned to see dwarves beginning to pour out of the magistrate's office into the courtyard toward his battlement and portcullis. The watch commander, fearing they were trying to link up with an outside force that had eluded his scouts, made a fatal error.

"Drop the portcullis!" he shouted.

The men operating the hefty metal-barred door took the heavy wooden sledge hammers and pounded the large curved hooks that held the brake. The portcullis lurched and fell with tremendous force, imbedding itself deep into the ground. Dust and rock shot up in a cloud from the force of the gate's fall. The watch commander ordered half the archers to watch west for the main force, and the other half to cut down the dozens of short stocky shadows that were flooding the courtyard. He watched in disbelief as hundreds of dwarves continued to pour from the magistrate's office and stormed the inner portcullis housing area. He smiled, for the weight of the portcullis's fall would make the gate impossible to be mechanically raised without being dug out. Digging it out would take hours and they would have crushed the tiny dwarven army that was within, and then dealt with the outside army that had somehow managed to elude his scouts. Then to his dismay, the dwarves started hammering and destroying the gears and cogs of the gate, even while archers rained arrow after arrow down on their heads.

The watch commander stared in horror. There were almost five hundred dwarves in the courtyard, and more continued to churn out of the tiny office. He realized in that moment this wasn't a force to link up with an outside army. This was the army. The dwarves did the unthinkable, they tunneled under three hundred miles of earth and stone. The watch commander staggered back against the cold stone rail of his perch, watching in disbelief as almost a thousand dwarves were now battling soldiers in the courtyard, and more still charged out. His heart sank, for he knew the Torrent would soon be lost.

*   *   *

"Cut down the dogs!" Amerix shouted as he charged into the dark grassy courtyard just outside of the magistrate's office. The dwarves' silhouettes in the flickering torchlight betrayed them as they charged through a storm of arrows. Amerix held his scarred and nicked shield high as arrow after arrow struck it. "Extinguish every torch yer eyes see!" he shouted as he led a charge to the battlement stairs with about thirty of his kin following him. The old general rushed by the bodies of the portcullis's guard that had stood against them. He hacked off one of the bodies' feet as he passed. Many of his men did likewise, chopping the dead into unrecognizable masses of flesh.

Amerix reached the large oaken door that led to the spiral staircase to the upper levels of the battlements and kept his shield above his head as arrows zipped past. He shouted out a roar to Durion and ducked further under his shield to protect him from the many arrows that flew down. His men also raised their shields as they peered around at the other wave that was now entering the north battlement. While Amerix furiously chopped down the door that led to the battlement stairs, dwarven screams and curses came from the north wall as dwarves burst back out the door they had just rushed in. Their armor was covered in a steaming, shiny black substance, and they clutched at their faces as they tried to rip their armor from their bodies. Some rolled around on the ground kicking and screaming. As they did, arrows embedded into their necks and chests. Soon the entire wave of thirty that stormed the battlement lay dead and burned.

"General, they will pour scalding oil down on us!" one of the dwarves shouted as he braved the downpour of arrows.

Amerix kicked in the remaining pieces of the chopped door and plunged in. "Aye, it'll sting, but me blade hungers for blood!" Amerix said as the dwarves hesitated but followed their general into the darkness of the stairs.

Amerix charged up the spiraling stone stairs. His shield was outstretched in front of him to deflect any attacks as he rushed up. As he rounded the top, Amerix witnessed six humans at the base of the stairs standing near a bubbling iron pot of oil. They pulled down on the iron rods and dumped five hundred gallons of boiling oil down toward Amerix and his brethren. The general put his shield up and charged through, ignoring the searing pain that ripped through his legs and neck. He could hear the screams of his kin behind him as they tried to charge ahead as he did. Scalding sticky oil dripped form his helm and his armor. Steam erupted from the patches of the oil that was on the ground, forming a swirling wall of mist that he stepped through. Despite his pain, he smiled a sinister smile. The six men had picked up crossbows and had them cocked and pointed at him. Amerix fearlessly charged into the room as the humans let the bolts fly. Amerix winced in pain as an arrow pierced his shield and stuck into his left forearm. Another ripped through his right leg plating and stuck a few inches above his knee, yet the old general charged ahead and brought his axe down in a mighty swing. The force of the blow knocked the man from his feet. He gasped in horror as he took his final breath of life, staring wide-eyed at the gaping wound that had once been his chest. The remaining men drew swords and attacked the dwarven demon. Amerix ducked a slice from the right as his shield caught one from the left. He swung his axe, hitting the next man in the head, cleanly cutting the top half of his skull off. He swung his shield in a backhand motion, knocking one man to the ground as he followed the swing and stuck his axe through the chest of the other. Blood and gore splattered Amerix as he fought on. One of the dwarves that charged up the passage behind Amerix had crawled to the top. He stared in disbelief and wonder as his general fought with such ferocity he had never seen. The remaining three human soldiers backed away in disbelief at the power the dwarf possessed.

"This is for me homeland!" shouted Amerix as he drove his axe down, shattering the blade of the human warrior, and slicing into his shoulder and neck. The dying man only gurgled in response.

"This is for me wife that died because of your precious sanctions!" Amerix said as he blocked the half-hearted strike with his shield and chopped the man's legs out from under him and brought the head of his axe down on the felled man's skull. The last man backed against the wall, he dropped his sword and went to his knees. He placed his hands in front of him and pleaded to Amerix for mercy. Amerix paused, then swung his axe and deftly cleaved the man's head from his shoulders. The skull rolled near the window of the stone battlement as blood and fluids gushed from the twitching body. Amerix didn't miss a stride as he walked toward the battlement door. He noticed a few of his men survived the scalding oil. They looked on in horror and admiration for their general. Never had they seen such heroism or such wickedness.

"General, what did the human say as he went to his knees?" asked one of the dwarves as they entered the room.

Amerix adjusted his oil-soaked helm, turned, and spoke through clenched teeth. "I know not the words from dogs!" he spat. "But it looked as if he begged to be killed mercifully," Amerix said, turning to pound his mighty axe into the next door that would reveal the archers atop the battlements that rained death down on his brother dwarves. His anger growing with each strike, Amerix tore large pieces of splintered wood from the door. In a matter of moments, the old general kicked the weak door in with his foot. Pieces of wood still clung to bent hinges as Amerix stepped through to the battlements. The cold autumn air felt crisp on Amerix's scaled skin. The old general glanced around the narrow stone battlement, axe ready to disembowel any humans, but there were none. He cautiously walked out onto the battlement railing with his shield up in a defensive posture. The entire north side of the keep was dark. Only a few torches remained lit. Amerix calmed and lowered his shield. Everywhere he looked, he witnessed hundreds of dead humans. He smiled and rubbed his singed, oil-soaked beard. "Summon my sergeants," Amerix stated flatly. "We will regroup and lay waste to the southern buildings."

The other dwarves nodded and departed as Amerix turned and regarded his sergeants.

"You all go round up some mead or some kind of drink. I won't entertain me sergeants without some drink," he said as the dwarves

71

all set off immediately. Amerix leaned back against the rail of the portcullis battlement. Everything was going as planned.

*   *   *

The watch commander witnessed the horror of his men being viciously cut down by the dwarven invaders. He tried to formulate some kind of a plan to stall the onslaught, or to allow the main of his force to flee to the southern part of the keep and develop some kind of a counter strike. The commander moved from the battlement to the walkways around the top of the wall. He watched as his archers shot down many a dwarf, but at least two thousand of the bearded folk had come from the hole in the earth, and still more poured out every second. The watch commander cursed himself for not heeding the warnings of his roving watch. If he managed to survive the battle, he knew he would be arrested and probably hung.

As he moved to stone walkways that would lead him safely down to the southern area that would give shelter, the commander spied the watch that had tried to warn him. "You!" the watch commander shouted as he pointed to the roving watch.

The watch turned and pointed at himself. "Me, sir?" the watch asked sheepishly as he glanced nervously over the rail at the approaching wave of dwarven death.

"Yes, you!" the watch commander shouted as he ran to him. "I want you to gather five men and make a stand at the first level of the battlement. When the dwarves . . ." He paused to help give the watch strength, hoping the dwarves would finish the watch off so it wouldn't be known he could have prevented the loss of the Torrent Manor. The watch commander began again. "If . . ." he stressed, ". . . the dwarves make it up the stairs and through your door, which is unlikely, dump the hot oil down on them as they come up the stairs. None of the bastards will survive. Then secure the door as best as you can, and flee down the battlements to the southern buildings for safety."

"Yes sir!" replied the watch as he and five other men began the task of rigging the cauldron of bubbling oil to fall down the stairs instead of over the side of the wall. The watch commander turned and took the remaining men with him. As he walked out of the bat-

72

tlement, he turned and secured the outer door from the outside by laying a large metal rod across the door's handles.

One of the men gave him a puzzled look. "Sir, won't they be trapped inside?"

The watch commander shrugged as he continued. "Yes, but so will the dwarves," he stated coldly.

The soldier turned his head and gave a final glance back at the doomed men as they ran down toward the southern buildings.

All over the Torrent Manor, flags and commands were given for the men to retreat to the southern quarter. Men, women, and children alike fled as fast as their legs might carry them to safety.

*   *   *

Amerix and his sergeants perched atop the tallest battlement in the Torrent Manor. Their bloodied plate-mail armor gleamed in the moonlit sky. They sat on small wooden barrels and feasted on fine wine, bread, and cheese. Amerix stood up and raised his armored hand, and holding a wooden mug into the air, proclaimed a toast. The other dwarves raised their wooden goblets in cheer as they toasted to victory. The old general watched from the battlement as the final few hundred dwarves came from the tunnel. They were each carrying a large wooden keg, topped with a black saturated cork. He turned back to his sergeants and began his speech. "Greetings me kin!" he began. "As we sit under the night sky of Leska, our enemies scurry like rats to hide from ye blades and hammers. Let us enjoy this moment before victory and know that Leska has blessed this battle. She came to me in a dream last night." Many of the sergeants gasped and leaned forward, not believing what they heard.

Amerix went on. "She came to me and said, 'Great general, I come to ye to bade yer blade to be swift on the morrow's night, for yer enemy will try to crush ye after victory . . .' "

The dwarves all smiled at the mention of the victory they had not totally achieved.

Amerix sipped from his mug, savoring the frothy drink before he continued his speech. ". . . After this fortnight's battle ye must march on to Central City and crush it!"

The dwarves all sat in shock and disbelief. Destroying an un-

73

suspecting keep of a thousand or so men was one thing, but attacking a large human city was another.

Yet, Amerix ignored their disbelieving looks and continued. "She said I will bless the great Amerix Stormhammer, for ye will lose not more than two hundred brethren, and in yer final siege, ye will lose none. Yer axe will be sharper than a demon's dagger, and no enemy will be able to kill ye," Amerix said, pointing at the oil that still clung to his armor and the crossbow bolt that was still jutting from his right knee.

"These are testaments to Leska's power!" he shouted. "I have suffered many wounds but I do not feel pain. The oil should have cooked me in me armor, but I pressed on, just as Leska ordained! Even as we speak, we are pouring thousands of gallons of oil around the southern buildings. We will burn the nasty humans in the fire of our vengeance!" Amerix shouted.

The dwarves glanced around. They had lost only a little more than a hundred brethren in the battle. Most were slain storming the battlements.

Another dwarf spoke up. He was badly burned and covered in bandages. " 'Tis true, me brothers! I stormed the stairs behind Amerix. He went face first into the burning oil! He ran through it, unhurt. The humans cried out in terror at the sight of him! They all attacked him at once, but in an instant he had killed them all! His axe even cut through their swords as if it was possessed by the gods themselves!"

Amerix smiled and seized the moment. "Aye me brethren, let us march to Central City. Leska has promised me that all who kill at least a score of humans in that battle will be given the gift of immortality!"

The sergeants were enthralled by the story and the personal accounts. They glanced around at each other looking for support. Soon, they were all eager to march. Amerix finished the meeting and began down the stairs to oversee the final stage of the battle: the burning.

The old general slowly walked down the oil-covered spiraling stone stairs of the battlement. His burns were beginning to blister, and the arrow protruding from his right knee was beginning to ache as the surge of battle drifted away from his mind, though it was a small price to pay to fulfill the lies he told his brethren. He

74

had lied in battle before. It didn't bother him. Amerix didn't like to deceive his own troops, but he realized that sometimes soldiers needed to believe in something if they didn't believe in themselves.

Amerix stepped into the cool night air. The coppery smell of death crept over him and hung in the heavy night air. He breathed a deep breath and exhaled in pleasure. It had been too long since he last knew battle. Oh how he missed her embrace! The smell of blood, the sting of a fresh wound, the sound of steel ringing on steel in the distance . . . Amerix turned abruptly and faced the south. He squinted, grabbing one of his sergeants by the beard, and pulled him close to his face. "What is going on?!" he screamed as spittle flew from his mouth and splattered on the sergeant's cheek.

The sergeant looked confused and motioned to the south quarter. "There is the human champion guarding the ones that are holed up in the buildings," the dwarven sergeant said calmly. "But no worry general, he has only slain about forty dwarves. We soon will reach two hundred casualties. Then the human dog will be powerless even to our weakest soldier. Leska has ordained it," the sergeant stated proudly.

Amerix shook his head in anger. "Wasn't anything easy?" he mumbled to himself as he placed his battered and dented helm back atop his head. He would have to slay this human champion, before he lost two hundred men. Amerix walked with a confident stride across the courtyard. He could see a large human sitting atop a giant white horse. Amerix hadn't seen a horse so large in all his years. It was almost twenty hands tall, covered in large metal plates that were strapped to head, shoulders and flanks. Amerix remembered mention of such armored horses. He thought it was called barding, though in truth he had difficulty remembering. What he did recall was that humans that adorned their mounts in such armor were well-to-do and almost always someone important. Amerix pushed his way through the dwarven crowd that held the human at bay. As he pushed his way forward he noted a few of the arrow shafts that protruded from many of his dead brethren were different than the ones that the humans used. These arrows were embedded all the way up to the fletching. Not only that, but the fletching was from some kind of green bird. As opposed to the humans' arrows that rarely ever penetrated dwarven armor, these arrows were almost all the way through.

75

Amerix strengthened his resolve and continued to press further. As he reached the front of the crowd, he witnessed the human warrior. He was adorned in full-plate armor from head to foot. He wore a long blue cape as opposed to the red ones the Beyklans so often wore. His armor bore runes like Amerix's but were elven in nature. He wielded a long sword that he had drawn, and it rested across his saddle. The sword was equally as ornate as the human's armor. Amerix studied this man closely. Both of his hands were armored in a gauntlets. His right gauntlet was leather on the inside with plating on the outside, while his other hand was completely housed in metal. His helm was full and complete with only a thin visor for his eyes. Amerix shook his head. Even the human champions were stupid in their choice of protection. They were so afraid of being wounded they often gave themselves severe disadvantages in combat. Getting hurt was some of the glory of war. How was a hero to tell his tale with nothing more than the imaginations of babes to fathom the great battle?

Amerix looked around for the archer. This human bore no signs of a bow or crossbow, and his helm was not suited for firing with any accuracy. Soon the old general saw a small slender woman atop the roof of a small building behind the armored human. Amerix pounded his bloody axe against his dented burnt shield in challenge. The entire dwarven army behind him hoisted their weapons high in the air and let out a mighty dwarven cheer.

*   *   *

Apollisian had rode many weeks to arrive in Torrent Manor from his Church of Justice in Westvon Keep. His squire, Victor DeVulge, and his elven friend, Alexis Overmoon, had arrived in the Torrent Manor over a week ago to investigate the accusations that the manor was in place to unjustly tax the dwarves of the Pyberian Mountains. Apollisian had made little headway after he arrived at the fair-sized keep. He was restricted from most areas of the keep, and locals were instructed not to talk to him. The Duke and his son were less than accommodating, and often forced Apollisian and his friends to camp outside. It was Apollisian's final day at Torrent when the dwarves attacked. Though his suspicions were then solidified, he faced a greater dilemma. The dwarves had for some reason disregarded his attempts to surrender, and marked him as an enemy. Apollisian wasn't aware the Pyberian dwarves were evil, and in fact, he knew their king, Tharxton Stoneheart. What was more unsettling to the paladin was the fact that he didn't see Tharxton anywhere, and the dwarves spoke of an Amerix as their leader. Apollisian was forced to kill two scores of the little folk, and Alexis shot a few that tried to flank him. Now they surrounded him and stood a safe distance away. The paladin sat on his mount and waited for this Amerix to show himself. His sword, "Songsinger," would sound a shrill hum when he fought evil enemies. What disturbed Apollisian was that his sword was yet to sing.

"He will come," the deep voice echoed in Apollisian's head. The paladin nodded in response to the voice of the sword—a voice that only he could hear. Sometimes it was more of a feeling than a voice. He seemed to feel the thought rather than hear it. The strange sword had spoken shortly after it was given to him from the church when he was knighted.

Apollisian helplessly watched the dwarves as they soaked the buildings with oil and placed wooden debris by them. Alexis had shot down any who approached with a flame, but the paladin knew they could not hope to escape or defeat this dwarven army. Instead he hoped Tharxton, or this Amerix, would show themselves. Justice was yet to be served.

Apollisian watched as a gruff dwarf approached. He could see the bearded invader towered over the other dwarves. He was almost five feet tall, with a black beard that was mottled with gray and swayed in the slight breeze of the night. As the dwarf neared, Apollisian could see grievous burns on the dwarf's face and neck, and black oil dripping from his armor in various locations. He had a broken arrow protruding from his shield and another from his right knee that bobbed as he walked. His thick, heavy shield bore a different standard than the other dwarves Apollisian had faced. It was a strange design of half circles and lightning bolts—not the banner of Stoneheart, which was a hammer encircled by a red sun.

Apollisian smiled to himself as his sword began to vibrate and hum. "King Amerix I presume?" called out Apollisian in the dwarven language.

Amerix's jaw hung open in surprise. In his four hundred eighty years of life, he had known only a few humans that could speak his tongue. "General Amerix to ye dog!" he spat. "Me King wouldn't soil his blade with the likes of yer human blood."

Apollisian's horse shifted its weight under the paladin and the stallion's ears flickered eagerly. The young paladin gripped his reins tightly and tensed his muscles to spring into attack at a moment's notice. His loyal war horse sensed the paladin was tense and prepared himself for the rapid commands that precluded a pitched battle.

Amerix continued. "How does a dung heap like yerself learn the likes of me tongue?" Amerix asked.

Apollisian did not respond. He gauged the dwarves' actions behind the gruff old general, trying to figure out how they were following the rogue general—whether they were loyal out of fear, or out of admiration and wonder. The young paladin sensed a little of both.

Amerix gripped his axe tighter and began to prepare for battle. It was obvious to him he would bear many a scar from this encounter. The human champion was but a whelp, but it was obvious he had seen more than his share of skirmishes. No matter. The gruff old dwarf had dispatched foes many times greater than this human boy.

"My name is Apollisian Bargoe of Westvon Keep. I came here to stop the unfair persecution of your people, but war is not the way. Depart general, spare the innocent women and children of this keep, and I shall lobby on you and your king's behalf to put an end to this injustice," Apollisian said with a grim smile.

Amerix said nothing. He just stared at the human for a moment. "You will what, human?" Amerix asked in a lighter tone.

Apollisian's spirit soared. Perhaps this Amerix was wise enough to listen to him. But his hope died quickly.

"Ye do too much talkin, and not enough bleedin!" Amerix said as he swung his axe and cut Apollisian's horse from under him. The heavy blade slammed into the left front leg of the steed and sliced cleanly through the cannon bone, severing the animal's leg. The horse toppled forward, sending Apollisian head first toward the ground. Amerix raised his shield up as two arrows with green fletching slammed into it with such tremendous force that they knocked the old general from his feet. The mortally crippled horse kicked and thrashed in terror while hundreds of dwarves, letting out a mighty battle cry, charged around it toward the buildings with torches raised high. Apollisian rolled from the fall and came up to his feet with Songsinger unsheathed. The finely crafted blade's wail echoed into the cool autumn night.

Amerix stood up slowly and looked at the human champion. The two circled one another, trying to weigh the other's strengths and weaknesses. Amerix wore a grim visage adorned with determination while his long black beard swayed in the night breeze.

Apollisian flexed his fingers that held Songsinger while he listened to the last dying moans from his faithful warhorse. Anger tore through his body, begging for his muscles to cut down this murderous dwarf, yet that wasn't the way of Apollisian. There was more at stake than vengeance for his horse, or the already slain men. He had to think about the still living women and children that were huddled in the keep's southern buildings—the buildings that were now beginning to burn. He had to offer this general one last recourse. Apollisian knew his own life was probably to end in this battle. Even if he did manage to defeat the dwarven nightmare that stood before him, he would not be able to stop the army that Amerix led. He must try to rationalize one final time with this demon dwarf.

"General, you have crushed this keep. It is no more. Its armies are vanquished. All that remain are the innocent. Show your men your true strength, and have mercy on the meek," Apollisian said along with a silent prayer, hoping to reach the rational side of his foe.

Amerix spoke through gritted teeth. "Mercy? What mercy did these scum show me wife? How about me boy? Where were you then, great paladin? Aye, I will show mercy to the human whelps; I'll show 'em all the mercy they showed me loved ones!" Amerix said as he charged in.

*   *   *

Tharxton was awakened by a voice that called into his tent.

"My king, scouts report the sun has set, we are ready to move," the voice said coolly.

"Aye, fetch the miners, we will set out in fifteen minutes,"

Tharxton said as he rose to his feet and tried to rub the sleepiness from his eyes. "I want to be at the end of the passage by midnight."

The dwarf stepped into Tharxton's tent, letting the heavy flap fall closed. He stammered and looked around at the ground uneasily. "Uh . . . my king, why do we need the miners? If you don't mind my asking, sire."

Tharxton stroked his beard as he gathered up his mail and began to don his finely crafted chain shirt. "To break through into the dungeons of Torrent!" Tharxton said angrily. He was groggy from sleep and was becoming aggravated at the guard's questions.

"But sire . . ." the guard stammered, ". . . Amerix departed an hour before sunset. He probably burst through over three hours ago. He said you were leading the second wave to finish off any stragglers that might have fled during battle and returned later."

"What?!" Tharxton screamed. He jumped up and quickly gathered his weapons and armor and placed them on. He burst from his tent into the cool thick air of the mine and glanced around at his army. Maybe a thousand of his brethren remained and they were just awakening. He shouted commands at them and dwarves scrambled up, beginning to put on their weapons and armor. The dwarves were confused, but followed Tharxton's orders.

"My king, why do we make haste?" one dwarf asked as he placed his heavy metal chest plate over his head and slid his thick muscular arms into place. "Surely Amerix hasn't finished the battle yet."

"Attention my kin!" Tharxton bellowed, ignoring the comments and questions of his men. "We have been double-crossed by General Amerix! I believe he will slaughter all of Torrent Manor, not just the soldiers."

The men all gasped and looked around in disbelief. One shouted above the others. "But my king? You ordered that earlier."

Tharxton shook his head in horror and disbelief. "Never have you heard those words from my mouth!" he shouted. "Surely such a cowardly act would bring the Beyklans to make war against us . . ."

The dwarf scratched his head in confusion. "Isn't that what we want?" asked another dwarf.

Tharxton did not bother to answer. He just began marching down the chamber toward the Torrent Manor. The other dwarves finished putting on their heavy weapons and armor and quickly followed the determined march of their king down the dark passage of the tunnel.

*   *   *

"Your life is now forfeit, Amerix," Apollisian growled. "But surrender now, and I shall spare the life of your kin," Apollisian snarled at the dwarf as he circled with his sword outstretched.

Amerix smiled wickedly. "Me life is forfeit?" Amerix chuckled. "I'll tell ye what, boy. I won't bury ye after I kill ye, so the buzzards will eat yer eyes and their droppings will pile on yer chin," Amerix bellowed as he charged in with his axe swinging high.

Apollisian brought up his shield to deflect the lightning-quick strike as the dwarf's razor-sharp axe bit into it. Sparks and chips of metal spewed from the force of the blow and cascaded around the two combatants in a shower of brilliant twilight. After deflecting the dwarf's strike, Apollisian brought his sword low at the head of the dwarf, who ducked and rolled, deflecting the slash with the top of his shield. As he rolled, Amerix pulled his axe from the shield and laid a thin slice across Apollisian's leg. The paladin glanced down at the cut and saw a small trickle of blood beginning to ooze from under his armor.

The two champions squared off and charged again. Amerix dove in with his axe in a whirling motion, his face bent with fury. Apollisian lifted his shield to deflect most of the blade, but felt its wicked edge as it bit into his shield arm. The paladin jabbed forward, over Amerix's shield, and into the dwarf's shoulder. Amerix winced in pain and disbelief as the sleek blade sliced his enchanted armor as if he wore none at all.

The two champions clashed and clashed again, their weapons meeting and nicking the other. Though each of them bore many wounds, none were crippling or fatal. Both warriors were mottled in blood, and Amerix's shoulder screamed in pain. The early wound he suffered was deep, but the mad dwarf drove on, placing Apollisian on the defensive. He wielded his axe with such uncanny precision that with each slash he came closer to striking down the paladin.

Apollisian grunted with each parry of the dwarf's blade as it

81

came ever so close to sending him to meet his god. With mad determination, Apollisian battled back. When Amerix would swing low, he would side step and strike a blow into the dwarf's weak side. Though the dwarf's axe was powerful, Apollisian knew it was not designed to deflect strikes as keenly as his enchanted blade.

The mad dwarf quickly recognized the paladin exploiting his weak side. Both bloody and weary, the dwarf was as close to defeat as he had ever been. He whispered a silent curse to father time. In his youth his strength alone would have cut down this human dog, but his youth had faded long ago. This babe he fought was but a whelp in dwarven years. Yet he fought with uncanny skill and resolve.

Amerix began to feel each and every pound of his axe. Every wound he had suffered screamed at him to lay down and die louder than they ever had. But just as the ancient dwarven general began to surrender to death, he caught himself, just as he had done a thousand times before. If he were to die, it would be after his enemy exhaled his last breath, and not before. Even as Apollisian slammed his streaking blade into the dwarf's axe and shield, he smiled. Apollisian charged with his sword low, forcing Amerix to stumble to his left as he slammed his shield into his face. The bone-crunching blow knocked Amerix to his backside. Without missing a stride, the old general rolled with the jolt and was back to his feet with a hellish fire in his eye. With axe and shield in an offensive posture, Amerix launched a barrage of dizzying attacks. Apollisian gazed at the tantalizing display in amazement. Amerix was bleeding from head to toe, bearing many deep cuts that the paladin had thought would be disabling, yet the dwarf stood before him grinning wickedly and twirling his axe in a myriad of strikes and feints. Apollisian had never faced such an unyielding foe.

The two champions circled and clashed again. The wound in Apollisian's leg was burning, and he was dizzy from the loss of blood, but he could not flee. He stole a glance over his shoulder and saw the southern buildings of the keep were almost all in a blaze. The roar of the fire was beginning to sound over the ringing of steel as heavy smoke hung in the cool night air.

Amerix saw Apollisian glance to the burning buildings. "Ye need not worry bout yer elf friend, me brethren have captured her without her dying, but she will beg to be killed after we haves our way with her."

Apollisian half turned, frantically scanning the rooftops, trying in vain to steal a glimpse of Alexis. All he could see were the wisps of flame lighting the night sky and the horrid black smoke that rose into the darkness.

That was all the distraction Amerix needed. He drove his axe forward toward the paladin's exposed shoulder. Apollisian tried to block the attack, but Amerix's axe struck his sword hand. The weak metal plates of the gauntlet surrendered to the axe's keen edge. Pain ripped through Apollisian's arm, forcing him to drop his sword. He bent over, clutching his severely wounded hand as warm blood streamed from the new wound and formed a steady drip that created a crimson puddle between his legs. Apollisian struggled to keep conscious while Amerix drove on harder, striking with his axe and shield, driving the human back toward the fire. Apollisian deflected each cruel strike with his shield as he frantically tried to flex feeling back into his wounded hand.

Amerix pressed Apollisian back to the double doors in front of a building that was ablaze from the blistering fire. The old general ignored the searing heat from the fire that raged around him while he feinted a low attack at Apollisian's wounded leg. As the paladin moved his shield low, Amerix drove his axe high, striking the paladin in the shoulder. The axe tore through Apollisian's armor and the force of the mighty blow knocked the human warrior through the crumbling, fiery doors of the rapidly burning building. Amerix started to follow the human into the fire, but the heat was too great and Amerix had always harbored a secret fear of fire. He looked behind him to see his men all were backed away from the buildings. The old general moved back from the fire and watched with satisfaction as the women and children of the Torrent Manor screamed in terror and agony as they were burned alive.

Amerix returned to his men while they enjoyed the spectacle of the burning keep. He smiled a wicked grin as he glanced around at the hundreds of slain humans being piled up in awkward and humiliating positions. Amerix glimpsed down at his many wounds that were bleeding the ground red under him, and he felt light-headed and wanted to lie down. His body ached from the battle with the human champion and it screamed out for rest, yet

Amerix forced his tired old bones to take step after step, trudging forward to his men. After a small but difficult march across the courtyard he addressed his sergeants. "We 'ave won the day, but we 'ave learned that Central City has already formed a large militia and sent the murderous dogs out against our homeland," Amerix said weakly. He tried to regain some composure from the battle but his ancient body was taxed beyond limits. The dwarves seemed not to notice and they were eagerly listening to the old general's every word. "We must set out at once for Central City. Gather yer brethren, have them grab whatever provisions they can find and muster outside the city's south wall in thirty minutes."

The dwarves all began to rush away to give the orders to their brethren while grabbing a few provisions themselves.

"Therrig," the old general called out as he weakly leaned on his axe for support. The top of the great weapon was buried in the courtyard grass from Amerix's weight.

A short squat dwarf who was wider than he was tall stepped from the masses. He bore a few minor cuts from the skirmishes with the humans, but if the small wounds bothered the stout dwarf, he showed no signs of it. His hair that was slicked back over his wide head was flaming orange as was his thick braided beard that hung down loosely from his solid chin. He had a deep purple scar on his neck from battling the dark dwarves that invaded his original clan when he was very young. The short boulder of a dwarf was Therrig Alistair Delastan, faithful follower of Amerix Alistair Stormhammer. Therrig didn't follow Amerix because he was a general, he didn't follow the old general because he was a member of his new clan Stoneheart, nor did he follow him because he was one of the last remaining members of his original clan. Therrig followed Amerix because the old general was as ruthless as he was cunning. Amerix had no friends, only enemies and allies that needed to follow his lead, or they might find themselves dying with his enemies. With Therrig, that kind rational was what made him one of Amerix's most devoted followers.

Amerix knew the wicked lawless dwarf held more than a few of his many hatreds for humans. Amerix took a moment to gather his fast waning strength. "Therrig, I want you to take the miners and drop our attack tunnels."

Therrig smiled wide at the notion, exposing thick yellow teeth,

84

while Amerix stared deep into the eyes of the dangerous ally. "Before Tharxton enters them?" Therrig asked.

Amerix nodded angrily while Therrig's shoulders slumped. He began to protest but Amerix cut him off.

"I may not agree with me king, but he is me king and the leader of the Stonehearts," Amerix said as he pointed to Therrig. "And Stormhammers . . ." he said as he pointed to his own chest. ". . . do not remove their kings in such a dishonorable way."

Therrig growled in agreement and hurried off toward the mine, forcing a path between the mass of dwarven soldiers that had began to gather around the pair, interested in what the two were talking about.

Amerix stood up straight and pressed his large hands into the small of his back. He felt a few pops and relief swept over him. He walked a little quicker, and more upright, toward the portcullis.

The old general stood by and watched his dwarves work. They had already enacted a work line and were organizing foodstuffs into various piles. He called out to one of his sergeants.

The eager dwarf rushed over to him. "Yes, me general?" the young dwarf asked.

Amerix turned and pointed to the portcullis. "Wouldn't it be grand if our enemies came to this destroyed keep to see their loved ones all slain, only to fall into a horrid pit trap as they approached the portcullis?" Amerix asked with an evil glimmer in his old blue eyes.

The sergeant nodded eagerly as Amerix continued. "And wouldn't it be even more grand as the ones who survived the pit trap navigated to the other side of the portcullis and hit yet another trap designed exactly the same?"

The sergeant now smiled and shook his head in agreement. "Aye, it would sir."

"Then grab some men and do it! You have twenty-five minutes! Do not fail me," Amerix said as he looked around at his army. It was possibly the greatest army he had ever commanded. He rubbed his long straggly beard and tucked it into his belt. He drew out a dirty blood-soaked cloth and began to wipe the oil and blood from his armor. As he ran his stubby fingers over the intricate runes along the thick plates, he remembered a time long ago when clan Stormhammer was thriving, long before the dark dwarves came from the bowels of the earth and annihilated them. His clan alone would have had a chance if it had not been for the great white dragon. Amerix strained hard to remember that one's name, though he could remember pale white scales and wickedly cold breath easily. He could remember the screams of terror from his brothers as they tried to vanquish the mighty foe, but he could not remember its name. The old general shrugged and dismissed the horrific memory. But every man, woman, and child of Beykla would surely remember the name of Amerix Alistair Stormhammer.

*　　*　　*

Apollisian lay motionless on his back in the center of the floor inside the burning building. He could see many fiery rafters above him that dripped a steady flow of burning embers and ash. He coughed on the smoke that was becoming thicker at every passing moment. Closing his eyes in defeat, the paladin prepared himself for death. He couldn't move either arm and was growing dizzy from the loss of blood. It was the scream that roused him from death's embrace. Apollisian cursed under his breath and forced himself to roll to his side. Though he could feel himself slowly dying, he wasn't dead yet, and many people sounded as if they were trapped inside the fiery tomb. The young paladin screamed as he forced his mutilated arm to his bloody, wounded shoulder. Struggling with every inch he moved, Apollisian managed to inch his numb hand onto the mortal wound. He tried to chant and channel the healing power of his god, but his lungs had filled with blood and the only sounds that passed his lips were sickening gurgles. Apollisian scooted across the floor and wedged his body against the stinging hot stone wall while pieces of fiery debris from the wooden rafters above him fell around.

Apollisian let out another gurgled scream as he forced his tortured body to sit upright. He could feel the blood from his lung clearing and tried the chant again. As the words escaped his bloody lips, he felt magical energy course through his hand and into the wound in his shoulder. The soft blue light reached deep into his chest and began to heal the grievous gash. Apollisian slowed his breathing, closed his eyes, and waited. Soon the wound was closed, but he still bore a deep scar that could easily be torn open if he overexerted himself. The paladin applied a tight bandage to his mangled sword hand and crawled slowly under the smoke. He made his way down the long marbled corridor that was filled with red hot oaken beams that led toward the screams he heard earlier. Huddled in a corner, he found two small boys. They were clinging to each other and choking in the thick smoke while tears streamed down their tiny faces. Apollisian rubbed his eyes and looked at the two again. They looked exactly identical! He had heard of such births, but they were usually feared by people and kept hidden from others. Often the youngest was sometimes slain at birth. But here sat both of them, huddled together in the crumbling burning building.

Apollisian weakly called out to them between coughs. "Come over here boys, but stay low, under the smoke."

The two boys ran under the growing layer of thick heavy smoke to him. They appeared to be almost six years old and were dressed in poor peasant rags that were scorched and burnt. Their long greasy brown hair hung to their shoulders and was mottled with soot and ash.

Apollisian motioned for the boys to follow as he led them out of the small room. The paladin could hear the support timbers collapsing and frantically searched for some kind of cover. When he reached the far end of the corridor, he witnessed a giant marble pillar that had fallen over and landed on another that lay flat. He crawled under the makeshift shelter and pulled the boys close. Apollisian pulled out his water skin and tore some clothing from the boys' shirts and doused it in water. He then wrapped the wet cloth around each of the boys' noses and mouths. Saying a prayer to Stephanis, he and the boys waited for the fire to subside or burn itself out.

*   *   *

"My Lord! My Lord!" the robed figure shouted as he entered the great marbled dining room of King Hector De Scoran. The two attendants that were standing by for the king jumped as the robed man ran by. "We have done it; we have deciphered the text's true meaning!" he shouted. Hector slowly took a sip from his golden flagon and took another bite of his mutton, ignoring the robed man. Hector casually leaned on the giant polished oaken table and continued to chew.

The man slowed his pace and spoke slower and softer. "My lord, we have deciphered some more of the text's meaning. When it pleases you, I would like to show you what we have found. I'm sure it would please my Lord very much," the robed man said. He brought his sleeve up and wiped away some sweat that was beginning to form on his brow when he realized he had interrupted the king's meal.

Hector rotated the leg of mutton and looked at the pinkish meat as he chewed. He swallowed his bite and took another long draw from his flagon, swallowing several times. He dropped the leg of mutton on his plate and wiped his mouth with a white silk cloth that was sitting next to his flagon. Hector stood and grabbed the towel he had wiped his mouth on. As he walked behind the robed man from the dining room, he wiped his hands off and tossed the towel to one of the dining attendants. The attendant didn't move until the door closed and the king was gone.

Hector followed the man down the hall to one of his private studies. He pulled out a small set of keys on a brass chain that hung loosely from his corded belt and opened the door. The study was completely circular and was adorned with beautiful tapestries depicting lush forests and magical runes. He led Hector over to a bulky podium that had many large wax mounds that had once been candles, littering the top portion of it.

The robed man opened the text and read the ancient prophecy as Hector looked on curiously.

"A day shall come to pass when the mother of mercy shall bear child. This child will be like no other, for Gods and men alike will seek to vanquish him. The hate from the hells dwells within his mind, as compassion for the meek guides his heart. If allowed to live, this child will bear the false testimony of the gods, as he ascends the throne of righteousness, while working the magic of evil. The evils of the realms will oppose him, but they will be crushed asunder as the scorpion under an anvil or fire, for he shall command evil and good alike unto his ascension . . ."

The robed man said as he pointed to the first section and read again, "A day shall come to pass when the mother of mercy shall bear child." The robed man read as he rubbed his hands together eagerly while thumbing through some notes, "The mother of mercy has already bore her child, my lord."

Hector shrugged. He had already figured as much. He had sent patrols out every time someone might fit the description of a mother of mercy and had her and her family slain. Yet it didn't surprise him this mother of mercy had eluded him thus far. "Who is she?" Hector asked with venom dripping from his words. "I will dispatch a raid and she will be no more."

The robed figure rubbed his hands more nervously. "We believe she is already dead, my lord, killed by one of your raiding parties almost eighteen years ago."

Hector smiled and crossed his arms. "Then we have nothing to fear."

The robed man nervously cleared his throat. "Well, not exactly, my lord. See, the mother of mercy was slain, but not before she bore a male child."

Hector was becoming more agitated. He already knew it was a male child because the prophecy stated "he" several times. The king, growing more impatient, spoke forcefully. "Then go and fetch some clerics. Find the woman's spirit in the afterlife and order it to divulge the identity of her son, so that we may slay him."

The robed man again became nervous. It was common for the king to have the bearer of bad news slain and the robed man knew of no worse news than the news he was about to give. "We did that my lord, but we believe the woman has no spirit."

"Nonsense," Hector said flatly as he waved his hand in disbelief.

"It's true, my lord. We figured out why she was called the mother of mercy," the robed man squeaked.

Hector's ever growing scowl began to frighten the robed man. "Why was she called the mother of mercy?" Hector asked as if on cue.

The robed man moved to the opposite side of the podium as Hector did, and he began his speech. "My lord, we learned recently that there was a fallen goddess named Panoleen. She was the goddess of mercy. She was forced from the heavens by the mandate of the council of gods for some kind of transgression. We are not sure exactly what. She was called what is known as a Breedikai, or original god. She was created by Dicermadon to preside over mercy. For some unknown reason, she was forced from the heavens and dwelled here in Terrigan. Since she was created as a goddess, she had no soul. When she died, she ceased to exist. Panoleen came to Terrigan and met a paladin named Trinidy. She married and bore a child eighteen years ago."

Hector frowned and rubbed his jaw. "Why is this child a threat?" he asked curiously. "Surely no boy could overthrow my empire."

The robed man shook his head slowly, fearing Hector would strike him dead at any minute. Beads of sweat were building up on his flushed forehead and beginning to trickle down his face. He wiped the annoying drops away with his sleeve as he continued. "My lord, Panoleen's child would be gifted with her innate power as a god. He would easily rise more powerful than any mortal that has ever existed, thus making him a threat to both mortal men and the very gods themselves, just as the prophecy states."

Hector pondered this new twist of information. Certainly this boy would prove to be dangerous, but he was just a boy. The wicked king smiled and turned to the robed man. "What is your name, young sage?" he asked with a cunning smile.

"Spencer . . ." the robed man stuttered nervously. Spencer was unnerved by Hector's depiction of him, calling him a young sage. Spencer was certainly a low-ranking sage, but he was far from young, coming close to his fiftieth birthday.

Hector rubbed his chin again as he went deep into thought. Who was this boy? How would he be a threat to a kingdom? Might he carry some plague to his mighty nation? Or might the wrath of the gods descend on his nation for some act or failure to act, that he might make? He had to know more. "Spencer, you said this son of Panoleen would be more powerful than any mortal?" Hector asked inquisitively as he stroked his chin.

Spencer's mind raced. Had he said that? Was Hector trying to trick him into something? He finally swallowed hard as he answered. "Yes my lord, that is correct," Spencer said meekly.

"Good, then no matter how powerful he is, he could be killed, because you said it yourself, he is mortal."

Spencer smiled and wiped another trickle of sweat that ran down the side of his face.

"You have done well, Spencer, but now the true question. I hope you came with more knowledge than the other sages gave you," Hector chided.

Spencer began to tremble uncontrollably as Hector went on.

"What is the name of this boy?" Hector asked grimly as murder danced in his dark eyes.

"I do not know, my lord. We are going to see the dragon, Darrion-Quieness soon. We hoped his ancient knowledge might aid us," Spencer stammered.

Hector's mind wandered. Darrion-Quieness was a great white dragon. He was the most powerful of all the white dragons on the continent of Terrigan. The name "Quieness" was actually a name of nobility among dragon kind. Hector knew he dwelled deep in a mountain lair in northern Nalir, and that any meeting with him was not inexpensive, usually costing at least one life, not counting thousands of gold and platinum pieces, or the dragon's favorite, diamonds. Yes, it was a dangerous meeting for any group of mages. Hector pondered who or what Soran might pay to appease the mighty beast to gain the information he sought about the fallen goddess. Hector was going to kill Spencer. In fact, he was looking forward to it. He didn't like bad news, and it always made him adjust better with the pleasant screams of death, but he was too intrigued with the interpretation of the text and the new addition of Darrion-Quieness. He had used the dragon in the past to wipe out a small clan of do-gooding dwarves in the Pyberian mountain range on the northwest corner of Beykla. Hector eliminated the dwarven clan of Stormhammer, and the dragon earned countless amounts of gold and jewels. A few of the clan had survived, but that had been many years ago and they had not surfaced yet.

"Go away from me Spencer. I should kill you for not being able to answer all of my questions, but today I shall not," Hector commanded.

Spencer didn't wait another second. He grabbed the folds of his robes in his thin delicate hands and ran. Hector smiled as he watched the back of the aging sage while he ran awkwardly out of the chamber.

Evil Amerix Stormhammer. That is what history called him. But if a slave rebelled against his persecuting master, is he then evil? If a man sought justice for the murder of his wife and child, is he then evil? Some say that justice and revenge are two different entities. I say nay, they are one and the same. Goodly men, hidden behind the mask of their own view of morality often cross this delicate line, becoming forever lost in the swirling quagmire of justice and revenge. They rationalize revenge as justice when they try to give back some of the pain they do not have the strength to bear. Often hiding this need of revenge behind a guise of justice. I say justice is not an action that "evens" the score so to speak, but more an ideal that goodly men possess. Justice can never be equal to the event that demanded it.

There is no justice anyone could ever extract on a demon or an evil god short of making it suffer the same endless torment it gave since creation. If that were justice, Amerix would be "just" in his brutal killing of the men at the Torrent Manor. Surely the lives lost, including his wife and child, were a direct result of the greed from the Beyklans. Though when Amerix mercilessly slaughtered the men and women of the Torrent Manor, he crossed that narrow line between justice and revenge. But why was that line crossed? It was crossed because Amerix could have killed every man, woman, and child in all of Beykla, and his wife and child would still be dead. Would that sedate his own ignorant need for revenge? No. The only justice that could come would be the renewed strength in Clan Stoneheart, by forcing the Beyklans to relinquish their taxes, an action Tharxton would have succeeded in doing, thus making the dwarven way of life better than it had ever been. That would have been justice. Every goodly man has the knowledge of the difference between justice and revenge. But when the soul is clouded with emotion and the searing white hot pain of those we have loved and lost, justice and revenge pervade into one emotion that we unintentionally create. What a sad irony, for there is no justice for a man wronged. I do not fault, or even hate, Amerix Stormhammer. For even Lancalion Levendis Lampara himself once became mired in that swirling abyss of emotions between justice and revenge.

—Lance Ecnal—

Three

Time for War

Lance awoke from his deep slumber to find a delicate slender hand shaking him softly. He strained his tired sleepy eyes through the darkness and saw Tamra's beautiful face. Her long red hair hung down from her face and her beautiful green eyes were alight with youth and vigor, though her whispered voice spoke with urgency. "Lance, get Jude up. You need to leave."

Lance propped himself upright with his elbows and rubbed the sleep from his eyes.

"What do you mean? What's going on?" Lance asked inquisitively.

Tamra climbed the rail to the top bunk and leaned closer to Lance. He could smell the sweet scent of her hair as her strong presence loomed over him. Lance struggled for a breath. Never had he been so close to a woman before.

Tamra leaned closer, placing her mouth inches from his ear. Lance could feel her hot breath against his cheek as she spoke. "My father's . . ." she paused. ". . . My father's friends from the northern farms report that the dwarves of Pyberia attacked the Torrent Manor last night. Central City will soon be closed to outsiders. If the dwarves somehow attack Central City, many lives will be lost. Central City is large and has many men in its militia, but the reports say the dwarves number over five thousand. If they were to attack . . ." she struggled to keep her voice steady. ". . . Many would die."

Lance pulled away and looked into her deep green eyes. "Why are you telling me? Shouldn't you be running and telling the farm to get your workers ready to run?" Lance asked.

Tamra looked down at the floor and struggled to find the words to make Lance understand without betraying her father. Lance recognized the struggle she was having. He wondered what truth she was dancing around. Both turned and looked down at Jude as he tossed and turned in his bunk.

"Lance, you must flee, go back the way you came. Go away from this place and Central City, away from the dwarves and away from danger," Tamra urged sincerely.

Lance frowned at her. He couldn't figure out why she wanted only him and Jude to flee. If there was any real danger to the farm, it would seem she would want the farmers to flee. Lance didn't know a lot about dwarves, but he did know they were not surface farmers. If the dwarves did come, and even if they burned Central City to the ground, he doubted they planned to inhabit the area. He kind of chuckled as he imagined a hundred of the bearded folk manning plows and sweating in the surface sun, but Tamra seemed truly worried about him. No one other than Jude or Davohn had worried about him, yet Lance was not trustful by nature. He decided she must have some hidden agenda. No matter, it must be close to sunrise. He and Jude would get a head start to Central City. If the dwarves were coming, he needed to hurry and get to the library before they had a chance to burn it down. "Okay Tamra. Jude and I will leave your farm. I don't understand why you are telling me, and want only me to run," Lance stated flatly, though he had guessed Jude's notions about the farm were not so off target. Jude had many observations about the farm and even came so far as to tell Lance he didn't think it was a farm at all.

Tamra smiled at Lance when he said he would leave. She was confused at why she worried about him. The young daughter of Master Hentridge had seen a hundred men as handsome as Lance, if not more handsome. Some even were important or wealthy, she just sensed something about him that made him seem important, something she couldn't place a finger on, but she felt it just the same. "We will be fine," she said finally as she climbed down from the bed and silently moved toward the door.

Lance noted that she moved with stealth and grace, another surprising revelation of beautiful Tamra. After he returned from the library, Lance decided that this farm needed another visit. The young mage climbed down from his bunk and reached to wake up Jude. To his surprise, Jude was getting up and getting his equipment together.

"Lance . . ." Jude said as he pulled out his chain armor and placed it over his head. "Why do I get the idea you just tricked that woman, the same way you always seemed to trick me over the years?" Jude whispered with a half smile.

Lance smiled back and hopped down from his bunk. "My friend, I didn't trick her. I simply told her I would leave the farm, and so we shall. We will leave the farm and head directly toward Central City." Lance paused. "How much of the conversation did you hear?"

Jude just smiled as he pulled the leather straps of his chain armor tight. "Enough," he said with a chuckle as he slipped on his backpack. "You ready?" Jude asked as Lance placed his much lighter and smaller pack on his back.

Lance pondered that remark for a fleeting moment. "Let us be off, my friend," Lance said with a cheery smile as the two headed out the door.

The two friends were greeted by the cool autumn morning air. They closed the door to the tiny building that housed thirty men. Lance wondered if any were awake as they departed. He figured a few were. He began to doubt this was an ordinary farm with each moment that passed as they made their way through the many small buildings that littered the farm. Lance looked at the stars that still hung in the deep blue sky as the glow of the eastern sun began to wash away the night. He and Jude went to the stables and found their horses were saddled and ready to go, tied to the thick wooden rail outside the large building. Jude checked over the tack to ensure everything was in place and in good order, while Lance scanned the silo, searching for some sign he might find to settle the unresolved matter about the farm, but he saw nothing unusual.

Lance and Jude rode swiftly away from the farm in the cold dark morning. Lance wasn't sure there was truth to the tale from Tamra. He doubted the Dwarves of Pyberia would ever come against Beykla. No race, nor country had ever succeeded in conquering the fierce nation, let alone a small clan of dwarves. Besides, from what Lance had heard about the dwarves, they were a peaceful culture of artisans and craftsmen, not warriors. Sure, there had to be a few warriors, if not several, but not enough to even humor the idea of a victory against Beykla. Yet try as he did, Lance could not come up with a plausible explanation of why Tamra would try to get them to leave. So Lance took the warning as misguided concern.

As the two companions rode west along the trail toward the road, the birds began to chirp at the eastern sky, and the forest became alive with sounds from the fast approaching dawn. Lance reached into his pack and removed a small lead chest. It was smooth on all four sides and was shaped like a book. It had two silver hinges on one side and a gold locking mechanism on the right. He ran his fingers across the deeply engraved runes that were on the top. Lance didn't know what they said, or if they were writing at all. He lifted the first of the four books. Its cover was black and it had silver runes about it. Lance had decided that the rune was a symbol for death or some likeness of it. Yet, he continued to open the ancient tome without worry. He was near to completing the study of the first spell in the book and was eager to try to mimic the dweamor.

Jude glanced over at Lance. The swordsman started to give a word of caution, but he knew Lance would dismiss the notion and Jude didn't feel like wasting his breath. He knew Lance would simply say, "Is a sword wielded by an assassin any more evil than one wielded by a paladin?" Jude couldn't refute his friend's logic, though in his heart he feared for Lance. Jude wasn't sure if it was because he feared magic or he had some kind of perception about evil that his friend did not.

The two rode for most of the morning. Lance studied his book in depth, uttering only a few words of recognition as he frowned and rubbed his chin. Jude continually scanned the horizon for an army of dwarves that he was reasonably certain he would never see.

The forest around them began to give way to open fields and small farms. The farmers paid the two little heed as they quickly moved about their respective fields. Jude noted with more than a passing interest that some of the farmers seemed to be packing things on their animals. Some farmers had grain, others had clothing and foodstuffs. Some had pots and pans and other important items, as if they were to survive away from home for a while. They didn't all seem to be packing, a fact that made Jude sit easier in his saddle, but none of the items that were packed by the farmers were placed on oxen or wagons. If the packed goods were for market, they would be in larger bulk and they would be mostly the same textile. Some might have a lot of leather goods, where some might have grain, but it seemed each one had packed a little of everything while their families continued to work and play.

"What do you make of that?" Jude asked Lance as he pointed to the farmers that were packing their belongings on a small horse.

Lance looked up, startled for a moment, oblivious to the question Jude had asked. "What was that, Jude?" Lance asked with a confused look. "Are we there?"

Jude lowered his voice and frowned at Lance. "It is a good thing I watch the road. A dragon would sweep down and swallow you whole and the only way you would notice would be because it would be harder to read that blasted book in gullet!" Jude roared as he threw his arms in the air.

Lance smiled and deflated his large friend's rage. "That is why I hired you, to watch the road for me," Lance said with a soft snicker.

Jude ignored the comment and pointed at the farmers. "Doesn't that strike you as odd," Jude said as he motioned to the horses many farms had packed with an assortment of goods.

Lance quickly glanced at the horses and then dove back into his book. "Nope," he replied as he retraced the page with his finger to find the most recent line he read. Jude sighed and shook his head. He decided that if there wasn't an army of dwarves coming, it was an army of something.

*   *   *

Tharxton and his men emerged from the far end of the tunnel. The young dwarf king stroked his braided red beard as he looked on the death scene in the dungeon under the Torrent Manor. It had taken his dwarves almost nine hours to burrow through the wall of collapsed rock that they surmised that Amerix had dropped for them. The stench of death hung in the air of the dungeon like a fog. Everywhere Tharxton looked, he witnessed torn, decapitated bodies of half starved men. He looked at how their bodies lay and realized the way of the battle. The human prisoners had clawed at their cell walls, or tried to force themselves through an impossibly thin space between two bars as they were cut down. Tharxton marched on slowly. He drummed his thick fingers across the pommel of his massive hammer. Shaking his head in disbelief, he walked up the stairs. From there he smelled smoke and heard the distant cackles of fire.

"Do you think Amerix is still here with our brothers?" one dwarf asked.

"No," Tharxton answered back. "If he were, he would have posted guards at our only path of approach," Tharxton said flatly.

The dwarf pondered a moment. "Maybe Amerix feared his guards would see their king and betray him," the dwarf offered.

Tharxton stopped and turned to face the dwarf.

The soldier stepped back a bit, surprised by the king's sudden movements. "Do you think the general is surrounded by dwarves that he cannot trust? Or even more disturbing, do you think the general is so foolish that he would post a guard that he is questionable about his loyalties?" Tharxton bellowed, his anger growing with each passing moment. The dwarf king raised his stubby finger and pointed angrily at the dwarf as he spoke. "You had better re-think your enemy! He is more cunning than you can imagine and more deadly than any enemy you have ever faced. He could cut you down with a thought. So until you understand the depth of our danger, do not open your fool mouth!"

The dwarf stood silently and embarrassed at his bereavement. Tharxton threw his arms out wide and stormed up the stairs shaking his head. The dwarves behind him followed cautiously, for they had never heard their king raise his voice and they knew the gravity of the situation they faced.

As Tharxton stepped out into the courtyard, he witnessed a spectacle he could not have imagined in his nightmares. Everywhere his stern eyes fell he witnessed slain mutilated bodies of women and children. Tharxton fought back rage and despair all at the same time. He realized that if he didn't find Amerix soon, he wouldn't have the forces to stop the humans from retaliating, and next he would stare upon a similar sight, but with slain dwarven women and children. Tharxton looked to the south, where he witnessed what was left of the once proud keep. Its buildings were made of pure marble and the highest quality wood. The Torrent Manor must have been beautiful indeed, save that it was made beautiful by the sweat and tears of dwarven blood. This keep was a testament to the dwarven losses by the Beyklan sanctions. Tharxton felt rage boiling inside of him—a rage that only death would sedate. But as he stared at death, he was merely repulsed.

Tharxton slowly walked around the courtyard of the fallen, burned out keep, taking in every gruesome scene. He had ordered his men to look for survivors. And as they milled about, he closed his heavy eyes, shaking his head slowly. No, he thought. This is not the way. Tharxton now understood the council's reluctance toward military action. The Beyklans were too proud to back down, and the dwarves could not hope to win a war against this powerful nation. Yes, they had dealt a decisive blow, perhaps enough that it might give the dwarves some bargaining power, but he knew the Beyklans would demand justice. He knew they would demand the head of Amerix. And as Tharxton looked around at the mutilated bodies of the human women and children, he didn't think the idea so wrong.

Tharxton was awakened from his thoughts by the call of one of his men.

"We have found a survivor," one dwarf yelled as he cheerily ran to Tharxton's side.

"One?" Tharxton asked incredulously.

The dwarf smiled and said, "Well, two actually, though only one is human."

Tharxton frowned. "Well what is the other one?" the king asked, growing more impatient with the report.

The dwarf eyed him cheerily. "An elf."

Tharxton growled. He never liked elves much. They were a goodly race for the most part, yet they were always too fancy for his taste. Tharxton liked races that liked to drink stout drinks, work hard, and fight, and of course nothing could be farther from the description of an elf.

Tharxton walked toward the rubble where they supposedly found the pair. He looked down and witnessed a young human with brown hair that was conscious. He wore padded leather armor, though it was badly burned. His face had suffered many burns that were blistered and his hands were scorched black.

The other was an elven female. She had long blonde hair that was braided in the back, though it was now singed and burnt. She clutched a white ash bow that appeared to have suffered little or no scorching. She was bleeding from a large piece of wood that protruded from her right shoulder. It appeared that her right leg was broken and that both legs had been buried under a mountain of burning stone and wood. When Tharxton approached her, the human jumped out and lunged at him. Though the chains that held his wrists and neck jolted taut, he was jerked backward to the ground. The human spat out some gibberish the other dwarves couldn't understand and they all had a hearty laugh.

Tharxton turned angrily toward them. They all became quiet and began to find some task to do to escape the scowl from their king. Tharxton stooped low to the elven woman. As he felt her cheek, the human ran out again at him, and again the chains jerked him back.

"Step away from her, you murderous bastard, or so Stephanis help me, I'll spend the rest of my days hunting you down, dog!" the human shouted through clenched teeth.

Tharxton kept his eyes locked on the elf as he responded. "You think the rest of your life will be that long?" Tharxton asked.

The human gasped in surprise that the dwarf could speak the common tongue. Tharxton turned and called out for one of his clerics in his native language.

The human calmed himself, though his words still dripped with venom. "You will do well to kill me, dwarf," he said. "For if you let me live, I will spend the rest of my days hunting you."

Tharxton just smiled and kneeled low, barely just out of the human's reach. "Again human, I am confused as to why you think the rest of your days will be long. If I wanted you dead, you would be dead," Tharxton said. The dwarf king had no intention of killing the man. He was hoping the man might give him an idea as to where Amerix went.

"I am searching for a rogue dwarf, named Amerix, that took a small portion of my army," Tharxton lied. Amerix didn't take a small portion of his army, he took just about all of it, but Tharxton hoped if nothing else could be gained from the conversation, when he released the man, he might well tell the dwarven numbers to be much higher, maybe buying his clan some negotiating time.

"He fled south, toward Central City, but he will soon be dead. Central City's militia is the size of his army, and many of the Beyklan western army is stationed there," the human said proudly.

Tharxton didn't disagree. He hoped that Amerix would soon be dead, but he learned long ago, as did many of Amerix's enemies, that the dwarf didn't die easy. Though the arrogant boast didn't fall on deaf ears, Tharxton motioned around him at the many thousands of dead human soldiers. "Does Central City have soldiers like these?" Tharxton asked. "How many did you say? Let me tell you something, boy. Though I hold no love for General Amerix, and I hope for his own sake he is slain in battle, his meager army lost only a hundred or so against the Torrent Manor. Do you think he will lose any more against Central City?"

The human winced at the thought. The dwarven onslaught had been unstoppable.

Tharxton smiled at the human's humbled pride, and began again, softer. "That is why I must catch up to Amerix, before more innocents are slain by his evil hands," Tharxton said, smiling as the human sat confused and his clerics removed the wooden stake from the elven maiden and healed her.

The human cleared his throat. "I am Victor De Voulge, Squire of Apollisian Bargoe of Westvon. She . . ." The human pointed at the elven maiden. ". . . is Overmoon, Apollisian's scout and friend," Victor said, standing up after making the proclamation and wiping as much soot and dirt from his pants as he could with his horribly burned hands. Victor then extended a hand to the dwarf king, after seeing the elf healed and tended to.

The young king turned and gently took the man's hand as the clerics approached to heal him. "I am King Tharxton Stoneheart, fourteenth King of the Pyberian Mountains. Well met Victor De Voulge, well met."

*   *   *

He had been following the Ecnal for over a week. Only that cursed Jude had prevented him from extracting his revenge on the damnable mage. The rogue knew that Jude was more than just a deadly opponent and his reputation around Bureland furthered the truth. He had witnessed the large man cut down many men in Bureland and they were not considered anything less than deadly themselves, so he knew to try to keep wide of his reach. But the stealthy rogue was watching and waiting, and soon he would be

101

able to sneak in and make the boy pay for his treachery. The swordsman couldn't remain next to Lance forever. And when he did leave the pitiful mage's side, he would slice the poor spellcaster from ear to ear.

The rogue took a deep breath and sighed. It appeared the pair was traveling into Central City. The strong guilds there would not likely approve of the slaying on their streets, and he had a long history with that guild. They would not be overjoyed to see him again, so he would have to wait until Lance once again came onto the trail. The rogue's mouth twitched in anticipation. He ran a finger along the scar that extended from his nose to his ear. He had been patient in revenge with the one who had caused this wound, and in time, it was avenged. The rogue had been operating quite comfortably in Bureland, and when Lance had double-crossed him, he was forced to flee his comfortable home. This wound too would be avenged. He turned and melted into the shadows, leaving no trace he was ever there.

*   *   *

Lance and Jude arrived in Central City late in the afternoon. They gazed at the magnificent city. As they rode from the south, they saw that the city was made up of small houses much like the ones in Bureland. There were many lower class people about carrying groceries and fresh goods from the many tent-like markets that littered the streets. Many of the citizens led mule-drawn carts in and out of the city—some carrying goods to sell and some buying goods to return to the farms with. The general mood seemed to be tense, but most of the people Lance smiled at, at least grinned back. But as the pair rode deeper into the heart of the city, the buildings became jammed together, creating a myriad of dark, twisting alleyways. The people rode in fancy leather-encased carts that were splashed with a myriad of colors and driven by armed men. The people that were walking around wore fine silks and made a wide berth for Lance and Jude. But while the streets seemed safe, the dark alleys held lurking shadows and dangerous figures that crept about, as if hiding from the very sun. Most of the buildings were two stories at least, and as many as thirty people lived in a single building. Lance gawked at the spectacle. Few buildings in Bureland were two stories, and fewer were three or more stories. Yet as Lance rode on, he could see many buildings ahead that dwarfed the ones they now rode next to.

The people of Central City were all moving about busily. Jude noticed more than one building with windows boarded up and many citizens openly carrying weapons. Most of the people took little or no notice of the pair as they rode in. Lance and Jude rode forward. Lance, seemingly oblivious to the distinct way the villagers were acting, plodded on with a smooth, calm smile. Jude, however, marked each villager's actions in a long list of reasons why he should have stayed back in Bureland.

The pair made their way steadily down the wide cobblestone road. It was wide enough for three wagons to travel abreast, and every hundred feet they passed a tall wooden pole with several lanterns affixed to the top of them. Lance paused at an intersection in the road. He looked west, then east, then turned to Jude.

The large swordsman shrugged his shoulders. "Could be any direction my friend. Perhaps we should enlist the aid of a villager," Jude said as he sat comfortably in his saddle, his massive hands resting on the saddle horn as they lightly held the reins. Lance didn't reply as he glanced around. The west road led toward a large building that was at least five stories tall. Across the street from it was a larger oval-shaped building made of pure marble that was at least twice as tall as the five-story one, yet it had no windows that Lance could see. The road between the two buildings curved in a northerly route. Lance looked east. He could see another large marbled building with giant pillars that rested atop a wide staircase. The windows were oversized and the glass was stained. He couldn't see any kind of a holy symbol, though he thought it to be a church of some kind. On the other side of the street he could see a large, three-story building that he immediately recognized as an inn. Lance motioned for Jude to follow as they made their way toward the building. They passed many men dressed in the Beyklan high guard uniform of brass-colored mail with red flowing silk capes and plumes. Lance waved to them, but as he expected, they made no attempt to acknowledge his presence. Jude stared hard at the men. He could see an eager nervousness in their eyes and in their stride. He knew these men were soon to be marched off to battle. He recognized that look well, for he remembered wearing it

103

many times as a young militia soldier marching off to battle orcs. Though he guessed Tamra's warning correct, these men wouldn't face orcs. They would soon face a merciless tactical army of dwarves.

Jude moved his large dun horse closer to Lance's steed. "I believe Tamra's warning, my friend. This city is on edge. Every man, woman, and child seems to be preparing for some kind of a defense. Even the guards march with nervous steps. I believe the dwarves are indeed coming," Jude said in a quiet voice.

Lance looked at his big friend. He too had noticed that the city seemed to be on edge, and perhaps his friend was right. "Then we must hurry before they arrive. I see an inn up ahead. Let us find someone there who might direct us to the library," Lance said as he urged his horse into a quicker step.

Jude gave a nervous look around and followed his friend east toward a large wooden building next to the inn that had thick, wooden double doors that were open wide. Lance could see many horses inside and tack strung along the walls in a rather disorderly fashion.

A small boy of about ten years old approached the pair. He had one front tooth and smelled as if he hadn't ever had a bath in his life. "Ye be stayin' a day, er a week?" the boy said as he reached for the reins of Lance's horse.

Lance dismounted and handed the boy the reins. "We will be here only for a short while," Lance replied.

The boy frowned and held out his dirty hand. "Gonna cost ye a silver as if ye stayed a'day," the boy said with a frown.

Jude dismounted and handed the reins of his horse to the stable boy. The boy stood tall, unimpressed with the size of the swordsman. "Then a silver, I guess, we will pay," Jude said, reaching into his pouch that the boy had been staring at greedily. He retrieved a silver and placed it into the boy's dirty hand.

"A silver fer each horse," the boy said as he pocketed the first silver and held his hand out for the second.

Jude began to argue, but he noticed Lance was entering the inn. He mumbled a few curses and gave the boy a second silver, then hurried to Lance's side. Lance glanced up at the sign as he entered. It read: Welcome to the Blue Dragon Inn. Lance and Jude saw that the sign had a long, narrow, blue dragon coiled about the words as they entered the common room, marveling at its size. It was the largest common room Lance had ever seen. It could easily house over three hundred patrons and had a polished stage at the far end. The bar was directly to the right of the entrance and it curved all the way around the west side. There were hundreds of different types of wine and whiskey stacked on shelves behind the bar, as well as many large wooden kegs of ale and honey mead. There were four bartenders and three times as many serving wenches that meandered through the tables. The ceiling was high, almost fifteen feet, and it held giant polished wooden rafters. These rafters supported about a score of candle chandeliers that hung down at the far end of the room, just above a bleached white skull that was about the size of a man. A bright brass plaque was hung under the skull with the name "Gorsaat" on it.

There were over fifty patrons and they ranged from royal guards to peasant farmers. Lance and Jude approached the bar and sat down. Soon a small but robust young man with thick uncombed red hair came to them. "Welcome to the Blue Dragon Inn. My name is Fifvel. What would you be drinking, my good sirs?"

Lance balked at the way the man spoke. He felt somewhat out of place. This was nothing like the Aldon Inn in Bureland, which was rough, more relaxed, and lacked any real luxuries to sell. This inn was bulging with class and prosperity. Lance guessed that for the cost of the chandeliers alone, they could buy the Inn of Aldon outright.

"I am looking for the library, good sir," Lance said in his best attempt at a nobleman's voice. "I have need of a scholar there."

Fifvel eyed Lance's strange black cloak and myriad of symbols at the hems of it. He stared at it suspiciously for a moment before he responded. "You one of them spell casters?" Fifvel asked with a rough accent that was nothing like the rehearsed greeting he spoke before. " 'Cause if you are, we don't take any spell casting in here. If you do try it . . ." He paused and pointed over to a big man sitting at the far end of the bar. ". . . Glaszric will rip off your arms."

Lance looked over at the large man and the back at Fifvel. "It's hard to cast spells with no arms," Lance said as he smiled at Fifvel.

" 'Tis true," Fifvel said flatly.

Jude took more than a passing look at the large man sitting at the far end of the bar. He was almost six inches taller than Jude, and had long black hair that he kept in a pony tail. His skin had a strange paleness to it, almost a green tint, and he had a large sloped forehead. He had a great sword that was almost six feet long that scraped the floor as he sat on the barstool. Jude watched the brute of a man take a sip from his large wooden flagon. He noticed a distinct under bite and two small yellow tusks protruding from Glaszric's lower lip. "Damn half-orc," Jude muttered under his breath. Half-orcs were usually not ones to be trifled with. They fought with the ferocity of orcs, but also had some of the intelligence of men, making them often quite deadly opponents. Jude had tangled with one in his day, and he barely survived. He had no inclination to tangle with another one. His skill with a sword must be quite accomplished for a half breed to be living in Beykla, since the orc wars were recent history.

"Well if you're looking for the library, it is right across the street," Fifvel said as he pointed out the window.

Lance leaned on the bar and peered out the window. He could see the large marble building with the magnificent pillars, and another smaller building with a statue of some kind of totem pole. "What is the larger building?" Lance asked.

Fifvel wiped some spilled ale from the counter. "Are you going to buy some ale, or continue to torture me with questions?" Fifvel asked with noted sarcasm.

Jude tossed three silver pieces down on the bar. Fifvel just looked at the coins.

"The first coin is for telling us where the library is. The other two are for whatever Fifvel deems them for," Jude said with a smile as he got up from his seat.

Fifvel slowly slid the coins into his pocket while Lance and Jude exited the common room.

*   *   *

Amerix stood motionless in the black of night. The heavy rain pounded his helmet and stung his face. A steady stream of water dripped from his elbows and landed in one of the many puddles that formed on the ground around him. Though the storm brought no wind, the rain was heavy and was making the ground wet and slippery. Amerix stood emotionless as he watched one of his sergeants approach. Each flash of lightning created a still image of the dwarven army. It never rained in the under mountain and the dwarves clearly were not enjoying the autumn storm.

"General, ye scouts report that the city has been warned of our approach, and even as we speak, the human dogs ready their defenses," the young dwarf yelled in the loud pounding rain as water ran down his face and into his eyes. The sergeant removed his horned helm and wiped the water from his face, then replaced the helm atop his head. "General, shall we advance? The city is only an hour's tromp. Though Leska curse this rain, it will probably take two hours." The sergeant spat as rain began to flow in his eyes once again.

Amerix remained emotionless. He ignored the stinging rain. He ignored his old aching bones. He ignored everything save for his vision of a burning, destroyed Central City. Even the stinging, humming sword he stole from the dead human champion that was strapped to his back was little more than a minor distraction.

The sergeant began to turn about when Amerix spoke. "The storm, sergeant, is because of me fury," Amerix stated flatly.

The sergeant looked confused and shifted. "What do ye mean?" the sergeant asked.

"It is spawned from me fury," Amerix said again.

The sergeant didn't respond. He just stood blankly staring at Amerix.

Amerix gave the sergeant such a murderous gaze that he stepped back in fear.

"Me axe will strike as quick as a lightning flash," Amerix said as he pounded his wet, metal fist against his breast plate. The gauntlet made a dull ringing sound as it thudded against his chest. "Me cry of vengeance shall echo like thunder across a barren valley," Amerix said in a louder tone, striking his fist against his chest again, causing a more acute ringing sound of metal upon metal. Many other dwarves looked over to see what was causing the noise. "The blood of the human dogs will bleed the ground red, choking the life from every plant miles from here!" Amerix screamed as he pounded his fist against his breast plate making a thunderous sound that was audible in the driving rain. Many other dwarves began to fall into rhythm with him. The sound of their pounding fists began to pierce the night. They pounded harder, chanting songs of

107

war and death to their enemies. They all abruptly stopped when Amerix struck his fist into the air. All were silent except for the constant sound of the driving rain. Small trickles of water streamed down his outstretched hand and into his thick, matted beard.

"This rain is a sign from Leska!" Amerix shouted. "She now washes away the evils that ye will soon be forced to commit! Let us all bow our heads and thank Leska for her cleansing rain!"

In unison the dwarves kneeled to the wet muddy earth, their heavy mail creaking in the rainy night. As abruptly as they kneeled, the dwarven army rose.

"There is a small cavern about an hour from here," Amerix said as he raised his armored hand and pointed to the southwest. He wiped away some rain from his face and beard and turned to his men. "This cavern leads back toward our homes in the Pyberian Mountains." Amerix paused and grinned wickedly, exposing thick yellow teeth. "It also leads us within a mile of the sewers of Central City. Come my brethren, let us march onward to victory!"

Led by the redoubled dwarf known as General Amerix Stormhammer, the dwarven army marched onward toward Central City.

*   *   *

"It is not Nalirian," the old man said after glancing down again at the ancient parchments that sat on his large oak desk.

Lance fumed. "They have to be!" he shouted as he tugged at the hems of his sable robe. Lance was beginning to fear he had been duped by the thief he had hired back in Bureland. Anger ripped through his body. He had to find out about why his parents were killed. Thoughts began to flood into his head. What if they weren't killed? What if they gave him up willingly because they didn't love him, or what if . . . Lance calmed himself and forced the irrational thoughts from his mind, though, in his dreams, Lance imagined he could feel their souls crying out for justice beyond the grave.

Jude placed his heavy hand on Lance's shoulder. "Well sir, so you say they are not Nalirian. So be it. But it is obvious it is some kind of writing. Do you know what kind of writing it might be?" Jude asked calmly.

The sage smiled and shrugged his shoulders. "I am familiar

108

with every text, rune and national writing throughout the land of Terrigan. And I assure you, this writing was not done by any man such as you or I," the sage said flatly.

"Then what kind of a man?" Lance asked, picking up on the game the sage was playing. The sage pointed at the small pile of gold coins that now sat on his oak desk. Lance and Jude had been playing this game with the sage with minor success at a cost to their purse. Jude sighed and placed another gold coin onto the ever growing pile.

The sage smiled at the newest coin added. "An elven man," the sage said as he crossed his arms under his thin chest and smiled.

Lance stared at the old man for a moment, then furiously grabbed the parchments from the desk and placed them back into his leather case. He stomped toward the door with Jude close on his heels.

"Don't you want to know any more?" the sage called out to their backs as they started out the door.

Lance turned furiously. "Sure, I would like to know the day of your death, that I might come to your funeral and give sneer at your lifeless body!" Lance said, his voice dripping with venom.

The sage said nothing. He just kept a wry smile and pointed down to a pile of coins. Lance bit his lip in frustration and slammed the door to the library as hard as he could. He even thought about opening the door again so that Jude might slam it hard enough to cave in the frame.

"Well at least we know it is elven now," Jude said in a soft tone.

Lance didn't reply. They had spent a small fortune at the sage and the task was becoming more impossible with the knowledge the writing was elven. How much, and how long would it take to find an elf that would translate it? Lance had never met an elf, but he heard numerous stories on how elusive and indifferent they were to humans. And even if he did find an elf willing to read it for him, Lance had no idea what the parchments might say. He surmised that when they finally translated it, it would turn out to be some kind of cooking recipe or some other stupid elven thing.

"What now?" Jude asked as he looked around the deserted streets of Central City. It was almost dark and the city was strangely vacant. He watched as a linkboy went about the streets, lighting the

109

many lanterns that sat on tall wooden poles. Lance just rubbed his chin, deep in thought.

"Perhaps we could return to the Blue Dragon Inn. We have paid for a night for our horses, might get a room as well," Jude said as he motioned across the street. Lance didn't say anything. He just continued to stare off to the east at the large stone columns of the river battlements. Central City was sitting next to the Dawson River. The Dawson River flowed from the Sea of Balfour, just north of Beykla, all the way to the bottom of Terrigan, crossing many nations. Central City was one of the few areas to cross the mighty river. They had constructed a magnificent stone bridge that spanned the river's width. It served as a by-way and also a defensive battlement from any invaders that may come from the east. Though no other human kingdoms dwelled in the east, there was a high elven nation. But high elves were not known for being overly generous to humans.

Jude was anxious to leave Central City as soon as possible. He was intimidated by the sheer volume of people, but he was more afraid of the rumored dwarven army. Jude had never seen an army of dwarves, but he had heard individual tales of dwarven warriors slaying giants in single combat. The thought of being caught in the path of an army of the little folk terrified him. The thunder and an occasional flash of lightning from an approaching storm made Lance and Jude realize that they needed shelter.

"Let us stay one night, Lance, then let's be off from this cursed city," Jude said as he grasped Lance's shoulder. Lance, deep in thought, only nodded as he slowly walked across the street to the inn.

*   *   *

Apollisian awoke to find him and the two young boys huddled under the wet, singed blanket. They were unconscious still but did not appear to have any severe injuries. Their hair was scorched and they had black splotches of soot all over them, but the young paladin was sure they would be okay. Apollisian rose and meticulously burrowed out from under what was once the great hall. When he poked his head above the rubble, his heart sank. All around the burned-out buildings of the Torrent's south quarter were the dwarves. He was relieved that he couldn't see Amerix, especially since he was without his sword, Songsinger. He would need the ancient blade if he was to face that demon again. Its enchantments were powerful, but the young paladin wasn't sure if it was powerful enough to dispatch such a mighty foe. He whispered to the twins to keep quiet while he took a deep slow breath, savoring each fresh draw of air like it was his first. The young paladin had been buried under the smoke and soot for many hours and his lungs burned with the foul gases he had inhaled. Though he longed to find and slay this hellion Amerix, his first duty was to get these two boys to safety, and then find if Overmoon and Victor were alive. He suspected that the elf had managed to slip away somehow, but he was sure that Victor, if left to his own devices, would have more than an easy kill of the mighty dwarves. Just as Apollisian was looking for an exit along the battered and collapsed south wall, he noticed two large forms among the dwarves. Pain shot through his blistered face as he recognized the pair. It was surely Victor and that wry elf.

*   *   *

Tharxton sat quietly on a wet pile of partially burned wooden timbers that served as a makeshift bench under one of the many tents he and his men had constructed as they searched for survivors. An autumn storm had soaked the remnants of the Torrent Manor, extinguishing most of the fires, and thick white smoke still erupted from the great pile of debris. Though the storm had passed, water still dripped from the edges of the tent and trickled down the rubble from the stone buildings and formed large puddles in the rain-soaked courtyard. Most of the bodies had been gathered, and a mass funeral was soon to be held. Despite the extent of the human casualties, Tharxton found his mind wandering to the identity of the elf. The young king's face was wrinkled up as he struggled with the elf maiden's name. He was certain he had heard of Overmoon, but he wasn't sure if it was a hero of history or if it had some political ramifications. Tharxton cursed himself silently for not listening better to his lessons as a child. The only lesson he could recall was not to call an elf by his first name. Only other elves were allowed to speak it. For a non-elf to speak an elven name was punishable by

111

death. Tharxton chuckled to himself at the absurdity of the idea of the elf trying such a thing with his brethren all around, but he had seen stranger things in his life, and creating yet another enemy on this day was not on his list of good ideas. He tried to discern from her actions if she was royalty, but he soon abandoned his observations. Those damnable elves were so prissy as a culture, how anyone could tell peasantry from royalty was beyond him. He thought back to the few words they exchanged since their initial meeting, but couldn't develop any conclusions one way or the other. Tharxton shrugged his shoulders in defeat and decided that regardless of her station as an elf, the farther away she was from him and his men, the better. The approaching dawn would surely bring troves of humans to investigate the great plumes of billowing white smoke that undoubtedly could be seen for tens of miles. Besides, word was three more survivors were found under some rubble in the south sector, a young warrior named Apollisian and two small children. Tharxton remembered Apollisian. He spoke to the human knight about ten years ago when he was in the initial negotiations with the Beyklans. He recalled that the young knight was from some church of justice, but was of little help to his king and his people. Hopefully this human would take the elf away from him and out of his hair.

The young king was roused from his mind's wandering as Apollisian entered his tent. Tharxton swallowed hard at seeing the man. He remembered a young boy, barely a man in chain armor the last time he spoke with Apollisian, but standing before him today was a full grown man. The young king knew humans aged much faster than dwarves but he was still amazed at the man that now stood before him. Apollisian stood much more confident now. His long blonde hair no longer carried the stain of blood and soot, and his armor had been cleaned up, though he was still battered and a little bloodied, and most of his wounds had been healed.

"Any word on the location of this . . . Amerix?" Apollisian asked as he nervously ran his fingers through his thick blonde hair.

Tharxton had explained the story of General Amerix Stormhammer, and Apollisian did not relish facing the deadly dwarf again, but he knew in his heart that if he did not, many more innocents might die by the renegade's wicked axe.

"He has fled into some caves south of here, no doubt back en route to the Pyberian Mountains, back to our home, to roust his supporters for a coup against me. So I will take the remainder of my army and march back through the tunnels and deal with the renegade there. After he is caught, I will try him for treason," Tharxton said with gritted teeth.

"And try him for the murder of the innocent people of Beykla," Apollisian quipped.

Tharxton nodded nonchalantly. He could tell Apollisian was afraid of Amerix. He commended the human for surviving a fight with the wicked dwarf. Not many dwarves could have survived, let alone a human. But as Apollisian dreaded a second encounter, Tharxton was frothing at the idea. He was sure Amerix would have cut him down a hundred years ago, but that was then. The young king was angry and wanting some justice—but not so much for the lost men of the Torrent Manor. No, he was on a mission to slay the lot of them anyway. It was the ruthless way the humans were killed. Tharxton wanted to sack the manor to send a message that the Stoneheart clan would be persecuted by the humans no longer. Instead Amerix sent a message of undeniable war—a message the young king knew would soon be answered.

*   *   *

As Apollisian left the dwarves' makeshift tent, he was deeply troubled. Could he trust the supposed king with the capture of Amerix, or should he seek the dwarf's head himself? Normal edict of the vow he took when he became a warrior of his church dictated that he hunt the scoundrel until either he or the dwarf was dead. But Apollisian had the young Overmoon in his charge, not to mention he had to get the orphaned boys to Central City first and foremost. Overmoon's father, King Minok, desired for his daughter to learn the ways of justice, not die in the pursuit of it. But how could she learn of justice if he ran from it? He had explained to King Minok the dangers his daughter might face, but he was sure the elven king did not imagine they might be hunting the most wicked and powerful foe Apollisian had ever faced.

It was a long slow journey for Apollisian and crew. They had but one horse and they let the two boys, Cerebron and Corwin, ride as they walked. They had to frequently stop and let their only horse

113

rest, and let Overmoon hunt. Had she not been so proficient at hunting, it would have been a much hungrier trip. Victor did his duties as a squire should during the three-day trip. Overmoon seemed cheerful and often tried playing with the boys. She had a childish nature that seemed more akin to the boys than to Victor and himself. Corwin warmed up to Overmoon during the day but cried for his lost parents at night. Cerebron, however, just sat in his own silent solace. Whether day or night, he ate only enough and drank only enough to sustain himself. Any attempt at conversation with the boy was met with cold resistance or a blank stare. Apollisian worried for him. He could see an inner fire in the quiet boy's heart. A fire that would not easily be quenched. The young paladin hoped the church of justice in Central City would help show the brothers the light of goodness.

"I'm worried about the boys," Overmoon said as she walked alongside Apollisian. "Are we to just drop them off at some church and abandon them?" Overmoon asked as she stretched her elegant arms wide, exposing the myriad of tattoos entwined along the inside of her forearms.

Apollisian only stared straight ahead. Overmoon gave the paladin a disapproving gaze. He turned and looked at her beautiful face and gazed deep into those compassionate brown eyes. The young paladin stared into them for a long moment, fully taking in her beauty not only as an elf, but as a woman. In that moment he was lost. There was nothing but him and her. No Amerix, no war, nothing but the ignorant bliss of a man staring into the deep void of what he could never have. Aside from the vow of chastity he made to Stephanis, the God of Justice, he could never marry an elf. Elves lived ten times as long as humans, and as he would grow old and weak, she would retain her youth and beauty—a curse, he thought.

"What is a curse?" Overmoon asked. "What are you talking about?"

"What?" Apollisian asked, somewhat embarrassed.

Overmoon just fumed. "I ask you a legitimate question, and you look at me as if I am an idiot, and say, 'a curse.' I know I don't know all of the human customs yet, but what are you talking about?" she growled. "And don't patronize me, I am three times as old as you and twice as smart."

Apollisian glared with anger. He could feel blood rushing to his face. "Save that tone for the children, elf. Perhaps you need to be reminded who is whose charge. If you dare to speak to me in such a tone again, I will send you back to your father. You can explain to him how your childish tongue ended your journey!"

Overmoon turned and sneered as Corwin snickered. She whipped back and was cut off by more of the paladin's condemnations.

"Furthermore, I care not for your age, and if I were you, I wouldn't mention it again, for your lack of wisdom is an embarrassment not only to me and my God, but to the entire Overmoon family." Apollisian paused and softened his tone as he continued. "Now, to answer your question, the curse I am referring to is the curse to do what is right. I would much rather chase the fiend Amerix to hell and back, but instead I am traveling with three children and my squire."

Overmoon squinted in a glare of such anger that Apollisian thought he might need to draw his sword, but she turned and walked back over near Victor, walking on in silence.

Apollisian rubbed his scarred hand over his empty scabbard. As soon as he dropped off the children he would return to Torrent Manor and reclaim his blade. Then he would claim justice for the slain innocents that were brutally slaughtered there.

Overmoon didn't speak the rest of the day or the night. She just sulked around the campfire. Victor tried to warm up to her, but whenever he spoke she never replied, just stared at him. The young squire dared not comfort her, though in his heart he was swiftly taken by her beauty just as Apollisian was. Unfortunately for young Victor, he had not the resolve nor the wisdom of Apollisian, and could not recognize how fruitless the dweamor he had with the woman would be. The young paladin watched in sadness as Victor struggled with her rejection. Yet he was glad for his vow, for never would his heart hurt so. He watched the squire sulk a while and decided that a walk might do him some good. "Do a walk around the camp, Vick," Apollisian said. "We will be going to sleep soon, and tomorrow we will ride into town."

"Yes, my lord," Victor said as he smiled and nodded, disappearing into darkness.

Apollisian unfolded his bed roll for the boys. Corwin smiled and crawled inside. Cerebron merely sat at the foot of it and stared into the darkness, hugging his knees into his chest. Apollisian leaned against a tree and sighed. His body ached from the fight. He had been healing himself each day, but he was still a few days from a full recovery. But he was recovering emotionally much slower. He often awoke at night to the screams of those that were burned alive, or tortured himself about the battle with Amerix, thinking that he should have done this, or if only he had said that; though deep in his heart he knew he did everything he could.

"Cerebron won't make it," a soft feminine voice said.

Apollisian turned to see Overmoon standing next to him. He marveled at the flickers of light from the fire as they danced across her almond skin. Her braided blonde hair coiled around her head in a tight circle. The young paladin looked at her with surprise, but she never returned his gaze. He looked back at the boys. "I agree he is troubled, but I believe it is early to make such morbid predictions."

Overmoon just stared at the pair. Corwin was fast asleep, but Cerebron sat staring blankly. "Once when I was a young child . . ." She paused and looked Apollisian in the eye. ". . . Long before your father's birth, my village was attacked by orcs. I lived a privileged life, but I remember a young maiden that lost her true love on the battlefield. She sat in the same chair that young Cerebron sits in now. She neither cared if she lived or died. It was soon after that she took her own life," Overmoon said while glancing at Cerebron as he sat next to the fire, then turned back to Apollisian. "Do you know why she took her own life?" she asked solemnly.

Apollisian paused and cleared his throat. "Because she felt with the love of her life gone that she could no longer bear to live," the young paladin responded.

Overmoon turned away and stared back at the boys as she replied. "No," she said flatly. "She took her own life because she realized that the tragedy she had endured had robbed her of her sense of right. She no longer cared for right or wrong. The two became blurred into one nothingness that she could not decipher or comprehend. She was so dead inside that she held no regard for her life or anyone else's. She knew that only in death her soul might be freed from the shackles that were leavened upon it. That child . . ." She pointed to Cerebron. ". . . Has no sense to even realize what he has lost. Evil will overcome him and he will most likely live a life of

116

crime, and commit many times over, the acts that he suffers for now."

Apollisian shook his head. "That is why I take him to the church of Stephanis, so that through worship he will learn about justice," the young paladin responded.

Overmoon placed her soft hand on his thick shoulder. He could feel the warmth of her touch through his light tunic. She leaned close and whispered into his ear. "Do you think Stephanis is known by humans only?" she asked as she walked away.

Apollisian lowered his head as he watched Overmoon's beautiful form disappear into the darkness. It was going to be another long night.

*   *   *

They worked feverishly night and day, digging and burrowing through hardened stone. Amerix had sent close to three hundred of the dwarves back down the passage that led to Mountain Heart, the underground village of his people, and instructed them to leave as many clues as they could that might lead Tharxton to think they marched onward to their home village. He had his miners burrow south instead, and then rigged the passage to collapse to cover their tracks. They now followed an old limestone deposit that ran parallel with the Dawson River. When the passage ended, they simply dug their way. Since the old cave was relatively close to the surface, they had faced few dangers that are normally encountered while traveling underground. It was well into their second night when they encountered their first dilemma.

"My lord," Therrig said as he roused the sleeping general. Amerix opened his weary eyes. He slowly rubbed the sleep out of them and yawned. Blinking several times, he sat up and looked around. Therrig cleared his raspy throat and rubbed the giant scar that ran along his neck. He had earned it in a battle with the dark dwarves when the Clan Stormhammer fell. "Are you ready for the report, my lord?" Therrig began again.

Amerix's thick black beard shook as he nodded slowly. "Aye, but me hopes it is better than the grim expression ye bring this day," Amerix replied as he rose from his satchel and began the tedious task of donning his armor.

117

"Well my lord . . ." Therrig began. "We have found a large cavern that is full of mushrooms and precious water. The lake is large and we suspect that there are many beovi swimming in its depths."

Amerix smiled. Beovi were underground fish that fed on algae and other plants. They grew to be quite large and were a delicacy to dwarven kind. Unfortunately, lakes of beovi usually attracted other humanoid races. "So who are our new neighbors?" Amerix asked dispassionately as he tugged on his dirty leather boots.

"A group of kalistirsts. Maybe one hundred, no more," Therrig replied with lust for battle in his eyes.

Amerix pondered the thought. Kalistirsts were a type of underground race that resembled the cross between a mole and a dwarf. They don't have eyes and are covered in a thin fur. They have three fingers and three toes that have six-inch long claws and can burrow through solid stone in moments. Their claws prevented the race from using tools or weapons, but the claws often doubled for both. They were generally a friendly race but often sided with whoever, or whatever, as long as the price was right. Amerix entertained the idea of massacring the group. After all, it was a group of the kalistirsts that helped lead to the downfall of Clan Stormhammer. Amerix let out a small sigh. It wasn't this group. "I will go down with two others and make contact with the kalistirsts. I will tell them we are going to fish and gather supplies, then be on our way," Amerix said as he rose and stared at his great helm. The ram horns were moldy and the iron spikes were beginning to rust, and aside from the many hundred dents in it, it was still in good shape. He placed it on his thick head as he did a thousand times before, and prepared for the meeting with the mole people.

"And what if they refuse?" Therrig asked in his raspy voice, drumming his fingers on the head of his mighty hammer.

Amerix turned, and with an evil calm said, "Then we kill them." Therrig smiled at the words his general spoke. He was tired of digging and gathering food. Rubbing his deep scar on his neck, Therrig wandered off with visions of kalistirsts running in sheer terror from his hammer.

The cavern ceiling wasn't unusually high, and walls were made up of soft limestone. There were many small sedimentary rifts that acted as ledges, but since they were made of limestone, they were fragile at best. The only real solid stone was the cavern floor. It was made of smooth black clay. A trickling sound of water seeping through the limestone walls and filling the pool echoed through the large cavern. Amerix carefully navigated his descent from the dwarves' rocky perch to the cavern's base. He recognized the limestone for what it was, and didn't spend any more time on it than was necessary. With a small grunt he plopped down from the final ridge onto the hard dirt floor. The old general glanced around as he approached the pool. Though he couldn't see any kalistirsts, he knew they were probably burrowed nearby. Their first reaction to any intrusion was to hide, often leaving whatever tasks they were doing at that moment unfinished.

Amerix walked slowly to the level base near the pool. It was murky with minerals from all the limestone, but it appeared to be quite deep. Amerix removed his battered helm and called out in his native tongue. "Show yerselves, mole people. I knows ye be hiding," Amerix bellowed. The ancient general waited a few moments, but none of the kalistirsts appeared. After a few minutes of listening for some kind of reply, he shrugged his shoulders, replaced his helm, and slowly trudged back up to the cavern his men had dug.

The dwarves spent the next day fishing and resting. The cavern was large enough to hold the five-thousand strong army comfortably for a few days. Though they suffered next to no casualties during the battle of the Torrent Manor, many of his men were wounded. The rest and relaxation in the confines of the caverns would help heal their minds as well as bodies. Amerix disliked the surface as much, if not more, than his men, so he opted to stay below as much as possible. He watched as his men caught hundreds of beovi. They cut the giant, pale, white fish into small strips and cooked them on calours, flat sedimentary rocks that were heated by fire. They then salted the strips and smoked them with smoke from the burnt cartilage and bone. The process took little time and effort, plus it bolstered the dwarves' morale to be performing activities they so often did while in their home stronghold of Mountain Heart. Amerix had many sentries posted to guard for the kalistirsts should they decide to take the lake back from them, but the mole people never showed themselves.

The old general roamed around the perimeter of the cave as his men readied their supplies. The cave wasn't overly remarkable, he had seen countless like it in his lifetime. It was formed when a large pocket of limestone was slowly dissolved by a flood or over a period of time by rainwater. The limestone eventually eroded away and left a cavern behind. The water that dissolved the limestone continued to flow into the cavern and large lakes where water formed. Amerix wasn't exactly sure where beovi came from, but he had learned that caves needed to be at least a thousand years old to have the large fish inhabit them. He guessed that some of the eggs had to have washed into a cavern after a large flood or some other significant ecological event.

Amerix had his miners collapse the tunnel, then burrow into this cavern to keep Tharxton from following them, though he explained to the miners that he feared humans might somehow follow them into the depths of the earth. The miners knew that Amerix didn't fear that event coming to pass, but could not guess the real motive behind Amerix's wishes. But in truth, they were not overly concerned with it. He gave the orders; they followed them. A few of the dwarves were grumbling about not hearing from Tharxton, but that was as far as it went. Though, Amerix knew his army was fickle at best, and he needed to strike Central City within the week or risk that many of his men that were loyal to Tharxton would become suspicious.

After the second day, the dwarven army was cramped in the cavern. Despite its large size, it could not comfortably house the enormous group for long. By the eve of the second day, Amerix decided to push on to the southern corridor. It was much smaller than the one they dug, but it was made out of weak clay and Amerix feared that it would not hold and shafts might carve into it. So they marched, single file in some cases, south toward Central City, toward what they felt would be another decisive victory.

What is the reason for war? Honestly, is there a reason? Could not ideas and influences be spread without the threat of death or dismemberment? I guess what the real question is, is how does one define a war? The popular belief is that it is a battle waged by multiple combatants. Could someone fight a war without killing anyone? No one has to die to win a military campaign. If a castle is under siege and the attacking army does not let any food or water get into the castle, the defenders would have no choice but to surrender. How could they not, unless they allowed themselves to starve to death? But if they did choose death over surrendering, then I ask: why?

Why do men and women choose to die rather than give up? Could a war not be settled by fighting dogs? Or by a sport of some kind? Could not a war be fated on a single battle, where each side places their trust in a champion?

The answer is simple: it could. The problem is men, as a society, lack honor. If all men had honor, or followed a set of humane rules, there would be no need to fight to the death. There would be no fear of losing that would be great enough to warrant giving one's life. Given that truth, why can't men create these rules? Men can come together to build towers that reach the sky. They can build ships that can sail to the far reaches of the world. They can even wield and control forces that are unseen and contain enough power to shape the very earth they live in. Yet despite all of these abilities they possess, humans lack the basic fundamentals to achieve the simplest thing of all: peace. Peace is not a structure to create or a spell to bring someone back from the dead. It is merely the omission of violence. Are humans so cruel and wicked that they cannot keep themselves from committing acts of violence? Strange how the simplest of tasks is so far beyond those that can achieve almost anything.

—Lancalion Levendis Lampara—

Four

The Foe Beneath

Hard driving rain pounded relentlessly against the shutters of Lance and Jude's tiny bedroom window. They had rented a quaint room on the second floor that had a window facing west. Thinking the bargain price was a steal compared to the other rooms, Lance soon learned why the room was so inexpensive. The young mage had wanted to move the bed away from the window because the relentless storm drove many spurts of water through the weak and splintered shutters, soaking the blanket, but the bed was secured to the floor by large metal plates. Jude slept against the door and Lance sat at the other end of the room wrapped in a thick wool blanket studying the Necromidus. He strained his bright, green eyes in the flickering candle light as the wind raced through and nearly extinguished the candle again and again. The pounding rain played out songs until Lance grew weary and drifted off into sleep.

The storm had been a fierce one. There was a large puddle of water under the window, and bright beams of sunlight jetted through the splintered shutters setting yellow dots of sunlight on the bare floor and walls of the sparse room. A cold stiff wind howled outside announcing that autumn was well on its way. Lance gathered his pack and roused his large friend, who was sleeping on the floor in front of the door.

Jude slowly opened his eyes and stretched his thick arms. With a mighty yawn, the big man rolled over and pulled the thick wool blanket tight around himself. "Come, my friend, today is the day we leave this city," Lance said with a smile. But it quickly transformed into a frown when Jude merely mumbled and shifted. "Come on Jude, I thought you'd be happy to leave this city. All you have done since we arrived was complain. Now I am ready to leave

122

and you sleep on the hard wood floor as if you were in the bed of a young princess," Lance said as he loomed over his friend.

Jude finally sat up after a few more prods. He rubbed his eyes and smacked his lips. Lance said nothing as Jude slowly reached over, rummaged through his pack, and pulled out his water skin. He took a long deep draw, letting water spill out the corners of his mouth and down his unshaven chin. When he finished, he tossed the water skin on top of his pack, belched, wiped the water from his mouth with his sleeve, and plopped right back down, pulling the blankets tight around him. Lance groaned in frustration and forced open the door, pushing hard against Jude's legs. If Jude noticed at all he didn't show it until the door slammed shut and Lance's footfalls grew quieter as he went down the hall. Then the large man cracked a smile.

As Lance descended the stairs to the common room, he was overwhelmed by the smell of venison and eggs. Lance was surprised to see the common room rather empty. There were a few tables of militia guardsmen and a few farmers eating, but other than that, the great room was empty. Lance strolled to a small table against the north wall and waited for one of the serving wenches to come over. After getting her attention, he ordered a plate for himself and one for Jude. He savored the fresh meat, while contemplating where he might go next to decipher the text he had gotten from the thief in Bureland. The old sage had told him the writing was elven, but little else. Lance doubted the sage could read elven and merely recognized the language. But there were many types of elven races, and each had their unique respective languages. Lance worried how difficult it would be to find an elf that could, or even would for that matter, read it.

Jude rose and dressed. He was happy to be leaving this city finally, even if it was early in the morning. Though their stay was a little over a day, it was a little too long for the swordsman. The large man donned his chain armor shirt and strapped his large sword over his back. Hoisting his heavy leather pack over one shoulder, he opened the door and trotted downstairs. He was a little surprised at how empty the common room was, but guessed the storm had forced a lot of patrons to head out early. He looked around the room and spied Lance sitting at a small table at the north wall staring intently into nothingness. Jude noticed that his wizard friend had already eaten, but had purchased him a plate as well. He dropped his pack on the floor and took his seat across from the young mage, staring at the food on the plate. The aroma of the fresh meat and eggs wafted up into his face.

Jude shoveled a heaping spoonful of egg in his mouth, he took a bite of bread, and while chewing the mouthful, he spoke. "Hey Lance, what's up?" Jude asked as he piled in yet another mouthful.

Lance shifted his gaze from the wall to the floor, but said nothing. Jude paused his chewing for a moment, then swallowed his mouthful. "We will find an elf to help us," Jude said as he placed his large hand on Lance's shoulder.

Lance shook his head from side to side. "No, my friend," Lance said. "We are human. They'll not willingly help us."

Jude just looked down at the small portion of food that remained on his plate. He guessed Lance was right. Elves rarely spoke to humans unless the humans were great kings or heroes. He and Lance were anything but that.

"Perhaps you could trick one, like you tricked me," Jude said with a smile, but Lance merely shook his head again. Jude frowned and sighed. "Well . . ." Jude said reluctantly. "I could put my ear to the street and see if there is anyone in the city that might be able to help us."

Lance turned to his large friend. He cracked a small grin. "We might be forced to stay in the city a few more nights," Lance said as he trailed off, his grin erupting into more of a smile.

Jude clapped his friend on the back, glad to see his spirits were lifted. "Well . . ." Jude said as he smiled and sat back in his chair, his massive arms folding behind his head and propping his feet onto the fragile table. "If I am to suffer a few more nights in this city, I will need better housing."

Lance grinned lightly at the thought. He preferred to purchase a better room anyway. "Let's go and rent us a fine room, my friend," Lance said as he finished the small amount of wine that was sitting at the bottom of his wooden flagon. Perhaps this would be a good trip after all, Lance thought. Just perhaps.

*   *   *

Amerix stepped through the small opening from the tunnel his men had dug, into a new one. His hard leather boots splashed down into a two-foot-deep stream of putrid water. The odor of methane and pneumonia hung in the stagnant air of the sewers under Central City. The sewer shafts were about nine feet high and twenty feet across. The gray stone walls were covered in a dark green moss that secreted an oozing slime. There were two three-foot-wide stone ledges that lined the slow flow of water down the passage. The passages were dimly lit from sewer grates located close to a hundred feet above the sewer corridors. The sunlight reflected off the moss covered passages, giving the entire sewer a soft green hue.

Amerix slowly waded to the ledge on the east side of the passage. Large masses of floating debris swirled in the putrid water as he waded by. A few of his commanders walked out of their tunnel and gagged on the noxious odor that was stirred up from the muck.

Amerix chuckled. "Ye gots the stomach for war, but ye can't deal with a little stench," Amerix said as he walked over to them. One of the dwarven commanders doubled over and vomited profusely. Amerix clapped him on the back and laughed again. "Let us be a movin' to a more favorable place so we can stage a command post and map this area."

The two commanders merely nodded in agreement as they covered their noses and mouths, fighting to keep the remaining contents of their stomachs in their bellies. As Amerix's leaders moved into the dark odorous passage, the reaction was much the same. Very few vomited, but all were more than disgusted at the task. Human waste clung to their legs as they slowly waded down the large sewer corridors. They carried their weapons high above their heads in an effort to keep the finely crafted blades from becoming soiled. Aside from the vileness of the wading in human excrement, the dwarves valued their weapons in a religious sense. They placed the utmost value on crafts and artwork and their weapons were surely works of art. Most of the commanders wielded blades and hammers that took decades to forge.

Many dwarven eyes scanned the long dark sewer corridors beneath Central City. And unbeknownst to the bearded invaders, there were many non-dwarven eyes scanning them from the shadows.

*   *   *

"What is it?" the hand signals asked from the shadows above the dwarven parade.

Ryshander impatiently signed back to Kaisha. "Dwarves," he signed.

Kaisha frowned. She had called the sewers beneath Central City her home for over ten years and never had she seen a dwarf there, let alone many of them. She strained to look past Ryshander toward the corridors. She could hear them splashing down the grinder, and her keen sense of smell detected heavily oiled weapons and armor. Though she could not understand what they were saying, her thin lips began to quiver in excitement, but Kaisha dared not move a single inch. She had learned from Ryshander long ago about hiding in the shadows. Often times even the slightest movement could spell disaster. And with well over thirty armored dwarves marching a few feet away, detection was the last thing she wanted.

Ryshander studied the dwarves for some time. His well-honed muscles clung to the thin crevices of the wall without complaint. He noticed that the dwarves were not familiar with the grinder or moving in the sewers. They splashed around and spoke out loud. Though Ryshander wasn't young by human standards, the fact that he and Kaisha were wererats kept them looking far younger than they were. Ryshander was almost thirty-five, and Kaisha was about twenty-seven, though they looked to be in their teens. And even though being a lycanthrope, or wererat, prevented them from being injured from weapons that were not magical or made of silver, the pair had long ago learned the value of caution.

They stayed motionless save for a few hand gestures here and there. When the dwarves were out of sight they both sighed softly. Ryshander slowly lowered himself from the small alcove near the base of the ceiling, and then offered his hand to aid Kaisha. Though in truth she was as skilled as he was in climbing, it was more a gesture of respect and emotion, than of necessity.

"We should alert Pav-co immediately," Kaisha signed.

Ryshander shook his head. "This may well profit for us. We should follow them and see who or what they are looking for. Maybe we can aid them and line our own pockets with gold, instead of Pav-co's."

Kaisha frowned as Ryshander stopped signing and moved

slowly and quietly down the corridor, his green cloak blending almost perfectly into the moss covered walls. She hurried to him. "My love, what if we find they are looking for Pav-co or some other of our kind because Pav-co wronged them? You would stroll into their numbers for the sake of a few coins and leave me alone in this world without you?" Kaisha signed as she pouted and poked out her lower lip while crossing her arms under her full breasts.

Ryshander slumped his shoulders and gently stroked her smooth cheek with his callused gloved hands, his dark brown eyes gazing into hers. "Let's go and poke around ole Pavie, and see if we can learn if he wronged any dwarves recently. Though, I know we are wasting valuable time that we could be using to line our pockets with dwarven treasures."

Kaisha merely smiled a thankful smile, and the pair hurried down the grinder toward Lostos, the sewer guild house of Pav-co.

*　　*　　*

Lance sat in the new room that he and Jude had rented. It had high ceilings with intricate designs of swirling colors. The floor was hard polished oak, with a singular plush rug in the center that extended just below each bed. There was a large cedar closet next to each bed that had ivory handles that dangled down like plump apples from a tree. This room had actual glass instead of rotting wooden shutters, and the large oaken beds were against each smooth wooden wall adjacent to the window. The mattresses were stuffed with goose down and had fine cotton sheets. The blankets were made of thick wool and were dyed red and gold, the colors of Beykla. Lance ran his delicate hand over the blankets. He didn't much appreciate the choice of color, but he realized that he was probably one of a very small group of people that despised their home country. Sitting on the bed, Lance leaned back and basked in the beam of warm sunlight that bore into the large room like a shower of golden bliss. He had been studying the Necromidus for most of the day while Jude was out looking for a renegade sage that worked the streets for a local thieves guild. Lance had heard of the renegade sages. He also knew of mages that sold their talents to the highest street bidder. A strange environment to study and practice magic, he thought, but not too much stranger than studying on horseback and in unfamiliar inns.

Lance was close to finishing the first book he had been studying. Yet he was not sure if the spells would work. The magic he was studying, the magic of the Necromidus, was inherently evil. It required the practice of weaving dark necromancies on live people to ensure the spell was being cast properly, and to highest effectiveness. Lance certainly wasn't going to try it on innocent people, so he felt the next conflict he had, he might try one then. Though he feared something might go awry, he was confident that he had learned the spell correctly. Plus, battle was definitely not the controlled median for learning spell casting, but he figured he had no other recourse.

Lance practiced the incantation several times as he awaited Jude's return from the streets. As he weaved his hands in the prearranged motions of the spell, he could feel a strange tingling at the end of his fingers as a celestial blue light enveloped them. He could almost sense the magical weaves around his hands screaming for release, pulling at his restraint to loosen them, but Lance resisted. He closed his eyes as he struggled to control the order of the ancient incantations. Large beads of sweat began to form on his brow and his body shuddered from the strain. Lance fought the sensation for several minutes before collapsing on his bed. He had withstood the pull from the spell but it had scared him. Never had any of the dweamors he weaved before fought against his cognizant will. Yet this spell from the Necromidus seemed to have a mind of sorts. Lance shook his head as he thought to himself: No, not a mind of its own, but more of a will, a pagan desire that lusted after the release of intense energy. Lance thought about the spell, and how to put the encounter into words. He then rolled over on the soft, plush bed, pulled out his pen and ink, and began to scribe in his notes.

*   *   *

His time for revenge was rapidly approaching. He had been trailing the mage and his swordsman for many days. He followed them around the alleys and streets of Central City patiently waiting for the mage to be alone. Yet, everywhere the mage went, the damned swordsman followed. Grascon was becoming more and more impatient. The longer he stayed in Central City, the more likely it was some of the thieves might recognize him, yet he could not let the mage live after double crossing him like he did. He rented a room across the hall from Lance and Jude. When they moved he moved. He didn't bring a lot of gold with him so he was forced to cut a few purses, and a few necks of course, to pay for the plush room before Lance and Jude found more accommodating living quarters. He became excited when Jude went out on his own, but it was during the day. Grascon didn't like operating during the day. His victims were at an extreme disadvantage during the night, and he had learned long ago, you don't underestimate any mage, regardless of age. They were a difficult lot to measure. He just hoped Jude didn't return until much later.

*   *   *

Jude wasn't having any luck. He had wandered through the back alleys of the city for most of the day. He and Lance had only nine gold and some change left and it didn't seem to be enough to buy any information about the guild or guilds. He had almost gotten into a score of sword fights and was growing tired of walking in the streets.

It was late afternoon when he decided to enter the sewers and see if he might find some guild contacts there. Jude searched the alleys for a grate that was not under the observant eye of the city guards. He surmised that the grate was not well watched, so he probably wasn't the only one that might use it. Jude knew that guilds often operated in the sewers, so it seemed to be a good place to look to finish out his day.

Jude grabbed the heavy rusted sewer grate and pulled. His long thick arms strained little as he hoisted up the moss-covered ladder that extended a hundred or so feet into the darkness. Jude climbed in, and carefully replaced the grate back over his head. Green slime and water dripped down in his hair and on his shoulders as he slid the grate back into place. He covered his nose and mouth as he lowered himself down the chute.

Jude climbed about one hundred feet down the ladder before he reached the passage. He had difficulty seeing very far in the dark and cautiously stood on one of two ledges that lined the dark, foul smelling passage. In the center of the passage was a slow stream of a green putrid water. It had large pieces of floating debris that appeared to be waste, and other foul smelling substances. Jude scanned left and right, his eyes struggling with the dim green glow of the sewers. He turned and walked down the right ledge, careful not to trip on anything that might send him headlong into the disgusting waters. Jude was an accomplished woodsman. He was no ranger, but his tracking skills were quite refined. However, he couldn't find any obvious tracks in the moss-covered ledge.

After traveling down a few hundred yards until he reached a "T," Jude looked long and hard down each passage, straining his dark brown eyes in the dim green light. He went left, then right, then left again, making mental notes of each turn, never marking the walls to keep any would-be thieves from tracking him should they stumble across the scars in the moss. He had just about decided to turn around when he heard the strange voices up ahead.

*　　*　　*

The two dwarven scouts had been walking for hours. Their short little legs were tired from the tedious task of walking on the slippery moss that lined the filth-strewn corridor of the under city. They wore fine chain shirts and bore large axes. They wore thick metal helms that were strapped to their chins, just under their short brown beards. They were stained with waste and excrement that clung to their armor and legs. As they walked noisily and clumsily down the corridor, the smell of the sewers, and the lack of meeting anything of consequence save for a sewer rat or two, had made them quite complacent.

"Bah, this stinks!" one of the dwarves called out. "We ain't seen a thing since we came into these Leska-be-damned sewers."

The other dwarf nodded in agreement. "There is no need to be quiet even. There ain't a single human down here in this rotten hell," the other said as he wiped his sleeve on his burning nose, and the other agreed. The pair turned the corner and stood motionless in surprise. Standing directly in front of them was a large human—probably the largest human the dwarves had ever seen. He stood six feet seven inches tall and was about three dwarves wide. He had a giant sword strapped to his back and wore a chain shirt that hung low below his knees. His hands were outstretched with his palms showing and he was speaking some rabble that they could not understand. There was a moment of hesitation by the dwarves. They gawked in awe at the giant that stood before them. Then in dwarven fashion, they did what any dwarf would do when faced with an enemy of sorts; they drew their weapons and attacked.

*   *   *

Jude advanced slowly and cautiously toward the voices. They were not exactly what he expected, but he thought perhaps they were some form of thieves cant. As Jude cautiously navigated the narrow ledge to a right turn in the corridor, he could hear the deep voices growing louder. Jude stood on the right side of the sewer corridor and waited as two dwarves rounded the corner and stood in shock. Jude quickly studied the dwarves. He noticed they carried their large double bladed axes in their right hands and they were facing with their weapon arms on the outside of the ledge. Jude was also right-handed, and his weapon arm was on the inside, therefore he had a distinct disadvantage if this encounter came to blows. What also worried the large swordsman was that due to the dwarves' small stature, they each could launch feints and thrusts without hindering each other.

Jude outstretched his arms and placed his hands palms out, showing that he bore no weapons. "Friend dwarves, I mean no harm. I am looking for a renegade sage or some other . . ." Jude was cut off by a low strike to his left knee. He raised his leg and twisted his body in an attempt to dodge the blow. The axe narrowly missed his hamstring and whistled past. The second dwarf launched his axe overhand, swinging down for Jude's head. Jude, off-balance, managed to avoid the brunt of the blow, but the axe tore a deep gash through his heavy chain shirt and into his chest. Searing pain erupted from the wound and the force of the blow knocked the injured swordsman backward. He lost his footing in the wet moss and tumbled headlong into the sewer. With a mighty cold splash, debris-filled water washed over Jude and he hit the putrid waterway's hard stone floor that was under the three-foot deep sewer rivulet. He drew his great sword while under the water and stood up as quickly as he could. His massive form erupted from the water in a defensive stance, and he held his great sword close to his body with the tip of the sword pointing straight up. The giant blade glinted in the pale light of the sewer as the fetid water cascaded down the polished blade. Jude's eyes were set aflame by the filthy water that dripped down from his long hair. He struggled to see through his tear-filled eyes as the two dwarves in the water advanced toward him. Jude tried to wipe away the stinging waste from his face as he backed away from his two assailants. With his left hand over his face wiping furiously, Jude managed to awkwardly parry another strike from a dwarven axe.

Jude backed against the stone ledge on the far side of the sewer. He didn't dare climb onto it, since the moss was much too slippery to navigate a battle on. Instead he grabbed his sword with both hands and took a wide stance. Someone was going to answer for the stinging gash in his chest.

*   *   *

Ryshander and Kaisha were having difficulty making their way back to Lostos. Every passage they took seemed to have dwarven patrols in it. It was as if the dwarves just magically appeared in the sewers. Each patrol was made of two or three dwarves wearing light armor and carrying large axes or hammers. Ryshander feared a confrontation might harm their chances for making any coin from the dwarves, and the increasing number of the bearded folk had Kaisha more than slightly concerned, so the pair rested under a grate that led to the surface. "We should flee the sewers, my love," Kaisha signed as she smiled warmly at Ryshander.

Ryshander's long brown hair bounced as he shook his head from side to side. "It is not yet dark, my love, and we would face more dangers than a few dwarves if we emerged from the sewers during the day," he signed urgently.

Kaisha frowned, folded her arms under her breasts, and leaned against the wall of the grinder.

Ryshander placed his gloved hand on her shoulder. "I know what you are thinking, my love," he signed. "But there are only four alley sewer grates, and we are nowhere near any of them. We can-

132

not come out of a street grate while it is light, so we either have to keep moving or wait here until it gets dark," Ryshander signed as he kind of smiled to himself. For once, he was the conservative one. Normally he is quite ready to take a few chances, but something was different this time. He couldn't put his finger on it, but he could tell something bigger than a few dwarves being in a sewer was occurring.

"What is it, my love?" Kaisha signed as she studied Ryshander's face. She could see the uncharacteristic concern in his eyes—eyes that were normally dreaming of riches, not contemplating troublesome events.

Ryshander returned her gaze and took a long look into her beautiful brown eyes. How he loved her. Without her, there was nothing in his world. His sun, moon, and stars all began with her name. He shook his head. "Nothing, Kaisha," he whispered with a smile as he gently stroked her smooth jaw line.

Kaisha's eyes went wide with Ryshander's words. He had broken a stalwart rule of the under city. Speech was strongly discouraged. Many who broke the rule found themselves cold and dead soon after. She frowned at him and began signing furiously. "How dare you speak down here!" she signed with great emotion. "I understand your passion for all things, but I will not tolerate such recklessness!" Kaisha's signs were almost audible due to the emotion she was instilling in them.

Ryshander could only look down and kick at the muck on the cold sewer floor. He knew it was reckless to speak, but he was so caught up in the moment. He wanted to explain to her that it was her beauty that forced him to speak. He wanted to scream at her that he could be at the end of his existence and if he could have but a glimpse of her smiling face, he could die knowing that his life would had been complete from simply knowing her. Instead he humbly looked up and signed an apology. She accepted with a half frown, half smile, and kissed him gently on his cheek. She started to sign again when the pair heard the sound of ringing steel echo faintly down the corridor of the grinder that sounded suspiciously like swordplay.

Without missing a beat, the pair rushed to the battle as fast as they could go while remaining silent. Cautiously navigating down the slick moss-covered passage, the pair neared, then slowed. They

133

didn't want to wander into any perimeter patrols in case this was some kind of planned attack. Pav-co would severely chastise them for their carelessness if he had set some sort of ambush.

After checking the ceilings and small alcoves of the grinder for would-be enemies, they approached the clamor. As they warily rounded the corner, the pair watched with deep interest as two dwarves battled a giant of a man.

"Who is the human?" Kaisha signed.

Ryshander shrugged. "Are you sure he is human? Never have I seen a human as big as he. Perhaps he is half ogre or some other half breed," he replied.

Kaisha shrugged in reply and the pair returned their eyes eagerly to the fight.

* * *

Jude clenched his large two-handed sword as green slime from the sewers dripped from his well-defined muscled arms. He held his sword out straight toward the two advancing dwarves. Blood streamed from the wound in his chest and ran down his stomach and onto his legs. He clenched his teeth and began a low growl. Jude knew the enemies he faced were not the drunken novices he usually fought in Bureland. He now battled two adversaries that had more than a hundred years to train and better their techniques than he did. But he was not about to go down without at least drawing some of their blood in the fight.

As soon as the first dwarf came into range, Jude circled his blade over his head with both hands and struck down hard from his right. The dwarf brought his axe up to intercept the heavy blade. The two weapons collided with a shrill ring and the force of the blow knocked the dwarf's weapon to Jude's left side. The dwarf tried to roll with the blow and return a strike but Jude had already moved to his right. The giant man continued to swing his mighty sword in a spinning motion, straining every muscle in his thick arms. He groaned and struggled against the inertia of the mighty sword to change its direction. Instead of bringing the blade, and momentum, into the side of the second dwarf, he brought the heavy blade directly down into the dwarf's head. The second dwarf tried in vain to move his axe from the right where he expected Jude's

134

sword to strike, to deflect the overhead blow, but he underestimated the large man's speed.

The great sword sliced deep into the dwarf's face. There was a dull melon-splitting sound, as the blade cleaved the thick metal helm and implanted itself deep into the dwarf's skull. The dead dwarf slipped under the disgusting waters and disappeared from sight. All that could be seen was the pommel of Jude's great sword protruding from the murky water. Jude gripped the impaled blade and placed his foot on the dwarf's skull as he pulled, trying to free his weapon from the fallen enemy, but his wet and slimy hands could not get a firm grip on the hilt of the blade as he took a slice across his left shoulder from the other dwarf. The bearded attacker was preparing a second strike as Jude clutched the new wound with his hand. His weak, numb, and wounded arm hung low as warm sticky blood streamed down from his shoulder and dripped into the stagnant water.

Stinging pain shot from his new wound and clouded his head. He stood with his feet wide in the knee-deep water of the sewer, trying to regain some balance. Glancing at the hilt of his sword that was firmly lodged in the skull of the first dwarf, he realized that he would not have enough time to free the weapon before the dwarf's second attack. Jude set his feet and waited. As the dwarf came in with a high strike aimed at Jude's neck, he ducked low and grabbed the axe just under the blade, at the base of the head, with his wounded left arm. Pain erupted from the wounded shoulder and sent the shock rippling through his body. The mighty swordsman didn't completely stop the blow as the bottom tip of the axe blade stabbed into his forearm, and he tried to hold onto the dwarf's deadly axe. As the dwarven soldier struggled to free his axe from the giant man's grasp, Jude brought his right arm around and struck him solidly in the face with an overhand right. The small nasal bone of the dwarf snapped under the force of the giant man's punch, sending red blood shooting out from the dwarf's nose. The bearded invader released his axe and staggered back in the water clutching his shattered skull. Jude transferred the dwarf's axe to his right hand and waded toward him. Realizing he was unarmed and severely wounded, the dwarf tried to climb onto the ledge and retreat. Jude followed, quickly closing the gap with his huge strides. The dwarf never looked back as his fingers frantically dug at the moss-covered stone ledge walkway. Jude brought the axe down into the back of his fleeing enemy. The keen dwarven weapon tore deep into the dwarf's back and lodged into his spine. Jude checked his many stinging wounds as he glanced at his enemy, whose body slid from the ledge into the sewer water, and then disappeared from sight under the sewer's shallow depths.

Ignoring the pleas from his wounds to stop and rest, Jude continued on, not knowing how many more dwarves might be lurking in the dark sewers of this under city. He was far from the last grate up to the street that he had remembered seeing. Jude was perplexed as to why there were two dwarven soldiers in the sewers of Central City. Regardless of the events that he concocted, Jude had nothing but bad feelings about them, especially because of the rumors of what happened at the Torrent Manor.

The large man placed the handle of the dwarven axe under his left arm and wrenched his two-handed sword free from the skull of the other dwarf. He placed the blood-soaked weapon back in the scabbard that hung from his backside and slowly waded over to the other side of the sewer. He was covered in spotted blood that had splattered from the dwarves, and heavy streams of his own blood soaked his chain shirt and arm. He could feel the sting of the filthy sewer water in his fresh wounds and knew that if he did not get them clean, he could die from an infection. Jude had seen many battles where the victors on the field lost their lives from infection that developed in dirty wounds.

The large swordsman slowly stepped back onto the ledge and continued down the grinder toward the ever dimming green glow up ahead. He hoped it was a sewer grate, for he knew he could not see in the dark, and that any dwarf he encountered could see well in total blackness. Plus, he was wounded to the point he could not defend himself properly and another battle with the bearded folk would most certainly have a different outcome. Jude forced the thoughts of another encounter from his mind and tried to focus on finding a way out of the sewers and back to Lance.

*   *   *

"Now what?" Kaisha signed to Ryshander. The battle was over, she could readily see that, but she didn't know whether they should search the dwarven bodies or intercept the large man. Certainly the sound of the battle was heard by nearby dwarves and they ware already rapidly approaching the area.

Ryshander shrugged. "I think we need to loot the dwarven bodies. We can pocket any coin or jewelry they may be carrying, and present the weapons to Pav-co and receive some recognition from him. Certainly he knows of the dwarves in the under city by now. We have seen enough of their patrols that they have surely been spotted by some other guild members," Ryshander signed.

Kaisha nodded slowly. "Yes, I agree. Plus I think now it would be very foolish to try to bargain with them. They will be angry at their losses, and there are too many of them for them to be some kind of adventuring group."

"Not only that, if the dwarves are agents or friends of Pavie's, we can blame the looting on the big man that killed them," Ryshander signed with his lust for gold in his eyes.

Kaisha nodded and the pair hurried over to the bodies. They quickly searched the two dead dwarves, but found no jewelry, no gold, no provisions, nothing other than their weapons and armor.

"This doesn't make sense," Kaisha signed and placed her hands on her hips, visibly frustrated.

Ryshander frowned. "Well, there is nothing for us here and we need to move before their friends arrive," Ryshander signed as he nervously glanced over his shoulder.

"Let's try to catch up to the big man and follow him. Maybe he will lead us to some answers," Kaisha signed as she picked up the heavy dwarven axe and handed it to Ryshander.

He nodded, taking the weapon and hurrying down the passage in the direction the human had gone.

*   *   *

Jude wandered down the dark moss-covered corridor. His wounds screamed for dressing, but he had managed to control his wits through the mind numbing pain. Though he was not out of the sewers yet, he was certain he was heading toward a grate. He played the battle over and over again in his mind as he raced down the passage. He was pleased with the outcome. Though he thought of many tactical changes he would make could he fight the battle again, he was more than pleased with himself. He had battled and defeated two well-armored dwarves in combat. And though he was profoundly wounded, he was certain the injuries would heal. Jude felt a little more confident. Before, he had only faced poorly skilled and very poorly armed men from Bureland. Though he had won those contests hands down, he had never truly been tested by serious combat. His mind wandered to the time he bested a half-orc in the common room of the Inn of Aldon, in Bureland. The half breed was extremely intoxicated and could barely stand unassisted. That was Jude's main claim to fame. The half-orc had everyone so intimidated that even the witnesses to the fight tremendously exaggerated the telling of the tale.

Jude reached a corner of the grinder. He paused and listened. He couldn't hear anything other than his own soft breathing. He ever so slowly peered around the moss-covered stone wall. His heart danced at the sight of a feint bluish green light cascading down from a sewer grate to the surface. The large man moved cautiously toward the ladder to freedom. With every step closer, he fought the overwhelming urge to break into a dead run. He didn't look back at the imaginary dwarven horde or other fiendish devils that he felt were stalking him. As he reached the rusted iron rungs that were embedded into the slimy moss-ridden stone walls, he stole a glance behind him. His muscles tensed as he half expected to be staring into the eyes of a dwarven army that stood poised to claim his life after he was so close to freedom. But when he turned, Jude saw only darkness and vague outlines of the empty sewer corridor. Jude easily ignored the pain in his shoulder as adrenaline pumped through his body and he climbed toward the grate. It seemed with each rung he climbed, the seconds dragged on. Finally he reached the final rung. Jude hung the dwarven trophy on the top rung of the ladder and peered at the sewer exit. To his horror a large wagon wheel was sitting on the rusted iron grate. Jude could see the dimly-lit sky from under the wagon and he could smell the sweet night air, but all he could do was helplessly touch it with his hand. Jude's heart fell into a dark abyss. How could he have come so close to escape, to fail at the verge of freedom. His mind raced as he imagined his predicament. Did he dare climb back down and stumble around in the darkness searching for another grate that could be anywhere in the stagnant tunnels of the under city? How long

138

should he wait? He couldn't tell if the wagon was attached to any horses. Was it merely stopped for a short time, or was it parked for the night? Jude wrestled with the decision of whether to wait or to press on when he heard many dwarven voices echoing from the dark passage below. Jude shoved up against the grate with all his strength, but he could not even budge it. Fear began to tear through him. He knew he could not defeat many more dwarves, and if he did, he would never be able to navigate the sewers in the dark. Jude exhaled softly, coming to the revelation that he would just have to wait until the wagon moved or he was slain. He figured if the dwarves tried to come up the rusted ladder he was perched on, he could kill enough of them to discourage them from climbing up to attack him directly. The group he encountered didn't have any projectile weapons and he doubted the dwarves could throw their heavy axes the hundred or so feet up at him. Jude thought if he was lucky, they wouldn't think to look up the grate and might not see him. He then glanced up at the wagon and rethought the luck idea. He had six hundred pounds sitting on the sewer grate proving he wasn't very lucky tonight. Either he would manage to escape, or he would die.

*　　*　　*

Ryshander and Kaisha hurried down the dark mossy corridor of the grinder. They figured the human would try to escape the under city at the first grate he came across, which was only a few hundred yards away. Their soft leather boots glided to a stop when they saw the human slowly climbing the rusted iron ladder toward the sewer grate about a hundred feet above the passage. They began to move more cautiously and measured their stride with each other to reduce the sound of footfalls that would hinder their ability to detect any ambient sounds. They could hear the human swordsman's labored breathing, and his fresh warm blood stained the mossy walls and pooled at the base of the ladder.

"What now?" Kaisha signed. She noticed the human wasn't opening the grate and she didn't want to risk catching an axe in the face if she or Ryshander tried to climb up behind him.

"We wait," Ryshander signed back as he moved to the edge of the grate passage. He positioned himself just to the point that the human wouldn't notice him. Though he figured the human couldn't see in the dark, he learned long ago that people were sometimes surprisingly resourceful.

Ryshander listened carefully while his keen hearing detected the sound of the human hanging the dwarven axe from an iron rung. Then he heard his faint groans as he tried to force open the grate. Ryshander turned and signed back to Kaisha. "I think the grate is locked."

Kaisha frowned. The city never locked them before, why now? "Perhaps it is barred or blocked," she signed to Ryshander.

He only shrugged in response and returned to listening intently to the top of the passage while Kaisha fidgeted nervously. She didn't like the idea of waiting at a barred or locked grate. They were in the middle of a corridor. If they needed to flee an attack from both directions, they were trapped. Avoiding being trapped is one of the first lessons learned in the under city. Not only that, but the thought of the city locking, or worse yet, barring the other grates gave her chills.

Ryshander was watching the silhouette of the human from a small metal mirror he had removed from his pack. His focus was disturbed by a tug at his sleeve. He looked up at Kaisha's frantic signing.

"Dwarves!" she signed hysterically and darted back toward the way they came.

Ryshander listened for a moment. He heard the dwarves talking as their clumsy footfalls echoed down the grinder, announcing their approach. He looked up at the human, and then looked back at Kaisha. She was urging him to follow her. Reluctantly he abandoned the human to his own devices and rushed back down the grinder toward Lostos, toward safety.

*　　*　　*

Therrig could hear something shuffling at the top of some chute that led to the city surface. When Amerix learned the patrol had not returned, the grizzled old general sent Therrig and a small band of fighters out to discover what happened to the two dwarves.

Therrig gripped his large two-handed enchanted hammer. The dwarven champion itched to spill some human blood and he hoped he might find the humans that killed or captured the missing patrol. Therrig considered himself Amerix's most trusted friend and his best warrior. He wore thick plate armor that had a large face shield that protruded from his right shoulder up to eye level. His helm was open-faced like most dwarves, and had a bright blue mohawk on the top that was held in place by a thick leather strap that ran under the solid jaw of the mighty dwarf. If there was a problem, Therrig would deal with it. But much to Therrig's disappointment, when he reached the chute, he found nothing except vivid red blood. Whatever it was, it had escaped. Therrig chewed on his lip angrily and shouted curses at his men for not catching the fleeing intruder. Amerix was not going to be happy to find out a human may have escaped after learning of their presence. But what angered Therrig more was the fact that he did not get to kill the intruder himself. It had been too long since the wicked dwarf had slain a foe, and his lust for battle grew stronger. The wicked dwarf decided to make a wider sweep of the under city. Perhaps he might find something to placate his ache for battle.

*　　*　　*

Jude stared into the blackness below him. He couldn't see the stone floor of the corridor but he could hear the dwarves speaking as they drew closer. Jude's heart began to beat so hard he feared the dwarves might hear it. He placed his sweaty forehead against the cool stone wall of the chute and said a silent prayer to the goddess of mercy Lance had spoken about. Jude had prayed to just about every god or goddess he knew of throughout his life and was yet to receive any kind of response or answer, so he figured since he hadn't ever prayed to the goddess of mercy, this certainly seemed like a good time. Just as he finished his silent plea, he heard the sound of leather creaking and the command for the horses to move. Could it be? Jude looked up to see the wagon riding off into the night. He didn't waste a second. With renewed strength he shoved the grate up and onto the cobblestone street. It made a loud clang as it bounded off of the hard cobblestones of the paved road. Jude hastily climbed out of the sewer chute and quickly replaced the heavy iron grate. He sat on the ground for some time to inhale the sweetest air he had ever breathed. The autumn night breeze washed over him like a cool towel in the hot summer. Jude stood up and stretched his tightening muscles, and began the walk back to the Blue Dragon Inn. He wasn't exactly sure where he was, but boy did he have a story for Lance.

*　　*　　*

Amerix sat in the large sewer room he had converted into a command center. He had posted detailed maps that his scouts had made outlining grates, ambush intersections, and dead ends, in case the battle moved back into the sewers. His men worked feverishly to remove the large growth of moss and scrape away the filth and slime that had built up on the walls and floors. The ceiling in the staging room was about twenty-five feet high, higher than other parts of the sewer. The dome-shaped stone ceiling still dripped an occasional drop of moisture, so Amerix had his men construct a canvas covering his command tent. The dawn was rapidly approaching and the grizzled old general still hadn't received any word about the missing patrol. He hoped the humans didn't move into the sewers. He saw no sign of the pink-skinned dogs in the under city, and every iron ladder under each grate had a steady growth of moss on it, indicating that the grates hadn't been used in some time. Yet, it was obvious his missing patrol had encountered something because the seasoned pair hadn't returned. Amerix entertained the idea they became lost, but that angered him, since the majority of the under city had been mapped. He made his patrols memorize every detail of the existing map before they went out. Amerix had sent Therrig, who he considered a loose bolt in the wheel of war, but the wicked dwarf was a proven ally who had a group of ten highly skilled fighters to search out the missing patrol. But with each passing minute, the old dwarf became more impatient for their return. The ancient general decided that he had spent enough time in the sewers, and called for a messenger.

"Yes, my general," the young dwarf, barely a hundred years old, replied.

Amerix scribed down a note on a damp parchment explaining that he intended to strike in a moment's notice and to have the army ready to march at any time. He then rolled the heavy scroll up and gently placed it in an old ivory case. He sealed the case with red can-

142

dle wax and affixed the Stormhammer seal to it. He handed the ivory case to the young messenger. "Take this scroll to Commander Kestish," Amerix said without looking at the messenger. The old general turned after handing the scroll off and began mulling over which grates he wanted to have his army emerge from. Before glancing up to see if the messenger was gone, he returned his thoughts to his battle plans. "Should we split our forces and have a surface unit hit them from the north while we emerge and hit them from behind? Or should we pour out of every west grate, trapping the human scum between us and the Dawson River?" Amerix asked aloud.

Commander Fehzban frowned. Though he was one of Amerix's most loyal supporters and skilled clerics, he had been more than a little apprehensive about trying to sack Central City. He wasn't sure what strategy would be the best. Never had a dwarven clan warred with a human city, so there were no battles to study, no experience to draw from. Commander Fehzban had been equally worried about the Torrent strike, and it turned out as a complete success in every definition of the word, but he doubted they would be that lucky twice. He knew that Amerix didn't worship Leska. He also knew that Amerix's account of his visions from her could be described as a drunken stupor at best, but he didn't dare cross his demonic leader. "Perhaps we come from the east grates, my general," Fehzban said in support.

Amerix turned and frowned. His old face wrinkled in derision. "Why in the name of Durion would we do that? That would leave the human dogs with a clear path of escape!" Amerix growled.

Commander Fehzban smiled disarmingly. "Well, my general, we would have much fewer losses . . ."

"So would the human scum!" Amerix spouted, cutting off Fehzban in mid sentence. Fehzban paused and gave Amerix an incredulous look.

"Go on," Amerix said finally.

"As I was saying, general, the humans would flee, leaving us to pillage and burn the entire city. Plus, without supplies the humans would be desperate and disorganized in the forest—much easier to defeat or scatter," Fehzban said proudly, though in truth he disliked any plan to attack a city as well-defended as Central City.

Amerix pondered the tactic a moment. "Well Commander, I

like the idea. I will look at the east grates and see if it is a feasible route of attack," Amerix said before he dismissed the commander and returned to his battle plans. He was certain about one thing: they would attack from somewhere tomorrow night.

*   *   *

Ryshander and Kaisha hurried down the small dark passage that led to Lostos. The secret door that led to the hidden guild hall had been a long trip from where they had encountered the battle between the dwarves and the human. Furthermore, Ryshander had to take time and find a secure spot to hide the finely crafted dwarven blade. He planned on selling it later and didn't want Pav-co to get his hands on it. Kaisha knew that they were late and probably were going to be reprimanded. But with the news they brought, she imagined it would be short-lived.

They came upon the small, intricately ornate wooden door. It had carvings in it depicting a beholder floating above a small city. This beholder was one of the most fearsome of kind. It was a large floating ball of flesh with a single eye in the center and a large mouth with a thousand dagger-like teeth that was gaping in mid roar. Its long thick tongue seemed to reach out from the carving, and it had many small tentacle-like stalks that protruded from the mass of flesh. Each of the stalks had a small eye on the end of it and the entire creature seemed poised to strike dead anything that might oppose it. Ryshander had never seen a real beholder and neither had Kaisha. But from the stories they were told about the horrible beast, if they did it was likely that either of them would survive the encounter. Though they had seen the door a thousand times before, it always gave them reason to pause and admire the craftsmanship that was required to carve such a spectacle.

The pair pushed through the door after disarming a number of deadly poison needle traps and re-arming them once on the other side. They walked down the dry marbled hallway of Lostos, while fellow guild members paid them little attention as they went about their nightly tasks. There were probably thirty or so wererats in the guild—more than adequate numbers to control all the streets and some of the politicians. Pav-co had created the guild some fifty years ago and he had become severely rich from operation. The re-

144

sourceful thief had survived seven coup attempts that Ryshander knew of and he doubted there would be more attempts anytime soon.

As they neared Pav-co's room they noticed there was a general anxiousness in the air. People were rushing about, ignoring Ryshander and Kaisha completely. Pav-co emerged from his room and began walking toward them. Both bowed low to their corpulent leader. Pav-co gently reached down and took Kaisha's hand in his and gently kissed the back of it. Ryshander knew Kaisha loved him, but he detested Pav-co's disgusting open invitations to her. Once Pav-co had flatly propositioned her. Ryshander was so enraged he was going to march down and duel the loathsome creature. Kaisha begged him not to. Though Pav-co was much older than Ryshander, she had seen the plump little man deal out death to the most experienced thieves. Kaisha loved Ryshander too much to let him risk his life over some twisted sense of her honor. She knew that if she needed to, she could lull the fat man into her bed and kill him with a well placed dagger. She always kept a long, sharp, silver hairpin for just such an occasion.

"My beautiful Kaisha," Pav-co said as his lower lip twitched with lust at the sight of the stunningly beautiful woman that stood before him. Pav-co looked her up and down, drinking in her beauty. Kaisha was about five-feet-six with long brown hair that cascaded down her solid shoulders. She wore a black cloak that overlaid a brown and green tunic sewn with a lighter green stitch. The tunic was low cut, revealing the deep crevice between her firm breasts. The tunic came to rest a few inches above her hips and tightly hugged her waist. Her breeches were a thick, dark green velvety material that made little or no noise when brushed together or up against something else. The snug breeches extended down to her dark black leather boots that rose up just below her knee. She wielded a short sword that she kept strapped to her right leg and she wore a thin black belt with many pouches that contained her tools of the trade. Pav-co salivated at the thought of bedding the gorgeous thief, but he valued Ryshander's talents too much to have to kill him. He knew that if he took her by force, the young wererat would certainly seek blood. And though Pav-co bore no doubt he could easily slay Ryshander, no bedroom event was worth endangering the operation of his guild.

145

"What do you have to report?" Pav-co asked. He looked at Ryshander and acknowledged him for the first time.

Ryshander glowered at him. "We encountered a giant man that slayed two dwarves," Ryshander said.

"We aren't sure what the dwarves are doing in the under city. They had no provisions and no supplies or tools, other than the weapons the human ran off with. We heard more dwarves as we tried to follow the human so we were not able to track him on the surface," Kaisha said.

Pav-co's face turned red in anger. "You let a human come into the under city and then escape!" Pav-co growled.

"We had no choice. Before we could kill him many dwarves came marching down the grinder. If we were killed, how would we warn the guild of the dwarven activity?" Ryshander pleaded.

Pav-co grabbed at his fat belly and chuckled. "Do you presume that you are my only patrols in the under city?" Pav-co asked. "I am already aware of the dwarves. They have cleared out the old construction room and made it some kind of headquarters or such. I am sure they are not looking for us. I think they are mapping the under city for some reason. There are about two hundred down here now. They burrowed into the grinder from some adjacent tunnel, so we know they are not sent by the magistrate. I first thought they were a group of misguided miners, but they are dressed for battle, not mining," Pav-co said, stroking his fat chin. "I do not want either of you to go against them for any reason. I have given a guild order to avoid them at all costs. They are no threat to us, and I suspect they are some raiding party that took a wrong left or something. They have many enchanted weapons and could easily cut our numbers in half. Unless they pose some direct threat to our guild, they are to be left alone. I suspect if given time, they will leave."

Ryshander and Kaisha pondered the news for a moment.

"Did you get a good look at the human the two dwarves were fighting?" Pav-co asked.

Both Ryshander and Kaisha nodded.

"Good. I want you two to follow this human and see what he is up to. It might tell us why the dwarves are here. If he appears to be unaffiliated to the dwarves in any way, teach him why humans are not allowed in the under city," the fat guild master said. Pav-co

146

reached down and gently took Kaisha's hand a second time. He kissed it again and winked. Then he hurried back to his room.

"I swear one day I will run my sword into the fat belly of that loathsome creature," Ryshander growled.

Kaisha smiled disarmingly and avidly kissed Ryshander on the mouth, taking time to nibble his lower lip in a playful kiss that always seemed to relax him. "There will never be a need for that, my love," Kaisha said with a vixen's smile. She gave Ryshander a long reassuring look.

Ryshander's face became flushed as the pair hurried out of Lostos back to the grinder. They only had a few hours to find the giant man that had eluded them.

*　　*　　*

Grascon slowly opened the door to his room. He had oiled the old iron hinges the night before to ensure they didn't make any noise. He had hoped that Lance's door would have external hinges but it seemed nothing was ever easy. The hinges to the fool mage's door were impacted.

Grascon examined the door again as he had done many times before. He checked it for any thin wires or other telltale signs of traps but he found none. Grascon wished he had found some. He would much rather diffuse a poison needle trap than stumble into a glyph or some other warding spell created by the mage. He wasn't sure if Lance knew how to cast such spells but he wasn't taking any chances.

Grascon reached into one of his many belt pouches, drew his dagger, and pulled out a thin needle-like wire with a small flat hook on one end. He looked at the dagger he drew for the killing deed. The thin blade was covered in black powder to take away any glint in the night sky. Pav-co had trained him well when he worked for him. Grascon had assassinated many people for the fat thief. Pav-co eventually betrayed him and nearly cost the thief his life. He bore an ugly scar in remembrance and vowed to kill the fat man one day, but Pav-co was still too strong. Another time, he thought to himself.

Grascon carefully placed the small tool into the door lock. He could feel the thin appendage slide into the tumblers inside the door. He then removed a shorter wider tool and inserted it just above, but overlapping, the first tool. He slowly worked the two tools, until he felt them silently fall into place. With careful breathing techniques he slowly turned the handle to the door, twisting the knob so slowly that it was nearly impossible to notice the movement from the other side. Slowly, ever so slowly, he turned the knob until he felt the resistance from the bolt being moved from the receiver. Using the notches in the back of the knob he placed the night before, he gauged how far to turn it without creating the resounding click from the bolt sliding back into the now unlocked door. The deadly assassin pushed open the heavy door and slipped inside like a ghost. Grascon easily scanned the large room in the complete darkness. He could see two large beds. One had a figure in it asleep. Instead of moving right toward the sleeping mage, he moved along the walls of the room. Measuring each step, he looked for any kind of traps or alarms. He found none. Grascon could not believe how easy this was. Lance should have been expecting him, yet the boy slept as soundly as a child in his mother's arms.

"What a fool," Grascon thought to himself as he crept ever so slowly toward the bed. He raised his finely crafted dagger over Lance's sleeping form. He would have his revenge tonight.

*   *   *

Jude staggered down the dark streets and narrow alleys. It took the wounded swordsman a while to get his bearings after emerging from the alley. He avoided anyone he saw as he made his way back to the Blue Dragon Inn. Fortunately it was the first clear night in a while and Jude could see the stars and the moon. Under different circumstances he would have almost enjoyed the night walk. Jude had survived a fight with two deadly enemies and even taken one of their axes as a prize. The swordsman studied the magnificently crafted dwarven blade in the dim moonlight. The weapon gleamed in the pale light and revealed many dwarven runes carved in it. The head of the axe was double bladed and the edge was precision sharp, despite the many nicks in it. Though the axe was heavy, it seemed it should be much heavier than it was. Besides that, the weapon was so well balanced that Jude felt it could be thrown as easily as it could be swung. The craftsmanship of the keen dwarven blade mesmerized the large swordsman. Though he favored the use of his two-handed sword, Jude entertained the idea of wielding the axe as his primary weapon. He put the thought out of his mind for now. He needed to get back to Lance as quickly as possible. He had been gone a long time and undoubtedly Lance would be anxious to see him. Jude knew Lance wanted to stay in the city to get his papers read, but after the fight with the dwarves, Jude just wanted to get out of this deadly city.

Jude lumbered into the common room of the inn. His chain armor was covered in filth, and dark red blood stained his breeches and dripped on the hard, polished floor. It was late evening and there were only three patrons in the large room. One was a poorly dressed man that was passed out at the far end of the room. His dirty brown hair covered his face, which was down on the table, and a flagon of thick mead was still in his dirty callused hand. He was mumbling something about crops and taxes. The other two were playing a game of cards near the bar. Jude noticed that the table they were sitting at gave them a complete view of the room. The first patron was a male in his late teens and the female looked to be about the same age. The male was dressed in a dark green outfit covered by a dark cloak while the female was stunningly beautiful. She was wearing a tight fitting outfit that revealed her voluptuous breasts. She also wore a black cloak that was held together by a thin, silver hair pin. Her long straight brown hair was pulled back in a ponytail that dangled from the back of her head. Jude tried to gain more of a look, but her revealing tunic had forced him to take more than a passing gaze. He silently cursed his lustful eyes, but quickly decided that neither of the two were a threat, as he hurried up the sturdy oak stairs. As Jude rounded the corner at the top of the stairs, he noticed his wet boots made little sound on the hard floor when he walked down the hall toward his room—a much better establishment than he had ever experienced.

Jude turned the polished brass handle of the door and noticed it was not locked. He couldn't believe Lance was so foolish as to leave the door to their room unsecured. Jude slipped into the room and closed the door. He walked over to the unlit lamp that rested on the small table next to his bed. His chest and shoulder stung horribly and he was in dire need of a bath. He needed to repair his chain shirt that had been sliced open by the keen dwarven blade.

Jude reached down and grabbed the flint and steel that sat on the small wooden table near the bed. He struck them together and lit the ornate lamp. Suddenly pain tore through the right side of his ribs. He felt the plunge of cold steel pierce his chain shirt just above his kidney. Jude thrashed out his right hand and struck something. He turned to see a small man clutching his face and tumbling back against the wall. Jude drew his two-handed sword as Lance awoke violently and sat up in his bed.

Grascon recovered from the crushing blow to his face and quickly rushed in to meet the giant man. Jude accepted a stab to his exposed belly as he drew his great sword from his scabbard. Jude felt the dagger pierce his chain shirt again, but the blade was too small to fatally penetrate the mail. Jude's massive sword came slicing down and caught the intruder between his neck and his shoulder. The sharp weapon cut deep into the thief and sent him sprawling onto the floor. Blood splattered onto the wall and onto the plush rug that was in the center of the room. The thief clutched the fatal wound with his hands as he writhed in the throws of death. Jude took a step toward Lance and swooned. He could feel sharp stinging pains erupting from the minor knife wounds, causing the room to spin. His vision failed and he fell to his knees, dropping his great sword in a clamor.

Lance leapt from the bed and rushed to his friend. "Jude, thank the heavens you returned when you did! Are you alright?" Lance asked as he placed his arm under Jude's, and tried to lift him.

Jude's eyes rolled back in his head. "Poison," Jude said weakly, and then he lost consciousness.

Lance gently lay his hulking friend on the floor. He frantically began checking Jude's wounds to see if they were fatal. After quickly glancing him over, Lance realized he would survive the wounds, but he wasn't so sure about the poison. Lance rose to his feet and gasped in horror. The thief Jude had slain was standing in front of the door. His clothes bore a long blood-soaked tear from the collar bone to his waist, but there was no wound.

The thief smiled a one-toothed smile. "Remember me, mage?" Grascon asked with a wicked grin.

Lance stood in shock at the recognition. He recognized the one-toothed grin and the long scar across the man's face. It was the thief he had double-crossed back in Bureland. Lance knew he had to act fast. Lance cast the same spell on Grascon that he had often

150

cast on his adoptive father to make him drop his axe. Normal mages, and even sorcerers, had to move their hands, recite chants, and sometimes use components to cast their spells. But Lance was always able to visualize the movements and chants in his head to cast them. He knew he was unique in this ability and it allowed him to use magic so that other people had no idea he was casting.

Grascon watched in shock as the slender dagger shot from his grasp, skittered across the floor, and came to rest near the wall.

"Impressive, mage," Grascon said as he chuckled. "But I do not need the knife to kill you," the assassin said as his face began to quiver.

Lance watched in horror as the assassin's face began to elongate and erupt with hair. His hands began to grow long thick fur, and his fingers sprouted sharp black claws. His body convulsed and changed rapidly. Lance knew he didn't have much time. He began reciting the movements and incantations of the spell he learned from the Necromidus. As Lance finished the spell, a strange energy began to fill him. He felt it building up within him, searching for release. The magic called out to him, building and growing, pleading to be loosed at an enemy, but Lance fought it. He struggled to gain control, but the magic was too great. He felt himself losing his grip, losing his restraint. He was semi-aware of the strange half-rat, half-man creature that was once Grascon, advancing toward him. Lance was more afraid of the magic that continued to grow within him. It screamed at him to be free, yet Lance did not know how to release it. He fell back against the wall, barely able to stand. His vision was changing to blue light as the energy that bubbled within him neared peak. Lance shook his head, as intense cold washed over him. His flesh tingled and his bones ached, and he could hear nothing but an all encompassing ringing in his ears. He didn't even care that the creature stood before him with deadly claws streaking toward his neck. He didn't care that his friend may be dead, and that he was soon to follow. All he could think about, all that he desired, was to release the pain, to release the energy.

Grascon brought his claws down and sliced into Lance's neck. Grascon's wicked talons barely cut Lance's skin when his monstrous body was racked by tremendous pain. Lance could feel the intense energies release. It was the greatest feeling he had ever experienced. There was a great explosion but no sound was made.

The blue energy fired from his body and ripped into Grascon's. The wererat was hurled back across the room. The assassin clutched his chest and stumbled to a sitting position. Lance slumped back against the opposite wall. His thoughts were clear. There was no pain, only a sense of euphoria. He looked at Grascon trying to recover on the floor. Lance walked over to him. He could feel the energy rebuilding. He could feel it strengthening.

Lance reached down and grabbed Grascon on his head. He relaxed the restraint of the energy, and loosed it again. Lance could see the few weaves shoot out from his fingertips and erupt into the wererat's body. He could feel the magic reaching deep into the Grascon's life force, pulling at it, trying to wrench it free from his soul. Again Grascon writhed in pain, crying out in ultimate agony. The assassin clutched his chest and violently kicked and thrashed on the floor, trying in vain to escape the suffering he now endured. Lance released his grasp and stared at the would-be assassin. Grascon lay panting on the floor, struggling for each labored breath. Again Lance could feel the energy building, and again he loosed it on his enemy. Grascon screamed in terror and pain as his life force was slowly torn from his soul. Moments later, his twisted existence was over; the wererat known as Grascon the nimble lay dead.

The door of Lance's room burst open. A man and a woman rushed in with their weapons drawn. The male was dressed in a black cloak that hung loosely around him, and the female wore a green tunic and pants, with a similar cloak as the man. She held a short sword and he wielded a longer thinner blade that Lance had never seen before. The hilt was made of thick wire-like silver that was woven around the pommel, and the blade was long and slender with a sharp edge on each side. The short sword that the woman wielded was relatively plain, save that it bore runes along the blade from the hilt about six inches up. The sword looked strangely familiar to him.

"What's going on?" the man asked as the woman sheathed her sword and approached.

"We were attacked by this thing," Lance said as he pointed to the body of Grascon that had changed back to human form.

Kaisha kneeled down by Grascon's body. She recognized the scar and the face. She turned and signed to Ryshander. "It is

152

Grascon. He is dead. They must have used magic to slay him, because I don't see any silver or enchanted weapons."

Ryshander pointed his sword to the dwarven axe that was lying next to the large man they had followed in the sewer. Kaisha shook her head that she didn't see any wounds on the renegade thief. She moved Grascon's body so that Ryshander could see the wound had healed up. Wounds caused by non-silver or non-magical weapons on wererats always healed immediately.

"My friend was poisoned, can you help him?" Lance asked as he kneeled and checked Jude for signs of life. To his relief, Lance felt the warm breath on the back of his hand as he watched Jude's chest rise and fall.

Kaisha leaned over and examined the large man. She stuck her finger into the tiny hole in the side of the large swordsman. She pulled her hand back and smelled the yellow sticky fluid that was on her finger. "He will live," she said to Lance before turning to Ryshander and signing, "Jahallawa extract."

Ryshander frowned. Jahallawa extract was a poison that was used to paralyze its victims. It was most commonly used by assassins like Grascon, to capture enemies that had wronged them, so they could torture them to death. Ryshander wondered what the large man could have done for Grascon to risk coming back to Central City to capture him.

"I am Kaisha, this is my partner, Ryshander," Kaisha said, gesturing back to the man holding the thin blade.

Ryshander bowed low and crossed his sword over his chest. "We heard the commotion downstairs and came up to investigate. We are glad you are okay. This one here . . ." he said pointing to the dead body of Grascon, ". . . is particularly deadly."

Ryshander walked over and picked Jude up by his shoulders. "Grab his feet, let's put him in bed," Ryshander suggested.

Lance picked up Jude's filth-covered boots and helped place him on his bed, while Ryshander covered his nose and mouth with the sleeve of his sable cloak. "Where on earth has he been to have become mired in such stench?" Lance asked, trying not to gag.

Ryshander chuckled. "Who are you?" Ryshander asked.

Lance smiled. "I am Lance Ecnal and this is my friend Jude," Lance said as he motioned to Jude.

"Ecnal, as in the house of orphans?" Ryshander asked.

Kaisha gave him a reprising gaze. "Ryshander!"

"What? I just asked him if he was from that house, that's all," Ryshander said in his defense.

Lance smiled disarmingly. "No need to dance around the question. I am from the orphan house of Ecnal. I was adopted by a woodcutter named Davohn Ecnal of Bureland," Lance said flatly.

Kaisha sat on the bed across from Jude and frowned. "I thought the house was eradicated by assassins from Nalir, or so I was told," she said.

Ryshander stepped forward. "Yea, that's what I heard also. I wouldn't go around proclaiming I was an Ecnal, those dogs might still be lurking around looking to snub you out," Ryshander said with mock interest.

"Maybe that's what Grascon was doing," Kaisha said, picking up on Ryshander's questioning antics.

Lance shook his head. "No, he and I had history in Bureland. He stole some items for me, and got caught with them. He tried to get me to cover up for him, but I wasn't going to go down with the fool. I didn't think he would try to kill me, though. I figured he knew it was part of the risk he took when I hired him."

Kaisha and Ryshander weren't convinced. They knew Grascon when he worked for Pav-co. He was a skilled cat burglar and an assassin. He wouldn't have gotten caught unless he was set up. But neither of them would have thought him to be killed so easily either. The one truth was that he wanted to repay Lance for something since he was using Jahallawa extract. The poison was quite difficult to prepare and very expensive to buy. It wasn't something you used on a job. It had to have been personal.

"What did he steal for you?" Ryshander asked boldly.

Kaisha felt her face go red. She couldn't believe he was being so careless. But to her delight, Lance didn't seem guarded at all. "Well I'll show you," Lance said as he fetched the leather case containing the elven writing. As he picked up the case he sent a myriad of small weaves into the pages, transforming them into portraits of what he envisioned his mother to look like. He handed the pages to Ryshander. "There are some pages missing, these are just the portraits. I was supposed to receive some records recorded in elven, but I haven't yet. I am waiting for the new thief I hired to retrieve

154

them. I left word where I would be staying, and I expect them at anytime," Lance said with a smile.

Ryshander skimmed through the portraits. "She is beautiful, a lost love?" Ryshander asked.

"You could say that," Lance replied as he gathered the portraits and placed them back in the leather case.

Kaisha could sense that Lance was becoming guarded. She decided to dress the wounds of the large man to try to regain some of his lost confidence. "He needs his wounds cleaned to ward off infection," Kaisha said as she went to the closet, pulled some clean towels, and started to create bandages and dressings. She poured water from a large clay pitcher into a wash basin and wetted some towels. She dabbed the wounds carefully. To her surprise, Jude started to wake. Ryshander stared in disbelief as Jude opened his eyes and began to speak.

"Lance . . ." Jude said weakly.

Lance rushed to his side. "I am here, my friend. You are going to be alright," Lance said as he grasped Jude's hand.

Jude looked at him distantly. "Some protector I turned out to be," Jude said with a half frown, half laugh.

"Just rest, you were poisoned, it will take a while for you to get your strength back," Lance said.

Jude smiled and closed his eyes, then drifted back into a deep slumber. While Jude and Lance spoke, Ryshander and Kaisha were stunned.

"How could he be awake?" Kaisha asked Ryshander in a flurry of signs.

Ryshander merely shrugged his shoulders. "How much did he get?" Ryshander signed back.

"Two full doses. Though they didn't pierce as deeply as Grascon would have liked I'm sure, the man still should have been out for at least a few days," Kaisha signed as she glanced back to Lance and Jude to make sure they were still talking and not watching their signing.

"Must have something to do with his massive size," Ryshander signed back.

Kaisha shrugged and looked away. She had watched the giant man defy the odds in the sewers against two dwarven fighters, and

155

now he awoke from two full doses of Jahallawa, more than enough to drop any man.

"How long will he be like this?" Lance asked.

"It depends," Ryshander said as he pushed off the wall and walked over near the bed.

"Depends on what?" Lance asked.

Ryshander bent down and pulled a thin silver dagger from under the bed. He held it up to the light and ran his finger along the edge. The sharp blade sliced a small cut on his finger. He held it up to Kaisha. She nodded in recognition.

"Well . . ." Kaisha said as she sat back down on the bed next to Jude. ". . . Normally I would say a week before he made a full recovery, but he seems sturdier than most. I'd say a couple of days before he can travel."

"A couple of days?" Lance said in disbelief. "I can't wait that long."

"What's so important?" Ryshander asked with a touch of skepticism.

Lance shifted uneasily on the bed. It was strange that these two seemed to show up and have so much interest in him and Jude. He didn't think they were working for the magistrate, but it disturbed him that they knew this Grascon. "Why the interest in me? I am just a traveler looking for a sage," Lance said as he began to envision the formation of another spell.

Ryshander looked at Kaisha and then back to Lance.

Kaisha shrugged. "I don't care, tell him."

"Tell me what?" Lance said nervously. He didn't have much energy left for a battle, and he was a dunce with a blade.

Ryshander went over to the small wooden desk that sat near the wash basin. He grabbed the chair and turned it around. He sat in it backwards and cleared his throat. "Kaisha and I are members of the thieves guild here in Central City. Grascon . . ." he pointed over to the dead wererat's corpse, ". . . was one of our assassins a few years back. We were never sure of the details, but he wronged our guild leader. He was then marked for death, but he escaped. He was scarred on his face from the encounter, so he fled Central City."

"Who is your guild leader?" Lance asked innocently.

Ryshander laughed, and Kaisha shook her head. "We don't speak his name to commoners," Ryshander said as he began again.

156

Lance made a mental note that the guild leader was male. "We were in the sewers checking out reports that there were some dwarves poking around down there and our leader wanted to know what they were up to. So we went to investigate. Not long after, we heard the sound of swordplay. We carefully snuck up and saw your hulking friend dispatch two skilled dwarves in combat. He was certainly interesting to us, not only because of his unusual size, but because of his battle prowess. We had hoped he was somehow connected to the little folk so we followed him. He led us here to the Blue Dragon Inn. We ate in the common room, he came upstairs. We heard a commotion so we came up to investigate, and here we are."

Lance nearly fainted at the mention of dwarves. "Dwarves! How many?" Lance asked as he jumped up.

Ryshander was a little confused by Lance's sudden interest in the bearded folk. Perhaps they were tied together somehow after all. "I don't know, thirty, maybe forty," Ryshander said.

Kaisha was a little surprised to see the young mage so visibly shook up. He had barely survived a deadly assassin, but he was more worried about a few dwarves. "What's the big deal about a few dwarves?" Kaisha asked.

Lance looked at her in disbelief. "You have got to be kidding me," he said. "Do you people not get out? Didn't you hear about the Torrent Manor?"

Kaisha looked at Ryshander and then back to Lance. "What about it?" she asked. In truth this was her and Ryshander's first trip from the under city in many days.

Lance shook his head in shock. "What, do you two live in a cave?" Lance asked. Then it dawned on him they probably lived in the sewers, and no doubt the guild was located there also. Lance kept right on talking, never missing a beat. "The Torrent Manor was attacked by an army of dwarves and it was burned to the ground. They killed every last man, woman, and child from there. Jude thinks they might come here and try to destroy Central City also."

Kaisha looked at Ryshander nervously as he laughed aloud. "Yea right. There is no way ten armies of dwarves could destroy Central City," Ryshander boasted.

Kaisha got up and walked over to Ryshander and lightly back-handed him in the belly.

"I'm sure that's what the people of Torrent said," Kaisha stated flatly. Ryshander stopped laughing, but an occasional chuckle still escaped his lips.

Lance looked around uneasily. "Jude told me of the dwarves attacking before we arrived, but I still pushed us coming here," Lance said remorsefully.

"What was so important?" Kaisha asked.

"Well I mentioned those papers that were coming, they are written in elven and I can't read them. I need to find someone that can. That's what Jude was doing when you saw him. He was looking for a renegade sage or someone that worked under the table so to speak," Lance said as he plopped on the bed next to Jude.

"What makes these papers so important?" Ryshander asked impatiently.

Lance paused for a moment. He was unsure if he should trust the pair, but it seemed as if Kaisha wouldn't let Ryshander attack him. He couldn't imagine someone as beautiful as her would try to harm anyone. "You know how all the Ecnals were being slain?" Lance asked.

Ryshander nodded. Lance looked at Kaisha. She nodded also.

"Well, I think these writings have something to do with it," Lance said.

Ryshander and Kaisha were both intrigued. Everyone in Beykla knew of the orphan killings. The problem was that because they were orphans, no one cared to find how or why. They had just assumed that all orphans had been killed. Their names were well recorded with the magistrates and it was difficult at best to hide the surname Ecnal. Yet, before them stood not only an Ecnal nearly grown into a man, but an Ecnal that had spell casting ability. That in itself was unheard of.

"Well, my friend . . ." Kaisha said as she rose from the bed and placed her soft hand on Lance's shoulder, ". . . we have some pressing affairs to tend to. We would like to return and aid you if we could."

Lance was puzzled. "Why would you aid me?" he asked innocently.

Ryshander placed Grascon's silver dagger in his belt. "Well Lance, we aren't going to lie to you. We could profit from it possibly. You never know when something might be worth something, but I tell you this, on a thief's honor, we will never turn you in to the magistrate. That is how we work."

"A thief's honor?" Lance asked almost in a laugh.

Kaisha frowned at him. "Do not think us backstabbers because we live in the night. There are rules for how we live," she said. Her warm smile lifted some doubts Lance had. "Plus, I can read elven," Kaisha said as she and Ryshander walked out the door of the room. Lance couldn't help but grin with anticipation. He couldn't wait for the devious duo to return.

*   *   *

Therrig walked back to the area where the battle took place and leaned down to examine the bodies of the two slain dwarves. He marveled at the massive strength it must have taken to cleave through the dwarven helm. The other body had a broken skull around the nose and eye area. It appeared as if he had been struck with a metal gauntlet that was shaped like a fist. Therrig turned the body over and examined the wound on its back. The slash was too short to have been made by the weapon that killed the first soldier. Therrig suspected it was done by the dead dwarf's own axe. The opponent the pair had faced was no novice to swordplay, that much was certain. Therrig studied the area for a long while, noticing slight scuff marks in the moss covered stone ledge that led away from the dwarves' bodies.

"Come on," Therrig said as he placed his heavy blue mohawk-covered helm on his head. The thick leather straps that held the helmet in place dangled unfastened from the sides of his dirty cheeks. The armored cap's bright blue plum bounced as Therrig walked steadily down the dark sewer passage. The other dwarves in the group dared not speak. Therrig was known to be much more ruthless than Amerix. He didn't tolerate questions or general rabble. Therrig felt ignorance was a sign of stupidity and often punished those who showed either. The group merely followed Therrig blindly down the corridor.

They walked through the putrid sewer passage for almost an hour. Therrig studied the trail as he walked, noticing that there were three separate scuff marks now, when before there had been only one. The cruel dwarf wondered who or what was following

159

the large warrior. Therrig fully expected to find two more bodies, but the trail led him to a rusted moss-covered ladder that went to the old iron sewer grate from below. The dwarven warrior checked the area and noticed that the tracks led back the same direction that they came from but on the other ledge. Therrig waded across the green debris-filled water and followed the second pair of tracks for almost another hour, going back the same direction they had just walked. The dwarves in the group were becoming impatient after walking in the sewers for more than three hours. Their legs were getting sore and their noses stung from the putrid smell they were stirring up, but they didn't dare speak up. Walking hours in the disgusting moss-covered passages under the human city was far better than crossing blades with their wicked patrol leader.

Therrig stopped walking in the middle of the corridor. The other dwarves paused, and watched Therrig closely. Therrig noticed the tracks stopped for a few feet then resumed. He wondered if there was some kind of a trap they were avoiding. He kneeled and checked the passage slowly and meticulously. Though he wasn't exactly sure what he was looking for, Therrig knew most traps had a trip or some kind of pressure plate. After examining the floor area for a while, he decided to do the same to the moss-covered wall. Therrig pushed and prodded the stones on the moss-covered wall. He felt one of the stones press in. The wicked dwarf winced and prepared his body for whatever trap he set off, but nothing happened. He opened his eyes and examined the mossy wall more closely next to the dull, gray, stone block that was depressed slightly. Therrig took a deep breath, reached up, and depressed it again. This time, the stone made a grinding sound and a small door opened up into the wall revealing a long hallway with a fifteen-foot ceiling. The other ten dwarves that were with Therrig moved out in a defensive fan, in case an enemy charged out.

The floor was made up of polished marble and the air was fresh. There were large granite pillars that lined the walls of the hall, and enormous tapestries hung in-between them.

Therrig and his soldiers carefully stepped through the doorway and walked slowly down the hall. Their thick leather boots made soft thumping sounds as they moved closer to an ornately carved wooden door at the far end. The door was made of wood and had an intricate carving of a beholder with mouth open displaying hundreds, maybe thousands, of razor sharp teeth. Therrig was torn. He felt he should return to Amerix and tell him of the hall, but he feared that there might be someone here that could alert the city of their presence. He was sure the warrior they were following before was working on that, but why should he help speed the process? Then again, Therrig was worried he would be called a coward for not routinely searching and destroying everything in the hall. Therrig bit his bottom lip as he thought about it for a moment. He was in the mood to kill someone anyway, so he decided to push on. Therrig wasn't very knowledgeable of human cultures, but he was sure this type of structure was not a normal occurrence in the sewers. Therrig surmised then that this area was of some importance. Destroying important human structures was generally a good thing.

Therrig looked for some kind of handle for the door, but he couldn't find one. After many unsuccessful attempts, a frustrated Therrig took his hammer in both hands and swung as hard as he could at the door. Large pieces of wood splintered away from the carving as the hammering echoed down the marbled halls. Again and again he struck the door, and with each massive strike more and more of the door was chipped away. Sweat beaded up on Therrig's forehead, and his blue plumed helm fell off with a clang. Therrig didn't even give the armored cap a second glance. He left it lying among the pile of splintered wood that littered the floor around him. After a few minutes he could see the large wooden door was about to surrender to his mighty blows.

"Get ready, me brothers! Time for killin'!"

*　　*　　*

Pav-co heard the large booming sound coming from the chamber door. He brushed the crumbs of his current meal from his protruding belly as he struggled to get to his feet. He stumbled among his many soft velvet pillows, trying to get to the door of his private quarters. Several half dressed woman scurried about looking for their tops to cover their exposed breasts as the obese guild leader reached his door. He stuck his chubby, syrup splattered face through the doorway. He could see many of his wererats scurrying about donning weapons and armor. Some had picked up bows and

161

crossbows and were heading up the marbled stairs that were on the east and west sides of the large room. Pav-co had never seen his men in such a state before. He could hear the booming much more clearly and noticed that the chamber door at the far end of the room was shuddering with each earth shattering blow. Large pieces of plaster and chips of marble were being knocked away from the frame of the door with each resounding thud.

"What is going on here!" Pav-co demanded.

No one seemed to pay the guild leader any attention as they began to slowly get into their positions.

"What is it, Pavie?" came the soft voice from one of the many concubines inside the plush pillow chamber. Pav-co turned and struck her in the mouth with his closed fist. The woman shrieked in pain and grasped her mouth as blood streamed from a deep gash in her lip.

"Shut up whore!" Pav-co screamed. He slammed the door to his quarters shut and slid a large iron bar across the thick wooden door. He stepped over the wounded woman, ignoring her while glancing around the room. Pav-co ignored the cries of his men from the outside as he gathered his belongings. He placed anything that was golden into a small chest and donned a silk tunic and breeches. He didn't bother to button up his shirt, and his hairy fat belly jiggled as he ran. He dropped many golden trinkets as he hurried to the back of his quarters. Pav-co grabbed one of the large silk tapestries that hung from the back of the wall. He grunted and pulled the heavy curtain down, revealing a small trap door. The door was made of polished wood and stained glass. It had a thin metal gate that was easily lifted to reveal a small platform hoisted to the surface by a thin chain. Pav-co glared in response to the screaming pleas of the concubines to take them with him. The guild leader coldly abandoned them, ignoring their prayers as he slowly hoisted himself, and many of his golden baubles, to safety.

*   *   *

Therrig's mighty war hammer smashed again and again into the splintering door. Large pieces of wood were broken away, revealing brief glimpses of the room on the other side.

162

"Get ready! As soon as I get this door down I want yees to attack!" Therrig bellowed.

The dwarves readied themselves. They were not overly concerned with the battle at hand. They were more concerned with what Amerix was going to do when he found out they sacked this structure.

Therrig used his sleeve to wipe a sheen of sweat from his brow as he backed away from the shattered door. Only small pieces of wood that hung from bent hinges remained. The expansive room on the other side was similar to the hall they were in, but it was much wider and the ceiling was much higher. There were many marble pillars that stood on each side of the room, and at the far end there were stairs on each side that ascended to a ledge lining the walls of the room. Tapestries hung in between each pillar, and the center of the floor was lined with a thick green carpet that went from one of the entrances to the door at the other end.

The dwarves rushed into the strange sewer dwelling. Hiding behind each pillar was a man with a bow or crossbow. Arrows and bolts rained on the dwarves as they silently took each one and continued on.

Therrig calmly placed his large plumed helm on and rushed the length of the room, trying to get to the stairs. Pain shot from his leg as he ran. He looked down and saw a small bolt protruding from his right thigh. Without pause he ripped the bolt out and started up the left stairs. He ducked behind the tip of the first pillar as arrows whizzed past. His leg was a little numb, but he was no worse for wear. Therrig was slightly confused. He had been shot a hundred times, but he never had a wound go numb before. The wicked dwarf thought maybe the injury was more serious than it appeared, but he didn't have time to ponder it now. The dwarven leader took a deep breath and ran out from around one pillar and darted to the other one. An arrow pierced his left forearm and another grazed his helm. He paused at this pillar and gazed down at the battle below. His men had just about cleared the room, but four dwarves lay dead or dying. Therrig was shocked. These were not just simple dwarves, they were battle hardened and extremely skilled fighters. These humans were definitely a spirited bunch.

As the dwarves rushed the stairs on the opposite side and the others began to batter down the door at the far end, Therrig watched with enjoyment before jutting out from the pillar he was behind and charging the humans that had been shooting at him. To his surprise, there was no one there. The wicked dwarf glanced over the ledge, and back down to the splintered door, and saw two humans running through it as fast as they could.

Therrig plucked the bolt from his forearm and slowly marched back down to the first floor. The six remaining dwarves were gathering the bodies of the slain humans. The dead humans dripped a trail of red, shiny blood as their bodies were drug into the center of the large room. The dwarves piled them up on the green carpet that was quickly staining red. Therrig counted all twenty-four of the bodies with passing interest.

"They use poison, sir," one of the dwarves said as he held a small bolt for Therrig to examine. Therrig looked at the crossbow projectile carefully. The shaft was made of wood and the head was made of metal. He scanned along the length of the shaft to the fletching. Nothing seemed unusual about the bolt as far as he could tell.

"Looks normal to me," Therrig said.

"The poison is in the head, sir. When the bolt is removed the tip tears away, releasing the poison," the dwarf explained. Therrig, enraged by the dwarf pointing out an obvious fact that he felt he should have known, threw the bolt on the ground and shook his finger at the dwarf.

"Ye think I don't know that?!" Therrig shouted. "I meant it looks like a normal poison shaft made by the humans, ye whelp!" Therrig bellowed as he pounded his finger into the chest of the wincing dwarf.

The dwarf bowed and apologized. "I'm sorry sir, I didn't mean to show disrespect. I . . . uh . . . was trying to show you that I discovered that fact. I was sure you already knew . . . I mean . . . that . . ."

The dwarf's feeble attempt to appease Therrig's ego was met with a gauntleted fist to the face. The dwarf's legs swooned and he staggered back, clutching his shattered jaw. Blood streamed from the wounded dwarf's mouth as he walked back toward the others who were gathering bodies. Therrig made note of many dead human females that were wearing scant silk outfits that revealed their soft forms. They bore no armor or weapons. None of the dwarves reported any spell casting, which led Therrig to presume that they were for someone's amusement. The wicked dwarven leader smiled to himself. They had killed someone important. Amerix was going to be pleased.

I vaguely recall the rumors I heard about the battle of the Torrent Manor. And my experience with the attack on Central City was one-sided at best, but both battles were won and lost by arrogance and confidence.

The battle for the Torrent Manor was lost by the humans because of their arrogance. They believed that the walls of their keep were impenetrable from the outside. And in truth they were, but they were also impenetrable from the inside. The humans did not consider all possible forms or methods of attacks, and in their arrogance, ignored the few warnings of danger when they received them.

The dwarves, through confidence and superior tactics, knew of their strengths and weaknesses and exploited each respectively. They did not have the force, or ability to siege the castle, so they struck in the dark from inside. Therefore their confidence in their ability to see at night allowed them victory over the humans, who arrogantly believed that they were invincible.

In the fight for Central City, however, the dwarves' arrogance that led them to not contain their foe as they had done in the battle for the Torrent Manor allowed for a second force to charge across the bridge. Had the dwarves been more aware of their weaknesses, they might have sealed the bridge, or destroyed it outright, thus eliminating any outside surge of re-enforcements. Alas arrogance and confidence are applied to more than just battles, and can be applied within one's life. I was fortunate enough within my adventures to have never been so arrogant that it overshadowed my confidence, yet being aware of the implications of such attitudes is what keeps each in check.

—Lancalion Levendis Lampara—

Five
The Unlikely Heroes

Apollisian, Alexis, Victor, and the twins arrived at the north gate house of Central City. The gate house consisted of two large stone towers that were well over thirty feet tall. They were made of large brown stone bricks that appeared to have been cut, rather than molded. On each side of the tower were six murder holes, two every ten feet or two on each story. The top battlement of the tower housed a bright, silk, flowing Beyklan flag that slowly tossed in the light wind. Between the towers, two guards normally stood their posts with little enthusiasm, but now they were uncharacteristically vigilant. Though there was no actual portcullis that would prevent entry to the city, the towers acted as a waypoint of sorts for the heavily traveled northern roads. The group was a little tired from their fast paced ride, and Apollisian's armor was dirty and he was in dire need of a new sword. His second weapon, a finely crafted short sword, was a sufficient blade, but Apollisian longed for the smooth touch of his enchanted long sword, Songsinger. The paladin was eager to find the dwarven demon, Amerix, and reclaim his lost weapon.

Alexis had taken a bath the day before in a small pond they had found near the road, but they didn't have the time for the others to bathe. They were in a hurry to get to Central City and long periods of rest were not feasible. The paladin had suggested that she bathe while the others prepared the food they ate. No time would be lost by her bath and the elf's constant complaining had been wearing on Apollisian and Victor alike. After frequent suggestions, Alexis agreed to the proposal. The elf didn't like the others working while she was bathing, but she liked being dirty and grimy even less. Alexis didn't bathe long and the group was back on the trail after a short rest and a quick meal. They had two horses left after the battle of Torrent and took turns riding to save energy, while keeping a steady pace. They had made the half-week journey in a mere two-and-a-half days. Alexis watched with great interest as they approached Central City. She was always amazed by human cities. They were so compact compared to an elven village. She often wondered what it was like to be human. If she were one, she would be dead or close to death from old age. Alexis couldn't imagine living such a short life, how terrible it must be to die so quickly. She guessed that having such a short life is what drove the humans to be so ambitious. She might feel more of a need to accomplish great deeds had she been born human.

Apollisian walked along the side of Victor's horse. The animal was about the same size as Apollisian's, but neither beast was accustomed to carrying armored riders. Apollisian occasionally stroked the tired equine's neck as he walked alongside it. Alexis rode her horse most of the journey, arguing that someone had to stay mounted in case the twins' horse became startled and fled. The twins rode double on Victor's horse, since it was larger than Alexis's, and more docile, and less spirited. Cerebron was in the front and Corwin rode in the back.

Cerebron appeared unimpressed by the large city. He made no comments as they neared, and showed no signs of interest. Corwin, however, was eagerly straining to see around his brother and take in all the sights and sounds. He was amazed by the giant battlements and the expansiveness of the large human settlement. They had spent their entire lives within the confines of the Torrent Manor. Their mother feared that they would be slain for being identical twins, but that was the least of the paladin's concerns at the moment, and he knew the children would be safe at the church when they reached Central City. The group approached the gate house as they neared the main roadway from the north side. The thirty-foot-high towers were made of thick brown stone. There were spiral stairs in the center of the tower that rose up to each of the three levels. The first two levels were made primarily of wood, and the top was made of stone. It had a large flagstaff mounted on top in the center of the tower that flew the Beyklan ensign, a half red, half white flag with a crown bridging the color contrast, and a sword slanted from corner to corner that went into the center of the crown. The battlements had many tall narrow slits in the side of them in which archers could fire arrows from, also known as murder holes. The top of the battlement was manned by two armored crossbowmen. They wore leather armor and their thin metal helms glinted in the bright afternoon sun. The lower guards sat on old wooden chairs and occasionally picked someone that was entering the city to question. They wore austere leather armor and wielded long spears. Their spears were decorated with ribbons they had earned from a rare orc attack, but those attacks were becoming less frequent with each passing year. The king of Beykla, King Theobold, had crusaded his knights and other warriors through all of the land, eradicating most of the evil surface races. An occasional orc tribe might try a raid against the city, but afterwards they were usually hunted down and killed to the last creature.

As Apollisian neared the gate, he removed his leather gauntlet from his hand and hoisted it in the air. "Hail guard!" the paladin called out.

The guard turned his head and stared at the approaching man. He squinted his weary eyes, trying to recognize whether the man bore a standard that he needed to acknowledge. The other guard recognized Apollisian's symbol and bowed low.

Seeing his partner bowing, the first guard followed suit.

"My lord, good day to you, sir," the second guard called out as he bowed deep. Apollisian just smiled and touched each of the guards on the top of their heads.

"Rise and greet me as men," the young paladin said.

Alexis rolled her eyes. She wasn't interested in stupid human formalities. All she wanted was to get to a room and take a real bath.

The two guards stood slowly and grasped Apollisian's hand firmly. "Good to see you again, my lord. I'm glad to see you survived the Torrent. We were certain you had been lost. Where is your steed?" the second guard asked.

Apollisian shook his head as a grim expression crossed his face. "He did not survive. He was intentionally cut from under me by a dwarven demon that I shall soon send back to hell," Apollisian said boldly.

"You may soon get your chance, my lord. We are on alert, but scouts report nothing in all directions," the guard said as he turned to the first guard who was busy standing in awe of the paladin. The second guard noticed his awestruck counterpart and ordered him on a task to relieve the embarrassment of his staring. "Stahlsman, go and fetch our finest warhorse for Lord Apollisian to ride while he is here at Central City."

Stahlsman nodded, carefully leaned his spear against the hard stone walls of the battlement, and hurried off to the stables.

"Listen to me well, watch," Apollisian said with cold seriousness. His change of tone caught the guard by surprise. "The dwarves, if they are to attack, would not march against you as any other army might."

"What do you mean?" the guard asked as he removed his brass-colored helm and scratched his sweaty head.

"They would tunnel under you and erupt from your innards, hitting you behind your front lines and burning the defensive retreats you might have established," the paladin said coldly. "I must go to your duke and warn him," Apollisian said, looking past the guard into the large city.

"Duke Blackhawk is not in, my lord. He is away at a meeting with King Theobold at Kalliman Castle," the guard said. "He isn't due back for a few days."

Apollisian shook his head. "Then who is here in his stead?"

"Colonel Mortan Ganover," the watch replied.

"Then I shall go to him post haste," Apollisian said while he waited for his horse. "I have one other need, good sir watch."

"Name it, my lord, and it shall be done," the guard said, dipping low again.

Apollisian gestured to the twins that sat on Victor's horse.

"These are the only surviving members of the Torrent that I am aware of. I need you to take them to the church of Stephanis and have them enlisted as my charges. Their names are Cerebron and Corwin."

The watch frowned as he looked at the boys who were completely identical. "How will anyone tell them apart?"

Apollisian chuckled. "They are as night and day. Cerebron seldom speaks and Corwin seldom keeps quiet," the paladin said as he pulled out a soft leather bag from his belt pouch. "Take this bag of gold coins and give it to the church. It should be more than enough to rear the children until they are old enough to fend for themselves."

The guard took the heavy violet and orange bag of coins,

placed it under his leather tunic, and hooked it to his belt. "I shall see it is done as you wish, my lord," the guard said as he dipped low.

Apollisian glanced over the bowing guard's shoulder at the second guard that was leading a large warhorse toward them. It was a pure black stallion that had three small white spots on its flanks. It was well over eighteen hands tall and was not as thick-chested as normal warhorses, but its legs were much longer and more muscular.

"Here you are, my lord," Stahlsman said as he handed the horse to Apollisian. The paladin took the black chain reins and stood in awe at the steed. "Never have I seen equal," Apollisian whispered softly in awe of the fine animal.

Alexis helped the twins dismount and led them to the first guard's position inside the battlement. She glared at Apollisian, aggravated at the human's love for animals.

"Just a horse," she said as she walked past.

Apollisian didn't appear to hear her as his eyes feasted on the magnificence of the creature. "What is he called?" Apollisian whispered to Stahlsman.

The guard shrugged his shoulders. "I don't know. He was in the stables when I got there. We ain't had him long, that's for sure."

Apollisian slowly stroked the neck of the majestic creature. "Then he shall earn his name in time while serving as my steed."

Alexis returned from dropping off the twins. She was not at all happy with Apollisian's decision to dump the children, but she could not think of any other viable choice. They couldn't take them with them. Her village wouldn't accept them since they were human, but leaving them with a church didn't seem much better than the other two choices. Alexis wasn't sure whether she was angry at the decision they were forced to make or just frustrated over the death she had witnessed at the Torrent. Regardless, she was happy to be back on the trail of that fiend Amerix. She owed him a few well-placed arrows. Alexis watched Apollisian as he gently stroked the neck of the new horse. She recognized the spots on the flanks. It was no doubt a type of Vendaigehn. Vendaigehns were a breed of horse from the plains of Vendaiga, a city in the queendom of Aten, far to the west, near the great sea. She knew the women of Aten were powerful spell casters who enslaved every male they encoun-

171

tered. Only elven males were tolerated, and only a few of those were allowed safe passage. Almost everyone avoided that deadly country, even females from other races. Aten women were born with a gift of innate spell casting ability and were known as sorceresses. Only purebloods had the right to citizenship, therefore females not born to an Aten family had no citizenship rights, though she doubted the paladin knew anything of that place.

Alexis climbed atop her horse as Apollisian mounted his. She was happy the squire remained quiet during the whole affair. Alexis was becoming more aggravated at his simple advances. They were nothing more than futile attempts at best, but the thought of marrying a human disgusted her.

The trio rode through the streets of Central City. They passed many people that were hurrying about. Apollisian marveled at how smoothly the strange horse moved. It seemed as if he sailed across the road on a cloud of air. Smiling, the paladin glanced around the city as they rode into the heart of it. He noticed that the general mood of the city guards was vigilant. Apollisian was pleased to know that at least the city was at a higher level of readiness.

They rode on while passing a large round stone building that bore no windows and was very tall. It had a large expansive set of marble stairs that rose from the center up into the building. The stairs stopped about midway up the structure and it appeared as if there was a large depressed flat area in the center of the building.

"What is that?" Alexis asked as she pointed to the round building.

Apollisian glanced over. "That is the coliseum," he said with a disgusted look on his face.

"What is a coliseum?" Alexis asked innocently. Her grasp of the human language was still weak. Victor chuckled until Alexis's venomous frown silenced him.

"It is a terrible place where criminals and prisoners are forced to fight each other and sometimes animals and monsters, for the amusement of the crowd," Apollisian said.

Alexis's jaw dropped as she stared wide-eyed at the building. "Why would someone be amused by another's death?" she asked innocently.

Apollisian struggled as he tried to think of how to respond. "Do you know how your race thinks alike and seldom attacks or hurts anyone or anything unless provoked, and orcs are just the opposite?"

Alexis nodded slowly as she studied the pained expression on Apollisian's face.

"Well, humans aren't born with those innate ideals. Each human is as unique as their faces. Some have ugly faces as well as ugly hearts," Apollisian said solemnly. "That is why I strive, every waking hour of my existence, to seek justice for those who cannot find it on their own."

"Have you ever been to the coliseum?" Alexis asked. Victor began to chuckle at the thought of it.

Apollisian gave her a reassuring smile. "My dear Overmoon, if I were to ever set foot in that abhorrent place, it would be to destroy its owners, and bring its walls crashing down atop the vile patrons," the paladin proclaimed.

Alexis smiled at Apollisian's decree as they continued their ride through the bustling streets of Central City.

They approached a large, several story building with a stable across the street. The trio left their horses at the stable and entered the large building known as the Blue Dragon Inn. Alexis took in the many strange sights and sounds that she was experiencing in the human settlements. She had never imagined the structures would be as large as they were. Her father had told her stories of how plentiful humans were, but she was just now realizing the depths of those truths.

They entered the building and stood in the common room of the Blue Dragon Inn. There were many people eating and drinking. Some bore weapons, some were militia guardsmen, and some appeared to be farmers. The overall mood seemed to be pleasant, and few paid the trio much attention.

"I'm going to find and speak with the acting magistrate," Apollisian said as he tossed Victor a small bag of coins. Victor held the small violet bag that was engulfed with a bright orange "A" that was embroidered on the side. "Get two rooms. One for us, and one for Overmoon. I expect to return sometime this evening. Probably after dark, so get something to eat and have your clothes laundered. I'll see you tonight," Apollisian said as he headed out the door.

Victor turned to Alexis. "Do you want to get something to eat after we get our rooms and bathe?" Victor asked with a warm smile.

Alexis studied his face as he spoke. He was so young, even for human standards, she wondered if he really comprehended the ordeal they had endured at the Torrent. She wondered if he fully appreciated how lucky he was to have not burned to death when the building that fell on them collapsed. "I'll meet you at your room when I am ready. I am dying to eat some freshly prepared food."

As they went to their rooms, Alexis eyed a young human sitting at the far end of the common room, near the wall. He had black hair and bold green eyes. He wore what appeared to be a Cadacka. A Cadacka was a ceremonial robe of mourning worn by elves when someone close to them was slain or murdered. They wore the robe until they found justice or were slain themselves. Anger began to flood through her. She fought the urge to draw her sword and spill the human's entrails on the common room floor. She realized that she was surrounded by humans, and that the chance the robe was a Cadacka was nearly next to none. Alexis took three deep breaths to calm herself and made a mental note of the man. She would look into this. If he indeed wore a true Cadacka, he would give it up, or have to be slain. Alexis forced her tired legs up the long stairway and settled into her room.

*   *   *

Ryshander and Kaisha strolled into the early morning light. The bright morning glow was just beginning to erupt from the eastern sky and wash away the dark blue ceiling that held the stars aloft. Robins and other song birds were alive with cheery melodies and the crickets were ending their songs for the night. The pair made their way down the cobblestone streets of Central City, enjoying an unusually warm morning for early October. There were a few farmers that had spent the night in the city, rising and heading back out to their farms. But for the most part, the streets were bare. Ryshander and Kaisha rounded a corner and hastily ducked into a dark alley. In moments, their vision shifted to acclimate to the darkness. They moved silently from shadow to shadow until they reached one of the four alley sewer grates. Ryshander hoisted the heavy grill up and gave an exaggerated bow as he motioned for Kaisha to enter. She curtsied with a quiet giggle and descended into the darkness. After Kaisha had climbed into the grate, Ryshander lowered himself down and replaced the heavy iron cover over them, and they climbed back down into the dark, damp under city.

Once in the sewers the pair changed from cheery to dutiful. They moved with precision and grace, ever diligent not to make a sound, becoming omnipotent of their surroundings. They moved quickly down the black corridors that were growing light from the green hue with every passing moment. They had rounded the corner that led to the entrance to Lostos when they first noticed something was wrong. They could clearly see the secret door was open, revealing the long passage to their home. Ryshander drew his rapier and Kaisha drew her short sword. They cautiously moved up to the side of the mossy wall next to the exposed secret door. Ryshander listened for a long moment but could not hear anything.

"I hear nothing," he signed to Kaisha nervously.

She looked back at him with an equal amount of fear in her eyes. "What now? Should we enter?" she signed.

Ryshander shrugged. "I'm not sure, I guess we should see what's going on. I find it impossible that someone just left it open," he signed.

Kaisha nodded. "I think something is terribly wrong," she signed tensely.

Ryshander slowly peered into the passage, making sure it was safe before he began to walk down the long hallway. Kaisha entered and followed backwards, guarding for a rear attack, as Ryshander nervously ran his thumb along his rapier's hilt and he cautiously moved forward. She held her sword tightly and slowly scanned the shadows of the grinder. Ryshander cautiously glided down the smooth marbled hall, looking for any threat that might appear. As he neared the large wooden door at the end of the narrow passage, he was struck with shock. The beautiful carving of the roaring beholder had been smashed and lay splintered on the floor around what used to be the oaken door. The splintered remains of the door hung from bent and torn hinges. Ryshander stared in disbelief at the destruction of the door that he had paused to admire every day. Kaisha bumped into Ryshander as she backed down the hall. She turned to see why he had stopped. The beautiful thief started to sign in protest when she saw the remnants of the once beautiful door. Kaisha fought back tears at the sight of its destruction. She feared what unseen horrors they might find as they continued deeper into their home.

"I don't know if we should enter, my love," she signed to Ryshander.

He looked at the door and then back the way they came. "One of us needs to go. I don't want you to be in danger, so you stay here while I investigate. If I don't return in a short while, flee," he signed solemnly.

Kaisha shook her head in defiance. "I'll not let you face whatever dangers lay in wait, my love. If death comes to claim you, it will have to go through me. I could never live my life if you were not in it," she signed back empathetically.

Ryshander smiled. He was torn between the need to protect his love, the respect to let her act as an equal, and the sheer admiration of her bravery. He made a silent vow to himself that if death came to claim them, he, not she, would face the reaper first. "Okay, my sweet Kaisha, but I'll lead. I'm better with my blade than you," he signed with a nervous but playful tone.

"After we find out what happened to our brothers and sisters I will make you eat those words," she signed back with a half grin. Kaisha was so thankful that she found someone like Ryshander to share her life with. She doubted there were any other men in the entire world like her love.

Ryshander silently placed many small spike-like appendages on the ground near the base of the shattered door. He hid them among the debris so that if anyone tried to sneak up from behind them, they would step on the nasty caltrops. He hoped they would cry out and alert Kaisha and him to their presence.

The pair advanced side by side, as equals, through the shattered door. Once on the other side they witnessed the most horrible, unimaginable sight they had ever seen. The magnificent tapestries lay torn, were strewn about, and were covered in feces and urine. There were spent bolts and arrows scattered all over the floor. As they moved deeper into the room, the most horrible sight was yet to be seen. All of their friends and loved ones lay dead. Some were stripped to the nude, their genitals removed and placed in disgusting positions. The female guild members were exposed and appeared as if they had been ravaged multiple times by their assailants. Their clothes were gone and their bodies lay sprawled and horribly wounded by vicious cuts and puncture wounds that appeared to have been made while they were still alive.

Kaisha hid her face in Ryshander's chest as she began to sob uncontrollably. Her once infallible composure shattered in a flash after the sight of the ghastly scene that lay before her. Ryshander placed his arm around her in comfort, but he remained cautious. He was not sure the attackers had left. Kaisha realized the potential danger that still lingered and forced herself to regain her lost composure. She pulled her face from Ryshander's chest and returned the blank stare of death that came from her fellow guild members.

Ryshander tightened his grip on his thin rapier and stealthily moved to Pav-co's chamber door. He noticed the door was cracked open slightly and he could see a few of Pav-co's concubines lying on the floor. He went back to Kaisha, who was still standing silently in wide-eyed horror. "They have been in Pav-co's chamber. I can see some of his concubines lying on the floor. I couldn't tell if they were breathing, but they were nude like the females here," Ryshander signed.

Kaisha winced as Ryshander referred to the dead guild members as "female." He knew their names as well as she did. She thought perhaps that was his way of de-personalizing the tragedy. "There are only twenty-four bodies here," Kaisha signed, trying to mimic Ryshander's way of referring to their dead loved ones.

"Who is missing?" Ryshander signed back.

Kaisha fought back tears. "Kellacun, Travits, and Miranhka," she signed.

Ryshander frowned. "Well at least Miranhka escaped. I don't really care about the other two. They weren't much better than Pav-co," Ryshander signed.

Kaisha nodded in agreement and moved toward Pav-co's chamber. She slipped through the cracked door and Ryshander was close behind. Once inside, the scene was much the same. The female concubines had been stripped, tortured, and raped many times. Ryshander and Kaisha searched the entire chamber but did not locate Pav-co's body, yet they did locate the chute and elevator the fat thief had used to escape.

"He abandoned everyone to die," Kaisha signed in disbelief.

Ryshander put his arm around her in comfort. "We should leave this place before we, too, become victims of his cowardice.

Let's go find that Ecnal and his swordsman. They seemed to know something about the dwarves. I bet the bearded folk were responsible for the murders," Ryshander signed.

Kaisha nodded blankly as the pair hastily departed the razed guild hall.

*   *   *

Lance had been sitting in the common room of the Blue Dragon Inn since Ryshander and Kaisha had left. He would frequently go up and check on Jude, then make his way back down to his table. He was excited about Kaisha's visit. He hoped she could read the elven pages he had gotten from the thief back in Bureland. Lance couldn't believe his luck when the beautiful woman burst into his room with her friend and later declared she could read elven. They helped him with Jude, and reported they had seen many dwarves in the sewers. Lance just hoped he and Jude would be able to leave before the dwarves decided to attack. Jude hadn't awakened from his poison induced sleep yet, and Ryshander suggested that he might not be able to walk for a few days, so Lance decided to wait in the common room. Just in case the mysterious pair returned, he didn't want to miss them.

Lance was sitting at a small round wooden table near the rear by the back wall, giving him a wide view of the entire room. He watched each person as they entered, hoping with each new patron it was Kaisha and Ryshander returning. But as time passed into mid morning, he decided that the couple wouldn't be back for a while. He had no idea what they were doing, but the pair didn't seem like the type that wasted time.

Lance was finishing his breakfast when a strikingly beautiful woman came into the common room accompanied by a young man, not much older than Lance. The woman was wearing a finely woven green cloak that hung loosely over a thin suit of tightly woven chain mail. She had a pure white bow draped over one shoulder and a dark brown leather quiver that was loaded with long arrows and had bright green fletching. She wore short riding boots that came up to the bottom of her slender calves. She had a strange looking belt that didn't seem to accent her outfit that much. It was much wider than most belts and was made of thick, tanned leather. It had

178

many small chains woven around it and the front buckle had a symbol or a word from some language that Lance had never seen. She was much shorter than most women, maybe a little over five feet at best.

The young man that was with her wore a suit of violet, padded, leather armor with a religious symbol on the front that was sewn in bright orange. He was maybe twenty years old but had striking features and held himself with a small air of superiority. He appeared to be intimidated by the woman, but the more Lance watched, he decided he was smitten instead.

The small woman purchased a room from the innkeeper and walked toward the stairs when she paused, looking Lance in the eye. She seemed to stare for a brief moment, as if contemplating something, then her expression turned to shock as she darted up the stairs. Lance felt the need to follow her, but decided against it. Jude hadn't eaten yet, and the small woman didn't quite look all that safe. Lance watched the man in the violet padded armor for a short while, then he purchased a meal for Jude.

Lance walked up the stairs toward his room after he had finished his meal. He carried a bowl of steaming hot vegetable soup, a loaf of bread, and a hock of mutton for Jude. He walked slowly up the stairs, careful not to spill any of the soup. Lance reached his room and struggled to open the door with his foot without spilling or dropping anything. After a short fight with the door, he entered and placed the hot soup on the wooden table next to his sleeping friend. Lance reached over and gently shook the large man's shoulder. Jude slowly opened his eyes and turned over.

"I brought you some soup, little bear," Lance said mockingly with a chuckle.

Jude propped himself up with his elbow. His weak arms strained and shook as he forced them to lift his body upright. "May the gods curse you and your childish mockeries," Jude said, panting from exertion.

Lance laughed and slowly dipped the spoon into the bowl, allowing the soup to slowly pool into the spoon before offering the large man a sip.

Jude frowned and growled low. "Get your damned hand . . . away from my mouth, or you will draw back a bloody nub," Jude said, narrowing his eyes at Lance.

Again Lance laughed as he tossed the spoon into the bowl of soup. A small amount splashed onto Jude and the table.

Jude wiped the soup from his cheek with his large hand and glared menacingly at Lance.

"I will remember these moments next time an assassin looms over you," Jude said.

Lance dismissed Jude's threat with a snicker and began to study the Necromidus.

Jude dipped the fresh bread into the hot soup and hungrily stuffed it into his mouth. He then took a bite of the juicy mutton and slowly chewed the concoction in his mouth. "Mmmh. Vis es goomb," Jude said with his mouth full, motioning to the bowl of soup with the hand that held a large piece of bread. He finished chewing and stuffed another oversized portion into his mouth. The large swordsman savored each delicious bite. A few heaping spoonfuls later, the soup and mutton were gone. Jude snapped the bone in half and picked at his teeth with the splintered end. Despite Lance's teasing, the swordsman was happy to have a friend that stood by him. He knew that no matter what happened, Lance would always be there for him.

Jude slowly rose from the bed and stumbled over to his gear, which Lance had neatly stacked against the wall. His massive sword was leaned against the closet where his laundered clothes hung. Jude fumbled through his dirty leather pack and removed his whetstone. He struggled to lift the heavy sword he had once wielded easily, and staggered back to bed. He plopped down and tried to catch his breath. "I had no idea there were poisons that could do this without killing you," Jude said as he sat exhausted from the small journey across the room.

Lance didn't look up from his reading when he replied. "Ryshander and Kaisha said a normal man would be unconscious for many days, and wouldn't be able to move for weeks. They were surprised by your great constitution. I, on the other hand, was surprised that the feeble concoction felled you at all. You must be getting weak in your old age," Lance said with a teasing smile.

"Come over here mage, and let me get my hands around your scrawny neck. I'll show you how weak I am," Jude said with a half-threatening glare. Lance just smiled and returned his concentration to his studies, carefully flipping each page of the ancient text.

Jude glared at Lance a while longer before scraping his heavy whetstone against the massive two-handed sword, making a shrill scratching sound.

Lance winced. "What on earth are you trying to do?" Lance asked.

Jude ignored him and forcefully rubbed the whetstone against the blade a second and third time. Lance fumed and tried to block out Jude's attempts to annoy him. He tried to concentrate a few minutes more, then slammed the book shut. He got up, snatched his cloak from the hook in the closet, and headed for the door.

"What?" Jude asked as he held his arms out wide, grinning from ear to ear.

"I'm going downstairs," Lance said as he slammed the door shut. Jude laughed for a good while.

*   *   *

Therrig and his six dwarves marched triumphantly through the sewer corridors toward the command room, nursing the few minor injuries they suffered in the fight. They carried the bodies of the four slain, two that died in the battle and the two they found dead, so that they could be laid to rest in a proper dwarven ceremony.

Commander Fehzban saw Therrig and the patrol approaching. The commander despised the wicked dwarf, but tolerated his presence because he knew Amerix considered him valuable. "Therrig Alistair Delastan! Where have you been? You were supposed to find the missing dwarves, not go gallivanting throughout the sewers!" Commander Fehzban shouted angrily.

Therrig ignored the revolting comment from the aging cleric and slammed his shoulder into the commander's as he brushed by.

Commander Fehzban recovered from the shoulder blow and started after the disrespecting thug. "How dare you insult me!" Commander Fehzban shouted.

Therrig turned quickly and swung his hammer at the angry dwarven commander. The hammer's head whistled and slammed into the commander's hard breast plate. There was a great thunder clap that emitted from the hammer as blue bolts of lightning ripped into the stunned cleric. Commander Fehzban stumbled back onto his rear from the force of the blow and struggled to stand. His legs, weak from the hammer's might, struggled to support his weight.

"It is you who insults me, commander," Therrig said, shaking his stubby finger at Fehzban. "You forget, I am not one of your lackeys to command. I am Therrig Alistair Delastan, and I obey no Stoneheart," Therrig shouted. He spit on the ground at Commander Fehzban, then turned and marched toward Amerix's headquarters.

Commander Fehzban struggled to get to his feet with the aid of some of his men, but resigned to sit a while longer until strength returned to his body.

"My lord! My lord!" a dwarf yelled as he came running into Amerix's tent.

The dwarven general looked up from his complete map of the under city that was laid out before him on stone block. He had marked many grates from the west in which he wanted to emerge from when he and his brethren attacked the surface. "What is it?" Amerix asked, annoyed that he was being disturbed.

The dwarf paused to catch his breath. "Therrig has returned. He lost four soldiers, he found the two missing patrol members dead, and now he fights Commander Fehzban!" the dwarf spouted out as fast as he could.

Amerix's face grew red with fury. "He what?!" the general shouted as he pushed by the dwarf and began to march toward the sewer corridor. Amerix could see Therrig angrily marching toward him. His deadly hammer was in hand, and he walked with a furious purpose. Behind him were about twenty dwarves, including two that were helping Commander Fehzban to his feet. Amerix marched toward the group. He was aware of the ever growing dissension between the wicked dwarf, Therrig, and the skilled cleric, Fehzban. He had made it abundantly clear to Therrig that although he may dislike the commander, he would not tolerate any more disobeyed orders from Therrig.

"Therrig! Where in the nine hells have ye been? I demand yer report!" Amerix shouted, his long silver-streaked beard shaking with each thunderous word.

Therrig narrowed his eyes. "I found the missing patrol, they were slain by a group of humans. One fled to the surface, the others retreated to some kind of church or other structure that was located down here. We stormed the structure and killed all of the inhabitants. There were . . ."

Therrig was cut off by Amerix's booming voice. "Ye what?!" Amerix shouted as he moved his face a few inches in front of Therrig's. "Who gave ye permission to engage the humans?" Amerix demanded as spittle shot from his mouth while he screamed at Therrig.

"No one. I took it upon myself to . . ."

Again Therrig was cut off by the ancient general. "That's right! No one gave you the authority to risk the lives of our brothers, and our mission," Amerix screamed as spittle sprayed in Therrig's face. Therrig's fist grew tighter around his hammer as rage built up inside him. He was growing stronger every day, and the thought of taking orders from some old has-been was taxing the young wiry dwarf's restraint.

"It was a successful . . ."

Therrig tried to speak but was again interrupted by Amerix. "It was nothing but foolish!" Amerix screamed. "And furthermore, ye insult your commander in front of his own soldiers, and worse than that, ye have committed a treasonous assault against him!"

"He is no commander of mine!" Therrig shouted back, his tone growing more and more bold with each passing moment. "And Leska and her mission be damned! Durion would not have us sulking around in these damned sewers. We would be defeating our enemies, not cowering below them like roaches!"

The ever growing crowd of dwarves gasped aloud at the blasphemous words that came out of Therrig's mouth. Even Commander Fehzban couldn't believe Therrig had spoken such atrocities.

Amerix moved quickly. He grabbed Therrig's hammer and at the same time he struck the young and powerful dwarf in the face with his gauntleted fist. He felt Therrig's nose crunch under the force of his mighty blow. Amerix kept Therrig from recovering from the quick strike by punching him a second time in the ribs, where his armor was linked together by soft, penetrable leather. It wasn't an area that could prove debilitating, but it distracted Therrig long enough for Amerix to pull his hammer away. The an-

183

cient general used Therrig's shifted weight and twisted the hammer up and along the back of Therrig's arm, forcing the young dwarf down to the ground. Therrig's chin struck the stone sewer floor hard. Amerix tossed the hammer to the side and hoisted the dangerous dwarf off his feet. He placed one hand around Therrig's throat, and the other grabbed his leather shoulder strap and held him aloft, squeezing Therrig's throat as blood streamed from the young dwarf's nose and mouth.

"Ye are hereby removed from rank, title, and clan. Ye are no longer a Stoneheart. Ye had better cling to the to the Stormhammer name, for it is as dead to ye as ye are to me. Ye will forever be the renegade survivor of Clan Stormhammer," Amerix shouted as he tossed the dazed dwarf to the ground.

Therrig hit the stone floor of the sewer and slid on his back. Blood streamed from his nose and mouth and soaked his beard. The young dwarf sat up and looked around for his hammer. He noticed it was behind the general and realized that he could not retrieve it and likely survive the encounter with the old dwarf. Therrig stood slowly and lifted his chin defiantly. No one could believe what they had witnessed. They knew Amerix was a skilled fighter, but to have dispatched a ruthless killer like Therrig so easily amazed even Commander Fehzban, who had served under Amerix since he came to Clan Stoneheart.

"Give him a pack and enough supplies for one week. Remove his armor and his weapons so that he may not make war," Amerix shouted.

The dwarves rushed to Therrig, stripped his armor, and left him wearing a dirty brown loin cloth. Therrig didn't resist. He just kept his deadly gaze on the old steel blue eyes of Amerix. The two remained locked in a deep gaze until the dwarves finished removing his armor and weapons.

"You cannot do this to me, Amerix," Therrig said with a deadly calm as he was restrained by several dwarves. "I will have my revenge. I will savor the thought of it as long as I draw breath," Therrig said with a wicked smile.

"You are right, Therrig," Amerix said softly. "I cannot do this to ye. No one could. Only a pitiful coward such as ye could have done it to yerself," Amerix said as he turned his back to Therrig.

"Don't you dare turn your back on me, Amerix Alistair

Stormhammer! Just like you turned your back on Clan Stormhammer the day the dark dwarves came," Therrig screamed. "I will have my vengeance in blood!" Therrig bellowed, his voice trailing away as he was escorted to the caverns, away from the army, away from Stoneheart, and away from Amerix Alistair Stormhammer. Though the young dwarf was gone, the truths he shouted at the old general echoed in his tortured heart.

*   *   *

Apollisian walked across the cobblestone street from the Blue Dragon Inn to the city civic building. It was a giant building that seemed more like a work of art than a functioning dwelling for governing bodies. It was four stories high and over three hundred feet long. It had a large round dome that rested in the building's center. It was made of a dark gray stone that was polished smooth around the doors and windows. The dome was highly decorated with precious metals and detailed designs. The main level of the building was on the second floor and there was a tall expansive staircase that led up to four large stone pillars standing on a balcony type area before the huge double doors leading inside. Many well-groomed people came and went carrying various papers and books, and all were dressed in the finest clothing.

Apollisian confidently entered the civic building and strode down its polished marble halls. Inside, people milled about performing their daily tasks. The men inside also wore fine robes or tunics and were clean shaven and well manicured. The entire first floor reeked of perfumes and scented soaps.

Apollisian approached the first person that he came to. His heavy armored boots clanged against the polished marble floor as he walked. The young paladin felt out of place with his unshaven face and soiled traveling appearance. All eyes watched him with an air of superiority and obvious scrutiny.

"Good day, sir," Apollisian said to a robed man who was speaking with another man dressed in a fine green silk tunic. "I was wondering who might be in charge of the city while Duke Blackhawk is away on business."

The pair didn't respond as they looked Apollisian up and

down from head to toe. They scrunched their noses in disgust while the one with the tunic turned and walked away.

The robed figure haughtily dusted off his sleeve as if the paladin had somehow contaminated it by standing too close. "Why would the acting Duke waste his time with you?" the robed figure asked with a disgusted look on his face.

Apollisian struggled with restraint. He took a deep breath and spoke again. "Good sir, I care not to dabble with the silly answers to your prejudiced queries. I only require the knowledge of the acting Duke's stateroom. If you do not wish to show me, so be it. But I shall recall your name, and call on you to explain to the Duke, when he returns, of your inability to recover nobility," Apollisian said with a more arrogant tone.

The robed figure appeared to be unimpressed but pointed to a stateroom down the hall. Apollisian said nothing and pushed his way past the frail robed man, and strode confidently toward the stateroom chamber.

The young paladin marveled at the blind arrogance of the officials in this civic building as he walked down the wide corridor, passing several offices and staterooms with men hard at work, filing papers and the like. He entered the large room and stood by a hefty wooden chair that was located just inside the door in front of an oak desk. The room was large and had thick oaken edges that were covered in ornate carvings. Bright colors, that were mostly reds and yellows, were plastered over wall tapestries, desk coverings, and any other item that could bolster such emblems.

An older man with gray hair and thin spectacle looked up from his paperwork at the imposing figure that stood before him. "Can I help you with something?" the man asked.

Apollisian looked down at the man and exhaled slowly. "Good day to you, sir. I am Apollisian Bargoe of Westvon keep. We have much to discuss."

*   *   *

Ryshander and Kaisha navigated the city streets, moving from shop to shop. The day was a cool one, much cooler than the previous one had been, and the kiss of autumn was about the air. They had pawned off a few items they had gathered from Lostos that

Pav-co had left behind and had lined their pockets with gold coins. They were beginning to believe Lance's story about the dwarves, or at least some of it. They had noticed how the surface guards were excited and seemed to be on alert. Kaisha suspected the dwarves were the ones responsible for the slaughter at Lostos, and the fact that they didn't take so much as a single one of Pav-co's golden trinkets that littered his chamber floor further proved it. Had the dwarves plundered the guildhall, it would seem they were not there for war. But the bearded invaders took nothing. Armies have no need for gold. They have a need for food, weapons, and armor—a fearful fact that loomed over the head of the thieving couple.

Ryshander surmised that if the dwarves could conquer Lostos, a strongly defended guildhall that stood for fifty years, they would have little trouble wreaking havoc in the city. The pair decided to gather as many supplies and as much gold as they could and flee the city. They had spent most of the day shopping and the evening sun was rapidly waning. The shopkeepers were closing their doors early, even though the sun had not yet set.

Ryshander and Kaisha walked down the dirt side street of the market. Ryshander had purchased many supplies, including some fine clothing and some traveling gear. He played with a brass-lined wooden spyglass he purchased while Kaisha wore a fine gold necklace and three gold rings. She had stolen them while the greedy shopkeeper focused on Ryshander and his fat purse, when the thief was thinking about purchasing the expensive spyglass. Kaisha also purchased some finer clothing and some traveling gear. They looked much more like a wealthy couple than a skilled, thieving duo.

They walked hand-in-hand down the side of the market street. The cool autumn breeze covered them in a gentle refreshing hood, as the evening sun painted a dazzling portrait of red, yellow, and orange in the west sky. They gazed into each other's eyes and became lost in the breathtaking moment that was theirs to share—a moment so intense that only two souls that are equally entwined by the shackles of love could even begin to fathom. The couple frequently shared these intimate looks and often laughed when others had no idea what they were saying.

A scream tore into the fabric of their heavenly reverie. The shrill cry ripped through the ever darkening alleys and echoed off of the many large buildings of Central City. Ryshander placed his hand on his finely crafted rapier that was hidden under his new silk cloak. Kaisha did the same with her short sword. They were not too far from the west side of town and were planning to leave from the east gate, across the Dawson River.

Ryshander strained his eyes and shifted from the colorful spectrum of daylight to the deep defined lines of his night vision. He could no longer make out specific colors more than a few feet away from his face, but he could see farther and more details in the night than the best humans. Kaisha focused her eyes and shifted her vision also. All around them they could hear strange voices and sounds coming from the darker areas of the streets and alleys. Kaisha turned her head to some movement she picked up directly behind them, to the west. She could see many dozen small stocky silhouettes rapidly moving from the shadows into the night.

"Dwarves," she struggled to say through the ever growing lump in her throat. Ryshander grabbed her hand and they ran east as fast as their legs would carry them, toward the Dawson River, toward freedom.

*　　*　　*

Lance sat in his posh room with Jude. The evening was turning colder and he decided to stay in for the night. He read the Necromidus and began learning another spell. The ancient text often amazed him. Its strange symbols, arcane writings, and diagrams seemed to talk to him sometimes. Though they never actually spoke, it seemed to Lance that they had a message that was meant only for him. Occasionally he would take a break from his reading and think about how he could twist or change the weaves of the dweamor to better fit his needs.

Jude had finished sharpening his sword and was napping again. He had regained some of his strength, but still could not wield the massive blade properly and had a difficult time keeping his breath when performing the simplest of tasks.

Lance had been waiting for Kaisha and Ryshander to return. It was starting to get dark and he wondered what was keeping them. He was hoping to depart in the early morning, but he wasn't going to leave until Kaisha deciphered his papers for him. He had endured an encounter with the Bureland militia, on the journey to Central City, and an attempt on his life by a wererat assassin. All Lance wanted to do was decipher the script he received and get back to his adoptive father, Davohn, who he hoped wasn't too angry by the letter he put on his bed when he left.

Lance heard an odd commotion from outside his window. He went to the shutters and looked down into the ever darkening street. He could see men with weapons running toward the west, and many town folk running east. Lance strained to see into the alleys, where he thought he noticed many small shapes moving about.

"Jude," Lance called out. He continued to stare into the near darkness, trying to see what was going on while he looked for his large friend to wake him. Lance grabbed the sleeping swordsman by the shoulder and gently shook him. "Jude . . . wake up," Lance said.

Jude opened his tired eyes and sat up. Lance noticed how much easier it was for his friend to sit up than it had been during the day.

"What is it?" Jude asked as he yawned and stretched his ever strengthening muscles. Lance moved back to the window and peered outside. "I'm not sure. There is a commotion on the street. A lot of people are moving down the street and the city guards are running toward the north alleys," Lance said, never taking his eyes from the scene below.

Jude got up from his bed and slowly went to the window. He looked down below over Lance's shoulder. They noticed a bright light flare up near the building just east of them.

"Torches?" Lance asked.

Jude stared a moment, then moved from the window and started donning his chain shirt and equipment. "Fire," Jude said as he slipped the chain shirt over his head and began to tighten the side straps.

Lance continued to watch out the window. "What do you think started the fire?" Lance asked as he spied a group of short, stocky silhouettes brandishing weapons while emerging from an alley.

"Dwarves!" they both said in unison.

*   *   *

Apollisian sat outside the office of Kreegan Malone, the acting duke, for most of the day. The would-be city leader chastised Apollisian for such a foolish notion as dwarves attacking. Apollisian demanded they claim Divine sovereignty to have some preventive measures taken. Divine sovereignty was an executive form of defense that any paladin in the kingdom of Beykla could enact. It gave the paladin the authority to control and lead a city militia until either the king or one of his generals arrived to relieve the paladin. By Beyklan law the local magistrate had until dusk of that day to relinquish authority of the militia to the paladin. The acting duke, Colonel Ganover, told him to wait outside his office and he would present the forms by dusk. So Apollisian sat outside the office on a hard oaken bench and waited. He had sat for almost seven hours when he first heard the commotion. The paladin slowly rose from the bench and stiffly walked to the giant front double doors of the civic hall. Peering out into the darkness he noticed a group of excited militia guards running west down the road in front of the Blue Dragon Inn. Apollisian watched a while longer and he witnessed many people fleeing from their homes in a panic. He drew his short sword, stepped to the balcony area, and stood in between the massive pillars while he focused his eyes on the small fire that sprang up from the building just west of the Blue Dragon Inn. The building wasn't a large one, but the flames were beginning to flicker and sprout up the side of it. The young paladin felt his heart beginning to race. He placed the tip of his sword between his feet and closed his eyes. He concentrated and began to focus his thoughts on the heart of his soul. He quickly scanned the area, his subconscious filtering through the crowd, searching the inner depths of all that was near to him. His soul touched on the vile blackness of evil once, then again, then many times. Apollisian awoke from his brief trance and rushed across the street to get Victor and Alexis. His worst fear had come to pass. The dwarves had arrived.

*   *   *

"General, what attack are we going to use?" Commander Fehzban asked as he entered Amerix's tent.

The old general continued about his tasks without answering

190

the commander's question. He was used to having to explain everything to Commander Fehzban, and it annoyed him.

Amerix finished the task at hand and turned to his commander. "Aye, Commander. Ye will take two hundred of yer men, and emerge from the east sewer grates as planned," Amerix said.

Commander Fehzban was visibly shaken. "I thought we agreed that attacking from the east was the best strategy," Commander Fehzban said nervously.

"Aye, 'twas a good one. I'll give ye that. But me thinks such an attack is better served as a diversionary scheme," Amerix said as he stroked his long, black, silver-streaked beard. "Ye and yer men will emerge from the east grates first and set as many buildings aflame with the leftover oil from the Torrent Manor. Then after ye runs out of oil, ye will attack and kill every human ye see. Then as ye are doing that, me and the rest of the army will begin a mighty sweep from the west grates and annihilate the humans," Amerix said with a proud smile.

Commander Fehzban just nodded, took the scroll detailing the emergence points, and headed to round up his men. He knew that disagreeing with the ancient general was futile and he had successfully led the battle of the Torrent Manor. Though Fehzban disagreed with both strategies, the commander didn't question this plan either.

Amerix took the next few hours organizing the move of the four-thousand-strong army to the many west grates that ran north and south of the city. He briefed each commander and gave them rallying points in the city. Amerix planned to use the sewer passages as communication lines as the battle progressed. That way, messengers couldn't be killed or intercepted as they delivered messages. He instructed his commanders to tell the men to attack mostly military units first. There were too many civilians here to spend valuable strategic time slaying them. Amerix stated that after the city was well within their grasp, they could go back and slay the civilians. It was close to dusk when Amerix received reports that there were several fires on the east side of town. The attack had begun.

*   *   *

191

Apollisian burst through the common room doors of the Blue Dragon Inn. There were a few patrons drinking and eating that quickly turned to see who came in. Some had moved to the windows and peered out at the commotion, but didn't seem overly worried about the fires. Apollisian paused and stretched out his arms to get the crowd's interest. He stood as a formidable figure, demanding the attention of all that were in the common room. His plate mail glistened in the setting sun and his silk cape flapped in the breeze from the door. He paused for a moment before he began.

"Listen to me, good people of Central City," Apollisian called out. Very few of the patrons appeared to pay any attention. Apollisian went on anyway. "Outside, the same dwarven army that attacked the Torrent Manor runs rampant through your city streets, killing all they see and setting buildings ablaze," the paladin announced, waving his outstretched arms.

With that proclamation, all the patrons refocused their attention on the strange man in armor that was preaching to them. The crowd had heard of the tragedy of the Torrent Manor and the mention of dwarves was enough to stir a reaction from them.

"Dwarves!" one man cried out. "What should we do?"

"Flee for your very lives!" Apollisian yelled. "Their numbers are in the fives of thousands and they will not rest until every man, woman, and child lay dead and burning!"

With that the crowd was set alive. Some ran screaming for the door, others went to windows to validate the paladin's claims.

Apollisian ran up the stairs. He didn't know where Alexis and Victor were staying, so he called out for them. Many opened their doors and stuck their heads out to see who was screaming in the halls. Apollisian merely yelled "dwarves" and moved on. Few comprehended the claim and most merely closed their doors. Apollisian reached the third floor of the large inn, when he recognized Victor. The young squire had already donned his armor and was making his way toward Apollisian.

"Victor!" Apollisian called out.

"Stephanis be praised!" Victor said, rushing to Apollisian's side. "We had feared you had already been caught in the fighting," the young squire said, bowing low to the feet of his lord.

Apollisian shook his head from side to side and urged Victor to his feet. "Not yet, though I am eager to find the demon responsible for this bedlam," Apollisian growled with a glare of determination.

"Alexis and I were planning on keeping the east road clear for innocents to escape. With you here, it just might work. We counted only three or four scores of dwarves. The rest must be attacking from another direction. Alexis thought to cover us from the roof of this building, and you and I might slay any advancing enemies that might try to harm those fleeing," Victor proclaimed, proud of the established plan. Apollisian said nothing. He just turned and headed back down the stairs to the street. There were a lot of people to help escape.

*   *   *

Jude and Lance had finished placing on their gear when they heard the shout of "dwarves" coming from the hall. The voice sounded urgent and somewhat panicked.

"What should we do, Jude?" Lance asked after hearing the man run by.

"Flee, obviously!" Jude said sarcastically as he opened the door to the hall and peered around, making sure that there were not any dwarves in the building.

"Of course," Lance said as he placed the Necromidus in his light, leather backpack and slid it over one shoulder. "But where? We don't know what direction they are attacking from."

Jude paused in the hall. People rushed by, dropping belongings as they ran down the posh corridor. They had apparently learned firsthand about the warning and were now deciding to listen to the paladin's advice. "Let's go to the roof of this building. Perhaps we can see where they are attacking from. Then we will obviously flee in the opposite direction," Jude said. Lance agreed and the pair was soon rushing up the stairs past fleeing patrons. They reached the flat rooftop door. It was made of wood and had thin metal bands that crossed it horizontally. The door's lock had been smashed and it was standing open. Jude drew his two-handed sword and stepped into the darkness. Though he wasn't fully recovered, he had enough strength to wield his sword for short stints of time. He glanced around the rooftop, scanning for signs of a struggle. On the north side he could make out a small form leaning over the edge, firing arrows down to the street. He started to charge, but he realized that though the form was short, it was too tall and slender to be a dwarf. Jude figured anyone who was not a dwarf was a friend at this particular time.

Lance came panting up the stairs after Jude and they made their way to the south side of the building, away from the mysterious shooter on the north.

"There!" Jude said, pointing his finger to the west. "You can see many buildings that are aflame. They must be coming from the west."

Lance just tugged at Jude's arm, pulling him back toward the open door as he regained his breath. "Then we go east," Lance said.

The figure on the north side of the building turned, and in a feminine voice spoke.

"Flee to the east. We are going to fight their lines and set up an avenue for retreat. Hurry!" she said.

Lance started to say more. He wanted to find out who she was and what correlation she had with the dwarves but this time it was Jude who pulled him down into the stairwell.

"I think that is the woman I saw come into the bar this morning," Lance said as he ran down the stairs toward the common room.

Jude didn't answer as he started back down the stairs. He took two and three steps with each stride as he hurried down. Lance had a difficult time keeping up with Jude's giant strides.

As they reached the common room they heard the sound of steel ringing on steel. Jude peered around the corner. To his horror, there were three dwarves already in the room and many townsfolk lay dead.

"Only one way out," Jude whispered to his friend. Lance nodded and gritted his teeth. This was going to be his first real battle.

*   *   *

Ryshander and Kaisha rushed through the dark and eerie cobblestone streets of Central City. They heard many screams of terror and agony behind them as the wave of dwarves advanced through the west side of the city. The distant sounds of ringing steel echoed through the night and ricocheted off of many burning buildings.

194

Guardsmen shouted commands and calls of warning as they tried to organize some semblance of defense in the murky blanket of confusion.

Ryshander and Kaisha could see fires on every side of the city now, but Ryshander felt that east was still their best chance for escape. He knew the Dawson River ran alongside the eastern part of the city—that if they needed, they could swim to safety.

The sounds of battle seemed to close in around them as they cautiously made their way around the meandering alleys toward the Blue Dragon Inn. They could see the building just a few hundred feet away, and beyond that was the great stone bridge that went over the Dawson River. Dwarven invaders battled militia lines that were forming as they tried to funnel people down the street and across the bridge. A small man wearing bright violet, padded leather armor was standing over a few dwarves he had slain while another man, wearing full plate armor and wielding a short sword, was on the other side of the street. They appeared to be commanding about a score of militia men as they stood against a tidal wave of dwarven attackers. The shadows of the human defenders danced across the road through the many raging fires that were beginning to flare up from surrounding buildings.

Ryshander and Kaisha rushed past the militia, following the crowd that hurried toward the bridge. Villagers were already fanning out into the darkness of the forest on the other side of the river. Some continued down the dark road, while others stood in disbelief at the siege of their beloved city. Some wept at the horrific sight, others shouted angrily, but none dared cross the bridge back into town.

Kaisha stopped dead in her tracks and kept her iron grip on Ryshander's arm, jerking him back violently. He turned to see her standing at the edge of the stone bridge. She was gazing off into the tremendous battle that was unfolding before them. Multitudes of people rushed by, clumsily bumping into them as they scurried to safety. Screams from other villagers were prompting them to continue, yet Kaisha stood still.

"Come on, my love!" Ryshander screamed as he violently tugged at Kaisha's hand. Kaisha resisted and kept her iron visage locked on the slaughter of her home city.

Ryshander moved up behind her and wrapped his arms

around her waist. He started to lift her, when she forced his arms away.

"No!" she screamed.

Ryshander stood in shock. He noticed that her tender eyes were red and puffy with tears streaming down her beautiful face.

"We cannot flee," Kaisha said softly while another person bumped into her as he went screaming by.

Ryshander gently grasped her arm and moved to the edge of the bridge to avoid being hit by more frantically fleeing townsfolk. "What do you suppose we can do?" Ryshander asked with his arms outstretched. "We are only two, and they are many," he said motioning to the dwarven horde.

Kaisha pointed to the man in plate armor, and then to the man in the violet padded leather armor. "So are they," she said.

"But, my love . . ." Ryshander pleaded.

Kaisha gently placed her delicate finger over his lips as she pursed hers and made a hushing sound. "I understand how you feel, my love," Kaisha said. "But I cannot let those two strangers battle the dwarves alone. Those bastards killed our friends and our family. They destroyed our home, and took our livelihood. I'll not let that go unanswered," she said defiantly with her fists doubled up at her sides. Her normally soft demeanor was replaced with the hardness for battle.

Ryshander slumped his shoulders. He loved Kaisha with all his heart, but sometimes she was foolhardy. Why would she want to risk herself for something that was already lost? Lostos was gone. Their friends were gone. Getting killed in a meaningless battle would do nothing. He loved her emotion, her vigor, but he hated times like this when she implemented those traits for the wrong causes.

Ryshander hung his head low and shook it from side to side. He slowly drew his shining silver rapier and pulled his cloak back. Kaisha gave him a long passionate kiss. Her hands delved deep into his thick hair and she seemed oblivious to the death around her as she drank in his lips. After she finished, she pulled away and silently gazed into Ryshander's eyes, while he returned her loving stare. The pair had a moment of utter silence. They heard no screams, no sounds of battle, no cackling of fire—there was only their love. Ryshander smiled uncertainly and Kaisha drew her short sword. The pair started back across the bridge into the battle for Central City.

*　　*　　*

Jude rushed down the flight of stairs and into the common room. On the floor were three dead farmers, and next to them two dead bar wenches that had suffered horrible slashing wounds. Another barmaid was being pulled down behind the counter by a short hairy arm. Across the room near the door, two dwarves wearing thin chain mail and wielding small axes were fighting four militiamen. The militiamen were bleeding from several wounds and the dwarves were laughing and mocking them.

Jude hurried across the room with a booming roar and drew his mighty sword. The two dwarves battling the militiamen turned in time to see Jude's massive two-handed blade come crashing down. The wicked sword laid a deep gash across the chest of the first dwarf. Bright red blood erupted from the gash as the dwarf screamed, clutching the mortal wound.

Still weak from the poison, Jude could not lift his sword to parry. The second dwarf smiled eagerly at the exposed ribs of the large man. But before he could swing, the tip of a thin spearhead erupted from his chest. The stunned dwarf clutched at the tip of the spear that one of the militia guardsmen thrust into him. His axe fell to the ground as he gurgled in protest. Jude swung his mammoth blade in a circular motion, striking the dwarf in the neck. There was a dull ring of steel striking bone, and the dwarf's head tumbled end over end through the air.

Lance rushed over behind the bar. He saw the woman was bleeding from her eye and her nose appeared to be broken. The dwarf was huddled over the top of her and had a handful of her hair. He was pulling her head back as he kissed and bit at her neck, oblivious to the battle behind him. His left hand was fumbling with his thick leather belt as he began to loosen his breeches. Lance imagined the motions of the spell he cast on the wererat, Grascon. The magical energy swirled inside of him, and raged to peak in mere moments, surprising Lance at how fast it surged. He reached down and grasped the dwarf by the back of the neck. The gruff dwarf turned and glared at the small stature of a man, not understanding

197

his inescapable peril. Lance loosed the magic that eagerly danced along his fingers. The strange blue energy erupted from Lance's hand and invaded the dwarf's stout body. The bearded foe lurched and arched his back in pain as the powerful necromancy ripped at his life force, pulling and tearing it from his body while his arms and hands recoiled in rigor from the intense pain that surged through him. Lance felt the magic rebuilding instantly. It did not call to be loosed like it did before. Though Lance could feel its lust, he was much more in control than the last time he wielded it. The dwarf screamed in agony as Lance loosed the magic into him a second time. The dwarf's eyes rolled to the back of his head. Drool and spittle dripped from his mouth as his soul was shredded by the powerful necromancies of the Necromidus. Seconds later, the dwarven soldier, turned rapist, lay dead.

Lance hastily glanced around the large common room. He noticed Jude had dispatched the other two dwarves and was beginning to barricade the common room door with tables and benches that the militia pulled over to him. The young mage looked back down at the barmaid he had saved. She was lying on the floor, half naked, covering her exposed breasts with her arms. She shook uncontrollably and rocked back and forth, seemingly oblivious to the bodies and the other men around her.

"What does it look like outside?" Lance asked as he continued to look at the woman who sat on the floor. He wanted to say something to console her, but he wasn't sure what he could possibly say to help.

Jude moved to the window and peered out as he placed a heavy table, which it took all four militiamen to drag over to him, against the window. "Looks dark," Jude said with a sarcastic smirk.

"Where did all the dwarves come from?" one of the militiamen asked as he nursed a deep gash in his right shoulder. The others fanned out and started dragging over more tables to place against the doors and windows.

"The sewers," Jude said flatly as he wiped the blood from his giant sword on the dead dwarf.

The wounded militiaman struggled to grasp the idea that so many dwarves got into the sewers. "How did hundreds of dwarves get into the sewers undetected?" the wounded man asked.

"Thousands," Lance corrected as he poked his head into the kitchen area.

The men pulling the tables stopped in mid-stride. "What?" the wounded man asked as he tied a thin, cloth strap around his bleeding wound.

"Thousands," Jude repeated.

The wounded man sunk to the floor. He stared at the far wall of the common room and did not speak.

"It can't be," the wounded man said. Jude ignored the militiaman's doubt, and finished barring the door.

Lance ducked into the kitchen as Jude placed his heavy pack on a table and walked toward the bar.

"What are you looking for, Lance?" Jude asked.

The militiamen still stood dumbfounded at the proclamation of the dwarves' numbers. They were seemingly oblivious to the ever growing sound of battle outside the inn.

"How do you know this?" the wounded man asked.

Jude ignored the wounded man and walked toward the door to the kitchen to see what Lance was up to.

"Just checking to see if there was a back door they might come through. There isn't," Lance said with a pause as he emerged from the kitchen door holding a brown cloak. He leaned down and placed it around the shivering woman. She recoiled at his touch, but Lance placed the soft cloak around her anyway.

Jude felt weak from the quick battle. His muscles hadn't fully recovered from the poison, and he felt sluggish. He walked over to the window and peered behind the table they had placed in front of it. Jude noticed that there were many dwarves that lay dead in the street. The felled invaders had arrows protruding from their bodies that were imbedded up to the bright green fletching. There were two men standing in the street, fighting to keep an alleyway open for fleeing townsfolk. One man was wearing plate armor that was covered in blood. The other was nursing a few minor wounds, but was also covered in splattered blood. He was wearing violet leather armor.

"Lance!" Jude called excitedly.

Lance ran to his hulking friend. "What is it?" Lance asked as he peered around Jude's shoulder into the now arriving night.

"Those two men are fighting to keep an avenue for escape for the fleeing townsfolk, but the dwarves are rapidly shutting it off. If we are to escape, we need to leave now," Jude said with a stern conviction.

"We must help those men," the wounded militiaman said.

Jude turned and laughed. "This city is lost. Your only chance is to flee," Jude said as he gathered up his pack and slid it over his shoulder. Lance pulled the woman from behind the bar up by her arm. She had placed the dark brown cloak on and allowed Lance to lead her, but she gave no other clues that she realized what was going on around her.

"You may not want to help, but we will not let those two brave men hold the line alone," one called out. Another stood and agreed. Jude exhaled in defeat as Lance, the woman, and the four militiamen entered the eerie twilight battlefield.

*   *   *

Apollisian burst into the street from the Blue Dragon Inn's common room with Victor right on his heels. "I'll stand on the north side of the road. You stand on this side, next to the inn. That way Overmoon's arrow can help you keep an axe from your gullet," Apollisian said as he ran across the street, drew his short sword, and waited for the first enemy to show himself, while Victor drew his long sword and mimicked the paladin.

Three dwarves came from an alleyway. They were carrying an empty keg of oil that they had dumped on the civic building when they noticed the lone human warrior guarding the fleeing townsfolk who were escaping toward the large stone bridge. The dwarf holding the empty wooden oil keg tossed it down on the cobblestone street and drew his axe. Then the three dwarves let out a battle cry as they charged the paladin as fast as their little legs would carry them.

Apollisian steadied himself and set his feet to receive the charge of the bearded invaders. The first dwarf came in with a high axe strike. Apollisian side-stepped the attack and stuck out his foot, tripping the charging dwarf. As the stumbling attacker went sprawling by, Apollisian ducked low under the second dwarf's slice and rammed the tip of his short sword into his belly. The sturdy blade sliced through the magnificently crafted dwarven

200

mail and lodged deep into the dwarf's stomach. The dwarf gurgled in protest as bright red blood spilled from his mouth and dripped on the paladin's helmet and shoulder. Apollisian released his short sword, rooted deeply in the dying dwarf, in time to grab the third dwarf's arm as he swung his axe in an overhead motion. The paladin's muscles strained as he shifted the momentum of the third dwarf and forced him to spin behind him. The first dwarf had recovered from the fall and was getting to his feet when he was hit by the body of the third. Both dwarves tumbled to the ground as the young paladin wrenched his short sword free from the dead dwarf's belly. As he dislodged the blade, the two remaining dwarves charged. Apollisian brought up his shield to block the first strike. The dwarf's superior blade sliced into the paladin's shield and the strength of the blow ripped it from his grasp. The dwarf tugged frantically at his axe, which was wedged in the stout shield, trying to free it before the human could strike him dead. Apollisian jabbed his short sword out at the enemy, who was struggling to free his weapon. The blade pierced the dwarf just under his nose and erupted from the back of his head, sending the dying dwarf into the troughs of death.

The third dwarf brought his wicked axe toward the paladin's exposed shoulder. Knowing he could not move in time to intercept the blow, Apollisian prepared his body for the shock of the weapon hitting its mark. Instead, the paladin was hit with a splash of red sticky blood that covered his face. He looked up in surprise to see the final dwarf lying dead from an arrow that pierced his skull. The tip was sticking out between his eyes, and his beard was already soaked with blood from the grievous wound. Apollisian didn't waste any time as he shot to his feet, picked up his shield, and hurried back to the street to intercept the endless wave of dwarves that were coming from the west. He decided to thank Overmoon, for the well-placed arrow that saved his life, with a firm handshake if they survived.

*   *   *

Victor drew his long sword and stood in the dark street next to the Blue Dragon Inn. The flickering light from the burning buildings danced and wavered their red reflections off of his shiny mail.

201

He motioned for patrons to flee toward the river whenever they ran out. Most didn't need any instructions on where to run, they just followed the crowd.

It did not take long to discover the man who was directing the humans they were trying to kill away from them. It was almost dark when four dwarves charged from the west road. They wore heavy chain armor that bounced when they ran. Victor thought it looked more like they were wearing silver cloth shirts than chain mail, but he had heard of dwarves' ability to craft immaculate weapons and armor.

The first arrow shot struck the lead dwarf in the left knee. The shaft made a hollow thud as it completely pierced his leg, lodging into the cobblestone street. The dwarf grabbed at his wounded leg, dropping his axe and tumbling to the ground. The second dwarf swung his axe in a horizontal strike, hitting Victor in the right hip. He cried out in pain as the weight of the axe tore through his padded leather armor and deep into his pelvis. The force of the blow knocked the squire from his feet as the third dwarf's axe sliced the air where Victor had been standing.

Victor weakly rolled to his feet with his blade set in a defensive position. The pain from his hip was clouding his mind, but Victor ignored the searing sensation and brought his sword down in an overhead strike, hitting the dwarf who had just missed him. The dwarf recoiled in pain and dropped his heavy axe onto the cobblestone road. The third dwarf was hit in the chest and fell dead before he could come any closer, as another of Overmoon's arrows hit its mark.

Victor scanned the area for more enemies when he noticed that Apollisian battled some dwarves on the other side of the road. He wanted to run over and help his mentor, but he knew his job was to keep to this side of the street clear. The squire hastily glanced down at his stinging wound. The blade had laid a fine slice completely through his armor and deep into his hip. He tested his range of movement, and made sure that no major blood ways had been hit. Victor hadn't been a squire long, but he had heard tales in which men suffered only minor wounds, but had one of their blood ways cut, and died a few minutes later. Victor wasn't sure where his blood ways were. He knew that he had some in his neck, and around his heart, but that was about it. After a quick assessment, the squire backed against the wall of the Blue Dragon Inn. It was almost pitch black now, and he could hear more dwarves coming from the west, and what sounded like dwarves inside the common room. The squire heard a woman scream and struggled with all his will to keep from rushing into the inn. He could hear the fighting and the woman screaming for help, but he knew if he left the roadway many more would die, possibly even Apollisian. Tears streamed down his face as he listened to the woman's screams and pleas for help. Then a sickening bulge rose from his belly to his throat when he heard her no more.

*   *   *

Alexis took position on the roof of the Blue Dragon Inn. She stood next to the small ledge that ran across the rooftop of the large inn. She placed her leather backpack next to the ledge and strung her white ashen longbow. The weapon had served her ever since she learned to fashion it as a child. As she aged she made many modifications, making the already deadly bow more accurate. She tested the air, and knelt down, ensuring her silhouette couldn't be seen from the ground as the waning sun fell under the horizon. Though the dwarves could see in the dark, they could only see nearly as well as elves. Alexis was hoping she was high enough from the streets that the stout invaders would have a hard time seeing her—a scenario she did not take into consideration at the Torrent Manor, a mistake she would not make again.

Alexis had a clear view of both sides of the road and even some alleys. She had well over sixty arrows and a grappling hook set on the side of the wall for escape when the time came. Two men had burst on the roof as she was shooting dwarves, before they reached Apollisian and Victor. She told them to flee and it seemed the pair had listened.

Despite the good position, Alexis was terrified at the sight that lay before her. It was like the slaughter at the Torrent Manor all over again, except on a much grander scale. As far as she could see, there were fires rising up and the militia was trying to organize a defense, but the dwarves would rise out of a sewer grate and cut their defenses in half. She watched helplessly as the dwarven onslaught slowly made its way east, toward her and her companions.

Alexis notched an arrow and brought the deadly shaft back to the corner of her mouth. She watched many dwarves as they poured into the street from the dark alleys. She slowly inhaled the scent of her bow string and the fletching of her arrow as she held her shot, waiting for the right time to loose it. When she inhaled all the way she kept the breath for a half second, then started to exhale, releasing the shaft. Before that deadly arrow traveled ten feet into the night, she had pulled another from her quiver and began to draw it back. She had loosed the second before the first had even hit its mark.

Alexis watched Apollisian and Victor become wounded time and time again, though she tried her best to cover both of them with a barrage of arrow fire. It seemed just as she would help one, the other would be overrun. And to make things worse, the building she was on had been set on fire. She was having no problem seeing, because elves, like dwarves, could see much better in the dark than humans.

Alexis was quickly running out of arrows and slowed her shots, trying to save her deadly shafts for the most opportune times. Alexis took hold of the grappling hook and made sure its sturdy iron hooks were set. Soon she would be out of arrows and would have to brave the deadly streets.

*   *   *

Lance and Jude burst from the common room doors and ran down the crowded cobblestone street that was dimly lit with torchlight that provided little light compared to the violently flickering twilight of the raging fires burning all around. Jude took the lead and Lance led the woman by her arm as best as he could toward the Dawson River bridge. The lines that the city militia had set up to allow people to flee to the east were all but broken, causing townsfolk to flee in a plethora of different directions, and the trio had more than a few dwarven pursuers.

Three squat dwarves clad in heavy chain armor, thick hammers, and heavy axes, rushed out from behind the small wooden guard house that was just before the bridge. Jude skidded to a halt and drew his mighty sword to face the attackers in front of them, oblivious to the attackers at their rear. He knew Lance was a poor swordsman and was certain the woman with him had no talent either.

Lance slowed, turning to face the four dwarves that were behind them. The dwarves smiled and taunted him in their gruff voices, no doubt making rude comments about his stature and his fine silk cloak. Though Lance could not understand their language, he was sure he was able to discern that they were certainly taunting him. The young mage glanced down nervously at the barmaid, who was cowering behind him as if he was the most powerful wizard in the realms.

Jude charged in and swung his massive sword down, hitting the first dwarf in the shoulder. The incredible force of the blow carried the blade down to the dwarf's waist, nearly splitting him in two. Blood and entrails spilled out from the dwarf as his two counterparts lunged in at the giant man. Jude side-stepped the second strike and shot out his foot, awkwardly catching the dwarf in the face. The bearded invader grabbed his bloodied, broken nose and staggered back. While Jude's thick leg was coming down from kicking the first dwarven soldier in the face, he suffered a wicked axe cut across his thigh. Jude growled in pain and swung his two-handed sword back, hitting the dwarf in the neck and cleanly severing his head. As the bearded cranium bounced down the road, it was kicked inadvertently by a score of fleeing townsfolk. The third dwarf, after seeing the ease with which his counterparts were dispatched, ran away clutching his bloody nose.

Lance envisioned his spell, forming a simple weave of magic in front of him. The first dwarf's axe shot from his grasp, sailing through the air, and landing more than thirty feet away from him. The dwarves yelled something that Lance couldn't understand, but he was sure it had something to do with the spell he cast. Two of the attackers roughly grabbed the woman by her arm and hair, pulling her away from Lance. He could see the unbridled lust for murder in their dark sinister eyes, and he heard their sick giggling at the way the poor woman screamed in horror.

Something deep inside of Lance was set afire. He was suddenly more concerned with the welfare of the strange woman that he had never met, than of his own. Lance didn't know her, he didn't know her family, and he didn't even know her name, but something was loosed from the young mage that he had never felt before.

Lance rushed after the two kidnappers only to be blindsided by another dwarven soldier that had joined the fray. He felt a searing hot pain in his left shoulder that silenced the world around him, making his body go weightless. He no longer heard the sounds of battle, the horrible screams, or the cackling fires that raged around him. He was no longer scared or angry. What little peripheral vision Lance had was in slow motion. He was at peace with himself in a semi-conscious state, seemingly unaware of the life and death battle that thundered around on the ground. When his body finally came to a stop, he could suddenly hear the battle raging all around him again. He smelled the thick pitch from the fires, he heard the screams of terror and the cries of death. Everything sped back up as his eyes readjusted to reality. Lance could hear screams from men, women, and children who were mercilessly cut down in the ever darkening street. As he struggled to stand, he could hear every raging fire and he felt the intense searing pain that was shooting from his left shoulder. Lance raised his head and was surprised to find himself lying on the ground. Blood soaked his robe and matted in his dark black hair. He couldn't raise his left arm and had trouble sitting upright. People ignored him as they ran screaming past him, trying to get across the wide stone bridge. He looked up and saw the dwarf that had blindsided him coming at him with a blood soaked axe. Lance tried to form a spell but he couldn't get the jumbled thoughts out of his head. He tried to stand and run, but he was too dizzy, and his legs didn't seem to obey his commands for them to stand. All he could do was watch helplessly as the murderous dwarf approached.

The dwarf raised his axe and brought it streaking down at Lance's head. Lance closed his eyes and prepared for the killing blow that he was powerless to stop.

*   *   *

Ryshander and Kaisha rushed back onto the city streets as scores of civilians ran past. It was almost dark and they could see many dwarves who had broken the militia lines and were wreaking havoc on the fleeing townsfolk.

"I'll go to the north side of the road and see if I can aid the man in plate armor," Ryshander said.

Kaisha nodded worriedly and pursed her lips, motioning for him to kiss her. Ryshander smiled after placing a gentle kiss on her warm lips and disappeared into the masses of townsfolk.

Kaisha watched him go for a fleeting moment, then turned her attention to the hysteria in the streets around her. She saw two dwarves, clad in heavy chain armor, dragging a woman into one of the alleys. Kaisha rushed over to the building and set herself against the cold stone wall. She stood motionless, listening to the dwarves' heavy panting and their excited voices. Kaisha could hear the woman's muffled screams and pleas for help. Kaisha stepped into the alley's shadows as silently as a falling feather and saw one of the dwarves on top of the woman, forcing her legs apart, while the other pulled his belt free and dropped his breeches to his ankles.

Kaisha stepped patiently closer, struggling to ignore the woman's screams for help. She could tell the dwarf's fingers were probing between her legs, but she could not help her without catching the bearded marauders by surprise. Kaisha inched closer to the horrific scene. With each step she could smell the growing stench of the dwarves and hear their disgusting grunts and groans. The wererat thief deftly maneuvered behind the dwarf who was standing, waiting his turn. She stealthily reached around and grabbed his beard with her left hand, while her right hand drew her wicked blade across the stunned dwarf's neck, slicing both arteries and the esophagus. The mortally wounded dwarf clutched at the horrific gash in his neck while Kaisha kicked the back of his knee, forcing the dying dwarf to the ground. He rolled over on his back as blood spurted from the severed arteries. The dwarf that was on top of the woman stood up and awkwardly reached for his axe, though his breeches were around his ankles. Kaisha dipped in with a low slash into the dwarf's unprotected groin. The dwarf dropped his axe and clasped his hands between his legs, screaming and rolling around on the ground.

While the dwarf rolled in the dark wet alley, screaming in pain, Kaisha grabbed the woman and pulled her out of the alley. The deadly thief thought about killing the second dwarf, but due to the nature of his injury, she felt life was much worse than death.

*   *   *

207

Apollisian was bleeding from more wounds than he could count, and his once shiny plate mail was now scuffed, dented, and bloody. He was tired and his muscles screamed for a moment of rest, but the paladin was surrounded by a horde of murderous dwarves. The attackers must have recognized him from the battle of the Torrent Manor, because none of them would advance any more. They kept their distance and Apollisian was managing to slowly force his way east toward the bridge. He could see Victor on the other side of the road, battling the dwarves, but he could not tell if his squire faired well. As Apollisian glanced around, he saw that virtually all the buildings were ablaze and the fighting seemed to be lessening. The paladin knew that if he faced Amerix in his weakened state, he would surely die. Though none of Apollisian's wounds were fatal, they slowed his movements and his reactions. He knew that if he faced a skilled warrior such as Amerix, he would need more strength and speed than he normally possessed, in contrast to the slow stiffness that now ravaged his body.

Apollisian watched the dwarves that were on the east side as they turned and began focusing their attention on a new foe. Steel ringing against steel echoed through the streets as the paladin noticed that many dwarves were falling. This new dwarven foe was wearing a dark black cloak and wielding a shiny silver rapier as he easily danced and glided through the dwarven ranks.

The man adroitly forced his way through the dwarven lines and burst into Apollisian's circle. "Ryshander Delastan, at your service, good sir knight," Ryshander said as he dipped low, but still kept a wary eye on the horde of dwarves that had paused when he reached the human champion who had cut so many of them down.

Apollisian eyed the amazing man up and down. His clothes were extremely tattered by many slashes from the dwarven blades and looked as though they might fall off of the man at any minute. He wore a dark black cloak and dark green breeches, and wielded a shining silver rapier with a thick wire-like hilt that spiraled around and ended at the pommel.

"Well met, Ryshander Delastan. I am Apollisian Bargoe, defender of Westvon, and champion of Stephanis," Apollisian said as he brought his bloody short sword up to his chest in salute. "How are you not wounded, my good man?" Apollisian asked as he cautiously eyed the dwarven mob.

"Well, I have certain enchantments about me that make their finely crafted blades next to useless against me. Though I dare not wait until I find one that is not hindered by my enchantment," Ryshander said, struggling to keep his face from twitching nervously. In truth, Ryshander bore no such enchantment. He and Kaisha were simply wererats. Wererats could only be harmed by magical and silver blades, and so far, none of the dwarves that he had faced wielded either.

"Shall we go, good sir? It seems we have worn out our welcome and you look a little tired," Ryshander said with a sly grin.

Apollisian nodded. He didn't appreciate the way this man made light of the senseless slaughter of thousands of people, but he certainly wasn't about to argue moral sensibility with him at this particular time. "Wait. We have to move across the street and get Victor," Apollisian said.

"My partner, Kaisha, is on that side. She will get him," Ryshander replied as he started wading into the east flank of the dwarves.

Apollisian launched himself into the dwarven horde with renewed vigor and followed his new acquaintance toward the Dawson River bridge.

*　　*　　*

"General! General!" the panting dwarven messenger screamed as he rounded the corner of the grinder. Amerix turned his head, climbed down from the bottom rung, and faced the messenger as he stood battle ready. He was adorned from head to toe in his ancient plate armor. The thick ram horns curved around the scarred helmet and large iron spikes protruded from the many dwarven runes that arched back over the top. His large steel shield was strapped to his arm and it bore more scars and had seen more battles than most dwarves had seen days. He carried his magnificent axe in his right hand as he towered over the other dwarves.

"What is it, messenger?" Amerix asked uninterested as his shoulders slumped lazily. The battle was going well. His army had suffered many more casualties than he expected, but overall the battle was widely a success.

"They have the human champion cornered, the one from the

Torrent," the messenger said as he propped his hands on his knees, fighting for breath.

"What champion?" Amerix asked as his posture straightened and he became more interested.

"The one you had slain at the Torrent Manor and knocked into the fire. He lives somehow," the messenger replied.

Amerix scowled and angrily stroked his long silver and black beard. How the human survived the fire, Amerix didn't know, but he was determined to kill him again. Amerix snapped out his hands and grabbed the messenger by his heavy chain armor, pulling him close to his face. "Where is he?" Amerix demanded.

"He is at the east side of town near the bridge. He is wounded but his skill is too great for us to overcome him. So Commander Fehzban ordered us to surround him until you could get there," the messenger replied nervously.

Amerix immediately started down the corridor with the messenger in tow. "Where is that elf and the human whelp that runs with him?" Amerix asked. "If the human champion survived the fire it is feasible that those other two nuisances survived also."

"The elf is on the roof of some large building by the east bridge. She rained arrows down, keeping us at bay for some time, but she slowed her shots enough that we set fire to the building she is perched on. We think she is running out of arrows," the messenger said, taking in labored breaths as he scurried behind, trying to keep up with Amerix's furious pace. "The human boy is surrounded on the other side of the street." The messenger was pleased to give his general such valuable information.

Amerix didn't respond. He just marched as fast as his stocky legs would carry him to the eastern-most grate.

* * *

Lance was too dizzy to move, and closed his pained, weary eyes. He lay wounded and bleeding, waiting for the keen dwarven blade to slice him in two, but all he heard was a shrill ring of steel on steel. He finally opened his eyes to see Jude's mammoth blade rising back from deflecting the dwarven strike.

"Get up Lance!" Jude screamed as he deflected another strike from the dwarven attacker.

210

Lance ignored the horrible pain in his shoulder and struggled to his feet. His arm hung limp and he staggered back a few steps, scanning the streets for the woman in the brown cloak. A feeling of profound loss crept over him. He feared the woman would suffer a fate worse than death.

Jude deflected another blow from the dwarf's axe, sending the wicked weapon wide, and stepped close, striking the dwarf in the face with the pommel of his giant sword. The dwarf clutched his broken nose and staggered back as blood poured down his chin. Jude pressed in with a horizontal slice, but to his surprise, the nimble dwarf recovered quickly, ducking under the blow and slashing a deep gash in Jude's already wounded leg. Jude howled and stumbled to his left. The dwarf followed Jude's momentum and struck again from the right side. The large swordsman just managed to bring his heavy blade up in time to deflect the deadly strike, but the force of the blow knocked him to the ground.

The dwarf attacked furiously. Jude weakly lifted his sword up to try to intercept another blow from the deceptively quick attacker, but as the dwarf raised his axe over his head, the weapon shot from his grasp and flew through the air, landing far away from the stunned soldier.

Jude quickly kicked up with his good leg, catching the short dwarf in the already bloodied nose. The dwarf grabbed his nose and staggered back as Jude forced himself to stand. The dwarf recovered from the kick in time to see Jude's mammoth blade slicing through the air as it struck him in the side. The dwarf tumbled to the ground, clutching a gaping wound in his ribs. As he stared wide-eyed at his own entrails, the bearded soldier died.

"Come!" Jude said as he limped through the crowd toward the bridge.

Lance followed reluctantly, constantly looking back, hoping to steal a glance of the woman in the brown cloak.

*   *   *

Kaisha fought her way west a few hundred feet. There were not as many dwarves on the south side of the road as the north, and when she could sneak by, she did. When she reached the Blue Dragon Inn, she noticed that there was a man wearing violet leather

211

and he was very bloody. She could tell he bore some wounds, but a lot of the blood was from the many dead dwarves that lay around him. She did not know who the man was, didn't know his name, and had never seen him before, but the sight of him standing alone against a horde of dwarven enemies, trying to help townsfolk to safety, ignoring his own wounds and danger, seemed to inspire her. Kaisha rushed in with her sword ablaze. She slashed many dwarves who challenged her, cutting them down quickly. Soon the dwarven invaders stepped back to assess the new enemy that seemed impervious to their weapons.

"Come on, this way!" Kaisha yelled.

Victor looked back toward the soft but commanding voice that called out. He was shocked to see a beautiful woman standing before him. She wore a dark black cloak that had many slash marks in it and wielded a short sword.

Kaisha took her finger and placed a lock of her long hair behind her ear that was hanging in her face, and held her blade in a threatening manner, daring the dwarves to press another attack.

Victor didn't hesitate and backed toward her, covering the rear as she fought a path to the east. Soon, they were out of the dwarven ranks and in a full sprint toward the Dawson River bridge.

*   *   *

Alexis climbed down from the flaming building and eased herself into the darkness of the narrow, debris-filled alleys. Apollisian and Victor were making their way to the east bridge and she knew she had to take a discreet route. Alexis placed her light leather quiver over her shoulder and secured the bottom strap to her belt to keep the quiver from turning over when she ran. She slid her bow over the other shoulder and drew her long sword. As she was making her way down the dark and narrow alley, she heard some voices in front of her. Alexis nimbly ducked against a wall and peered into the darkness. She saw many dwarven forms coming from a sewer grate ahead. Hoping to avoid a confrontation, she doubled back toward the street. As she rounded the corner, more dwarves appeared in front of her. The bearded soldiers cried out at the sight of the woman and seemed as surprised to see her as she was to see them. Alexis slashed out, catching one in the shoulder. The dwarf howled and dropped back as another slashed forward at her right side. She ducked the axe and stabbed low, but at the same time she took a vicious slice across the back of her shoulder. She ignored the searing pain and backed up, parrying another strike. The wound in her shoulder was shooting mind-numbing pain through her body. She fought her attackers from both directions for many minutes, wounding several of them. But her strength soon failed and she lost the grip on her sword. The weapon clanged to the alley floor as she was overcome by her enemies. Alexis took a wicked slash across the midsection that cut through her finely crafted elven chain armor and into her belly. She felt sick, and doubled over clutching her wounded stomach.

The dwarves called out and heckled her as they kicked and beat her with their fists. She fought back as best she could, trying to defend herself, but soon she knew only darkness.

*　　*　　*

Apollisian and Ryshander were in a full run toward the wide vine-covered bridge that spanned the Dawson River. They were about one hundred yards away when Ryshander spied an unusually large dwarf standing in the black of night. He was adorned in full plate armor and wielded an axe and a great metal shield. His long silver-streaked black beard jostled in the night breeze as he stood between the wererat and freedom.

"One more, then we are home free," Ryshander announced as he and Apollisian slowed to a walk. Apollisian strained his eyes, but he could not see far into the deep black of night.

As they neared the large dwarf, Ryshander arrogantly flicked his thin rapier around, taunting the dwarf. "You are an awful big dwarf," Ryshander chuckled. The irony of the statement was not lost on his ears.

Apollisian could hardly see in the black of night, but when he heard Ryshander's words, his heart sank. He knew of only one big dwarf, and that dwarf bore the name Amerix. "No!" he screamed, and raced forward into the night, hearing the ring of steel on steel as the man who helped him escape clashed with the renegade general.

*　　*　　*

213

Amerix emerged from the eastern-most sewer grate with several of his officers. The renegade general quickly sent his officers on other menial tasks as he spied the human champion from the Torrent Manor. He slowly inhaled the wonderful smell of death and battle that hung in the night air. His ears swallowed every jovial ring of steel against steel and he relished every human scream that echoed in the crisp autumn night. The ancient general slowly stood by the bridge. He could see a few humans still fleeing across, but his eyes were scanning for a particular foe. The old dwarf cracked a half grin when he saw the bloody paladin being led through the night by a lone human with no armor. Amerix stepped in front of the strange human and watched the human confidently stride up to him. The strange man didn't seem afraid like the others. On the contrary, the man said something in his disgusting language and chuckled to himself. It made no difference to Amerix. The thin, weak looking man wielded a small thin sword that the old general doubted would pierce his skin, let alone his thick chain armor. Amerix didn't understand what the man said. The old general only understood two languages. The dwarven language, and the language of war.

*   *   *

Ryshander squared off what he thought was a good distance to attack the dwarf, but before he could react, Amerix moved with lightning speed, lunging out with his axe and jabbing Ryshander in the face with the tip. The sharp serrated shaft ripped a deep gash across Ryshander's nose and tore the corner of his eye. Ryshander howled in pain and shock because the weapon had actually hurt him. Holding his bloody eye, Ryshander lunged in with his rapier. His small sword slashed through the air, but to his surprise the blade hit nothing, while a horrific pain ripped through his ribs as the dwarf's axe tore a large hole in his side. Ryshander's legs buckled under him and he tumbled to the ground.

Ryshander ignored his pain and surprise at the dwarf's fighting prowess as he struggled to see through his left eye the next strike coming down. His right eye was full of blood. He managed to deflect the blow, but the heavy dwarven axe shattered the blade of his thin rapier and made a cut in the wererat's hip. There was a flash

214

of brilliant yellow light as the enchantment on Ryshander's shattered sword escaped into the night.

Amerix smiled, preparing to kill the arrogant human, when he noticed movement in the corner of his eye and instinctively ducked a strike from his left. His shield took a portion of the strike and deflected it wide. He pulled his axe free, swinging it from the right. Amerix felt the keen blade bite into the shoulder of the paladin. Apollisian ignored the minor wound in his shoulder and circled, drawing Amerix away from the downed thief.

Ryshander managed to weakly sit up. He was amazed as the two champions squared off in the dimly lit city street that had shadowy flickering twilights from the many raging fires.

Each seemed to hate the other. It was then Ryshander realized there was a past between the two that he knew nothing of. The thief knew his wounds would kill him if he moved much, so he sat back and watched the epic battle unfold, hoping Apollisian would emerge the victor.

"How many times must I kill ye?" Amerix growled to Apollisian, knowing the paladin could speak his tongue.

"Know this, evil Amerix, when I kill you, you will remain dead," Apollisian said through gritted teeth as he feinted in, drawing the dwarf's shield down, then striking high.

Amerix was prepared for such tactics and deflected the strike with his axe. He then lunged forward with his shield, but Apollisian had moved and Amerix's shield hit only air.

The battle raged on, neither combatant gaining an upper hand, and each sporting more than a dozen minor wounds from the fight. Amerix's mind wandered as he fought the champion paladin. He struggled to understand why the human called him evil. He wondered if it was a contextual error he may have made in the dwarven language but he didn't think so. The ancient general was amazed that the human had the gall to think him evil. It was the humans that were the evil ones. They had persecuted his people and caused the death of his beloved wife and child. Had the evil Beyklans not imposed the embargo on goods to Andoria during the civil war, his wife and child would have received the necessary medicines they needed to treat the illnesses they had. Instead they received no medicines and, as a result, died. His family died as a direct result of

215

the Beyklans' greed. Now only Beyklans died as a result of their own greed.

Apollisian attacked and moved, repeating the movements as he maneuvered himself closer to the bridge and away from the severely wounded Ryshander. Amerix followed the paladin blindly, striking hard and fast, unaware that he was being drawn backward toward the bridge.

*   *   *

Lance stood at the base of the large stone bridge and looked over into the growing darkness. The bridge spanned a deep chasm that the Dawson River had formed from centuries of erosion. The cliff face was sheer and well over a hundred feet high. The many docks at the base of the cliff were well lit by hundreds of torches, and Lance could see where the city was constructing a larger dock and a retractable platform to raise and lower goods. There were a few townsfolk who were climbing into the small boats and other water crafts that were moored.

Jude limped along the bridge, occasionally glancing back at the battle line many militiamen had formed to protect the stone pathway. The bridge was about sixty feet wide and its sides were covered in thick green moss that dangled over the edge and hung down. In the center of the bridge were two small ten-foot-high battlements that a few militia guardsmen had manned in case the dwarves tried to follow the townsfolk across the bridge.

Lance paused and gently pressed his hand on his wounded bloody shoulder. The pain from the wound was excruciating and caused him to swoon.

Jude stopped and pulled his pack from his shoulder, dropping it next to the stone rail. "We are a safe enough distance away," Jude said as he leaned against the rail of the bridge near the battlements and pulled some cloth strips from his pack, gently lifting Lance's sable robe. The axe wound had severed many tendons and bit halfway into the bone of his arm.

Lance winced as Jude tightly tied the bandages around his arm and shoulder amid the chaos of fleeing townsfolk. "Well what's it look like, leech?" Lance asked with a halfhearted chuckle.

Jude half smiled at the title "leech." A leech was another term

216

for doctor, and the swordsman had never thought himself as a doctor before. "Well . . ." Jude said with a pause. "It's not good, my friend. I have seen similar wounds in swordsmen, and they would never wield a sword again with that arm. I have even seen some lose the arm," Jude said solemnly.

Lance studied his friend's face. He noticed deep remorse in his eyes, and knew his friend believed the worst. He looked away and tried to think of solutions. He wondered if there were any healing spells in the Necromidus. Lance knew that so far every spell he reviewed was for war, and more than likely that was all the magic tome contained. Evil mages were not known to study healing magic. Lance thought about purchasing some healing from a church, but it was likely the spell would cost more gold than he and Jude had combined.

Jude finished the wrap and Lance decided to focus on getting across the bridge to safety before he worried about something that had not even happened yet. He pulled the knot tight that he had tied on the bandages that were wrapped around Lance's arm when he saw Ryshander and a man in plate armor squaring off against a lone dwarf. The dwarf was the biggest dwarf Jude had ever seen and he stood almost five feet tall, if not taller. He was adorned in plate armor and wielded an axe and shield.

"What do you see, Jude?" Lance asked, seeing his friend's eyes were fixed across the bridge.

"It's that thief we met in our room," Jude said, never taking his eyes from the impending battle.

"Kaisha?" Lance said excitedly.

"No, the other one," Jude replied distantly, keeping his eyes fixed on the unfolding battle.

Lance's shoulders slumped as he looked over the rail to the north side of the road. He watched the thief get cut down in a few quick strokes while Jude's breathing quickened at seeing the battle prowess the dwarf possessed.

"That dwarf just cut him down!" Lance screamed.

Jude unconsciously took a few steps back toward the city. "Look, he lives, the other warrior has stepped into the fray," Jude said as he drew his giant two-handed sword.

"What do you think you are doing?" Lance asked weakly as he slumped against the thick stone rail.

217

"The same thing you were doing when you ran after the girl that the dwarves grabbed," Jude responded as he hurried back toward Central City.

"Getting your fool self cut down?" Lance groaned as he fought to his feet to follow his friend.

Jude half smiled as he charged into the battle. "No, growing a conscience," he countered.

Lance grinned through the pain from his shoulder and envisioned the motions of a spell in his mind. "We have very poor timing at developing these things," Lance said with a halfhearted smirk. Jude just smiled in return, then broke into a run.

*　　*　　*

Victor pushed and fought his way through the crowd to the base of the bridge where he saw Apollisian battling a dwarf clad in full plate armor. The dwarf's armor was adorned with runes and battle scars, and topped with a helm that had ram horns on the side. Victor immediately recognized the dwarf as the renegade general, Amerix. The squire rushed to the battle as fast as he could. He ducked in and around the crowd that was running to the bridge. Just as he neared the fight, he lunged in with his long sword, swinging it wildly at the dwarf.

Amerix easily caught the blow with his shield, ducking away from Apollisian and swinging his hefty, double-bladed axe low at Victor. The squire was amazed at the speed and fluidity of the dwarf's attack. Frantically swinging his long sword, Victor managed to deflect most of the blow, but the wicked axe still laid a deep cut across his calf.

"Victor, get back!" Apollisian screamed at his squire as he pressed his attack.

"I'll not let you face this demon alone," Victor shouted while he limped a few steps back as bright red blood ran from his new wound.

Apollisian didn't respond, he just focused his attacks to Amerix's right side, hoping that Victor might gain less of the dwarf's attention.

Amerix recognized Apollisian's barrage of thrusts as a ruse and continued to shift his attacks and movements, forcing the pala-

218

din where he wanted him, as opposed to where the paladin wanted to go.

The dwarf cracked a wicked smile. "I can dispatch yer whelp at me leisure," Amerix taunted.

Apollisian's heart raced. He didn't doubt the dwarf's claim.

"He is not your foe, Amerix," Apollisian grunted as he deflected a fierce blow from Amerix's axe. The shrill sound of ringing steel echoed into the night.

"Nay are ye," Amerix responded. "But ye refuse to let me get the justice my people deserve, so for that ye must die."

Victor didn't understand what Amerix and Apollisian were saying. The young squire didn't speak dwarven. He guessed the paladin was trying to distract the demon dwarf, so Victor pressed his attack. Victor leaned most of his weight forward into his thrust and lunged in with his long sword. Amerix quickly side-stepped the thrust and attacked Apollisian high. Victor's wild stab went just under the dwarf's armored arm. Amerix clapped his thick plated arm down on the squire's blade, pinning it under his shield arm and his body. Amerix twisted his body and struck his axe out at the paladin while driving his shield around and ramming the edge of it into the squire's exposed hand. Victor shrieked in pain and dropped his long sword that was pinned under the dwarf's arm.

Amerix raised his shield arm slightly and let the sword fall at his feet, then swiftly ducked a strike from Apollisian.

Victor backed away and drew his short sword as his gaze shifted to a young woman helping the man away that Amerix cut down earlier.

"Ye see, that is all the mercy ye will get from me. Turn away and let me have me justice, or ye and yer whelp will die," Amerix bellowed, motioning to the squire's blade that lay at his feet.

Apollisian felt his heart race with fear and his stomach go queasy. He couldn't leave, and he couldn't let Amerix slay the innocents of Central City. "Victor, go help the militia, I've got the dwarf," Apollisian shouted.

Victor ignored the paladin's command. He knew Apollisian would die to protect him and he wouldn't let that happen. One good thrust and the evil dwarf would be no more. The squire watched the thrusts and feints of the two champions and waited before thrusting his sword in, catching Amerix under the shoulder plate and laying a deep puncture wound.

Amerix howled in pain as the squire's short sword ran deep into his shoulder. His cold, murderous, steel blue eyes fixed on the boy-squire. He cocked his shield arm back, and thrust the battered metal plate with all his strength at the paladin. The shield hit Apollisian, knocking him off balance while Amerix pushed forward and knocked the paladin from his feet.

Apollisian adjusted quickly and rolled with the blow, stabbing upwards under Amerix's shield, piercing the dwarf's thick breast plate. The paladin couldn't believe a skilled warrior such as Amerix had made such a mistake. In the next instant the paladin knew it was he that had erred.

As the paladin's sword came stabbing in, Amerix made no attempt to avoid or deflect the strike and accepted the blow with grim determination. After the short sword hit his mark, Amerix turned and laid a deep slice along the back of Victor's shoulder.

Victor cried out and dropped his short sword, clutching the crippling wound. Apollisian watched in helpless horror as he struggled to get to his feet in time. Yet, the paladin knew in his heart he would not.

Amerix feinted low. Victor, not understanding the feint for what it was, moved his leg and dropped his arms. Amerix shifted his weight and brought the wicked double-bladed axe high, laid a horrific slice across the chest of the squire, and easily sliced through the thin leather armor. Blood streamed out from the grievous wound as Victor stumbled backward from the force of the blow.

Again, Amerix swung his axe in a deadly arc, catching Victor in the neck. Apollisian watched in horror because he knew Victor was dead before his body hit the ground.

*   *   *

Jude ran through the fleeing crowd as fast as his wounded leg would carry him, hopping over bodies of dead humans and dwarves alike. Lance hurried after him, keeping an eye on the front lines in case the dwarves managed to force their way through. The militia was holding for now, but there were only a few hundred

220

fighting, and Lance knew they would soon be overcome by sheer numbers alone.

Amerix attacked with such ferocity that the air whistled with each deadly strike. Apollisian had suffered a severe gash across his right leg and he could feel his toes going numb. The paladin knew his leg was soon to follow and he tried to lead the dwarf close to the bridge.

When Jude reached the pair, he swung in with a huge overhand slash at the large dwarf. Amerix raised his shield and deflected the blow, whipping his axe across his body, knocking away a thrust from the paladin.

"Get away! You don't know his skill," Apollisian called out as he tried to maneuver between the dwarf and the large man.

Jude said nothing, keeping his eyes locked on the dwarf's deadly visage, and backed away as Amerix glared at him. The renegade dwarf was just far enough away from the swordsman that he couldn't get a good attack without making himself vulnerable from the skilled paladin.

"Tell yer friend to come closer, I'd like to cut him down like I did to yer whelp," Amerix said with a wicked, yellow toothed smile.

Apollisian said nothing; he backed onto the bridge, drawing the dwarf closer. The paladin launched several feints and thrusts at Amerix as the two took their battle over the Dawson River.

"Lead me where ye will, human. I will cut ye down were ever ye flee," Amerix taunted with each attack.

Apollisian fought his way to the rail of the bridge. The deadly dwarf had scored too many hits and the paladin felt his strength waning. He knew he had little time to defeat the dwarf, but Amerix seemed to gain strength as the battle raged on. His strikes were becoming more focused and precise and he had an easier time defending the paladin's ailing attacks.

Jude watched the battle a few feet away. He had followed the paladin as the fight moved from the cliff face onto the bridge. He honored the man's request to stay back. Jude recognized the dwarf's skill with his axe and knew it was superior to his own, but the swordsman stayed close in case the armored man fell. Jude wasn't sure how long he could last against such a foe, but he was not going to let the man die.

221

As the battle raged on, it soon became obvious to Jude that it was coming to an end. The warrior's attacks were becoming labored and weak. He threw fewer strikes and his defenses were becoming sloppy. Jude glanced over at Lance, who was standing at the base of the bridge watching the epic battle. The dwarven soldiers were making a push and the militia was falling back. Across the bridge almost all of the fleeing townsfolk were out of sight and a few militia were futilely firing arrows at the dwarven front lines.

Jude took a deep breath and unsnapped the leather strap holding the thick rope and grappling hook that hung at his waist. He ran to the edge and swung the grappling hook over the rail, pulling up fiercely. The thin teeth of the grappling hook bit into the under side of the bridge and the rope groaned as Jude strained, setting it deep into the under side of the bridge. He then quickly tied the rope around his waist, pulled it taut, and turned to face the epic battle as it came to an end.

*   *   *

Apollisian cried out in pain as the dwarf's axe ripped a deep gash across his shoulder. Blood erupted from the crippling wound and splattered on the moss-covered rail of the bridge. Apollisian watched helplessly as his finely crafted short sword tumbled over the edge of the bridge and dropped a hundred feet, to splash into the swift river. Seeing the human champion near defeat, Amerix swung his axe down again. Apollisian tried to avoid the blow, but the wicked axe tore a gash in his armor and bit deep into his lower back. The paladin fell to his knees, struggling to stand. Blood streamed from his wounds and pooled under him as he tried to keep conscious.

Amerix launched a kick and struck the paladin in the mouth with his metal shin plate. Blood splattered from the paladin's mutilated lip as he tumbled to his back. Apollisian lay on his back staring at the night sky. He gazed for what seemed like an eternity, at the thousands of stars that were visible for only fleeting moments through the dark black smoke rising from the burning buildings of Central City. He struggled with the thought of dying—though he could heal himself, that took a few minutes, and Apollisian knew the dwarf would strike him dead in just a few more moments.

Apollisian couldn't understand why the dwarf was waiting. The kick had left him stunned and he couldn't hear the battle well. It seemed as if all sounds around him were muffled and quiet. He wondered if he was already dead, and his soul just hadn't left his body yet. Apollisian tried to raise his head. He managed to lift his chin a few inches. He glanced around the bridge and noticed a strange woman kneeling over him. She had long brown hair and beautiful eyes.

Apollisian smiled as best he could. The seemingly angelic woman said something to him but he couldn't make it out. Behind her stood a bizarre man wearing a black cloak with silver trim and elven runes on it. The man had a vicious wound in his shoulder and his arm hung limp. He didn't seem to be much older than a boy, but the paladin stared at an ageless look in his eyes that seemed to show thousands of years of knowledge and wisdom. The boy's hair was wild and unkempt, held in place by dirt and sweat from the battle.

Apollisian figured he wasn't dead yet. He tried to gauge where the dwarf had gone, but the strain was too much for him and he had lost too much blood. The paladin watched helplessly as the two people slowly drifted from view, and he slid into the darkness.

*   *   *

Jude double-checked the rope and took a deep breath. He watched helplessly as the paladin's sword was knocked over the edge of the bridge. In the same swift series of attacks, the dwarf cut the paladin down, and as the helpless man tried to rise, the merciless dwarf kicked him in the face. Jude winced as blood splattered from the man's shattered jaw, knocking him to his back. The murderous dwarf stepped over the downed man and raised his axe.

Jude rushed forward ignoring the searing pain in his leg as he forced his tired, wounded muscles to trudge on. As he rushed across the bridge, he gained speed and momentum, lowering his broad shoulders, and outstretching his thick powerful arms. When he neared the dwarven general who was perched atop the downed man, he growled and his tired legs shot his body like a catapult into the stout dwarf. He caught the dwarf around the neck and shoulders as the force of the blow carried them both into the rail vehemently. Jude hit the stone ledge and his momentum carried him up and over it. He desperately clung to the dwarf's beard with his left arm and hooked his right arm around the dwarf's back, grabbing his shoulder plate with his thick dirty fingers.

Amerix growled as he struggled against the immense weight of the huge man pulling at his beard and shoulder. His back hit the moss-covered rail and his feet lifted from the ground. His shield arm tugged at the iron grip on his beard while his right arm released his axe, and he clung by his fingertips on the edge of the rail. The enchanted weapon fell to the stone bridge with a loud clang.

"Throw him over!" Jude screamed as he hung, suspended by the dwarf's beard and shoulder plate.

Amerix twisted, and with brute strength, forced Jude's hand from his shoulder plating, then twisted his body and turned his stomach to the rail. He grabbed Jude's wrist with his right arm and the iron muscles contracted as Amerix hoisted Jude up, relieving pressure from his beard.

Jude watched the dwarf's strength in disbelief as he was held suspended over the edge of the bridge by the dwarf's right arm.

Kaisha ran up behind the dwarf who was leaning over the rail. She reached down, grabbed his legs, and rammed her shoulder into his buttocks. Amerix easily launched over the edge of the bridge. She watched as Jude and the dwarf tumbled head over heels through the air, and the dwarf fell over a hundred feet into the Dawson River. Jude fell about thirty feet and was jerked violently as the rope went taut, holding him above the river.

The dwarf hit the river and disappeared under the black depths of the water in a shimmering white splash.

Jude hung suspended from the bridge by the rope that was tied around his waist, moaning and grabbing at his rope-burned waist and sore ribs. "I thank you, my lady. Now if you could just somehow hoist me up," Jude said through clenched teeth.

Kaisha grabbed the rope and pulled while Lance pulled with his good arm and helped Kaisha raise Jude back to the bridge. When Jude slowly climbed over the stone rail, he untied the rope and quickly bundled the lifeline up, placing it back on his belt.

"We have got to hurry. The dwarves have pushed the militia to the bridge. We haven't much time," Lance said.

Cries of anguish from the militia echoed in the night as they tried in vain to hold the front line.

Kaisha helped the wounded Ryshander to his feet. He was badly injured, but she had dressed his wounds, and he was well enough to travel. The pair stared long and hard at the burning city. It had been their home for so long, and now it was in ruins. Kaisha tried not to think of the thousands still trapped in the city, fighting for their lives.

"How are we going to move him?" Jude said as he motioned weakly to Apollisian. Lance looked around. Ryshander was too injured to move anyone, and Jude's leg kept him from helping. Lance couldn't even move his arm. It was then they heard a trumpet sound and heavy horses running toward them.

"More dwarves?" Kaisha asked as her voice cracked with fear.

Jude limped by her and stared into the blackness of the east road. "I don't think dwarves ride heavy horses," Jude said with a hopeful smile.

Lance stepped forward clutching his wounded shoulder. "Then who?"

Just then their question was answered as a score of mounted heavy lancers erupted from the blackness and onto the bridge. They were wearing brilliant, brass-colored plate armor with long, red, flowing, silk capes. Their hoof beats thundered on the bridge's stone floor as they charged toward them.

"Get against the rails!" Jude yelled. All three moved next to Apollisian, who lay motionless. Kaisha kneeled down and tended to the fallen paladin as the others watched in awe of the riders. They wore full plate armor from head to toe and large helms that sprouted thick red plumes. The plumes danced and bounced around their shoulders as they thundered by. Their silk red capes danced in the rushing wind behind them, and their horses were barded in bright, shining plate armor that hung down over their heads and flanks. The horses and riders charged forward fearlessly. The first horseman bore a flag attached to the end of his lance, the flag of Beykla.

Another trumpet sounded and the few remaining militiamen holding the edge of the bridge parted. The unsuspecting dwarves rushed in, thinking they had broken the human resistance. The first dwarf looked up as a heavy lance lodged into his chest. The thin metal tip of the lance easily pierced the dwarf. The remaining attackers turned and fled when they saw the blood-soaked banner of

Beykla erupt from the back of the impaled dwarf. Militiamen let out a heartfelt cheer into the night as hundreds of heavy horsemen charged across the bridge. They raised their wounded and bloody arms in triumph. Jude, Lance, Kaisha, and Ryshander watched as hundreds of armored men began to march across the bridge. They bore the banner of Beykla, and some bore a strange blue banner with a depiction of a bright yellow battlement.

"The banner of Westvon Keep," Kaisha whispered under her breath.

Lance turned and looked at her. She was staring into the black of night. He couldn't see any other banners anywhere. He was amazed at how she could see so well in the dark. A few moments later the large blue banner erupted from the horizon, carried on the end of a pikeman's weapon.

"How can you see so well?" Lance asked.

Kaisha flushed in the night. She hadn't anticipated his human eyes. She said nothing and tended to the fallen paladin. Lance frowned, trying to solve the riddle.

"Didn't you hear the trumpets?" Ryshander said, stepping forward. "Those are the Westvon trumpets, had you never heard them before?"

Lance stammered. "I am from Bureland, I have never been to Westvon," he admitted sheepishly.

"We should go there sometime then, to thank them for saving our city," Ryshander said as he moved back and kneeled down to Kaisha. When Lance turned back and watched the soldiers as they marched by, Ryshander began to sign. "You need to be more careful, my love. We are not in the company of our brothers and sisters. There are things we unconsciously do that they can not. We do not know how they are to react to our bloodlines."

Kaisha nodded and lifted the paladin to an upright position. She dabbed his head with a dry rag, while Ryshander looked around at the ragged group. He and Kaisha had made a life of looking out for themselves. But when their way of life was attacked, they fled. It wasn't until they witnessed firsthand the fate that was befalling their city, that Kaisha had stirred a deeply repressed emotion known as empathy. The haggard thief looked solemnly at Lance and Jude.

Lance was a mystery in himself. He wore a strange robe and

226

claimed to be a wizard, yet he bore no spell components or other items that Ryshander was used to wizards carrying. Lance was barely a man, yet he seemed so able and fearless in seeking out his own agenda. Ryshander didn't know anything about his writings that he needed deciphered, but when the time arose, the mage put himself in harm's way to protect a woman he had never met before. Jude, the giant of a man, seemed to care for nothing but the safety of his friend. Yet he too risked his life to save the strange warrior that battled the large dwarf.

Ryshander smiled as he watched the soldiers battle the dwarves on the eastern edge of the city. What a bizarre group of unlikely heroes they were. The young thief stared warmly at beautiful Kaisha as she tended to the paladin.

She felt his loving eyes on her and met his loving stare with hers, smiling as she rose to stand by his side. Ryshander placed a gentle arm around her waist as the pair watched the soldiers establish a firm hold in the east part of town. For the soldiers of Beykla, it appeared the battle for Central City was far from over—it had just begun.

*   *   *

He looked at the downed paladin. Amerix decided not to slay the man. He was not his enemy. The defeated man that lay before him was a champion of justice. Though Amerix thought him confused, his intentions were honorable. Amerix raised his axe above his head to give thanks to Durion, the mountain god, when he was struck in the side by a tremendous blow. He felt the weight forcing him over the railing of the bridge. Amerix reacted instantly, twisting his body and struggling with all his strength to keep from being forced over the mossy edge. His back lay against the cold bridge railing and his thick metal armor squeaked under his weight against the hard rail. Something had a hold of his beard and was twisting his head to the side, while strong-feeling fingers tugged at his right shoulders. Amerix strained his muscles and let out a roar. The mighty dwarf turned his body and faced down over the edge of the bridge. He stared straight into the eyes of the large human that attacked him during the fight with the human champion. Amerix reached down with one arm and hoisted the human closer to him,

227

smiling when the man bore a look of pure astonishment at his power. He noticed the human was anchored to the bridge by a rope that was tied around his waist. The dwarven general reached down to cut the rope and send the doomed man down into the murky depths of the Dawson River when he felt someone grab his legs, and then a shoulder hit him in his rump. Before he could react, Amerix tumbled over the bridge and zipped by the dangling human. He tried to reach out and grab the man, but he tumbled past. Amerix knew he didn't have much time to react. He used the razor-sharp knife he held in his hand to cut the laces of his armor as he tumbled down. He cut the side straps and then his leggings, waiting until impact to cut the rest, hoping the armor would take some of the impact of striking the water from such a high fall.

Amerix hit the water with a tremendous clap. Some of his air was forced from his lungs when he hit, and Amerix felt himself sinking rapidly under the depths of the mighty river. He thought about just letting the ancient armor pull him into the pits of his watery grave. He had lived a long life, longer than any dwarf should have. Normally dwarves died of old age by the time they reached their four hundredth year of life, but somehow the ancient general kept on living. He wasn't young by any standards but he still had more vigor than some dwarves who were two hundred years his junior.

As he slowly sank into the depths, Amerix struggled with losing the armor that had been handed down through his family for over a thousand years. It was not only a symbol of the Alistairs, Amerix's family, but it was a symbol of the last remaining members of Clan Stormhammer. The armor had been handed down from generation to generation, some three thousand years. As the grizzled old general floated slowly to the bottom of the river, he gazed off into the black depths of the murky water at an image that seemed to call to him. He stared for a moment, his powerful lungs holding the giant breath of air they stole before he hit the water. The image floated closer and outstretched a hand. It was a dwarven woman, her skin was murky white, and she was adorned in silk robes. She had bright blue eyes and was clad in fine jewelry made of gold and precious gems. Her long straight hair floated and danced in the murky depths as she stood watching the old general. Next to her stood a tall but much younger dwarf, not nearly as tall as

228

Amerix, but taller than most dwarves. He wore sparkling chain armor that bore the symbol of Stormhammer. Amerix strained his old eyes as he recognized the pair. It was Seraneen and Torgalt, his wife and son. Amerix smiled and outstretched his bloodied old hand. Amerix felt a wave of warmth fall over his body, despite being at the bottom of the icy cold river. His heart soared and he felt a sense of completeness that he had not felt since their deaths. He was glad to be dying, to be re-uniting with them, but they did not take his hand. Seraneen smiled and shook her head slowly from side to side. Her thin brown hair waved in the depths of the water.

Torgalt stuck his chest out proudly and spoke. "I wear not the plate armor of Stormhammer, yet would ye deny me family's honor?"

Amerix unconsciously shook his head from side to side as the sound of his only son's voice made him want to weep.

"Then why, Father, do ye deny yerself that same honor?"

Amerix stared for a moment as the pair faded from vision. He violently roared a muffled bellow of despair as he tried in vain to grab them and they disappeared from sight. Suddenly it was as if his lungs screamed for air. He realized that he was on the muddy silt-strewn floor of the Dawson River, being bounced and dragged down river by the strong undercurrents. Amerix ripped his armor off, and with a mighty thrust off of the river floor, his thick muscled legs launched him up toward the surface. He kicked and paddled his arms as he fought for every moment of air, trying to hold his breath in. He felt his limbs going weak, his lungs burning, and his mind tingling from lack of oxygen. The renegade general stared up at the black water above him as he frantically searched for the surface, but he couldn't determine how far he had to go before he would reach the cool night air. Just when he thought he couldn't hold his breath any longer, he erupted from the river's deadly grasp to feel the crisp freshness of the autumn night and to smell the muddy odor of the river water. He looked around, searching for the bridge he fell from, but could not find it. He floated down the river, exhausted. In a few minutes he reached an area of the river with a slower current. He just lay exhausted on the small cold beach. Amerix's thick, padded underclothing clung to his wet body as he mulled over the encounter he had under the depths of the river, ignoring the battle just before. Amerix had been in thousands of battles before. Near death experiences were nothing new to the old renegade. He wondered if it was real or a hallucination from the lack of oxygen. The exhausted dwarf quickly drifted off into a deep sleep before he thought out any answers. He had survived once again when any other dwarf would have died. Would death ever claim him, or would it merely mock him, teasing him until he was feeble and crippled, begging for it, rather than fighting it as he had done for over four hundred eighty years? As Amerix contemplated the battle and what kind of dwarf Durion was, the old renegade general drifted off into a deep sleep.

What is a hero? I often struggled with this title given by men to other men. The title earns benefactor no wealth, no land, and no advantage. In fact, it often makes the title bearer a target for those who are cowards and resent the courage they cannot ever possess.

Then I ask what makes a coward? Is a man that flees from battle a coward? Some say yes. But what if he fled the battle out of wisdom? Is fleeing from fear a cowardice act, or is fleeing as a whole? I believe that allowing fear to overcome in so much as you run in terror, is cowardice. A man who flees with the knowledge he cannot influence the battle at this time is wise. In truth I have learned that men cannot make cowards and heroes by labels. You already are either a hero, or a coward, merely undiscovered. It takes a crisis event to find which. A man cannot ever know what he is until he has been tested.

But the mantle of a hero is a grave one indeed. Most say it is not a title that you can give yourself. I believe it revolves around some unwritten edict based on the sense of honor. But can a man without honor be a hero? Again, I say yes. Being a hero is not someone else's perception of your deeds, but an inner force that compels people to act in a way that is unselfish. An orc that is raiding a village could be a hero, even if he is slaying innocent women and children of the village he is attacking. If a comrade of his is surrounded by the defenders of the village and the orc charges into the face of certain doom, and fights to free his comrade from the villagers, I believe he could be called a hero, though certainly not by the villagers' standards. But, placing his life on the line for a friend is, in a sense, heroic. I believe most men fall between the lines of cowards and heroes, never excelling beyond one or the other. I think perhaps a man who has the wisdom to know he cannot save a loved one, and retreats to save himself, is a form of a hero. It is not because he saved himself—that is surely a selfish act—but because he had the courage to face the nightmare of accepting their fates, knowing that his death would leave others alone who might need him to survive.

Most men would disagree with me. But I have never been like other men and few think as I do—the single greatest compliment the human race could afford me.

—Lancalion Levendis Lampara—

Six

Darrion-Quieness

He awoke from his deep slumber and his thick pale lids fluttered, slowly revealing his vivid green eyes. Darrion-Quieness, the great white dragon, licked the outside of his giant tooth-filled maw and yawned. The ancient beast stretched his limbs and rolled over on his giant pile of gold and jewels. His pointed nostrils sniffed the frigid air and detected some intruders in his cave. They were at the entrance of his lair, and he lazily decided he had a while to wake up before he devoured them. Darrion-Quieness was a white dragon, one of the weaker of the dragon races, but he had survived a millennia and grown to mammoth proportions. He was three hundred feet from head to tail, and his scales had changed from gleaming white at birth to a pale, murky opaque. His dark black claws were long and hooked, protruding several feet from his scaled toes. His thick, oversized head was well armored, and he had a single spine with a sail crest that angled back toward his body. His long white leathery wings permitted flight, but he certainly was not the most agile creature in the air.

Darrion-Quieness stood and glanced around his ice-covered lair. There were many frost giants frozen in solid ice that littered his cave. They were his favorite food, and they were in abundance in the tallest peaks of the mountains. Darrion-Quieness had the ability to control the weather and he elected to make it a perpetual winter around his small mountain home. The cold weather attracted many colder clime creatures such as frost giants and other beings on which Darrion-Quieness was more than happy to feed. Occasionally adventurers or other humans would wander his way, but most intelligent beings stayed far clear of his mountain home. Sometimes some foolish hero, usually a human, would try to rid the

232

world of the horrible evil named Darrion-Quieness, and the dragon usually toyed with the foolish morsel before he ate him.

But something was different about this group today. The giant dragon could smell many humans and he didn't detect any weapon oil or armored men. This troubled the great white. If they did not have swords and armor, they were probably spell casters, and wizards posed the greatest threat to the dragon. He hated fighting wizards because he had difficulty discerning how powerful they were. Darrion-Quieness sighed as he silently positioned his back to the wall of his sleeping chamber. He wasn't about to provoke the mages, so he would have to barter with them rather than battle today. He would rather battle, but he didn't get this old by foolishly fighting the spell casters.

The ancient dragon sat on his pile of gold and jewels and waited for the intruders to show themselves. They sheepishly rounded the corner to the main cavern. He counted seven in all. They wore long black robes and bore the mark of Nalir. Darrion-Quieness smiled a pearl-toothed grin. Though he wasn't going to eat today, he was going to get many diamonds as payment. The old dragon loved diamonds more than anything else. He scanned the humans for several seconds, trying to see the pouch where the diamonds were kept, but he could not see it. He decided that the humans were crafty for hiding the treasure because he was known to just take the diamonds and eat the people rather than speak to them. The dragon thought he might just decide to test their might and get both dinner and diamonds.

One of the humans stepped forward. Darrion-Quieness could smell many magical enchantments about him. He was small for a human, and kind of old.

"Darrion-Quieness, it is I, Soran, that calls your name today. We have sought you out so that you might aid us. We have brought the usual payment. It will be delivered upon receiving answers to the questions we seek," Soran said. His voice quivered with fear from the mere sight of the powerful beast. Soran had cast spells to protect himself and the other mages from the dragon's aura of fear. Yet, he could still feel the great white's powerful magic prying at his mind's defenses.

Darrion-Quieness didn't respond. He ignored whatever the human was saying and thought about the wonderful diamonds he would receive from the day's transaction. Soran took the dragon's silence as permission to continue.

"Before, we came to you and asked about the prophecy. You told us that a man was born that would crush the kingdom of Nalir. You said he was an orphan with the surname Ecnal. We have slain every Ecnal in the land of Beykla, where the orphans have such a surname. What . . ." Soran was cut off by the dragon.

"How many beautiful shining diamonds did you bring?" Darrion-Quieness asked, picking his teeth with his giant black talon.

Soran stammered. "Y–you will be p–paid when our question has been answered and we are safe from your lair."

The dragon frowned. His glaring emerald visage made all of the mages gulp with fear. He stared at the small group of wizards and watched sweat drip from the brows of many of them. He was sure his cave was cold, and if they were sweating it was surely out of fear. With amazing speed the giant creature zipped forward. He inhaled deeply and his throat swelled as he lowered his head. A giant cone of blue air rushed from his mouth and covered the frigid breath. The dragon paused and raised a wicked claw to smite any of the mages that were still alive. To his pleasure, only Soran had survived his horrible breath. The wizard was pinned in a coffin of ice. Only his head and one of his arms were free. Soran tried to speak but could not. He fought for consciousness as his traumatized body slowed from being half frozen. He stared helplessly at the terrible beast that stood before him.

"Hector!" the dragon called out. "I know you can hear me. I can sense your weak crying. How dare you send your goons to disturb my sleep and have the gall not to send any diamonds. I know of your talents, king. I demand payment now!"

A strange blue light formed and an image of Hector De Scoran appeared. The king was adorned in black and silver plate armor. The armor had intricate designs of scorpions on the shoulders and their tails stretched down the king's arms.

"Fitting that you show a weak image instead of coming yourself. Afraid you will suffer the same fate as your lackeys?" the dragon taunted.

"Do not tempt me beast, I have allowed you to make a home on my land. The only time I will come to your lair will be to claim your hide as my trophy."

Darrion-Quieness spread his wings and roared. The cave shook and small rocks and debris fell from the thunderous sound. He despised the human king and he despised being taunted even more.

"But for now, you are useful to me. I have brought your diamonds and I offer these men as tender morsels to placate your perpetual hunger."

Soran gasped. He didn't understand why his master would do this to him. Kalen, he, and his colleagues had done as the king had asked. They had deciphered the prophecy, they had . . . deciphered the prophecy. It made perfect sense to the doomed wizard. His group was no longer useful and the knowledge they had of the prophecy made them a liability to the wicked king. The trapped mage struggled against his frozen prison, but he could not move.

The image of Hector produced a large bag of diamonds and dropped it to the floor of the cave. The bag slowly transformed from a glowing image to a tangible bag. The dragon reached out and tore open the bag with a single claw. He purred in delight at the hundreds of diamonds that spilled out.

"Ask your questions, Hector, and then be gone," the great dragon said as he plopped down on the icy cavern floor in delight.

Hector De Scoran smiled and paced the cavern floor. "Did we succeed in slaying all of the Ecnals in Beykla?"

The dragon lay on the cavern floor, slowly counting his wonderful diamonds.

"No."

"How many did we miss?" Hector asked.

"One."

"Where is he?"

The dragon stopped counting for a moment. "You waste your time, Hector. The more you seek to invalidate this prophecy, the more you will enforce its validity."

"So it can be changed?" Hector asked eagerly.

Darrion-Quieness exhaled and resumed counting. "All prophecies can be changed, but they always seem to have a strange way of fulfilling themselves."

Hector pondered the dragon's words. "Where is this Ecnal?"

"He is in the Beykla, in Central City."

"What is he doing there?" Hector asked eagerly.

"One hundred thirty-seven."

Hector frowned. "What?"

"One hundred thirty-seven. That is how many diamonds you have given me."

"What does that have to do with anything? That is more than enough payment for these simple questions."

"Good-bye, Hector. Do not disturb me again for one hundred thirty-seven days, or I will fly to your castle and test your boasts of power." The dragon waved his hand and the image of Hector was gone. The mammoth beast walked over and looked down at the terrified wizard.

"What is your name?" he asked the imprisoned man.

"S–S–Soran," the man stuttered from both fear and the temperature of his rapidly freezing body.

The dragon shook his head. "No, your name is lunch," the dragon said as his massive jaws snapped on Soran's half frozen body. The dragon crunched and chewed the wizard as he climbed back on his mound of gold and jewels. After his nap he was going to have to take a trip near Beykla. He wanted to see what was so special about the son of a fallen goddess. He swallowed the small meal and drifted back into his deep sleep.

*   *   *

"Damn that lizard!" Hector screamed as he tried to re-establish the link that took him to the dragon's lair. He focused his mind and channeled many powerful weaves into the spell. After several unsuccessful attempts, he turned his attention to what he learned. The king recalled that the dragon said the Ecnal was in Central City, so that is where he would start looking.

"Guard. Send for a sage or one of the wizards," Hector commanded. The guard nodded and left the king's chambers.

Hector thought about his many agents he had in Beykla. His favorite was the wererat guild that was run by Pav-co. Perhaps he would see if the fat thief might know of the Ecnal's whereabouts.

A few minutes later a young sage rushed into the room. "Yes, my lord. You sent for me?" the man stammered, falling to the feet of the imposing king.

Hector looked down at the kneeling sage with an arched eyebrow of superiority.

"Spencer, is it?"

"Y–yes, my lord," the sage whispered.

"I recall you have always served me well," Hector said with an evil grin.

Spencer thought to mention when he had failed to answer a question Hector had asked him, but he didn't want to bring up the fact, if Hector didn't remember it. The king had threatened to kill Spencer on a later day for not knowing the answer. Certainly Spencer didn't want his king to remember his promise of death. That was the only promise the king always seemed to keep.

"I always serve with my all, my lord," Spencer said as a trickle of nervous sweat ran down the side of his face.

"Well Spencer, I have a minor task for you," the king said haughtily.

"Yes, my lord?" Spencer asked as he scooted on the floor closer to Hector's feet.

"It is an easy task. Perform it expeditiously and I will forget I planned to kill you."

"Yes, my lord. Name it and it will be done," Spencer said as his voice cracked with fear.

"I want you to go to the library and tell my first wizard, Kalen, that I need to get a message to Pav-co," Hector said as he stroked the blade of a silver curved dagger. "Tell Pav-co that I want him to find the Ecnal and kill him. He is to return the Necromidus to me as proof of the deed."

"Yes, my lord," Spencer said, and the sage scurried from the room.

Hector sat back in his throne and smiled, pondering the Ecnal's death as Spencer hurried from the chamber. Regardless of what the dragon said about the prophecy, the Ecnal could not harm him, or his kingdom, if he was dead.

*   *   *

Spencer rushed into the posh room located in the top of the

southern tower. He closed the heavy wooden door and tried to slow his breathing. Across the table a young gray elf laughed and closed his ancient tomes. The wind from the shutting book mussed his long silver hair.

"Spencer, my good man, what brings you to my room?"

Spencer frowned and wiped the sweat from his forehead. "I deliver a message from Lord Hector, and you would be smart if you heed it. He is a thousand times more powerful than you."

Kalen smiled and stood up, shaking his slender head. He walked over to the obstinate messenger. "Spencer, Spencer, Spencer. Just how long do you think that silly old man will live?" the gray elf asked.

Spencer glared at him. He hated it when the elf mocked the king like that. "Go on fool, mock him! One day you will wear out your usefulness, and he will kill you."

Kalen smiled as he wiped the long silver hair from his narrow face and turned back to the sage as he spoke. "Who do you think is more important, sage? You or me?" Kalen asked.

Spencer tried to respond but he felt an incredible force tightening around his neck. His hands clawed at the invisible force, but they merely passed through air.

"Spencer, your silence shocks me. Do you really think I am as important as you?" Kalen said sarcastically.

The sage merely struggled in vain against the ever tightening grip around his throat as Kalen continued. "Why would he need you? I can do everything you can. You have no real magic. You just have knowledge. Anything you can find, or remember, or decipher, I can too. Plus, I can kill any man as easy as I am killing you. Can you do that, Spencer?"

Spencer only gurgled in response as his face turned purple from lack of oxygen. "I can even read your mind, you pathetic creature." Kalen paused for effect and smiled at the dying sage. "So our mighty king wants me to send a message to Pav-co to kill the Ecnal?" Kalen asked rhetorically.

Kalen strolled past the nearly unconscious sage and waved his hand at a small crystal mirror. Its sides were made of some small jagged bones that bore many small intricate carvings. He waved his hands and recited a brief chant. Suddenly the vacant mirror began to swirl and take shape. Kalen stared into the mirror that showed a large room laced with golden trinkets and adorned with red velvety pillows.

"Pav-co. I have an assignment for you," Kalen taunted before he turned and looked back at the sage.

"Oops. I'm sorry, Spencer. I forgot about your little breathing problem," Kalen cackled. The elf waved his hand and dismissed the incantation that held the sage's throat. Spencer collapsed to the floor gasping for air. He gently rubbed his throat and weakly stood up.

"Tormenting the sages again?" came a voice from inside the mirror. Kalen turned to see the cherub face of the wererat guild leader known as Pav-co. He was a fat man with much jewelry piercing his face and body. His bald head glistened under the candle light that lit his lavish room. The gray elf smiled and softened his tone.

"Ah, my dear friend," Kalen began.

Pav-co merely frowned. He was no friend of the wicked elf. He just received great amounts of wealth and support from the king of Nalir, therefore he tolerated the elf's intrusions. "We are not friends, elf," Pav-co said. "Why is it you disturb my tedious efforts of relaxing?"

"Well, my fat little cohort, our master wants someone dead."

Pav-co winced at the words "our master." The thief had no master and would die before he had one. He dealt with Hector and his minions for personal gain only—a relationship that seemed to call on him more and more as of late. "Find some more `dangerous' orphans that you need slain?" the fat man mocked.

"The motive behind our tasks is unimportant to you," Kalen retorted. "You will do as you are told."

Pav-co glared silently at the image of the gray elf in the mirror. "And if I don't?"

Kalen smiled deviously. "Then you shall no longer receive the business of Hector the Great. And if we don't deal with someone, they are not our allies. Need I explain what we do with `non-allies'?"

Pav-co didn't respond for a few seconds. He pondered the elf's unspoken threat and decided that the wicked king's occasional missions were more than worth the inconvenience. "Name your task. It will be done."

"I thought you would see it my way," Kalen mocked. "There is a man coming into town. He is very young, maybe eighteen years old if even. He travels with a large swordsman. The youngster wears a black robe with silver on the cuffs. The swordsman wields a great sword and wears chain armor. We do not know their names, nor do we wish to learn them. We just want them dead."

"It might be beneficial for me to know their names," Pav-co said as he rubbed his fat belly.

Kalen narrowed his eyes. "Then go and ask them."

Pav-co started to respond, but Kalen waved his hand and dismissed the dweamor that activated the mirror. He sat back in his soft chair and thought about the specifics of the pair. They were certainly interesting at least. A human boy with a Necromidus was something he didn't hear about every day. A Necromidus in itself was very rare. The complete collection of the basic Necromancy incantations was very expensive and it took years of study just to be able to read it.

After the image of the thief vanished in the mirror, Kalen scratched his head and pondered whether the boy had any ability to cast any of the spells. Certainly if he did wield the necromancies that were in the book, he might be called an ally rather than enemy. The gray elf shrugged his narrow shoulders and returned to his studies. What threat the king saw in a mere human boy was of no consequence to him. The old pink-skinned man would soon be dead, replaced by a much more decisive ruler.

*   *   *

Pav-co screamed and slapped one of his many concubines in the face. She recoiled in shock from the unexpected blow.

"Damn that elf!" the fat thief screamed as he walked over to his chambers and placed on his silk robe. He turned and looked at the many concubines that stood quietly looking at him. "Out, out, get out! All of you!" he screamed.

The concubines hurried out of the room, grabbing clothing and robes as they left. The fat thief placed on his belt and his boots. He checked himself in the looking glass one final time before he stuck his head out of his chamber door.

"Kellacun!"

A nimble woman about five-and-a-half feet tall walked over. She was wearing a long, black, shimmering cloak that seemed to float about the air as she walked. She kept her long black hair tied in a knot behind her head, held by a single silver hairpin that doubled for a knife. She had many small belt pouches attached to her belt that held various poisons or potions, whichever she preferred. She kept her steel blue eyes fixed on the fat thief as she walked over. She didn't trust the fat guild leader any farther than she could throw him.

"Yes, your fatness?"

Pav-co's face immediately flushed red with anger. He reached up and grabbed the woman by the hair on the back of her head. Pav-co forcefully pulled her within an inch of his face. She could smell the stench of his foul breath as he spoke.

"You are lucky you are so valuable to me, bitch, or you might find yourself in a riverbed one morning," Pav-co said as he pulled her into his chambers. He forcefully tossed her forward as he closed and locked the door.

Kellacun gingerly readjusted her hair and stretched her neck. "And how important are you to me, thief?" she asked.

Pav-co winced at the title "thief." He knew she was reminding him that without the guild he was nothing more than a cutpurse himself. "Damn you, wench, why are you so insolent? I pay you twice as much as I ever paid Grascon and four times as much as I pay my other thieves."

Kellacun just smiled and delicately sat on the fat thief's desk. She crossed her shapely legs, revealing her slick black boots that had the depiction of a red spider just under the knee.

Pav-co glared and shook his head. "I need two men killed. A young man that wears a cloak and a large swordsman with a great sword."

Kellacun stood up and started walking out the door. "That is a job for one of your less skilled thugs, not an artist such as myself."

Pav-co rushed in front of the door, blocking her exit. "Not so. I need you to find out about them first, what their names are, if they are important, and what connection they have with Nalir."

Kellacun's eyes lit up. "Nalir? Working for Hector again?" she asked.

Pav-co nodded. "And getting a pretty penny for it too."

241

Kellacun folded her arms and shifted her weight to one foot. "So why not send a cheaper thief?" she asked honestly.

"Because I know nothing about the pair, not even their names. I don't want to take any chances. And even with your high cost, I should make a few coins from the deed."

"Since the work is for the mighty king of Nalir himself, I would hope to get a little more than the usual," Kellacun said with a wry smile.

Pav-co walked across the posh chamber and opened a thick book that rested on his large oaken table. He didn't look up from his writing as he spoke. "You are not a freelancer, Kellacun. If you think you can make more coins on the streets, I can put you there."

The sly woman didn't respond. She stared with evil contempt at the fat man as he wrote in his charge book. She contemplated walking over and sticking the thin blade of her cutlass into his pig heart, but instead the skilled assassin walked out of the guild leader's chambers.

*　　*　　*

Spencer rushed into the king's bath house. Hector lay comfortably in a steaming bath. He rested his feet up on the end of the emerald-colored marble and sipped wine from a golden goblet that rested on the rail near his head. There were many attendants helping with his bath, including many scantily clad women.

Spencer quickly kneeled down at the base of the tub. "You sent for me, my lord?" the messenger asked eagerly.

Hector took a long sip from his goblet before answering. "Yes, Spencer, I did. I need for you to go find out how the tasks fare that I asked Kalen to do."

Spencer gulped hard. He hated Kalen. The evil mage always tormented him whenever he went to his chambers. Spencer wanted to tell the king all the horrible things Kalen said about him, but Spencer feared that Hector might become angry at him for some reason, so the meek sage-turned-messenger kept the comments to himself. It had been a few days since he had to go to the gray elf's chambers, but he vividly remembered the last unpleasant encounter and he wasn't eager to repeat it. "My lord, I am sure that elf has done as you wished. He is very competent at what he does."

"Did you tell him my instructions?" Hector asked as he sat up suddenly in his tub. Water from the overfilled vat spilled out and splashed on Spencer's arm.

"Yes, well, kind of. He took it from my mind. I hate it when he does that," Spencer said as he wiped some of the sudsy water from his sleeve.

"He read your mind?" Hector asked, more elated than surprised. "Good, his studies are paying off. He is progressing faster than anyone I have ever known. He will be a powerful ally one day."

Spencer winced. He knew that Kalen had no intention of being Hector's ally. He decided that he must tell his king of the mage's backstabbing intentions.

"My lord, I do not wish to bring bad news, but for my lord's sake I think you should know," Spencer said with a cracking voice as sweat began to drip from his forehead.

Hector chuckled at his young sage's anxiety. "And what devastating tale will you spin for me today, my faithful servant?"

Spencer wrung his hands before he started. "My lord, the mage has intentions of taking over Nalir when you die. He told me so. He said you were weak and he . . ." Spencer was cut off by Hector's booming laughter.

"Spencer, my most loyal servant. Do you presume to think that I do not know my allies' intentions? I know all of them. Of course he desires my kingdom. If he did not, he would not be useful to me at all," Hector bellowed.

"But, my lord, I don't understand. I thought . . ."

"Do not think, my faithful servant. You do not have the mind power to understand the tasks of running an empire. But alas, you are very loyal. Mark my words, dear Spencer, one day I will make you more powerful than Kalen ever will be. Until then, however, you will serve me here. Now go and find out what I asked."

Spencer nodded and slowly backed out of Hector's chambers. He closed the door and ran as fast as he could to the mage tower. His mind raced as he contemplated what kind of power Hector would give him. Would Kalen still be around? Spencer hoped he would be so he could use some magic of his own against the tormenting mage. What a glorious day it would be.

Spencer reached the chamber door of the mage tower. He

opened it and barged right in. He knew there would be a horrible consequence for intruding without knocking, but it was okay, because he knew that one day he would return the pain tenfold to the tormenting mage.

"Who dares disturb my work?" Kalen growled as he lost his concentration and the sparkling drops of magical energy that floated in front of him spiraled out of control before popping into nothingness.

"I bring a message from the king, mage," Spencer said confidently.

Kalen studied the messenger very closely. Never had he seen the messenger so confident. The meek slave would expect a horrible thrashing for such an intrusion, yet there he stood as if he were telling a sibling that he had work to do. Kalen slowly walked from around his desk. He cast a few quick spells to see if it was the king disguised in some magical illusion, but as far as he could tell it was the foolish sage. Kalen probed Spencer's mind for a few moments before he realized that it was indeed the sage that had rudely intruded on his studies.

"Fool," Kalen said calmly as he waved his hand and began a spell. "You will pay for this intrusion."

Spencer stuck out his chest defiantly. "Do your worst, wizard. King Hector told me one day he will make me more powerful than you will ever be, and you had better be long gone or I'll make you suffer for whatever you . . ." Spencer stopped his sentence short. He looked down in horror at the strange bumps that were beginning to grow on his hand. "What are you doing to me?" he asked as pain ripped through his side, forcing him to his hands and knees.

"Just making you a little more appealing," Kalen chuckled.

Spencer stared in horror as his fingers turned green. They then curled up into the palms of his hands and fell off. He slapped his knobby hands at the severed digits, trying in vain to pick them up. His skin stretched and pulled taut over his face as his eyes bulged and moved farther apart. He cried out in pain and anger at the smiling face of the gray elf. He tried to lunge forward but he could no longer feel his legs. He tried to look down at them but was having difficulty moving his neck. Spencer's mind was nearly torn in two from intense searing pain. It felt as if his body was being ripped and stretched from the inside out. In a few seconds the former sage lay on the ground of the mage chambers. His once soft skin had been replaced by hard scales. His eyes had shifted to each side of his narrow head. His arms had shifted and withdrew into large fins and his legs merged, forming a webbed tail. The pain had finally ended. Spencer tried to speak, but he could not. He couldn't stand or move his arms. He just felt his body involuntarily flopping on the hard stone floor. Terror gripped the sage. He couldn't breathe. He struggled for a breath but he could not get one. He felt himself slowly losing consciousness.

Kalen smiled in glee at the large fish that flopped on the stone floor of his chambers. He watched with a morbid pleasure as the once sage, now fish, struggled to breathe the air of the room. The elf walked over to the mirror that he used to communicate with the fat thief from Central City. With a wave of his hand he activated the two-way mirror. In a few moments the magical energies took hold and the chambers of the guild leader shone from the other side. What he saw did not bode well. The entire chambers was in shambles and there were many half dressed woman that were lying in twisted disgusting positions. They appeared as if they had been raped many times and their bodies bore wounds that would have taken a few hours to kill them. The gray elf scryed the area, searching for a conscious mind to detect, but all he felt was death. The elf dismissed the mirror and turned to the fish that lay still on his floor. There was a fluttering gill every few seconds or so. Kalen pondered the sage a few moments. The walk to the king's chambers was so far, and he hated climbing the stairs. With a heavy sigh he waved his hand and dismissed the magic that had transformed the sage from man to fish. In a few seconds Spencer lay on the ground gasping for air.

"You are lucky today, sage, for I need to relay a message back to our king. Go and tell him Pav-co's guildhall has been sacked. I do not know by whom or why. Tell him I am awaiting his wishes on how to follow up on our tasks that we incurred prior to this event."

Spencer nodded quietly and stumbled from the room. His arms and legs were sluggish from the transformation.

"Where is your bravery now, sage?" Kalen mocked.

Spencer collapsed outside the closed door of the mage tower and wept. He didn't weep out of pain or fear. He wept out of complete and total despair at the evil that surrounded him. It was at that moment that he knew that Kalen would kill him at his first opportunity and Hector would do nothing to prevent it.

Spencer took a long walk that day to Hector's chambers. He had never thought the elf's powers could do something like that. He didn't even think Hector could do that. Now, he struggled with the realization that perhaps the elf would someday soon make good on his boasts for taking over the kingdom. Spencer shuddered at the thought of answering to the vile wizard.

After a long walk to the king's chambers, he decided that no matter what happened, if he could escape Nalir, he would.

Spencer knocked on the king's chamber door. He pushed the large heavy wooden door open and slowly plodded down the slick marble floor. He walked past the intricately carved throne of gold and onto the stone balcony. Hector sat in his leisure chair and gazed off into the horizon of the vast swamp.

"My lord, I bear message from Kalen," Spencer said solemnly.

Hector turned and looked at the sage who stood before him. He was usually wracked with fear, bowing and trembling. Now he stood apathetic before him.

"What news, Spencer?"

"My lord, Kalen reports that the guildhall in Central City has been destroyed. He says he doesn't know how or by who," Spencer said as he stared blankly at the swamp that was a few hundred feet below him. The forlorn sage thought about jumping. He doubted he would survive the fall, which was precisely what he was hoping for. He fantasized about the peace of death, about not having fear or pain anymore. He had no ambition, no desire to see another day. Spencer knew he was nothing more than a tool to be discarded when he was no longer useful.

Hector could detect the sullenness in Spencer's voice. He didn't know what to make of it, but in truth he didn't care. He had many more important matters to attend to than the everyday ramblings of a depressed servant.

"Good job, Spencer. You may take your leave for the rest of the day."

Spencer paused for a moment, taking one final glimpse of freedom that was a few hundred feet below, before he turned and left the chamber.

Hector sipped wine from his goblet as he gazed over his kingdom. It was mostly swampland with a few patches of fertile ground. These patches were densely occupied by small cities that grew crops and mined resources for the small kingdom. Though Nalir was small in land area, it was one of the most populated cities, and had vast resources to fuel his army.

Hector rose from his leisure chair and walked into the throne room. "Guard," he called out.

A man wearing scale mail armor and wielding a wicked falchion rushed over. "Yes, my lord," the guard said with a deep bow.

Hector paused for a moment with a stern look of abstention on his aging face. "Go and fetch the priests, I have need of them. Tell them to meet me at the altar."

The guard nodded and rushed out of the chamber.

Hector strode to the far end of his throne room and slid one of the heavy tapestries back that hung from the ceiling to the floor. He stepped behind the arduous curtain and walked to an iron door that was in the middle of the stone wall. The door was small but was covered in strange divine runes that ran in three circles. He traced his armored finger along the dark symbols that were etched in the door. They were put in place to keep creatures that were pure of heart from entering, and they kept creatures from the abyss from escaping. Some of the runes had rare crystals and gems placed into them with minor arcane enchantments. The whole concept was a little confusing for Hector. While he was an accomplished wizard, he had little understanding of divine magic. What amazed him more was how the priests used arcane and divine magic together to bind the creatures they summoned to the room.

Hector removed his gauntlet and traced his bare finger over the encrusted symbols again. He smiled as his skin tasted the warm heat the gems emitted.

"You sent for us, my lord?" came a raspy voice from behind the king.

Hector turned to see four of his priests entering his throne room. The lead priest was adorned in a deep violet, almost black, robe with bright red symbols on the back and around the cuffs. The others were similarly dressed, but did not wear robes as ornate. Hector outstretched his arms at the sight of the priests. Hector worshipped Rha-Cordan, the god of death. Though the god himself wasn't inherently evil, many of his followers were. Rha-Cordan de-

247

termined where all souls went when they died. Hector, understanding all men die, ascertained that the god of death had the ultimate power of soul decision. Although Hector didn't understand the details of how the other gods influenced Rha-Cordan, he knew that ultimately the god of death had the final decision.

"Resin Darkhand, good to see you, my friend," Hector said as he bowed low.

The priest said nothing in return, but bowed much lower than his king. "Why have you summoned us, my king?" Resin asked.

"We must summon the arch demon Bykalicus once more," Hector said nonchalantly.

Resin shook his head and sighed. "My lord, Bykalicus is no lesser fiend. He is a mighty demon and has a kingdom himself in the deep abyss. He will not take this summoning lightly."

"But you can keep him in the summoning ring by the will of Rha-Cordan?" Hector asked.

Resin nodded his head slowly. "Yes, that is correct, but there is much more to it than that. If he were ever to escape the abyss and come to our plane of existence, he would wreak havoc on his enemies. If you continue to summon him, taking him away from his duties against his will, he will undoubtedly call you his prevailing foe."

Hector chuckled. "He cannot come to our plane of existence unless he is invited or brought, correct?"

"Yes, my king. But . . ."

"And the only way he can move or perform on this plane by his own free will is to kill his summoner?"

"Yes, my lord, but you are not understanding," Resin pleaded.

"Can any mortal scry on the mind of a demon and his power?" Hector asked with his hands on his hips.

"None that I am aware of, but . . ."

"And would a demon allow any other mortal, or fiend, to get revenge on those he hates?" Hector asked, folding his arms under his chest.

"No, he would not, but you do not understand. Demons with his power are resourceful beyond our comprehension."

Hector waved his hand in dismissal. "I understand completely. No fool that has the power to summon a demon will allow himself to be slain, just to gain revenge against me. And no demon will reveal his enemies to any other creature. So we are perfectly safe. Plus, Rha-Cordan guides our souls after death. And since we are in his divine favor, there is nothing to worry about," Hector rationalized.

"As you wish, my king," Resin said in defeat.

The group of priests walked into the summoning chamber. Its four walls were made of solid stone. There were no windows or furnishings of any kind. In the center of the floor was a circle that was fifteen feet in diameter that was composed of large runes much similar to the ones that surrounded the door, except they were on a much grander scale. The stone floor was made of rough stone, not like the smooth stone of the rest of the castle. The runes were deeply carved into the hard stone and were covered in strange red dust and dried blood.

Hector went and stood at the far end of the room and prepared some of his basic spells. His priests encircled the runes and began chanting. They raised and lowered their arms several times, citing the greatness of Rha-Cordan. Hector finished his protection spells that shielded his mind from scrying, from magical fear, from charms, and other spells that would render him helpless. Demons were more skilled than powerful human wizards, and arch demons were more powerful than most.

The priests finished their chanting and dances. The four stood, arms outstretched, with their heads tilted back. A frigid wind ripped through the chamber, blowing their robes up around them. The runes began to glow red hot as a bright scarlet light appeared in the center of the summoning circle. The light rapidly stretched and grew, forming a vertical ring. In the center of the ring, Hector could see the infinite wasteland known as the deep abyss. Small demons scattered from the portal dragging half eaten bodies of men and women who screamed for help, who would not, and had not come, for an eternity.

"Bykalicus," the priests whispered in unison. The demons on the other side hissed and growled at the announcement of the fabled abyssal king.

"Bykalicus," the priests said slightly louder than before. The wind picked up in the room and it made a shrill howling sound as it tore around the priests.

"Bykalicus," the priests said louder, their voices echoing

249

throughout the entire abyss as dark sulfurous clouds started churning.

"Bykalicus!" they screamed, reaching up to the ceiling with their outstretched arms. The wind in the abyss howled and the sulfurous clouds bubbled and frothed within them in an excited storm of hellish fury. Then, as suddenly as the storm began, it stopped.

The priests looked into the shining crimson portal they had formed. There was nothing on the other side, save for the barren wasteland of the abyss. The priests began chanting again, very softly.

A large, muscular clawed foot stepped through the portal. It was dark red and covered in protruding veins and sinew. It had thick black claws that erupted from scaled toes and a large black horn that protruded from one knee. As the imposing figure stepped all the way through the portal, the priests gasped aloud. The demon stood well over fifteen feet tall. His dark red skin had flames trickling all over his incredibly burly body. He had giant bat wings that were tucked behind him and wielded a giant great sword that was aflame with blue fire. The demon's eyes were bright yellow and had an aura that extended horizontally past his face. He had two giant goat horns that protruded from his head and curved over his back, and his large canine maw dripped an acidic drool that burned and singed the stone floor where it landed. The powerful demon slowly stretched his neck and looked from side to side chuckling.

"Sloof uoy ot htaed," the demon growled, then paused and watched the foolish mortals as they struggled to understand the abyssal tongue.

Resin waved his hand and chanted, sending waves of divine energy around the demon to convert his language to one they could understand.

Bykalicus smiled, knowing the humans would have to create a magical weave for them to understand him. In doing so, he could determine their power with the arcane arts. To his surprise, the humans wielded divine magic. "The power of Rha-Cordan," Bykalicus grumbled, knowing he couldn't cross the mighty god of death, or his disciples while still partway in the abyss. He took a deep breath and decided to see what these fools wanted. Perhaps he might trick them into releasing him on the prime material plane. He would love to crush a few human kingdoms. It had been over ten thousand years since he was last able to do that. "This is the third time you have summoned me with your puny mortal magic," Bykalicus said as he stared down at the intricately crafted protection runes around the circle.

"If they are so puny, demon, then sever the bonds that hold you and kill us," Hector taunted.

The priests all turned in astonishment at their king. "My lord, you should . . .," Resin was cut off by the booming voice of Bykalicus.

The demon's fists were clenched and his rippling muscles went taut with fury. "Do you think that death is what you have to fear from me?" Bykalicus asked.

Hector shook his head from side to side. "I fear nothing from you, slave. You will serve me as commanded and then return to serve your dark gods."

Bykalicus tucked his head back and outstretched his arms. His arms extended out, wide from his body, and his fists tightened. The arch demon's body quivered as he roared in such a fury that the chamber walls shook, knocking the priests from their feet. The flames that danced across his body flared up to white hot fire, forcing Hector and the priests to shield their faces from the intense heat. Bykalicus glared at the pathetic human that stood before him. The massive flames that sprouted up around his body subsided back to the small wisps that were there before, but they danced more rapidly across his body now. He smiled at the image of the number of foolish mortals that thought they were intelligent, wise, or powerful enough to taunt him, but in the end, he always feasted on their souls, as he would feast on these morsels, in due time.

"Where is the Ecnal?" Hector asked confidently.

"You presume I know much, fool," Bykalicus retorted.

Hector narrowed his eyes. "I command you to answer, demon. Where is the Ecnal?"

Bykalicus smiled, his face distorted unnaturally into a sinister guise of wickedness. "He stands atop a cliff looking out on your vast swamp-filled kingdom. Behind him stands an army that defies Rha-Cordan as a storm of vengeance brews behind him. I can hear the thunder of his voice and feel the reign of his power. Though Rha-Cordan screams for his army's soul, they refuse him, as he offers the souls of your soldiers instead. The Ecnal stands poised full

251

of a hate-filled power that you could never dream of. He plans to kill you, and it would prove an easy task for him. But I assure you, Hector De Scoran, you will not succumb to his power."

"Power? Is this the son of the mother of mercy?" Hector asked in disbelief.

Bykalicus chuckled. "You see me as I am standing before you, mortal, yet you are as a blind man. You are responsible for the slaying of thousands of innocents on a whim that one might be the son of the departed mother of mercy. Yet you knew not who she was. For the purposeless slaughter to further yourself, your power—a deed of complete vileness—I will answer but one more question."

Hector was silent in thought. It was the Ecnal that was prophesized to destroy his kingdom. Was the identity of the orphan's mother important? He suspected the Ecnal might be the son of the mother of mercy. If she was indeed dead, she posed no trouble to the living. Hector lifted his head. "How do I defeat the Ecnal?"

Bykalicus grabbed his belly with his clawed hands, bellowing so deeply, mortar from the bricks in the summoning room fell to the floor in large chunks. "Find his father's body, and have your priests perform the DeNaucght."

The demon turned and stepped back through the portal. Many lesser demons, that had gathered near the portal gate, fled in terror at the sight of Bykalicus. They bounded over the dark desolate land, kicking up small rocks under their clawed feet as they clambered away. Once the demon stepped through the portal, the top of it narrowed as the bottom raised up to the top, until a small scarlet horizontal line floated about three feet off of the stone floor. The line then collapsed within itself until a small red dot remained suspended in the air. Then the sparkling crimson spec of magical energy popped into nothingness, and the portal was no more.

"My lord, I tried to warn you," Resin said as he picked the many ice crystals out of his hair that had formed from the frigid air of the abyss.

"Warn me from what?" Hector asked. "The demon has said nothing that I have not heard before, except the DeNaucght. What is that?"

The priests looked at each other worriedly. Resin straightened his robe and knocked some of the ice crystals from his hair. "We know not what the DeNaucght is, my lord, but be rest assured, we will research the matter thoroughly. But my lord, I feel I must caution you not to anger the demon lord so. It can bring nothing but ill events for us."

Hector waved his hand in dismissal. "I know what is needed to get onto this plane. The foul beast is well kept in the abyss. And after I die, Rha-Cordan will keep my soul from such tyrants as he, because I have served the god of death so well," Hector said as he walked from the room, undaunted, as drops of melting ice dripped from his hair and onto his shoulders and face.

"My lord, shall we work on interpreting what the demon said?" Resin called out as he and his acolytes walked from the summoning chamber.

Hector shook his head and waved his hand in release. "There is nothing to interpret. The demon said it clearly. Obviously he was speaking of the future. The Ecnal cannot kill me, though we must perform much research on the fate of my kingdom."

"As you wish, my lord. What of the DeNaucght?" Resin asked.

"I will expect you to find how to perform it as soon as possible," Hector commanded.

"As you wish, my king," Resin said as he bowed out of the throne room.

Hector walked back out onto his lofty balcony. He sat in his plush velvety chair and placed his weary feet up on the stone rail. The cool autumn wind washed over his wet face as the king gazed out on his land. He imagined the Raynard cliffs that separated his boundaries from the fertile lands of the elven kingdom of Vidora. He supposed the Ecnal would look off of those cliffs. Hector tried to imagine how Ecnal's army would deny Rha-Cordan, the god of death. He wasn't sure how anyone could deny the dark reaper their souls. The weary king mulled over the demon's words as he drifted off into deep sleep.

*   *   *

The great dragon, Darrion-Quieness, soared high above the fertile kingdom of Vidora, known as the land of the elves. He gazed at the sparse clouds that floated well below him like hundreds of giant balls of cotton. He didn't dare soar much lower than he was flying. Though the powerful wind currents made flying more tiresome at this height, the elves didn't take too kindly to white dragons taking perch on their lands. Though he could easily wipe out any elven village he encountered, Darrion-Quieness knew that attracting the attention of the elven nation was not a wise decision. The elven heroes and powerful mages often crusaded for hundreds of miles to rid the world of those who threatened their lands. He knew of a great green named Yohr-Acht. The ancient green dragon had decided to make a lair on the fertile lands of Vidora. The damnable elves marched against him and had nearly slain the green as they drove him out. He wasn't sure exactly where Yohr-Acht had moved to, but the great white thought it was somewhere near the Vidorian border. Darrion-Quieness decided that, too, was not a good place to land. He feared the power of the green dragon. Greens were more powerful than whites, and Darrion-Quieness despised the odor of their nasty chlorine gas breath weapon. It took days to rid his hide of the awful smell. In fact, even if he stumbled upon a much weaker green dragon, he tried to avoid the encounter because of his dislike for their breath attacks. He had endured the taunts of many greens that survived the encounters with him only because of his dislike for the chlorine. Had the dragon any pride, he might have killed the weaker greens for their insolence, but Darrion-Quieness had learned long ago that pride often coincided with death.

The great white flew for several days until he found a fairly large mountain range that was in the middle of the Vidorian kingdom. The range was not a tall range, and it seemed to be only a few hundred miles long, as opposed to the many other ranges on Terrigan that were usually twice as tall and long. He slowly circled down, carefully searching for signs of any elven villages. When he was satisfied that there were none, Darrion-Quieness landed atop the largest snow-covered peak. The mountain top had pierced the cloud veil and was covered with many layers of snow and ice. Though the weary dragon couldn't find a cave at the mountain's peak, he was more than camouflaged in the deep snow he had landed in.

Like a cat stretching before he went to sleep on a soft pillow, the great white made a bed in the giant snow drift. He folded his wings around himself, creating a buffer from the wind, and tucked his long thick tail around his muscular body. He closed his deep green eyes and summoned the innate power to control the weather. The great dragon imagined thick clouds forming above him and then a great snow. He concentrated on the large snowflakes that cascaded down from the billowing cloud cover that hovered above him. In a few minutes, a storm had formed just above the mountain peak and a heavy snow began to fall, just as the beast had imagined. The summoned storm did not move with the wind or dissipate until Darrion-Quieness dismissed it. Soon the dragon was enveloped in a soft, white blanket of cool, refreshing snow that covered him just like the many large rocks that rested atop the great peak. The dragon snuggled under the comforting layer of snow and he quickly slipped into a deep sleep.

Darrion-Quieness awoke from his long peaceful rest. He poked his head out from under the snow that had fallen over his body. The large brick of crumbling white snow that had formed on his wide-scaled head while he slept, tumbled and fell into pieces, causing his bright emerald eyes to flutter until the snow had all fallen away. The peak had sustained just about its limit for snowfall, and the dragon surmised he had been asleep for a couple of days. The great white climbed from under the icy white blanket and slowly stretched his ancient muscles. He hadn't eaten in about a week and his stomach was protesting angrily. He stretched his fantastically immense bat-like wings wide and stuck out his thick, scale covered, barreled chest as he gazed over the great peak. With a mighty leap the dragon launched from the face of the mountain, sending large icy boulders cascading down its side as he began to soar toward the valleys below, searching for something to eat. He preferred the taste of frost giants, but the great white wasn't sure if there were any of their kind living in this mountain range. The dragon hated frost giants, unless he was eating them of course, and he scanned the area for any sign that the gray-skinned giant race may have made a home here. The wicked race of giant kin often killed or enslaved younger white dragons to use as food, or made to serve as mounts. Darrion-Quieness often went hundreds of miles in search of the cursed giants to line his lair with them as frozen tasty snacks.

After a few hour of searching, he spotted some movement in the snow near the base of one of the valleys. Using the low-flying mountain clouds as camouflage, the unnaturally stealthy beast glided within a few hundred yards undetected. He gazed down at what he hoped to be a frost giant hunting party. But to his dismay, he saw seven large humanoids that only stood about eight feet tall and had blue skin, rather than gray. They were very muscular and wore only large loin cloths made of animal hides. Their blue skin was callused and their heads were bald with strange tribal tattoos on their faces, chests, and arms. Their foreheads were sloped back and they had wide, plump-lipped mouths with yellow flat teeth, save for two large canine teeth that they probably used for cutting flesh. They were all male and wielded either a great stone axe, or large tree trunks they used as clubs. The largest one, that seemed to lead the group, appeared to be the chief. Directly behind him were two smaller ones that dragged the bodies of two armored men, an armored elf, and a tied-up halfling.

Darrion-Quieness smiled as he soared undetected above the blue-skinned giant kin. He wasn't overly fond of mountain ogres, but they were distant kin to the frost giants and were kind of tasty if they were frozen solid enough. The great white guessed the ogres had caught some unwary adventurers, and planned to eat them. Darrion-Quieness smiled wide as he pondered the irony of the situation and started his descent from the clouds.

He tucked his powerful wings close to his body and lay his arms and legs back toward his tail. He straightened his long neck and plummeted at unearthly speeds toward the unsuspecting ogres. The wind rushed past the colossal beast as his descent increased rapidly. His bright green eyes watered from the rush of the wind, and the dragon smiled just before impact. He decided he hated frost ogres too.

*   *   *

Stieny Gittledorph was quite possibly having the worst day of his life. And by the looks of things around the little thief, the day was most likely to be the last day of his life. The tiny halfling had made quite a name for himself in the elven village of Navlashier. He had lived comfortably for some time by lifting unguarded jewels and other trinkets from unsuspecting adventurers. He was even a skilled cutpurse and had made quite a fair sum at that trade as well. The thief thought about the events that led up to his current predic-

256

ament, rethinking the encounter with a few 'ifs' and several 'maybes.'

All was going well until those darned adventurers got a little testy when he took a jewel from them. Granted it was the largest emerald the little thief had ever seen, but it was still just a rock. If they didn't want him to steal it, they wouldn't have left it so unguarded. They had left the magnificent crystal hidden in a secret pouch at the bottom of a small silk bag hat they kept under their pillows when they slept. That was mediocre security as far as Stieny was concerned, and they had only placed three magical wards on the door and four simple locks. Any self-respecting thief could do no less than lift a jewel with such poor security. The irresponsible adventurers had never thought to check the ceilings for hidden doors, or they would have discovered Stieny's favorite method of relieving local adventurers of valuables. The halfling had a network of tunnels in the ceilings in every inn in town and frequently helped himself to whatever valuables the newcomers had. This group at least had to have some kind of expert tracker with them, Stieny figured. With his luck there was always something bad.

He had fled the town to lay low in his little cave hideout when the troublesome adventurers appeared in the mountains. Stieny fled out the back through a secret door, but that darned elf in the group spotted it right away. The halfling was just about to make his escape when he was ambushed by a large group of mountain ogres. He would have escaped, too, but he dropped the jewel in the deep mountain snow. While the adventurers were fighting the ogres, something hit him in the head and knocked him unconscious. When he came to, he was tied up from head to toe and was being dragged through the cold icy snow behind the disgusting mountain ogres. Stieny noticed the adventurers had met a gruesome fate—at least they looked dead to the little thief—but what troubled him the most was he noticed that the huge emerald was missing from his pouch. The nerve of those disgusting ogres; it was one thing to be captured and taken home to be eaten, but the little thief drew the line at being stolen from.

"Stupid thieving ogres," the little thief said under his breath as he struggled to look around. He was tied up with thick, waxed rope that held his hands at his sides and wrapped around his thin little body. Halflings were not normal commodities for ogres, so he guessed he had been captured by the adventurers before the ogres had captured them. Stieny had managed to free his right arm and could wriggle out in a few seconds, but the halfling knew he could not outrun the fiendish beasts, so he elected to wait for a more opportune time to escape.

"Well, at least it can't get any worse," Stieny mumbled under his breath, sure to not let the ogres know that he was awake.

As the halfling had lain on his back being dragged through the snow, he had spied a large, pale white object shooting from the sky. The object had been coming in so fast Stieny almost didn't recognize its reptilian features.

"Me and my big mouth," he said to himself. "Me and my big mouth."

*   *   *

Darrion-Quieness tucked his giant wings tight against his body and dove down with blinding speed. He could feel the wind rushing past his scale-encrusted face, causing his bright green eyes to water as he watched the snow covered gully rush up to meet him. When he was about a hundred feet from the lead ogre, Darrion-Quieness shifted his massive body back and extended his giant wings. The dragon's massive leathery wings caught air and slowed his plummet as he stretched his claws and prepared to tear into the flesh of the lead ogre. The dragon's sword-like talons ripped into the dark blue hide of the unsuspecting ogre, and the force from the blow shattered the beast's bones. There was a great explosion of snow and ice as the dragon's body crashed into the earth. The other ogres covered their faces and heads as the thick pieces of snow and dirt fell onto them. They slowly lowered their arms and peered at a massive crater that had suddenly appeared before them. The blue-skinned ogres growled back and forth between themselves, trying to determine who should investigate the crater, when a giant pale white scaled hand with long black talons crunched into the hard snow. The ogres looked at each other hesitantly and started backing away, ignoring the halfling and the dead adventurers' bodies.

Darrion-Quieness slowly raised his thick head until his bright green eyes barely broke the edge of the crater. He smiled a wide

258

toothed grin as the ogres turned and fled with their arms raised in terror.

Darrion-Quieness climbed halfway out of the hole and sucked in a deep breath. His long neck swelled and his head reared back. After a few moments, the colossal beast violently threw his head forward and thrust his wings wide as he expelled his glacial breath attack.

A cone of blue air erupted from his mouth and spread over the terrified ogres as they howled in pain. The dragon swept his head from side to side, completely covering all of the giant kin with his icy breath. The two remaining ogres ran away in terror as they tried to crawl up the side of the deep ravine. Their skin was more of a violet hue than the original blue and they had difficulty moving their arms and legs from the exposure to the abyssal cold. Their skin was cracked and blistered and bled everywhere it had to stretch to move. One of the ogres rubbed and clawed at his face and eyes as he stumbled around blindly in the snowy valley.

The dragon flexed his powerful legs and leapt over to the top of the ridge just as the pair of fleeing ogres reached the peak. Snow and ice from the top of the ridge cracked and tumbled away from the giant dragon's weight as the beast smiled an evil grin, bearing his long sword-like teeth. The two mountain ogres fell backward and tumbled down into the snow. Darrion-Quieness shot out a clawed hand and snatched one of the falling ogres by its blistered leg. As the ogre tried in vain to break free of the dragon's iron grasp, the dragon hopped down from the ledge in pursuit of the remaining ogre, crushing the one he had in his claw under his tremendous weight as he landed on the frozen tundra. The ogre's body made a sickening pop and went limp as the great beast crushed the life from it.

The last ogre fled as fast as he could, screaming in terror down the middle of the ravine. He kicked up large chunks of packed snow from under his fur covered boots as he fled. Darrion-Quieness paused to take a bite out of the ogre he had pinned to the ground while waiting for the last one to get far enough away that he could lash out at it with his heavy tail. The heavy scaled tail shot out like a giant whip, catching the ogre in the midsection. The force of the blow knocked him from the trail and his body hit the side of the rocky ravine. The ogre fell limp and was quickly covered by a pile of snow that fell from the top of the small overhang.

Darrion-Quieness paused and scanned the area for more enemies. After a few minutes he was certain that there were none and he began to pile up the ogres' bodies. The dragon packed them in the deep snow drifts to freeze them for later and he quickly ate the ones that were frozen solid by his frigid breath weapon. After the dragon finished eating, he began to pile up the gear of the ogres and the dead adventurers that they seemed to have caught. He counted the gold coins each had and wished he had time to fly back to his lair to save the loot. But the great beast knew he did not have time for such endeavors, so he resounded to burying the fair amount of gold coins in the snow bank, then freezing it solid with his icy breath. He was just about to take flight and begin the three day journey out of Vidora, when he noticed a single set of tiny footprints in the snow leading away from the battle, over the ravine, and down the steep hill on the other side. Darrion-Quieness narrowed his eyes as he thought for a moment, trying to figure out who had been watching him. After a few minutes, he noticed the dead halfling that was tied up and dragged behind the ogres was missing. He contemplated just leaving the pathetic creature to his own devices in the frozen mountain wasteland, but the dragon imagined a legion of great elven wizards that were friends to the halfling coming to hunt the dragon for treating their little friend so poorly. The dragon shook his head from side to side, sending spittle flying from his mouth as he snapped out of the daydream of battling scores of elves. Though the prospect of a small war was somewhat inviting, the great white had a mission, and battling leagues of elves was not in it. So he elected to hunt down the little bug, before he became a problem.

With a mighty leap the great beast was in the air soaring east above the tracks that led down toward the base of the mountain.

*   *   *

Stieny's large round eyes had spotted the dragon only an instant before the gigantic creature crashed into the lead ogre, crushing the monster instantly under its tremendous weight, sending up a shroud of snow and ice from the force of the impact. The earth

260

shook under the blow and the other ogres were knocked from their feet while rocks and other small debris fell from the tops of the ravine. The ogres scrambled to their feet as a giant cloud of snow and ice drifted down in front of them, obscuring their vision.

Stieny, however, worked feverishly at freeing his other arm and cutting the thick, coarse rope that bound him. In seconds, the tiny halfling was free from his bonds and running as fast as his little legs would carry him. He plodded through the deep snow, scurrying toward an alcove in the side of the rocky ravine the ogres had been traveling in. Though it didn't offer one hundred percent protection, he hoped it would be enough to survive the horrible breath of the ice beast that would surely come at any minute. As he trudged through the waist-deep snow, he could hear the familiar sound of a great breath being taken in. The little halfling winced as he felt the air beginning to tighten and expand from the wicked force of the expulsion of the dragon's icy breath. He squeezed as much of his little body behind a small rocky outcropping as he could as the abyssal cone of cold ripped past, freezing even the very air it rode upon. The wind howled and screamed and he could feel the horrible coldness that was just a few inches away. His black furry tunic that was exposed to the valley air began to harden and crack. The thin leather straps that held his knives and his short sword cracked and froze and his hair hardened and broke apart in the abyssal wind. Stieny could feel the bone chilling, cold rippling behind him, coating the rocks near his face, turning them into a dullish blue-gray. A thin layer of ice made popping and cracking sounds as it formed all around him.

When the air began to turn back to normal temperature, the chilled halfling turned to inspect the effects of the great dragon's breath. To Stieny's bewilderment, the soft white fluffy snow had frozen solid. It was no longer compiled of a thousand tiny flakes of ice, but was a sheer sheet of white frozen terrain. Every rock, tree, and bush sagged under the weight of inches of ice that clung to their surfaces and branches. It seemed as if the very air itself had frozen around everything that had been in the path of the great white's breath. There was a deadly calm and a great fog floating softly over the newly frozen ravine that slowly began to dissipate before the halfling's eyes. Stieny was terrified to venture out, but he knew that if he remained where he was, it was only a matter of time before the

261

dragon would find him. Just when he had mustered the courage to try to make a run for it, Stieny's sharp little ears heard the sound of the ogres slipping and sliding on the icy ravine floor. They were screaming in fear and fleeing for their lives. The tiny halfling poked his red chubby face from around the corner of the rocky alcove. His rosy cheeks were blistered and red and he had small icicles hanging from his brown curly hair. He witnessed two of the ogres trying to climb the ravine wall to escape the wrath of the voracious beast. Their skin was blistered and cracked and it appeared as if they did not have much use of their fingers or their arms. Stieny gasped, clutching his neck with his thin little fingers as he looked at the great white dragon. It was the largest beast he had ever seen. It was at least a hundred yards long from the tip of its massive head to the end of its spine-riddled tail. Its large white scales were a murky white at the apex and a light blue just near the base. He could see many gold coins and other precious metals and gems that had become embedded in between the scales near the dragon's underbelly from spending hundreds of years lying on a horde of treasure. The dragon's head was covered in a large white bony sheath that made it seem almost as if his skull was just under the scales. He had a great ebony spine that splayed back from the top of his head toward the base of his skull, and over the back of his neck. There was a large flap of thin white skin affixed to that spine, forming a small sail. The dragon's eyes were an effervescent green that seemed to pierce into the halfling's soul as they evilly watched the ogres futilely climbing the ravine wall.

Stieny watched the colossal beast for a few more seconds before he noticed he had started running down the other side of the ravine as fast as his short little legs could carry him. As Stieny reached the bottom of the slope, he stopped and glanced around. He had no recollection of climbing out of the ravine or even running this far. He had no idea what direction he was facing and he wasn't really sure where the ravine he ran from actually was.

The young thief dabbed the sweat from his forehead and slowed to a walk, pondering the event. He had heard that the most powerful dragons emitted some kind of a fear aura. He surmised that he must have somehow fallen prey to it. The cries of the helpless ogres echoed across the valley and Stieny knew he had not run far. He reached back and grabbed his ice-covered hood, pulling it over his head the best he could. As he pulled the cover up to protect his head from the cold wind, the frozen leather shroud shattered in his fingertips. The confused halfling studied the remains of the hood in his hand. The leather was dry and cracked and covered in a thin layer of ice. The little thief knew he didn't have much time to find somewhere to hide. Stieny hoped the dragon wouldn't miss him, but he knew that the giant lizards were quite gifted in the powers of recollection when dealing with numbers. The fiendish beasts often sat and counted their millions of coins every day, never counting the same coin twice.

Stieny struggled through the deep snow as he rounded a rocky outcropping on the trail he had been dragged down when the adventurers captured him. He turned up the tiny rabbit trail that led to a small cave at the base of the rocky extension. Huddled in the dark, the cold, scared halfling sat and waited.

* * *

Darrion-Quieness glided down the trail, following the tracks of the tiny halfling. The dragon had a full belly and was really wanting to relax on the mountain peak before he flew off toward Beykla instead of chasing the worthless halfling worm. But the dragon knew he couldn't let the halfling wander into town—he might alert someone to his presence, and the dragon hated having enemies following him. And if there were any enemies that the dragon didn't want, it was enemies from Vidora. The damnable elves would seek to vanquish him for no other reason than he was a white dragon—the racist, pointy-eared hellions—and they called *him* evil.

He tracked the halfling a while longer before he came upon a small rocky outcropping that the tracks led into. The dragon looked around the other side and saw that there was no other exit from the cave. The beast scratched away at the base of the boulders and was delighted to find that they sat on the surface, rather than extended into it. That told the dragon that the cave didn't extend into the earth, but merely a few feet under the rocks. He decided that with one quick burst of his frigid breath into the hole he could be assured that the halfling would be no more.

Just as he started to suck in air, he heard the squeak of the little voice.

"Please, great dragon, don't kill me. Perhaps I could be of some use to you," Stieny said, knowing that the beast was probably full from eating the ogres, and hoping it could speak common, the generic language of surface dwellers.

Darrion-Quieness cocked his head to the side and marveled at the stupidity of the foolish creature. "Don't you know you have nothing to offer me, save for some diamonds. But if you had any, I'd just kill you and take them anyway," the dragon said as he noticed the halfling's cloak had been frozen from his breath.

Stieny gulped and re-adjusted his collar. "Well, I am sure there is something I could do for you, great and majestic beast."

Darrion-Quieness sat on his haunches and scratched at his chin while he pondered the thought for a moment. Eventually he was going to have to find some humanoid to infiltrate Beykla and find the Ecnal. He figured since this halfling was already afraid of him and was not from the city, the halfling could not summon any powerful friends to save him. All he had to do was fly him there and he was set.

The dragon unconsciously dug at his underbelly with one of his sharp claws, knocking a few coins and jewels into the soft snow. "I noticed you have been mildly exposed to the power of my breath attack."

Stieny didn't reply, he just sat motionless in fear. The dragon pulled a bright gem away from his underbelly and lightly breathed on it. Stieny could see the very air around the gem harden and grow heavy as great particles of ice fell around it like a miniature snow storm. The beast then showed the gem to the halfling and dismissed the fear aura that surrounded him, knowing the halfling would no longer be affected by his magical fear.

"I have trapped your soul in this gem, little one," the dragon lied as he held the large emerald before the halfling's little face. "Notice that you no longer have that gnawing fear pulling at your insides?"

Stieny nearly burst into tears. All he wanted was not to lose his life. Instead he had now lost his soul. He knew it was so, because he could indeed no longer feel the presence of that gnawing fear.

"I will return your soul to you in good time, little one. But first, you will accompany me to Beykla. I will explain more later. But know if you ever flee I will find you, and if for some reason I cannot,

I will crush the gem, thus destroying you and your soul," the great white said, lowering his shoulders and motioning for the halfling to climb onto his back.

Stieny merely nodded weakly and climbed aboard the great beast. He marveled at how soft the dragon's smooth white scales were. Then in an instant, the giant beast exploded into the air, and for the first time in his life, Stieny was flying.

Ultimate despair: a point in which a being can no longer descend, a shallow where he can only stay on the same level or begin an ascension. I believe every great man or woman that has ever lived has suffered from this plight at one point in their lives. Some may have reached it as children, others not until the day of their deaths, but all have some form of ultimate despair. What makes a person great though, is not merely reaching this point, but reaching it and going beyond; it is understanding oneself and developing a kind of reprise that can never be challenged.

Too often men are fooled by vengeance or love and think they have this reprise, but they have yet to begin to achieve the self-actualization that is necessary to reach this higher being. It is difficult to explain how the transformation comes about, and impossible to describe. It cannot be purposefully sought and cannot be artificially created. It alone is more powerful than all the magic of all the gods in Merioulus combined. Once attained, this personal state of well being can never be stolen, crushed or changed, it will always remain unchallenged. Even in death, it is the single most powerful core of existence. Unfortunately, all too often, a person is lost before they come to this higher being.

The transition of one's soul is never immediate. Frequently one begins the journey to this higher being, only to die long before reaching it. Only the greatest of all beings complete the cycle. However, once completed, the person knows they have reached a pinnacle in their lives, reached an apex of their soul that can never be bound, broken or destroyed. It is a feeling of such euphoric proportions that there is not a combination of words in all the languages of existence combined, that can describe it. I simply refer to it as a true birth.

—Lancalion Levendis Lampara—

Seven

Plight of the Stormhammers

Amerix awoke face down on the shore of the sandy beachhead and stared at the fine granules for a few moments before raising his sun-scorched head. He rolled over on his back and weakly stretched his stiff muscles. He looked down at his many wounds that covered his old withered body. The wounds were covered with many small, thin, yellow spores. "Damn flies," the dwarf said to himself as he began the arduous task of sweeping the larvae eggs from his infected wounds. When he was sure he had gotten them all, the old dwarf gingerly rose to his feet. He coughed up some muddy brown water and didn't bother to wipe the soupy concoction from his long, silver streaked beard as he plodded to the edge of the river. In front of him, the cold Dawson River curved around the beach he was on, and splashed against a large rocky cliff on the other side. The cliff was covered in thick leafy green vines in some areas, and many birds of prey nested and perched on the vast rocky ledges. There was a large stork-like bird that prodded its dagger-like beak into the shallow water near the edge of the river, pulling out a long slender fish it had speared. The bird didn't seem to mind the large dwarf as he kneeled down at the water's edge and sipped.

Amerix paused for a moment and stared at the reflection of the old dwarf that gazed back at him from the water. The old dwarf looked into the eyes of his father, his father's father, and beyond, yet he only saw grief and hardship. Try as he might, Amerix could not locate any real success. There were countless victories in battle, but each of his ancestors had died in battle. The glorious mail of Stormhammer was then passed on to the firstborn son. This tradition had survived tens of thousands of years, but no longer. It had ended when Amerix's only son fell to an illness that could have been cured, had it not been for the politics of the Beyklans. Suddenly the old face had returned. He finally recognized the dwarf that was staring back from the water. Though it seemed still distant, he recognized the burning hate for the Beyklans. His mind quickly shifted into the thoughts of their screams and his sadistic pleasure with the emotion he felt when his wicked axe sliced deep into the flesh of one of the Beyklans. Ah, his axe, what a fine weapon he possessed. The weapon was forged by some distant father, probably twenty times removed, and it had been passed down to each son until it was given to him by his father.

Amerix reached down to feel the enchanted weapon, but he grasped only the dry leather sheath that once held the pommel of the ancient blade. Despair again washed over the ancient general. He had nothing. He had squandered everything his fathers had passed onto him. He had lost Clan Stormhammer to a white dragon and an army of dark dwarves, and he had lost his armor, his axe, and his great helm. He couldn't even protect his only son when the boy needed him most. And now, he sat defeated on the shore of some unnamed beach, crushed and broken. The powerful dwarven general, probably the greatest dwarven warrior to have ever lived, dropped his forehead on the sandy beach and wept. He wept from the bowels of his soul. The wailing was so intense, every bird, every frog, every insect—even the plants shifted their leaves—to alleviate themselves from the sound of ultimate suffering; the sound that now came from the belly of the old defeated dwarf. The wailing drifted from the valley into the forest, echoing far across the land and into the twilight of the day. And as the sun set on Amerix Alistair Stormhammer, it set on the great general, father, and king. Once the red sun of the day that was vanishing into the dark horizon of the western sky had set, all that was left was an empty hollow of a dwarf that could never be filled. The great warrior lay defeated on the sandy beach—not defeated by any enemy he had ever faced, but defeated by the blinding hatred that had nearly consumed him from the inside.

As the waning light of the day shifted into darkness, the dwarf cried himself to sleep. He slept only because, try as he might, Amerix could not will himself to die.

*   *   *

268

He was led down the unlit passage, back into the under dark. The group of dwarven miners took him to a small cavern with a single pool and tossed him in. The young red-haired dwarf tumbled down the rocky slope about thirty feet and came to rest at the base of a small pool. Therrig Alistair Delastan sat up and glared at the Stoneheart dwarven miners that collapsed the tunnel behind him. He was exiled in the small underground cavern, bound, bleeding, and with no food, weapons, or armor.

The wounded dwarf examined his clothing. He still wore the padded undergarments that he normally wore under his thick plate mail to soften the burden of the heavy steel. The padding was worn, but it still would function as some sort of protection, should he meet some underground beasts. Therrig wiped the small trickle of blood from a gash that had opened above his left eye when he had been tossed into the cave. The small cut continued to bleed despite Therrig's continual attempts to staunch it. After his shirt sleeve was soaked with blood, he managed to stop the bleeding, and rose to his weary feet. Therrig didn't bother trying to climb back to the passage the miners had collapsed. He knew quite well of the prowess of the Stoneheart miners, and that if they sealed the passage, it was indeed sealed. The outcast slowly walked over to the pool and knelt. He cupped the crystal clear water with his hands and began to wipe his face and arms, being careful not to get the cut over his eye wet. He had grown accustomed to being clean over the years and being dirty was aggravating to him. After he washed his face and hands, he sat at the base of the pool and chuckled to himself. He knew better than to chuckle out loud, for there were many monsters in the under dark that would love to find an unarmed dwarf and have a nice little lunch. Yet, the irony of the situation wasn't lost on him. He had been a faithful follower of Amerix, and even followed his orders to the letter, yet it was his own kin, Amerix, that had ordered him banished, not the good, loving Stoneheart Clan. But who was responsible meant little to him. He would have his revenge on the entire clan. Clan Stormhammer was no more, and if he had any say in the matter, Clan Stoneheart was soon to follow.

Therrig was sitting on the shore eating some beovi that he had caught in the small pool, when his keen hearing detected two sets of footsteps coming from a passage that was on the north side of the cavern. Therrig tossed the remnants of the white pale fish into the water. He knew the splash would attract the attention of the pair while he rushed over to a dark alcove and waited for the trail blazers to show themselves.

Two well-armed dwarves emerged from the north passage. The passage was higher than the cavern floor and had a small ledge that led down to the pool. The dwarves were wearing thin chain shirts and bore large hammers that they carried with both hands. Their skin was a dull gray, their eyes were murky white, and they had thin gray beards that barely touched their chests.

The pair looked over the ledge down at the pool and scanned the cavern for the source of the splash. "You sees anything, Artone?" one of the dark dwarves asked the other, who shook his head. He scanned the cavern floor for signs of life but located none. His murky white eyes that were designed to see only the infrared light spectrum picked up on a warm spot on the rocky floor next to the pool. He pointed to the warm area.

"You sees the body mark?" Artone asked while his pupil-less eyes scanned the cavern looking for the humanoid that made it.

"Yea, I sees it. Kalistirsts?"

"Nopes, not none of dems. Theys don't sits on the shore. Theys get dems fish and eats dem elsewheres," Artone said. "Plus theys don't travel by demselves. Theys always go wit dems friends."

The other dwarf nodded in agreement and looked at Artone.

The older dark dwarf shrugged his muscular shoulders and started down the slope.

"Whats ever is, ain't no big. We's can go kills it."

Therrig hugged the wall of the alcove, keeping his body behind the large boulder as the pair of dark dwarves walked by. He didn't hear all of the conversation, but he knew the dark dwarves were coming to find him. Therrig hated dark dwarves more than anything. It was their kind that attacked and wiped out Clan Stormhammer with the aid of a white dragon named Darrion-Quieness. Therrig was not sure why the dark dwarves or the dragon were interested in Clan Stormhammer, but he had vowed to kill either of them whenever he saw them again.

Therrig gathered a small rock and placed it in the palm of his hand, stepped out from the alcove, and cleared his throat. The dark dwarves, who were just reaching the cavern floor, stopped in surprise, and whirled round to see the dwarf who stood behind them.

"Who be's yee?" Artone asked nervously.

Therrig stepped forward with the palmed rock facing behind him. "I am Therrig Alistair Bigbody. My clan is just a click away," Therrig said as he pointed back behind himself, continuing to approach the two dark dwarves.

Artone examined the clothing that Therrig wore. Though he could not see anything but the heat spectrum, the dark dwarves were adept at identifying the slightest variations of it. He noticed that Therrig wore no armor and no weapons. As Therrig came within a few steps of him he spoke again.

"If yous from Bigbodys, why yous got no armor or weapons?" Artone asked.

Therrig smiled wickedly. "I have a weapon. It's right here!" Therrig said as he lunged forward and swung the rock down, catching Artone in the face. Blood shot out from the gruesome wound and the older dark dwarf fell to the ground clutching his broken nose. The other dark dwarf swung his heavy hammer at Therrig, but the cumbersome weapon was too slow. Therrig ducked the clumsy strike, grabbing the hammer Artone had dropped, and leaped into the icy water. He splashed into the pool and stood chest deep in the frigid subterranean pool.

Artone winced as he held his hand against his bleeding nose. "He's gots me sledge, fool, goes and gets it!"

"But he's in the pool," the younger dwarf protested.

Artone growled in response, and the younger dark dwarf sighed as he began to slowly wade into the icy water. Artone picked up the rock and heaved it at Therrig. Therrig just submerged as the rock splashed harmlessly on the surface where he had been standing. He resurfaced a second later smiling confidently.

"You throw like a kalistirsts," Therrig taunted.

Artone screamed in rage. "I'sa kill yous, Bigbody!" the dark dwarf screamed, his voice echoing off of the cavern walls.

Therrig chuckled in return and submerged again.

"He's gone and wents under again," the younger dark dwarf said, looking back at Artone.

"Don't tells me, fool! Finds em!" Artone screamed, shaking his fists violently in the air. The younger dwarf turned back around as Therrig erupted from the pool behind him. He hooked the handle of the sledge behind the dark dwarf with his powerful arms and pulled back, forcing the cold steel shaft into the dark dwarf's throat and cutting off his air. The dark dwarf struggled against the weapon and managed to slip his hand between the hammer and his neck.

"Helps me, Artone!" the dark dwarf grunted as he struggled to free himself from the hammer.

Artone rushed forward into the pool, but only waded in ankle-deep. "Come ons fool!" Artone shouted. "Gets loose and splits his skull!"

Therrig could hear the splashes of Artone in the water. He shoved forward, forcing the dark dwarf under the surface. The icy water rushed around Therrig's face and head. He knew he couldn't spend too much time in the water or the cold would dull his movements. He pulled with all his might on the hammer, forcing the final breaths from the lungs of the dark dwarf he held. When he felt the dark dwarf's muscles relax, he released the dead dwarf and emerged from under the surface.

Artone held the other dwarf's hammer in his hands and growled. "Yous killed me scout. Nows I'sa going to kills yous!" Artone screamed as he rushed in with the dead dark dwarf's hammer.

Therrig waited for the charging dwarf to close in on him. Artone's hammer came down in an overhand strike. Therrig side-stepped the heavy hammer as it slammed into the shallow pool. It made a loud clap and water splashed away from the hammer's stone head. Therrig held his hands far apart and brought them together as he swung. The hammer came down rapidly and struck the dark dwarf in the knee. A resounding snap echoed off the cavern walls, followed by a shrill scream as Artone's knee shattered. The wounded dark dwarf fell in the knee-deep water clutching his morbidly broken leg. He tried to stand on the broken leg but it twisted and bent under the weight of his body. Therrig clutched and circled Artone. The wounded dark dwarf shifted his weight to face Therrig, much to Therrig's delight. Each time Artone had to move to face Therrig, he had to hop and briefly put weight on his broken leg. He would involuntarily yelp in pain as he shifted.

"Comes on dog," Artone taunted, hoping Therrig would rush him. His mind was going numb from the pain, and he wasn't sure how much longer he could stand on the broken leg, but to his dismay, Therrig said nothing. He just continued to show a sinister smile and stayed true to his circle.

Therrig circled the dwarf for almost an hour, taunting him and giggling with sadistic glee as Artone tried to remain on his feet. Eventually Artone couldn't tolerate the horrific pain and he collapsed. Therrig walked over and looked down at the grimaced face of Artone, the dark dwarf.

"This is for Clan Stormhammer!" he shouted as he brought the heavy hammer down on the unprotected head of Artone. The dark dwarf's skull shattered, killing him instantly. Therrig pounded the lifeless body for twenty minutes until splattered blood dotted his face like a hive, and blood ran from Artone's pulpy body like a tiny crimson river on its exodus to the sea.

Therrig removed the undamaged armor from the drowned dark dwarf and placed it on. The armor was tight, since dark dwarves weren't as strong as normal dwarven kin, but it was better than the rags he had been wearing. He meticulously hooked each leather strap and hoisted the stone hammer over his shoulder as he walked north through the passage from the pool. He had gathered a few supplies and made a few coins from the kill. Therrig hummed to himself a dwarven battle tune and hoped he might come across some more dark dwarves. He had a lot of rage to vent.

*   *   *

Amerix awoke on the sandy beach again. He spit out a few large green beetles that had crawled in his mouth while he was asleep. The surprised beetles scampered away from their warm hiding spot as the old dwarf sat on his butt and stared at the tranquil river scene that lay before him. The sun was high in the sky and it hurt his eyes, but he made no attempt to shield them from it. He was barely conscious of the plethora of insects that landed on the back of his neck and arms to feast. The old dwarf just sat and thought of nothing, and everything, at the same time. He stared at his thoughts that seemed to visualize on the rocky cliff that stood before him. He counted the cracks, the number of vines, how many sticks floated past. He watched the birds of prey dive in and out of the water, snatching fish and other aquatic animals. He watched a large line of ants march over his thigh and continue across the beach. Amerix sat all day and well into the evening, though to him it seemed that he merely blinked a couple of times and it was dark. He glanced down at his red, blistered skin that had been scorched from the sun, but ignored the painful rash and lay back down. He closed his eyes and thought about his wife and son, praying to Durion to send an army to slay him. Yet as the night progressed, only the birds and crickets seemed to answer his silent prayers. Amerix lay on his back, unaware of the hundreds of dwarven bodies that began floating past his sandy bed. He soon drifted off into deep sleep and was happy to know peace there.

*   *   *

"These are the heroes who helped hold the bridge," a militia sergeant said as he pointed to Lance, Jude, Ryshander, Kaisha, and an unconscious Apollisian that was being tended to by the surgeons. Lance started to protest, but got a quick elbow in the ribs from Kaisha. He looked at her with a frown that quickly melted away against her wry smile.

"He was the true hero," Kaisha said as she pointed to the ground where Apollisian lay with his head propped under a soft pillow.

"Is he dead?" the militia sergeant asked as he motioned to a powerful-looking armored man and a group of similarly dressed soldiers. The front man wore a great helm with black hawk wings that were outstretched as a bird in flight. His armor was thick and he wore a long red silk cape with the banner of Beykla draped down his back. The men behind him wore bright brass-colored scale mail of the Beyklan high guard, with similar silk capes, and red tunics.

"No, he is just wounded and exhausted, but if he doesn't see a healer soon, he might be," Kaisha said.

Ryshander shifted forward, adjusting his tattered clothing. "We all could use a good healer. We have gold to pay for services."

Lance winced. He and Jude had little gold left. He thought about sneaking off and checking the dwarven bodies, but Jude had explained that soldiers don't usually carry gold with them into battle.

"There is no need to pay. You have already paid with blood," the man with the hawk helmet said.

274

Jude nodded. "Thank you sir, my companions and I are grateful. Where might we seek these healers of yours?"

Lance fumed. He despised Beyklans, and did not feel grateful. He had tried to save some innocents, not preserve their morbid sovereignty. Had he given it more thought, he wouldn't have tried to rescue the stupid girl behind the bar. All that got him was a severely wounded shoulder.

Ryshander seemed to be having equal difficulty with Jude's words. He despised the local magistrate as much as Lance despised the country. He didn't intervene to save any innocents, just to make Kaisha happy. Plus, he was no companion to the barbaric swordsman or his slick mage. Yet the armored man seemed oblivious to Lance's and Ryshander's contempt. "There is no need to seek them out, noble hero. I have already arranged for them to come here. After I heard the tales of how you rallied the soldiers and made a stand on the bridge, I ordered the clerics to come here after they tended to their own church."

Lance frowned. "You ordered? Who are you?"

The man chuckled and feigned a slight bow. "Why I am Duke Dolan Blackhawk," the man announced. "And who might I be speaking with?"

All four of the heroes stammered in surprise. "I am Lance Ecnal. This is my friend, Jude," Lance said. Jude bowed low and saluted with his massive two-handed sword. Lance pointed to Ryshander and Kaisha. "And they . . ." He was cut off by Ryshander.

"I am Ryshander and this is Kaisha," the wererat interjected as his lower lip began to quiver and twitch from anger. Kaisha bowed low, but Ryshander held his gaze.

"And who is that noble hero?" the duke asked, as he motioned to the downed paladin, seemingly oblivious to the wererat's glare.

"We know not his name, my lord," Kaisha said.

Ryshander glared at her. How dare she refer to the man that had killed or imprisoned their fellow guild members as lord?

"Well, citizens, we will learn his name when he awakens. After you receive your healing, I request your audience in city hall. That way we can prepare the ceremony for your medals." With that announcement the duke turned and started back toward the large city hall building. It had suffered some scorching, but it was no worse for the wear.

"We need to leave," Ryshander said as he grimaced from the pain that came from his many wounds when he tried to sit on the burnt porch of the Blue Dragon Inn.

"Why should we leave, my love?" Kaisha asked as she kneeled and grasped his gloved hands. "We could rebuild, start a new home, or maybe Pav-co will return."

Ryshander shook his head. "That fat thief will not return, at least not for a long while, and I do not wish to do all the work of rebuilding just so he can return one day and reclaim it for himself."

Kaisha nodded her head in defeat. "Then where will we go, my love? Dawson?"

Ryshander often thought about going to the great city that was at the base of the Dawson River, hence its name. But the city was full of dangers that just didn't exist in Central City. There were many guilds larger than Lostos ever could have been, but the price for failure was death. "I do not know, Kaisha. I just want to be rid of this place. I nearly lost you several times in the last two days. I just want to go away where I can never fear of losing you again," Ryshander answered truthfully. He surprised himself at his honesty and then felt foolish for sharing his emotions in front of the others. He stared down at the earth in an attempt to hide his embarrassment from the woman he loved. He felt warm soft hands grasp his face and lift his head. He raised his chin and stared deep into the beautiful brown eyes of his one true love. She smiled at him in such a way that seemed to melt away his anger and fear. Her smile sang a thousand-word song that made it okay for him to say what he felt and not be ashamed for it.

"I love you," she whispered and gently kissed his lips. He returned her kiss and weakly hugged her.

*   *   *

"When they come to get their medals, kill them," the duke said as he marched down the marbled corridor of the city hall. The clacking of his metal plates echoed down the singed corridor.

"But sir, I thought you said . . ." a robed cleric began to protest. "It is not just."

The duke whirled around. His long red cloak spun around him. "You want justice?" the duke asked, jabbing his index finger into the face of the violet-robed cleric. "Fine. Ryshander and his girlfriend, Kaisha, are thieves of the guild Lostos. They are wanted on too many charges to mention. I am sorry if you were planning to make a grand ceremony for five heroes. You will just have to have it for three," the duke said as he turned from the hallway and entered his stateroom.

The cleric lowered his head and nodded. "Yes, my lord," he said as he turned and made for the door of the burned office.

"Also . . ." the duke called out. The cleric paused as Duke Blackhawk finished his order.

"Find that viper, Ganover, his pride nearly cost me my city. Put him in chains and bring him to me for trial. He must pay for denying the paladin," the duke commanded as he sat on a partially burned oak desk.

"Yes, my lord, I will make it so," the cleric said as he bowed low and backed out of the duke's office.

*   *   *

She awoke to find herself being dragged on her back down a moss covered stone corridor. Both of her eyes were swollen shut and she could not see. Her deep slash wounds ached and she could feel the taut ropes tied around her body, arms and legs. She noticed there was a horrible pungent smell accompanying the wet moss that seemed to come from her left. It was then that Alexis Overmoon deducted that she was in the sewers of Central City.

Alexis pretended to be unconscious as the dwarves dragged her further down into the sewer. She expected she was being taken to General Amerix for execution or some kind of trial for trumped up war crimes. She didn't dare tug at her bonds, at least not yet. She didn't want to risk the dwarves realizing she was conscious. If she was going to somehow escape she needed to learn more about her captors and her surroundings, and she needed to try to get her eyes to open.

She was dragged for another ten or so minutes before the dwarves stopped. They roughly dropped her feet, which were tied to the lead rope. Alexis strained her ears to listen to what the

277

dwarves were saying through the constant ringing that echoed in her head from the many blows she had taken that rendered her unconscious in the alley.

"We need to take her to the rallying point," one dwarf argued.

"No, we need to take her to Commander Fehzban. It makes no sense to go to the rallying point with a prisoner," the other retorted.

Alexis listened intently to the two dwarves arguing and lightly struggled against her bonds. She surmised that as long as they argued she might get a chance to test the ropes that bound her, hoping they would be too engrossed in their disagreement to take notice. Alexis knew it was risky, but she figured she would have few opportunities before there were many eyes upon her.

Alexis first lightly pulled against the ropes that bound her hands and discovered she had no extra movement. In fact she noticed that the ropes were slowly cutting off her circulation. She could just begin to feel the telltale tingling in her fingertips, but when she checked her legs, she found that the ropes were quite loose from her having been dragged. Given the right opportunity, she would be able to stand and run, though unless she figured out how to get her eyes open, she knew she wouldn't get far. Alexis heard the dwarves reaching a conclusion so she relaxed and waited for another opportunity to test her ropes.

"Fine, we will take her to Commander Fehzban, but I'll have you know, it will be your beard in the shaving chair if Amerix gets mad, not mine."

The other dwarf smiled at the small victory and roughly jerked up on the rope holding Alexis's legs. "And I'll have you know that when Commander Fehzban hands out praises like dolgo seeds it will be me standing with my hands out."

Both dwarves paused as they looked at each other. "Boy, a good handful of dolgo seeds would sure hit the spot."

The other dwarf merely nodded as he imagined roasting the mountain nut over a slow fire. Both dwarves seemed to have similar fantasies for a moment, and then they smiled, shaking their heads as they started back down the moss-strewn corridor.

"I can't wait until this war business is over with. I have been having forge withdrawals," the dwarf chuckled.

The other nodded and smiled. "I hear that. I would have never thought I would miss working. But as they say; the grass is always greener, but it still has mites."

Alexis noticed the closer the pair got to the familiar areas of the sewers, the more lighthearted they became. She was dragged another thirty minutes down the moss covered corridor, then they stopped.

"Go and fetch the commander, I'll wait here," one dwarf said. The other nodded in delight as he imagined the comforts of home that he hoped were only a few weeks away.

Alexis tugged at her bonds once again, though she did so with care. She didn't notice any new weak spots from the trip, much to her dismay, and she still couldn't get either eye open and her hands were close to being numb from poor circulation caused by the tight knots. She resounded to wait. Getting killed here in the sewers would help nothing and she hoped she might be able to reason with this Commander Fehzban. She was glad at least they weren't taking her to Amerix. Alexis was sure that demon would remember her well-placed armor, and she recalled Apollisian talking about how the dwarves themselves were not evil, though he was sure there were a few among them that were. She hoped that Apollisian was right about the majority of them. She also hoped that the commander could recognize her royalty and that she might use it to gain favor with him. But her general pessimistic side figured he would have some kind of personal grudge with her family. That was just how her luck seemed to go of late.

*   *   *

"What do you mean you can't find Amerix?" Commander Fehzban yelled to the haggard messenger. His armor was bloodied and dirty and he walked with an obvious limp.

"We can't find him. He was last seen near the bridge when the re-enforcements came from the east. Our lines were scattered and many of the men fear he is dead. Our entire eastern front has been decimated and the rest of the army is fleeing to the rallying point, near the entrance back into the under dark."

The battle was a huge success for the dwarves. They had split the humans' defenses, pushed to the bridge, allowing the weaker groups to flee to the west, and slowly crushed the strongest group

279

that was making a stand on the bridge over the Dawson River. They had set ablaze buildings of strategic position or buildings that would hurt the humans' morale by being burned. It seemed as if the battle was going to be another easy victory. Amerix led the charge on the final push when he learned that the human champion from the Torrent Manor was alive and leading the resistance, and that was when things began to fall apart. The humans had a wizard, a giant of a man, as well as two swordsmen that seemed impervious to attacks, and the champion from Torrent, holding the bridge. Amerix ordered the majority of the front into battle and the humans had hidden horsemen on the other side. The heavy lancers charged across the bridge and in seconds wiped out the eastern front the dwarves had established. Behind the thunderous hooves were a flood of pikemen who hit the fleeing dwarves in their backs. Commander Fehzban still didn't understand why the humans had such a force on the eastern side of the city, but that didn't matter now. The battle had been lost and Fehzban was waiting for a word from Amerix before he sounded the full scale retreat to Mountain Heart, their home city in the Pyberian Mountains.

"Sir, with all due respect, Amerix is dead, or captured at least. Let us flee to our homes and prepare for the humans' counter strike. We can make it home in a week or so. I'm sure the king will be glad to hear of our victories," the messenger pleaded.

Fehzban stroked his long beard. "So be it. Sound the retreat. We will make haste back to Mountain Heart and plan our defenses there. The Beyklans have learned we can strike anywhere. Perhaps their people will fear our might and force their leaders to leave Clan Stoneheart to their own devices."

The messenger's face cracked into a huge smile. "Yes sir! I will make it so," he shouted as he eagerly ran from the command chamber.

Fehzban gathered his gear and looped his thick leather backpack over his left shoulder. He rolled the maps and battle plans onto the wooden table and piled them up. Fehzban reached into his pack and removed a small wooden flask. He placed the brown cork in his mouth and pulled until the wooden flash popped open. After pouring the thick syrupy brown liquid on the parchments and the table, he set them on fire. The commander stared quietly at the small fire as it spread to the table and slowly engulfed it. He worried that this was merely the first defeat in a series of defeats that would eventually lead to the demise of Clan Stoneheart. Fehzban stood mesmerized by the fire for many minutes until the table was nothing more than a pile of smoldering ashes, then he turned from the chamber and started down the corridor.

As he rounded the corner of the command room he heard his name being shouted by a dwarf that was dressed in chain armor and wielded an axe—the same armor the front linesmen wore when they were sent into battle on the eastern front. Fehzban's spirits soared at the possibility that he had news of Amerix.

"Commander Fehzban!" the dwarf shouted as he ran up to the commander.

"What news do you bring of the front lines?" Fehzban asked eagerly. "What of Amerix?"

The dwarf seemed confused. "What do you mean; *of* Amerix? I am sure he has a fine grasp on the bridge and is preparing to burn the city down around the foul human scum. We have returned because we have captured a prisoner," the dwarf said happily.

Fehzban became enraged. The stupid front liner had no idea of the battle status and he left the battle because he caught a prisoner. "I hope you are trying to make me laugh, front liner, and that I am just in a foul mood, because I am becoming angered that you have left the battle since you caught a damned prisoner," Fehzban shouted with his fists tightly clenched at his sides, his unfastened helmet straps shaking as he spoke.

The dwarf took a step back as all the color drained from his face. "Not just any prisoner sir, but the elven archer from the Torrent Manor. And sir, we were ordered to bring her back," the dwarf pleaded more than announced.

Commander Fehzban shuddered. He remembered Amerix speaking of the elven archer back at the Torrent Manor. The commander feared that she was royalty or someone of significance. Rarely did elves travel with humans, unless one or both were of great importance. The thought of angering an elven nation on top of the human one gave the old commander a shiver.

"Bring her to me and be gone. Go to the rallying point and meet up with the remainder of the army, we are heading home," Fehzban said.

The dwarf was visibly shocked. He had no idea why they were

heading home so soon. Surely the razing of the city could not have been completed so soon. Fearing the worst and feeling defeated, he did as ordered. He turned and slowly plodded back down the sewer corridor, to his companion.

"I can see by the long face, we should have went to the rallying point," the dwarf chuckled in victory as he clapped his friend on his shoulder.

The dwarf merely shook his head from side to side. "We have lost the battle I believe. We are to meet at the rallying point as soon as we deliver the prisoner to Commander Fehzban."

The other dwarf's face turned sour. "What do you mean we lost? How can that be? We had them pushed back to the bridge," he argued.

The other dwarf just shrugged his shoulders. "Perhaps we didn't lose, perhaps Amerix feels that we need to leave soon. All I know is that Commander Fehzban gave us orders to meet the rest of the army at the rallying point."

"Was he mad at us for coming here?"

The dwarf shook his head. "No, he was pleased at our captive, I think. He just seemed defeated to me."

Neither dwarf said anything else. They bent down and picked up the rope that held the feet of the elf and started to drag her down the corridor.

Alexis was elated at the news she heard from the dwarves. If in fact the dwarves had been routed it was a mammoth victory. She couldn't imagine how Apollisian and Victor had succeeded, but she found herself surprised at how uplifted she was when she imagined the paladin alive. She was happy for Victor too, but that happiness was nothing like the strange feeling she had when she thought of the paladin. She dismissed the jumbled mass of emotions when she felt her feet being roughly thrown down.

"Here she is, commander," the dwarf said sullenly. Fehzban nodded and dismissed the pair with a wave. They silently turned and hurried down the corridor to the rallying point as ordered. Fehzban paused until he was sure the pair had left. When he was satisfied they were gone, he leaned down and whispered to Alexis.

"Stay still if you can hear me, elf. I mean you no harm." Fehzban wasn't sure his grasp on the elven language was firm so he repeated the phrase in dwarven, just in case she was conscious and could speak both languages. He paused for a moment and watched the elf. She was bound tightly by the rope and wrapped from neck to ankles. Her feet were a little loose, but the ropes around her wrists were extremely tight. Her face was purple and swollen from being beat and he doubted that if she were conscious she would be able to see.

Alexis didn't know what to think of the dwarf. He spoke a little elven but she wasn't sure exactly what he meant. She thought he mentioned something about harming her, but it was not in the tone or the context she would have expected. She wasn't sure how she would defend herself if he was going to harm her. All she could move was her legs and she could only thrash them about at best. She listened instead, but heard no one else but the dwarf that had spoken. She used her keen hearing to scan the passages for footsteps or weapons being drawn, but she heard nothing except the rhythmic breathing of herself and the dwarf that stood before her.

Fehzban kneeled down before the elf and placed his hands on her face. He closed his eyes and began chanting softly to himself. "I call forth the power of Leska, and in her divine might, that she cast out the pain and heal the injuries that have befallen the child that lays before me." After his chanting, his stubby hairy hand turned warm and began to show a soft white glow. Magical energy erupted from his hand and flooded into Alexis. She wanted to cry out, but the warm energy was soothing to her battered face. In a few moments the pain was gone and she opened her eyes, staring at the bearded face of Fehzban. He was an older dwarf and his beard extended just above his waistline and was braided in three braids that hung down. The ends of them were decorated with bright green wraps that held the braids to keep them from unraveling. He wore a small metal helm that was open faced, revealing a bright smile and deep blue eyes. He wore thick plate armor that bore a large dent in the center that seemed to have been made recently. Alexis said nothing to him. She just stared intently at the face of her rescuer or her executioner, though she doubted the latter.

Fehzban smiled at the elf. She was beautiful, even for an elf, and he noticed a mark of superiority on her. It was subtle at best, but he could detect it nonetheless. Even bound, gagged, and beaten she emitted an air of superiority that could come only with nobility. Most dwarves lacked the wisdom to discern the difference between

283

elven commoners and nobility. It wasn't an easy task for any dwarf. Elves were so lucid that it was nearly impossible to discern their hierarchy, but Fehzban had dealt with elven nobility in the orc wars and had learned the difference through many embarrassing trials and errors. The old commander stared down at his elven captive. Her blonde braided hair was long and stained with blood, though her wounds were all healed. She stared at him with her beautiful brown eyes that seemed to soothe him. He reached down and cut the ropes that bound her.

Alexis rubbed her hands together vigorously, trying to get the blood flowing to them as quickly as possible. She was certain the dwarf that stood before her was not an enemy, at least not at the present moment. He was obviously a cleric of some kind. She stared at the dwarf again, but this time without blurry vision. He was adorned in full plate armor that bore a great dent in the chest. His armor was dull and grimy, but appeared as if he kept it polished and clean under normal circumstances. He wore a small helm that had an open face, but she noticed, through her clear vision, that the helm bore a few scars from untold battles. Under his armor he wore a finely woven green tunic that was held together by gold-colored seams. His short cape was made of green silk and depicted the gold emblem of Leska on the rear of it. He wore thick metal plates that extended from just below his knees to the tops of his heavy walking boots. He was a formidable looking adversary to say the least, but Alexis detected a glint of deep-rooted passion in his steel blue eyes that was not characteristic of the blood thirsty dwarves that she had seen ravage the Central City and the Torrent Manor. She noticed a gleam of empathy and caring that she had not seen in the diminutive people.

"Well are you going to just sit there or are you going to introduce yourself, elf?" Fehzban said in his native dwarven tongue. He was not sure how well she understood his elven, but her reaction from the first time he spoke was that she seemed quite confused.

Alexis slowly rose on unsteady feet and dusted herself off. Though she was covered in the grime from the sewer, Fehzban was amazed at how much dignity she managed to restore to her stature by the simple motion. "I am Alexis Alexandria Overmoon, first daughter of King Christopher Calamon Overmoon of Minok Forest," she said as she raised her chin in the air with pride at the announcement of her titles.

Fehzban seemed unimpressed at her titles, but he was astonished at her ability to speak dwarven. He kept his tone soft and soothing. "Your equipment is there." He pointed to a dirty sack that was lying next to the wall. Her sleek white ash bow poked out from the sack that was full of her chain armor and other equipment. "You need to take your leave, as I am taking mine. You are not an enemy of Stoneheart or any other dwarf kin. My deepest apologies for any wrongs you have suffered. I would like to extend to you some sort of retribution for all that you have suffered by the hands of my men, but alas, I do not have the means at this time. Someday, *Alexis Alexandria Overmoon*, I shall compensate you," Fehzban said, over-pronouncing her name. He turned and quickly hurried down the corridor. His back hid the deep smile he wore from speaking her full name. His heavy plate armor jingled and rattled as he ran, but he didn't seem to mind as he disappeared into the darkness.

Alexis fumed. How dare that dwarf call her by her full name. Alexis started to protest, but she had little time to don her gear and she was afraid she might be caught unaware in the dark sewers and needed to get back to Apollisian as quickly as possible. She opened the dirty bag, placed on her thin chain armor, grabbed her long sword and composite long bow, and darted down the sewer corridor.

*   *   *

Amerix awoke face down in the crusty sand for the fourth consecutive day. He opened his heavy eyelids and gazed cross-eyed and expressionless at the many fine granules of sand that rested before him. There were a few dark-colored grains, but most were light brown or tan. The old dwarf stared, fixated on the tiny rocks, until a small ant wandered by. It zigzagged its way across the rough terrain, pausing to hold on whenever Amerix exhaled. The small black insect didn't seem daunted by Amerix's breath, which acted like a frequent windstorm that ravaged the land around it. Whenever the wind stopped, it paused a while longer to make sure it was safe, then would start again, only to be blown away by an unsuspecting breath a few moments later. Amerix closed his eyes after the ant was blown away, seeing nothing else worth staring at, but he was not tired enough to sleep. The intense hunger he felt the first and second days had given way to a general cramp that constantly gnawed at him, but his great despair seemed to shield his mind from any pain or hunger he might have normally felt. The old dwarf lay face down on the beach for many hours before forcing himself upright. His once powerful arms were weak from starvation and shook with fatigue when he used them to prop himself up. The dwarf seemed undaunted at his own weakness and even cracked a small smile at the thought of himself wasting away. His head was light from malnutrition and he felt sick to his stomach. He was covered in a thousand tiny insect bites and the renegade general was sure he had many mites that had made a home in his hair and beard. Amerix chuckled at the thought of how a week ago he would have never allowed himself to be so dirty, even if he was a dwarf. Now he wasn't even sure if he wanted to be a dwarf anymore. He was pretty sure he didn't want to be alive, despite the fantastic hallucination he had had under the river. He knew it was just that, a hallucination. Amerix placed no weight on what was said to him, knowing that it came from deep in his own mind and not from the lips of his departed wife and son.

As he sat on the sandy beach with his legs outstretched in front of him, Amerix occasionally wiggled his toes to ward off flies, and watched the many beautiful birds that hunted and swam in the river bottoms. Amerix was in no fear of being attacked by anything, though he would likely not care if he were, since it would end the dilemma of life for him. He didn't fear attack because the Dawson River was so ancient it had carved a deep crevice in the earth over the last ten thousand or so years. The small beachhead he was on was rare in the great river bottoms. Usually the only dry spot was a large rock that had fallen from the cliff and jutted up from under the river's edge. And as it was, the rocky cliff on the eastern side of the cavern was only a few hundred feet away, so Amerix was quite secluded in his tiny world.

The renegade general sat on the beach most of the day baking in the warm autumn sun. His light skin became blistered and red, but as the days wore on, it was replaced by a golden bronze. His body soon depleted the fat reserves he had built up, and his once somewhat flabby arms wore away to a tight iron-like sinew.

286

Amerix repeated this process day in and day out, occasionally munching on a large beetle when the hunger pains seemed to rouse his brain from desolation, but he did little else.

*　　*　　*

Therrig cautiously navigated down the gloomy tunnel that the dark dwarves came from. It was a small passage that appeared to have been a string of limestone at one time, that had been all but worn away over time from a small trickle of water that ran down the center. The stream slowly filtered by like the dawdling drain of a sewer that was about one foot wide and no more than a few inches deep. The walls of this particular passage were made of thick clay, with small patches of limestone. Therrig followed the passage for a few hours until he noticed the ceiling was expanding. The renegade paused and ran his hard-callused finger over the stone surface of the passage. He detected many unnatural grooves and nicks that made him suspect that the corridor had been widened unnaturally. Therrig paused and studied the walls and rocky crevices that extended several feet in front of him where the ceiling jumped from seven feet to thirty. He noticed several small ledges that seemed just the right height to conceal a sentry and just low enough to allow an attack on any unwary passersby. Under the largest ledge, bright yellow mineral deposits marked a small trickle of water coming out of the wall that formed the tiny stream that ran down the passage he had jut come up. Therrig slowly made his way under the rocky ledge and focused his ears, trying to hear the faintest sound, but heard nothing. After a few moments he was satisfied that there were no enemies about, and continued on into the large corridor. In the distance, Therrig could see the passage turned to the right and still continued to enlarge. It was readily apparent now that the passage was not natural, and he even noticed a crude pickax that was resting against the wall near the end of the corridor. The pickax was not crafted well and the head was made out of some kind of dark metal. The shaft was also made from the same metal, but was very thin, making the tool unbalanced. Therrig smiled a yellow toothed grin. He knew the pickax was made by the dark dwarves. The inferior race usually didn't have access to the finer ores, and their weapons and tools, if made from metal, were usually weak and dark colored. The shaft was made of the same metal, because the dark dwarves didn't have access to wood to have any wooden shafts in their tools or weapons. So the dark dwarves made their shafts of the same ore that they used to make the tool heads. In order to make the weapons or tools practical, they had to make the shafts thin and narrow in order to keep their weight down. This thin shaft often made the weapon awkward and unbalanced.

Therrig slowly walked up to the crudely made pickax that was resting against the wall of the cave. He carefully placed each foot softly in front of the other. The young dwarf wasn't a master at moving silently, but on the smooth stone of the passage he was confident at his ability to do so. As he reached the pile of tools, he looked down and examined the thin metal handle. He could detect slight variations in temperature on the handle where it had been held recently. Therrig reached down and felt the narrow shaft. It was impossible for him to feel the temperature difference, but he could plainly see the distinct lines between the shades of blue.

As he looked down the ever expanding cave corridor, Therrig noticed its ceiling rose to sixty feet. At the top he saw many long stalactites hanging down, indicating that it was a natural corridor. The young dwarf paused and leaned against the cold stone wall, pressing his back against it in an attempt to hide. Therrig slowed his breathing as he tried to detect any would-be enemies that might be making their way down the large passage. To his surprise, he could hear many voices coming from around the corner in the corridor. Therrig stalked forward, keeping his back against the wall, and his eyes ever scanning forward. As he rounded the corner, the corridor opened up into a huge expansive cavern. There was a passage that zigzagged down the ledge that he was standing on. At the bottom of the ledge were thousands of stone dwellings that had been crafted in a marvelous underground city. He could see many giant towers that were hundreds of feet tall erupting from the stone dwellings, that at their peaks had stone bridges leading into passages carved into gigantic stalactites that were hanging from the ceiling. The huge stalactites had many windows and other constructs in them. To the far north of the immense city, there were large mushroom fields that were being tended by scores of goblins that were often beaten with whips by dark dwarves. There was a great river that ran down the center of the city and it came from the wall on the north side of the cavern and exited on the south side of the city into a deep tunnel. There were beautiful bridges that spanned the river at several points. It was uncommon for dark dwarves to build anything that even remotely resembled a work of art. Disregarding the immaculately ornate buildings and structure, Therrig took a deep breath and moved closer to the edge of the rocky outcropping that overlooked the city. His eyes darted over the streets and alleys searching for a secluded spot to make his descent into the large city. Everywhere he looked, Therrig saw dark dwarves. He noticed temples that were constructed in the honor of Durion, the mountain god, the same god that the Stormhammers had worshipped. Though the dark dwarves were often at war or at least at odds with the Stormhammer Clan, Therrig found the thought of revenge much greater than the irony of working with the race that wiped out his friends and family hundreds of years ago.

The crazed dwarf known as Therrig Alistair Delastan began his descent into the city of the dark dwarves, hoping to either forge a new alliance and have revenge against Clan Stoneheart, or kill as many of the light-skinned dwarves as mortally possible.

The passage into the dark city was narrow and steep. Large boulders covered in small cracks lined the edges of the path, and small rocks skittered under Therrig's feet, threatening to topple him. He steadied himself and slowly made his way to the bottom of the passage seemingly undetected. As he neared the base of the trail, he could hear steel ringing against rock from behind a large stone wall that divided the trail and then a small courtyard. The wall was finely crafted, but age and wear had rounded off its fine points. Therrig quietly walked along the base of the wall listening to the ringing steel, taking steps with each ring. The wall was made of large stone bricks that were covered in a dark green moss. The moss was overlaid by thick black vines that grew from the base wall and rose up and over the top of the stone structure. The vines had many small white flowers that budded, but Therrig was unable to discern the color with his infravision. Infravision, the ability to see in complete darkness by the use of the heat spectrum, prevented the dwarf from seeing colors, unless they were in conjunction with a heat source.

Therrig ignored the flowered vine and circled around the far side of the wall. Once he rounded the corner, the wall was tiered, becoming smaller the further he went, and he soon could glance over the top with little climbing. Therrig lightly rubbed his hands together and pulled himself up ten or so feet, to the top of the stone wall. He could see about thirty small humanoids breaking rocks with large hammers. The humanoids were about three feet tall and had long pointed noses and ears. Their heads were scaly and riddled with small bumps. They had dark beady eyes that could see as well as any creature that lived in the under dark. Their skin was green and they had only four fingers on each hand. The creatures, which Therrig recognized as goblins, hammered at the rocks as four dark dwarves drove them on with the threat of a whip strike. The four taskmasters were wearing chain armor and no helms, showing their pale, thin, ugly faces and small beards. The dark dwarves wore black tunics that appeared to be made out of some kind of leather. They had large black whips in their hands and bulky metal hammers hooked to their sides through thick leather loops. Occasionally one of them would strike out and lash a goblin for no apparent reason other than their own sick entertainment. Then all four would laugh when each goblin cried out and worked furiously for an hour or so, thinking he might avoid another lashing if he worked harder.

Behind the four dark dwarves was a large stone building that was protected by the wall. There was a great doorway that extended beyond Therrig's ability to see in the dark. The frame was ornate and covered in intricately carved stones. The structures looked very familiar to Therrig, but he couldn't place his finger on why. The roof of the building was made of stone also, but it was constructed with thin rock-like slabs, much like the humans' wooden shingles, to displace any water that may drip from the giant stalactites that hung overhead. The buildings were amazingly crafted and there was not a single square inch of them that had not been carved by an artesian.

Therrig paused at the thought of how long it would take to carve such designs on an entire building. Many of the designs were worn or damaged and it was obvious that the dark dwarves had nothing to do with the artwork of the city. He surmised that this was probably the home of some other dwarven clan that the despicable dark dwarves had conquered. Therrig fought the strong urge to leap over the wall and cut down the dark dwarves where they stood, but he knew that would solve nothing, and only alert the masses to his arrival before he could make his way into the heart of the city. Therrig wasn't exactly sure how he would enact his plan, but he knew that the dark dwarf leadership was set upon the "might is right" principle. He hoped that he could somehow overthrow the current leader and take charge of the city—quite a difficult task, he reminded himself, and he decided that getting accepted in the general culture would be his first priority.

Therrig slowly climbed down from the wall and made his way along the southern part of the city. Everywhere he went there were amazingly crafted buildings and structures. He saw countless tributes to Durion, the dwarven mountain god, and even a few altars. Therrig struggled to understand why the dark dwarves would have altars to the mountain god. Dark dwarves usually worshipped sinister gods, like Kobli or Rha-Cordan, not a surface dwelling god. But as Therrig passed by countless altars to the mountain god, it was undeniable to him that his dark cousins had taken a liking to Durion.

Therrig was almost halfway around the southern tip of the city when he saw it. It was as if he had been stabbed through the heart with a molten hot stake. Standing before him was the depiction of a great dwarf. The statue was almost forty feet tall, and though it had been severely damaged and defaced, there was no mistaking it. The figure wore a great helm that had horns jutting out from either side. It was an open-faced helm that revealed the steady face of a proven warrior, yet the gentle, kind-hearted eyes of a father. The dwarf's thick beard was long and unbraided, extending well below his belt line. He wore a glorious suit of finely crafted plate armor that bore many nicks and scratches in it from the dark dwarves trying to deface the imposing figure. The legs were severely damaged, with most of the stone around them knocked away revealing a solid core of trinium, the strongest known metal. The base of the statue was torn away, revealing the thick trinium core that extended below the surface, keeping the statue from being knocked down. The figure held a great hammer that housed a huge blue jewel on each side of its head. The jewel still shined brightly, illuminating the area with a soft azure hue in all directions. Therrig stood before the awe inspiring statue of Midagord Milence Stormhammer, first king, and founder, of Clan Stormhammer. Suddenly a torrid of emotions

291

ripped through the renegade dwarf. He recalled playing around the statue when he was a small boy after he and some of his friends had completed their lessons for the day. He chased his friends, and they chased him, in a never ending game of tag. Therrig remembered sitting at the base of the statue when he first heard the screams. His family ran around their buildings frantically trying to hide, while his father rushed out of the house in his armor and held the family hammer. It was a brilliant war hammer that glowed scarlet at the head. Therrig could taste the danger, and ducked behind the base of the great statue. The statue of the king always made him feel safe.

Therrig could see thousands of figures erupting from the north passage, followed by a great beast. The creature had a long serpentine head and great wings that were twice as long as its body. The heat spectrum of breath was so cold that it was black. It was so black it seemed to draw in all the light from around it. Therrig had never seen such cold in his young life. He remembered the sound of steel ringing against steel and the anguished cries of women and children as the dark invaders swept from house to house killing all of the inhabitants. Yet, Therrig remained hidden in the southern-most part of town, behind the feet of the great king and warrior, Midagord. He watched as a small faction of his kin formed a line of defense atop the hill on the west end. They were outnumbered one hundred to one, but they fought valiantly. For every one that fell, fifty of the enemy fell, but soon they were forced to withdraw further south. It was as if the plague of dark dwarves, led by the white dragon, methodically purged the city of his kin from north to south. Yet, Therrig had been undetected under the watchful eyes of his king. The young dwarf saw the last of his brethren fall at the western front that they had held for so long. He saw hundreds of dark dwarves rushing down the eastern trail toward his house. Therrig stared in utter fear at the horrific beast that unleashed a breath attack that was so cold it was as if the abyss itself had opened up and begun to swallow the buildings and towers of his home city. Yet he hid, cowering under the feet of his king. Therrig knew that his king would save them. He would stride up confidently and challenge the evil beast, just as he had done in the past to invaders. Therrig had no doubt his king would slay the white lizard with a single blow and then glare at the dark dwarves so menacingly that they would either throw down their weapons and flee in terror, or weep and cower, begging for forgiveness for their evil deeds. The king did not come, yet still, he waited.

The sound of fighting grew ever so near, so close that the copper smell of death assailed his nose as it floated past him, and still he waited. He could see the dark dwarves as they kicked in the door to his home and entered. He heard the screams of his mother and sisters as they were cut down, and he watched in horror as the dark fiends erupted from his home with his mother's head on a pike. He watched as they laughed and kicked his sisters' heads around on the ground for sport.

Therrig buried his face in his hands, not able to bear the memory of what he had witnessed. The young dwarf's spirits were lifted somewhat when he saw his father run to him from the west trail. His father was covered in blood and bore wounds in many places. There were seven other dwarves with him, including the king and his son, Prince Amerix Alistair Stormhammer. He told his father that he had been brave, but he had not. He wanted to tell his father that he tried to stop them from killing his ma' and his sisters, but he had not. He tried to speak but all that came out of his mouth was a pitiful cry of defeat. Tears streamed down his bare face and soaked his shirt as he moaned in agony at the horror he had endured. His father grabbed him firmly by his shoulders and looked him straight in the eye. Therrig could hear his father as if he was there again. His father's voice was as angelic as a choir of angels to the renegade dwarf.

"Son, always know that I love thee. Go with Amerix and the others. Yer ma' and sisters have been wronged. The king and I cannot let that crime go unanswered. We will catch up as soon as we are done," his father said as he drew his hammer and started off to his house with the king. Therrig remembered seeing the king wearing little armor but wielding the mighty hammer he was known for. Therrig recalled nodding his head slowly as he reluctantly began talking to the others. They roughly pulled him into a small boat and frantically started rowing into the southern cave of the river that ran through his home city. He remembered looking back the whole way, desperately searching for his father, who Therrig would never see again.

Therrig came to his senses as wet tears ran down his dirty, blood-stained face. He glanced around again and realized where he was. He was cowering under the base of the statue again; only this time, the statue's legs were smashed and damaged. The beautiful golden plaque had been ripped off and defaced, but the hammer still shined bright as it did when he was a boy. Therrig wanted to cry, to hide, to run away again, but he glanced down at the stone hammer that was in his hands. He looked at his once weak and boyish arms that were now strong and powerful. Hate filled his heart. He stood fully erect and stepped out from behind the stone statue and stared at the house that was his as a boy. As he placed one foot in front of the other he could hear again the screams of his mother and his sisters. Therrig took deep breaths as he walked up to the doorway. The portal had never been repaired. He could still see dried blood on the inside of the walls when he walked in. The renegade dwarf's knuckles turned white from gripping the stone hammer so tightly. He could see a female dark dwarf standing in the kitchen area where his mother once stood. She was singing while he could hear two small children playing in the other room.

I'sa gots a pie for yous, my dear, my dear.
I'sa cooks it hots for yous, my dear, my dear.
and evens thoughs hots, hots
and the stoves I'sa foughts n' foughts
I'sa do for yous, my dear.

The singing was cut short by a wicked slice from Therrig's stone hammer. The heavy weapon hit the woman in the back of the head, splattering blood all over the wall and sending her lifeless body headlong onto the counter. The renegade dwarf smiled in satisfaction as the twitching body of the female dark dwarf convulsed and fell onto the floor. He quickly stepped to the side of the doorway and placed his back to the wall that led to the living area of the home. He recalled walking into the kitchen from that area as a small boy to ask his ma' what she was cooking for dinner. She would shoo him out with a laugh.

A small boy walked in from around the corner. He looked like any other small dwarf, except his skin was a pale gray and his eyes were without pupils, designed to see only with infravision. The boy started to cry out at the sight of his mother on the floor bleeding, but

294

Therrig's hammer silenced him before he could utter a single sound.

Therrig roughly kicked the body of the small boy next to the woman and it thudded sickly on the stone floor as he headed into the living area. The room was nothing like he remembered, except for the design. The once grand stone furniture was worn to indiscernible shapes, and there were no tapestries hanging on the walls like when he lived there. He could hear a young girl singing in the far room that was his as a child. A sense of jealousy pervaded him and baleful revenge wafted over the renegade dwarf. He stepped into his old room and silenced the little girl as she played with a wooden doll, oblivious to the murder she was about to fall victim to.

Therrig carried the body of the small girl into the kitchen by her hair and tossed her lifeless form to the floor. He imagined that his mother and sisters were piled in a similar way when the dark dwarves killed them. Therrig stepped over the dead and placed the heavy stone hammer on the counter, removing a sharp dagger from the drawer next to the wash basin. He turned to the bodies in remembrance of the fate his mother and sisters suffered, though he was sure to have more sport than they did.

*　　*　　*

Lance shook Ryshander's hand firmly. "Well if you must be off, my friend, it was a great pleasure meeting you. Had it not been for you and Kaisha, I might not have survived the battle with Grascon."

Ryshander nodded his head slowly. He was a little uneasy at being called anyone's friend. "I am sure you had the battle well in hand, my young mage. All we did was help tie a few loose ends for you," he said as he motioned over to Kaisha, who was taking a deep draw from her flagon of cider. "She promised to decipher some elven for you. We cannot stay here any longer, but we are heading south, towards the southern part of Beykla. It seems they feel the way the king had dealt with the dwarves has been wrong and they blame him for the war. Whether it is true or not is no concern of mine, but I tend to agree with them. We will spend a few days in

295

each town, until we reach a small settlement north of the great mine. It is called Terrace Folly. Have you heard of it?"

Lance frowned and turned to Jude. The big swordsman shrugged his shoulders and waved his large hand, trying to get the barmaid's attention so she would refill his mug.

"Well, I guess we haven't, but as soon as we are done here, I hope to look you up," Lance said as he placed his right hand on Ryshander's shoulder. He hadn't received any clerical healing on his left arm yet, but the clerics were supposed to be at the Blue Dragon Inn soon. The inn hadn't suffered much damage, and the innkeeper, who never missed an opportunity, set up shop, hired new barmaids right away, and began to get as much of the Westvons' gold as possible.

Ryshander uneasily accepted Lance's hand and stood up from the charred table. The wererat thief gave a farewell wave, then he and Kaisha departed out the front door of the charred common room.

"Strange pair," Jude said as he took a sip from his newly filled mug.

Lance turned his chair and faced his large friend. "Yea, you would think they were related, with that same nervous face twitch."

Jude took another large draw from the mug and shook his head, spilling some of the contents from the corner of his mouth. He wiped the froth away from his chin with his sleeve and smiled. "Nah, I was talking about the way they fought. They weren't that good of sword fighters, but they were seldom wounded from the dwarves' weapons. In fact, I think Ryshander hadn't been hurt at all until he fought that big dwarf next to the bridge—ya know, the one Kaisha dumped over the edge," Jude said as he made a heaving motion.

Lance frowned and rubbed his forehead with his good hand. He was tired from the fighting, and some of the militia reported that there were still dwarves barricaded up in some of the eastern buildings near the coliseum. The whole event was very taxing on the young mage.

Jude sensed his friend's exhaustion, which made the large swordsman more aware of his own. He leaned back in his chair and propped his feet up on the charred table, causing dark soot to crunch under the weight of his boot. "Ya know, my friend, I don't care if they were parishioners of the dark gods themselves. They helped us out of a tight spot and even saved that knightly fellow. In my book, face twitching or not, they are all right," Jude said as he took a final draw from his third mug of ale. He hammered the flagon down with a smile and let out a light belch.

Lance nodded distantly. "But don't you think it was kind of strange that they seemed to appear at the most opportune times?"

Jude shrugged his thick muscled shoulders as he held his mug aloft for the serving wench to refill. "You mean stranger than a thousand dwarves spilling from the sewers of a Beyklan city and killing hundreds of townsfolk?" Jude asked cynically.

Lance chuckled, but didn't reply as he rubbed his aching shoulder. What Jude said rang true, but it still seemed to Lance as if the pair were following them, although he could not figure out why.

Jude leaned forward after the serving wench refilled his mug. "Look Lance, I find this whole stinking city strange and twisted. I want to leave as soon as possible and return home. We are lucky we didn't get ourselves killed with this fool adventure."

"You are right, my friend. I no longer have the money to pay your wages. You are free to go home to the squalor you were living in," Lance replied bitterly.

Jude frowned and slammed his mug down, sloshing ale on the charred table and the floor. He raised his large hand and shook his thick index finger at Lance. "You damnable ass! I didn't come on this little trip because of your gold. I came because I knew you would go on this fool journey with or without me, and I knew someone was going to have to save your puny neck, and I'm quite pleased at the many times I have successfully done so," Jude growled.

Lance was surprised at Jude's anger. He hadn't meant what he said the way it came out, and offending his lifetime and only friend was not what he intended. "Look Jude . . ." Lance offered softly. "I didn't mean to insult you. I . . ."

Jude cut in and held his hand up to stifle any response from Lance. "Say no more, my friend. I was needing a little adventure in my life, whether I was willing to admit it or not, and I would be glad to travel with you and save your neck as many times as need be—all in the name of friendship," Jude said as he leaned back, placing his feet back on the old burned table.

Lance smiled wryly. "You mean like the time Grascon came into the room and you were lying on the floor while my superior skill and power overwhelmed the enemy that felled you?" Lance said with a chuckle.

Jude frowned at first, but could not contain a chuckle himself, and soon both had a hearty laugh. "Don't get me started," Jude gurgled and raised his mug in the air. "A toast to friendship," Jude offered.

"To family," Lance corrected him.

Jude nodded. "To family."

The pair finished their mugs and were sitting contentedly in the burned out common room of the Blue Dragon Inn when three men in brass-colored scale mail and long red silk capes came in. They had long swords that hung confidently at their sides and their helms were opened-faced with chain bishop collars around their necks. Three men strode in behind the armored soldiers wearing thick violet robes with bright orange fringes and cuffs. The robed men each displayed a holy symbol depicting golden balancing scales, crossed by a gavel, and they were in their early to late twenties. Another man stepped into the room behind them wearing a green silk tunic and breeches. He held a scroll case in one hand and a strange looking rod in the other.

"I am looking for Lance, Jude, Ryshander, and Kaisha," he said.

Lance raised his good arm and winced as the movement hurt his injured shoulder. "I am Lance," he said, then motioned to Jude, who was soliciting the serving wench for another mug of ale. "And this is Jude."

Jude nodded his head as he took a drink from his flagon.

"What can we do for you?" Lance asked.

"The duke sends his regards and offers healing services from the church of Stephanis. Where are your companions?" the man asked.

Lance sat forward in his chair. "They left already—said something about going to Westvon. Why do you ask?"

The man in the green tunic displayed a look of anger and dis-

298

appointment that didn't seem to coincide with his response. "They were to receive accommodation for their bravery."

Lance nodded hesitantly, but Jude studied the armed men. They began a sweep of the common room and then started up the charred wooden stairs to the inn's rooms. Jude motioned to Lance and twitched his head at the men as they started up the stairs. Then the priests laid their hands on Jude and Lance. They could feel the bizarre warm sensation as their wounds were magically healed, and Jude focused on the armed men as they disappeared from sight.

"Where are they going?" Lance asked as he marveled at the complex weaves of magical energy that the priest used to heal him. What fascinated Lance the most was that the priest didn't seem to guide the weaves at all—they seemed to move on their own, as if they understood the command and were simply following a routine order. For all of Lance's spells he had to guide each individual strand.

The man in the green tunic shifted uneasily. "They are checking to see if there are any dwarves left in the building—just a common procedure that you needn't concern yourselves with."

Lance shrugged his shoulders, but Jude kept his muscles tense, prepared to draw his great sword if needed.

Soon the priests were done healing them and the three armed guards came back down the stairs. "If you see Ryshander or Kaisha, send them to city hall so they can pick up their reward," the man in the green tunic said as the group turned and exited the charred common room.

Jude shook his head as he held his mug aloft for yet another refill. "Those men were not looking for dwarves and I seriously doubt they were hoping to give Ryshander and Kaisha any kind of a reward that they might have wanted."

Lance nodded. "I figured that group had a different agenda. That's why I told them they were heading to Westvon, though I doubt they believed me."

Jude shook his head in agreement. "No matter. Let's get out of this Rha forsaken town. I don't care where we go, as long as it is away from here."

Lance pondered the encounter for a moment. "Why didn't that group question where that knightly fellow was?" Lance asked.

Jude smiled as the serving wench refilled his mug. He took a long deep draw and wiped his mouth with his dirty sleeve. "I don't know, maybe he was part of the city's fighters and they already took care of him," Jude asked more than said.

Lance stared at the black charred table in thought. "Maybe, but I doubt it. This whole city has a hidden agenda if you ask me, but I don't really care, so long as it doesn't involve us."

Jude nodded.

"That's no way for a group of brave freedom fighters to talk," came a voice from the doorway of the common room. Lance and Jude turned to see the knightly figure that battled the dwarf on the bridge. He stood a full six foot two inches tall and was adorned in his plate armor. The slash wounds were repaired and the dents had been pounded out. The armor was polished bright and he wore a vivid violet cape with the symbol of the scales and the gavel, like the robed men that just spoke with them wore. His short sword was in a scabbard that was lashed tightly against his leg, and an empty scabbard for a long sword hung at his side.

Lance smiled and stood up, extending his hand to the imposing man. "Finally I get to learn the name of the mysterious champion that battled the dwarven nightmare."

The armored man took Lance's hand and shook it. "I am Apollisian Bargoe of Westvon and champion of justice," Apollisian said with an iron smile.

"I am Lance Ecnal and this is my friend, Jude," Lance said as he pulled out a charred chair and bid Apollisian to sit.

The paladin sat down and placed his armored hands on the burnt table. "I wish I could visit and trade tales, but I am looking for a friend of mine, who I fear may have perished in the fight. Her name is Overmoon. She is an elven archer and I hoped you may have seen her."

Jude said nothing and took another drink from his flagon. When he finished he sat up in his chair and puffed out his chest, obviously intimidated by the imposing figure who sat at their table.

Lance tapped his head as he replayed the events of the battle over and over in his mind.

"I don't think I recall any archers during the battle, let alone an elven archer," Lance said remorsefully. He could see the disappointment in Apollisian's face.

"I'm sorry," Lance said.

Jude cleared his throat. "What about the woman who was on top of the inn when we were fleeing. She was very small and was using a bow."

Apollisian nearly knocked the table over as he leaped to his feet. His chair tumbled behind him. "Yes! She was on top of the inn laying cover fire for me and Victor. Where did she go?" Apollisian pleaded.

Jude leaned back in his chair to distance himself from the excited paladin. "I don't know where she went. We saw the fires in the west and decided that east was the best way to flee town. So Lance and I darted back down the stairs."

"How do you get to the roof from here?" Apollisian asked.

Jude motioned to the stairs, and before he could say anything else, Apollisian was in a full run. When he bounded up the stairs Jude shook his head and took another drink. "That fellow gets excited easily."

Lance nodded. "But surely you would be excited, too, had we been separated in a terrible battle."

Jude shook his head as he finished the mug of ale and plopped it down on the table.

"Nah, I would be counting my blessings to be rid of the bane known as Ecnal," Jude said with a chuckle. Lance flicked a piece of burnt wood at his friend and they shared an enthusiastic laugh.

*   *   *

Amerix awoke to another bright shining day in the hot sun. The weather was progressively turning cold and the trees near the edge of the river seemed to have lost a third of their leaves in the last few days that Amerix had lain on the small sandy beach. He rubbed his dry callused hands over his cold bare arms. The old dwarf was, for the most part, a victim to the elements without his clothing. He glanced over to the blood-stained leather tunic and breeches that lay in a heap where he left them when he emerged from the cold swift river. He considered placing the ragged clothing back on, but it was as if he was donning a former skin of his old self. Amerix found it odd, but he had no desire to even resemble that creature that was formerly called Amerix Alistair Stormhammer.

The renegade dwarf stared off into blank nothingness as he recalled the day his home city was attacked by the dark dwarves and the white dragon. The invaders erupted from the northern river cave that cut the large dwarven city in half. He had been at the palace when they hit, training with his axe and a hammer. While his father rushed out to meet the invaders, young Amerix was sent to oversee the evacuation of the women and children. His father's commands had infuriated him. He had just graduated from the academy in top honors and no dwarf in all of Dregan City, save for his father and some of the top military commanders, could best him in combat, yet he was sent to do a whelp's job. Looking back, Amerix had the wisdom to see it was just a father looking after his only son, but at the time, Amerix saw it as his father lacking any faith in his battle prowess. Amerix realized later that if he had fought in the horrible battle, he would have surely died. Every dwarf who fought on the front lines died, save for his father. The king of Clan Stormhammer battled all the way to the final dwarf at the southern end of the city. Amerix recalled back to when they reached the southern river cave and spied a young whelp cowering under his father's statue. One of the masters-at-arms, Vrescan Alistair Delastan, Amerix's older cousin, cried out that the whelp was his son. King Midagord and Vrescan exited the boat, scooping up the boy and placing the whelp in the boat. They then went off to fight side-by-side against the dark invaders. Amerix pleaded for his father to flee with them, but the old king smiled sadly into his son's eyes and said he could not. Amerix recalled his father's voice on that frightful day all too clearly.

"There is a duty that I must do, my son—a duty that you are just beginning to remotely fathom. The mantle of a king is a heavy mantle indeed. Vrescan's family has been slain, as has our own. Take the boat and sail south. The river will open up into a valley near the human kingdom of Adoria," Midagord said as he hastily removed his plate armor. The old king placed them at the feet of his only son and fought back tears of pride as he recalled when his father had given him the very same honor by bequeathing him the family's breast plate and helm.

As he stared up into the cold blue eyes of his father, Amerix knew at that moment he would never see him again. He started to protest, but he was silenced by his father's stern raised hand.

"Take this wisdom with you as you take the armor of

Stormhammer, my son. For one day, you may be a king. Always know that any man can wear a crown, but know that only a king can hold his head up high when the fates of his people are his to bear," Midagord said as he grasped his son by each shoulder sternly. After a long pause of staring into the young blue eyes of Amerix, Midagord turned and purposefully marched past the great statue that was erected to depict his strength and honor.

Amerix watched helplessly as his mentor, his king, his father, charged into a battle that could not be won, with the cry of vengeance on his lips.

Amerix did as he was told. He sailed south into the valley and eventually settled with a clan of dwarves in the Pyberian Mountains called Stoneheart. He married and had a son. Amerix never forgot what his father said to him, even though he had changed in ways his father would never understand. The world was different now than it had been when he was a whelp. The renegade general stared as he had a few more fleeting thoughts, then glanced down at the pile of rags that was once a fine set of padded armor he wore the day he sailed out of Dregan City. He found it fitting that the rags now lay soiled and dirty on the shore of a nameless beach of the Dawson River. Amerix had spent all of his adult life trying to seek personal atonement through battle for the loss of his entire way of life. The old dwarf chuckled when he realized that only in defeat had he achieved atonement. Amerix cracked his first genuine smile in so long that he couldn't recall the last one he had. He had managed to find reprieve in the knowledge that his soul was not determined by the battles he won, not by the enemies he slew, or the great armies he crushed. He realized that his soul was determined by no one other than himself. The ancient dwarf rubbed his arms in an attempt to warm them in the cool autumn morning.

"I'll come home to you soon, Father," he whispered to the wind. "But first, there are two enemies I need to slay."

*   *   *

Tharxton sat on his magnificently crafted throne in the grand palace ballroom that was located in the middle of the fabled dwarven city of Mountain Heart. In front of him, the polished marble floor was filled to the brim with politicians and other influential

303

persons of Clan Stoneheart. The young king rested his weary head on his ceremonial armored hand as he listened to the ramblings of three thin, astute looking dwarves dressed in fine blue tunics. His other hand methodically twisted and pulled on the ends of the braids of his thick red beard. The face the young king wore was one of great sadness and vicious contempt. He had returned to his home to find that the renegade general had led his army further south and into a second battle with the humans. The old dwarf had met defeat and had most likely been slain. The remainder of the army returned to Mountain Heart at the instruction of their commanders and now faced trial for treason and desertion. The king had weathered the other trials with patience and sullenness, but now he had reached the commanders of the army. They were second only to Amerix himself. The voices of the pleading barristers that surged in the commander's behalf echoed in his unconsciousness as they announced the last commander to be tried. Tharxton forced his weary mind back into the chamber and clear from his intermittent doldrums.

"My king, Commander Fehzban was to follow all of Amerix's orders. Amerix was the first general, and the commander had no other recourse except to follow the general's commands," the thin dwarf said as he paced back and forth before the chained commander who merely stood in silence in the great hall with his greasy, dirty hair covering his face as he stared at the polished floor. Behind them hundreds of dwarven officials and cabinet heads listened on intently, occasionally muttering to themselves about well-placed strategic arguments from both sides. Tharxton had spent the last few weeks listening to the pleas of the army's officials. He had ordered only a few executions of soldiers that he was sure, beyond a reasonable doubt, had committed atrocities in the eyes of Leska. The young king had the aid of his clerics and priests in the trials, but he issued at least some kind of punishment to each and every dwarf who had participated in the battles. Some ranged from dismissal from the service and loss of weapon privileges, to banishment. But a few not only were banished, but had their names stricken from the clan's records as if they had never existed.

Tharxton had worked his way from lowest in command to highest, next to General Amerix Alistair Stormhammer, who was considered dead. That left only Commander Fehzban to stand before him and be judged. The young king asked for personal accounts from other officers and soldiers alike. He used the magic of his priests to ensure the truth was being told, and had executed anyone who tried to lie during the proceedings. It soon became unnecessary to use any truth spells after the soldiers witnessed the results of lying, but the king used them anyway. He wanted no doubt as to the accuracy of his verdicts. Tharxton became enraged when he learned that the paladin, Apollisian, the elf, Alexis Overmoon, and the paladin's squire, Victor, had blood shed by his troops for a second time. He was even more outraged at the retelling of the story when the elf was brought before Commander Fehzban. Tharxton cursed aloud in the presence of the clergy and threw his goblet of wine in the face of the commander. Fehzban merely closed his eyes and accepted the taint of wine as Tharxton announced his judgment.

"If the damned general would have ordered ye to leap into a pit of vipers, me thinks you would have smiled as ye fell," Tharxton screamed as he rammed his fist into his hand. Fehzban shook his head slowly from side to side and started to respond, but when his ashamed eyes met his king's, he silenced himself in shame and hung his head low, staring at the floor once again.

The weary king shook his head and began again more slowly and solemnly. "The most grave punishment will befall you, Commander Fehzban. For your sins against Clan Stoneheart, you are hereby banished. Your name will be blotted out of every book, every tablet, every plate that exists in Clan Stoneheart's archives. Your family will be mandated to move from your home and it will be destroyed. They will destroy everything they've owned from this day and before. They are not to have one single token of your existence. You are to leave Mountain Heart, never to return under penalty of death," Tharxton commanded as he looked over the astonished crowd that had jammed into the room of the palace. "And further, if the name Fehzban ever escapes the lips of any persons, regardless of age, race, or clan, in our great city of Mountain Heart, from this moment to the end of time, their fate will mimic his. So teach your children well, and make them mind the law, for I will not be lenient to any violators."

The onlookers and other dwarves in the hall all mumbled and gasped in shock. They obviously felt the punishment was grave and not befitting the crime, though Tharxton was not issuing the sentence based on the crime Fehzban committed. He issued the order based on the result that was sure to come from the crimes that were committed: undeniable war with the humans. "The law shall remain until our grandchildren's grandchildren cannot recall the horrors that Commander Fehzban has committed in this clan's name." The king turned his head, regarded the teary eyes of his once faithful commander, and spoke much softer. "There is a price to pay to be a leader of our brethren, Commander. I pay this price now, as do you."

Fehzban lowered his head and wept as the king finished his sentence. His tears ran down his dirty face and soaked into the filthy gray prison rags he had worn since his return to Mountain Heart weeks prior. Fehzban knew he would face grave charges, but he felt he had no other recourse than to follow the orders of Amerix during the mandate of war. Looking back, he realized that his actions would probably lead the Beyklans to make war with Clan Stoneheart until the clan was no more. Yet Fehzban kept his head lowered, unable to look at a single face that bore down on him as Tharxton finished his declaration of castigation.

"Fehzban Algor Stoneheart, you are hereby denounced from Clan Stoneheart, and denounced from the dwarven race for crimes against Leska's divine teachings, and crimes against the morality of good. You will be forever known as the nameless and you will be stripped of everything that was yours before today. Your hair and beard will be burned off with acid, never to be grown again. You will be branded iniquitously so that wherever you go, those that have reason will see your mark. May Leska send your soul to the dark clutches of Kobli for the damnation you have wrought on us all," Tharxton announced as he slammed his gavel down on the arm of his throne and stood erect, eyeing the cowering, weeping Fehzban. The crowd stood up, quietly mumbling as Tharxton slowly rose from his desk and walked past Fehzban toward the door of the palace throne room.

Fehzban wanted to look at the face of his king one last time, but he could not. Instead he stared at the hardened boots of a king that was no longer his.

Fehzban was roughly pulled down a dark corridor from the throne room. The passage reeked of feces and urine and Fehzban could hear the moans and shouts of prisoners who littered its halls. He was blindfolded and shackled, not even allowed to look upon the walls of his once loved city's dungeons. The ringing of his short shackled steps echoed in his mind, as he was oblivious to where he was being taken. He felt himself being led into a small room that had a strange pungent odor. He was roughly forced backward into a greasy wooden chair as large metal clasps were locked around his legs, arms, and waist. He felt no panic, no fear, no remorse, and Fehzban cared not if he lived or died. Though he was saddened to a state of shock, he could sense the movement around himself and could hear the pop of several corked bottles. When the dwarven sentries removed his blindfold, the dirty rag fell around his neck and Fehzban looked around. He was in a small room that had no doors or windows. The walls were stained with dried blood and had small patches of dark green moss that grew on them. The ceiling was bricked stone, just like the walls, but there was no moss or dried blood on it. There was a large wooden table at the far end that contained many small leather cases with large metal instruments sticking out, and one bull's-eye lantern with its shield facing out from the room, making the light reflect off of the walls, giving the room an eerie kind of glow. Some of the instruments on the table had sharp, knife-like edges, and some were serrated like a tree saw, but each leather container holding them was covered in blood stains. Next to the leather instrument packages there were three small dark glass vials. Their corks had been removed and placed on the table. The bottom of the corks were more sponge-like than cork-like. Fehzban's chair was against the wall near the only entrance into the room and was made with a strong sturdy wood. The metal shackles that were affixed to it must have been bolted in the back, because Fehzban couldn't so much as budge them.

The door opened up and a squat-looking dwarf came in. He was an old dwarf and had white hair and a beard. He was bald on the top of his head, and his beard was long but thin, hung loosely from his chin, and bobbed when he spoke. Fehzban focused more on his rotten yellow teeth and his pungent breath than on what he said.

"Ye has been bad boy? Yes?" the old squat dwarf said with a wicked smile.

307

Fehzban scrunched his nose at the foul odor that came from the old dwarf's mouth.

"Yes, ye had been bad. What's yer name, bad boy?" the old dwarf asked.

Fehzban said nothing. He was more fixated by the dream-like events that were unfolding before him.

The squat dwarf tightened his fist and struck Fehzban in the face. Pain erupted from Fehzban's mouth as his tongue swished his broken front teeth amid a mouthful of blood and saliva. The once proud commander's eyes went wide as if the punch had ripped him from his mind's secure hiding place. The fallacies that he clung to, as he hoped against hope that he was dreaming, came to an abrupt end. He smelt the strong acrid odor from the three vials on the table. He noticed the thick layers of dried blood that lined the walls of Fraitizu's workshop. Fraitizu—the name echoed through the corners of his mind. The old dwarf was the clan's interrogator of prisoners who were sentenced to die. If the clan cared little what happened to the prisoners, they sent them here. A profound sadness swept over him as he knew no dwarf had ever been sent to Fraitizu's lair before. The place was reserved for orcs, goblins, and other wicked creatures. Fehzban quickly pushed the thought from his mind. It had to be a trick or some kind of mind torture. Surely he wasn't really meant to be here.

Another nefarious punch landed against Fehzban's right eye. A plethora of lights erupted in Fehzban's mind as his head snapped back from the blow and crashed into the hard wood backboard of the lockdown chair. Hot sticky blood dripped from a small cut under his right eye, and thin runny blood poured from his mouth and ran down his chin, before dripping on the dirty gray prison tunic he had worn for weeks.

"I asked ye a question, you stupid orc lover. But by all means, keep quiet. I heard what ye did, and I hope to beat ye until ye die. Now I asked ye, what yer name is."

Fehzban looked at the squat dwarf. His skin was pale and he wore a pair of thin spectacles. He had a strange red spot on the top of his head, where he probably once had hair when he was younger. Fehzban became so angry he wanted to leap from the chair and beat the treacherous little fiend.

Another punch struck Fehzban in the chin. He felt a large pop as his jaw was rammed hard into the back of his head. Shooting pain ripped through his jaw as he lost muscle control in the lower part of his face. His front teeth slid out of his mouth in a tiny stream of blood and spit. Fehzban vomited from the severe throbbing that was erupting from his broken jaw, and swooned. His vision became fuzzy and he could hear a steady ringing in his ears.

Fraitizu frowned. "Ah no ye don't. Ye ain't leaving my party so soon." The squat dwarf turned and went to the bench and retrieved a small white vial that was sitting behind the three black ones. He picked up the vial and uncorked it. He placed a small dirty rag over the top and briefly turned it upside down, soaking the rag with its contents. As he walked back over to Fehzban he spoke to the guards. "Ye can leave if ye want to. I'm about to get into me work."

The guards nodded and eagerly departed from the small stone room as Fraitizu waddled up to Fehzban, placing the soaked rag under the commander's nose. Fehzban tried to turn his head away from the foul smelling concoction, but he was held steady in place. To the commander's surprise, the concoction cleared his head, but the intense pain still remained. It then became clear to him that Fraitizu wanted him awake for whatever plans he had in store. Fehzban felt more hate rip through his body. He quickly dismissed it though, and rationalized that many thousands had sat in the chair before him, and surely hate had helped none of them.

Fraitizu grabbed a fistful of Fehzban's hair and jerked him close to his pale, wrinkly face.

"I am only going to ask ye one more time, then if ye doesn't answer I am going to break out my squealers," Fraitizu said as he motioned to the table containing over ten small blood-soaked leather pouches. "What is yer name?"

Fehzban wanted to spit in his face, to break the bonds that held him, reach out and crush the throat of the old evil dwarf that stood before him. But he knew he could not. So the only recourse was to placate the squat little demon until he was free.

"Ma name ith Fethsban Algo Thonhar," Fehzban tried to say through his slack broken jaw.

Fraitizu sighed and shook his head. "I figured ye to be smarter than that," he said with mock sadness that was replaced by a wicked grin. "Didn't ye hear the king say that it was a crime to say that name? Now I am going to have to punish you."

Fehzban glared as menacingly as possible for a dwarf with a right eye that was bleeding and swollen shut, who was tied down in a chair, completely immobile, and missing his front teeth, with a steady stream of drool and blood pouring from his mouth.

Fraitizu turned and walked over to the wooden table containing the many leather pouches. He mulled over them for a few moments, then made a happy sigh when he located the one he wanted to use. The interrogator meticulously opened the pouch ever so slowly and procured a long corkscrew-looking wire that was about an inch in diameter. The end had a flat, horizontal wooden handle, and the tip was serrated like a saw. He returned and stepped in front of Fehzban.

"Open yer hand and flatten it over the end of the chair," Fraitizu said with an eerie calm.

"You ticked ma," Fehzban muttered in response.

Fraitizu said nothing. He reached down and tried to move Fehzban's hand where he wanted it. Fehzban jerked his wrist and grabbed the small frail hand of Fraitizu. Fehzban squeezed with all his might. Fraitizu shrieked in pain as the bones in his hand popped and snapped. The interrogator dropped to his knees and fumbled at his belt. Tears welled in his eyes from the iron grip of his captive who shook his hand and arm. Fraitizu fumbled at his belt, removing a small hammer from his waist, and struck Fehzban in the wrist. Fehzban involuntarily let go of the wicked dwarf and cried out as the pain shot up from his newly shattered wrist. Fraitizu rubbed his limp broken hand and glared at Fehzban.

"Ye stupid ox. Now I am going to make ye wish ye were dead!" Fraitizu growled as he brought the steel hammer down time and time again on the commander's hand. Bones splintered and poked through the top of his wrist and hand, as blood dripped down the chair like a water root that had been severed by a miner's pickax. When Fraitizu finished the vicious attack, he huffed and wiped sweat from his brow as he stared at Fehzban's viciously mutilated wrist and hand. He tossed the hammer onto the wooden table with a disgusted look on his face. The small iron tool clanged and bounced around before coming to a rest near the wall. The old interrogator retrieved the corkscrew-looking tool and placed the tip on the back of Fehzban's broken hand. He slowly twisted the screw and watched in cruel satisfaction as the serrated head of the tool slowly burrowed way into the back of Fehzban's hand. Fehzban screamed in severe pain as the wicked tool burrowed into his flesh. Fehzban vomited a second time when the tip of the screw pushed against the skin on the palm of his hand. He felt his skin stretch, resisting the screw until it could hold no longer, and the tool ripped through the palm of his hand with a sickening pop.

"Ye like that, bitch?" Fraitizu asked as he spit at the feet of Fehzban.

The pain-riddled dwarf tried to answer, but his tongue only let out a pitiful moan of pain and despair. Fehzban tried to formulate a spell in his mind, but he couldn't focus through the pain. He tried to laugh defiantly, or make some other sound that was more attune to triumph, or at least a sound that would make him feel like he had some form of conquest in the face of his wicked captor, but he found he could only cry.

"Yea, ye likes it," Fraitizu said with an evil grin. "I've got some more toys for ye. Don't go nowhere, little traitor. I'll be right back," the interrogator chuckled as he turned to the wooden table loaded with the leather pouches of torturing tools, leaving the drill securely in the commander's hand. Fraitizu rubbed his chin with his good hand as he mulled over which pouch he wanted to select next. Each time he started to get one, he shook his head and looked at a different one. He suddenly smiled as an idea entered his mind and he knelt down in front of the table and opened the cabinet that was below it. He pulled out a large, rusty looking iron device. It was larger than a man's head and had knobs and screws at several joints. There was a large bar that rested horizontally under the main chassis and many leather straps ending with thick buckles on the back. The inside of the iron contraption had hundreds of tiny iron spikes that had long since rusted. Each spike was affixed to a screw and had a tiny barb on the end. Fraitizu hefted the bulky device over to Fehzban and placed it on the ground in front of him. He weakly flexed his broken hand, seemingly relishing the pain that erupted from the motion, and he gazed at his captive, who was helplessly strapped into the chair.

Fehzban didn't stare at the device in terror like most of the victims he used it on, although every person he used it on, man or beast, shrieked in terror when they saw it for the second time. Fraitizu knew he could not use it a second time because that usually

311

meant death, so he was going to make the first usage last. He hoisted the heavy iron device up and placed it around Fehzban's head. Fraitizu strapped the thick leather laces in the back and pulled them tight until he could see the skin discolor from lack of blood. The wicked interrogator liked it that way, because when he screwed the spikes in, the blood often popped out like the insides of a slug when stepped on. After he fastened the long iron bar just under the commander's chin, Fraitizu strapped it into place. He adjusted the screw on the bottom until the thick iron bar rested tight under Fehzban's chin. He then went to the back of the iron contraption and fastened it to latches located on the back of the chair, like he had done countless times before. Fraitizu hummed a little tune and smiled as he tightened everything down and made sure the head piece was securely affixed to the thick wooden chair.

Fehzban's mind raced despite the numbing pain from his hand. He closed his eyes and began a prayer to Leska. "Oh great mother of mothers, keeper of the mountains, tender of the greatest trees, honor be thy oath and deed. I ask you . . ."

Fraitizu frowned at the prayer and quickly screwed a tiny screw into Fehzban's face. Blood spurted from the wound and ran down his prisoner's cheek, but the prisoner continued his prayer undaunted.

". . . For strength to sever these bonds in thy glory . . ."

Fraitizu's eyes went wide and his jaw hung open. He quickly rushed to the front of the mask and tightened the screw that was under the iron bar resting against Fehzban's chin. The bar made it impossible for the captive dwarf to speak. Fehzban continued the prayer in his mind, though he was unsure if the spell would work, since he could not speak.

Though you cannot hear my speech from my throat, I know that you see that which is hidden and my faith is resolute. I thank you, mother of earth, for setting me free, Fehzban whispered in his head. He then opened his eyes and grinned at the nervous Fraitizu as he quickly screwed a fourth screw into Fehzban's face. Fehzban slowly flexed his powerful arms and raised them against the thick iron shackles that held him. He felt the shackles give slightly and he increased the pressure. His smile of hope quickly transformed into a torrent of despair. The once proud dwarven commander struggled to force the shackles open and tried to rip free of his evil captor, but he could not. It was in the next instant he felt the touch of Leska leave him. She had turned on him just as the multitude of his people had. He had nothing, had no one, and was completely alone. Suddenly all the pain from his body returned. He felt each tiny barbed prod that had been jabbed into his face. He felt the hot sticky spurts of blood shoot down his cheek when a new barb was slowly stabbed into his flesh. He simply wanted to die.

"Kill me, you coward," Fehzban tried to say, but the iron bar under his chin kept his mouth closed exceptionally tight.

Fraitizu walked to the front of his prisoner and gazed at his handy work. The iron mask-like structure, called a "bordeck," was perfectly in place, and the needle-like iron barbs were all deep into Fehzban's face. Many tiny streams of blood streaked down his prisoner's cheeks and soaked into his dirty prison rags. Fraitizu snickered evilly as he watched his prisoner struggle with the obvious revulsion of his fate. The wicked captor stepped closer, reached under Fehzban's chin, and began to slowly tighten the screw. The old bordeck squeaked as the iron bar under Fehzban's chin began to slowly tighten. Fehzban struggled against the pain in his jaw. He tried to shift his weight, or move his head in a futile attempt to alleviate the ever growing pain, but he could not. Fraitizu chuckled when he heard a muffled pop when one of Fehzban's teeth shattered as his bottom jaw was forced into his top by the crushing bar. Fehzban's muffled screams of pain seemed to drive the sadistic dwarf to move faster as he continued to screw the bar tighter and tighter. In mere moments, all of Fehzban's teeth were shattered, and he began to choke on the blood that was rapidly rushing down the back of his throat. Fraitizu, fearing the death of his playmate, quickly loosened the bar and looked in horrific satisfaction at Fehzban's mutilated face. He removed the bordeck from his prisoner, ripping the deep-rooted barbs out as he pulled it off. The barbs left deep lacerations in Fehzban's face from the iron mask shifting when it was tightened down. Fraitizu gently placed the iron contraption on the table and slowly picked the large pieces of flesh from the hundreds of barbs that clung to them like a hooked fish. He hummed a tune to himself that seemed to coincide with the unintelligible moans from Fehzban.

"Tomorrow, my pet, we will work on yer other hand. Ye see, ye are scheduled to be with me for some time. The king has stated that

313

I can do as I wish with you, as long as I do not harm your ears. I asked if I could remove your eyes and he nodded. I asked if I could rip out your tongue a little each day, and again he nodded," Fraitizu said as he walked over and grabbed Fehzban's face in his unbroken hand and roughly pulled it close to his.

Fehzban's eyes rolled around in their sockets. He was seemingly oblivious to the horrid captor that spoke to him. "I asked the king: Why can I do all of those things to the rest of him, but not to his ears? Do you know what the king said, my little traitor? He said: Because I want the filthy murderer of women and children to hear the screams of every man, woman, and child that comes in sight of his hideous shell. He said he wants the sound of their terrified voices to echo in his beautiful ears for all of eternity. The king said he hoped that the horrid deformities that I leave you with are so severe that you are forced to live alone and in hiding from all that you may find any solace in; that you may die alone, wounded and lost, just as you have left Clan Stoneheart," Fraitizu finished as he spit in Fehzban's face. Fehzban was oblivious to the spit that ran down his cheek. He did not take any notice of wicked Fraitizu as he blew out the lantern and left the room, locking it behind him as he went. Had Fehzban been conscious, he might have felt some kind of comfort in the darkness, but instead his mind was far away, being saved from the horrible torture his body was enduring.

Unconditional love. Women and men alike seek this out. They believe this supposed emotion can heal all wounds, win all wars, and defeat all enemies. They think the emotion has the ring of a euphoric power, though I learned long ago, it lacks any foundation more solid than the breath it takes to say it. Though many will disagree with me, there is only one setting in which unconditional love exists. That is the bond from mother to child. Notice I do not say mother and child, for the child, if horribly wronged or abused by the mother, can withdraw his or her love. Yet a mother, regardless of the evils done to her by that child, can no easier cease to love him or her, than she could make the sun cease to shine. All other kinds of love are most certainly conditional—some more than others of course, but when measured, all are conditional. I hate the phrase: blood is thicker than water. It is the sound of a fool trying to spout wisdom. In my life, as well as others, a friend is easily more trustworthy than any family member. Family members too often fall back on the adage: whatever I do, he will always be my brother. I can think of no other friendship, other than a family member, that takes the platonic love for granted. It is true when I say: one family member can do more harm to you than a thousand enemies. Believe me, it is a fact. You see, it is not the dagger that an enemy slashes at your chest that utterly defeats you. You anticipate such an attack from an enemy. There is no betrayal, no sadness; it is, in a way, expected. It is the dagger that is plunged deep into your back that can wound you to your core existence. Though pain from the stab in the back is undoubtedly severe, it is the horrible pain of the ultimate betrayal that can crush your soul.

Yes, in my life I could have counted all of my friends on each hand, and they were willing, and sometimes did, give their life for mine. Though I would have given mine for theirs, I was so unfortunate to never have had that opportunity. Yes, you see true friendship is like a soft ember glow from a campfire. It is seen best only when it is surrounded by darkness.

—Lancalion Levendis Lampara—

Eight
A Paladin's Plea

Alexis slowly climbed from the open sewer grate that led to a dark alley between two large stone buildings. The buildings were made of light brown stone that lined the foundation. The walls were made of thick wooden planks that bore many burnt patches from the battle. The alley was littered with bodies of dwarves and humans alike. Alexis stepped alongside the wooden walls of the alley and crept toward the bright street. It was mid-morning and the sun lit the cobblestone boulevard well. The elf drew her long sword, slowly making her way to the edge of the street, and peered out into the cobblestone byway from the dark alley. She saw human patrols marching through the streets calling out to any citizens that seemed to be alive. There were other groups of militiamen picking up bodies and throwing them onto hefty wooden carts. She noticed that the carts were either exclusively for dwarven bodies or for human bodies, and were thick, sturdy and made of wood. The carts' wheels squeaked as they were drawn down the road by a single horse. The horse was in poor condition and appeared old, but it was suitable for the task they had chosen for it. The humans seemed diligent in their duties, and somewhat cheerful, despite their onerous task: picking up the victims of the tragic attack.

Alexis quietly sheathed her sword, pulled her cloak over her head, and slipped into the street. She walked quickly with her head down and made her way east, away from the human patrols. The further east she went, the more sporadic the damage was. Some areas were barely damaged, and the citizens were out in force repairing their own dwellings. Other areas were so badly damaged that the duke's men were pulling any standing structure down with thick warhorses and strong iron chains. Few tried to hail her, and when they did she pretended not to hear. The militia who survived the battle were so busy with the task of cleaning up the city that they paid her little more than an afterthought.

Alexis rounded the corner by the city hall when she came to a large structure that was badly burned on the outside. Its walls were severely scorched and had gaping holes in them as well. She recognized the damaged building immediately. The Blue Dragon Inn had suffered a lot of fire damage. Structurally it appeared as if it would stand, but it had been rigorously burned. She walked to the front and saw three figures in the brass-colored scale mail armor and red silk capes of the Beyklan high guard. Behind them were three men in brightly colored robes. The robes were thick and looked as if they kept the wearer warm in the harsh autumn winds. The robes were a deep violet and bore many strange swirling patterns on the sleeves and the cuffs of the neck, near the collar. They bore religious symbols that Alexis did not recognize, while in the front of the group a small thin man wearing a silk green tunic walked purposefully across the street and led his unique looking entourage toward the city hall.

Alexis avoided making eye contact with the many militia soldiers that roamed the streets outside the inn, and gripped her cloak tightly about her face while she ducked into the common room of the Blue Dragon Inn. The common room was not as she remembered it. The once bright and vibrant room was now black and charred. All the tables and chairs were covered in a thick layer of charred wood and soot. Large tapestries that once hung from the walls were piled up in the corner, burned almost beyond recognition. There were only two patrons in the area. They were sitting at a table at the far end of the room. One had his massive feet propped on the burned table that they were sitting at, holding his mug aloft for the serving wench to fill, while the other sat across from him sipping a flagon of his own. The pair appeared deep in thought and seemed oblivious to her presence. She started to turn to the barkeeper, who was eyeing her suspiciously, when she noticed that the man sitting across from the large swordsman was the man she had seen a few days earlier in the Cadacka. Alexis could feel the instant rage beginning to build in her. She placed her hand under her cloak, readied her sword, and walked over to the pair. The large one had a great sword strapped to his back and wore a thin suit of chain armor that bore many thin cuts. One of his muscular arms rested at his side, and his weapon arm was held aloft in an attempt to fetch the serving wench. The man in the cloak didn't seem to be armed and looked up at her over the brim of his mug as he sipped. She paused involuntarily when her eyes swept across his. She was held by his gaze, taking a long look into the man's deep green eyes. She was shocked at the inner fire that danced in his emerald orbs. It was as if the human who sat before her, with the chiseled, childlike face, had an indwelt fire that he did not know he possessed. His boyish features hid the wisdom and strength that only an eternity of challenges and struggles could create. She recalled seeing the same indwelt strength in her grandfather's eyes before he passed, but to her dismay, she recalled her grandfather having only a fraction of the power that she saw in the eyes of this boy. Alexis held her hand on her sword, not drawing the blade or striking down the human as she had originally planned. Instead she just stared as if in a daze at his sparkling emerald eyes.

Lance shifted uncomfortably as the short woman stood before him. She was certainly attractive, perhaps a few years older than he. She had long blonde hair that was pulled back and hidden under the hood of her green cloak. Her eyes were an almond brown that flickered back and forth across his face rapidly. She was maybe five feet tall and her slender green cloak was draped loosely around her body. She held one hand inside, and the other was in at her side. Lance stared at her uneasily for a few moments before Jude spit out a mouthful of ale on the table. Lance jumped from his chair and looked angrily at his friend. Jude leapt up from his chair, knocking it over backwards, and drew his sword.

"Lance, step away from her, she is armed!" Jude yelled, kicking over the charred table. Lance backed away slowly and readied a spell in his mind, though he doubted she was any threat.

Jude stepped in between her and Lance. "Take your hands slowly from your cloak, madam, or I will cut you down where you stand," Jude commanded.

The woman didn't reply. She just followed Lance with her eyes wherever he went. Alexis's jaw did not close, nor did she blink as she watched Lance.

Jude nervously stepped toward the small woman. He cursed himself silently for not noticing her weapon hand under her cloak earlier. Her small stature and the way she deftly moved across the room should have alerted him that she may be hiding some kind of a sword. He could tell from her stance that she was no dunce with a blade.

"I have warned you, my lady. Now step away and show your hands or you will be cut down from where you stand."

Alexis did not move. She was barely conscious of the large man who stood next to her. She did not notice if he was armed, and she didn't care. She wrestled with the voices she could barely hear that were seemingly emitted from Lance's eyes—sounds she had never heard before; sounds that were older than time; sounds that were so muffled to her soul that she could not discern if they were sounds of laughter or horrifying screams. She stood transfixed on those dazzling emerald orbs.

Jude did not know what to do. It was obvious this woman was a threat to Lance. The swordsman was certain by the way she stood that she was indeed a danger to anyone she attacked. Jude knew if he allowed her to draw the blade that he could not see, but was surely hidden under her cloak, she could be a deadly opponent. He could wait no longer. Jude flexed all the muscles in his powerful arms. They propelled his great sword on deadly arc toward the unyielding woman who stood before him, with blinding speed. Jude watched as he struck at her, waiting for her to even slightly shift her weight in an offensive manner, but she did not. His sword whistled harmlessly past. The mighty swordsman could not bring himself to strike down a helpless woman regardless of what imaginary threat she posed. He waited for her to react to his strike and slip a blade into his unprotected ribs, but she did not move. Jude quickly regained his stance and stood amazed that the woman did not even flinch as his great sword whistled inches from her head.

"Lance, did you cast a spell on her?" Jude asked in a confused manner.

Lance shook his head. "She seems spellbound, but not by my hand," Lance said as he walked up to the strange woman. He bent down and looked into her eyes.

Alexis gazed into Lance's brilliant emerald orbs. She ignored the sword that whistled by her head. Though every instinct that dwelt within her screamed to parry the strike, she could not. Now the boy stood before her, staring intently into her eyes. The voices were becoming more audible. They were sounds of millions of souls crying infinitely for mercy that they would never receive. It seemed as if all the souls suffering from eternal damnation in the deep bottomless abyss cried out from his beautiful, but sinister eyes.

"Overmoon!" Apollisian shouted as he jumped down the bottom four stairs and ran to her. She turned her head slowly and blinked her stinging eyes repeatedly.

Apollisian ran up to her and grabbed her by both cheeks. "I thought you lost! What happened? Why didn't you come to the bridge like we planned?"

"I . . . I . . ." she stammered, trying to recall the exact events that just took place. "I was captured by dwarves," she managed to say.

Apollisian shook his head in disbelief. "How did you escape? Were you harmed? Where did they go?" Apollisian asked excitedly.

Alexis placed her delicate finger over his lips before he could go any further. "I am okay. They did not harm me past enduring. Their leader, named Fehzban, freed me as they were marching back into the under dark. I think they do not know where Amerix is," Alexis said calmly.

Apollisian glanced around the room and peeked suspiciously at the table that was flipped over. He eyed Jude's great sword that was loosed from its sheath.

"What is going on here?" Apollisian asked accusingly.

Jude stumbled over his own tongue. "Uh . . . we uh . . . she had a sword . . ."

Alexis cut in. "They thought me a threat, but no more. Tell me of Amerix. Is he indeed dead?" the elf asked, trying to distance herself from the boy.

Apollisian eyed Jude a second longer before he answered as if to convey to the giant man that if he tried to harm Alexis he would defend her with his life. "He is indeed dead. Thanks to this man," he said as he motioned to Jude with an obvious grimace on his face. "And a woman named Kaisha. They forced him over the bridge into the icy waters of the Dawson River."

Alexis turned to Jude and looked at him as if it were for the first time. "I thank you, swordsman, for your bravery."

Jude flushed at the praise from the beautiful woman. He mo-

320

tioned to Lance. "If it was not for him, I would not have been able to aid Apollisian."

Apollisian recalled the aid Jude gave him when he battled Amerix before the bridge, and how Jude had saved him there. He relaxed his glare, but he still kept a leery eye on the pair as he righted the table and pulled over two slightly burned chairs for him and Alexis.

Alexis sat in the burned chair and looked around the room. "Where is Victor?"

Apollisian glanced down and paused before answering. "Amerix killed him. He tried to aid me, even when I told him not to. I knew Amerix was too skilled for him, but he would not listen. His body is buried in the cemetery," Apollisian said remorsefully. He closed his eyes and whispered a quiet prayer. "Stephanis guide his soul to Yahna. Let him frolic in your glory and may justice prove his heart throughout."

Alexis placed her hand on the armored shoulder of the paladin. "My friend, we must talk about matters that are private."

Apollisian nodded and stood from the table. They walked up the charred stairs to the room they once rented.

When they were gone, Lance turned to Jude. "I thought you were going to kill her. Why did you swing your sword at her?"

Jude exhaled deeply as if some profound weight was lifted from his shoulders by the pair leaving the room. "She was poised to strike at you quickly. She had a sword under her cloak and she was almost ready to use it," Jude said as he tried to dry the wet spot where is ale had spilled when he kicked the table over.

"Why would she try to kill me?" Lance asked doubtfully.

Jude shrugged his shoulders. "I don't know. Why not? There are a lot of crazy people in this town. Look at that assassin. What was his name? Grascon, I think. Why would he want to kill us?"

Lance cringed. He had not told Jude that Grascon was the thief he had double-crossed to get the papers he had that were in elven. "Well, my friend," Lance stammered. "You see, the papers I have . . . they are stolen."

Jude shook his head slowly from side to side. "Figures you would keep something like that from me. Anything else I need to know about?"

Lance shook his head as Jude held his mug aloft for the serving wench to fill. "Anyway, it seems strange for someone to try to kill you over some stupid papers. I wonder, what makes them so important?" Jude asked.

Lance shrugged. "I'm not sure. I thought they were some kind of execution order or some other connection to my parents' deaths. But now, I have learned they aren't even written in Nalirian, they are written in elven. I have to wait to travel south to Terrace Folly, to meet up with Kaisha and Ryshander, before I can even read them."

Jude sighed and placed his heavy hand on his friend's shoulder. "Patience, my friend. We will find someone who can read them, rest assured."

                    *   *   *

Alexis and Apollisian stood in the dark, burned out stairwell that led to the many rooms of the Blue Dragon Inn.

"We have to go back to see my father. I think he might be connected to the Abyss Walker. I have seen it in his eyes!" Alexis pleaded.

Apollisian motioned for her to calm down. "Quiet. Do you want them to hear? Who is this Abyss Walker?" the paladin asked.

Alexis took a deep breath. "I do not know. I remember my father mentioning it when I was much younger."

Apollisian ran his hand through his long golden hair. "Alexis, we have to travel to Dawson City and avert a human counterassault against the dwarves. They will be undoubtedly prepared, and the Beyklans have seriously underestimated their number. It is obvious that the dwarves can strike any Beyklan city if given enough time. The south, who is not in favor with the king's decision about the civil war in Andoria, and not in favor with his treatment of the dwarves, is growing restless. The rumors of a coup are gaining ground, so we need to travel to Dawson and plead to the king to swallow his pride and let the dwarves be. If he presses an attack and another Beyklan city is assaulted, I feel the south might act against his throne."

Alexis's face flushed. "You humans and your ignorant priorities! I am talking about all races of the realms being slain by the Abyss Walker, and you assume that a stupid human kingdom that has stirred up a bee's nest is more important. If this man is the

322

Abyss Walker, he is prophesized to single-handedly annihilate half of the world and all of the heavens. It is written that he will bring about plagues as never seen before the beginning of time. Surely that has to rate somewhere in that moronic paladin code of yours."

Apollisian took a deep breath and closed his eyes briefly. He fought the urge to lash out at Alexis's attack on his faith. Instead he calmed himself and spoke softly. "For someone as old as you are, you act as though you are some ridiculous child who needs a good paddling. I understand that you believe in this Abyss Talker . . ."

"Abyss Walker," Alexis corrected with a stern glare.

"Whatever. You have no proof other than some feeling you got when you looked in his eyes. You want me to risk the lives of thousands of people because you say you saw something in an orphan's eye? That is ridiculous. You give me one shred of hard evidence and I will consider speaking with the Minok nation."

Alexis started to respond only to cut herself off. "I don't have any proof and I don't remember the text my father talked about word for word, but I know there is something strange about him and I believe that he is the Abyss Walker. He wears an elven Cadacka, for Leska's sake."

Apollisian exhaled slowly. "I recognize there is something strange about him, but he is no threat. I searched his soul several times. There is no evil there. He is quite selfish, but nothing evil. Nor his large friend. The fact he wears a ceremonial elven mourning cloak is no proof that he is in bed with Rha-Cordan himself."

Alexis nodded reluctantly. She did not like conceding to Apollisian. It wasn't so much that he was a human. She had gotten used to the fact that he possessed wisdom that even some of the elven elders did not have—a trait that was quite exceptional for any human. It was more the fact that he was a man. She had a strange rancor towards men. They were rash and bold, often suffering or acting of their own pride rather than of their intelligence, yet more often than not, they ruled over women. She fought the urge to shout at the paladin and instead took a deep breath to strengthen her resolve. "Okay. Let us go and plead the dwarven case to the king, but after that, I insist we travel to Minok and speak with my father, but let's ask them to accompany us so I can keep an eye on him."

"We will not waste a single moment from now until then," Apollisian said, smiling. When they walked out from the stairwell,

Jude was standing facing Lance. The two were an odd pair to say the least.

Apollisian extended his armored hand in front of them. "Lance and Jude. I am needed to speak with the king on some urgent matters. Myself and Overmoon . . ." He motioned to the elf who was standing next to him with an aggravated look on her face. She still wore her cloak up, hiding her pointed ears under thin silk folds. "We would like it if you accompanied us. The king no doubt would like to hear other firsthand accounts, and I am sure the High King of the Elven nation would like to know the pair that had helped battle the dwarven onslaught that had nearly killed his daughter."

Lance nearly swooned. Apollisian wanted to take them to see the king? The king of Beykla? The thoughts of the grand castle began to flood through his head and he was completely oblivious to the mention of the elven king.

Jude, however, was not overly impressed with the mention of kings and found it strange they had helped an elf in the battle against the dwarves.

"Are you suggesting that Overmoon is an elf?" Jude asked skeptically.

Alexis slowly removed the hood of her thin green cloak. Her long blonde braid spilled out and fell across her chest, exposing her narrow, pointed ears. Lance nearly had to catch his jaw to keep it from hitting the floor. He couldn't believe he was standing in front of a real live elf. Elves rarely ever spoke to humans, much less allowed two to travel with them. Lance made no attempt to hide his excitement, but Jude nonetheless was more than suspicious.

"Why is an elf fighting a battle that concerns the lives of only humans?" Jude asked skeptically.

Apollisian started to answer but Alexis cut him off. "My father is High King of the elven nation and has asked his personal friend here . . ." she motioned to Apollisian, ". . . to teach me the ways of Stephanis, that I might learn the rigors of true justice."

Jude was reserved, but could not deny the elf's beauty. She was small in stature, but she held herself with such an air of superiority that he did not doubt her claim of royalty.

Lance stood wide-eyed in disbelief. He wanted to rip the pages from his pack and hand them to her, hoping she would read them on the spot, but something inside of him stayed his hand. He wasn't sure what it was, but there was something she was hiding from them. Jude looked at Lance. "Well Lance, what do you say? We were getting ready to move on."

Alexis cut in. "Where were you going?"

"Back home to Bureland," Lance replied. "My father is surely worried about me. I have been gone a long time."

Apollisian nodded. But Alexis prodded further. "We could send a messenger to your father that you are safe, and that you will return home as soon as you can. I can even arrange for some monetary compensation for him if you wish. Call it a reward for helping us in battle," Alexis offered.

Lance nodded eagerly. He longed to travel with her and the paladin. She could decipher his letters a few days after they got to know one another, and his father could surely use any money he could get. "What do you think, Jude?" Lance asked.

Jude looked at him and then at Apollisian and Alexis. The elf was surely beautiful, but there was something hidden that he could not put his finger on. Jude could see the eagerness on Lance's face and he reluctantly agreed.

"Okay Lance, I'm with you wherever you need me, but I am not sure any king will find us as complimentary dinner guests."

"It is settled then," Alexis said. "We will depart early in the morning. Do you have any horses?"

"We had two," Lance said. "But I am not sure where they are or if the stables were damaged."

"The stables were unharmed. We will meet you there tomorrow at dawn. Good day," Apollisian said as he and Alexis made their way out of the common room and into the street.

Lance sat back down at the burned table. Jude sat down also and rubbed his tired brow.

"What adventure are we headed for now?" Jude asked wearily.

Lance seemed ignorant to his friend's exhaustion. "I hope you are hungry, Jude, because we are about to dine with kings."

*　　*　　*

They had flown for a few weeks, occasionally stopping to rest on top of large mountain peaks along the way. Stieny had survived on what little game he could catch with the dragon never letting

325

him wander far. The halfling had no intention of trying to escape as long as the dragon held his soul in that cursed jewel. They had finally landed on a large mountain peak in the Pyberian range. Stieny was sure the peak had a name, but he had never been to this area of the world. The halfling stood on the edge of a steep cliff looking out over a vast sea that stretched out to his north, and he gazed at the water that glittered like a myriad of shining specks of light reflected from the rapidly waning sun. The red globe, that was halved by the watery horizon, set the twilight sky aflame with deep reds and yellowish hues. The thin clouds that streaked across the sky were colored purple in the pneumatic evening canvas.

Stieny sat on the rocky face and let out a resounding sigh. The air was much crisper in Beykla than it had been in Vidora. The trees that were below him all shined amber and crimson hues from their autumn leaves. Checking his gear, Stieny removed a piton from his pack and hammered it into the side of the rocky face. Small pieces of stone splintered away from the thin crack as the metal teeth bit into the cliff. The halfling laced a thin, waxed rope through the eye, placed it around his torso harness, and wrapped it around a thin metal clip that was hanging from the back of the canvass harness next to his other coiled length of rope. He let the rope fall from behind him after he had secured a tight lashing in the piton. The rope skittered and tumbled down the cliff and jerked violently when it reached the end of length. The halfling slowly began the arduous task of repelling down the steep cliff. It wasn't that the rock face was too far for the nimble halfling to climb down that made it difficult; it was the knowledge that if he fell, he would surely perish from the plunge.

Stieny reached the end of his rope and stared up at the distance he had descended. The snow-covered peak was well over three hundred feet above him and the wax line he descended down was wavering and bouncing along the side of the cliff as a light breeze blew by. The halfling hammered in a second piton and repeated the process, descending down another three hundred feet before stopping, then removing the harness and climbing down the remaining forty feet.

When he reached the ground he tossed the leather pack containing the small metal hammer and the pitons behind one of the many large boulders that rested at the foot of the steep cliff. He had no problem finding one, as some were larger than the mountain ogres that had captured him. The ground descended rapidly from the cliff but Stieny deftly maneuvered his way between the giant boulders and thin evergreen trees that littered the side of the mountain. The halfling hiked for most of the night, stopping for only brief rests, then pushing forward. When the night sky turned into a deep azure hue, he stopped and made camp. Robins and other song birds began their songs of the day, while Stieny unpacked his bed roll. He wearily tossed the bedroll open and plopped down on it, not having the energy to crawl inside, despite the chilly autumn wind that whipped through the thick trees of the mountain plains. The little halfling closed his exhausted eyes and in seconds was fast asleep.

*   *   *

Apollisian slowly chewed his eggs and tapped his cracked wooden fork on the thick oaken plate that sat before him. He had purified the food before Lance and Jude came down, in case of poison. It was not uncommon for evil denizens to try to poison the champion of justice whenever they got the chance. Alexis stared quietly at her breakfast, humbled by the feeling of tremendous peril she got when she looked into Lance's eyes. However, Lance and Jude conversed eagerly as they enjoyed the fine breakfast that the paladin had purchased for them. Their money situation had become bleak, and they were eating leftovers from the specials of the day.

"Overmoon, did you send the messenger to Master Ecnal in Bureland?" Apollisian asked as he ate another small bite of eggs.

The elf nodded, averting her eyes from Lance. "Yes, the messenger was sent out this morning. He was pleased to be traveling south, away from the conflict. I believe he was equally happy to be delivering a message that was not military in nature."

Apollisian nodded in approval and glanced at Lance and Jude. Jude was sizing up the bar wench and paused, staring blatantly at her. She had long black hair that was pinned behind her head and wore a heavy overcoat that seemed an odd attire for a serving wench. When she finished serving, the wench awkwardly left the dining area and went into the kitchen because she noticed she was being watched.

327

"You fancy the serving wench, Jude?" Apollisian asked.

Jude turned back and picked through his eggs slowly as if searching for something. "No, not exactly. Lance and I have stayed here since we arrived in Central City. I don't ever recall seeing her, and I noticed she had a long thin dagger under her tunic, strapped tightly under her arm, as if she was trying to conceal it. It was much in the shape of an assassin's dagger. I am sure I would have remembered her long black hair," Jude replied.

Apollisian said nothing in return. He merely closed his eyes and hummed softly to himself. Alexis got up from the table and made her way to the door of the kitchen. She positioned herself on the hinge side, so if the door opened up, she would be behind the potential enemy.

Lance noticed Apollisian's and the elf's actions and readied a spell in his mind. Jude went to the front door of the common room and scanned for potential enemies outside. After a few brief seconds, Apollisian stood up from his chair and drew his sword.

"There is evil afoot in the kitchen," Apollisian proclaimed.

Alexis drew her bow and kicked the thin wooden door in. She leveled the narrow shaft around the room. It was a long room with a long flat cooking surface that lined the south wall. The cooking surface was littered with kitchen pots and pans, and on the far end were many vegetables that were being prepared for the lunch meal. There were many large wooden cabinets that rested above the counter, and a large stand-up closet that stood at the end of the room, and probably housed aprons and other cooking apparel. There were some scattered dishes on the floor and a trail of spilled ale that led out the east door into the scullery. A figure shot out from behind a large cabinet and rushed for the door. Alexis raised her bow and fired two arrows in a blink of the eye. The slender shafts whistled toward their target at blinding speed. One of the shafts hit the figure in the side just under her armpit. The green fletching barely protruded after the shaft had sunk almost completely in. The other shaft lodged deep into the figure's hip, making a sickening thud sound as it pierced bone. The figure let out a feminine cry and stumbled into the scullery room.

"Intruder in the kitchen!" Alexis shouted as she hurried to the door the figure had darted into.

Apollisian charged forward, lowered his shoulder, and

knocked the thin wooden door from its hinges as he burst into the kitchen. Small pieces of splintered wood erupted in the air as he emerged into the room. He saw Alexis rushing through the east door with her bow drawn and an arrow notched.

Jude was standing in the doorway when he heard Alexis shout from within. He heard the paladin's heavy footfalls rushing toward the kitchen so he bolted out of the common room door and ran around into the alleyway on the east side of the inn. His boots crunched under charred wood from the fires that had not been cleared from the alleys yet. Lance hurried behind his large friend, trying to keep up with his huge strides.

Alexis burst into the scullery with her bow drawn and up. She slowly stepped forward, scanning the dark room with her infravision. She didn't see anything but steadily advanced. The room was dirty and smelled of mildew. Hundreds of dirty dishes were piled up in a large wooden tub that was filled with brown stagnant water. The tub was sturdy and re-enforced with large iron bands that ran horizontally around it to keep it water tight. The water-filled tub rested against the east wall, next to the wooden door that was cracked open. Light seeped in from the door, making it difficult for Alexis to use her infravision. There was a thin wall that didn't connect to either side of the room, but acted as a partition, dividing the one room into two. There was a large counter with clean towels neatly folded next to hundreds more clean dishes that were efficiently stacked on the large counter.

Apollisian focused on his inner thoughts and hummed quietly again. He felt his soul floating from his body and drifting around the room briefly. It swooped and glided around the large room and came to rest on the black vileness of evil. He recoiled from cold touch and his face grimaced as he came out of his succinct trance. He pointed to the southeast corner of the room with his sword. Alexis nodded and advanced around the large tubs of dishes on the east side, and the paladin advanced around the piles on the west.

Jude rushed down the alley and slowed when he neared the southeastern corner. He leaned against the charred building and strained to listen as Lance came panting up next to him and placed his hand over his mouth to try to quiet his breathing in response to Jude's angry glare. Jude looked down the alleys in all directions. The Blue Dragon Inn towered above the other buildings, but the buildings were still two stories each. The alleys were dark, even in the day, and reeked with the smell of rotting flesh. The bodies were bloated and swollen and many large, late season blow flies crawled on their rotting faces. Jude ignored the repulsive sight and focused on the back door. He kept his weapon raised, and turned the weapon sideways to bring the flat of the blade down. He intended to take this person alive. This was the second unexplained attack on him and Lance, and the swordsman wanted answers.

Alexis rounded the corner and saw the serving wench huddled in a corner. She was shivering with pain, but she was not bleeding. The only part of either arrow that could be seen was the bright green fletching that was hanging out of each wound. The wench sat with her eyes closed, panting with quick short breaths as beads of sweat lined her forehead. Apollisian rounded the other corner and sheathed his short sword. He took out a fine set of polished steel manacles and placed them on the woman's wrists. She seemed oblivious to the elf's and the paladin's presence.

"Why is she not dead?" Alexis asked. "The first arrow has pierced her heart and both lungs. The other arrow perfectly stuck into her hip socket, freezing the movement of her leg, yet she lives, and look, she doesn't even bleed. What manner of wicked creature is she?"

Apollisian frowned. "I know not, Overmoon, but she surely intended our deaths," the paladin said as he removed a thin glass vile from her small belt pack. He smelled the liquid and quickly replaced the cork. "Surely some kind of poison."

Alexis kept an arrow notched in case the woman rose up, but the captive merely panted and sweat, with an occasional face and nose twitch. Apollisian searched her person and found a long thin dagger, neatly tucked under her arm near her side. He pulled the thin blade from its sheath and examined it. There was a small wooden plunger at the pommel of it, and the blade had a hollow recess at the end. There were three thin red lines on the hilt with a heart in the background.

"She is an assassin," Apollisian growled.

Alexis nodded, never taking her eyes from the strange woman. "It seems she was up to no good, but how can you be sure she is an assassin?"

Apollisian stepped away from the woman and held the dagger

up so Alexis could see it. He pressed the wooden plunger on the pommel, and dark blue liquid dripped from the hollow area near the end of the blade.

"What is it?" Alexis asked.

Apollisian kneeled down and took the sheath from the woman's side and placed the dagger in it, then stuck it in his belt line. "It's called a venom dagger—a very dangerous weapon used by skilled assassins. Rarely can a single person afford one. They are usually owned by guilds and loaned to assassins when they are assigned a job. There is a crest on this one, though I do not recognize who it belongs to. I'm sure the local magistrate will be able to tell me where it is from."

Jude could hear the elf and the paladin inside talking and motioned for Lance to enter. They pushed through the back door of the scullery and Lance crunched his nose at the odor of mildew in the room. Alexis spun around quickly, but relaxed when she saw who it was.

"We were waiting in the alley in case she tried to run out the back," Jude said as he pointed to the back door.

Apollisian nodded. "Thank you, I am glad to see you have some combat sense about you. It will surely be a benefit to have you along on the journey."

Jude nodded in thanks, sheathed his great sword, and looked at the small woman who was in shackles. Lance stared at her intently, trying to recognize her face, but he could not.

"Who is she?" Lance asked.

"An assassin of considerable skill. In fact, had I not used my ability to neutralize poison this morning before we ate, we would undoubtedly be dead," the paladin said. "I tend to attract many enemies due to my plight to seek out justice and serve it where it is needed, but rarely have I made an enemy who I have not known. And I do not recognize the guild insignia."

Jude frowned at the mention of another assassin and looked at Lance. Lance returned his look and shrugged his shoulders, then looked back at the assassin and watched as her face twitched.

"Her face just twitched!" Lance exclaimed.

Apollisian looked at the woman and back at Lance in confusion. "So?"

"She is a wererat," Jude said, remembering the way Grascon's face twitched when they battled him in their room. Lance cringed at the thought of a second wererat assassin sent for him, not the paladin.

Apollisian nodded his head in recognition at the mention of the wererat and rubbed his chin.

"That explains the lack of blood from her wounds," Alexis said. "Had I not hit the mark exactly she would have shrugged off my arrows and escaped."

"Good. That means all I have to do is remove the arrows and her unnatural healing abilities will take over, correct?" Apollisian asked.

"I think so. That is what happened to the last one that attacked me," Jude said, wincing before he finished.

"What do you mean the last one that attacked you?" the paladin asked.

Jude kicked at the ground nervously under the angry gazes of Lance and the paladin. Lance spoke up before Jude could respond. "We were attacked by one of the rat people in our room one night. Jude and I fought him before we killed him. Kaisha and Ryshander said he used to be a member of the thieves guild here in Central City years ago. We are not sure why he attacked us," Lance lied. He knew he had double-crossed the thief in Bureland, but he had only double-crossed one thief. Why was this one here trying to kill him?

Alexis frowned. "Assassins don't randomly kill or rob people. They are paid to kill, they kill for a reason."

Apollisian nodded. "Overmoon is correct. They don't choose their targets randomly. I will remove the arrows and use the zone of truth to interrogate her. She cannot lie, nor refuse to answer my questions. We will get to the bottom of this."

Lance shivered nervously. What if she was in leagues with Grascon? Blast! Lance had never thought of the thief having a partner. Lance cursed himself for not thinking of every possible outcome.

The paladin tugged and pulled at the arrow that had pierced the woman under her arm. She writhed in pain and hissed as he slowly pulled the white ash shaft from her body and marveled at the gleaming shaft, devoid of any blood. Apollisian closed his eyes and chanted. "Oh Stephanis, champion of justice, I ask that thee take away the shield of deceit that lies in this room. I ask that ye

332

open the grasp of justice and compel this being of the dark to answer my queries true as if she were filled with righteousness. In thy light I shine." When Apollisian finished his chant, Lance could feel the air thicken around him, giving him goose bumps and making the hair on the back of his neck stand on end. He glanced at Jude, who seemed oblivious to the magical change in the air around them. Lance could see millions of tiny specks of energy floating around from the corner of his eyes, but whenever he tried to look directly at them they were gone. The woman quickly came to and opened her eyes, glaring at her captors.

"Who are you?" Apollisian asked.

The woman hissed and laughed mockingly at him. "I am . . . I . . ." The assassin's eye went wide with disbelief as she struggled against the magic that compelled her to speak. "I am Kellacun," she said finally as if the struggle against the magic was exhausting.

"Why did you try to kill me and Alexis?"

The assassin grinned. "I was not trying to kill you, fool!" Kellacun said.

"You lie dog!" Alexis growled with rage as she rushed the assassin. Apollisian held his hand up, motioning for her to stop. Alexis held herself but gave the assassin a threatening glare.

"She is bound by the magic of Stephanis," Apollisian said. "However difficult for us to understand, her responses are truthful." The paladin turned and began again. "Who were you trying to kill?"

Kellacun struggled a few seconds against the magic that surrounded her, but her strength quickly waned. "The Ecnal," she said.

Lance swallowed hard and Jude angrily fought the urge to draw his sword and cleave her head from her shoulders.

"Who is the Ecnal?" Apollisian asked.

Kellacun pointed a slender finger at Lance. "He is."

Apollisian turned and looked at Lance, then turned back to the assassin. "Why did you want to kill him?"

"Because I was paid."

Lance relaxed a bit. He was comfortable in the fact he doubted Grascon would have paid anyone to help him. But then the dreaded thought of who else might want him dead replaced his previous fear.

"Who paid you?" Apollisian asked. "Was it Grascon?"

Kellacun wrinkled her nose at the mention of the exiled thief. "No, had I seen him, I would have likely killed him first, just for fun. I was paid by my guild master, Pav-co."

"Why would Pav-co want him dead?" Apollisian asked.

Kellacun shrugged her shoulders. "I'm not sure, but I think the King of Nalir was paying well over a thousand gold crowns for his head."

Lance balked. Who was the King of Nalir? He had thought he had papers from Nalir, but they turned out to be elven. Perhaps Nalir was connected to his parents' deaths after all. Perhaps it was Nalir that had ordered his whole family killed, but he had escaped. Now eleven years later, they were trying to finish the job. But why? The questions rocketed around in Lance's mind.

"Why would the King of Nalir want him dead?" Apollisian asked.

"I don't know. He probably found out that he was one of, if not the last, Ecnals alive. Since he paid us, and everyone else under the sun, huge sums of money to kill them all years ago."

Lance felt his knees waver and he had to sit down. Jude placed a reassuring hand on his friend's shoulder.

Apollisian rose, dismissed the zone of truth, and turned to Lance. "I am sorry to hear that you are an Ecnal," he said somberly. "I hope that your parents' passing has been eased by the hand of time."

Lance took a deep breath. "It has been very difficult for me. My mother and father were murdered when I was but twelve cycles old, or six years to you northerners." Apollisian nodded in recognition of the southern Beyklan ways of measuring years by the two moon cycles that take place every four seasons. Lance continued. "I managed to escape the house out the back. I ran and ran until a woodcutter named Davohn took me in. I had a sufficient life, but I am here in this city searching for answers to their deaths," Lance said, leaving out the papers he had and the fact that they were cut down by men in Beyklan high guard uniforms.

"Well, when we travel to Dawson, perhaps the king's records can shed some light on the Ecnal murders. I was but a squire when they were happening, but I remember them as if they were yester-

334

day. Perhaps the king's investigations can shed some light on them, and perhaps allow your grief to finally rest."

Lance nodded. "My thanks to you already, Apollisian."

"Mine too," Jude said. "Lance has been my friend since he came to live in Bureland. He is a good man."

"Well it seems our departure has been postponed a few hours. Alexis and I will take this prisoner here to the magistrate for trial. We will return shortly and begin our journey." Apollisian and Alexis walked back through the kitchen into the common room, and out into the street. Lance and Jude plopped down in the chairs they had been eating in. They looked at their plates and then at each other. At the same time they got up and sat down at a different table.

*　　*　　*

Amerix walked around the edge of the small sandy beach. He followed the sandy shore as it curved around the undersized river flat he had been living on, and he smiled as the warm sand crunched between his toes and the tepid autumn air gently warmed him between cold breezes. The old dwarf came to a place where the river flat ended and the cliff face began. It was a tall cliff probably some two hundred feet up, but the climb was not sheer and there were many hand-holds in which he could use to pull himself up. He was checking around the ground to find a good place to start his ascent, when he spied one of the dwarven bodies that had been tossed over the cliff and into the river. It had been swept down current and became lodged in a group of logs and rocks in an eddy created in the bend of the river.

Amerix rubbed his cold arms as he stared longingly at the thin chain armor and the heavy leather padding that the dwarf had been wearing underneath. Most dwarves were poor swimmers, and Amerix wasn't exactly skilled at it either. He argued with himself for several minutes on whether or not to retrieve the body. The chain armor was rusted from being submerged for so long. It wasn't until the body had become bloated that it had risen from the river bottom to the top. And even then, the chain armor seemed to keep the body from fully reaching the surface. The body floated just under the top of the water as it bounded back and forth against the rocky shore from the river current. Amerix made his way over the precarious rocks and lay on his belly. He grunted as he reached down and hoisted the wet, bloated body of one of his kin from the river. Amerix ignored the horrid look of death from the body as he dragged it to shore. To his surprise, when he got it to the sandy beach he noticed the body had a long sword in a fine leather sheath that hung from its back. Amerix recognized the damnable blade immediately. He grabbed the long sword by the pommel, drew it, and hoisted it over his head. He drew back as if to hurl the cursed weapon back into the river, then he paused. He had carried the damned sword since the battle of the Torrent Manor, and the sword never ceased making unbearable shrill noise. Yet as he held it aloft, staring at its beautiful craftsmanship, and the water glistening on its perfect, flawless blade, the sword made no noise whatsoever. Amerix pulled the sword close and examined it. He cautiously turned it over, waiting for the damnable shrill to begin at any minute, but it did not. Amerix shook the sword angrily. "Come on ye damn sword. What's the matter with ye? Why ain't ye screaming?" Amerix said as he stared at the wet blade as if it would respond, but instead only the chirping of birds and the constant trickle of water running in between the large rocks that lined the edge of the river flat and the cliff wall answered.

"Well if ye ain't gonna hum, then I'll carry ya. I could use a good blade," Amerix said as he piled up the leather clothing and the rusted chain armor. After scrubbing the filthy clothing in the edge of the river to get as much of the stench off as possible, the old dwarf put the suit of padded leather armor on. He then slipped the rusted chain shirt over his head and strapped to his back the leather scabbard that held the sword he had gotten from the paladin at the battle of the Torrent Manor.

Amerix spit on his hands and wiped them in the rocky dust near the base of the cliff. The chalky sand-like dust from the broken stones that fell to the river flat acted like a gripping agent for the dwarf. Once he was satisfied he had as much grip as he could get, he began to climb the sheer rocky wall.

It took him almost two hours. The climb wasn't overly treacherous, but Amerix was not a skilled climber and he often had to stop and ponder where he wanted to place his next hand hold. Once he reached the top, he pulled himself over and lay on his back breathing heavily. His malnourished body was weak and the climb had exhausted him. He lay panting for many minutes and finally sat up. The trees at the top of the cliff were beautiful. They were cloaked in many colorful oranges, reds, and yellows from the autumn season. Squirrels and other tree creatures skittered about the tops of the trees, sounding alarms announcing the appearance of danger on the forest floor.

Amerix dusted the chalky residue from the cliffs, and off of his pants and shirt, and began his trek into the forest. The dead dwarf's clothing was too small for him and it chaffed his underarms and the inside of his legs when he walked. The boots were impossible to force on, so Amerix walked barefoot. He winced occasionally when he stepped on a sharp rock, or when he walked too close to a bramble patch. Amerix knew little of the surface animals or plants. He had no idea which ones were poisonous and which ones were not. When he was a member of Clan Stoneheart, they had hunters and gatherers that had that sort of task. When he was younger and lived underground, before the attack, he seldom, if ever, ventured to the surface.

The old tired renegade general walked south, knowing that the war was north and southern Beykla was sympathetic to the dwarven plight. Amerix walked for the rest of the day, taking frequent breaks and chewing on an occasional piece of bark, or a beetle when he found one. The old general wasn't exactly sure where he was going, but he knew he was walking in the right direction.

*   *   *

It had been a few hours since Apollisian and the elf had left the burned out inn. Jude had spoken to the barkeep, Fifvel, about hiring assassins, jokingly, and the barkeep nervously laughed with the large swordsman. Fifvel's strong man, Glaszric the half-orc, had not been seen since the fighting, and the barkeep feared him dead. Lance and Jude recommended that he speak with the militia guardsmen who were assigned to retrieving the dead, thinking that they would remember picking up something as unique as a half-orc's body. Fifvel agreed and offered Lance and Jude free drinks for the afternoon. The pair were sitting at the bar, and a merchant and four of his workers had begun unloading new tables and chairs into the common room, when the paladin and the elf walked in.

"Good news and bad news," Apollisian said as he marched into the room, giving the workers ample space to unload their wares. Alexis slipped past and walked near Lance but she did not look at his face.

"What's the good news?" Jude asked as he sipped his flagon of ale with his left elbow leaning back against the bar.

Apollisian patiently waited for the men to put down a new table, then walked over to Lance and Jude. "The king is now on his way here to see the damage firsthand, so we do not need to travel to Dawson after all."

Lance said nothing and stood emotionless, trying to discern why the elf acted so strange when she was near him.

"What's the bad news?" Jude asked as he suspiciously looked over the rim of his ale-filled mug.

Alexis piped up as she stared at the floor near Lance's feet. "You will not have a journey in which to accompany us on. That means no gold."

Jude spit out his mouthful of ale and sat forward, trying to keep the liquid from dripping from his chin to his tunic. "You mean you were going to pay us in gold?" Jude asked with a hint of disappointment in his voice.

Lance looked at Jude and smiled. Despite what his hulking friend might say, he loved gold. He would save his mother from a rampaging orc if he had to, but he would also allow himself to be paid if someone offered it.

"How much gold?" Jude asked as he wiped his mouth with his sleeve and took another deep draw from his mug.

"Ten gold crowns per day," Alexis responded flatly, as if the sum was nothing that an alley man couldn't get begging.

Jude spit out a second mouthful at the announcement of the fee he and Lance would have received.

Alexis fought to keep from grinning at the large swordsman's greed for the coin. Lance looked at Apollisian, but the paladin said nothing when it came to the pay and seemed unaffected by the announcement.

Alexis paused for Jude to wipe his mouth a second time. "But after we speak with the king, we are headed to Minok, the capital city of my great people, and we could use your escort on our way there."

Lance eyed the elf suspiciously. He didn't trust her. It seemed as if she had an agenda of her own. The paladin seemed uninterested either way, but the elf lingered on Jude's response.

"Thanks but no thanks," Lance said, and watched in satisfaction as the elf's smile changed into a scowl.

However, Jude sported a scowl of his own. "Lance! Are you crazy?" Jude said, getting up and pulling Lance to the side part of the bar, away from the paladin's and elf's ears.

"Ten crowns a day? That is a lifetime of pay we could make in a single day. More than our fathers will probably ever see, and you want to turn it down?" Jude asked incredulously.

Apollisian turned and started toward the door. "You work out the details with them, Overmoon. I am heading to city hall."

Alexis suddenly stiffened. "You want me to stay alone? With him?" she asked as she motioned to Lance.

Lance frowned and looked at Jude. The large swordsman shrugged his shoulders as the elf turned back to them.

"You work it out. We can negotiate pay later," Alexis said as she hurried out of the inn.

"Negotiate?" Jude asked rhetorically. "We could get even more money each day?"

Lance frowned. "She is up to something. And what do you think she meant when she said she didn't want to be alone with me? What was that about?"

Jude laughed. "You just don't know women. They are always up to something, and as for her not wanting to be left alone with you, I figured you would be used to that response by now."

Lance punched Jude in the arm. "Ha-ha. Very funny. I had better not forget this day."

Jude stopped chuckling. "Why is that?"

Lance gave a wry smile. "Because it will probably be the only day in our lives when you say something witty."

"Have your laughs," Jude said, finishing his mug of ale. Even Fifvel was chuckling at the pair's verbal sparring.

Lance walked over and grabbed their packs. He tossed Jude his dirty leather pack and placed his on his shoulder. "We had better decide how much gold we want to extort from the royal elven coffers, but I think regardless of what she pays us, it is us who will be extorted."

*   *   *

Alexis ran and caught up with Apollisian. "Why did you leave me in there with him?" she asked.

"I do not approve of your deceitful tactic of encouraging them to accompany us to Minok," the paladin said flatly as he strode down the road.

"What is deceitful about it?" Alexis asked. "I have offered them pay to travel with us. Is a merchant that charges twice as much for an item as he paid for deceitful?"

Apollisian said nothing as he walked. Alexis continued. "I can't very well say: Hey, I think you might be the man prophesized to bring doom on the world. He might not even be the Abyss Walker, but my father's elders need to at least see him."

Apollisian stopped and turned to face Alexis. He started to chastise her for rationalizing an act that was certainly not the way Stephanis wanted tasks performed, but he was stopped dead in his tracks when he looked into her beautiful almond eyes. Her hair was braided back from the top of her head and its tail hung loosely across her chest, cluttering in the soft autumn breeze. How could he be angry at such beauty? "I am sorry, Overmoon. I just think it is deceitful, that's all. There is no need to get defensive. I wasn't naming you the heiress of Rha. I just disagree. Okay?"

Alexis nodded. "I will be honest in every question they ask."

"I would hope so," Apollisian said as he draped his arm over Alexis's shoulder. She started to protest but it felt nice to have a friendly arm around her. "The duke awaits," Apollisian announced as the pair turned and marched down the dirt road toward the large stone building that was city hall.

Apollisian and Alexis walked down the marbled corridors of city hall. The debris from the attack had been all but removed, and there were little, if any signs that a battle ever took place inside. Apollisian rounded the corner and stood tall and proud in the doorway of Duke Dolan Blackhawk's chambers.

The duke glanced up from his desk. "Apollisian and . . ." The

340

duke drummed his fingers on his heavily bearded chin. ". . . Overmoon, is it?"

"Yes, my lord," Alexis said giving a shallow bow.

"What can I do for you?" the duke asked as he quickly slid some parchments into his desk drawer.

"We are to speak with the king when he arrives," Apollisian said in a commanding tone. "I will not be denied."

"I see that you will, paladin. The king is due in sometime this afternoon. Shall I send a messenger for you or . . ."

Apollisian interrupted. "We will wait here for his arrival."

"So you shall," the duke said as he narrowed his eyes. Duke Blackhawk was a proud leader and he despised the way the king allowed holy champions of justice to walk around as if they were born noble, because the fools owned neither claim to land or titles.

"You may leave my office now."

Apollisian narrowed his eyes in return. "So we shall," he said as he and the elf left the duke's office.

The pair walked down the corridor and turned into a small room. It had a man behind a single desk. He was about thirty years old and his fat belly was smashed against his desk as he leaned forward to write on the parchments that sat before him. He looked up at the paladin and the elf. The fat man glanced back and forth, quickly sizing them up. When his eyes rested on the holy crest on Apollisian's shoulder plate, he jumped.

"You need a room, my lord?" he asked as he quickly pulled out a small wooden box containing many keys. "We have a few left."

"Yes sir, but we need them for only a few hours, at least until the king arrives," Apollisian responded politely.

The man blushed at being called sir. He started to make a joke about Apollisian and the elf only needing it for an hour, but quickly changed his mind. He handed Apollisian a small, brass-colored key. "It is just down the hall," he said pointing to a door that was behind his desk.

Apollisian and Alexis walked through the hall and checked each door until the number scrolled on it matched the key. The paladin unlocked the room and they entered. It was a small room, but was nicely furnished and smelled of rose petals. He sat down on the bed and began removing his armor.

"What was that about?" Alexis asked as she placed her back to the door, folding her arms under her breasts.

"Large cities have rooms for politicians to stay in if they do not want to stay at an inn. Sometimes . . ."

Alexis cut in. "Not that. The duke and you. I thought you two were going to draw blades."

Apollisian smiled as he hefted his heavy breast plate over his head and let it clang to the floor. He mussed his blonde hair with his hand and wiped it backwards out of his face. "I despise men of his nature. They are in power only because they were born into it. They too often feel that people exist to glorify their position; when in truth, his position exists to glorify them."

Alexis stared into Apollisian's deep blue eyes. She marveled at the unyielding sense of morality that danced within them. Her father had indeed chosen a remarkable man for her to travel with. "But why shouldn't he be glorified by his people if they love him?" she asked.

Apollisian nodded solemnly. "I do not say Duke Blackhawk is an unjust man, but I say he has many moral shortcomings that prevent him from being a great leader."

"But can everyone be great? If that were true, no one would be great. Everyone would be ordinary, despite how smart or wise they were," Alexis chided as she stepped closer to the bed. Apollisian stood and started unbuckling the straps to the heavy metal plates that protected his arms.

"Not true," Apollisian responded as he stared into Alexis's beautiful almond eyes. He almost stuttered in his response. "Every leader should be great. They should be the greatest person of the group they lead. That is why . . ." He paused. He became lost in her beauty. He longed to lean forward and kiss her soft supple lips.

Alexis didn't seem to notice that he didn't finish his sentence. She was staring up at him. Her eyes danced across his chiseled features. His mussed blonde hair dangled about his face in long heavy streaks. His skin glistened and his deep blue eyes seemed to sparkle more vibrantly as she became lost in them. She leaned closer, longing for his embrace. She had never felt this way in all her years in Minok. She had always found males to be ignorant and petty, often boasting more of their own conquests than speaking of anything intelligent.

Apollisian leaned closer to her until he could feel her hot breath against his face. It seemed the closer he got to her the more perfect her features had become. He had traveled with her only a short time, but during that span it seemed as if he had known her for a lifetime. Cold shivers erupted down his spine. Never had he longed for someone the way he longed for her. He stared into those beautiful brown eyes as she stared into his. Just as they both abandoned cultural boundaries and leaned forward to embrace in a kiss, there was a loud knock at the door.

"My lord, the king arrives!" the fat man that they had met from behind the desk announced from the other side of the door.

"Uh . . . thank you sir, I will be right out," Apollisian said as he awkwardly stepped back and began placing his armor back on.

Alexis also walked in a circle, confused and flushed. "Uh . . . shall I go with you?" she asked.

"No, it isn't necessary. My meeting will be brief. Go and secure our escorts if you like. I shan't be long."

Alexis nodded and picked up her pack. She opened the door and turned back, looking at the handsome man she had traveled with. She wanted to rush into his arms and kiss his face for eternity. She wanted to wrap her arms around his thick chest and never let go, but instead she smiled and walked from the quaint little room.

Apollisian ran to the water basin, splashed water on his face, and began wiping some of the grime away with a towel. He took a brick of lye that was sitting in a dish and wiped his underarms with it, then rinsed with a wet corner of the towel. He wished he had time to actually bathe, but he had to have first audience with the king.

After he wiped himself down, he took the wet towel and wiped the inside of his armor clean. Then he quickly slipped the heavy plate over his head. He swiftly fastened the side straps, grabbed his sword belt, and rushed from the room.

Once the door closed Alexis exhaled deeply and went back inside of the room. She sat on the edge of the soft bed and let herself fall back.

What am I doing? she thought to herself. *He is a stinking human for Leska's sake. He will die in about forty years or so. I won't even be out of my centennials. Plus he will be as old as an elder in twenty years,* Alexis thought as her mind drifted back to his chiseled smile and his steel

343

blue eyes. *But he is so handsome, and how can he be so wise for so young? But stubborn. Way too darn stubborn,* she thought.

Alexis lay on the bed thinking of a hundred reasons why she shouldn't have feelings for the paladin, but despite every one of those reasons, she could no more deny her feeling for him than she could deny her heart its beat. In a few minutes she was fast asleep.

Apollisian took a deep breath as he darted down the hallway to the central corridor. He chastised himself under his breath for getting so close to the elf. Not only would she live five or six times longer than he, but her father, King of the Minok nation, would order his head on a plate if Apollisian became involved with his daughter. Plus, he had taken a vow of celibacy when he became a paladin of this church. He was wed to Stephanis in a matter of sorts. If he wedded as a mortal, he would lose the ability to wield his god's divine power. Stephanis would not grant him the divine protection that was necessary to hunt down and smite those who were unjust.

Apollisian rushed into the corridor and witnessed chaos. Men were rushing around with stacks of papers while others were trying to tidy up. Apollisian navigated past them as best he could. Occasionally he bumped into one, but the frenzied man didn't even seem to notice. When he got outside it was a spectacle to see. Apollisian had met the king only once in his life, when he was a squire. His paladin went before the king to address the remnant fighting of what was left of the orc wars that were occurring at the time. Now the grown paladin marveled at the sight as if it was his first time again. Fifty men with shining red lances held high rode in the front. They were adorned in brass-colored plate armor that gleamed in the autumn sun like sparkling flecks of gold under a trickling fresh spring brook. They wore red silk tunics under their mail that glistened as if they were wet, and they wore full faced helms that had bright red plumes that draped along their backs. The thick plumes bounced and waved as they rode while each lancer held a shield in their off-hand that was painted with the Beyklan crest. The long narrow shields were made of thick steel and reflected the sun as brilliantly as the plate mail. The lancers held the reins of their warhorses proudly and the horses pranced with their heads held high. The horses were large, thick-chested creatures with legs that were powerful, but slender, and their coats were dark, sleek, and trim. The horses were covered in thick barding that matched the mail of the lancers, and the heavy metal plates that covered the animals' heads, necks, chests, and flanks were equally adorned. Behind the lancers were four carriages that were surrounded by men wearing the same armor as the lancers, except these men bore finely crafted long swords that gleamed like polished chrome. The carriages were so adorned that they seemed to be made of pure gold, and they sparkled like a jeweled ring on a bride's wedding day. Huge patches of brass-colored metal held a thousand rubies that were in the shape of the Beyklan crest, a crown tilted on its axis with a long sword through the middle of it. The carriages' wheels were made of wood that was painted red with many thin spokes that were red and yellow, alternately, and lined with various jewels.

As the carriages rolled down the street, Apollisian could see there were fifty lancers, dressed the same as the front lancers, who covered the rear of the entourage. The carriages slowed and stopped in front of the steps that were before Apollisian's feet. There were many city officials that were eagerly awaiting the king's arrival and they danced nervously in one place as if they were trying to warm themselves on the cusp of a great blizzard.

The royal guardsmen who were armed with the long swords dismounted and opened the carriage doors. Many servants and noble women stepped from the carriages, but he did not see any man who was wearing a crown. The many silk-clad perfumed men and women walked past Apollisian as he looked back and forth wondering if he had missed the Beyklan king.

After the ladies had exited the carriage, the front lancer dismounted and removed his thick armored helm. His long brown hair spilled out from under the visage, revealing a middle-aged clean shaven face. He handed the reins of his warhorse to the man behind and tucked the red, velvet lined helm under his left arm, as Duke Blackhawk bowed before the man.

"My king, I have eagerly awaited your arrival," the duke said without looking up.

"I doubt that you have, Dolin. We have matters to discuss in reference to your replacement while you were away. I am displeased with his handling of the dwarven attack. Which means I am displeased with you," the king said as he scanned the crowd standing atop the marble stairs in front of the city hall building.

"My king . . ." the duke began without lifting his head or rising from his kneeling position. ". . . I must apologize for . . ."

The king interrupted the duke when his eyes met Apollisian's. "Go to your quarters, Dolin. We will address your apology there," the king said, never taking his eyes from the paladin.

"Yes, my lord," the duke replied as he hurried up the stairs, never looking back.

Apollisian wanted to look away from the king. Never had he met such a penetrating gaze. The king's dark eyes seemed to invade, judge, and protect, all at the same time. Apollisian swallowed hard as the king approached slowly with an aura of superiority. The paladin could feel his nose tingling with anticipation and he was sure his feet had left the ground. The tyrant who stood before him seemed to emit an awe-inspiring power that he had never been witness to. The paladin waited at the top of the smooth marble stairs.

When the king reached the top he paused and looked Apollisian up and down, and Apollisian never released his gaze. The king was a large man, probably a few inches taller than Apollisian. He wore the full plate of the Beyklan high guard, just as the other lancers, but his seemed to shine more brilliantly. He was no smaller than six-foot-five inches tall and was thick chested, holding himself with his shoulders back, and chin out. His mere posture screamed royalty louder than any crown ever could have. Neither of the two men bowed. Apollisian prayed his memory of ceremonials was well intact from the church. He was about to perform one of the most important of all.

"You dare not bow to a king?" the king asked, arching an eyebrow.

Apollisian held that iron stare. "I bow to only one king," he said unyielding.

"And who is this king who is mightier than the king that stands before you? How dare you make such a claim?" the king replied with an angry tone. The crowd seemed to gasp and mumble amongst themselves.

"I make no such claim. He can never be claimed by one man. His power is supreme and unforgiving. The wrath of his greatness can only be served by him and him alone," Apollisian replied without pause.

"Then why serve him at all? How can he protect you?" the king asked as he drew his sword and stepped back in a defensive posture.

Apollisian kneeled as he spoke. "He cannot protect me, nor will he. He is not about protecting any one man. He is the unyielding right to justice that no man can take away, nor any man hide from," Apollisian said as he outstretched his arms and placed his empty hands up toward the sky. He leaned his head back, exposing his neck, and he closed his eyes as he continued. "His sword is mightier than all the swords combined, and his wrath is as a wave of cleansing water, washing away the taints of those who have been wronged. Those who would wrong me shall drown in an endless sea of despair for an eternity."

The king placed the tip of his sword at the feet of Apollisian and he leaned on it as he kneeled with the paladin. "Then let us thank this king for his wisdom, and hope that he shall guide our hearts to carry out that which those who have been wronged cannot," the king said as he bowed his head before the paladin. Apollisian placed his armored hand on the head of the king and they prayed. After a short while Apollisian stood while the king still kneeled at his feet. The crowd gasped aloud. The king's guards held their stances, eyeing the crowd suspiciously. They had heard of the ceremony though they feared the crowd might not have.

Apollisian ignored them and placed his hand on the king's head a second time. "Then rise, brother, and bask in the light of justice knowing that Stephanis shall watch over you and yours."

The king rose and smiled. Apollisian visibly relaxed as the king spoke. "It is good to see you again, Apollisian. I haven't had the pleasure of meeting you since you were anointed."

"The pleasure is all mine, though I must admit that being able to recall the formal greeting between you and a champion of the faith, knowing I never have to perform it again for some time, is no pleasure."

"Is Victor not following along in his studies as well as you liked?" the king asked as he glanced around with a frown.

Apollisian lowered his head. "I'm afraid Victor was slain during the battle trying to hold the east bridge."

The king shook his head from side to side. "We lost too many good men in that battle. I understand the duke's lackey, Mortan Ganover, had resisted your call for the militia."

"He didn't resist per se, my liege. The law allows him until sunset to relinquish command. It is just that the dwarves attacked just before sunset," Apollisian said.

"We will address the duke's inability to appoint proper leadership later. You have my ear, paladin. Is there anything you have witnessed about the dwarves? I trust your judgment over all else. I did not decree such authority over champions of Stephanis to ignore them."

"Well, my liege . . ."

The king interrupted. "There is no reason to call me *liege*, Apollisian. We both serve the same king. We are brothers. You may refer to me in familiar as Thortan Theobold."

"Thortan . . ." Apollisian paused, adjusting to referring to the king in the familiar. ". . . My revelations in regard to the matter of the dwarven conflict are not necessarily what you may want to hear. They are unbiased, however, and offer what I believe to be a great political insight into other areas that are of interest to you."

King Theobold did not respond as he waited for Apollisian to continue.

"You see my . . . er . . . Thortan, I believe that Stephanis has disagreed with the sanctions in regards to the Adorian civil war. The dwarves have suffered by the taxation our kingdom inflicts and we have obviously suffered under their attacks. The south, who are rumored to not hold you in high favor, are threatening a revolt, and it will be difficult, to say the least, to stave off a revolt and a dwarven nation that has numbers in the tens of thousands. I think in order to have true justice for both sides, we need to lift the sanction and never tax the dwarves again. They, in turn, will de-escalate the war and cease to attack. This leaves your kingdom to concentrate on the revolt and quell it before it grows, thus giving justice to a people that I believe have been wronged, and keeping this great nation intact at the same time."

The crowd mumbled amongst themselves at the boldness of Apollisian. King Theobold raised his hands and hushed them. They immediately fell silent.

"Your wisdom is above reproach, my young paladin. I shall do as you suggest. I will send a message to the king of Clan Stoneheart and I have already dispatched a legion of royal soldiers to keep order in the south. You made your case well, young paladin. I thank

348

you for your time. You are free to seek out justice where it eludes others," King Theobold said as he simply walked away and entered the civic building.

Apollisian sighed in relief and slowly made his way back to Alexis. They were setting out on their journey to the Minok nation this afternoon, and it was not a small one.

Leadership. Many men have been leaders, but few have truly possessed leadership. King, general, chief, and any other title given by men to other men is just that, a title. It has no bearing on man's ability and offers him or her nothing more than a burden. People do not actually seek out leaders. They seek out security. The masses, in their own ignorance, do not look for the greatest person or the best leader. They look for someone that has the same ideals or beliefs as they do. Too often the masses ask a question, not seeking the correct answer, but merely any answer, as long as it is feasible and provided. Any one person could spout lies and foolish banter as long as the people he or she speaks it to have no knowledge of what he is speaking of. Rarely does one person stand up and challenge the masses and their ignorance.

I have noticed that crowds are fickle creatures. A single person can rise up and coerce the masses with little more than a random direction, and that crowd will blindly charge into the fray without thought of the danger or whom they are following. Some would argue that the masses follow the leader because he has leadership ability. I disagree. I say that a true leader doesn't give speeches, he doesn't inspire fear or awe in order to get the masses to follow him. A true leader simply does what he or she feels is the right thing to do. It is the masses that then follow suit behind him. It is not the fact that they are looking for an idea or that he or she rose from the depths of a crowd and shouted passionate commands. He simply and quietly chose a path. The crowd merely recognized the path and chose to follow. Those types are great leaders. These "true" leaders will never be abandoned by those that follow them, and they will never be victims of a coup against them. They may lead the masses for a short time however, because true leadership is not the same as a title longevity. As I have said before, the masses are fickle and ignorant. If his followers somehow abandon a true leader, it will be because he simply decided to go another direction. Their rejection will mean nothing to him, because he was not intending to lead them in the first place, he was merely traveling down the road he believed was correct. Alas, I feel there is no such thing as a "true leader," but merely true followers.

—Lancalion Levendis Lampara—

Nine

Children of the Forest

Kellacun was roughly thrown into a dark, dirty cell. The sable-haired woman skidded along the bare stone floor that was covered in filth and a dark green slimy residue that reeked of feces and urine. Many rusted iron shackles hung from bulky steel hooks that were about ten feet up on the far wall. There were a few bleached white skeletal arms that hung from the shackles and dangled directly above several piles of moldy bones. Rats and other vermin had long ago eaten the flesh from the skeletons that were piled up in gruesome heaps of decaying frames. There was a single window that was set about thirty feet up the moss covered wall. The small portal was riddled with thick iron bars that appeared to be well maintained. The rusted chains holding the dangling shackles were attached to small pulleys that were secured just a few inches below the bottom of the window.

Kellacun felt her arms being grabbed by rough powerful hands and hoisted up. "Up we go, you dirty little bitch," the coarse voice whispered in her ear. She could smell the fetid odor of ale and rotted onions that wafted from his breath. Kellacun did not resist the man as her wrists were roughly shackled. She had been severely beaten and clung to consciousness like an insect on a log in a gale wind. The assassin was barely aware that the skin of her wrist had been pinched in the shackles when it was closed. A small amount of blood dripped from her fresh wound as she felt herself being lifted to her feet. Out of the corner of her eye she could see the guard. Her vision was a little blurry after her beating, but he appeared to be a burly, obese man. He was wearing a dark brown, sleeveless leather tunic that was soiled with grease and sweat near the armpits and just under his chin. Rings of dirt that had collected in the wrinkles of his arms and legs covered his fat body. He had long dark greasy

351

hair that clung to his sweaty face and neck in clammy strings. His plump arms jiggled as he quickly pulled the rusty chain taut, hand over hand, hoisting Kellacun to her feet. The guard slowed and then strained as her body weight pulled against the chain. Once he had hoisted her a few inches above the ground, the guard hooked one of the chain links around a smaller iron hook that protruded from the wall.

Kellacun winced in pain as she tried to cling to the ground with the tips of her toes, but soon her entire body weight rested on her frail, thin wrists. The fat guard chuckled as he finished securing the rusty chain that held her aloft. Kellacun kept her eyes closed, trying to ignore the growing pain as the shackles ripped open the delicate skin of her wrists. Though the wounds would soon heal, the wererat still felt the stinging pain. The guard waddled over to the thick wooden door of the cell and fumbled through his pockets. A few seconds later he procured a set of brass keys on a large steel ring. The guard locked the heavy cell door from the inside and placed the keys back in his pocket with his thick fingers.

Kellacun gripped the rusty chain just above the shackles and pulled, relieving some of the pressure that was on her arms. She had not recovered the strength to hold herself long, but the pain in her wrists was becoming unbearable. The fat guard chuckled again and wiped his dirty arms across his mouth as he waddled toward her. He waited for a few moments and Kellacun could no longer hold herself up. Her muscles went slack and she yelped in pain as her wrists supported her entire body weight again.

"Hurt?" the guard asked with a rotten, yellow toothed smile. He didn't seem much interested in her reply, it was more a question of stupidity than of merit. When Kellacun didn't answer he looked her up and down. She was strung up by her wrists with her head hung low. The fat jailer knew she was due to be executed in the morning for attempted murder and a plethora of other charges for alleged crimes that occurred over a seven year period. His sick brown eyes took in the prisoner who hung helpless before him. She wore a light brown prison tunic that was too big for her small frame. The oversized neck hole hung down in front of her, exposing her deep pale cleavage. Her breeches were loose and slack, made for a male prisoner, and clung to her shapely hips by a thin twine that had been crudely wrapped around to act as a belt. Her face was bruised from the beating she took and her long black hair hung down in front of her chest.

The fat guard loosed her breeches and rubbed his hands together in anticipation as the filthy garment fell around her ankles. He bent down and eagerly removed the wide-legged pants and tossed them behind him. Her sleek, shallow legs shined in the pale light that fell through the tall window. The fat guard began to unfasten his own breeches in such a haste that he ripped the leather belt loose more than unfastened it. Looking back at the locked wooden door to ensure he was not to be disturbed, he spread Kellacun's legs and stepped between them. She cried out in pain from the shackles but seemed oblivious to the corpulent guard that groped her buttocks.

"You be a good girl and I'll finish quickly," the portly jailer said as he licked his three fingers and ran them up and down between her legs as his fat, coarse digits slightly penetrated her.

Kellacun was vaguely aware of what was going on. She had been in and out of consciousness since her beating, but she was being rapidly brought back to awareness by the corpulent guard's molestations. After he finished wetting her, the guard lifted her up by her buttocks and drew her hips near to him. He guided himself in easily, and vigorously ravaged her.

Kellacun began to rush back to her cognizant mind. Something was not right. She was in pain, but it was not like the ache she had prepared for. Something was wrong, different. She struggled to speak and mumbled a jumble of incomprehensible words. The fat guard seemed to be excited by her mumbling, mistaking it for moans of pleasure, and continued his vigorous violation.

Kellacun suddenly opened her eyes. She glanced around the room in a confused state for a moment, as she struggled to understand the rapid jerking motions her body was being subjected to. The assassin felt the pain in her wrists, though her body weight was being supported slightly. She blinked again and everything came crashing back. The obese guard who had brought her to her cell now stood between her legs violating her. She could smell his filthy stench and feel his cold, clammy sweat as it dripped on her bare legs. Though she was repulsed at the disgusting creature that was pleasuring himself on her, she almost grinned at her luck. She had endured much worse in order to get close enough to a victim she

353

meant to assassinate, and now she would endure this in order to escape. Men were easy prey to her and she had no doubt how to use the fat jailer's lust to her advantage. She thought quickly, because she suspected the plump man did not have interludes often and would rapidly satisfy himself.

Kellacun began moaning, feigning pleasure. "Lick me, you ox."

The fat guard seemed oblivious to her speaking.

The assassin said it again, but more loudly, though she was careful not to alert anyone who might be standing outside the cell door.

The portly jailer stopped and looked at the woman in disbelief. "What did you say?" he asked as he wiped his glistening forehead with his greasy forearm.

Kellacun wrapped her legs around the fat guard's waist and wiggled her hips in anticipation. "Lick me, you ox, I want this to last as long as it can. If you lick me, I'll be sure to take care of you in the same way," she whispered with a vixen's voice.

The fat guard's eyes went wide as he stuttered. "Uh . . . like . . . you mean . . ."

"That is exactly what I mean. What harm can I cause you? I am shackled and have no weapons. I am to be executed in the morning. I would like to have one night of pleasure before I leave the world of the living," she said as she nibbled at the fat man's lip. The assassin held her breath as not to take in the repulsive odor that erupted from his rotten mouth.

The fat guard pulled away from her and roughly hoisted her up by her buttocks. He placed her right leg over his left shoulder and her left leg over his right shoulder. Scooting her hips toward his face, he began to pleasure her orally. Kellacun ignored the burning pain in her wrists caused by the shackles. She could feel warm sticky blood dripping down her forearms, but she kept telling herself she would soon be free.

The guard spent a few minutes pleasuring her and lifted his head. "Now me. It is time for you to do it to me," he said eagerly.

Kellacun bobbed her tongue sensuously and bit her bottom lip. "I can't wait to taste you. But I can't do it chained up here."

The guard glared. "I can't let you out," the fat man said angrily. "What do you think . . ."

354

Kellacun interrupted him. "You don't have to release me, you silly ox, just let me down from this perch."

Before she could finish her sentence she watched as the guard's pale white buttocks jiggled and bounced as he ran to the chain he had secured on the iron hook that held her aloft. He unfastened the heavy chain and she roughly slid down the wall and landed on her bottom. The guard ran back over and put his hands on his hips expectantly. Kellacun scooted over and took him in her mouth. She struggled to perform mediocrely and almost vomited several times due to the stench of his unclean body. The fat guard seemed oblivious to her disgust and tightly gripped a handful of her sleek black hair. Kellacun deftly ran her hand into his pocket and withdrew a shiny steel ring with several brass keys attached to it. She took her time, careful not to clink the keys together, and placed the ring in her armpit under her loose fitting prison tunic. She finished a few minutes later and kissed and caressed the guard's legs. "How was it?" she asked as she shifted the keys from her armpit to her hand. While she held them under her breeches, which she picked up from the floor. She slipped on the oversized prison breeches as she waited for the fat guard to respond.

"I have had much better," he said as he roughly grabbed the rusty chain attached to her shackles. The fat guard didn't bother putting his pants back on as he dragged the chain over to the hook to hoist her up a second time. Kellacun backed against the wall as he lifted her up and secured the chain on the iron hook. Kellacun winced in pain as she dangled with her bodyweight on her shackled wrists again. She didn't worry about real injury, since she was a wererat and could only really be harmed by magical or silver weapons. Her shackles were neither. Though she bled, her wounds healed almost as quickly as they were formed. Had she not been beat with that silver gauntlet, her eye would not be swollen either.

The corpulent guard fumbled with his pants as Kellacun quietly shuffled in the dark room with the lock of her shackles. She tried several times until she found the key that slid into the lock. The fat guard walked over to the cell door and tried to lock it. He cursed and reached into his pocket for his keys to resecure the door. When he searched one pocket and found it empty, he checked the other. When he didn't find the keys he turned around and began looking on the floor of the cell. He kicked at piles of excrement with

355

his leather boot in the dim light, turning over the disgusting mounds of debris, but didn't find anything.

"Where in the hell are my damned keys?" he said under his breath as he heard a familiar click. He jerked his head up toward Kellacun in time to see her scampering up the thick chain that had held her shackles.

Kellacun smiled as she felt the tumblers turn and heard the click of the lock. The shackles opened and she grabbed the chain with both of her hands and began climbing up. Her bare toes slipped into the smallest crevices in the smooth prison wall, and with the aid of the chain, she scampered up the wall easily.

"You'll never get out of those bars, bitch!" the fat guard yelled as he opened the wooden cell door and slammed it shut. Kellacun could hear him screaming for more guards on the other side. Once she reached the top of the chain she climbed onto the windowsill. The ledge was about eight inches wide and the iron bars were thick, but the stone around them was worn and weathered. Kellacun grabbed the bars and sucked in a deep breath. She exhaled long and softly, pulling with all her strength, but the bars would not budge. She sighed, and closed her dark dangerous eyes, loosing the primal rage within her that she continuously kept at bay. She growled deeply as her arms shook and trembled, while long dark hair replaced the fine angelic wisps that covered her arms and delicate face became twisted, and a long snout erupted from her nose. Her ears became pointed and the hair on her head shifted and erupted from her body. In moments the transformation was complete and the once beautiful assassin was replaced by a half woman, half rat-looking beast. She glared at the bars that were before her with red vibrant eyes. She grabbed them with her now muscular fur- and claw-covered hands, pulling with all her might, but even in her hybrid form, the bars were securely anchored in the stone. She glanced back at the door and could hear men rushing down the hall. She knew she didn't have much time.

*　　*　　*

Kalen sat in his easy chair and studied the many spells he had been trying to learn. He grew weary of not having the luxury of casting them on live people, and Spencer hadn't come by in days.

The gray elf slammed his book shut and sighed. He leaned back in his soft velvety chair and propped his head up with his hand as he leaned on the plush arm rest, drumming his fingers silently on the soft blue felt fabric that was sewn around the expensive piece of furniture. Kalen twirled his long silver hair in his hand, smiling suddenly when an idea crossed his mind. He hadn't heard from the thieves guild since it was sacked, but he could try scrying on the assassin, Kellacun. He wasn't too familiar with her, but he had seen her on a couple of occasions.

The gray elf jumped from his chair with new vigor and selected a book from the expansive oak shelves that lined his study from floor to ceiling. He took the thick tome over to the polished white ash table that served as his workbench, and opened it. After a few minutes of drumming through the pages, he stopped and clapped his hands. "Ah-ha. Found it," the elf mumbled to himself with an evil grin.

Kalen studied the spell for a few hours, stopping only to take a drink of wine from the golden goblet he had left over from lunch. He walked over to the scrying mirror and chanted softly. In a few moments, the cloudy mirror began to take shape. The image came so dark that had Kalen not had infravision he would not have seen much. To his surprise he found the assassin barely clothed and chained up. She had no pants on and there was a fat man between her thighs having his way with her. The assassin appeared to be unconscious or oblivious to what was going on. Kalen, disgusted, started to end the scry, but the assassin came around and feigned to be interested in the fat guard. He kind of chuckled at the events as they unfolded, sitting back down in his plush chair to enjoy the show.

"Don't be a fool, you corpulent slob. She has as much interest in you as she has in staying in those chains," Kalen chuckled as he watched. "Surely he doesn't believe . . ." Kalen was cut off by the man as he hoisted the assassin to a more comfortable position. "Now why on earth would the fat idiot do that?" Kalen asked himself aloud. "He has no need to . . . ohhhh," Kalen said as the portly guard let the assassin down from the perch so she could accommodate him in the same manner he had just accommodated her.

"You stupid fool, I hope she kills you slowly," Kalen said to the guard as he watched the events unfold.

The gray elf sipped his wine and watched in pure amusement as Kellacun lifted the keys to her shackles from the guard's pockets as she finished accommodating him. The guard then searched for his keys while she escaped her shackles and climbed to the windowsill. The fat guard screamed something Kalen couldn't understand and he tried to rush out of the room while the assassin climbed the chain but could not get the bars from the window to give. The gray elf sighed and began chanting. He had never cast through a scry before, but he had watched Hector perform it and it did not seem that difficult. He just modified the weaves and merely projected, rather than wove them. Kalen watched as the guards burst into the room as the assassin stepped into a shining blue portal that quickly closed once she had stepped through.

A bright blue dot appeared in Kalen's chambers. The magical energy expanded from a small spot to a long horizontal line. That line then stretched and grew until it created a large oval portal. It was not long before a frantic woman stepped through. She had long sleek black hair that hung down around her. She wore a dirty light brown prison tunic that was much too big for her. One of her naked shoulders poked out of the neck as the shirt hung from her shoulders awkwardly. The light brown breeches she snatched from the floor were also too big for her and clung to her waist loosely by a thin piece of brown twine that acted like a crude belt. Her face was swollen and she had many small bruises around her left eye.

Kellacun frantically scanned the room. It was a small round room with a tall ceiling. There were bookshelves on each wall that were loaded with thousands of books and tomes. On a polished white ashen desk sat an open book with no doubt arcane writings, and sitting in front of her in a dark blue silk cloak was a thin, yet nimble looking gray elf. He had long straight silver hair, though it was not as long as hers, and bright blue eyes. He sat imposingly in a felt chair with his thin arms crossed under his chest.

"Who are you?" Kellacun asked as she kept one eye on the mage and one eye around the room. She struggled to understand why she was in human form again, but she figured it had something to do with the portal.

"I am your employer's employer," Kalen responded surreptitiously. "And it seems you are now out of work."

"How so?" Kellacun asked as she glanced to the ceiling, trying in vain to locate a door to this cursed room.

Kalen paused and a disgusted look crept onto his face. "Please look around, you act as a rat trapped in a stew pot, but I assure you the only door out of here lies with me, so be a good little vermin, and I will let you get back to your work."

Kellacun reluctantly stopped looking for an exit and gave her full attention to the elf that sat before her, but she glowered menacingly at him, though she could not tell if he even noticed her expression.

"I would have sent you a portal earlier, but it seemed you were rather enjoying yourself," Kalen said with a chuckle.

"Pray, elf, that no one hires me to see you dead. I am an efficient killer," Kellacun retorted as anger flared through her at the elf's mockeries.

Kalen nodded and smiled. "I see that you are, but I thought you were hired to kill the Ecnal, not roll in the hay with fat disgusting guards."

Kellacun fumed. She could feel the need to release the rage, to release the beast that was within her, and to drink the blood of this miscreant who sat before her.

Kalen sensed her anger and continued. "Tell me, did he taste as yummy as he looked?" Kalen taunted.

Kellacun snarled, and in a flash she transformed into her hybrid form. She leapt over the table, her claws and teeth bared, but before she could sink her teeth into the elf's soft flesh, ten tiny green specks of light formed in front of her. The lights flashed and the specks encircled her, leaving her held immobile by the powerful magical rings.

"Temper, temper," Kalen taunted as he got up from his chair and circled the magically held wererat that was on top of his desk. "You transformed pretty fast. I suspect if you are injured or angry it is easy for you, yes?" Kalen asked, knowing the assassin could not reply. "Cat got your tongue?" he asked again, laughing out loud at his own wit. "As I was saying before your pitiful outburst, your old employer is no more. His guild has been wiped out and every one of his members has been killed. So that means you now work for me, or I kill you. I assume you will choose the first. Any objections?" Kalen asked again and chuckled knowing Kellacun could not respond. "Good. As you may know, and perhaps you do not, the man you were being paid to kill is named Lance Ecnal. I know not how he managed to escape the orphan killings ten years ago, but the fact remains you are as sloppy now as you were then. I am more than displeased at your pitiful attempts at assassinating him. Perhaps you should seek another profession. One that employs your better talents," Kalen said, pausing briefly while rubbing his smooth chin in mock thought. "A harlot's dress would suit you nicely after witnessing your performance with your jailer. I am sure he has fewer complaints about your job performance than I," Kalen mused.

Kellacun struggled against the magic that held her. Anger flared through her veins as she imagined ripping Kalen's throat out and feasting on his blood. But try as she might, the magic held her as easily as the sky held the clouds.

"Strain all you wish, fool. You are too stupid to slip through the spell that binds you. If I were you, I would hope the spell holds, for I hunger for a reason to kill you. But alas, I need that orphan slain. If I were not so busy here, I might do it myself. Perhaps if you fail a second time, I might seek out this troublesome youth," Kalen said as he stood up slowly from his old chair and wandered to his bookshelf. He pressed his narrow finger on his bottom lip as his eyes darted among the vast volumes of knowledge that rested on the old oaken shelves. Finally he came across an old book that was bound with four golden rings. Kalen carefully took the tome and placed it on his desk in front of Kellacun. The cover was made of wood and had many demonic symbols and arcane runes about it. He slowly lifted the cover, sliding it gracefully on the thick golden rings, revealing the first page of three that were also made of wood. The front page was much thinner than the cover, but thick enough that it remained rigid when lifted. This page also had many strange symbols and writings on it. Kalen paused and rubbed his manicured finger over the engravings as he read aloud.

A day shall come to pass when the mother of mercy shall bear child. This child will be like no other, for gods and men alike will seek to vanquish him. The hate from the hells dwells within his mind, as compassion for the meek guides his heart. If allowed to live, this child will bear the false testimony of the gods, as he ascends the throne of righteousness, while working the magic of evil. The goods and evils of the realms will oppose him, but they will be crushed asunder as the scorpion under an anvil or fire, for he shall command both of them alike unto his ascension . . .

Kalen finished reading and turned to the magically held Kellacun. "Do you know how long it has taken me and the scholars to decipher this text?" the gray elf asked. Kellacun, still held by the powerful holding spell, could not respond. Kalen did not seem to notice her lack of response as he ran his fingers worshipfully along the wooden carvings on the ancient page. "It has taken me well over thirty years. It may seem a long time to yourself, human, but in fact, it is an amazing feat of wizardry and intelligence. Deciphering a single word should take decades of study in the meaning of the old tongue, yet we did an entire page in thirty years!" The elf gloated. "The elders of Minok covet these writings so much that none may even glimpse the magically sealed scroll case that holds them, let alone lay their eyes on the tome itself, but I have a copy. I'll not tell you how I have come across such a coveted treasure, just know that I have. Know that if I can steal that which has been kept safe since the dawn of time, I can easily claim your life should you disappoint me," Kalen said as he shook his fingers in an odd display of movements. In moments the green rings of magical energy that held Kellacun tight, began to glow brighter until the glimmering bonds enveloped the wererat and then she was gone.

Kalen leaned back in his velvety chair and stared longingly at the pages that were before him. He tapped his index finger against his thin bottom lip as he whispered to himself. "Hector has his own agenda, and is confident that the child of mercy can be found and slain, saving himself and his reign. Still, I fear time has run out for us. I know the child is not merely the executioner of Nalir. I know from teachings that even as a child he is much more than that. Indeed, the Abyss Walker has been born, and his time of mourning comes to a rapid end."

*   *   *

"A storm is coming," the raspy voice of the elven ancient known as Eucladower Strongbow announced. The venerable elf sat on the giant root of an Illilander tree, the largest and oldest tree in all the realms. The gnarled, twisted roots of the great tree weaved in and out of the lush forest floor as they snaked down a gentle slope that ended at the base of a shimmering pond. Orantal Proudarrow, lord ranger of the Darayal Legion, said nothing as he gazed at his ancient friend. Eucladower was clothed in a green silk robe that hung loosely on his weak frame. His thin silver mustache trailed down his face and blended with his long, straight, sleek beard that hung past his knees. His perky elven ears protruded from his silver hair that was laid back revealing a deep widow's peak hairline. The tips of his silk robe were embossed with a shimmering golden hue that seemed to sparkle in the few beams of sunlight that managed to jut through the dense forest canopy. The elder leaned on a long wooden staff with a gnarled head that seemed too heavy for Eucladower's frail body, yet the ancient elder lifted it easily. The tip of the gnarled oak staff resembled an eagle that was perched atop the staff, yet it bore no profound features.

Orantal gazed out across the shimmering lake that was at the foot of the Illilander tree, pausing a moment to see if his longtime friend was going to say anything more. He had grown accustomed to the Eucladower's labored speech and it saddened him to know the elder's natural life would soon come to an end. The ranger lord sat down on the giant gnarled root, next to his ancient friend, and smoothed the silk breeches that were under his thin mail. He glanced at the armor he had bore through countless trials and tribulations. The thin chain shirt hung lightly from his green silk tunic. Great spider webs of yellow danced across the chest of his garb and almost appeared as the rays of a setting or rising sun. He wore a single shoulder plate that was strapped to his left shoulder tightly. The plate was also green with the splash of the yellow spider pattern. Orantal's blonde hair was pulled back in a ponytail held by a long green ribbon that hung between his shoulder blades and the end of his hair. His long pointed ears, though not nearly as long as Eucladower's, poked from under his sleek thin hair, and his twin narrow swords hung tightly at his sides. The ranger lord sighed and looked at Eucladower. The ancient elf began to speak again in his old raspy voice.

"Yes, a storm *is* coming, Orantal. I see the damned shall have their voice on our world, but first, the storm comes to us," the elder said.

Orantal shot to his feet and scanned the forest around him clutching his twin sword hilts as if the enemy might be near. "What do you mean, elder? What storm? Are we in danger?"

The elder groaned as he leaned on his gnarled staff to help him stand. "Yes, my friend. We are in danger. Help as we might, try as we must, there is no stopping the Abyss Walker. He has been born and now he comes to us."

Orantal nearly stumbled forward in shock as he hopped down from the Illilander root. He and all the elves were taught about the Abyss Walker as children, though they knew not much more than that he could bring the end of the world.

"How can this be? There have been none of the signs. At least none of the ones that I know of," the ranger lord proclaimed. He knew only two of the signs: like the dead that defy Rha-Cordan, he shall come of mourning that knows not why he mourns. There were many more, but Orantal was not on the elder council and he knew of at least two other signs, though he knew not what they were.

"We may not see all the signs, my young champion. But they will come to pass nonetheless. We must remain vigilant. The signs will come soon, if they have not already, but I cannot deny the Abyss Walker comes. I can feel his wrath in my soul," Eucladower said in a low raspy whisper as he slowly walked from the tree aided by his gnarled staff. Orantal merely walked alongside the elder elf and nodded with his hands grasped behind his back.

The pair plodded down from the majestic slope pausing briefly for the elder to rest. The sounds of the virgin forest seemed more loud to the ranger lord, who knew that they could very well be a wasteland soon. It was said that the Abyss Walker would bring about a blight to the land.

Orantal and Eucladower walked from the base of the hill and entered a thick vale. The vale bore no underbrush and the trees were large and perfectly straight. They showed no scars or ill branches, and animals roamed nearby, uncaring about the many elves that milled about. The Minok Vale was one of the largest elven cities in the realms. To any but an elf, the Vale merely appeared to be a group of perfect trees that were exceptionally tall and blotted out the sun, though few humans had ever been to the Vale and could see it for what it was. Each tree bore the markings of many thin doors that were all but concealed to the untrained eye. Each

363

tree housed an elven family that had as many as fifty members each. Some noble families were known to have many trees, but they were often found at the heart of the Vale, not on the edges. At the top of each tree, there were sentries posted who were hidden so well that many birds perched among the branches did not know they were there. The sentries were armed with deadly bows of the finest craftsmanship. The elven weapons were superior to the humans' in every way, from beauty to balance. It was not uncommon for an elven weapon smith to spend a hundred years forging a sword, whereas humans spent months at best.

Many elves milled about doing their daily routines. Some paused to offer a bow of respect to the elder, and others offered a quick, but respectful dip, as they hurried past in their own tasks.

Eucladower turned to Orantal as he breathed heavily from the short, but tiring walk.

"Go, lord ranger. Round up the Darayal Legion. Though we cannot stop that which already will be, we can help preserve that which we might lose."

Orantal bowed low. "As you command, Elder Eucladower," Orantal said as he hurried off into the forest beyond the Vale.

Eucladower slowly strode through the vast elven city. The elder smiled at the children who ran through the bottoms, and then he grimaced at the thought of what the Abyss Walker might do. Certainly the Vale would oppose him, but the elder knew it would be futile. He had not broken the prophetic seal, but Eucladower knew that foretold a horrible reckoning that the dark one would bring about the land. He hoped that the storm he felt was not the true Abyss Walker, but merely an agent of the damned, trying to earn favor of his dark lords. They had faced a few of those over the centuries, but he had never felt the powerful presence before that he now felt. He could usually feel the taint of lesser evils from a few miles away, but he knew that this taint came from hundreds of miles away.

"At least we have time," Eucladower mumbled to himself as he pushed his way into the elder chamber that was located at the base of the largest tree in Minok Vale.

"Time for what, Elder Eucladower?" an old elf asked.

Eucladower glanced up and noticed he had walked into the chamber of the wise without knowing it. He was planning on going there anyway, yet he was so deep in thought he must have wandered in. Cursing his old mind, he regarded the man who had spoken to him. King Christopher Calamon Overmoon sat in his polished oaken chair wearing his golden crown. The crown bore eight thin horns that represented each of the eight vales that dwelled under his rule. At the base of each horn was a jewel that bore the symbol of the respective nations. The magnificent crown of Minok rested on King Overmoon's formerly blonde hair that was now more silver than blonde. His deep blue eyes bore the wisdom of nearly eight hundred years of rule. He wore a bright blue robe, streaked with silver elven runes, and a bright silver shawl that ran around his neck and down the front of him, bearing ancient cobalt runes. His fingers were encrusted with many rings, though he wore them out of symbolism rather than out of vanity. The room the king sat in was more long than it was wide and had a beautifully polished red wood table shaped the same as the room where the entire council of wise, save for Eucladower, now sat. The venerable elf slowly made his way to his seat, resting his gnarled staff against the table and folding his knobby hands before he answered.

"Time to prepare, time to flee, or time to fight," Eucladower said in his raspy voice through labored breaths from his long walk.

"Why would we do these things, Elder Eucladower? Has another claiming to be the dark one come close to our vale?" the king asked. "We will merely crush this one as we have the others in centuries past."

Other elders murmured amongst themselves in the room, but none spoke aloud.

"This one cannot be slain, my king. I fear he is the true Abyss Walker, and he is undoubtedly coming," Eucladower announced.

The council of wise murmured amongst themselves more loudly.

"How can you be certain, Elder Eucladower?" one of the other elders asked. "Many feel the Abyss Walker is more legend than truth, created to scare small children into behaving."

"Yes, how can you be certain?" King Overmoon said as he rubbed his head under his crown.

Eucladower took a deep breath. "I know the same way I know when water falls from the sky it is rain, even if I cannot see the clouds. I know, for when a breeze blows against my face, it is the wind, even if I cannot see it. I know these things because he is over a hundred miles away, yet I see every feature of his face."

The room gasped at that announcement.

"What does he look like, Elder Eucladower?" one of the other elders asked while wearing a red robe that was adorned with yellow runes.

"Yes, tell us of him," another shouted.

Eucladower took a deep breath and began again. "He comes as a storm, violent and deadly. I can hear the voices of the damned crying out from him as if he carries their tormented existences in his pocket and their cries for mercy on his breath. He is but a babe, a human babe, but his soul is that of the gods," Eucladower proclaimed.

The other elders relaxed and murmured to themselves.

"We cannot abandon the Vale on Eucladower's visions, my king," an older elf in a blue and yellow robe pleaded as he rubbed his creased forehead.

"Yet we cannot stay, nor can we risk doing nothing," another elder put in. All the elders seemed to nod their heads in agreement.

Eucladower took a deep breath before he spoke. "I ask for a reading, my king. The ancients will attest to my sight."

The room gasped again and became completely silent. No one stirred, no one seemed to breathe, save for King Overmoon.

"We can do no such thing, Elder Eucladower," the king said. "There are the four signs the Abyss Walker is coming. All of them, we, as children of the forest, would experience firsthand. We have not had a single one. Elder Humas, would you kindly recite the first passing of the Abyss Walker."

The elder with red and yellow robe stood up, straightened his collar, and cleared his throat. "The son of a Vale, not by blood, will turn his back on his brethren and embrace the shadow," Humas recited.

"Elder Eucladower, the ancient tongue referred to the son of the crown as the son of the Vale. As you know I have been married twice. My first wife, Surelda Al-Kalidius, a gray elf, was slain, Leska bless her soul, before she bore me any children. And now, my wife, *your queen*, has bared only a daughter that is, as we speak, traveling with the human paladin, Apollisian, as she learns the ways of justice," the king said confidently.

"What of her son, Kalen?" Eucladower asked.

366

The elders whispered amongst themselves.

"How do you know of Kalen?" the king asked with an elevated tone, on the edge of anger. He leaned forward and arched his eyebrows with more than passing interest.

Eucladower settled back in his soft chair and folded his ancient knobby hands. "My king, you forget I am almost two thousand years old. There is much I have seen. I remember Surelda well. She was quite beautiful and wise, my king. She complimented you tenderly."

The king sat back in his throne, more relaxed. "It is true she had a son, though he was not of my blood, therefore he could not be a son of the Vale."

"Elder Humas," Eucladower spoke with his raspy voice. "Could you kindly recite the passing a second time?"

Elder Humas cleared his throat again and recited the passing more slowly than he had the first time. "The son of a Vale, not by blood, will turn his back on his brethren and embrace the shadow."

When Elder Humas finished, the entire room was buzzing with whispered talk. The king rubbed his head under his crown. "This may appear as if the passing could be satisfied, but Kalen is no longer a son of the Vale, even under the old code. Even if he were to embrace the shadow, which I would wager my crown he has not, he cannot be named a son of the Vale."

Elder Humas spoke. "We as Elders of the Vale must vote on the passing. It is my contention that this passing is plausible."

"Agreed," the other elders said in solemn unison.

The king leaned back in his polished oaken chair and rested his head against his hand.

"Elder Bartoke, would you kindly recite the second passing?" the king asked wearily.

An elf rose in a blue and yellow robe and did not look much younger than Elder Eucladower. "A babe, half not of this earth, and half damned by the gods themselves, and feared by the children of the forest, will carry his own proclamation naming him not for who he is, but for who he will become."

"A babe is what I have seen, my king. I can hear the damned crying out for mercy, when his vision comes to me. He is a human boy, though I know not of this proclamation the passing speaks of," Eucladower said.

367

"The Elders of the Vale must vote on the passing. It is my contention that this passing is plausible," Elder Bartoke said as he sat back in his chair.

"Agreed," the other elders said in solemn unison.

King Overmoon, seeing the elders were serious about the readings, relaxed, but exhaled deeply. "Elder Varmintan, could you kindly recite the third passing?"

An elder stood who was wearing a violet robe that bore many green runes in it, very similar to the king's robe, but not nearly as ornate. "He who walks with wrath, shall stride into the vale as a guest wearing the Cadacka, though he knows not why he mourns. If the children of the forest do nothing, they will surely perish," Varmintan recited slowly.

"I guess we will know soon enough if the false bringer wears a Cadacka," Humas said gravely. "And what are we to do if he is wearing a Cadacka? How is it possible a human babe could come across one?"

"The Elders of the Vale must vote on the passing. It is my contention that this passing is plausible," Varmintan said solemnly.

The other elders spoke amongst themselves for some time, though no conclusions were reached. Finally they elected to discuss those options should the bringer prove to be true.

The king removed his crown and set it on the polished oak table. He stared for a moment at his reflection in the mirror-like surface of the table. Each jewel seemed to shine at him, mocking him, challenging his wisdom, his strength. He sighed and ran his fingers through his sleek hair, exhaled and straightened his posture. "Elder Darmond could you kindly recite the fourth passing?"

The elder wearing a red robe with a blue sash that crossed from shoulder to hip leaned forward. His hair was uncharacteristically dark for an elf and his bright green eyes shined in the dim light of the council room.

"Woe to the children of the world, for after he who walks with wrath stands among the mothers without children, he will slay that which is already dead. He will shed his mourning and walk among them saying: `I know you fools, now you shall perish,'" Elder Darmond recited.

There was a long silence in the room. The elders weighed the passing and contemplated it. It had been nearly fifty years since the passings had last been recited and the elders tried to take all possible meanings in.

Finally Elder Darmond broke the silence after almost an hour.

"The Elders of the Vale must vote on the passing. It is my contention that this passing is plausible."

The king nodded slowly. "Since the passings are contented plausible; I, King Christopher Calamon Overmoon, High King of Minok Vale, submit to you, Elders of the Vale, to read the prophecy that our great forefathers, in their wisdom, did graft for us in that when the day of the Abyss Walker is at hand, we could be prepared."

"So be it," the elders said in unison.

"Ancient Elder Eucladower," Elder Humas said. "Would you honor us with a reading of the great prophecy?"

Elder Eucladower slowly pushed back from the table and leaned on his gnarled staff to rise. He stepped awkwardly toward the king, who produced a small ivory scroll case that looked fragile and old. It was about a foot long, round, and covered in ancient runes that were hundreds of times older than Eucladower himself. The venerable elf staggered back to his chair but he did not sit in it. He rested his gnarled oaken staff against the polished table and opened the ivory case. With his knobby old fingers he lightly pulled three parchments out that appeared to be written on some kind of leather. He unrolled the parchment and cleared his throat. All the other elders and the king sat tight-lipped when the ancient elf began to recite the prophecy with his old raspy voice.

> . . . A day shall come to pass when the mother of mercy shall bear child. This child will be like no other, for gods and men alike will seek to vanquish him. The hate from the hells dwells within his mind, as compassion for the meek guides his heart. If allowed to live, this child will bear the false testimony of the gods, as he ascends the throne of righteousness, while working the magic of evil. The goods and evils of the realms will oppose him, but they will be crushed asunder as the scorpion under an anvil or fire, for he shall command both of them alike unto his ascension . . .

Eucladower took a deep breath and dabbed his forehead with the sleeve of his green silk robe. His labored breaths slowed as he

369

carefully passed the fragile parchment to the elders. Each one read the parchment and handed it to the next until it reached the king. King Overmoon read the parchment, then placed it on the table in front of him.

"Do read the second passage, Elder Eucladower," the king said in an almost whisper. The entire room sat in awe as the ancient elf began again.

> . . . Let it be known to all who have wisdom that this child, the Abyss Walker, will have the knowledge and power of a thousand lifetimes, though his mortal body will be younger than the trees he walks among. He will be betrayed by blood that is his own, when he fights that which cannot be fought. He shall defeat that which cannot be defeated and he will ascend that which hath no ascension. He will rise up for forty-two cycles, the last eight will bring about a plague on the land that has never been seen before, nor will be seen again. His emerald eyes will bear the pain of an eternity of damned souls that only the children of the forest may see. His mouth will shed forth such fire that any opposing him will be charred to dust from which they were created . . .

Again Eucladower passed the parchment to the closest elder to read. When he had finished reading it he passed the parchment along until it reached the king. King Overmoon did with the second parchment as he had done with the first.

"Do read the third and final passage, Elder Eucladower."

Eucladower nodded and began reading the final parchment with his old raspy voice.

> . . . He shall wear the cloak of mourning until his forty-second cycle. When he mourns no longer, the world will begin its mourning, for his wrath will be unleashed on all the world. When his fury is sedated, the kings of the Abyss will bow to his feet and call him lord, though he will reject them, saying: "You bow to me out of fear. That is all you know, therefore you are not worthy to kiss the bottom of my feet." The Abyss Walker will then turn to the heavens and all mortals dwelling in Yahna will tremble, for they know he is coming, and his wrath is renewed. That will be known as his true ascension . . .

Destiny. A simple seven letter word. Simple to pronounce, yet profound in meaning. Many pay a life's wages to learn their destiny and then destroy their lives trying to avoid it. Most people seek it out, but the wise fear it, and the brave accept it. But does destiny really exist? Often lovers say if we were destined to be, we will be. In a way I believe this to be true. But I argue this; someday you will die, is that destiny? Some say yes, it is a form of it. But what if you drank some poison today, would you then die, regardless of when you would have died if you did not? Of course you would die today. Did I then change destiny by drinking the poison? In a way. The end result of destiny is the same, but the means to it did not occur like it was thought to come to pass.

I say be wary of those who claim they are destined for anything. They are most likely fools merely trying to convince others of their own greatness, when in fact they have none. I was told my destiny many times, though in a way I fulfilled it, but mostly I did as I pleased, forcing destiny to bend around me, not me around it. But as always the end result was the same. As mortal men, we all will die. Many men learn of their destinies, but it is just the wise ones who depict which path they will take to get there.

—Lancalion Levendis Lampara—

Ten

And So He Shall Be Bound . . .

Deep yellow sulfuric clouds raged in a black sky that hung over a barren rocky waste. There were no plants, no animals, no water, just miles and miles of endless jagged onyx rocks and arctic cold. This is the deep abyss. A place to house the ultimate evils and the souls they damn. Dark silhouettes of sinister winged creatures dotted the infinite sky, and screams of pain and torment occasionally echoed across the barren landscape. Lightning flashed across the sulfuric atmosphere and the black clouds violently rolled and tumbled. The tumultuous scene was highlighted by the silhouette of a single man as he ran barefoot over the jagged terrain. His feet bled profusely and his eyes were wild with terror. The man was completely naked and bore many wounds on his soft pale skin. He was about thirty years old and his oily brown hair bounced stiffly in great greasy strings as he ran. His dirty hair was stiff and frozen and his body was covered in blisters from the abyssal cold, yet he did not have frost bite anywhere. No, in the abyss, nothing would inflict the damned that numbed any pain they might have. The only definite in the abyss was pain itself.

The man was well muscled and easily scampered up small rocky embankments, ignoring the ripped skin on his knees and hands from climbing the razor sharp rocks. His eyes watered and his lungs burned from the sulfuric air of the abyss as an occasional bolt of lightning flashed, showing a narrow path for the naked man to follow. He had no idea where he was running to, yet he ran. There was no place, really, for him to run. Everywhere he looked there were endless miles of rocky waste that were littered with the foulest beasts and demons the mind could comprehend.

The naked man stumbled and fell face first, sliding on the rough rocks that made up the ground beneath him. Stone debris scattered across the ground making grating noises from his fall. The naked man did not cry out in pain as his soft flesh was torn and cut. Blood ran from his fresh wounds and pooled on the rock-strewn wasteland beneath him. He merely started to get up when his eyes saw three shadowy, black, twelve-inch claws that dug into the hard stone. The claws were attached to a dark red foot that was more reptilian than human. Hard bony scales rose from the bottom of the shin to a knee that had a dark black horn protruding from it.

The man's eyes drifted higher up the beast and fear riddled him. He muttered a half-curse, half-cry at the sight of the fiend that stood before him. The demon had flames that danced and flickered across his massive muscular chest and down his thick arms and legs. His head was shaped like that of a man, but he lacked any hair, and deep black goat horns protruded from his head and curved down toward his back. The demon's great bat wings were outstretched behind him. His eyes were set afire with an amber aura that extended horizontally past his thick muscled face, which possessed such a penetrating gaze that anyone who met it, cowered in fear. The great demon chuckled as the human hung his head low and cried.

"Where were you going, Trinidy?" the great demon asked as he towered some fifteen feet high over the frail naked human. The human did not respond with anything other than uncontrollable weeping.

"Did you think you might escape? You have been here, oh, say ten mortal years or more. Yet, in your foolishness, you have not learned that there is no escaping my grasp. Your god has abandoned you, paladin. Why else would you be here?" the demon taunted.

"No!" Trinidy screamed as he leaped up and threw a punch at the demon's abdomen. The demon's mighty hand caught and smothered Trinidy's tiny fist and hoisted him in the air. With one powerful arm, he shifted momentum and sent the naked man head first back into the ground. There was a sickening crack as Trinidy's neck and skull collapsed from the force of the fall. Blood spurted from the fresh wound and splattered across the barren land. Small six-legged insect-like creatures erupted from the tiny cracks and began feasting on the fresh blood. Trinidy moaned in pain and sat up. He struggled to see out of his eyes as blood and tissue dripped into them. His head hung limp to the side from his broken neck, and horrible pain ripped through his body. He tried to ignore it. He had learned that the body cannot be killed or destroyed in the abyss. His wounds could easily be healed by any lessser demon so they could be re-inflicted again. That was part of the torture they reserved for the damned. Trinidy has seen Panoleen, his son, and everyone he has held dear, come to him and betray him in the abyss. They hated him, mocked him, tortured him, laughed at him, though he knew it was not them at all, but merely demons in disguise trying to hurt him beyond his body, and the champion paladin resisted. The demons were masters of lies and deceit, he had learned that quickly. Trinidy knew that as long as he held on to who he was, the demons could not break his soul. That was all he had left. If he lost that, there was no path for redemption. The paladin had no idea why the demon Bykalicus had gained control over him when he had died. Trinidy followed and worshipped Dicermadon, the god of magic and knowledge often referred to as the god of gods. He knew he was in good favor with his god at the time of his death, yet he awakened here, in the foulest place in existence. Trinidy imagined it had to be a test from Dicermadon, his god, before he was allowed to ascend with him. Trinidy had stayed true, despite the horrible trials he endured, yet his god never came for him. Trinidy knew that the demons were trying to break him for some reason, trying to crush his spirit. He had seen those who had been broken. They were never healed and often crawled about the abyss missing their lower torso with their entrails dragging behind them, or some were merely heads that were often chewed on by larger demons or kicked about by the smaller ones. They kept him whole for some large plan, he surmised. If he could discover why, he knew he could break free of their control and return to his god.

"Again, tell me where you were to run, mighty paladin?" Bykalicus mocked, knowing that calling the weak helpless Trinidy *mighty* was a great stab at his soul, for the paladin had once been mighty.

"Away, stupid dog, is it not obvious? I was running away," Trinidy retorted through his crushed skull and broken neck.

Bykalicus outstretched his arms and roared such a roar that every demon that was within eyesight fled in terror at the rumble from the abyssal king. The flames that flickered across his body erupted in a jet of violet flames that emitted such a cold that Trinidy could feel his skin freeze and crack right off of his face. Bykalicus shot out his hand, jabbing his clawed finger into Trinidy's chest. The paladin went wide-eyed as the demon's finger pierced his body. Bykalicus hoisted the paladin up to inches from his face. Blood dripped from the wound and froze before it hit the stone ground, making a tapping sound when the frozen pebbles of blood bounced on the hard gray slate. Trinidy could smell the acrid odor of Bykalicus's breath, despite his crushed skull and broken neck.

"Do you still pray, paladin?" Bykalicus bellowed. Acidic spit from the demon hit Trinidy's face and sizzled the already frozen flesh. The wound in his chest screamed at his mind as he felt his internal organs tear and pull from his body weight hanging against the wound.

"Can your god hear you, fool? Pray to him. I dare you. I will prove once and for all that he has abandoned you, champion," the demon king taunted.

Trinidy's mind raced. Was he really going to be allowed to pray? Every time he had tried in the past, mind numbing pain ripped through his head, rendering him either too stunned to think, or unconscious. He had tried to pray every day, or at least what resembled days in the cold dark abyss, until he lost count of the time he had been there. And then the forsaken paladin still tried to establish that link with his god to no avail. Every now and then, despite his perpetual failure, Trinidy thought he felt something, perhaps a link or sensation, but he often disregarded it, thinking he was fooling himself or it had been a demon's trick. He had learned how atrocious their tricks could be.

"Do not mock me, Bykalicus. I will not be tricked. I know you are planning something," Trinidy struggled to say through his broken neck. The paladin knew that if he had been in the mortal realm, his wounds would have easily killed him, but here, in the abyss, nothing could kill you. Wounds were merely another form of torture.

Bykalicus rocked his head back in a deep bellowing laugh. He folded his thick red arms and peered down at the broken paladin with his intense, raging, yellow eyes.

"You make me laugh, fool. How long will you be here before you break? You cling to something, some false hope perhaps, that you will be saved. No one will save you. You are mine. If I wish to devour you, it will be done. If I wish to throw you in a deep crevice and allow the gweits to feast on you, it will be done. But believe it or not mighty paladin, your god has offered me a hefty sum to speak with you. I had hoped to have you do the disgusting task through prayer, then I could say I lived up to my side of the bargain, and gain his offer. I know not why he has bothered with a fool like you, but alas it has been done. Perhaps you are stronger than I had thought."

Trinidy tried to lift himself upright. The paladin took the demon's compliment as an acknowledgment of his perseverance, lost in the mention of his god. Trinidy failed to recall that in his entire time in the abyss, the demon had never so much as offered a word of weakness about himself, let alone offer the paladin a statement telling of his own strength. The demon had done nothing except try to break him down. The paladin's head hung low on his chin and hot sticky blood froze to his naked body as it drained from the ghastly wound in his chest, where he had been impaled by the demon king's finger. Behind Bykalicus, Trinidy could see countless shapes of lesser demons looming in the shadows, hungering for him, no doubt smelling his wounds.

"You lie again demon," Trinidy said with a haggard voice. "If my god had a single inclination of my whereabouts, he would come here and smite you and your kind. You would beg him for mercy, but he would not . . ." Trinidy struggled to speak louder as Bykalicus bellowed in hideous laughter. ". . . even give you a passing thought as he destroyed you."

"Your god has no power here, fool," Bykalicus mocked, enjoying how well he had baited the hook. The paladin had been a worthy opponent for some time. Bykalicus could only count on one hand the number of those who had lasted as long as the paladin did before falling prey to his trickeries. But the demon knew that eventually he would. They always did. "If I chose to pull your god apart it would be so. The fool stays where it is safe. He has no real power here."

Rage ripped through Trinidy. He felt no pain, no fear. The mere mention of his god, Dicermadon, had lifted his spirits to unimaginable heights. The lack of despair lifted him and fed his strength. Bykalicus was pleased to see the paladin fighting back.

Pride, the demon king thought to himself. *The fool still has pride.* "Come, my pets," Bykalicus said as he waved his hands at the dark shapes that were looming in the shadows around them.

"Come and feast on the blood of my slave. He is wrong in his thoughts and must be punished."

Trinidy tried to look around, but his injuries kept him from seeing very well, although he knew the demons were there. He could feel them coming, feel their lust for his flesh. The paladin felt fear, but pushed it aside as he had done when he had battled evil in the flesh. "Come on, sons of the dark. I will kill the first that approaches. I know you can die here, so come, that I may end the world of your evil."

Bykalicus struggled to keep from smiling. The cowering, fleeing paladin of days past now stood defiant in the face of a horde of demons while he was naked, weaponless, and broken, yet he decided to battle them. The demon king had spun his web well. The fly lay trapped before him and now it was time to spin him up.

"What in the cursed name of Leska is going on!" Bykalicus roared.

Trinidy felt warm trickles of magic surge through his body. Bright white tendrils of energy whipped around his arms and legs as the gaping hole in his chest closed and the muscles in his neck strengthened, lifting his head upright. The white tendrils heated the air around him, forming the metal armor he wore when he walked the earth. The armor was polished and clean, bright like it was the day it was forged. The chest of the great suit of full plate mail bore the symbol of the god of magic and knowledge, Dicermadon. Trinidy felt his heavy blue cape dangling down his back and fluttering in the wind. The tendrils twisted and roamed their way down his arm and warmed his hand as they shot out past it, forming a white hot blazing sword that cackled and popped in the frigid air of the abyss. Trinidy's being glowed in a blistering white light that forced the horde of demons back, and they shielded their eyes and ran away hissing. Though he could not see their faces, Trinidy knew the demons were afraid, he could sense it. Trinidy looked at his feet as he felt the power surge through him. Hundreds of gweits twisted and rolled on the rocky barren ground at his feet in the troughs of death. The tiny abyssal insects, some a foot long, sizzled and smoked in the searing heat of righteousness that beamed from him. The paladin raised his sword in the air and then rammed it into the rocky ground at his feet. The glowing blade sunk into the rocky floor of the abyss as if it had been stuck into soft mud. Trinidy kneeled at the blade. Bykalicus' eyes went wide, then narrowed as a booming voice permeated the abyss.

"Rise, my child. Do not ever touch your knee to the abyss. It is not of the earth and its taint should only defile the bottom of your boots," the deep booming voice echoed. Bykalicus raised his elbows up as if to shield his face from it.

"He is mine, god of gods!" Bykalicus screamed at the dark sulfurous clouds in defiance.

"No, you have stolen him," the voice corrected. "Trinidy, my warrior, my faithful, my son, why have you remained here with the foul company of this lord of deceit? Why have you not called out to me?"

"I have, my lord, but you could not hear me. Every day I cried out to you, but the foul demons . . ." Trinidy responded as tears of joy streamed down his face.

"You must release him, Bykalicus, or face my wrath," the voice commanded.

"You have no power here, god of gods. He has been mine for some time, and mine he shall stay. I do not . . ." Bykalicus clutched his chest and roared in pain. Flashes of black erupted from the flames that danced across the demon's dark red skin. The demon lord fell to his knees growling in pain.

"Damn you, Dicermadon! He cannot leave the abyss without my invitation. Rip at my insides forever, he will not accept anything from me," Bykalicus chuckled through clenched teeth.

"Make the offer, demon, or I will make good on your request for an eternity," the voice boomed.

Bykalicus' chest heaved as he breathed in ragged gasps while he looked into Trinidy's stern steel eyes. "I offer you to return to the mortal realm, *paladin*. To right that which is wrong, but pray your god does not forget you again. My god hungers for your eternal soul," Bykalicus said as he spit at the feet of the paladin. The spittle sizzled and burned the rocks it lay on.

"Quiet, dog!" the voice screamed. "You shall never inflict your tainted voice on his ears again, and if you or yours ever again take one of mine, I shall come here with my angels and destroy this cursed place," the voice boomed.

"I accept your offer, beast," Trinidy said as he straightened his shoulders.

"Dnuob eb llahs uoy os dna," Bykalicus said with an evil grin as he rose to his feet.

The armor Trinidy wore turned black and shriveled into sable wisps of impermeable tendrils that swirled around him. Terror tore through Trinidy as he tried to shake the black snake-like tendrils from his arms and legs, but the spindly wisps whipped around, ducking and weaving as if they were alive. He felt the horrible cold burn his bare skin, and his lungs burned from the sulfuric air again as his sword and armor melted away and left him naked before the demon lord. Trinidy stumbled to the jagged rocks and looked at his bare arms and legs, where his magnificent armor had been a few moments earlier. The paladin gazed up from his hands and knees at the mocking demonic face that stood before him. Then suddenly he felt himself breaking apart. His skin bubbled and tore, tumbling away into a thousand tiny black pebbles. The abyss melted away from his eyes and he was warm again. Trinidy could see the barren landscape as it fell under him, and he rose to the air. He could see the ever shrinking demon as he gazed upward toward him. Trinidy's fear evaporated as he felt himself leaving the abyss.

"Thank you." He prayed to Dicermadon as the abyss fell away into nothingness and was replaced by calm darkness. "Thank you."

*   *   *

Hector walked determinately down the polished marble corridor of his dark expansive castle. His thick blue velvet cloak flowed in the breeze from his resolute walk as the leather under his heavy metal plate armor creaked. The halls of the corridor were littered with great tapestries that hung from golden rods affixed to the tops of the stone wall. Servants and guardsmen dropped whatever they were doing and fell to their hands and knees as he walked by. If Hector noticed them, he didn't show it. The evil king wore a grim visage of determination and vigor. His priests had summoned him in his chambers and Kalen had surprisingly discovered the name of the child in the prophecies and located him in Beykla. The gray elf

379

still wasn't sure who the mother of mercy was, but he was rapidly narrowing it down. It seemed whenever the elven mage was certain he had discovered the identity of the woman, the priest would point out a discrepancy and they were back to the beginning. Hector hoped the dark priests had discovered something instead of giving the same report he had received the past few weeks. The king was ready to begin executions for failure, but he didn't want to kill any of the priests. Not because he held any attachment to them, but because they were quite useful and it would take a long time to replace any of them. If they had nothing of value to report, he might just execute a servant or someone. Spencer had been lagging in his duties. Perhaps he would slay the pitiful wretch.

Hector rounded the corner of the corridor and paused at the ornate double doors to the church of Rha-Cordan that was inside of his great castle. The flamboyant doors to the god of death's house were made of thick oak, that was varnished to the point of being black, and they were re-enforced with huge iron plates that stretched across them horizontally. At the end of the plates, where the doors met each other, two huge iron rings hung down that were used to pull the doors open. Two royal guards stood watch in front of the church, and they were garbed in the deep black chain mail and leather tunics and breeches that bore Rha-Cordan's symbol, not the symbol of Nalir. The guards were tall and thin, wielding long bec-de-corbans, a long pole arm with a spear tip and a hook on one side that resembled a small axe, that they crossed in front of each other to prohibit the passing of unintended guests. Hector paused as the guards slowly and ceremoniously lifted the weapons to a vertical position. They did not drop to their knees or even bow. The king did not expect them to. He had learned long ago they considered their god their only king, and that Hector was merely their employer. Hector tolerated them as he often tolerated the church: as a small means to get to his ends. He knew he could have them executed at any time he wished. He was sure they knew that fact too, but they were devoted to their beliefs. Hector found that trait almost admirable, but he believed it more foolish than anything.

Hector tossed the edges of his blue velvety cloak over his shoulders, pushed the two great wooden doors open, and walked inside to the worship chamber. The chamber was about ninety feet long and forty feet wide. The walls were covered in dark tapestries depicting the god of death sitting on a throne of bones and in a few other positions. There were many candles sitting on ledges at each thick wooden beam that lined the walls. The beams were fifty feet high and led to a circular dome in the center of the room. The dome was covered in divine symbols and carvings made of gold and other precious metals. At the far end of the chamber four priests, including Resin Darkhand, the high priest, and Kalen, sat in chairs at a small table that had been placed in front of the altar for this apparent meeting. When Hector strode forward, they all stood and bowed deeply. Resin started to speak but Hector cut him off.

"Be quick with this report. The body of the Ecnal's father has been located in a mass grave near the Nalir-Vidorian border. We have over four hundred skeletal remains to search through and I need you priests to go speak with the departed souls and find which bones belong to who," Hector demanded coldly.

"My master . . ." Kalen began with an exaggerated bow and deep sinister smile. ". . . we have much to . . ."

Again Hector cut in. "I care not for what you have to say to me, fool elf. You have my manservant, Spencer, so rattled his heart is not into living most of the time. I will deal with your torture tactics after this meeting is adjourned," Hector said with an evil glare.

Kalen merely smiled and bowed as he whispered to himself, "I grow weary of you, master. Soon you will be old and feeble. I shall teach you then, the cusps of my torture tactics."

"What do you have to report, Resin?" Hector asked.

Resin straightened his robes nervously. "We have discovered much once we began to study with apprentice Kalen."

Hector raised an eye at his elf apprentice. The gray elf merely smiled and nodded his head submissively. "Go on," Hector commanded.

"We found the DeNaucght that the demon spoke of. It is not a ritual that we can perform. In fact, it is a ritual that angers Rha-Cordan more than commanding the undead to rise and walk from their graves. The DeNaucght is a ritualistic spell that requires three powerful goodly priests in order to cast it. It will summon the soul back to the body it came from and allow the person to live again as though he never died. If it is cast on a child, he will awake as the child he was when he died. If it is cast on an old man who was on his death bed, he will awake as the same old man, and would

381

surely die again soon. We know not what the demon meant, but surely we could not use Rha-Cordan's divinity on such a spell. It would surely not function as it was intended to," Resin stated flatly.

Hector frowned and rubbed his chin. "Perhaps the demon knows that it will not function the same."

"We had anticipated that, my lord, but we searched through every archive from every priest in the nation and we found nothing ever mentioning the ritual being performed by priests of our order," Resin offered.

Hector sat down in the soft plush chair that was placed at the head of the small table.

"You heal sometimes Resin, but is that not against the order?" Hector asked.

"Yes, but if it is to further the goals of our god, it is overlooked," the dark priest responded.

"Good, it is settled. There is no other kingdom in the realms that has followed and maintained the principles of the god of death more than Nalir under my rule. You and your priest will perform DeNaucght as soon as we sort out the skeletal remains. Surely you cannot argue that furthering the kingdom goes against the wishes of Rha-Cordan," Hector said.

"We cannot argue it at all, my king. Your rule is a bright beacon in the eyes of Rha-Cordan, but there is information that Kalen needs to speak of that relates to the prophecy and the Ecnal," Resin said.

Hector looked at the thin gray elf with his blue robes and long silver hair. "What do you have to say, elf?" Hector asked angrily.

"There are two other pages to the prophecy that we have not been able to decipher yet, and will probably not be able to in many years to come, but there are four semi-prophetic passings of elven culture that coincide with the prophecies themselves," Kalen said.

Hector didn't reply. He just folded his arms impatiently at the priests and opened an ink bottle while unrolling a parchment to scribe the words the elf spoke.

"The son of a Vale, not by blood, will turn his back on his brethren and embrace the shadow. I believe that passing refers to me. The self-righteous elven culture believes that Rha-Cordan is evil. As you know I was the stepson of King Christopher Calamon Overmoon for a short time. That would make me son of a Vale, but not by blood."

"What is a Vale, and what does it have to do with the Ecnal?" Hector asked impatiently.

"The Ecnal you seek is also known as the Abyss Walker in elven prophecy. He is foretold to bring plagues and other horrific things to the world. A Vale is a great elven city, but elven cities are hidden among the trees so much that if you walked in one, you would not even know you were there. These passages refer to Ecnal, which also is the son of the mother of mercy," Kalen explained.

"Go on with the other three," Hector commanded.

"A babe, half not of this earth, and half damned by the gods themselves, feared by the children of the forest, will carry his own proclamation naming him for who he is not, but for who he will become."

"What in Rha's underworld does that mean?" Hector asked angrily.

Kalen shrugged his shoulders. "It makes no sense as far as we are concerned, but I would suspect it will be meaningful to the Vales."

"Perhaps it has something to do with giving himself a title," Resin chided in.

"Perhaps. What are the others?" Hector asked.

"He who walks with wrath shall stride into the Vale as a guest wearing the Cadacka, though he knows not why he mourns. If the children of the forest do nothing, they will surely perish," Kalen recited slowly.

"Another one that means nothing to us. What is a Cadacka?" Hector asked.

Kalen frowned impatiently. "It is a cloak worn by those who are in mourning."

Hector merely showed a puzzled look and shook his head as Kalen recited the fourth passing.

"I do not know the fourth passing Hec . . ." Kalen corrected himself, ". . . King De Scoran. But I have agents working on getting it as we speak. These are elven secrets that are guarded more heavily than an arch-mage's tower. But fear not, my king, I will learn them."

"Believe me, elf, it is not I who should fear your failure," Hector threatened, then turned to the priests. "Do you have anything else?"

"Yes, my king. We believe the Ecnal's father's name is Trinidy. You had the family ordered murdered for worshipping another god other than Rha-Cordan. He was a paladin of the great god Dicermadon. His wife's name was Panoleen, but she did not worship Dicermadon. She was slain for blasphemy. The records show she spoke of a goddess of mercy," Resin said as he dabbed the sweat on his forehead with the sleeve of his robe.

"Why is his mother's name important? Was she some kind of merciful person, or is the Ecnal the merciful one?" Hector asked.

Resin shrugged his shoulders. "I do not know, my king, but I suspect that because the Ecnal's mother worshipped this false goddess, she might be the mother of mercy."

Hector sat up in his chair. "Is there a goddess of mercy?" Hector asked.

"If there is, I know not of it," Resin admitted.

Hector turned and looked at Kalen. Kalen shrugged his shoulders. "I have never read anything that refers to a goddess of mercy, but there are passages in the elven scrolls that refer to a forgotten goddess, and in the ancient scrolls there are missing sentences and some even half-pages that seemed as if they were magically erased somehow. It could be that these missing areas contained information about her. I do not understand how the same passages could have been erased worldwide, but they are in every ancient scroll that I have read," Kalen chided. "What is the most surprising, is that many scrolls I memorized word for word, have changed."

"Changed? How?" Hector asked inquisitively.

Kalen shrugged. "I do not know, but the name Panoleen just recently re-appeared. Still massive amounts of information are missing, but now the name Panoleen seems to be quite predominant, when before, it did not exist."

"No matter," Hector said as he stood up from the small table in the chamber room. "I will take my leave. Praise to you for your efforts. We shall be rewarded. I will have the excavators deliver the bones from the grave here. I want them sorted out as soon as they arrive. Be diligent, priests. Do not incur my wrath."

"We will complete your task as soon as possible in

Rha-Cordan's name," Resin said to Hector's back as the king walked from the chamber room.

"Be mindful of your loyalties, priests," Kalen said as he rose from his chair when Hector had left the room. "You might be surprised when they might be called upon."

Resin and the others looked at each other in confusion, but did not respond. It was no secret among the clergy that Kalen held no love for the king. But neither did they, save for when he demanded the masses to embrace the will of their god. That was the only loyalty they would acknowledge. The only loyalty that mattered.

*　　*　　*

Large wisps of dust and dirt blew like tiny storms across the barren plains. Gentle rolling hills of brown grass that were almost as high as a man, littered the ground like small patches on a pair of breeches. There were little or no trees, save for an occasional bush that had grown large enough to provide shade. Had it been summer, the plains would have been unbearably hot, but now with the embrace of autumn in full swing, the cool breeze was a friendly kiss under the hot sun. The land hadn't seen rain in weeks, but so was the way with the Serrin Plains. It rained seldom here, though no one knew why. Some said it was a curse from the gods, others claimed it had something to do with the wind currents from the Balfour Sea, north of Beykla. Regardless, the plains were intolerably hot in the summer and endurable in the fall and spring. In the winter, the snows would all but seal off the road with the great drifts that would rise from the never ending winds. But now, in early autumn, small animals scampered around in the safe grass and some zipped across the trail. The horses were spooked at the tiny animals always darting in front of them, but after the second day, they seemed to accept the furry little monsters as harmless, though they still would tense when one scampered across.

Lance enjoyed the slow paced ride. They had been on the trail for nearly a week. The paladin was paying them each day at nightfall and the elf did all the hunting. The Ecnal had studied his spells every night before he had gone to bed inside one of the small one-man tents that Apollisian had provided for Jude and him. Jude had declined to use his, saying that a tent kept him from seeing his enemies and allowed them to see him easily. But Lance had enjoyed the seclusion from the prying eyes. After the first week, Lance had just about learned every spell in the Necromidus. The collection of necromancy spells were complex at first, but the basis for all of the spells was the same. After Lance had worked out the first few, he had learned the pattern to the others and mastered the book in no time. Lance shuddered at some of the descriptions of the spells, and at what weaving certain patterns did. Most of the dweamors resulted in the painful death of the target, and a few did worse, ripping at the enemies' souls. There was a spell that caused nearby dead creatures to rise up and walk on the command of the caster. Why anyone would want to make the dead walk was beyond him. There was even one that allowed the caster to drain the life force of the victim and heal his own wounds from that energy. That was the closest to a healing spell that was in the book.

They rode for most of the day and made camp on a small hill at the base of a much larger one that was a few hundred feet from the trail. Apollisian and Jude began digging a fire pit and Lance would set up his tent and tend to the horses while Alexis grabbed her bow and went on a hunt. Once the fire was set and the horses were attended to, they mulled around the camp while their supper cooked.

Lance sat around the campfire on the cool autumn night. He held his cloak tightly around himself and scooted his feet close to the fire. The once cool breeze that had blown by had turned into a cold wind that chilled the young mage to the bone. Alexis had done well in hunting and the smell of the cooking rabbit made Lance's stomach growl. Apollisian sat on a log away from the fire with Jude. The pair had seldom talked, but they sharpened their swords at the same time each night. Alexis always asked Lance a lot of questions, mostly about his parents and where he was from, but she always stayed far away when they spoke. If Lance tried to come closer, she would get quiet and look away. Lance had asked her similar questions and learned a great deal about her culture in doing so.

Alexis sat down on a small rock that was next to the fire and warmed her hands and feet, occasionally turning the rabbit that roasted on the fire. She seemed distant tonight and often glanced into the darkness as if she were expecting something to emerge from it and attack them.

"You expecting company?" Lance asked sarcastically as he rubbed his socked feet together near the fire.

Alexis looked around again, as if Lance had reminded her that something was out there. After a short look, she turned back to him and stared at the ground when she spoke. She seemed to always stare at the ground. "We are in the Serrin Plains. There are many creatures that call this place home. Many of which do not take kindly to trespassers, and others that like trespassers, thinking they taste good. Either way, if we meet some of them, it will not be a pleasant encounter."

Lance looked around nervously, suddenly more aware of the dark than he had been a few moments before. "Like what kind of creatures? Like orcs?"

Alexis turned the rabbit again and stirred the fire with a small stick. Bright burning pieces of ash erupted into the air and rose above the fire, burning out after rising a few feet. "There are a few orc tribes that live in here. The plains are vast, but they stay away from the trails and live in seclusion for the most part. Our main concern is the hill giants."

Lance blinked in astonishment. In Bureland, long before Lance had come to live there, a hill giant attacked the town. The townsfolk said it killed twenty militiamen and ten royal guardsmen before it died. It is said that its club is the main beam that holds up the roof in the Aldon Inn. Lance had often rubbed the gnarled beam, doubting the stories, thinking drunkards had concocted it to attract patrons. Lance tried to imagine what a hill giant looked like, and how a man could even fight a beast like that.

"How do they live?" Lance asked. Alexis gave him a puzzled look. Lance frowned. "I mean, what do they eat? There aren't many game animals in the plains, and I don't think they could live off of rabbits and squirrels."

Alexis smiled nervously. "Why, they eat travelers like us, orcs, whatever they can get their hands on. Sometimes, they probably eat each other."

Lance felt queasy at the thought of being eaten and his own hunger subsided a little.

"Shouldn't we put out the fire or something like that?" Lance asked as he looked out into the darkness again.

"No, they do not hunt at night. Their vision is too poor to compete with the animals so they only hunt during the day."

Lance nodded his head and curled up by the fire. Alexis got up and took the rabbit down and cut it into four pieces. She handed Apollisian and Jude a piece each and then walked over and handed Lance one. As soon as Lance took the meat from her hand, she reached back quickly and sat down on the other side of the fire. Lance shrugged his shoulders and ate the juicy meat. It was not seasoned like he was accustomed to, but it was cooked on an open fire, which always seemed to make the meat taste better to him. His adoptive father often cooked out on an open fire with him when he was a boy. As he ate, Lance wondered if the letter he wrote Davohn had gotten to him yet. He hated to make the woodcutter worry, but he knew he had to investigate his parents' deaths. It was as if something pulled at him to do it.

Lance finished the rabbit and tossed the bones in the fire. He licked the greasy juice from his fingers and lay back on the ground, folding his hands behind his head. He gazed at the thousands of stars and wondered if Davohn were on his rooftop star gazing like he used to.

"Where did you get your robe?" Alexis asked bluntly as she chewed. Lance looked down and grabbed the front of his black and silver robe.

"What? This?" Lance asked pointing to his chest. "My mother gave it to me when I was very young. She said I should wear it when I got older. She said it would save my life. I never really gave it much thought. I kept it in a pack that was stored in a chest on the back porch of our home. When the men came and murdered my parents, I grabbed it when I fled. I didn't remember it was in there, I just kept a knife and some other stuff I had as a boy. It is a strange robe, I have never seen one like it before. I think some of these symbols are elven, I am not sure."

Alexis stared at the black and silver Cadacka. She felt her cheeks flush with anger, though she held it in, trying to keep her tone soft. "Why do you think the runes are elven?" she asked, knowing the runes were indeed elven, though she could not read them. She had studied a few scripts in the ancient writing, but she had no idea what the complex symbols on Lance's Cadacka meant.

388

Usually runes were designed for each individual, telling the story of why they mourn.

Lance sat up and shrugged his slender shoulders. "I don't really know, I have these writings that I thought were Nalirian, but a sage told me they were elven. Some of the markings on my robe are the same as the ones in the parchment."

Alexis's eyes lit up and she scooted closer to Lance, though still keeping a safe distance. "You mean you have some elven writing?" she asked, hoping it would shed some light on why the human was wearing a Cadacka that he knew nothing about. Perhaps his mother was the thief, or his father. Regardless, Alexis figured the explanation was in those papers. "Perhaps I could see them, maybe read them for you?" she asked with a wry smile that put Lance on edge. Lance indeed wanted the pages read for him. Kaisha was supposed to read them, but she was a long way away. Lance reluctantly reached for his pack and pulled out the leather pouch. He stared at it uneasily for a few seconds. It was in good order, though a little dusty from the trail. It was as if he almost feared what it might say. He had grown accustomed to not knowing what it said, and now, when faced with the chance to know, he had second thoughts.

"Perhaps we should read it another time. It is late and . . ." Lance was cut off when Alexis reached over and snatched the case from his hands. He surprised himself when he did not try to stop her.

Jude walked over with a piece of the rabbit in his mouth. He was trying to eat every small morsel of meat from its bones. His hands shined in the fire light with grease and his face glistened also. He studied the portion for a few moments and decided there was nothing left worth picking at and tossed the bones into the fire. He wiped his mouth with his sleeve and glanced down at the elf opening the parchment. The large swordsman quickly glanced at Lance and then back to the parchment. His friend did not look to be upset so he sat down and crossed his legs in the dirt.

"She's gonna read it for you, huh?" Jude asked as he licked his fingers clean.

Lance nodded nervously. Alexis didn't seem to notice the big man's presence, she was intent on the package. With nimble fingers she drew the parchments out from the case and stared at them. She said nothing, only stared stunned at the pages.

Apollisian came over with a piece of his plate armor in his hand and a polishing rag.

"What's so interesting?" the paladin asked.

Jude leaned over and whispered softly. "The elf is going to read some papers that my friend has been trying to understand for a long time. Those parchments are the whole reason that we left our happy little town on this fool adventure."

Apollisian backed away a few steps and whispered back to Jude. He covered his mouth with his hand in an attempt to muffle his voice. "What is so special about them? Do they explain his cloak?"

Jude frowned in puzzlement. "His cloak? No, he hired a thief a while back to steal these papers from a politician in Nalir."

Apollisian's eyes arched up at the mention of thievery. "He hired a thief, huh? Why would he do that?"

"Because he thinks the Nalirian government had his parents killed. He hoped the papers were some kind of murder order or something like that, but it turns out that they are written in elven. A very strange turn of events I must say," Jude noted. "Why did you ask about his cloak? He has had that since he was a boy. I assure you it is not stolen. He says his mother left it for him."

Apollisian shifted his feet. "The runes on the cloak and the colors are very similar to an elven robe of ceremony. Overmoon thinks that it means something."

"Like what?" Jude asked, looking back at the elf sitting on the small rock, reading. Apollisian shrugged his shoulders and continued to polish his armor.

"Beats me. Some silly elven thing, they are fickle creatures," Apollisian said as he wandered back over to his horse.

Jude stood and watched for a moment longer, then returned to his new friend to sharpen their swords. Jude liked the paladin, but he didn't agree with the way the paladin solved his problems. It seemed as if the man made them more difficult than they actually were, but Jude could tell he was a good man nonetheless.

Alexis examined each parchment carefully. "I cannot make much of these out," she said with a defeated tone. "They are in elven, but the text is so old I cannot understand it. I know of a few village elders that might be able to read this. I know my father can."

Lance sighed and slumped his shoulders. "Do you think they

390

mention my mother's or father's names? My mother is Panoleen and my father is Trinidy."

Alexis shook her head. "There are no special symbols for names, they are written the same as if they were in present day writings. I am sorry, but I see nothing that mentions any names."

Lance moaned, got up from the fire, and gradually wandered to his tent. Alexis watched as he slowly climbed inside and lay down. She stood looking at the writings, confused. Shaking her head she placed them back into the leather case and then put them in her pack.

"We are turning in, Overmoon. You still want first watch?" Apollisian asked.

She nodded back and drew her finely crafted bow. Notching a bright white arrow with the green fletching, she headed up the base of the large hill. She moved as silently as the wind, not even rustling the tall brown grass, and quickly ascended the small peak. With the moon bright in the sky, she could watch the camp and the surrounding areas much better than on other nights. Apollisian climbed into his bed roll and Jude sat up a while longer sharpening his sword, before he too turned in and drifted to sleep. Alexis sat on the hilltop listening to the sounds of the night. Crickets chirped their songs and an occasional wolf howled at the moon in the distance. She smiled to herself and thanked Leska for the beautiful night. She had spent enough time in the human cities to last her a lifetime. She was finally going home.

*   *   *

"My Guidance . . ." the acolyte said as he bowed low to Resin. The high priest looked up from the edge of the great book. His deep violet robe hung over his face and his dark sinister eyes peered from under the hood and just above the ancient tome.

"Yes, Pockweln? What is it? I hope it is important."

Pockweln dipped low, his blonde hair fell down over his eyes and he quickly wiped it away. "We have discovered what bones are Trinidy's. We did as the DeNaucght requires and set his agreement for resurrection."

Resin stared at the young priest for a few moments before answering. "I suspect that you did as I commanded and disguised yourself as his god?"

Pockweln nodded. "He did as you said he would, and there was another voice, we could not drown it out, or prevent its speech. It was as if he had more power than we did combined. We tried many times to silence him, but we could not, though he didn't interfere. It almost seemed as if he helped in some way. There were things happening that we could not see. I could tell from the fluctuations in the paladin's voice."

"There was much going on that you could see, my apprentice. You could not silence the voice in a hundred years. It has more power than you ever will. Even I could not muffle him, even if I studied for ten lifetimes," Resin said flatly as he glanced back down at the pages of the tome he had been reading. "I have made an arrangement with Bykalicus that need not be discussed. You and the others did not hear his voice, nor was he present. Do I make myself clear?"

Pockweln visibly stiffened at the mention of the arch demon. "My mentor, I hope you have the power of Lukerey with you when you make such deals with the denizens of the deep abyss."

Resin chuckled to himself at the mention of the god of luck and mischief, but did not look up from his reading. "My faithful apprentice, I do need his power on my side, though using caution is an understatement when dealing with his kind. A wise man understands that luck is when preparedness meets opportunity. And my good apprentice, I am very opportunistic," the high priest said, as his thick tome hid his wide grin. "Was there anything else to report?"

"Only one other thing, my mentor. There is one set of remains that gives us difficulty. They are from a female, a human we suspect, but we are unable to make contact with the soul."

Resin arched an eyebrow and set down the tome. He did not expect that response. He rubbed his chin and stepped away from the dark polished podium. "What do you mean, you can't make contact with the soul? No soul is forbidden to Rha-Cordan when the body is possessed. Are you merely weary? Perhaps you should try in the morrow," Resin suggested as he walked over to a small table that was set against the wall. The high priest opened a flask of fine red wine and poured it into a silver goblet. The red fluid sloshed up around the brim and the dark priest slowed his pouring when the goblet filled. He raised the silver chalice to his lips and sipped.

"High priest, I know that I, and the others, are not weary. It is as if the remains have no soul. Is it possible for a soul to be destroyed?" Pockweln asked.

Resin took a long sip and placed the goblet back down onto the table. The sound of the hard silver hitting the wooden table seemed to echo in the high priest's chamber. "No, it is not possible. Take me to the bones and I shall see for myself. For your sake, I hope that there is something prohibiting the casting, for if it is your ineptness, you shall be punished."

Pockweln bowed and led Resin to the large examination room. If the young priest had fear, he did not show it, though that was the way of their order. They did not fear death. They knew that in their demise, they would be rewarded by Rha-Cordan, and he would shelter them from the dark abyss. They believed that no other deity had the power to control the afterlife like he did. And in truth, they were somewhat correct.

The priests walked into the bone chamber. The room was over a hundred by a hundred feet and there were many large tables that were littered with bones and small parchments with names and other material written on them. Pockweln led Resin to a small table in the back that contained a single set of female remains. The skeleton was not complete, but the skull and most of the torso were intact. Resin took down his robe's hood and began chanting. He began with rhythmic movements of his hands and his aging voice rose and fell a methodic tune that seemed to enchant and inspire. Weaves of wispy black magical energies swirled around the dark priest's old knobby hands and fell around the remains that lay on the table. Resin moved his arms as if in a dance, dipping and twisting around in front of him, while he softly chanted the words of his spell. The aging priest's voice was harsh, but not yet raspy. He had somewhat of an angry expression on his face that poked out from under his long hair. His acolytes had been ordered to cast a few simple spells that allowed them to speak with the souls that had once belonged to the bones. After a few weeks they had identified all but this last set. It appeared to belong to a young woman, perhaps Trinidy's wife. Her name was Panoleen. Such an unusual name. Resin doubted he had ever heard the name in his entire life, or any other like it. His acolytes had difficulty speaking to her soul from beyond the grave. It was a relatively easy task. He surmised that perhaps they were tired from the taxing duties of summoning all the other souls.

The high priest finished his casting, but nothing happened. Resin frowned in frustration. He knew he had performed the spell correctly, yet he did not even sense the soul that belonged to the bones, let alone make contact for speech. He took a deep breath and exhaled slowly. Rubbing the beads of sweat from his creased forehead, he began chanting again. The sable cusps of magical energy whipped around him, just like before. His voice was louder, more focused, more angry, yet after a few minutes of focused casting, he achieved nothing. Anger flashed in the composed priest's eyes. He looked down at the remains that lay out before him. The bones were indeed real. They had not been fabricated, or cast. Yet he could not summon the soul that once dwelled within them.

Pockweln adjusted the front of his smock, and wiped his greasy hair back from his face.

"Did you make contact, my savior?" the young priest asked.

Resin seemed not to notice being called savior. It was the highest accolade to give to a leader of the church who followed the god of death. To be called savior meant that the person was responsible for saving their soul, and that without him or her, they would have been lost. Yet the praise fell on deaf ears. "Get out!" Resin shouted as he hastily removed his dark violet robe and tossed it on the table that was next to him. The high priest didn't even look to his acolytes as they bowed and started for the door. Resin wiped the sweat from his forehead and began chanting a third time. Pockweln motioned to the others and they quickly departed the room. When he heard the heavy door shut, Resin took a deep breath and began casting a third time, refusing to accept the possibility that the carcass had no soul. Even those who sold their souls to the gods could be summoned from their remains, yet this set of bones denied him.

He tried again and again, and each time he failed. A small candle was lit and set on the edge of the old table. Sweat ran down the side of his face and his back. His violet robe had long since been removed and lay on the table crumpled in a ball. He had the sleeves of his white silk tunic, which he wore underneath, rolled up to his elbows, he had unbuttoned the tunic to the bottom of his chest. Resin

394

placed his hands on the edge of the table and leaned over the bones. Sweat dripped from his chin and he breathed heavily. The high priest stared at the remains and the lifeless skull stared back, mocking him. Resin grabbed the dark brown cranium with both of his hands and drew it near his face. His hands shook with anger and his eyes flared with fury. "How do you deny me?" he shouted, his voice echoing across the large chamber. The skull only stared back in silence. Shaking his head, Resin placed the skull gently back down on the table and sat back in one of the many hard wooden chairs. He picked up a plain wooden goblet and waved his hand over the top. With a brief chant, the goblet filled with sparkling clear water that was chilled as if it ran from a mountain stream. Resin gulped the refreshing water down and wiped his mouth, letting his weary head fall back against the stone wall. The high priest rolled his head to one side, facing the chamber door when he heard it creak open. He started to protest in anger, thinking one of his acolytes had entered the chamber without his permission, but his anger subsided when he watched the nimble gray elf, known as Kalen, stroll in.

Kalen turned and slowly shut the door, careful not to make too much noise. He was dressed in a dark gray sleeping tunic and baggy brown breeches. His silver hair was tidy and pulled back against his head. His brown fur slippers glided across the stone floor of the chamber. Resin watched as he approached. Kalen scooted some of the bones over on the table that was next to Resin and hopped up, sitting while his feet dangled off.

"Having some difficulties, priest?" Kalen asked with an evil grin. Resin turned and regarded the mage. His face bore a sinister look that made Kalen lean back slightly.

"I am not in the mood, mage, for you or for yours. I am trying a task that you could never perform," Resin said as he stood up, stretching, and leaned back against the cold stone wall.

Kalen regarded the haggard priest with mild amusement. A thin wry smile crept on the gray elf's face. He sat on the small wooden table with an air of pompous authority that enraged the dark priest to near violence. If Kalen noticed the priest's angry glare, he ignored it. "Why is it so important to speak with these remains? We have Trinidy. That is what is important. In the morning you will perform the DeNaucght, just as the king wishes, and all

395

will be well. You can return to this chamber and question the bones till you wither and die," Kalen said with a mocking tone.

Resin shot forward and pointed his finger a few inches from Kalen's face. "I will perform that which is necessary to further the needs of Rha-Cordan. I will do nothing more. I am no puppet that dances on the strings of some king!" Resin shouted angrily.

Kalen smiled, ignoring the shaking finger that was a few inches from his face. Resin had become angry before, but Kalen knew the human priest was more than intimidated by his power. Kalen feigned a yawn and slowly patted the palm of his hand over his mouth. "So you say, priest. I need not see the wind to know it blows, and I need not see the strings that make you dance like an adolescent jester, to know they are being pulled."

Resin backed away and flexed his fists. He glanced around the room and took a deep breath before turning back to the gray elf who sat before him. "You will not weave me in your webs, Kalen. It is no mystery that you knit plots and schemes better than a jealous mistress."

Kalen did not lose his smile, though his face flushed with anger at Resin's comparison of him to a woman. The gray elf paused to regain his composure when Resin cut him off.

"Now, mage, you will leave my chambers immediately for I am finished with this verbal tirade. If you do not, I shall bring the wrath of Rha-Cordan down upon you," Resin commanded.

Kalen glanced around the room involuntarily, making frequent looks to the ceiling as if the priest were going to make good on his claim. Kalen hopped down from the table and walked toward the door timidly, half expecting the priest to retaliate in some fashion, yet he reached the ornate wooden door without incident. The gray elf turned and spoke to Resin before he ducked out the chamber door. "Know your place, priest. You never know when the toes you stomp today will be connected to the ass you will kiss tomorrow," Kalen said wryly as he turned and confidently walked from the chamber. There was no stir of air in the stale room, but his robe seemed to flow around him when he walked, as if his own private breeze followed him about.

Resin wanted to reply, to fire a few parting remarks, but by the time any had come to his mind, the gray elf had left. The priest jabbed his fist into his hand. Kalen was the one that needed to know his place. He was merely a foolish mage, caught in an epic plight that involved the very gods themselves. Resin didn't know how deep this plight ran, but the more he learned of it, the more he decided that the king was in over his head. There was something much deeper here than was let on.

Resin straightened the bones that Kalen had scooted aside and prepped them for yet another spell. He would not try casting it tonight. He was exhausted from the many previous attempts and he didn't know of anything to do differently than he had already done. Resin sat alone in the chamber for many minutes in the darkness staring at the remains. It confounded him how these bones resisted his attempts. Never in his life had he even heard of that happening, let alone experienced it himself. Yet there they lay before him on the old wooden table, mocking him. The dark priest slowly shook his head, pulled his robe close around his neck , and casually walked from the room. The morrow was certainly going to be interesting.

Kalen strode down the dark marbled corridors of Hector's dark sinister keep. There were a few sconces aflame, but the mounted torches bore little light as they were close to being burned out. The long dark velvety tapestries that hung down from the polished stone walls seemed to stare down eerily at the gray elf as he strolled by. Kalen ignored the thick hanging rugs he had walked thousands of times. He casually turned down a south corridor that was lit even more dimly than the one he had just walked down. He walked slowly, scooting his fur slippers across the marbled floor, alerting the two guards that he was approaching. He could easily see the two humans who stood watch outside the king's sleeping chambers. They were large for humans, and were no doubt accomplished fighters. They wore polished plate mail armor and long, blue, silk capes. Their gauntleted hands gripped their halberds tightly as they stood at full attention, straining their inferior eyes to catch a glimpse of the man who was scuffing his feet, but they could not see the gray elf. Kalen chuckled to himself at how deplorable humans were. They could not even see in the dark. He could have been an assassin and the pitiful whelps would not even know he had been there until he gutted them both.

The guards relaxed their stern glares when they recognized the gray elf. They said nothing to Kalen, for it was not uncommon for him to call on the king at late hours. The pair stood rigidly and raised their halberds up in a saluting position and stepped to the side to allow the elf entry. Kalen shook his head in disappointment. He could have been a rival mage magically disguised or some clever thief. The stupid oafs would never know until they found their king dead in the morning. Kalen silently made a mental note of their lack of attention to detail, hoping it would come to use in the future.

The gray elf stepped through the thick wooden double doors and entered the room. It was a massive room, but small in comparison to the other chambers that the king often held. Its ceilings were almost twenty feet tall, and tapestries and ornate carvings and statues littered the room. Large green plants from strange lands sat on thick marbled stands, and the king lay on the bed, propped up by thick pillows, reading some parchments. The bed was made of thick wood from the Vidorian forest. It was covered with silk sheets and the plethora of silk and satin pillows that seemed to engulf him. He placed the parchments aside and took a sip of wine from a jeweled chalice. He gulped down several large swallows and set the cup back down on the bed tray with a resounding clink.

"Kalen, what pleasure do I have with this meeting? It has been a busy week, has it not?" Hector asked, sitting up in the bed and shifting his feet so that they hung from the side of the bed.

Kalen bowed low. His long silver hair, that was combed back behind his narrow head, tumbled down in front of him. The gray elf raised his chin and forced his lengthy thin silver hair behind his long narrow ears with his delicate fingers. "It has, my lord, it has. We are very close to creating a being of power to hunt out this Ecnal and eradicate him like a mouse in a burrow. Soon, he shall trouble you no longer," the gray elf said with an evil tone.

Hector got up from the bed and stretched. He was getting older and the long days performing the duties as a king seemed to become more and more taxing. He rubbed his sore shoulder muscles and walked over to a large, ornate oaken dresser. "I agree, soon the orphan will be no more, but is he really the son of the mother of mercy? We have used a lot of resources and time, I hate to waste them on some boy that is of no use to me," Hector said as he removed his tunic and placed it on the top of the desk. He glanced down at his own arms and looked at his reflection in the mirror. His once powerful body was withering with age. Though still muscular, his skin sagged and his muscles had weakened. What a waste, Hector thought to himself. For a man to work so hard and to achieve so much, to lose it all in death.

Kalen leaned against the bed and folded his arms. "My king, I assure you that the Ecnal is the son of the mother of mercy. The fact that she worshipped a goddess of mercy is proof alone. If we . . . you slay him, you will void the prophecy against yourself and ensure the propagation of our kingdom."

Hector removed his breeches and tossed them on top of the dresser. He opened the bottom drawer and removed a silk sleeping suit and unfolded it. Carefully placing the soft tunic and breeches on, he turned and regarded the elf. "What are your stakes, elf? Surely you know I will not pass the kingdom on to you."

Kalen sarcastically feigned injury. "I would never think such a thing. You have no son, or heir. I know Spencer would undoubtedly rule after your death."

Hector's face flushed red with anger and he started to argue when he noticed the thin smile on the elf's face. He relaxed and changed his tone knowing the elf was mocking him in a friendly way. "You are lucky I appreciate your humor, elf, or you would sing at the gallows for a comment like that. Anyway, I may have an heir after all. It shows how much information you get from bedding the serving wenches."

Now it was Kalen's turn to flush. He had bedded many of the serving wenches that worked directly in the king's working areas, trying to get information on his routines, in case he felt the need to remove the aging human from power. If Hector knew of him bedding the women, what else did he know?

Kalen stammered. "My . . . king , I uh . . . needed to sew my oats so to speak. Surely you do not . . ."

Hector cut off the stammering elf. "Worry not, Kalen. I am not angered by your promiscuous nature, though I have seen some of the kitchen help. I guess the elven culture like women on the plump side, or is that merely your personal fancy?" Hector chided with a deep laugh.

Kalen relaxed a little. "Well my lord, a little ale and I . . . well, let's just say I become less particular than I usually would be."

Hector straightened his bed suit and climbed onto the bed. "Well, my elf friend, one of my concubines is expecting. I usually have the seed rooted out you see, but I have gotten rather fond of the little vixen, so I have decided to let her have it. If it is a boy, I shall keep it. If not, well, I will have her and it thrown to the rocks. Normally I would just dispose of the babe myself, but I have learned in the past that women tend to make a big deal of that sort of thing. It is a wonder how that Kingdom Aten gets by with only women. Sorceresses or no."

Kalen nodded. Half listening to the king and half thinking of some excuse for getting out of the chamber. The king's knowledge of his exploits had unnerved him. "Well, my king, I came to state that if you need my services during the DeNaucght, I would be available," Kalen said hoping that Hector did not detect any quiver in his voice. The elf hated being off balance and unsure of himself around Hector. He was confident that if they came to battle at this moment he would win. But the gray elf never left anything to chance. He needed to know everything and cover all angles so that when he decided to claim victory there was no way anyone could snatch it away from him.

Hector waved the elf away in dismissal. "I will call on you if needed, elf. Now be gone. I am weary and have a busy day tomorrow."

Kalen bowed and backed out of the chamber, closing the door. He hurried down the halls in relief. He had to start being more careful.

Hector knew he had to keep an eye on the elf. Every wench he bedded, thin or thick, was directly involved with his daily activities one way or the other. Hector knew the elf was not to be trusted, but it seemed the thin little pest was becoming dangerous. He would have to deal with him soon. Hector imagined a hundred plots to erase the elf before he managed to drift off into a deep sleep.

*   *   *

Trinidy opened his eyes. They burned and stung horribly, but he felt no cold, though he felt no heat either. The paladin quickly realized he was lying on his back, and his vision was blurry and dark. He could hear many loud heartbeats from around him and he could . . . smell them, smell their . . . life. It bothered him, though he knew not why. He tried to rise up, but he could not. His body seemed stiff

400

and rigid. He could make out a stone ceiling that was about fifteen feet above him and supported by thick wooden rafters. He tried to inhale and smell the room, but he couldn't force any air into his lungs. He expected fear to rip through him, but it did not. It was as if it were natural for him not to be breathing. This was strange to the paladin. Even in the abyss, he breathed, but here, wherever he was, he could not. Trinidy could hear faint sounds that he thought perhaps were muffled voices, but he could not make them out. The paladin wondered where his god had summoned him to. Trinidy tried to move his head, but his neck was stiff, yet it did not matter to him. he was not in the abyss, and Bykalicus was not around. That was all that mattered.

Trinidy could see the faint outline of his nose. It was dark, not pale like his skin normally was. He guessed it was bruised or he had dirt from his trials still smeared about his face. As Trinidy tried to speak, he quickly noticed he could not force any air out of his lungs, but he could make a guttural sound with his throat. He wasn't sure how intelligible it was, but it was better than lying on his back paralyzed. He couldn't make out what the people around him were saying, but they were rushing about. He could taste the fear in the air, and it tasted good. It made him desire more.

"Rise."

It was a simple command that echoed in his ear. To his surprise he sat up easily. He saw three men standing before him. They were dressed in robes and bore a holy symbol that hung loosely from their necks. Trinidy's poor vision prevented him from seeing what symbol it was, but he knew it was not the symbol of Dicermadon. These priests wore dark-colored robes. Priests of Dicermadon did not.

Trinidy glanced around the room, trying to turn his head again, but his muscles didn't seem to obey him. The paladin soon realized he was wearing the armor he wore before his death, though it was horribly rusted and in bad repair. In fact, his arms and legs were covered in dirt and soot. It looked as if he had been taking a bath in a freshly tilled garden. It was strange, but he couldn't smell anything, or really hear anything except the blood that was pumping through the priests' veins in front of him. He could hear their damnable hearts beating loudly and the sound almost seemed to hurt his ears, yet he didn't really feel pain. It was more like the sensation of fingernails grating against an instruction slate. Trinidy could tell the priests were speaking, but he could not make out what they were saying. Their words seemed to be drowned out by the indecent thumping of their hearts. The smell of their life seemed to cause him to hunger, it . . . mocked him somehow. Trinidy endured it patiently, waiting for this new environment to unfold.

*   *   *

The priests all gasped aloud, Resin probably the loudest. He, Pockweln, and Dorcastig had spent most of the day chanting and reciting the ceremonious spell known as the DeNaucght. Resin had prayed for a divine sign that he should perform the rites, and had received it in the form of a dream. It showed the paladin's body walking around in a state of undeath, carrying out his wishes. The beast had unbelievable power and he led an army against the enemies of Nalir. Why the king did not lead the armies himself, Resin didn't know, but sometimes dreams just didn't make sense. When Resin awoke, he knew he and his acolytes had Rha-Cordan's blessing in the rite, but the vision of the undead knight, and the reality that lay before him, were two different things. The beast wreaked of rotting flesh that had appeared out of nowhere and covered the skeleton when the spell was being woven. The wooden table that the skeletal remains had lain on had rotted and crumbled under the remains, and when the other three acolytes tried to pick it up and place it on the stone slab it now rests on, their skin was badly burned with cold and they clutched their insides and screamed, falling unconscious. Resin wasn't sure if it was due to the spell being incomplete or the nature of the undead being that lay before them. Regardless of the cause, the high priest knew that there would be many more revelations from this being of uncharted magic.

"Can you command it?" Dorcastig asked. The tall, dark haired, dark skinned priest seemed the most unnerved of them all, but each were more than dismayed by the vile creation.

"I know not," Resin said softly. "I am not sure if it is a being of its own volition or it has to be commanded. Ready your spells, in case it turns violent. I'll not have us injured or slain by a mockery of Rha-Cordan, even if he blessed its creation."

The others nodded slowly and began chanting a number of protection spells and other spells that did damage to undead and other creatures that were linked to the negative energy plane. Though priests of Rha-Cordan never created or controlled undead beings, they often battled them, seeing them as mockeries of their god. Only the god of death had power over souls. Undead beings were souls that were trapped in the rotting twisted bodies of their former selves—beings that the priests of Rha-Cordan took upon themselves to destroy whenever possible. Yet sitting on the stone table before them was an undead being of unimaginable power that they created. The thought of what they had done unnerved them.

"Rise," Resin commanded.

The three priests jumped back and readied their spells when the creation sat up and stared at them. They felt magical energy whipping around the protective barriers they had placed around their minds, yet they could feel it prying, trying to loose the shields and wards.

The undead creation had red, glowing eyes that seemed sunken into its skull. The creation's face had tight blackened skin that was drawn across it, barely making it more than a simple skull that was housed in a rusted great helm. Its lips were stretched and tight, exposing thick long teeth that were imbedded in a gum-less jaw. Hundreds of tiny stinging insects rolled around in the creation's mouth, occasionally crawling out and re-entering through the ear or nose holes. The three priests stared at the monstrosity for minutes before Hector entered the bone chamber. He gasped aloud at the hellish creation that sat on the stone slab. It was as if a dead rotting corpse had been dressed in a rusting suit of armor and propped up on the stone table. The king glanced at the rotted pile of crumbled wood that had been the previous table and walked up next to Resin.

"Is this what was supposed to happen, Resin?" Hector asked uneasily.

Resin didn't take his eyes from the hellish nightmare when he responded. "I know not, my king, but it seems as if it is under my command," Resin answered.

Hector looked around the room at the other acolytes.

Dorcastig, the Kai-Harkian priest, seemed the most terrified, but held his fear in check. He glanced back at Resin. "Tell it to kill Lance Ecnal."

Resin took his eyes from the monstrosity for the first time since its creation. "Should we tell it where he is?" Resin asked.

Hector shrugged his shoulders. "I know not, priest. This is a creation of you and yours. You command it. Besides, Kalen is out in the hall. He has readied a teleportation spell to send the rotting heap to task if need be."

Resin slowly turned to the undead beast. The high priest hesitated before he spoke. "You are to go find Lance Ecnal and slay him."

Trinidy heard the perfect words echo in his head. He could not understand anything else they had said until then. He could not move on his own accord, or even speak, yet it felt as if his bounds were loosed. He tried to stand up, and was amazed when his muscles did what he asked. He stood up slowly and gazed down at his arms. They were his again, fresh and new, just like when he was alive. He seemed oblivious to the men who stood before him. He could hear sounds, and smell odors. His brain was flooded with hundreds of sensations, but the most predominant one was the sound of the beating hearts of the men who stood before him. Smells assailed his nose, but the smell of their coppery blood stood out like a rose in a field of rocks. The men seemed to mock him, yet they said nothing. They seemed to fear him in some way, even the armored man who stood with an air of superiority. Trinidy guessed him to be a king or lord. They often stood that way he remembered. Trinidy frowned at his command. He was a champion of law and order, a paladin of the great god Dicermadon himself. He was no assassin, or bounty hunter.

"Who is this Ecnal, and what has he done, that he needs to be slain?" Trinidy asked, but he could feel something compelling him toward the double wooden doors of the chamber.

Resin glanced at Hector, who put his hand on his sword and backed away slowly. The other priests backed away too and seemed to be getting ready to defend themselves. Trinidy wasn't overly concerned with them for the moment. He did not understand why they seemed so afraid of him. He had not made one threatening movement and they didn't strike him as vile men.

Resin loosened the neck to his robe and wiped away sweat that was beading up on his forehead. "Because I command you to," Resin replied with mock bravery.

Trinidy chuckled, though the door pulled at him more strongly now. "I kill no man, save he who has done evil."

Resin quickly backed up against the wall and looked at the other priests in surprise. It seemed as if the once mighty paladin did not realize that he was nothing more than an undead beast. "I think something has gone awry."

The other priests nodded and began chanting protective divinations. Resin straightened his back and stepped forward, remembering his conversation with the demon lord. "Trinidy, you are to right that which is wrong," Resin said as his voice cracked and wavered.

Hector said nothing, he just watched the exchange with interest, though he too felt the magical fear aura that tugged at his mind.

The undead paladin turned and regarded the priest again. "Yes. I am to right that which is wrong. I remember that. I pledged that oath when Dicermadon rescued me from the abyss," Trinidy said as he glanced back at the door. It pulled at him violently.

Resin spoke again, seeing Trinidy was being pulled by some unseen force. He was certain now that the paladin did not know what had happened to him. Resin did not understand how he was oblivious to the state of his own body, but he guessed it had something to do with the way the DeNaucght was performed. It normally restored the man to his natural form just before he died. The high priest pulled his robe down and straightened it. "Lance Ecnal is the wrong. He must be slain for the wrong to be made right."

Trinidy did not waver, despite the visible struggle he was having against the magic that was compelling him to the door. "What wrong has he done?" Trinidy asked, his voice cracking from the strain of resisting the tremendous magic that pulled at him to leave.

Resin swallowed and stepped up, gaining confidence in what Bykalicus had told him. "He is the son of a goddess that was banished from the heavens. It is forbidden by Dicermadon, your god, the god of gods, for a Breedikai to reproduce. It normally is impossible, but the goddess of mercy was banished to live her life as a mortal. That way when she died, she would cease to exist, for Breedikais have no soul. The goddess married a paladin of Dicermadon to mock him. They had a son named Lance Ecnal."

Trinidy struggled with what the priest was saying. He knew almost every paladin of Dicermadon, or at least he thought he did. He was the only one that he knew of that chose a wife.

Resin noticed Trinidy was deep in thought. He continued. "The paladin was used by the goddess of mercy. She chose him out of spite, not love. Her name was Panoleen."

Trinidy was roused from his thoughts. The pull from the magic at the door had no strength against the love Trinidy had for his lost wife. He ignored the ripping magic and took three strides toward the priest. He drew his sword and leveled it at Resin, forcing the high priest back against the wall. The blade was black and it radiated such a deep cold that Resin's face stung and his robes stiffened and froze. Black tendrils whipped around the blade randomly like tiny circling dragons made of smoke. Frost whipped through the air around the sword from its abyssal cold.

"She used you, Trinidy," Resin said softly. "She used you to destroy your god," Resin said as he turned his head to try to get away from the cold of the evil blade.

Hector narrowed his eyes at the proclamation Resin was making. He didn't know who the dark priest had learned this information from, but he was going to find out after this creation was sent to task. And Hector doubted Resin was going to appreciate his interviewing methods much at all.

Trinidy narrowed his eyes. Their red glow intensified. "How do you know these things?"

Resin swallowed as he still tried to maneuver away from the stinging blade of absolute evil, with its frost biting into his skin, raising many small blisters. "I think you have been tricked, Trinidy," Resin whispered.

"And so you shall be bound," echoed in the paladin's head. The pull for the door became too great. "You are the one that has been fooled, priest. It is true I married a woman named Panoleen. And it is true we had a son, but his name is not Lance Ecnal, and she loved me with all of her soul. I'll not believe she would betray me or my god," the undead creation proclaimed. Trinidy let the sword down and he sheathed the evil blade. The air popped and sizzled until the entire blade was housed in its case. Trinidy turned and strode toward the door. The paladin did not look back as he spoke. "This is not over, priest. I will return." The wooden door twisted, crumbled, and cracked as the undead paladin walked past. The stone on the wall turned white and flaked away and the tiles under his feet blackened wherever his feet fell.

The priests ran to the doorway and watched as Trinidy strode down the chamber toward the wide double doors that went to the courtyard, near the portcullis leading out of the keep. The large iron portcullis was locked high in place to allow free movement in and out of the keep, but Hector had placed guards at the front gates of the courtyard to keep out unwanted visitors. The king knew the magnitude of this day, and he did not want to be disturbed by anything.

As Trinidy passed, the stone in the floor blackened like the stone in the chamber had when he passed. The walls crumbled when he walked by and the tapestries that were fastened on the walls rotted as they hung. The priests could see a rippling haze of corruption that danced around Trinidy as he walked. They all watched as a soft blue light erupted in front of the undead paladin, forming a small portal. Trinidy, undaunted, stepped through the azure door, the portal closed, and then he was gone.

Hector shook his head as Kalen stepped from the other side of the crumbled double doors, near where Trinidy had stepped into the portal. The gray elf strolled up in his quizzical way. He scrunched his delicate nose at the foul odor of rotting flesh that followed the undead knight.

"He is on his way, my lord," Kalen said with an exaggerated bow. "I have sent him to the Serrin Plains just outside of Central City so he is unlikely to be detected. I doubt the creation will be easily defeated, but Beykla does employ powerful wizards. Now if you people would be so kind as to tell me what that was?"

Resin cleared his throat. "That was a champion of Rha-Cordan. A champion of death."

Hector turned to Resin angrily. "You have been keeping secrets from me, priest. We will address your lack of loyalty another time. But for your sake, I hope your champion of death, your . . . *death knight*, succeeds. Your life may depend on it," Hector said as he turned and angrily stomped down the corridor with Kalen smiling mockingly over his shoulder. When they had rounded the corner, Resin slumped down against the wall, wiped the sweat from his forehead, and exhaled deeply. "If the death knight fails Hector, it will not be I who must fear, because the wrath of a half-god will be evoked, and Rha-Cordan does not hold you in the regards you might think," Resin said to himself with a relieved chuckle. "No, your soul is not well kept, my king. Not well kept at all."

Past. Everyone has one. Some cannot remember their past, others would just as soon forget. It seems though, that it creeps up on you and rears its ugly head when it is least desired. Even if a Kai-Harkian knows not his past, he knows what race he is by the look of his own reflection. He is usually a short, thick chested man with bronze skin and thick black hair. They are natural swordsmen and are immune to almost every kind of ingested poison. The mountains the Kai-Harkians call home are native to extremely poisonous plants.

The same recognition goes for the Andorians, though they are next to extinct. The Andorians are generally tall, fair skinned men that have long powerful arms used for wielding heavy swords in each hand without difficulty.

Men of all races, such as Kai-Harkians, or elves, or any other kind of humanoid, learn of their heritage and embrace it. But what if a man does not know his heritage when he is born, and does not learn of it until he is a man? Will he have difficulty accepting who he is if he did not know until he was grown? I say yes. A man develops his image as he ages. Call it a sense of self. It cannot be undone or changed because of an unknown truth. Really there are two truths: the truth of his heritage and the truth of who he is. Yet on the inside, all men bleed red. From orcs to Beyklans, they cannot change who they have grown to be. I could have no sooner sprouted wings and flown than I could have fathomed what men claimed I was. My name was Lance Ecnal. I lost my parents who I loved dearly. They were stolen from me by a vile and evil man who feared what I was to become, instead of what I was. Strange how that man single-handedly created exactly who he hoped to kill. Had my past been shaped by those who loved me, rather than by those who hated me, would my life have turned out the same? I will never know. But of all the souls that were ever lost, I pity his least of all.

—Lancalion Levendis Lampara—

Eleven

Proclamation of Doctrine

Alexis sat on an old rotten log and nervously watched Lance as he slept soundly in his tightly wrapped bed roll. Jude was reining the horses and getting them ready for the day's ride while Apollisian started cooking breakfast. Lance had last watch with Jude, and now he slept while the bright morning sun started its ascent into the sky. It was still very dark, but the eastern sky was aflame with the morning glow as it fought to erase the black of night. Crickets were chirping in the tall grass and a few birds started their morning songs while Apollisian sat on a large rock at the base of the hill, next to the warm fire that they were cooking breakfast on. The paladin stirred a large iron pot with a thick wooden spoon that was cracked on the ends from years of use. The pot was filled with stew from a rabbit Alexis had caught in the night while on watch. It bubbled from the fire and warm wisps of steam rose into the cool morning air. Apollisian watched Alexis reach into her pack and pull out a few of her tightly woven bowstrings. She moved from the old log to the ground, sitting with her legs folded, waxing the string of her long bow. She kept the string well waxed to prevent it from rotting and to increase its strength. Her long blonde hair hung overhead as she rubbed the yellow block up and down the taut twine, covering it with a thick coat. Apollisian watched her intently, soaking in her beauty. Neither he, nor Alexis, had mentioned the day they had in Central City just before the king arrived. It was an awkward moment for them both, and he knew there could never be anything between them. She was an elf. She would live a hundred of his lifetimes. While he grew old and feeble, she would remain young and full of vigor. He wouldn't curse her with the burden of loving him, though he knew he could not change the fact that he was indeed falling in love with her. She was such an amazing woman. Her

410

long blonde hair glistened from the red flickers of the campfire. She would wax her bow string for a while, then stare at the Ecnal intently for a few seconds, then return to her waxing. Occasionally she would catch the smitten paladin looking at her. Alexis would smile and glance back down at her work, but she kept her eyes on him for a second after. The smile would remain on her face until she happened to look back at the sleeping Ecnal.

Apollisian also looked at Lance, but all he saw was only a sleeping boy who was barely a man. Though he surely had a powerful look to his boyish eyes, the paladin doubted he was the monster Alexis had made him out to be. He imagined that she, too, was having second thoughts. Other than being self-absorbed in his journey, the boy was quite thoughtful and considerate. Not exactly the traits of a vicious killer that was supposed to murder hundreds of thousands like she said was prophesied.

Apollisian glanced over at Jude, who was still tending to the horses. Apollisian admired how well the man seemed to take care of the animals. He seemed to have some form of affinity for them. Once the paladin was certain the large man was occupied, he moved to sit next to Alexis. He inhaled deeply when her perfumed scent wafted over him. She looked surprised, but smiled, touching her knee to his when he sat down. Apollisian accepted the ginger touch and leaned over, speaking softly enough that Jude could not hear.

"I don't know, Overmoon. I know you have said he is this Abyss Walker, but he seems every bit the average boy to me. In fact, his heart has not even the twinge of evil to it. I have checked every night since we have left Central City. Are you sure he is this beast you claim he is?"

Alexis frowned and stopped waxing her bow string. She stared at the taut waxed line for a moment in thought, before looking up and meeting the handsome paladin's strong, blue-eyed gaze. "I, too, have my reservations about him. He seems very innocent, but I cannot deny what I see every time I look into those wicked green eyes of his. There is an evil lurking there greater than I can describe. It is as if every damned soul screams out to me for mercy when I meet his gaze. I can hear their voices so loudly I want to cower and cry," Alexis said as her voice cracked. She paused and glanced over at Jude. The swordsman was gathering grain from the packs and

411

tending to the animals. The horses were calm and whined softly at the anticipation of the treat he was bringing. Once satisfied he was not listening, she continued. "I cannot determine if he is who he seems to be, but the elders can. That is why I must take him there. As a prisoner, or guest, it makes no difference."

Apollisian shook his head. "I cannot allow him anyway, other than as a guest. It is unjust to imprison a man on mere suspicion alone, let alone suspicion of deeds he has not, nor might never commit."

Alexis stared deep into his steel blue eyes. She became lost in an azure sea of euphoric bliss. She had to force herself to keep from wrapping her arms around the handsome man, though she quickly regained composure and spoke with an eerie calm. "Apollisian, you are my mentor and beloved friend, but I will deliver this man to the council of elders in Minok Vale. Any who try to stop me will be seen as enemies to the elven nation and will be treated as such."

Apollisian was taken aback by her half threat. How dare she threaten him? He was a champion of justice. Few that breathed air had the wisdom to recognize true justice, and she knew he was sworn to uphold it. Yet, she sat before him, spouting idiocies as if he were a child to be spooked. Apollisian renewed his strong visage and stood up, forcing her to look up at him, which added to his powerful presence. His thick metal armor creaked and popped from the quick movement. "I am sworn to uphold justice. That young man shall not fall to the unjust while I'm still breathing, and mind you elf, I am not slain easily. If he is taken from my care by deceit or trickery, I will hunt down the kidnappers, regardless of race, religion, or creed, and send them to their maker. This I swear by the long hand of Stephanis, and so it shall be fulfilled," he stated loudly.

Apollisian stormed over to the fire, jerking up the stew pot, and slammed it down forcefully on the large rock. Some of the stew splashed up from the side and splattered out. "Soup's done," he said coldly as he walked past a confused Jude to his horse and began cinching up the saddle.

Jude looked over and frowned, trying to understand the angry exchange between the two. They had been like flirting lovers most of the trip, before this proclamation. He didn't hear all of it, something about swearing and being fulfilled. Jude guessed it was some sort of lovers spat, but he was sure it was directed to Lance. He decided to keep a closer eye on those two. If they moved against his friend, they would find his sword equally deadly.

Alexis glared at the paladin's back as he stomped off. Her face was flush with anger and she stood up, wiping the dust from her pants. Lance opened his eyes, yawned and stretched.

"Everything alright?" he asked lazily, stretching his arms as he finished his yawn. Alexis turned to him. Her frown had softened, but was still readily apparent across her face.

"Everything is fine. That bull-headed paladin just needs to watch his tongue."

Lance looked over at Apollisian, who was angrily packing up his things, and then back at Alexis as she started to do the same. Lance looked over at Jude, who mouthed "lovers spat."

Lance nodded his head in recognition as he slowly climbed out of his bedroll and started gathering his belongings in the cool morning. Getting in the middle of a lovers spat was the last thing he wanted to do. When the young mage finished gathering his belongings, he poured himself and Jude bowls of soup.

Jude sat down next to Lance and they ate while Alexis and Apollisian finished picking up camp in utter silence.

"I think they are up to something that involves you," Jude whispered to Lance.

Lance stopped chewing and took a swig from his wine skin. He finished the long draw and wiped his mouth. "Yea, I figured as much. I think she might know what the elven parchments I carry are. It's okay. I have a spell that will turn them into ordinary pieces of paper whenever I wish. If it is some crime to carry them, her people will be none the wiser until we are long gone. If I can't get them read there, I will go some place else. With all the gold we are earning on this journey, it should prove to be an easy task to pay a scribe to decipher them."

Jude nodded and took another big bite of stew. Breakfast was the only warm meal they got to eat on the trail, and they enjoyed it dearly.

The four were in the saddle before the sun rose from the eastern sky. Lance was becoming accustomed to riding every day. In fact, his horse had become spooked several times during the trip, and he was getting used to getting it under control himself without aid from Apollisian or Jude. Alexis never offered him aid, but always seemed interested in what he said or did. Lance thought perhaps that was the way elves were, but he suspected it was something deeper than that, especially after the spat between her and Apollisian.

The sun was near the middle of the sky when Apollisian called for them to stop. Lance reined his horse in tight, while the paladin dismounted and began examining the ground. Alexis was off hunting from horseback, so Jude rode up and dismounted also. The leather from his saddle creaked when his weight was placed on one stirrup, and the horse was shifted slightly when the large man fully stepped to the ground. He noticed Apollisian was kneeling down at a patch of flattened grass that was probably three feet wide and about five feet long.

"What is it?" Jude asked.

Apollisian said nothing. He moved about twenty feet to the east in the tall grass where he located another patch of flattened grass.

Jude frowned and rubbed his head.

"What are you looking at, Apollisian? Is this flattened area caused by deer?"

The paladin shook his head slowly and tested the dirt around the grass. He pulled up the grass stalk and noticed the browning grass still had moisture near the break. "This does not bode well for us."

Jude frowned. "What does not bode well for us?"

"These tracks are fresh," Apollisian said.

Jude rubbed his head and mounted his horse. The beast lurched to the side from his weight until he was fully in the saddle. The horse moaned from the heavy swordsman. "Isn't that a good thing? The deer can't be far off," Jude asked.

Apollisian mounted his horse and shook his head. "We need to keep our voices low from here on out. The grass was not broken by bedding deer. Those are footprints."

Jude's eyes went wide with astonishment. He started to reply but he heard hoof steps pounding from the east, over the side of the hill. Apollisian also heard the galloping horse and turned his gaze to the east. All he could see was the tip of the hill, the bright blue sky beyond, and a few white clouds that floated overhead. The wind blew the dry grass in small waves across the land.

"Overmoon must have found the same prints we have," Apollisian said calmly.

Jude glanced back down at the huge tracks. They were the largest tracks the swordsman had ever seen. What was more surprising was that it appeared the beast that made them wore some kind of boot. "What makes footprints that big?" Jude asked in disbelief.

Apollisian started to answer, but turned his gaze to the hilltop. He put his hand to his sword when he saw Alexis come charging over the hill. Her eyes were wide with fear and her horse was wet with lather. She was leaning over the front of the saddle, and her legs were flailing wildly into the side of her mount, immediately urging the horse to run faster, though it seemed the beast needed no encouragement for that. Large clods of dirt flew up behind her horse as its heavy hooves thundered against the dry ground.

"RUN!" she screamed as she ran by. Apollisian and Jude watched her ride toward Lance, then they looked back over the hill in disbelief. A large giant broke the horizon of the hill. It was almost twelve feet tall. Its skin was a dirty bronze and it wore many dozen animal hides that were crudely woven together to make a loin cloth. It had very muscular arms that seemed too long for its frame. It had thick, stooped shoulders and a prominent brow line with a low forehead. The giant's long, brown, greasy hair bounced across its face and shoulders as it ran. It held a massive club in its right hand that looked like the trunk of a small tree. The ground shook and thundered as it stomped toward them with its monstrous strides.

Apollisian and Jude turned and spurred their horses down the base of the hill to the road. Lance and Alexis were a few hundred feet ahead of them riding in a fury away from the hill while Alexis was riding smoothly and glancing back at Apollisian and Jude, and Lance seemed to bounce roughly about his horse's back, barely able to cling to the saddle.

"We can't outrun it!" Apollisian cried, drawing his long sword. "Split up and circle. We must wound it, then try to flee!"

Jude glanced back at the horrible creature. It had a great brass-colored nose ring and it smiled a rotten yellow-toothed grin as it gained on his horse. The giant knew it was going to overrun him. Jude jerked up on the thick reins of his horse. The leather reins creaked and popped under the strain of the horse's thick neck, and Jude's powerful arms, but they did not break as the terrified horse jerked its head back twice before coming to a complete stop. Jude ripped the reins around the horse's neck, turned it in a tight circle, and faced the beast. If he could not outrun it, he would fight. Running was not Jude's way.

The swordsman drew his great sword from its scabbard. The large blade glinted in the bright sunlight like a jewel under lantern light. He held the sword high in the air, spurring his reluctant horse toward the thundering beast. After he quickly wrapped the reins of his horse around the saddle horn, Jude waved the heavy blade two-handedly over his head in a circular motion, cutting the air, and making the blade whistle as he neared the thundering hill giant. As he closed in on the giant, Jude's horse resisted the charge and reared up on its hind legs. The swordsman fell from the back of the mount as the beast ran off, riderless. Jude hit the ground hard on his right shoulder but rolled with the fall and came up to his feet quickly. The pain seemed to ignite something deep within the large man. Given the tense situation, he barely sensed the deep sensation, pushing it back down inside of himself.

"Run, coward!" Jude screamed at his horse as the ground shook from the giant's nearing footsteps.

Alexis, noticing the giant was squaring off with Jude, stopped her horse and drew her bow hastily. The white ash bow, made of masterwork quality, creaked and bent as she notched an arrow and let it fly. The green, fletched missile whizzed through the air. Before it even neared its mark, she drew and loosed another with rapid precision. Her horse remained perfectly still, as if it knew she needed a steady platform to shoot from.

Apollisian also turned his horse and charged the giant, eager to smite the evil beast, and to aid the foolish swordsman.

Lance stopped his horse and turned to the battle at hand. Jude had fallen from his horse and the giant would be on him soon. He envisioned a spell in his mind. He pictured the magical energies that flowed around the air of the giant. Lance could see, even from the few hundred foot distance between him and the beast, the bright yellow magical weaves that erupted from the air around it, nearly engulfing the creature's thick wooden club. Lance struggled with the magic to create an invisible barrier that would force the club from the giant's hand. Lance called the unique dweamor "Lance's Prevention." There was no real name for the spell. He had developed it as a child to play pranks, but as he aged he found it had practical uses as well.

Jude winced as the giant brought his huge club over its brown greasy head in an overhand slam. He could see every crack, every old blood stain on the deadly trunk as it came crashing down. The swordsman realized his error when it was already too late. The giant could hit Jude when he was about fifteen feet away, long before he was able to get in close enough with his great sword. Just as the deadly club rocketed toward Jude, an arrow with bright green fletching embedded itself into the beast's head. The giant roared in pain, and thick red syrupy blood shot out from the hole in the beast's forehead. The arrow strike forced the club high, as Jude ducked low. The giant club hit Jude's great sword and tore the heavy weapon from his grasp. Pain erupted from Jude's wrists and he tumbled to the ground and landed roughly on his back, knocking the air out of his chest. A second arrow hit the creature just above its knee. The giant howled in pain and lost its grip on the great club just as the mighty weapon passed over the top of Jude. The club twirled end over end through the air and landed in the tall grass, hundreds of feet from where the giant stood. The giant held his knee gingerly with one hand and his forehead with the other. Jude sat up and struggled to regain his breath. He could see his great sword a few feet away so he began to crawl to it. His wrists were numb from the weapon being violently torn from his grasp and he was a little dizzy, but if he reached the weapon, he could still hold it weakly. Just as Jude grabbed his sword, he felt a strong arm hook him under his shoulder, and he was hoisted to the back of Apollisian's charging mount. The paladin's spotted horse ran faster than any horse Jude had ever been on. They both watched as the giant howled in pain and clutched at the arrow that was sticking out of its thick forehead. Long streams of blood poured from the wound and dripped off of the giant's chin. Two more arrows struck the beast in the right leg, just above the second arrow that hit. The giant howled in pain and backed away from the elf and her stinging arrows. Alexis notched a fifth arrow, but the discouraged giant hurriedly limped away muttering curses in its native tongue. Jude sheathed his great sword and clung to the paladin's waist until he reached the others. Lance hung his head low and pushed his thumbs against his temples.

417

"Thank you," Jude said softly as he continued to rub his sprained wrists.

"It is okay," Apollisian replied. "But, you should heed our warnings, Jude of Bureland. We have traveled this path many times. It is deadly to face a hill giant in melee. They can hit you with their long clubs before you can get in with your sword. It is best to wound them from a distance, then flee. If we had fought it, one of us would most likely be seriously injured or dead, even though the clumsy beast dropped his club."

Jude ignored the paladin's reference to where he was from. He no doubt understood the man was trying to belittle him by speaking of his home town. Jude looked to Alexis to see what the elf's opinion was. She sat on her horse confidently with another arrow notched, looking past him into the vast grasslands. He knew she was a skilled archer, but he had not fathomed the depth of her talent until today. She had hit the giant with near precision from almost two hundred feet away, while the beast was in combat with him. Never in his life had Jude seen such marksmanship. He wondered how far her talents went with the bow. She fired twice as many arrows as he could fire in the same time span. The elf surely was a force to be reckoned with.

Jude looked back at Apollisian while he waited for his horse to trot back to him. The horse had fled from the battle and was understandably afraid to run back to the group. Jude felt uneasy with the way the paladin chastised him. He was no fool, but his ego was wounded.

Jude cleared his throat and fired back at Apollisian. "It was no accident the beast dropped its club," Jude said as he pointed to Lance while the young mage pinched his fingers at the bridge of his nose, grimacing in pain. "My friend has many talents. Do you think he gets random headaches from nothing? Between his magic and my sword, we can fell most enemies, though I'll be sure to heed your warnings in the future."

Jude walked over, grabbed the reins of his horse and calmed the beast by gently patting its neck. The small speech helped soothe his wounded ego, but he didn't look to see if the elf or paladin took him seriously. He knew what he said to be true, to a degree.

Apollisian said nothing in return. He understood the reason

for the large man's claim, but he felt there was some truth to what he had said.

Jude took his terrified horse by the reins and unwrapped the reins from the saddle horn. The horse was panting and frothing from the attack and was quite nervous. Jude gently stroked the horse and spoke some soothing words before mounting.

Apollisian and Alexis turned and eyed Lance suspiciously. They both looked at him in a new, dangerous light. They guessed he was some kind of mage, but neither of the two had ever heard of a spell that could do such things—at least not so specifically. He had not demonstrated any great power, but the fact that the spell was unknown surely did not sit well with them. Apollisian was familiar and trained in the arcane arts. Though he could not weave arcane magic, he could recognize a spell if he saw it being cast, and so could Alexis. What bothered the paladin was that he did not see any gestures made by the young mage, and by the look on the elf's face, neither had she. Only the most powerful spell weavers had the ability to create dweamors, but none could cast them without verbal or somatic components.

Alexis looked back at Apollisian as if to say *I told you so,* before turning her horse up the trail. "We need to get moving before that beast finds his club and decides my arrows didn't sting that bad," the blonde-haired elf said as she turned and started to ride back up the trail.

Apollisian didn't respond. He watched his friend ride onward as the soft wind from the plains gently blew her long hair about her. He gently urged his horse onward. The Vendaigehn stallion pranced eagerly and followed the elf's horse.

Neither Jude nor Lance said anything in response. They just galloped their horses up the dirt path toward the ever expanding horizon line with the endless waves of flowing grasslands beyond, each hoping this journey would come to an end soon.

*   *   *

He stepped from the flashing blue portal into the blinding sunlight. The brightness of the sun, in contrast to the darkness of the portal he came from, was like night and day. The dark, calm portal gateway was serene and safe. This atrocious light of day seemed to assault him at every level of his consciousness. The glaring sun burned and singed his dark, decaying skin.

Trinidy raised his shield over his head to shadow the light. Never had the sun had such an adverse effect on him. It beat down on him like soft clay in a baker's oven. Trinidy looked around, wondering where in the realms he was. There was nothing but great rolling hills that were covered by endless waves of tall amber grass. The sky was a light parched blue, with thin white wispy clouds that seemed to be frozen in place. As far as his eyes could see, there were no trees to be found. The tall grass seemed to blanket the land from horizon to horizon. The light brown dirt that lay beneath his armored feet was cracked, dusty, and littered with small insects and bugs that seemed to scramble from under his boots. The insects were coal black and of every stinging type he could think of. He thought he saw a few scorpions and many spiders. They were larger than the other sable creatures that spawned under him, some as large as the palm of his hand. He started to lift his feet in fear of being stung, but the creatures didn't seem to pay him any heed. They darted from under his boots into the expansive grass. Trinidy shook his head as he ignored the bugs and continued to glance around the desolate land. How insects of that order survived in these harsh temperatures was beyond him.

Trinidy was not standing still more than a few minutes when he felt the arduous draw again. He could feel the pull, the voracious call of the same magic he felt in the keep. It was pulling him, calling him onward over the next rise, to the north. Trinidy turned and looked behind himself again, and his ancient armor creaked and popped as he turned. The death knight saw nothing different than what was in front of him, save for the magical pull. He shrugged his shoulders and stepped toward the hill, toward the magic that led him like a dog on a leash. Trinidy despised the mysterious call, but at least he was no longer in the abyss. He would tolerate chains in the dungeon of any king over that unforgiving, torturous hell. He was finally back in the world of the living. Back to do the works of his great god. Back to right that which was wrong. *To right that which is wrong.* The thought echoed in his head over and over again like a chorus of a favorite song.

The death knight plodded forward, over each hill, only to cross yet another. The brown scorched grass turned black and died about thirty feet around him as walked, leaving a trail of black rotting grass. Trinidy seemed oblivious to the foliage's change. Once he passed by, the grass crumbled to dust, leaving a long path of decay in his wake. The death knight held his shield above his head, protecting himself from the despicable sun. It seemed to mock him with brightness, and scorch his skin whenever his arms or legs accidentally stepped from the shadow of his large steel shield.

"Curse this damnable sun!" he barked with a guttural growl, surprising himself with the utterance. Almost immediately as he barked the curse, he was shrouded in a dark bliss. He could not see, yet he knew where he was walking and he did not stumble on the earth, nor trip over a rock or rise. And when the ground seemed to ascend to another hill to cross, it did not surprise him, as though he knew the hill was there. Trinidy lowered his shield arm as he walked in the sable paradise. His shoulder did not ache as it should have for holding the heavy steel shield above his head for so long. The shield was made of a thick steel that could stop a charging lance. It was surely heavy. Trinidy moved his arm up and down, testing to see if his muscles were indeed stiff. But to his surprise, they were not. He felt as if he could easily hold the metal shield up for hours more if need be.

Trinidy wasn't sure how long he had walked. It was at least several hours, but not more than ten, he guessed. His mind seemed to wander and he frequently lost track of time. His legs were not fatigued and his feet didn't ache as they should have from walking long distances in his full plate armor. He decided to stop and rest. Though he wasn't the least bit exhausted, he did not want to have fatigue creep up on him. Trinidy sat down in the grass, and was surprised when he didn't feel any of the dry brown foliage around him. His shield dropped to the earth and he removed his gauntlet from his hand. The death knight felt the grass, but all that remained were the ashes of the decayed undergrowth. He struggled to look around, but the impenetrable darkness still shrouded him. It wasn't normal darkness. He couldn't see an inch in front of his face. It blocked every ounce of light, or maybe it enveloped the light. Regardless of how it happened, there was no light to be found around him. Before he could wish the darkness away, it was gone as abruptly as it appeared. Trinidy realized he was sitting in a burnt clearing atop a small hill. The grass around him was gone, replaced by crumbled grassland that had been all but turned to ash. There were hundreds of stinging insects crawling around him on the ground again. They were all coal black and seemed to reflect the red sun of the autumn twilight on their glossy shells. Trinidy ignored the bugs and glanced to the rapidly setting sun. It would soon be below the horizon. The crimson orb was cut in half by the darkening skyline. The heavens were aflame with reds and yellows, as the thin wispy clouds bore a violet hue from the setting sun. Trinidy had always loved the sunset in the past, but now he seemed more relieved of passing than enjoying the sight. In fact he felt himself becoming angry at the sun for not going down more quickly than it was. The fading bulb seemed to mock him by going down slowly, though at least it did not sting his eyes or his skin, like it had when it was midday.

Trinidy felt the breeze that rolled over the darkening plains. He could not feel if it was a warm or cool breeze, he just felt the breeze. He felt the wind blowing his thin stringy hair and the resistance it made on his face. That lack of sensation puzzled him, but he did not dwell on it. He had not sat for more than a few moments before the magical pull tugged at him once again. He tried to fight it but he soon found himself on his feet and plodding north, into the night, answering the invisible beckoning from the unknown that seemed to lay just over the next hill.

Trinidy walked for many more hours into the darkness of the night. He liked the night. It was not because it was cooler, or because the sun was set—though he did not miss the stinging glowing orb—it just seemed more comfortable to him; more friendly in a strange way. There were no stars. It was a cloudy night with an occasional flash of lightning from a faraway storm, but he could see well in the dark. It didn't really bother him that he could see as well in the night as in the day. It was somehow second nature to him.

Trinidy came to a small dirt trail that led north and south. The pull from the magic urged him to go north. He looked south, though his bright red eyes glowed with wonder at what lay in that direction. He almost wanted to turn that way to defy the insatiable call, but he did not. Trinidy did not see reason to battle the unyielding urge just yet; no sense in wasting energy fighting the unseen leash. There would undoubtedly be a time for fighting, and now was not then. He slowly started up the dirt trail that led north, placing one foot in front of the other in his steady amenable trek.

He walked for the rest of the night and well into the next day, surprising himself that he was not tired, nor hungry. His feet did not hurt, nor did his muscles ache. He couldn't remember eating since he awoke on the table in that keep, nor drinking a single drop of water for that matter. He guessed he had been blessed by some sort of spell to aid him in his long journey. Trinidy decided that he would eat when he was hungry and not before. The sooner he answered the call, the sooner he would be loosed to pursue other interests.

The sun was high in the sky on the second day, stinging his arms and legs just as it had done on the first. He held his shield above his head again, wishing he had that dark shroud for a second time. He wasn't sure how he had summoned it the day before, if he had indeed summoned it at all. Yet he plodded on, often pausing perplexed at how the sun seemed to mock him. It seemed to taunt and ridicule him as it held itself aloft in the great perch in the sky. He glared at it, that damned yellow orb. Why did it taunt him so? Trinidy shook an angry fist at the sun. He stared at it while it burned his face and scorched his skin, but he continued to stare. The bright globe did not seem to burn his eyes despite the fact that he stared at it directly.

"Why do you mock me, sun? How dare you? Do you not know who I am? I am the will of goodness. I bring the sword of righteousness to the evils that hide under the rocks and in crevices to avoid you, yet you mock me!" Trinidy screamed. He drew his long sword from its sheath and held it aloft. The sword made a shrill ringing sound as it was drawn, and the air cracked and popped from the intense cold that wafted from the wicked onyx blade. Great wisps of frost and steam coiled around the sword as he held it high overhead. The cold cascaded down the sword, onto Trinidy's arm, and over his head and shoulders. The death knight felt a wash of coolness over his entire body. It was not as cool as he remembered, but more calm, like an inner serenity that had escaped him without his knowing.

Trinidy's tirade was interrupted by a new taunting. It came from over the next hill. He could hear its ignescent pounding. Thump-thump, thump-thump. The sound was like grating fingernails over a raw slate. Thump-thump, thump-thump. Mocking him, laughing at him. Rage washed through the death knight; rage like he had never felt before. It felt good. It was as refreshing as cold, crystal, clear spring water in the middle of the Great Desert of Tyrine. The pull of the magic called him away from the sound, but he easily ignored the insatiable pull. The rage was with him. Thump-thump, thump-thump.

Trinidy stalked over the hill, his wicked long sword in hand. Thump-thump, thump-thump. There it was, the object of the unremitting reverberation. Kneeling over a slain gazelle was a large brown-skinned hill giant. Trinidy knew the beast to be inherently evil, but he didn't lust to kill it because of its racial trends. It was the relentless pounding of its despicable heart that drove him onward.

The giant wore a blood-soaked bandage on his forehead and one around its right knee. The dark furs from the grassland animals it had slain in the past acted as the coverings for its wounds. Dark, crusted blood still clung to the giant's tan skinned leg, as the stupid creature had not yet wiped it off. The beast seemed about twelve feet tall when it stood erect, though now it kneeled over the felled gazelle, chewing on the deer's hide. Trinidy calmly walked toward the creature. The burning sun no longer seemed a hindrance to the death knight. The grass turned dark brown as the death knight passed and then turned to black ash, crumbling, leaving a wake of destruction behind him. Trinidy walked as silent as death, then stopped just behind the beast. The giant shivered visibly and rubbed its arms from the abyssal cold that wafted from the death knight.

"Stand and arm yourself, beast," Trinidy said as he held his wicked blade horizontally in front of himself.

The giant leaped to its feet, whirling around to face the voice that had somehow snuck up on him. The giant could feel the tendrils of fear ripping around his puny brain at the sight of the new enemy. It was a humanoid of some kind, dressed in dirty black plate mail armor. The armor bore many ornate skulls about it, at the knees, on the chest plate, on the shoulders, and on other areas. The man wore a tattered black cape that draped down his back, flowing softly in the breeze. He held a sword in front of him that smoked, sizzled and popped, though it was as puny as the swords the elves used. But it was the face of the creature that gave the giant pause.

He had long black hair that was thin and stringy. The top of his head was near bald, revealing pale white flesh underneath. The skin on the man's face was taut and skeletal-like, with no eyes, save for a small beady red glow. His lips were narrow and tight, unable to cover his dull gray teeth, giving the man a seemingly permanent smile. And the stench! The man smelled as if he had been dead for months. Large black bugs crawled from his mouth, into his nose and out again. It surely looked like any corpse the giant had seen before, yet there it stood before him, speaking in some language the giant did not understand. The giant beast studied the man for a brief moment before picking up his hefty wooden club. When the giant picked up his tree trunk of a club, it seemed to hurl the diminutive enemy into a fury.

Trinidy rushed forward, hurling himself abidingly at the giant, ducking a great sweep of the creature's club that would have surely killed any man. The death knight launched in with a barrage of attacks, slicing the beast's hamstring, then cleaving a horrific slice up the inside of its thigh, severing the femoral artery. The death knight's sword popped and sizzled, burning the wound of the giant with its abyssal cold. Warm blood erupted from the arterial wound and spurted the ground red. The giant howled in pain and smashed his club down at the death knight in great overhand strikes. Trinidy avoided each strike as it hit the hard earth, sending vast showers of dirt and debris into the air with the mighty blows. Trinidy backed away and stood staring at the giant. The beast panted and sweat, holding its severely wounded leg as its precious life's blood spurted into the earth. The giant looked behind himself, looking for a way to flee from this hellish enemy that stood three spans away from it.

Trinidy watched the giant as it stood there gasping from fatigue. He could hear its heart growing fainter with each passing second as the giant bled the ground red. Thump-thump, thump-thump. Yet the heart still mocked him. Hate tore through the death knight. How dare this beast try to live. It was dead already, it just didn't know it. Trinidy opened his mouth and let out a roar of defiance against the damnable thumping of the giant's heart. When he did, hundreds of black beetles and other insects shot from Trinidy's mouth, swarming around the giant's wounded leg. The hill giant swatted at the tiny insects as the stinging creatures bore into the giant. The hill giant roared in pain and fright as the insects burrowed under his skin, making hundreds of fast moving bumps up the inside of his leg. The giant pounded his fist at his leg, dropping his club and howling in terror and pain.

Trinidy watched on in utter satisfaction. He wasn't sure where the insects came from, but he felt a certain kinship with them, a brotherhood so to speak. He was pleased when he could hear their buzzing and the chomping of their wicked little jaws as they burrowed toward the giant's heart.

The hill giant dropped to the ground and began thrashing about, howling and screaming. Then, as abruptly as it started, it stopped. Trinidy stared in wonder at the giant as it lay still on its back. He could not detect the rising and falling of the beast's chest as it drew breath, he couldn't see any movement in its limbs, and best of all, that beating heart was stopped. It would mock him no longer.

The death knight approached the body of the giant. It lay still on its back. Its face was contorted with pain in the grimace of death. Its eyes were frozen wide with horror and fear. A single beetle crawled from the giant's mouth and disappeared into the grass. Then another, and another. Soon the entire swarm erupted from the giant's mouth and vanished into the underbrush as if they were never there. Trinidy kneeled down next to the dead giant and looked at the gazelle. It was partially eaten, but its skeleton was intact. The death knight reached down and gently stroked the gazelle's bloody cheek. He felt a flash of cold that was not cold, then the beast opened its eyes. It blinked several times and awkwardly stood on its own. To Trinidy it seemed as if the beast was healed. It bore no wounds that he could see and acted submissive to him, nuzzling its soft cheek under his arm. Trinidy gently stroked the gazelle and spoke to it soothingly.

"You are alive again, my friend. Go! Roam among the grasslands as you once did."

The gazelle reluctantly bounded off to the north, until it vanished over the hillside. Trinidy turned and searched the giant for any signs that he may have belonged to a raiding clan. He would not tolerate such evils roaming free to prey on those that were weak. But after a brief search he found nothing, save for three large boulders that the giant no doubt used to throw at unwary victims. He started to track where the beast came from, when the pull from

426

the magic became too strong. He reluctantly turned north and began his slow but steady trek across the plains. He enveloped himself in the shroud of darkness a second time as he disappeared over the rise of the hill, leaving a wake of burned and crumbling grass that was infested with black stinging insects.

To the north, a gazelle with its insides trailing behind it, and its hide mostly ripped from its body, left a bloody trail as it bounded lifelessly across the grassy plains.

To the south a hill giant opened his lifeless eyes. He had no heartbeat nor took any breaths. His skin was a pale white, instead of the light brown it had once been, and he stood in a pool of his own curdling blood. Maggots festered in a grievous wound on the inside of his leg, but he seemed oblivious to the larva as they devoured his flesh. He did not blink, or move. He just waited for his master, who had created him to return, so he could give him a command. Until then he would wait.

Can a god be killed? Surely a difficult query. I am positive its answer lies within the depths of the question. What does someone mean by killed? Do they refer to death as a mortal imagines death? If so, then I answer no. Not exactly. If a god, or goddess for that matter, takes the mortal form, after having been shielded from his or her own innate abilities, then yes. Their new mortal forms can be destroyed, and without their godly abilities to restore the body they will cease to exist. You see Breedikai, or original gods, have no souls. They have no inner beings that rest at their cores. They are, and always will be, the shell that surrounds them. That is why Panoleen, my mother, was destroyed. When she was shielded from her innate magical abilities and was made into mortal form, she still lacked a soul. When her body ceased to exist, she ceased to exist. But that is the only way I have ever learned to destroy a god. Usually the way gods and goddesses eliminate one another is to shield each other in their native planes, or shield them and make them serve in Merioulus as slaves, though this is never permanent and rarely has ever happened.

I learned that Breedikai feared the risers. The risers are men and women who, through arcane means, have risen to such power that they tried to be accepted by Merioulus. They somehow managed to live for hundreds or thousands of years with the aid of spells and dweamors, but they were always denied acceptance. Even with the power these risers possessed, they could not match the power of the weakest god. Some in their pride attempted to battle the gods, trying to force them to let them enter the great city of the gods, but they were all defeated and destroyed. Their souls were always given to Rha-Cordan for punishment. Rha-Cordan, the god of death, hated those who lived unnaturally long lives and he punished them so. The reason that the Breedikai feared the risers was that the risers had a soul. They could not be disposed of, shielded, or destroyed. Their soul would always exist. Rha-Cordan had control of a soul when it passed, and he did not belong, participate, or even agree with the laws of Merioulus. And though not since the beginning of time has Rha-Cordan ever fully released a soul to its own devices, he would not vow to the Breedikai that he would not ever. Who would have ever thought that a riser could be more powerful in death than he ever was alive? The Breedikai did, a fear of theirs I would one day learn for myself.

—Lancalion Levendis Lampara—

428

Twelve

Wrath of the Gods

Leska marched purposefully through the garden that was littered with large rows of green bushes carved into depictions of heroes and heroines. There were great marble statues of monsters and men alike carved with lifelike perfection unseen by the mortal world. Small ornate walls of stone, a few feet high, surrounded each fertile green bush like a thin shroud. Bright flowers of every kind and shape grew plentifully in this magnificent garden. Animals of every kind bounded from her path, sensing her anger, but following curiously once she had passed. The goddess's velvety green dress clung to her angelic body, revealing enough to show her femininity, but covering enough to prevent wandering eyes. Her dress was long and flowing from her waist, with light browns and yellows intertwined with the greens, though with each passing day, the browns and yellows became more predominate. She wore her hair braided back from her head and the soft tail bounced and waved as she marched with her delicate hands clenched into fists. Her bright green eyes radiated a flash of dangerousness that she seldom showed, and the rocks under her feet seemed to growl and shudder as she passed over them. Leska, the Earth Mother goddess, was not happy.

She had been overseeing the growing of a great vale in the southern reaches of Vidora, when she sensed the DeNaucght, a secret ritual that a few good sects of mortals knew about, and even fewer knew how to perform. The chant was reserved for the more powerful mortals so that they might allow a hero, or champion of righteousness, to rise from the grave, and right that which is wrong. But the sacred ritual had been perverted into some despicable act, drawing the soul back into a rotting decaying body, binding it with magic, and filling a once righteous man with a taint of evil that he

429

would eventually succumb to. It was true, Leska had no love for this mortal. In her eyes, and most of the eyes of the Breedikai, when he was alive he had broken the oath of celibacy and married. This violation did not go unpunished. The mortal lost the powers his god had bestowed upon him, but the fool seemed relieved. *Love, Pah!* Leska said to herself as she marched through the great garden. That witch, Panoleen, knew nothing of love. She did not marry the poor, foolish soul out of love. She wanted to get back at the Breedikai for banishing her from the heavens. Goddess of mercy indeed. She merely used her station to work her own sinister plots, but no longer. Dicermadon was hers now, but Leska was angry with the god of magic and knowledge. She knew of his silent workings. There was no other way for men of Rha-Cordan's sect to learn the DeNaucght than if Dicermadon, the god of magic and knowledge, had intervened. She had learned he was speaking with the arch demon, Bykalicus, but she overlooked the outlawed deed. She believed that his station often required him to operate outside of the laws from time to time, but once this sacred knowledge had been dispersed, the god king had gone too far.

Leska stormed from her garden, ignoring the questioning eyes of the other gods and goddesses as she stalked toward the god king's chambers. The very stone that lay under her feet growled and rumbled as she reached the door of Dicermadon's chamber. The great double wooden barrier was well over twenty feet tall and each half was well over ten feet wide, with every single inch of the wood touched by a master craftsman's hand. Leska pushed on the great door but it would not give. She felt the god king's magic holding the wooden portal fast shut.

"Open this door!" Leska demanded, though she received no response. She noticed out of the corner of her eye, many of the gods had begun massing around the chamber, sensing the confrontation between the Earth Mother and the god king.

"Be gone, Leska. I have matters that are more important to tend to," Dicermadon's voice boomed like a thunder clap from the other side of the great door.

Leska's face bore a deep scowl. She outstretched her arms, closed her beautiful green eyes of fury, and tilted her head back. It started as a dull rumble in the very stone of the temple that steadily grew into a loud roar. The temple shook and vibrated as the pieces

430

of mortar and plaster fell from the ceiling. Great waves of power ripped through the air around her like a heat wave. The ripples grew and grew, becoming more rapid and narrower. She stretched her fingers out from her hands as if in pain, and her body shuddered violently. The thunderous rumbling of the stone ceased abruptly. The waves of power dissipated, but Leska held her pose. Nothing stirred for moments, then suddenly there was a great eruption. A violent shock wave tore through the hall like an immense explosion, but without sound. There was no wind, no force, yet all the gods standing outside the chamber felt the powerful flow of magic rip by them. The doors of the chambers, that Dicermadon had sealed, burst into hundreds of pieces. Large chunks of wood and debris shot out from the doorway and scattered over the great chamber's polished marbled floor.

Dicermadon stood with his back to Leska. He was garbed in heavy gray robes and his wavy silver hair was unkempt. There were flecks of ice that clung to his collar and littered the floor. She could smell the strong stench of the abyss that hung in the air like a thick fog. She noticed a bright red flash of magical energy that vanished in front of the god king. Leska ignored the odor and the magic. "I'm no child to be kept from the cupboard, Dicermadon," she growled.

The god king turned slowly. His face was riddled with anger and hate and his steel blue eyes glowed with fury, while his wild silver hair began to dance from his power. "You dare interrupt me, woman. I ordered you to wait outside. You will soon see why it is unwise to command my attention when I do not wish to give it," Dicermadon shouted angrily.

The other gods that had assembled in the hall outside the god king's chamber coughed and covered their mouths as the stench of the abyss floated into the corridors. Some muttered angry curses. Others mentioned fetching the more powerful gods that sat on the council. Something was amiss in Merioulus.

A blast of force shot out from the god king, ripping pieces of the stone floor loose, striking Leska and sending her sprawling back into the hallway. She skidded to a halt at the far wall and jumped to her feet, just as Dicermadon was walking to the shattered doorway. He stood defiantly with one of his massive hands clenched in a fist at his hips, the other pointing a shaking index finger at Leska. He glared with hate at the interfering Earth Mother.

"Go away, witch, and I shall forget your trespasses here. As you see, it takes more than a childish trick with a door to harm me," Dicermadon taunted.

Leska stood up quickly. She wasn't hurt by the blast, but his power had surprised her. She had not battled another god in millenniums, let alone one as powerful as Dicermadon, but the Earth Mother knew that the god king was making deals with devils and demons. This could not, and would not, be tolerated.

"You shall be still until the council decides what to do with you. Making oaths with devils and demons is a serious crime," Leska shouted as she rose to her shaky feet. The other gods, that had given the pair a wide berth, gasped at the charges Leska leveled at the god king.

Dicermadon laughed in response. "The council are fools. They have no power, save for that in which I give them. I am Dicermadon, god of gods, lord of lords, king of kings. I have to explain nothing to you feeble Breedikais. I am the first and I shall be the last. My breath is the beginning and the end. My dealings with demons are none of you pitiful wretch's concern!" Dicermadon gloated.

The other gods gasped in horror. Most fled down the corridor to alarm the other gods, though they feared that even combined, they could do nothing to harm him.

Leska stiffened her shoulders and narrowed her eyes bravely. "I will do nothing that you command. You are out of order, and surely mad. You have broken the sacred law and you will be held accountable."

Dicermadon chuckled and folded his muscled arms. "Mad? Sacred law? Fool woman, who do you think made that law? I can unmake laws as easy as I make them. Do you not realize I am the king of kings, lord of lords, god of gods? There is no hand above my own. My eyes, my words, my very thoughts are pure manifestations of the will I deem to impose on the world, on the realms, on you."

Leska took a brave step forward in the face of the god king's wrath. "Panoleen was right about you. I should . . ."

"Panoleen? PANOLEEN! You dare speak her name in my presence! She is dirt under the heel of an ass. She is no more, as you soon will become!" Dicermadon screamed as he flung his arm at Leska, hurling a bright blue force of magical energy. The deadly sphere cackled and popped as it rocketed toward the Earth Mother. Leska ducked low and took a deep breath, sucking the iron from the very stones that she stood upon, making a large wall of wrought iron erupt from the ground in between her and the sphere. The powerful ball hit the iron wall in an explosion of magical energy. Great sparks showered around the Earth Mother, singeing her hair and putting small burn marks on her dress. She quickly released the hold on the stone and the iron melded again into the floor.

"I control all that which is of the earth, Dicermadon. Enchanted iron is impenetrable to energy spheres. I expected more of a fight from you," Leska taunted, though she truthfully doubted how long she could last against his immense power.

Dicermadon summoned a great blue shield of glowing energy and a sword to match. The godly weapons cackled and popped in the air as he rushed to cut the Earth Mother down. He charged in and let out a fitful roar as he quickly closed the distance to Leska. The Earth Mother hummed softly as the raging god king bore down on her. The stone floor in front of her came alive as two creatures formed from the floor. They were made of solid stone and stood about twenty feet high. They were covered in great rocks that formed spikes that protruded from mace-like appendages.

Dicermadon paused to weigh his new adversaries. "Elementals, and elder ones at that," Dicermadon chuckled as he deflected a powerful strike from one of the creatures. Its massive fist pounded the stone floor, sending up a shower of rocky splintered debris. "It will be a pleasure to destroy these ancient beasts," the god king taunted.

Leska jumped to her feet. She did not doubt the elementals would perish at the hands of the god king. The elementals could easily destroy entire kingdoms if she so set them upon the task, but they were nothing in comparison to Dicermadon's power. She regretted summoning the apparitions to merely die in such a way, but they would buy her time until she could rush to her garden. There she was, the most powerful Leska, wincing in sorrow as she ran when she felt both of the noble creatures being cut down.

Dicermadon started past the elementals to catch Leska before she could reach her garden. He knew she could summon more power there than she could anywhere else in Merioulus. Suddenly a giant fist of stone and sharp rocks struck him in the shoulder, knocking him to the side. He hit the thick stone wall roughly as it cracked and splintered from the force of his iron body. Large pieces of rock and mortar from the bricks popped and crumbled, falling to his feet. The god king wiped his long silver hair from his face, revealing a strong square jaw that grinded in angry determination. His steel eyes locked onto the two apparitions that dashed toward him, unaware of who they were battling. They knew only that their goddess had called them to slay the creature, and that they would do so. Dicermadon, the lord of magic and knowledge, knew that the elementals were creatures of magic. Their bodies were made of earth and stone, but the life force that coursed through the creatures was raw magical energy. Dicermadon, the lord of magic, outstretched his hand with his palm open. He closed his steel blue eyes and hummed, focusing on the magic that dwelt inside the beasts. The elementals rose their huge spiked stone fists into the air. They had no eyes and no mouths, but they fought with the tenacity of a man defending his true love. Yet, as soon as the giant fists came streaking down for the god king's head, he drew the magic into himself. Cloudy white tendrils of a thick milky glow erupted from the great elementals. They stood, motionless, as the weaves of energy that held their life force were pulled from their rocky earthen bodies. Dicermadon took a deep breath of satisfaction as he basked in the magical weaves that enveloped him. He inhaled the white milky tendrils that danced around his body, ignoring the shock of the other onlooking deities. In moments, the great elementals, that had the fury to topple mortal kingdoms, shuddered and shook, then collapsed into themselves. There was a great shower of rocks and earth until only a large pile of earthen debris remained.

Dicermadon flexed his powerful arms and shook with power. His sleek silver hair shuddered as his muscles strained, and great veins in his neck protruded as he flexed. The very halls of Merioulus shook verdantly as the lesser deities backed away from the god king. Many had already left the battle-ridden corridors, but many remained. Dicermadon shook out his arms and rolled his head around to loosen his tight-corded muscles. He weaved a flow of magical energy around himself, forming a great suit of plate armor that had hundreds of glittering diamonds and other precious gems embedded into it. There was the mortal sign of his followers on his chest, a great moon overcast by two towering pillars. He created a giant tower shield that was made of what appeared to be a white jade. The shield glistened in the pale light of the corridor and it, too, bore his symbol. Dicermadon raised his right arm into the air as white milky tendrils twisted down his arm and passed it, forming a great sword that was as long as he was tall. The blade was ridiculously wide, shimmering like polished chrome, and had a razor sharp edge on each side. The hilt and pommel were made of polished platinum. The pommel bore a great protruding azurite spike, and at the end of the spike was a serrated edge that glistened with a black fluid that clung to the wicked end like a thick syrup.

Leska gasped for breath as she sprinted through the long corridors of Merioulus. Lesser deities stopped what they were doing and watched in confusion as the Earth Mother darted in and around the complex corners of the great city of the gods. While she was running she had shifted her clothing to a dark green that was mottled with brown. It had a high neckline that consisted of bright white lace decorated with many brilliantly shining jewels that were interwoven. The silk-like outfit seemed to cling to her figure, revealing a perfectly chiseled body that would make any mortal stand and gaze in wonderment at her stature. Leska bounded out of the main doors of Dicermadon's great palace in a dazed rush. The frantic Earth Mother ignored the many confused looks and stares she received from the other gods that happened to be about. She did not have time to explain, and she doubted she would gain any allies in doing so. Few of the Breedikai could stand up to Dicermadon's power for a short period of time, let alone pitch a battle. The earth elementals would not last long against the might of the god king. They just had to occupy him long enough for her to reach her garden.

She took the small steps to the palace doors in a great leap and landed gracefully without missing a stride. Magnificent birds leapt to take flight to avoid the Earth Mother as she sprinted by confused onlookers.

In the wide meandering streets of Merioulus, a few lesser gods watched with interest about why Leska was sprinting so. Her soft leather-like moccasins padded down the polished cobblestone streets. She moved her arms up and down in sync, with her churning legs of the fluid run. She strained to force her legs faster, to draw

435

more ground between her and Dicermadon. She would have simply created a gate to cross through, but the streets had been sealed from those kinds of spells since the fall of Panoleen.

Some of the gods that walked the streets called out to her, but she did not respond. They muttered to themselves in nervous excitement at the terrified, yet determined look that shone on the Earth Mother's face.

Dicermadon burst through the wooden doors of the great palace. His magnificent armor shined like a great beacon in the night. The great sword sizzled with power and his long silver hair waved about his head like a thousand tiny snakes writhing in anticipation. Dicermadon noticed the many gods that stood in the street in puzzlement. He thought about ordering them to aid in the capture of Leska, but the god king knew that they would capture her, and she would be heard. She was one of the most powerful Breedikai. Only Surshy, the goddess of water and oceans, Whisten, the god of air and storms, and Flunt, the god of fire, were her equals. He did not want her captured. He wanted her destroyed. The little witch would cease to exist. How dare she try to order him about? She and all of the gods were under him. They would do well to remember that.

Dicermadon soon realized he would not catch her before she reached her garden, so he elected to march confidently to her. Let her prepare whatever defenses she thought might help her. Her strength was pale in comparison to his and it had been too long since he crushed an enemy. He would savor the battle.

The god king's chamber sat silent. The heavy stench of the abyss hung in the air, seemingly clinging to the thick furnishings that decorated the magnificent quarters. There was a flash of white energy that lit up the room. Wisps of bright light flickered from the corner of the god king's chamber near the bed. The light twisted and turned over itself until the image of a man began to form. He was taller than most, and thin, wearing a thick gray robe that cascaded around his lanky body. He wore silver sandals that poked out from under the edges of his robe, and a bright platinum chain, with a giant pearl mounted on the end of it, hung from his neck. His eyes gleamed a bright blue and his hair was pale white. Whisten stepped from the magical weave he had woven around himself and dismissed the energy. Making himself invisible was one of the many skills he had learned from Sha-Shor'Nai, the goddess of the sun. She taught the elemental god how to bend light, using a form of his abilities with air, to allow the light to pass through him, making him seemingly invisible. He had never imagined when the ability would be useful to him, until he had learned of the god king's double dealings. Dicermadon, had he not been so arrogant, could have detected his weave, despite how well he tried to disguise it, but the god king was too full of himself to even check for such things. Whisten knew that a fool's pride had brought down many a mortal king, so why not the king of the Breedikai?

Whisten channeled a stiff stream of wind, locking the stench of the abyss in the god king's chamber, and wrapping the rapidly fading residue of the portal around the abyss. It was an easy task for him to wield the magical energy of wind in that way, though he doubted Dicermadon could have done it as well. After a few moments of casting, he whispered a message and let it hang into another flow he made. The energy floated in front of him as he duplicated it several times. When he was finished, Whisten sent his spoken words along a line of wind to the gods he wanted to hear him. He was sure Leska did not have much time.

An endless ocean of magma slowly shifted and bubbled. When the bubbles burst, it sent a great shower of molten rock cascading through the air. Small islands of dull rocky mountains floated in the magmatic seas in the distance. These volatile mountains were home to some of the creatures that dwelled naturally in the plane of elemental fire. The sky was full of hues from bright oranges to deep reds, and held thick clouds of steam that would boil the skin of any normal creature. In fact the general temperature of this plane would kill any normal being in seconds, causing their fragile bodies to burst into flames and burn, as soon as they arrived.

Flunt stood at the edge of the great sea of magma, gazing out into the fiery paradise. His great cape of molten lava hung over his thick and powerful body. His eyes, which were afire with a bright yellow flame that danced along his face, narrowed as he sensed the approach of a magical energy that entered his home plane. It was traveling to him at remarkable speed. Flunt, the god of fire, had started to form a shield of magical energy when he recognized the particular weave. It was undoubtedly from Whisten, and the god of fire expected that it had something to do with Dicermadon. The god king reined supreme in Merioulus, but here, in his native plane, the god king had no power. Well, little power, Flunt thought to himself.

"I have your proof, come to me, but make haste. Time is not a luxury," the deep raspy voice of Whisten said flatly when the message hit the god of fire.

Flunt sighed heavily. He never seemed to get much time in this fiery paradise. The god of fire took his finger and placed it into the air, even with his head, and slowly drew it down toward his feet As he moved his hand, the air seemed to open up, creating a gateway into the god king's chamber. Flunt stepped through the portal, and into what he knew could be the beginning to an end of an era.

She swam through the endless blue of the perpetual ocean. There was no surface, no floor, just an endless sea of infinite water. Her long blue hair waved and glided behind her as she swam in the aquatic paradise. There was no sun to light the waters, but they remained a pale blue that emitted a soft light, elegantly flowing through the watery vastness of the aquatic plane. Her soft blue skin seemed to shimmer as she swam. She wore no clothing. There was no need for it. There were no intelligent creatures that dwelled in the plane of water that wore clothing either. Truth be known, she despised wearing clothing even when she was not in the elemental plane of water. She usually garbed herself in a thin watery shawl that clung to her every feature, often gaining her disapproving looks and stares when she was in Merioulus, though she wore her shawl more thickly when in the presence of Dicermadon. It was not that she felt as if she owed the god king some measure of respect. She merely disliked the way his eyes seemed to soak up her form. Surshy was definitely the most free spirited of the elemental gods, though she admitted that Lukerey was the most free spirited of all the Breedikai.

Surshy twisted and turned, rolling over herself as she swam in acrobatic arcs. She paused and pursed her thin azure lips as she detected a disturbance in the plane. A powerful magic had entered and was streaking toward her. She immediately wove a shield and readied herself. There were a few in the plane that had the ability to cast underwater, but she could tell this weave was not cast here. It had a small shield around itself, and its weavings were too intricate to be a mortal's. As the energy neared at immeasurable speed,

438

Surshy lowered her shields. She recognized the trace of it and allowed the dweamor to approach.

"I have your proof, come to me, but make haste. Time is not a luxury," Whisten's deep raspy voice murmured in the watery plane.

Surshy frowned and looked around at her aquatic paradise. Had she been anywhere else, the tears that welled up in her big green eyes would have rolled down her cheeks. She knew she might never get to swim here ever again. Her heart pounded and fear trickled through her veins. It had been a long time since she felt fear. Surshy bravely pushed the thought aside and readied herself. The goddess of water knew what lay ahead, though she knew nothing of what outcome was in store for her, or the Breedikai. She took some flows of water and twisted them into a small shield, creating an immeasurably miniature void in the plane, where no water could touch. She opened a portal to the chambers of Dicermadon. Taking a deep breath she stepped into the chamber of the god king, and stepped into the unknown.

Whisten wove a thick stream of air around the door of the god king's chambers. It would not take Dicermadon long to disrupt the hold of the door, but it would give them enough time to leap through a portal. The god of air placed his arms in the sleeves of his thick robe as portals began to open in the room.

Flunt slowly stepped through the first portal that appeared. His dark red and black molten cape immediately began to distort the air around him from the volcanic heat that wafted from it. Flunt's eyes flickered nervously and his narrow pointed nose twitched as he inhaled the wicked stench of the abyss that hung in the air of the god king's chambers. Both Flunt and Whisten turned to regard Surshy as she stepped through the portal she had summoned. Her bright blue skin seemed a stark contrast to the bright reds and whites of the room. She wore a thin shawl of water that barely covered her voluptuous body. The shawl seemed to flow about her person like a tiny stream that was cloudy enough to distort the shape it covered. Her dazzling blue hair clung to the contour of her head in a perpetual wetness.

Surshy glanced around the chambers with her beautiful emerald eyes that shined of anger and fear. "The foul stench of the deep

439

abyss looms here," she said cautiously as she began to weave many protective dweamors about her.

Whisten raised a calming hand in reassurance. "There is nothing to fear here now. The demon is long gone. Dicermadon's dealings were interrupted by Leska some moments ago," the god of air said, noticing that Flunt also had cast some protective barriers around himself.

Surshy fixed her cold eyes on him. Whisten had always been trustworthy since the beginning of time, but the elemental goddess had seen many gods that were thought to be trustworthy stab others in the back since the beginning of time. She stared at his unreadable face. He could match Durion's cold rocky stare easily. In fact, she was not sure the god of air could not harden his face more than even the dwarven mountain god.

"What happened when Leska interrupted his ... meeting?" Surshy asked with a barbed tone. It was no mystery that the Earth Mother was smitten with the god king, despite him being open and vocal about using her as mere entertainment only.

Whisten looked at Flunt, who was waiting patiently for the reply, and looked back to Surshy. "Believe what you will, brother and sister, but he attacked her. They battled, and she summoned two elder elementals to hold him off while she fled."

"Battled?" Flunt asked incredulously. "I thought the pair twined as lovers?"

Surshy chuckled and scoffed. "Even the god of fire is as thick-headed as any man. To quote a mortal, 'marriage is made in the heavens, but so is thunder and lightning.' "

Flunt glared at Surshy. The fire that flickered around his face brightened and quickened as he narrowed his eyes. "I apologize, sister," Flunt said with a sarcastic bow. "But we men are not as knowledgeable about deceit and trickery as women," the god of fire said as a thin smile crept on his face.

Surshy started to respond when Whisten cut them off. "Come now, this is not the time for sibling rivalries."

Both Flunt and Surshy turned a hard eye his way.

Whisten ignored them and continued. "I believe Leska was fleeing to her garden."

Flunt nodded slowly. "Yes, she would be the strongest there."

Surshy nodded as did Whisten before he started again. "I was

440

shielded with a powerful weave from air. He could not see me unless he strained to see the magical energy. A risky endeavor I know, but I am past lecturing at this point. The truth is, I witnessed him making a deal with a arch demon named Bykalicus. The demon is quite powerful and I speculate he has been around since the beginning of the abyss. I could not detect all that was said, but I know he gave the demon the knowledge of how to cast the DeNaucght."

Surshy frowned. "What is the DeNaucght?"

Before Whisten could answer, Flunt spoke. "The DeNaucght is a divine ritual that Leska allows only her most coveted priests perform. It usually gets her an intense argument from Rha-Cordan, but she sometimes allows it anyway. He really can't do anything about it since he left Merioulus," Flunt said with a satisfied smile.

"What does it do?" the goddess of water asked, turning away from Flunt and facing Whisten in aggravation.

Whisten sighed. Even at this hour of need his siblings could not keep from picking at one another. "The DeNaucght allows he who performs the ritual to summon the soul of a mortal who has passed back into its body."

Flunt stepped forward and explained to Surshy. "He means it will raise the dead."

Surshy clenched her fists and stepped toward the god of fire angrily. "Continue to mock me, brother, and perhaps Whisten and Leska will have need of this DeNaucght for you."

"Enough!" Whisten yelled. "We need to make haste to the garden. Leska is surely about to battle Dicermadon, if she isn't already. He is in violation of sacred law. He has confided with demons and given away secrets. Panoleen did the latter and look what he did to her. I have sent messages to the other gods. We will converge on him and take him there. The proof is trapped here with flows of air, though I am sure, in his own superciliousness, Dicermadon will volunteer the needed evidence. You know how arrogant he has become since the birth of Lancalion."

Surshy narrowed her beautiful green eyes. She donned a frown of grim determination that is seldom seen on her carefree face. "I agree we must make haste. I will summon the others and meet you at Leska's garden."

Whisten looked at Flunt. The two usually worked well together during typical duties or projects. Though Whisten disagreed

441

with Leska as much as Surshy battled Flunt, when times called for the four to work together, they banded like a close-knit family.

The god of air and the god of fire hurried out of Dicermadon's temple, and through the golden streets of Merioulus, toward Leska's garden.

*   *   *

Fehzban opened his tired, stinging eyes. He stared dumbly at endless blackness that was capped by indistinguishable flickers of light. The flickers danced and twirled around the corner of his dull blinded eyes. When he tried to look at the flashes directly, they would vanish as quickly as they appeared. Perhaps he was not really seeing the flashes at all. Perhaps the flashes were remnants of the burning hot pokers that Fraitizu had seared his eyes out with. Perhaps they were tiny angels that were trying to communicate with him somehow. Perhaps . . . Fehzban tried to silence the rapid thoughts that bombarded his mind incoherently. It seemed as time went on, he had more trouble keeping his mind focused. He found himself entertaining outrageous ideas and other nonsense. Fehzban knew these ideas and thoughts were surely false, but for some reason he still found them creeping into his head when he least expected them. The tormented dwarf pushed the thoughts away and focused on the sequence of the shrine that held the Heart of the Rock. He was one of the four keepers that held the combination to the magical lock that sealed the enchanted stone door. Fehzban ran the sequence over and over in his head, repeating it and repeating it again. The dwarf had done this for hours upon hours as he tried to fight the thoughts that welled up in his tortured mind. The intense pain and torture he had suffered at the hands of Fraitizu had severe effects on his brain. Fehzban knew his thought process was different than it had been. Though conscious of the distinct change as he was, he could no more correct it than a man falling could sprout wings. Fehzban linked his sanity to the combination of the sealed chamber.

He would find himself chanting the combination until he would drift back into unconsciousness. He tried to droll himself to sleep once more, but he could not find the dark bliss he had been able to in the past. The constant squeaking and rolling of whatever he was lying on seemed to prod his mind into perpetual consciousness. Fehzban tried to move his arms and legs, only to discover he was held fast by a thick rope, though in his weak state it could have been twine. He could hear the squeak of a wagon's axles as the hard wooden wheels bounced over the tough rocky terrain they were riding over. The hard wooden board he lay on was undoubtedly the wagon bed. Though uncertain if he was fastened to the floor directly, he could smell the thin, cold mountain air, and feel the crisp wind on his bare face. He surprised himself that the image of his bare chin did not shame him as he thought it might. Perhaps not having to face the image in the mirror saved him the humility.

Fehzban lost track of time on how long he rode on the back of the wagon. Neither hunger, nor thirst, seemed to assail him with any vigor, and darkness came and went several times before the wagon finally came to a rest. Fehzban listened intently as two men from the wagon, obviously dwarves by the pitch of the sounds they emitted, lowered the back wooden gate of the wagon and dragged him out. They roughly pulled him out by the ropes that bound his feet. Without bothering to grab his upper body as they dragged him out, Fehzban plopped onto the hard, frozen, rocky ground. He felt the hot stinging sensation surge up his arms as the two dwarves cut the ropes that bound his hands. They then quickly ran to the wagon and rode off, leaving his feet bound.

Fehzban lay quietly on the frozen road, wearing barely enough furs to keep him alive in the frigid temperature. At first the cold snow seemed to burn his hard callused skin, but after a few moments the stinging turned to a pleasant numbness. His perfect ears listened as the wagon hurriedly squeaked and bounced back down the mountain pass they had just come from. Part of Fehzban wanted to feel sadness at the wagon leaving. It was the last remaining morsel of his former self. Though in truth, he felt little more than gratitude for the wagon's departure. The intense cold seemed to affect him little as he lay there in the middle of the rocky trail.

Fehzban rested motionless in the frozen rocky path for the rest of the day. Though he could not see the sun directly, he could feel heat on his face and skin. Being blind, he was at a severe disadvantage during the day. He would wait for nightfall before trying to find shelter. Fehzban twisted and turned until his exposed skin was covered from the snow. The pain didn't bother him at all, but he

443

knew that if he were to get frostbite, he would have a more difficult journey than it was already going to be. *Journey.* He said that word over and over in his mind. What journey? Where would he go? He couldn't see, his hands were next to useless, and he could not even speak to ask for help if he heard someone nearby. Had he not gone over these questions in the long weeks he was in Fraitizu's chamber, the hopelessness would have overwhelmed him, but now he merely closed his useless eyes and lay his head back in the cold snow.

Fehzban drifted back into unconsciousness while he lay on the rocky trail. He dreamed of the battle at Central City. Amerix came back from the human surge at the east bridge and led a second charge that proved to turn the tide against the humans. He and the army returned to Mountain Heart with a hero's welcome. The king rewarded him and Amerix for their bravery, and the humans, fearing the dwarves might attack again, asked for unconditional peace. The clan was saved, and he went rushing to the waiting arms of his beloved wife. He could smell the sweet perfume he had brought her from the Andorian merchant, which she had dabbed on her neck for him to nuzzle in. He pictured her beautiful face but it seemed to fade from him. What was her name? Slowly Fehzban struggled to remember the simplest detail of her. He loved her more than life itself, why could he not remember her name? His son, what was his face like? He stared at the pair, seeing their faces but not being able to recognize them. He knew who they were, yet he did not. Suddenly he was snatched around the neck. His family drifted off into the background to be replaced by the dirty grease-stained walls of Fraitizu's chamber. The stench of dried stale blood assailed him as Fraitizu's wicked laugh echoed in his ears . . .

Fehzban shot up to a sitting position and lashed out at the darkness. His mangled fingers failed to make a fist as he tried to strike the nightmares in front of him. He screamed out an unintelligible yell at the night. After sitting for a moment to calm himself, Fehzban frowned and reached into his mouth to feel his horrible, mutilated tongue. He faintly recalled the day Fraitizu had cut it to pieces. He did not recall the pain, it was more of a recollection of the loss to himself, knowing that he would never speak again.

The banished dwarf climbed to his weary feet. He could not feel the warm kiss of the sun, and the air was cool and crisp. All around him the dark mountainous forest loomed over. The forest consisted of thick, dark-colored coniferous trees. They were spaced far apart and there were many thick bushes and rocky juts protruding from the thick, white, snowy blanket that covered the ground.

Fehzban plodded on into the night, climbing higher and higher into the mountains, sometimes scaling fifty-foot cliffs. It was slow going. He had to feel for each hand-hold instead of seeing it ahead of time. His mangled hands were next to useless, acting more like hooks than hands. He climbed until he eventually found a large rocky overhang. The overhang was on the edge of a large shelf on the side of a mountain. The shelf was almost a square mile covered with trees and snow. Climbing inside to escape the frigid wind, he lay down, exhausted. The underside of the outcropping was deep and offered good protection from the elements. Fehzban knew he would have to wait until morning to find which direction it faced, but he had good direction sense and was sure it faced east. Almost all storms came from the west, so this shelter should be sufficient. This was going to have to be his new home for a while, he thought to himself as he closed his weary eyes. He wondered why he even opened them since he could not see. It seemed natural to him he guessed. Fehzban curled his knees into his chest to conserve heat in the mountain air and drifted off into sleep.

*   *   *

Men garbed in fine silks and linens busied themselves about the polished marble floors of the Central City great hall. Servants rushed back and forth from offices carrying letters, orders, and sometimes even refreshments. The great hall had been busy from sunup to sundown since the king removed Duke Dolin Blackhawk from power. He was still noble and was allowed to keep his estates, but he would no longer head the council at Central City. Since then, every viable noble with the most remote claim to the office had busied their houses with the preparations needed to request the title. Oddly enough, House Ganover, the house directly responsible for the king ousting House Blackhawk, had prepared quite a strong bid for the title. With the paladin, Apollisian, gone from the city, King Theobold held no notions to humor him and his ways of justice. In truth the king despised Stephanis and all of his foolish followers.

445

The problem was that the overwhelming majority of the masses embraced the god of Justice, leaving the king no recourse but to don his facade whenever a warrior of the church was near. Fortunately for the king, few politicians embraced Stephanis, and the foolish few who did seemed to have untimely accidents that ended their tenures rather quickly. King Thortan Theobold believed that Justice had no business within politics. However, Thortan was no fool. Despite wearing the crown of Beykla, the masses still held a considerable amount of power; power that was rapidly dwindling, and power that he hoped would be completely diminished when he handed the crown to his son, Darious.

Thortan chuckled and rubbed his clean shaven chin as he gazed down at the reports sitting on his desk in his makeshift office in the great hall of Central City. Send a treaty of peace to the dwarves indeed, he thought. "Not likely," he mused to himself. The only foreseeable event that could lead him to such a spineless treaty would be if the southern portion of the kingdom seceded. Then he would have no choice but to make peace with the dwarves to keep his nation intact. But as soon as the south was secure again, he would wipe his royal bottom with the treaty and make the foolhardy dwarves pay for their attacks. Bykla had never been defeated in any war or conflict since time was recorded, and he was not about to be the first ruler to allow it. Even if he did lose some land temporarily through the treaty with the dwarves, Adoria seemed to be on the cusp of winning their civil war, and their lands would be poorly defended, ripe for the taking. His western army alone, led by General Erik Stromson, the well-known warrior of the orc wars, could easily take and hold the weak Andorian lands. All he had to do was secure the southern portion of the kingdom. He was close to succeeding until those damnable dwarves sacked the Torrent and then hit Central City. Thortan wondered if the full-bearded folk had a political agenda. He doubted it. It was probably just dumb luck they attacked when they did. His difficulty with understanding the dwarves' respective targets was that he could not plant any spies among them. The entire clan was like some small family unit, close knit and unyielding. The offer of coin for betrayal of any sort always failed. In fact most of his agents who attempted to hire one of the little folk to do such spindly tasks, were usually slain. It did not take long for the underground network to get wind of the dwarves' reactions, and soon no one would take such jobs. But Thortan didn't dwell on the things he could not change, he opted to seek out the positive of every event. In this affair, the dwarves had drawn first blood, giving the green light to eradicate them from the ore-rich Pyberian Mountains. Second, the dwarves had rooted out the wererat guild that dwelled under the city, something that the local magistrate had been unable to do since they were discovered some thirty years before. The true challenge was going to be getting the masses to embrace the wiping out of Clan Stoneheart. The south was certainly sympathetic to the bearded folk's plight and it was unlikely that the dwarves would ever be able to strike any cities there. Thortan did not have any villain or counter attack to strike the fervor of battle here in the north, and had learned of the General Amerix from some of his advisors. They said he was the leader of the attack and was the dwarven king's most trusted ally, yet reports hinted the dwarven general was slain in the battle at the bridge.

Thortan ran his callused hands through his long brown hair. He sipped cider from a golden goblet that bore carvings of dragons and knights while he pondered the problem in his head. Perhaps the dwarf was not slain at all. He could set a hundred rumors that the great general who had the Beyklans hiding in fear at the mention of dwarves was running like a fox, no, like a wounded rabbit, and that it was only a matter of time before he was brought to justice. He would set an insurmountable reward to excite the people to hunt for him, and he would set a great posse to capture or kill the renegade. He would tell no one that the dwarf was actually dead. After some time, preferably a lengthy time, a dwarf would be supplanted in the dead general's stead. The captured dwarf would be tried and sentenced for his crimes against the people like the renegade Amerix. The people would feel a great victory at the dwarf's capture. Thortan would then make peace with Clan Stoneheart for the time being, thus securing the south. He would seem sympathetic to the south for sparing the dwarven nation and he would appear a great protector to the north for capturing the wicked general that had mercilessly slain so many innocents. After the south was secured, Thortan would dispatch agents to remove and break up the current noble house that held such influence and was sympathetic to the dwarves, and slowly plant nobles of his own who were

447

eager to quell resistance as he started the campaign against the bearded folk.

Thortan sipped his cider again slowly, draining the goblet as he pondered his devious plans. It would take a great deal of work to plant the rumors of the dwarven general, and he had little time left here in Central City. He could delay naming the new duke only so long before the nobles began to become suspicious. If he were going to enact this new plan he would have to begin immediately.

Thortan pulled his heavy fur cloak about himself and began scribing orders of the day. He dabbed the gray goose feather quill into the small, dark-colored ink vial several times and scribed several more lines on the thick parchment. He paused for a moment, then looked up, mulling over his thoughts, when a rap at his door broke his concentration. Thortan looked up at the servant who poked his head inside. Edgar was not a young man by any means, but he was far from the autumn of his life, and more importantly, he certainly was no servant. Edgar had been the king's advisor for almost fifteen years and was the closest thing to a friend that Thortan had. Edgar was born of Motivas, a relatively large community in the southern portion of the kingdom. He spent a large portion of his life fulfilling the will of the church and participating in the ever revolving political field there. He quickly rose through the ranks of the locals and eventually came to be employed at the king's castle just east of Central City. Soon after, Thortan was named to the crown. After the king's passing, during the orc wars, Edgar made himself readily available to the young king. Edgar had a fine grasp on the south's politics and their nobles, helping Thortan hold together an already decaying field of trust.

"Edgar, my trusted advisor, how fares the city?" Thortan asked as he stood up from his desk and extended his hand.

Edgar took it warmly and grasped his other hand to cover both of theirs, shaking them lightly while staring into the king's eyes. Edgar had taken the king for a foolish prince when he was first crowned, but since then, the cleric had learned the man had a fair head about his shoulders, and was ruthless in dealing with those he saw as enemies.

"It fares as can be expected, my lordship, but the nobles grow eager to learn of the naming for a new duke. I have seen packs of ravenous wolves that were more receptive than that bunch," Edgar said, smoothing his dark blue robes with a red frill around the cuffs and cowl, marking him as Beyklan.

Thortan nodded as he spoke. "I agree that I need to name a duke soon, if for nothing else, to get me back on the track of dealing with the foul dwarves and quelling the rebellion in the south."

Edgar crossed his legs tentatively and leaned forward, interested in what new insight Thortan must have gained. The man's wisdom for scheming seemed to grow with each passing day. "I had thought you planned on sending an emissary to make peace with the bearded folk," Edgar said honestly.

Thortan nodded his head in agreement. "I certainly plan to, the south is very sympathetic to the little people's plight. Making peace with them will certainly take some of the fuel from the rebellious nobles' fires."

Edgar smiled and leaned back. The hard wooden bench made his rump sore. He was used to much finer seating and hoped the king would solve the dilemma fast, so he could return to his posh living in Dawson or the king's castle. "I agree, my lord. That it will. But, will it not also fail to placate the northerners here, that spilled the blood of their fathers, their brothers, and their sons fighting the bearded demons?"

Thortan grinned, leaned back in his chair, and placed his heavy leather booted feet on the desk in front of him. He cleared his throat and intertwined his fingers as he spoke. " 'Tis true, Edgar, they will be angered by the treaty." Thortan paused, waiting for the cleric to respond.

Edgar, sensing he was supposed to question the king's statement, sighed before he spoke in a sarcastic tone, waving his hands in a circle. "So what do you plan to do about the northerners and their thirst for vengeance?"

Thortan frowned and leaned forward in his chair, placing his boots on the floor and angrily planting his hands on the edges of his thick desk. "Do not mock me, Edgar!" Thortan shouted before softening his tone and relaxing a bit. "We have been friends long, but know I am your king."

Edgar leaned forward submissively. "I am sorry, my lord, but I do grow weary. I am no novice to politics."

Thortan nodded slowly and sat back down in his chair. "We will give them an object to hate. The masses will be told the mastermind behind the dwarven attack was the General Amerix. My reports tell me the general was slain when he was thrown from the bridge on the east side of the city, near the Dawson River."

Edgar interrupted. "But was the dwarven general slain? Some reports stated that he was seen floating down river."

Thortan frowned, annoyed at the interruption, but continued. "Truth is what we make of it. When we are finished, this Amerix will be able to slay a hundred giants by himself, and will be running in fear of my might. I will make an incredible reward for his capture, or proof of his death, inspiring the masses to pick up swords and hunt the foul creature. No doubt the mobs will slay any dwarf they see, hoping it is Amerix, but of course it will not be."

"Not until you decide it needs to be," Edgar put in.

Thortan smiled, placed his feet back on his desk, and relaxed once again. "And when I decide that the dwarf has been captured, he will be slain and his body will be put on display for all to see, making the north worship me as a hero, and the south happy with the treaty. In the meantime, my . . . under workers so to speak, will be rapidly removing southern nobles who are not in favor with my policies. After a short spell, I will renew the war with the dwarves, conquering them and what is left of the Andorian lands, thus carving out a place for me in history as one of the greatest Beyklan kings," Thortan boasted.

Edgar merely smiled. His longtime friend, and king, was really beginning to understand the ways of being a king. "Now, my lord, all we have to do is begin planting the rumors about the dwarven general escaping alive."

Thortan grinned lightly and rubbed his clean shaven chin, staring down at the parchments that lay on his desk before him. "Yes, I agree, my friend and advisor. That is why I have taken the liberty of drawing up these wanted petitions. I will have them hung in every inn, tavern, and shop from the northern reaches of Dawson to the lands we hold south of Motivas. I was careful to keep Amerix's description vague, other than saying he is large for a dwarf."

Edgar nodded, reached over, and examined the petition of arrest. He scanned it up and down for a few moments before speaking. "What of the few men that have actually seen Amerix? What if they decide to answer the petition?"

Thortan grinned as he stood up from his chair and pushed his arms through the sleeves of his heavy cloak. "All the better if the real Amerix is found and brought to me, though it makes no difference. Once any dwarf is brought before the masses, they will scream it is the renegade general. They will lust at want of his capture."

Edgar nodded in agreement and picked up the small stack of parchments. "I will see that these are dispatched immediately," the cleric said as he stepped from the king's makeshift office with a thin smile of satisfaction. He held no favor toward the dwarves and in fact would enjoy seeing the expansion of Beykla. Since the taming of the world, there was little land left to be gained by exploration, save for the wild lands to the far southwest, but the terrain was so rough, it hardly seemed worth the trouble to anyone. Yes, if Thortan's plan worked he most likely would be the last king ever to add lands to the great Beyklan nation. Edgar was saddened by the thought. Surely they were seeing an end to a great age. As he walked down the great hall in Central City, arrest petitions in hand, Edgar wondered what achievement the next age would bring.

Unselfish acts. Do they exist? Men claim that when they're in love they perform unselfish acts. Mothers and fathers claim the same. But I challenge their way of thinking. Are their acts indeed unselfish? I say that no man can perform an unselfish act, save for one. Many argue they have performed many unselfish acts on a multitude of occasions throughout the year. But I defy each of these supposed acts, and expose them for the true underlying selfishness that dwells.

A man gives a gift to a woman he is courting. Why is he courting her? Is he doing it for her? No, he is courting her because she makes him feel good, maybe even loved. If she did not create this sensation within him when he was around her, you can bet he would be off courting another.

Gifts on birthdays and holidays, are they unselfish? Does not the giver receive a pleasant feeling when they distribute the gifts? Of course they do. If they did not, they would certainly not give the present. A man would never give a gift to another man he hated. This selfishness in gift giving goes as far as to make the giver angry sometimes, when he or she is not thanked for the gift in which they gave. Plus, they sometimes feel inadequate if the gift they gave is placed lower in comparison to another's gift. In a way, they base their own self-worth on their gift. Self-worth, in a gift? Very selfish.

How often in a man's life has this simple wisdom eluded him? These are some examples of why man can never rise above his mortal self. His mind is flawed. He cannot see the world past what lies on the surface. Even the wisest scholars cannot admit this, and many other facts. They are too afraid to face the weakness of their race. Strange though, that true compassion comes from this selfishness. Love. It seems to permeate and fill someone with such euphoric proportions that the soul cannot contain it any longer, so it begins to leak out. This, and only this, is when a mortal man can begin to perform an act totally unselfishly.

Giving one's life to save another. There is no definite reward. There are hypothesized rewards, depending on the god who is followed, but no concrete evidence that the sacrifice won't be for naught. It is usually performed out of a great empathy that extends beyond one's ability to recognize. Yet again, only in death can a man achieve something he could never achieve while he was alive. Strange. The human race is a collection of good and evil beings that all fall short of the strength and wisdom of the gods they scorn, or sometimes worship. But what is stranger yet, is that I am often proud to call myself one.

—Lancalion Levendis Lampara—

Thirteen
Those Who Are Hunted

Myson Strongbow and Eulic Overmoon camped in a tall thicket of grass, southeast of the Minok Vale. The two Darayal Legionnaires bundled their gear into small thin backpacks, which were light to say the least. These elves were better adapted to living in the wilderness than their brothers, who at best are described as being at one with the forest. The Darayal Legion consists of one hundred of the top elven rangers of the Minok Vale. They travel the Vales seeking out evil denizens of the forest, such as orcs, ogres, and giants. Since the orc wars, during the only times in history that have been recorded in which elf and man have fought side by side, there have been little of the evil races left for them to hunt. Nevertheless, the legion has remained vigilant in its patrols, endlessly searching for evil to root out. The lands of the Minok Vale were vast, and still many orc tribes remained, though in truth, the orcs warred with one another more frequently than they warred with others. The humans the elves fought beside were long since aged, and most were now into the winter of their lives, where Myson and Eulic themselves remember some of the brave champions as if they had shared the same fires in recent moons.

Myson circled the perimeter of the small camp checking his snares. He had netted two large rabbits that would serve as their lunch and supper later on the trail. Myson was young for a legionnaire, as was Eulic, but Eulic was near royalty, being a first cousin to the Overmoon family, even bearing their name. They had been raised from the brotherhood of the sword, just before the orc wars in which King Kalliman Theobold led his men in the crusade to wipe out the green-skinned beasts from the face of his kingdom. Kalliman was a good man as far as the elves were concerned, unlike his scheming son. The elves did not think him evil so to speak, just selfish and calculating.

Myson hung the rabbits by their feet from his thick leather belt. His long blonde hair was braided in many hundreds of thin narrow strands that bounced along his head as he walked. The legion called it a varmin. They had worn the braids since their creation some millennia ago. The soft leather beads, or symas, that were fastened at the end of some braids represented lives he had saved during his tenure. Few legionnaires wore any silver rings, which marked selfless heroism, and even fewer yet bore gold. Usually the event that earned you a gold syma fastened to your hair was your funeral.

It was the smell of rotting flesh that drew the legionnaires' attention. They were in the Serrin Plains, the most deadly lands left in the northern Minok region. Rotting flesh could mean the remnants of an attack, some orcs, or a giant battle. Myson drew his finely crafted scimitar and his masterwork short sword. The scimitar blade was magically enchanted, giving the blade an unnatural balance that could never have been crafted from mortal hands, and the edge was so keen that it could slice into heavy mail that normal swords could not pierce. The scimitar's pommel was round polished brass and the hilt bore two winged horses, one on each side. His short sword was no less ornate, but lacked the magical enchantment the scimitar had.

Stalking over the hill, Myson witnessed a large deer that was walking toward him. At first glance he was not alarmed and lowered his weapons, taking an easier stance. But as the deer closed in on him, he could clearly see it was a walking carcass. It bore a deep maggot-infested wound on its neck and in its side. Rotting festering entrails dragged on the ground behind the beast, and its eyes were dull, glossy, and lifeless.

Myson moved slowly away from the animal. But as he moved, it moved. The deer lay its ears back and lowered its head, much like it might treat a threat from a wolf or other predator. Myson tried to back away again in another direction, but the deer again moved to intercept him.

"You desire a fight then, beast?" Myson called out as he approached the undead deer.

"You are not a natural thing. I shall rid . . ."

Myson was cut off as the deer lunged at him. The ranger

454

dropped to one knee and raised his scimitar up to catch the antlers and keep them from impaling him. Spinning, he slashed with his short sword behind his back, cleaving off the front legs of the animal. The deer stumbled and fell forward. Myson stood, turned, and faced the deer anew. He had never seen the undead before, but he had surely heard their tales. The deer acted as if it felt no pain, and was oblivious to its own missing front legs. It crawled and lunged at him, trying to kill him. Myson doubted the beast could see out of its eyes, it just seemed to sense him wherever he moved. With a clean swipe, Myson beheaded the deer. The rotting head hit the grassy earth with a dull thud. The body still quivered and twitched as black curdled blood slowly seeped from the wound. Wiping the gore from his sword onto the grass, Myson turned and hurried back to where he and Eulic had been camped.

Eulic saw Myson sprinting into camp with a worried look on his face. "What is the matter, brother?" Eulic asked. The long brown braids of his varmin bounced around his face as he turned.

Myson paused to catch his breath. "I encountered an undead deer in the plains. At least I think it was undead . . . no, I am certain it was. The beast actually attacked me."

Eulic frowned and looked around as if to see more undead descending down around them. When he did not see any he relaxed visibly. "Is it still there?"

Myson turned back the way he came. "I think it is. I cut off its front legs and then its head. If it is not there I do not think it could have gone far."

Eulic nodded and the pair hurried toward the area where Myson had battled it. Soon they came to the rise, where he met the deer. Sure enough, the beast lay like it had been dead for many days. Its head was severed and lay a few feet from its body. The front legs had been cut off, and maggots and other festering insects crawled in and over the body. The stench of rotting flesh hung in the air, making the two elves cover their noses and mouths with their light brown cloaks.

Eulic peered around the area of the ground until he located the animal's tracks. Myson scanned the area for any more undead creatures that might be approaching.

"How do you suppose it . . . you know, came to be?" Myson asked uneasily as he scanned the horizon.

Eulic did not look up as he answered. "I do not know, brother. It is said that a mage or priest, powerful in their magic, can command the dead to rise and walk. Certainly they must be dark of heart to do such a thing, and I know of no such evils intelligent enough to do these things in the Serrin Plains."

Myson nodded as he looked around. "Perhaps a dark mage or priest has made a home of our vast grasslands?"

"Perhaps," Eulic responded. "Look," the elf said as he walked along pointing at the tracks in the grassy ground with his nimble finger. "The beast came from the due south. No wandering, no zig-zagging. A perfect straight line."

"No deer travels like that," Myson replied as he followed Eulic, tracking the animal.

Eulic stood up and stared south into the rolling plains, tapping his lower lip. "Indeed. Perhaps we should back track this beast, dear brother. Maybe we will run into the evil that spawned such a horrific abomination."

"What of the legion? Should we not report our findings to Master Orantal?" Myson asked reluctantly. He wanted to hunt the malevolence as much, if not more than Eulic did, but such a finding was important to report.

Eulic did not respond. The ranger could sense his friend's desire to hunt down the vile mage or cleric as much as he did.

Myson met Eulic's gaze squarely. "We will advance to the south. If the fiend has established some sort of living quarters, then we will report it," Myson proclaimed.

Eulic smiled and drew his long and short swords. "Agreed, brother. Shall we?" he said as he motioned to the south and began walking. Myson smiled, drawing his two wicked blades, and started south, stride for stride, with his companion.

*　　*　　*

Amerix wandered through the dense forest for many days. He sustained himself on mushrooms and some roots from what few plants he could recognize. A few of the berries he had eaten had left him somewhat ill, and he was feeling weak.

As the venerable dwarf wandered further south, he noticed that the forest became thicker and more lush. The normally decidu-

456

ous forest gave way to a thicker and more jungle-like terrain. Though the trees remained deciduous, the underbrush was much thicker, making traveling through it more difficult. There were many broad vines that sprouted from the ground and entwined themselves in the thick canopy. Sounds of ground animals and birds that Amerix had never heard before seemed to echo around him, making him more nervous with each passing second. The ancient general had felled hundreds of enemies, but dark denizens of the upper world he had never faced. He had no idea what mysterious powers they held, or how big they might be. Amerix had faced most of the monsters of the under dark in his long life, but he had never ventured far on the surface. It was not like he was one of the dark dwarves who had trouble seeing in the bright surface light, but he had spent most of his surface life in the cold mountains.

As Amerix ducked under a thick vine that hung from the top of two trees, the long sword he had strapped to his back began to make the shrill hum. Amerix paused and took the sword off his back. The old dwarf held the blade in front of his face and gazed down at the finely crafted sword. The shrill hum did not seem to annoy him like it had done in the past. It seemed somehow foreboding to him.

Amerix studied the strange weapon for a few moments. The long sword was surely elven crafted. It bore many elven runes down the side, and had a blade that reflected the thin rays of sunlight that poked through the thick treetops like a beacon of light in total darkness. The craftsmanship was so magnificent, the sword seemed to tantalize him where he stood. Amerix wondered why he had never noticed the beauty of the sword before now. He had carried the foul weapon since defeating the paladin at the Torrent Manor, yet it never struck him as beautiful until today.

Amerix was roused from his inattentiveness by a crunching sound in the distance. Ducking down the best he could, the renegade general waited for whatever it was to come closer. Squinting his old wrinkly eyes, Amerix spied a green-skinned humanoid running recklessly through the woods. It had thick yellow tusks that protruded from its lower lip and extended well past its upper lip. The creature was wearing some kind of sleeveless hide jerkin that exposed its thick muscular arms. The creature's long tangled hair, that clung to tiny pieces of branches and leaves, hung wildly in its face. The thing would stop occasionally and turn, yelling something in a deep guttural language.

"Orcs," Amerix muttered under his breath. He hated orcs, as did almost everyone and everything. They were a horrible and vicious race that loved war, killing, and maiming. Plus, the green-skinned monsters were remarkably good at it.

Amerix watched the orc curiously as it neared at a hurried pace. It frequently stopped and turned, motioning for it to catch up. Amerix decided to wait until the green-skinned demon got a little closer before he erupted from the underbrush and cut it down. Just as the orc got close enough that Amerix could have charged out and run it down, he noticed the young orc seemed to be leading something along.

The orc whelp was almost as tall as he was, and seemed to be quite muscular. It whimpered and whined as it pitifully tried to push thorny branches and vines from its path. The adult orc, that Amerix decided must be female, looked about nervously as if the pair was being pursued. Her eyes darted around as she impatiently tugged at the younger whelp. She would pick him up and carry him briefly, but he was obviously too big for her to carry him long.

Suddenly Amerix heard a loud deep horn sound from the west. The female orc let out a guttural cry and scooped up the whelp, running as fast a she could, while branches and vines smacked her in the face. She ignored them and hurried past Amerix, often stumbling to the ground. Seconds later, crunching underbrush and the sound of many heavy footfalls pounded the earth. Amerix heard the sword again, or rather felt it. Its shrill hum echoed in his mind, warning him of the approaching pursuers.

The renegade general glanced to his left to see the female orc slowly making her way, despite the obvious efforts of haste she was making. The pursuers burst into the dwarf's view moments later. He counted thirteen of the green-skinned monsters. They were about six feet tall, and extremely muscular. Their long black hair was worn in many different styles and it bounced along their heads and shoulders as they charged wildly ahead. Some held wicked axes that were oversized for their bodies, with nicked rusted blades, while others held clubs with giant metal spikes driven into them to act as some kind of pickax. Others yet held rusted swords with equally nicked and scarred blades. Their bodies were covered in thick hide armor, though a few wore patched metal plates that seemed to be strapped to them with no apparent thought about protecting vital areas. The heavy metal plates hung loosely from worn leather bindings that clanged and bounced as they ran. When they saw the female orc running west, they began to hoop and holler in their guttural language, fanning out to overtake her on all sides.

Amerix waited. Though he despised orcs, he was not here to fight thirteen of the powerful creatures. Orcs were warriors by blood, and even half of their numbers would give the most seasoned dwarf some pause. Amerix slowly moved closer to the confrontation. In truth he was more curious than anything, figuring they could not hear him, while he walked casually through the underbrush, with all the yelling they were doing.

The female realized she was not going to escape. Amerix watched as she transformed from scared to fleeing, to angry and vengeful. She stopped, grabbed a small sapling, and snapped the bottom of it off with her foot. She pulled the string bark away with a roar and hastily ripped away the upper branches, making a crude club. If the other orcs were taken aback by her strength or repose, they showed no signs that Amerix noticed.

The orcs surrounded the female and the pair called out, back and forth, in their guttural language, all the while she held the young orc behind her, trying to keep the horde in front of her. Suddenly they all rushed in. The female ducked the first overhand attack of a wicked rusted axe and brought her thin club across the monster's neck. The force of the blow would have shattered any dwarf's or human's neck, but the orc merely howled and dropped to the ground, rolling around grabbing his throat, gasping for air. The second attack came from her left as a rusted sword thrust at her unprotected midsection. She partially deflected the strike, but the blade dug deep into her thigh. She ignored the wound as attack after attack rained down on her. Amerix watched as the female fell under the attackers. The orcs giggled as they hacked and chopped the female into an unrecognizable pile of flesh. The young orc howled and screamed as he was restrained by two of the other beasts. Once the attack was finished, the orcs fanned out and began gathering wood they found along the forest floor. They quickly started a fire, occasionally punching the young orc in the face when he would not stop crying. Amerix watched with slight anger at the treatment of the whelp, but more out of curiosity. He had never known orcs had the ability to sense loss. The fact that a female orc, even a mother, if that was what she was, would give her life defending her young, perplexed the renegade general. Orcs did not care for their young when the whelps were old enough to walk and talk. If the whelp died, it was because he was weak.

Amerix watched the orcs for a few hours. They managed to start a fire by rubbing two sticks together and then promptly ate the female orc they had just slain. They frequently fought each other, especially when they started feeding. All the while the whelp cried incoherently. Amerix had managed to ignore the sword's constant humming, but it seemed to irritate him now.

"A fine time to start bothering me, sword," he thought to himself while anger seemed to creep into him, with a deep longing for the destruction of the foul green-skinned beasts. The thought surprised him. He shouldn't care whether or not they killed and ate every one of each other, yet there he sat, on the edge of the underbrush, fighting the urge to foolishly charge out from the thicket and slay all of them. Amerix found his mind wandering to what the young whelp was thinking. He remembered when he was a young dwarf, not a child, but not much older than one. He recalled when the shimmering white dragon, who would have been beautiful under different circumstances, attacked his home city. There were a thousand scores of dark dwarves that followed the dragon as they invaded his home. Hacking and slicing, the dark dwarves carved their way into the heart of the city, while the dragon burned the outskirts with his unearthly arctic breath. No, arctic did not describe the coldness of the beast's breath attack. Amerix pondered it in his mind for a few moments as he reflected. There was nothing cold enough to accurately compare to the dragon's breath.

The shrill hum of the sword grew louder and more intense, waking Amerix from his daydream. The renegade dwarf had surmised the ringing was in his head now, but before others had clearly heard it. Amerix watched the orcs as night approached. The dark blue sky hung overhead and the cold chill of mid autumn sent his breath out in front of him in light frosty wisps.

One of the orcs reached over and grabbed the terrified whelp by the hair and roughly dragged him kicking and screaming to a

460

large stick they had broken free from one of the larger tree branches around their camp. They roughly lashed the whelp to the branch and carried him toward the fire. Amerix had had all he could stand. Though he cared little for the orc whelp, it was all the excuse he needed to charge in and cut the green-skinned beasts down. The renegade general hoped for death in battle, and every passing day he became further from that possibility. Gripping the sword handle tightly and adjusting the rusty chain mail that hung about his shoulders, he took a few deep breaths and broke from the underbrush in a mad rage, yelling an unintelligible battle chant that sounded more like a deep snarl than anything else.

The orcs stood confused and startled for a fraction of a second. They were battle-hardened creatures, fighting and dying was their way of life, but the hesitation was all that Amerix needed. With an overhead slice with the long sword, he cut a cavernous wound down the shoulder and deep into the chest of the first orc. It roared and clutched the gash, falling to the ground in disbelief at its indelible death. Steam rose from the fresh wound in the cold night as the beast gasped for breath. Amerix turned without hesitation, kneeled low, and sliced another of the green monster's legs in two, just above the knees. The magnificent long sword cut into the green beasts like a warm spoon into fresh dolgo nut pie. The second orc dropped his crude, rusted sword and grabbed his severed legs with both hands, letting out a blood curdling howl that pierced the calm night.

One of the orcs with an oversized axe swung it at the short dwarven hellion who attacked them. The wicked weapon came streaking down toward Amerix's exposed ribs. The renegade general shifted his feet to one side, moving closer to the orc, and away from the fulcrum of the swing, halving the blow's power. He reached out his old, but muscled hand, and caught the shaft of the rusted blade. Even with the orc's blow at half strength, Amerix nearly toppled from the force. His shoulder ached and he was knocked off balance from the beast's monstrous strength. Amerix spun, gripped the orc, using his shorter stature as leverage, and heaved the green-skinned beast over his shoulder. The orc, refusing to let go of his axe, left a clear kill shot as it lay on its back, stunned from the throw. But Amerix was forced to release the crude weapon and deflect a strike from another orc that lunged in. As Amerix par-

461

ried the rough, rusted blade with the fine long sword, he side-stepped toward the prone monster as it tried to regain its footing. The renegade dwarf plunged the keen elven blade into the downed orc, then stomped on the dying beast's head while wrenching the fine blade free from the monster's chest.

The orcs squared off against the renegade dwarf, showing more respect for their new adversary, but they quickly surrounded him, allowing no avenue for escape either. Orcs were stupid, but they were not cowards.

Amerix stood over the body of the orc he had just slain. He said nothing and glared menacingly at the now ten green-skinned beasts that were attacking him. The dwarf's hot breath erupted from his mouth as he exhaled forcefully from the exertion he had just performed. Two hundred years ago, he could have fought for hours without breaking a sweat, but not now. Amerix felt a sting in his shoulder and warm sticky blood dripping down his left arm. He did not have time to inspect the wound, but he doubted it was serious. That last attack he had side-stepped must have still landed, though he didn't feel it at the time. *Must protect me axe arm,* he thought to himself. Amerix chuckled when he remembered he carried a sword. A sword. If anyone would have told him that when he was over four hundred fifty years old, he would be fighting more than ten orcs to save an orc whelp with a long sword instead of his family's axe, he would have called the dwarf a plain fool. Yet there he stood in a dense forest in late autumn, wearing rusted chain mail and wielding a long sword. He guessed he probably wasn't even using it right.

Amerix kept flowing in a tight semi-circle while surrounded by the orcs. It made it difficult for them to tighten the trap, and kept them indecisive about who would charge in. The renegade general figured only five, maybe six could come at him at once, and was glancing around at the orcs, looking for the biggest one to kill. The largest was usually the leader, and if he slayed him, it would not take long for the others to lose interest in the battle. It would take them a good while to fight out a new leader, perhaps even killing a couple more in the process.

*   *   *

462

The orcs' bright yellow eyes studied the dwarf nervously. Their Kar, or war party leader, had gone down under the dwarf's first strike. They didn't understand why the dwarf had attacked them, especially alone. They were near no mountains, and in fact a few of the younger ones hadn't even seen a dwarf in the flesh before. Yet, the orcs were still more than confident they could kill the grizzled old dwarf that stood before them, even though he displayed a good sense of skill in battle. Their hesitation was from more of a desire to be the new Kar. The first one that rushed in would no doubt fall to the stocky demon's sword, but while he was slaying the first, another could get in a good strike and kill the dwarf, making a strong claim for Kar. The orcs were happy to have a successful hunt, capturing and killing the witch Valga. She had claimed that clan chief Slargcar had fathered her whelp. That actually was more than likely true, though no one cared. It was that Valga spat at the clan chief's feet and called him a weakling. Any normal orc would have been slain on the spot for attacking the clan chief's strength, but Valga was the clan shaman. She had dark powers that many orcs feared. It wasn't until clan chief Slargcar declared her a traitor and elf friend that she fled with her son, Vlargcar. Orcs hated elves most of all, and being declared elf friend was about as low as you go as an orc. Plus the witch's son, Vlargcar, had been born with blue eyes! No pure blood had blue eyes, let alone the blood of a clan chief. It had to be more of her dark magic, though it was all done with. They had killed the witch Valga and nullified her powers by consuming her body. All they had to do was kill this wretched dwarf and then sacrifice the whelp spawn to Drunda, the orc god, and all would be right. But before one of the orcs could get the courage to attack, the dwarf chose to attack them and rushed in.

*   *   *

Amerix waited impatiently for the orcs to attack. He guessed that one would eventually close in, but none of them seemed to want to be the first. They probably wanted to be the second, hoping they could sneak in a lucky shot and claim the killing blow for themselves. While they stood glancing nervously back and forth to one another and then back at him, Amerix chuckled. He would be

463

here all night if the orcs were trying to think up a plan of attack. Orcs thinking. The very notion lifted his spirits as he nearly laughed aloud.

Amerix shifted his tight grip on the long sword and he lunged at the orc that seemed the largest. The green-skinned beast was quite surprised that the short bearded creature would dare attack them, but Amerix made the surprise more apparent as he drove the sword home into the creature's chest. The orc stared wide-eyed and merely gurgled in response at the keen blade that was already wrenched free and set about some of his other comrades.

Amerix ducked low and brought the razor-sharp blade around his body and up the groin of the nearest orc. The sword slashed the beast deep from its groin to its chest. Clutching the grievous wound, the orc fell to the ground in howling pain as tears filled its eyes and its bright red blood spilled onto the leaf-covered forest floor.

The orcs seemed to recover from the shock of the dwarf attacking them when the bearded foe was surrounded and they quickly redoubled their efforts in new attacks. Amerix continued to stay low to the ground as he ducked and spun, carving a swath of death among his green-skinned enemies.

The battle raged on. The orcs fought with renewed fury each time they scored a hit. Amerix bled from many wounds. Though none were crippling or life threatening, they were beginning to slow him down. He had slain, or crippled eight of the thirteen orcs, but the remaining five seemed to attack with a structured unison. They had created a flow, one attacking, then parrying, allowing another to attack immediately after, giving them a balanced flow of attacks and feints. It gave Amerix little time to counterstrike each attack as he had to deflect or duck the next one. The orcs reveled in the notion they had outsmarted the dwarf and were going to wear him down. Yet, Amerix was no fool when it came to battle. Blood dripped from many wounds, as if the dwarf had spent more hours in the heat of battle than these orcs had spent breathing. An intelligent enemy would shift the attacks so that the next was never predictable. Though the shift might confuse its comrades and leave a short time when there was no attack, it was more likely to confuse the enemy more. Second, by performing the attacks in the same order, it taught Amerix where the next attack was going to come from after the first. Grinning with a blood-soaked beard from a thin slice across his forehead, Amerix spun, cleaving the hand off that held one of the orc's great rusted axes. The heavy weapon skittered into the thick leaves that lined the forest floor while the orc stood in shock holding his bloody nub, where a powerful hand that gripped his axe had been. The next attack was an overhand slice, which the renegade general rolled under, and the razor-sharp blade sliced across the midsection of the unsuspecting orc. The beast howled as the keen blade smoothly sliced into ribs, severing them, thus spilling its entrails out onto the ground before it. The remaining three orcs turned and fled. They had had enough of the demon dwarf.

Amerix plopped down against the tree as his chest rose and fell in great heaves. His breath seemed to send out a steady fog into the cold twilight air. Around him on the ground, some of the mortally crippled orcs mumbled to themselves and tried to crawl away but would not go far before death claimed them. The renegade general dabbed the warm blood from his forehead, careful not to tear open the thin cut any more than it was. After applying a thin dirty cloth as a bandage to his several wounds, Amerix let his weary head fall back against the tree. The cool bark felt soothing against his sweaty head. Glancing over at the whelp that was tied to the stake, Amerix noticed something peculiar about the little beast. Every orc he had ever faced in his four hundred fifty odd years of life had bright yellow eyes. That was always a sure way to mark an orc in the darkness, by his sinister eyes. Yet the whelp who sat bound to the wooden stake stared at him intently with crystal blue orbs. The renegade general had seen many strange things in his long life and paid the blue-eyed orc little attention. The dwarf focused more on the horizon, wondering if the green-skinned beasts might return with friends. He was in no mood to fight anymore of the potent monsters, and in truth, doubted he could last long against any further attacks. Each incredible strong strike he deflected seemed to suck his strength from him.

Amerix rose from the tree and adjusted the rusted mail that hung from his old body. Despite all he had just endured, at least the damned sword was not making that cursed shrill noise again. His head hurt enough as it was. Walking over to the whelp, Amerix leaned down and cut the thing free. He hated to let an orc loose, but it seemed foolish to risk his life battling its captors only to leave him bound up for more to return and kill him later. If the whelp was afraid or surprised, he showed neither. He merely continued to stare at Amerix with those steel blue eyes.

"What a ye lookin at ye green-skinned freak? Think I'm gonna eat ye, like yer pals?" Amerix asked rhetorically.

The orc didn't respond, he merely stood up slowly and rubbed his wrists. Amerix gazed at the green-skinned whelp wearily. The orc stood almost as tall as him and was very muscular despite his young face, though the dwarf knew little about how to tell how old an orc really was.

"Brohe-tah," the orc stated in a deep guttural voice.

Amerix stared at him with a confused face. The orc frowned in what appeared to be confusion. He tilted his head to the side and bared bright yellow teeth. Two large tusks protruded from the creature's massive under bite and his long black hair hung about his thick neck.

"Brohe-tah," the orc repeated, but more forcefully this time.

Amerix shrugged his shoulders, staring intently at the whelp who stood before him.

"What in bloody Durion's name do . . ."

That was all Amerix managed to get out of his mouth when the orc lashed out a quick powerful punch that caught the renegade general square in the chin. Bright stars erupted in the dwarf's mind as he staggered back trying to regain his balance. His feet were wobbly and anger flooded into him. He started for his sword when he realized that the orc still stood before him looking more puzzled than before.

Amerix had difficulty controlling his fury. "Brohe-bah to ye too, freak!" the dwarf shouted as he slammed a bone crunching fist into the orc whelp's face. Amerix felt the incredible hardness of the beast's skull against his knuckles. The orc fell back onto the ground, landing roughly on its rump. His bright blue eyes crossed with dizziness and he held his head in his hands. Amerix looked down at his bloody knuckles in amazement. The creature's skull was so hard, it split the skin on his hand as if he had punched stone. Yet, the whelp merely sat stunned on the ground. The renegade general placed his hand on his long sword as the whelp slowly stood up.

"Punch me again ye green-skinned baby, and I'll run ye

through like I did yer cousins," Amerix stated flatly, never releasing his hold on the sword's hilt.

The orc seemed unfazed by the threat, and walked over and retrieved one of the crude axes that had been dropped by its felled captors. The whelp picked up the oversized axe that seemed too heavy for him to wield effectively and hefted it over his shoulder. The axe was as long as the whelp was tall. The head was thick and rusted, with hundreds of nicks and chips in the blade. It was obviously poorly balanced, yet the orcs seemed to use it with great proficiency.

Amerix tensed and started to cut the beast down when an unexpected rush of serenity swept over him. There was a strange voice in his head that simply said, "Hold." Amerix paused as the strange sensation slowly passed. The whelp stood with a calm, non-threatening posture, looking around with its bright blue eyes. Shaking his head, the dwarf started walking south into the night, occasionally turning to try to run from the unwanted follower. But to his frustration, the orc seemed unwilling to leave him. Amerix muttered something under his breath about the next time he was at the bottom of a great river, he was going to stay there. The orc did not understand the dwarven tongue and only followed in silence.

*   *   *

Eulic and Myson followed the tracks of the undead deer diligently. They paused to rest seldomly and their trek took them most of the day and well into the dark hours of the evening. The thick grass plains waved softly in the cold autumn night under a bright starry sky. The two legionnaires relaxed sprawled out on a large hilltop, enjoying the rabbits they had caught earlier in the day. They had cooked their dinner before the sun had set, and now ate without fear of any attacks from the denizens that roamed the Serrin Plains. Myson roughly pulled the last bits of charred meat from the leg he was eating and stuffed them into his mouth. He chewed for a bit then tossed the bones to the side.

"Ya know, I was thinking," Myson said, wiping the grease that was at the corner of his mouth with his sleeve. "Perhaps we don't find the source of this zombie deer tomorrow. Then what?"

Eulic finished chewing the bite that was in his mouth, giving

467

Myson a look of disgust at his eating habits. Eulic cleared his throat. "I suppose that we head back to the Vale and report our findings."

Myson nodded reluctantly and roughly tore another large chunk of meat from his rabbit and crudely stuffed it into his mouth. "I suppose you are right," Myson said, rolling the chunk of meat in his mouth from one side to the other when he spoke. "But it sure would be nice to present the Vale with the necromancer's head."

Eulic nodded, then shook his head in disgust. "Have you no manners?"

Myson shrugged. "Who am I to offend? We are deep into the plains. We are not before the council or at some public function."

Eulic started to reply when Myson cut in. "Besides, I rather enjoy your hundred and one faces of contempt at my eating habits. Just when I think I have seen them all, a different one pops up," Myson said, trailing off at the end from laughter.

Eulic growled and stood up. "I'm going to set snares for tomorrow's food. Do get some rest."

Myson grinned and finished eating his meal. He occasionally smacked his lips, or licked his fingers loudly enough to get a revolting groan from the darkness. After he finished eating, Myson leaned back in the soft grass, crossing his arms behind his head. He stared up into the twinkling stars that hung bright overhead, and soon he drifted to sleep.

Eulic took his time wandering around the base of the hill, setting snares for rabbits and other small ground animals. He hoped he dallied long enough that Myson would be asleep, or had at least finished eating. The elf was as uncouth as a dwarf sometimes.

*   *   *

Trinidy wandered into the night. He was unsure how long he had been following the strong magical pull that led him almost due north through these thick plains. Strangely enough he had seen little wildlife, though he noticed fresh tracks and even fresh droppings. It was almost as if the animals sensed his coming and fled. He was glad he no longer needed to eat or drink on this journey, something that had to be tied with the quest, though he didn't specifically recall the blessing being cast on him. The fact that he did not need sleep did not sit well with him, though. He knew of spells that

468

sustained a man so he did not need food or water, but he was unaware of any magic that made sleep entirely unnecessary. Even the strongest spells required the target to get at least a few hours of sleep a day, yet he had gone well over four days without sleep, maybe more, and he did not feel the least bit fatigued. Trinidy would have spent more time pondering the fact but he had difficulty thinking clearly and the tug from the magic was so strong it often disrupted the easiest of thought processes. Trinidy feared what would happen if he needed to cast some protection spells to help an innocent or cause healing. Surely this great evil he had been summoned from beyond the grave to destroy would have persecuted thousands that would now need aid.

The death knight marched well into the night. He crossed over hill after hill, never losing sight of the forever expanding northern horizon, obeying the pull that led him on. It was almost daybreak when he sensed it. The sky was a dark blue and the stars were beginning to melt away. The eastern atmosphere held a crimson glow from the sun that seemed to glow brighter with each passing moment. The death knight stopped in his tracks, ignoring the pull that commanded him to march forward. He could sense two separate evils over the next rise. One was moving slightly to the west, where the other lay still. He could not see the evil, but he surely felt it. Trinidy frowned. He had never sensed evil before without actively pausing and meditating to find it. Either the evil was very powerful, or his senses had been enhanced. By the way he had sensations about the evil hill giant, he surmised his senses were somehow improved by the spell. The death knight drew his sword. The dark azure blade emitted a thick frost that wisped around it, cascading down the blade and enveloping the hilt and Trinidy's hand. Dark and sinister runes glowed bright blue on the blade near the hilt that was comprised of hundreds of tiny skulls. His shield, which held a giant skull affixed to the outside of it, emitted a similar frost, and the eyes of the shield began to secrete the deep azure hue.

Trinidy stalked forward. His rotten twisted face formed an impossibly distorted frown and the many dark stinging insects, that normally roamed from one empty eye socket to the next, now skittered across his visage as if they were disturbed. As he crested the horizon he paused in confusion. An elf kneeled at the base of the hill pulling a rabbit from a snare. The elf was not a dark elf, the only elves that Trinidy knew were evil. He wore finely crafted chain armor that clung to his slender form. His light blonde hair was braided into hundreds of tight weaves that dangled about his neck and shoulders, some of the weaves containing leather hoops at the end. He wore a finely crafted scimitar at one hip and a similarly crafted short sword at the other. He had a dark green flowing cloak that was thick, but seemed malleable as it hung loosely over his back. Though in every outward appearance the elf seemed to be a goodly elf, Trinidy knew different. He could feel the great evil that emitted from the animal. The dark notion was so great it took vast restraint from the death knight not to rush out and slay the elf where he stood. How dare the evil elf disguise itself as one of the goodly races. Then the horrific sound of mockery started coming from the elf. Thump-thump. Thump-thump. He remembered the same sound coming from the hill giant. The sound seemed to mock him then, to insult him somehow, but this sound went beyond that. The very fact that the elf sat there taking breath seemed the greatest attack on humanity that Trinidy could ever remember.

The death knight took the first step toward the elf. Then another. It took all of his composure to march to the elf instead of slaying it. He did not retain the paladin stature he had when he was alive the first time. He had always rushed in against evil, but he always made sure beings were evil before he slew them, just as he would ensure this elf was evil. Despite how strong the magic screamed the elf was, despite how strongly the pull ordered him, he ignored the elves and continued to move forward. There was no magic that would keep him from evil. None.

*   *   *

Myson kneeled before the last trap Eulic had set before he went to bed. Only the south traps had animals in them, and there was a large amount of those southern traps. Myson had gathered enough rabbits that they would not have to hunt for a week. It seemed as if something had herded the rabbits from the south, to the north, into their snares. Surely he would have to wake Eulic and see what he thought of the strange events.

Myson took the last rabbit from the snare and affixed it to his belt. He tied the two rear feet, just as he had done the others, and as

470

he hooked it to the leather strap that hung down, he felt a cold wave come over him. Myson shuddered. It was strange for a wave of cold like that to hit him when it didn't seem to travel on the wind. It was autumn after all, but the wave didn't move his hair, it didn't hit his skin, it was more of a sensation. There was movement to his left from the hill to the south. He turned and froze. The most ghastly scene he had ever witnessed in his life walked toward him. It was a man, or at least had been a man. It was well over six feet tall, indicating to the legionnaire that it had been human, but its face wore a glare that was unnaturally exaggerated. The frown creases started high on the forehead and the under-turned mouth extended well into the jaw line, exposing two rows of rotten, decaying teeth that were either dark yellow or light gray. Hundreds of large black insects erupted from his mouth and crawled to its eye sockets or to its ears like an ant hill that had been roused. Its eyes lacked anything but deep empty sockets that had a blue supernatural glow. Its hair hung down in thin black streaks across its face, which was devoid of muscle as if it had tight decaying skin drawn across it. The apparition wore thick rusted plate armor that bore twisted religious symbols and hundreds of tiny skulls. The armor bore hundreds of scars from countless battles and seemed as if it would crumble off of the undead beast at any moment. The thing held a great blade that was described as sinister at best. Its blade had an azure glow that radiated thin wisps of frost that cascaded down the sword, enveloping the monster's gauntleted hand. It carried a shield in the other hand that bore many twisted religious runes. It had a great skull of some unnamed beast affixed to it that had empty sockets that glowed as cerulean as the sword did.

Myson wanted to scream, he wanted to run, he wanted to draw his blade and attack, all at the same time. The undead monster emitted an essence of such absolute evil that the legionnaire had difficulty forcing breath from his lungs to shout at Eulic.

"Brother, to arms!" Myson shouted hoarsely as he slowly backed up the hill toward camp.

Eulic rushed over the rise wearing his dark green cloak and his bedding clothes, long sword and short sword in each hand. He cursed himself for not sleeping in his armor, but the chain was uncomfortable and was difficult to maintain if it was slept in.

"Do I have time to . . ." Eulic's voice trailed off as he gasped in

471

horror at the creation that stalked up the hill toward a backpedaling Myson. The beast seemed to leave a wake of decaying grass with each horrible step it took. The apparition stopped at the sight of the two elves at the top of the hill. It stuck its wicked blade into the dirt and pointed at them with its gauntleted hand.

"Yhw od uoy edih dniheb eht esiug fo yldoog sevle."

Myson glanced over at Eulic nervously. "Do toss on your armor, brother. I suppose this is our necromancer."

Eulic nodded, stabbed his blades into the earth, reaching down to his bed site and picking up the lightweight smooth set of glimmering elven chains.

*   *   *

Trinidy neared the elf that was kneeling near the trap. The creature seemed to sense him as he approached. He cursed to himself silently. The beast must have had a method to detect goodly beings. The elf seemed horrified at his sight. Evil always ran and cowered when confronted by good.

Trinidy followed the elf as he slowly backed up the hill calling something out in a foul dark language he did not understand. The death knight glowered his deep blue eyes. They were certainly evil now. He had heard the tongue of the damned escape from their lips. It was almost certain he would have to slay them now, though he would give the elf one chance to spare his life. Trinidy started to speak when a second elf came from over the rise wielding a long sword in one hand and a short sword in the other. It, too, had a similar haircut to the first elf. Trinidy figured they were part of some kind of cult, though he knew of no cults that wore such styles. The two elves conversed in the sinister tongue from the abyss. He had heard the language spoken when he spent those years under the enslavement of the arch demon, Bykalicus. The mere thought of the demon seemed to send Trinidy into a murderous rage, but he fought to suppress it. The elves emitted that horrible taunting; thump-thump, thump-thump, that nearly drove him mad, but he clung to his disciplined mind. He would not slay them out of hate, regardless of how evil they were. He offered them one chance to save their lives. He pointed his gauntleted finger at the pair.

"Why do you hide behind the guise of goodly elves?" he asked.

The elves did not respond right away. They just stood defensively and watched him. Then the blonde-haired elf with the rabbits tied to his waist spoke something in the abyssal tongue. The other stuck his swords in the ground and donned some chain mail. Trinidy smiled. The fools wanted to fight. That was fine with him. He needed any excuse to slay these children of night so he could get on with his quest for his god. The magical pull commanding him north was growing stronger and more difficult to ignore with each passing moment. When the dark-haired elf finished donning his chain armor, Trinidy gave them one final chance for salvation.

"Throw down your swords and I shall let you live," Trinidy said calmly. The two elves looked at each other, then the blonde-haired one drew his swords and stalked to Trinidy's left flank. The brown-haired elf drew his swords from the ground and stalked right. Trinidy smiled and prepared to rid the world of the evil vermin. Finally he was going to get to do something worthwhile.

*   *   *

Eulic quickly donned his chain armor. Just as he fastened the side straps with his nimble fingers, the undead apparition spoke again. The monster's voice seemed to echo within itself in a deep demonic sound.

"Worht nwod ruoy sdrows dna I llahs eraps ruoy sevil."

The elves shivered. The thing appeared to have once been human, but it was obvious to the legionnaires that any remnant of humanity left in the magically animated corpse was long since lost.

Myson drew his scimitar and short sword, circling the foul creation, while Eulic pulled his blades free from the hard clay earth and circled the opposite side. The two elves decided to fight in a flanking nature, in case this creation had some skill with a blade. The two legionnaires doubted the thing carried the wicked sword for posterity.

Myson flashed in with a feint from his short sword and low slashing attack with his enchanted scimitar. Eulic lunged in with his short sword showing a low attack, then twisted, striking high with his long sword. The two moved as one, striking just where the other was feinting. The calculated attack would have felled almost any opponent. Few were as skilled with blades in all the realms as a Darayal Legionnaire, and a pair of them set upon a single opponent was a force to be reckoned with. But to the legionnaires' surprise, their attacks were deflected. The feints were ignored as what they were and the low strike from Myson was deflected with a crushing down stroke from the heavy broad sword Trinidy wielded. Eulic's feint was also ignored and his high strike was deflected to the side with a powerful sweeping motion from the dark and sinister shield.

Pain shot up Myson's arm from the bone rattling block. His scimitar shook from the horrific strike that he was sure would have shattered any normal weapon. He watched in disbelief as Eulic's strike was deflected easily by the apparition's shield, sending the brown-haired legionnaire's arm wide, exposing his underside. Trinidy spun his heavy broad sword around his back, cutting into Eulic's chain shirt, laying a neat slice under his arm. Eulic winced in pain as the abyssal cold from the weapon sucked his breath and shot stinging magical energies into his flesh. Though the wound was far from fatal, far from crippling for that matter, the elf could feel the dark magical energies swirling into his body.

As Trinidy spun to strike Eulic with his broad sword, he brought his heavy shield around, striking Myson in the head and shoulder as he stood low after his strike was deflected. A surge of blue energy blasted out from the mounted skull that was on the shield, and hit Myson, knocking him backwards into the tall grass. He landed with a hard thud, which knocked the wind from his lungs. He had managed to hold onto his blades, though as he started to rise, he realized he had been knocked back a dozen feet.

Eulic clutched the wound in his side for a brief moment before resetting himself. He knew the wound was not fatal, and was little more than a scratch, but he could feel his strength waning from the wound. It burned cold and the legionnaire could feel his side going numb. He had little time to react as he was put on the defensive by a barrage of attacks from the undead creature. Eulic worked his blades in a magnificent dance, blocking and ducking the corpse's wicked attacks. The elf was amazed at how quickly the creature moved. It was impossible to move the way he did in the heavy plate armor, impossible to wield such a heavy sword that was designed to cut through plate armor, but not to fence with any precision. Yet the legionnaire used every ounce of energy, every ounce of skill he possessed, to keep the deadly blade from striking him. The corpse attacked with such perfect flow, he had no opportunity to mount any kind of attack of his own. It seemed as if he were merely delaying the end. Never had he faced a foe so skilled with a blade. Fear began to well up inside him. It was not fear of death, not fear of injury. The Darayal Legionnaires had long ago given up fear of those things. The thing a Darayal Legionnaire feared was failure. Eulic feared he might fail his kinsmen or worse yet, the Vale.

Myson flipped to his feet, swords in hand. He rushed forward slashing and stabbing. Trinidy deflected each strike, though it was obvious the pair attacking him strained his abilities. The elves ducked and struck with uncanny precision. Trinidy danced among them, though now his armor rang from an occasional elven strike.

Deep crimson blood streamed down Eulic's side from the wound that ran across his ribs. This apparition was dangerous indeed.

*   *   *

Trinidy deflected each strike with harrowing precision. He marveled at how well he moved with his armor on, and how light his heavy broad sword felt. Normally the elves, with their lighter weapons and thinner armor, would have been somewhat difficult for him, but he seemed to match them stroke for stroke. He felt himself take a few hits, but strangely enough, he didn't feel any pain. He knew he had hit the elves. The brown-haired one with the long sword and short sword bled from his side from a thin slice he had managed to lay just under the elf's arm. They were good, deflecting most of the death knight's attacks, but Trinidy could plainly see the elves could not hold out forever. He laughed aloud as he fought.

"You fool elves. Did you really think evil would triumph over good?" Trinidy bellowed.

The elves responded in the twisted abyssal tongue that infuriated Trinidy. How dare they speak their blasphemous language to him.

Trinidy growled and focused his attack on the brown-haired elf. The death knight could see the wound in his side was weakening him, causing him to lessen his guard with that weapon arm. The battle would soon be at an end.

Steel rang on steel across the early morning plains. The elves danced swords in a game of death among a circle of black dead and decaying grass, that rotted with each passing moment. Eulic and Myson fought for their lives. Their thin braided hair bounced about them as they twirled and ducked low. Large beads of sweat had formed on their brows from the great exertion of the battle, despite the frosted cold air of mid-autumn. The two elves were vaguely aware of the rapidly dying and decaying grass that encircled them like a small battle arena. Myson could tell that Eulic was growing weak from the wound in his side and he was losing a lot of blood. Myson could tell the corpse they battled also detected a decline in Eulic's ability to defend himself, because he suddenly shifted his tactics and focused on his wounded brother. Anger welled up inside Myson. This necromancer's pet was not going to slay his kin. He was not! Myson renewed the ferocity of his attack. He pressed harder, faster, whirling his blades like a court jester might whirl a baton. He ducked and struck, each time coming closer to hitting home on the apparition. He had scored a dozen hits against the thing, but it seemed impervious to minor blows. It bled only a little from the wounds, and it was not really even blood. A thick black substance trickled out that had the density of pine tar on a cold day.

Eulic was tired and hurting. The pain in his side grew more intense. The wound itself was very cold and numb, but great tendrils of white hot pain erupted from the edges of the wound and shot into his arms and down his legs, making it difficult for him to move with great precision. The corpse seemed to detect his weakness and it pressed harder. Eulic tried to circle, to keep the power stroke away from his weak side, giving Myson a greater line of attack. Eulic doubted the corpse was as skilled in life with his sword as he was now, in undeath.

The death knight pressed harder and faster. Each sword stroke from the wicked sinister blade that the death knight wielded came closer to hitting home, yet Eulic fought on. Eulic felt a sharp sting on his leg as he backed away from the death knight in a defensive dance of death. He glanced down to see many small black stinging insects crawling on his leather breeches, trying to bite and sting him. The ground seemed to be alive with hundreds of the tiny bugs.

Myson pressed harder. He struck faster and with more meticulousness than he ever had before. Narrowing his grim determined eyes, he saw an opening and took it. He slammed his scimitar home into the thick armored plate that covered the death knight's back. The enchanted blade easily sliced through the rusted mail and rammed to its hilt. The death knight raised his hands up into the air and arched his back as if in great pain. He dropped the wicked broad sword and his shield arm went slack. The sinister blade clanged to the cold hard earth. Eulic paused to begin clearing his breeches from the many scorpions and spiders that had crawled up them. Myson tried to wrench his sword free, but it was held fast in the thick armored plate that covered the death knight. The corpse turned with a look of shock on its twisted rotted face. Its cold blue eyes still glowed, but it appeared as if the battle would soon be over.

*   *   *

Trinidy pressed the attack. He knew the elf behind him was pressing his, but he needed to finish off the weak one before the damnable elves got in a lucky strike. Despite them being evil, they were remarkable swordsmen. Trinidy had to focus all of his attention on battling this pair. It was a pity these blade artists had to be slain. Their skill was surely dizzying. The death knight noticed, however, that while he fought these two denizens, the magical pull that seemed to almost force him to go north, had subsided completely. Perhaps these two were who he needed to slay. Maybe they were this great wrong that needed to be righted. That seemed too easy, but he had performed other tasks in his past that were thought to be impossible, that were just as simple. The one thing that still clouded his mind was that cursed thump-thump that echoed in his head. There were clearly two separate thumping sounds, though now they reverberated much faster and blended together, but Trinidy was sure the sounds were the markings of evil. They had to be, the way he despised them so.

Trinidy had pressed the wounded elf to circling, making his attacks one dimensional and easily predictable. He started to focus more on defending against the elf who struck at his back. That one's strikes were getting too close. That was when he knew he had erred. Trinidy felt the tip of the elf's sword pierce the plate armor that covered his back and he watched in horror as a sharp scimitar blade erupted from his chest. He arched his back and he dropped his sword and shield in anticipation of the incredible pain that was sure to follow. How could he die like this? How could he fail his god? Would he be sent back to the abyss? The thought of Bykalicus's hideous laugh and the cold sulfuric air of the great underworld launched him into a fury. If he was going to die, he was not going to die until these two elves were long since dead! He turned and faced the blonde-haired elf that had just stabbed him in the back—a definite sign of the evil elf's cowardice.

Trinidy angrily reached out with his gauntleted hand. With the rusted fingers outstretched, the old armor creaked. Trinidy felt a great rumble from inside, like a hunger, but not. It seemed to be some kind of force that dwelled within him; a force that cried out to be sated. It felt as if it bulged and grew inside him, like an ever growing bubble about to burst. The elf stood wide-eyed and stepped back.

"Necropium Nectues," Trinidy said. The words seemed to crawl out from deep inside him, almost as if someone else had said them. He did not know exactly what they meant, nor what language they were in. They were more a culmination of each language at the same time, separate in their uttering, but united; as if a thousand condemned voices cried out, rather than the deep growling voice of Trinidy. He had never cast any spell in that manner, nor commanded the wrath of his god, without first grasping his holy symbol. He did neither, yet the flash of dark black and blue swirling weaves erupted from his finger and shot into the blonde elf's body.

The wispy tendrils poured themselves effortlessly into the elf, like wind might blow through the leaves of a tree. Myson gasped and grabbed at his chest, writhing on the ground, twisting and rolling in the decayed ash that had once been tall grass, while hundreds of stinging scorpions and venomous spiders swarmed his body.

Trinidy turned and faced the wounded elf. He did not know how much longer he had before the sword sticking into him took his life, but he had only one more to slay; one more evil; one to vanquish to fulfill his quest. As Trinidy started toward the elf, he marveled at how his wound did not hurt. He could feel the sword protruding from his body, he could feel its weight in him, but he did not feel weaker, and there was no pain. No pain at all. How much time did he have? Probably not much. The lack of pain in a mortal wound was always a bad sign.

*   *   *

Myson backed away wide-eyed as the creature did not even cry out when he impaled it. He could see the tip of his enchanted sword sticking out of the creature's front breastplate, dripping a thick black ooze that seemed to sizzle when it hit the ground. Tightening his grip on his short sword, he prepared to either finish the undead denizen, or let it finish him. Eulic was safe for the time being, though he seemed to be slapping his legs for some reason.

Myson pushed his blonde braids behind his ear with his free hand. Gripping his short sword tightly he decided to try to draw the apparition away from Eulic until his friend could right himself. It was then that the undead extended his hand. His rotting fingers, covered by the creaking gauntlet, pointed at him. The black insects rocketed in and out of his eyes and his nose, some even going in his ears as if they were more excited than they had been moments ago.

"Necropium Nectues," the death knight said in a dark low growl that seemed to echo in Myson's ears. Suddenly Myson felt stabbing pains in his chest, as if something were being ripped out of it. His body shook with pain, and unimaginable cold rocked his muscles, causing them to tighten and curl up. He fought to stay conscious, but the pain increased. He wanted to cry out, to scream, but the legionnaire could not make his throat utter a single sound. His lungs held his breath and his very thoughts seemed to become sluggish. He was barely aware that he was lying on the ash-covered earth when he lost consciousness, oblivious to hundreds of tiny black scorpions and spiders that swarmed his paralyzed body.

*   *   *

Eulic swatted the pests away quickly. The wound in his side seemed to level off for the moment. Though his right side still was a little sluggish and cold, at least the shooting pains had subsided. He

479

scrambled out of the ashen ring that seemed to follow the death knight wherever he walked. The thing seemed to cause the plant life around him to die and turn to ash whenever he came near. The great many stinging and biting insects seemed to stay within a close proximity to the creature also.

Eulic watched as Myson ran the creature through. The thing seemed to arch its back and drop its weapon. A rush of triumph washed over Eulic. He hoped beyond hope that the wound would finish the beast, but in the back of his mind, he was certain it would not. To his horror the beast righted itself, and pointed a single finger at Myson. It said something, perhaps some kind of chant or command. Eulic could not tell which, but he watched Myson suddenly fall to the earth. Eulic hefted his swords and charged the undead apparition. He had taken a few steps when he skidded to a stop. Myson's body was instantly covered with hundreds and thousands of scorpions, spiders, centipedes, and other insects that stung him countless times. The little beasts crawled into his mouth and burrowed under his skin. Eulic cried out, half in terror and half in rage, as he charged into battle. This evil would die today.

*   *   *

Trinidy turned as the elf fell to the ground. He did not know what he had done, he only knew that it was fatal and the evil elf would soon be dead. Instead he turned and faced the other elf who was standing a few dozen feet away watching the scene. The brown-haired elf screamed in a twisted rage and charged. Good. If the elf had decided to run, Trinidy wasn't sure he would live long enough to pursue him, but now, he would either complete the quest his god set him on by killing these two evil elves, or he would die trying.

*   *   *

The two met in a shower of sparks, swords hitting swords, swords hitting mail. Eulic's finely crafted blade hit home again and again. Great gouts of sticky black fluid erupted from the death knight's wounds. Some landed on the ground and some landed on Eulic's hands or breeches, but the elf ignored both, despite the stinging pain he felt as the acidic fluid burned him. Each strike did

480

not seem to slow the corpse. Though Eulic felt himself slowing, he had taken many nicks from that sinister blade. Though the wounds were superficial at best, he could feel the evil magic boring into his flesh from even the tiniest of scratches. If the blade had even touched his skin, a festering wound would rapidly grow.

The death knight pressed the attack, its blade coming closer and closer to hitting home. On the rare occasions Eulic managed to strike at an exposed area of the corpse, the ominous shield seemed to shift faster than comprehension, deflecting his strike. It was becoming apparent that he could not defeat this monster by himself. Glancing over the undead monster's shoulder, Eulic could see Myson's body lying still. His face was covered with hundreds of purple welts that dripped yellowish fluid from the bites and stings, and his chest did not rise and fall with any breath. Muttering a curse, Eulic broke away from the fight, turned, and ran. He hated leaving his kin's body, but he needed to warn the Vale. This monster was beyond any Darayal Legionnaire. It would take the elders and the wise ones to defeat it. Eulic did not know if the creation held a keep or commanded an army, but he doubted it. He turned to see the creature following him at a slow pace. The grass around it quickly died, decayed, and turned to ash with each of its steps. Sheathing his swords, Eulic darted as fast as if they were getting worse. It seemed once he disengaged from combat with the monster, they stopped and leveled off.

The legionnaire had a fair journey ahead of him, though he did not pause, nor did he hear the hellish ball of fire that was rapidly descending on him.

*   *   *

Trinidy turned and strode toward the other evil elf. The brown-haired elf's wounds had weakened him, but Trinidy knew he was still a threat.

Amazed that the sword that was rammed through him did not cause him any pain or discomfort, Trinidy pushed on. Could it be by the grace of Dicermadon that the sword missed all of his vitals? If that were true, why did he not feel any pain? He didn't even feel weaker. He should have at least been weaker. The death knight didn't have much time to ponder the wound as the elf attacked. The elf

481

fought ferociously though his attacks were labored and his defense was poor. Trinidy managed to score a few minor hits as they battled. Why didn't the elf run? Evil ones were always weak when faced with adversity, and they would rarely risk themselves to save another. Perhaps the elves feared failing their evil master more than they feared dying by his blade. It did not matter to Trinidy. He would slay him soon. Just as the elf's defenses weakened enough that Trinidy planned to make the killing strike, it ran. How dare the despicable little beast run? Trinidy started after him, but quickly realized he was not suited for running in his heavy plate. He watched helplessly as the elf bounded up and over the rise on the hill. That was when it started again, the incessant pounding that echoed in his ears. Thump-thump, thump-thump. It was louder and faster than it had been before, but as the elf moved farther away, it grew fainter.

Anger welled up inside Trinidy that he had never experienced. How dare that evil beast think of running away and spoiling his victory. It was then he felt it. Another bulge inside of him. Like a great hunger that grew rapidly. It burned hot and demanded release. The death knight raised his hands in the air. Great weaves of magical flows erupted from his hand and shot into the sky. They swirled and twisted, drawing in great amounts of energy from the sun, intensifying rapidly until a great sphere of flames hung high overhead. Trinidy gazed to the north and stared at the hill. He could feel the great sphere hanging overhead. He could feel the link from it to his mind, like a leash to a hound. When the elf rose to the top of the next hill, he released it. No, it was more like a launch. The great flaming sphere plummeted from the sky and crashed into the elf. A great flash erupted from the explosion and the ground shook. Great chunks of dirt and ash erupted into the sky, slowly cascading back down to earth as the sphere died out on the hill's peak.

Trinidy casually walked to the area where the fireball had hit the ground. There was a large hole a dozen or so feet in diameter. It was about four feet deep at the center, and there were no remains of the elf. At the bottom of the crater, Trinidy could see pieces of red hot melted metal pooled up, and a bit of chunky ash. Thin wisps of smoke slowly ascended into the cold morning air. Trinidy smiled. The damnable thumping was gone and he felt the magical pull to the north again. Pulling the blade from his back and tossing it on the ground, he was oblivious to the wave of maggots and other larvae that spilled from the open wound and wiggled around on the ground as he strode away. Creating the veil of complete darkness to protect him from the sun, the death knight continued on to the north, answering the never ending pull that dragged him onward.

Prejudice. Such a horrible thing, or is it? Is it merely a product of a human's ability to protect itself? Why do humans fear orcs, ogres, and others of the evil races? They fear them because they are prejudiced. The preemptive dislike or hate comes from the basic emotion that all creatures despise. Fear. No creature that has a mind at any level likes to be afraid. Fear crushes the strong-willed, it stupefies the intelligent, and enfeebles the wise. It can override any basic emotion in any intelligent being. Few human emotions are as strong, or overpower sense as quickly.

A man who had never seen nor had heard of an orc might not be terrified of him. He might not be even afraid. But a man who had heard the tales of the wicked beasts, or witnessed their malice firsthand, will surely hate them as much as he fears them. The hate derives from the fear. No one enjoys being afraid, so they in turn become angry. I cannot fault anyone for being prejudiced, though it surely is not a position that should be taken by the wise. Though, prejudice is still an important tool. It is important when it becomes an overlying issue of hate and persecution that is transformed into a hindrance. Some may argue that imprudence based off of prejudice is the real cause of the inability to be cautious. I say nay, for even then, if discriminatory nature overrides thought, then much is missed, and much evil is done. It is dangerous for any man to try to give every orc the benefit of the doubt when the beasts are encountered, but if the man is in no danger from the orc, I say; why not? Much could be gained, and much could be lost.

Thousands of years before my birth, the elves had visions of me, of what I was, of what I would become. But in their ignorance, they never tried to understand why I became what I was prophesied to be. Surely that was no fate anyone would choose. Had the elves been as wise as they had claimed to be, they would have searched to understand the factors that drove me to what I would become. Instead, they feared me and feared the title that was given to me thousands of years before my birth; a title that had no meaning to me, nor that I was even aware of. My name was Lance. I was an orphan. I loved my parents dearly before their deaths and I loved my adoptive father, despite how much our views differed. It was the men who feared what I was to become and what I was prophesied to do, that actually set my feet upon the very path to become what they sought to vanquish. Strange, but through their attempts to prevent what was prophesied to be, they actually created what they sought to defeat: prejudice, a gift only to those with wisdom to understand its true meaning.

—Lancalion Levendis Lampara—

Fourteen

A Prisoner's Welcome

The bright glaring sun was set high in the barren sky. No clouds floated by, and the heavens were bare, save for a few white wisps that resembled thin feathers more than clouds. At first glance, the day might appear to be a bright, warm summer day, but the cold autumn air stilled the atmosphere. Long blades of tall brown grass bore many ice crystals, despite the noon sun, and a cold chilling wind swept across the endless plains. Lance sat lightly in his saddle as his horse plodded on to the north. The inside of his legs hurt constantly from the long hours in the saddle each day, and despite his growing tolerance, he doubted he would ever get used to it, despite what Apollisian, Overmoon, or Jude said. He was just not built to ride. Lance pulled his thick heavy cloak around himself to try to keep the chilling wind from his skin. They had woken before the sunrise, and Lance thought there were few things worse than climbing out of his warm bedroll to move around in the cold morning air. But they had camped in the valley of a fair-sized hill. Now the chilling wind was much worse, and his cursed horse made his legs and butt hurt. He was sure he had sores on the crowns of his rump and he probably wouldn't sit right for weeks. Reaching up and pulling the hood of his shimmering black Cadacka, Lance lowered his head and tried to recapture some of his lost sleep.

Jude rode on comfortably. He inhaled the chilly morning air deeply and exhaled. There was nothing like the air on the open plains. He was a little chilly, but some good riding and the rising sun would take the bite out of an otherwise good day. He glanced over at Lance and chuckled at the miserable sight. The poor mage was riding with his head nearly completely covered by that shimmering cloak with the strange runes. He would slowly lean further and further forward, until he was just about to fall from the saddle,

485

then jerk upright, muttering a few curses under his breath and adjusting his cloak. Then he would start the process again.

The battle with the hill giant had given the party a little cohesiveness, but Jude still noticed that Apollisian and the elf kept to themselves. Jude was a little distrustful of them—more of the elf—but Apollisian was a paladin, and Jude knew them to die before breaking their word. Readjusting the thick leather jerkin that rested under his chain armor, Jude rode on quietly, humming a tune to himself as he enjoyed the calm autumn air.

Apollisian rode silently. As they neared the Vale he became more uneasy with what the elves would do with young Lance. The boy had done no wrong as far as he could tell, and he knew next to nothing about this so called "Abyss Walker." Alexis did not speak highly of the title. Apollisian was torn between loyalty to the elves, and awareness of the fact that Alexis had an ulterior motive to get Lance and Jude to accompany them. The elf asked for the pair to be escorts, and she paid for their services, thus making the statement true, but her underlying motive was to get Lance to the Vale to go before the elders. It was the underlying issue that upset Apollisian. True, she spoke nothing false, but the paladin found it difficult not stating what was omitted. It was like lying without actually being mendacious. Certainly there would be a trial for his inner character. After many days of pondering, he decided that Alexis hadn't committed any untruths, though he would scrutinize the treatment of the boy, and his large friend, personally. If the elves meant to treat him unfairly, he would step in and prevent them. If the elves thought to take the boy by force, they would have to do the same to him. Apollisian doubted that the elves, regardless of how wicked they perceived the boy, would dare disrespect a champion of Stephanis.

The paladin looked over at Alexis as she rode quietly next to him. Her long blonde hair hung down from behind her in a single thick tight braid. She wore a dark green cloak that hung over her back and draped over the rump of her horse. Her quiver of arrows jutted out from a thin pocket in the back of the cloak, and her bright green fletching stood out in the plains over the never ending brown. She kept her white ash bow strapped behind the saddle, unstrung, next to her tightly packed bed roll and bouncing water skins. What a magnificent woman she was. Blushing, Apollisian looked away.

486

She was not a woman. She was an elf. She was his charge, a friend to the crown of the Vale, not some lady in waiting that he could court at his leisure. Cursing himself for being foolish, he looked back at her. Was there a chance? No, how could there be? She would live ten of his lifetimes. He would grow old and feeble, while she would remain spry and young. How could he condemn her to love someone that would grow old and die before her very eyes? Chastising himself for such foolish thoughts, Apollisian scanned the horizon. He would have much to explain if enemies managed to lay an ambush because he rode smitten-eyed at Alexis like some lovesick child. Tightening the reins to his warhorse, he jaunted ahead a few paces, his eagle-like visage ever bound to the horizon.

Alexis rode on into the day lost in thought. She fought herself to keep from daydreaming about her encounter with Apollisian at the city hall in Central City. Had she really almost kissed him? The fool man probably didn't even notice. Men were more than inept at noticing things like that. She had been alive for over two hundred sixty years and she had yet to kiss a man. She wondered if Apollisian counted as a man. He wasn't elven after all, so he wasn't much in her society's eyes. But his eyes, and his . . . Alexis blushed under her cloak. She had tried thinking less of the fool human and more of her task at hand. She had the Abyss Walker traveling with her for Leska's sake. She should keep her mind on that.

Alexis peered over to her right at Apollisian from the corner of her eye, just around the edge of her bright green hood. He rode looking straight ahead, scanning the horizon. His long blonde hair bounced around his face as his horse plodded the ground. The thick-headed man probably didn't even look her way once since they left Central City, she thought.

Alexis was startled by Jude's deep voice to her left. "How far do you suppose we have to go? I have been seeing a few more birds in the air of late and I suspect that there are trees up ahead. I doubt there is much area left in these plains," Jude asked as he rode, keeping both of his hands in front of him gripping the thick reins that held his horse's head.

Alexis tried to hide her flinch when he spoke. She had been so caught up in thoughts of the fool paladin, she hadn't noticed the large swordsman approach from behind her. Muttering a silent curse under her breath that was meant for her own ears, she turned.

By the expression on Jude's face, her curses must have been a little too loud. Blushing again, she placed her hand across the front of her cloak, just above her breasts. "Perceptive swordsman," she said turning and facing forward, lifting her chin in a regal pose. "We are indeed approaching some forest, but we will have a day or two ride yet once within. Do not worry, when we arrive at the Minok Vale I will tell you."

Jude frowned and looked forward, straining to see what she was looking at. After a quick scan and seeing nothing, he glanced back at her, more annoyed than before. "That will be worthless. Once we are there, I am sure I will know," Jude said condescendingly.

Alexis turned her body to face the swordsman as she rode. Her pompous face turned to wrought anger. Her bright green eyes flashed to a cold glare that would have given the most menacing men pause. "You are sure you will know?" she asked angrily. "I bet your pathetic human eyes couldn't see a single elf if you stood in the center of the clearing, you big lummox."

"Pathetic human eyes?" Jude asked incredulously. "I do not have to tolerate such speech. Woman, where I come from . . ."

Alexis cut him off. "I don't care where you come from, you stupid oaf. Wherever that backwoods hamlet is, it is not here. You are in the Serrin Plains, just at the foot of my Vale. You will do as you are told, or you will face the laws that govern all creatures here, and the elven nation does not take kindly to any humans, let alone loud-mouthed fools such as yourself."

Jude merely sat flabbergasted at the woman's barbed tongue. His jaw hung open at a loss for words. Seeing the swordsman's unevenness, she continued. "Now fall back and do as you are told. You have been paid to do a service and I intend to hold you to that."

Jude slowed his horse, astounded. He had never been spoken to like that by any man, let alone a woman. Had he not been so close to the elven lands, he might have wrenched the fool wench from her saddle and paddled her bottom, like she obviously needed.

Jude glanced over at the paladin. He wore an angry face, but he said nothing, nor did he look at either of them. Jude did not like the situation one bit. As soon as Lance got his script deciphered, they were going to head back home as fast as possible. These fool elves were pompous enough for ten kings! Jude glimpsed over at Lance.

The mage sat slumped over the front of his horse in his perpetual slouch, then made jerking upright motions. Shaking his head, Jude chuckled despite his confrontation with Alexis. Lance may be a refined city lad, but he could sleep just about anywhere. Jude remembered one time back in Bureland, Davohn had Lance cutting wood most of the night to fill an order he had from the mayor for the Freedom Festival. The Freedom Festival was a celebration of the victory over the orc horde in a war that lasted almost twenty years, though most of the vicious fighting took place in the first five. Lance had split a whole wagon load by himself, trying to cut more wood than Davohn had. No one thought he could have beaten the seasoned woodcutter, but come morning, Lance had almost as much and a half again as Davohn. When Jude and Davohn went to congratulate Lance on his hard work, he was nowhere to be found. It wasn't until later in the afternoon when old Morilla went to fetch some water from the well out behind her shop, that she found Lance asleep on top of a second pile of wood that he had cut, but did not have the time to pile up in the wagon. Jude chuckled softly to himself as he recalled Lance walking gingerly for the rest of the week from splinters in his behind from the split wood.

"Something funny, swordsman?" Lance asked, peering out from under the hood of his thick sable cloak.

Jude jumped, not thinking his friend was awake, but quickly regained his composure. "I was just thinking back to the Freedom Festival when you fell asleep on the wood pile and got all those splinters in your behind," Jude said with a brazen grin.

Lance grimaced and slowly shook his head from side to side, pulling down his heavy hood and sitting upright in his saddle. "That was a horrible day," he said rubbing his behind as if it hurt. "And then, old lady Morilla and Davohn held me down while that accursed Sespie Twinner pulled out all those splinters. I don't know what was more red, my face or my bottom. She would jump at any chance to torment me."

Jude smiled warmly. Despite the tragedies they had witnessed since leaving Bureland, they could still joke about their childhood, though Jude was a few years older than Lance. "You know she practically begged to help old Morilla pull them out of you, don't you?" Jude asked as his smile grew to cover his entire face.

Lance gave him an incredulous look, then faced forward on the trail a moment before turning back to Jude with his hands on his hips. "What do you mean, she practically begged?" Lance asked.

Jude chuckled, shaking his head in disbelief. "You would sooner know how to swordfight than you would know a girl's interest."

Lance frowned. What was that supposed to mean? Whoever knew what a girl thought? They seldom made sense, and if you seemed to have an idea of what they meant, they would change their own meaning in mid sentence, just to keep you from thinking you knew what the heck they were talking about. "No one knows what girls think," Lance said angrily.

Jude seemed to chuckle again. "I know she may have been a few years older than you, but she could not have chased you harder or made it more obvious without being the scandal of Bureland."

Lance seemed to lose his smile. It slowly faded and was replaced with a serious scowl that seemed deeper than the mere expression on his face. "I suppose I spent too much time studying. It is just like I knew one day I was going to find my parents' killers and bring them to justice."

"Whoa, whoa, whoa," Jude said as he put his hands up in the air. "We set out on a journey to decipher these papers of yours, not put our necks in a noose. Let's find the identity of the killers and let the local magistrates deal with the dogs. They are better equipped to handle such things. You are a beginner mage. Despite what you say, I think some of the things you do surprise you as much as they do me. Sometimes I think you need to go study under a real wizard before you hurt yourself."

Lance lowered his voice. "I know you are concerned, Jude, but I do things that wizards cannot. It is hard to explain. Wizards take pre-existing magical energies that dwell around them. By moving their hands, or chanting a few words, they have learned how to manipulate those energies. I can do that too, but Jude . . ." Lance trailed off nervously.

"Not only can I weave those energies, I do not have to chant or move anything. It is like I look at them and command them with thought. It is hard to explain. Just imagine that you could draw your sword and swing it with your mind, while other swordsmen still have to use their hands. To make things stranger, I feel the same magical energy inside me sometimes. Like a hungry feeling, or a

490

worried feeling. It seems like I can channel that energy out of myself, or I use it to manipulate the natural flows around me without using my hands. I'm not sure what that means, but I am afraid that if I went to a wizard, he would find out I do it differently."

Jude said nothing. He just rode forward staring at Lance's pleading face, listening.

Lance continued. "Jude, you know how those wizard guilds are. You have to join a guild just to follow their order to learn their schools of magic, and people seem to disappear from those schools all the time. I think that finding out about my parents will shed some light on why I can do what I do. Jude, I think that is why they were killed. Maybe they could do the things that I do."

Jude nodded slowly. "You had better not mention that to anyone else but me, Lance. I agree, someone might try to do something to you. I don't know what, but as soon as we get those papers deciphered, let's go far away from elves. I have had my bloody fill of the one we are traveling with, I don't need a whole city of them."

Lance nodded and rode next to Jude quietly.

Jude sighed deeply to himself. It must be tough being a mage, he thought. Lance always seemed tired, and what was that elf up to? She acted like she had a separate agenda than the paladin, and Jude could detect a stress between them, though he knew not of what. Though, if he had to ride with the pompous elf, he would have more than a little unmentioned stress, and she would have been turned over his knee long ago. Let that cursed pair watch their own backs. Gold or no gold, he was going to look after his only friend, and it seemed Lance had a strong need for watching.

Alexis glared at the hulking oaf of a human as he trotted his horse away. She figured given the chance, the fool might try to remove her from her steed and make good his threat. Human women were so weak. They were nothing like elven maidens. Elven maidens were strong and fierce, bright and wise, while human females were submissive and foolish, led by emotions rather than by intelligence and logic. It probably had much to do with the pitiful creatures' short life spans. Alexis couldn't imagine living such a short life. How would anyone get anything done? A good suit of elven chain would take almost twenty years to create, a human would be nearly a quarter dead by the time it was finished. Why the gods ever created the weaker race was beyond her. What made matters worse, her father seemed to have a soft spot for their plight. True, Alexis didn't judge every human the same, but she still had a good general idea of what and how they acted. "Brazen and foolish," she mumbled under her breath.

"What was that?" Apollisian asked turning his head as he easily swayed in his thick leather saddle. His Vendaigehn mount from Central City seemed much more agile than a normal horse; its thin slender legs seemed to flow across the land rather than walk.

Alexis felt her face flush. "Nothing," she said as she became lost in his deep blue eyes. How could a human man have such perfect eyes, set in such a stern gaze that seemed inviting to friends and deadly to enemies?

Apollisian narrowed his eyes and firmed his jaw. "I was sure you had referred to Jude as brazen and foolish."

Alexis's flush of embarrassment turned to hot anger. "Of course, aren't all human males?" Alexis cringed before she finished speaking. In her haste and anger, she had forgotten Apollisian was a human male. But he never acted like one, he acted more elven than a lot of elves, cool and calm in the face of danger, always thinking of the greater good rather than what was at risk at the moment.

If the paladin was angry, he didn't show it. Smiling, he slowly shook his head from side to side. "I can think of a friend elf that acts that way sometimes. Especially when she is in defense of her friends."

Alexis frowned and pondered the thought, then turned back to look at Jude. He was riding side by side with Lance, and seemed to be offering some words of encouragement. Though elves were known for expert hearing, she could only pick out small parts of the conversation. She turned back and glowered a glare of near-hate. Apollisian swallowed hard and leaned away as if the glare would lash out at him. "A friend to Abyss Walker is merely a pawn to be cast aside when his usefulness has run out."

The paladin gathered himself, leaning forward, to match her glare. "You may not judge a man for crimes he has not yet committed. Stephanis does not allow it." He paused then quickly added, "I will not allow it."

Alexis growled. Had she not felt a deep kinship to the man, she probably would have crossed blades with him just then. "It is not my place to judge anyone," she said furiously. "Nor is it your place to question the elders. Justice comes in many guises, human. You'd be best to learn that," she said, riding ahead angrily.

Apollisian ground his teeth together. The nerve of that fool woman. She dared to think she could lecture him on justice? Only a fool believes it has more than one meaning. Justice is justice, it is nothing else. Too many times, people think they are getting justice when they are in fact getting revenge, but the paladin was at a loss for how to comprehend this event. How could anyone think of trying a man for a crime they think he might commit, regardless of how heinous?

Apollisian started to work himself into a fervor, and then he calmed himself. King Overmoon was a wise man, he had been alive longer than some countries' historians can remember. He surely would not make such a grievous error in judgment. In fact, he would go to the king with the boy and plead his case if necessary. Apollisian could detect evil hearts, and though the boy surely had many dark emotions sometimes swirling about him, he was, without a doubt, not evil. Setting the plan clearly in his mind, Apollisian let his apprehensions about the Minok encounter slide away. He was revered by the Vale, and his word was as strong as some laws. He would voice his objection, and he would be heard.

Jude moved his horse away as the group continued north into the early afternoon sun. The wind was soft, though cold, and the air was crisp. The waves of dark brown grass that covered the plains seemed to move slowly with the wind, like many waves on the open sea. All the bugs had surely died or burrowed deep into the ground, yet his horse swished its tail occasionally out of habit. A few light wisps of clouds were frozen in the bright blue sky, and seemed to streak from horizon to horizon. The air had a definite autumn smell to it.

"That seemed to go well," Lance chuckled. "You have such a way with women." Jude gave him an angry glare. "That fool elf needs her bottom paddled."

"That one is worse than a pit of vipers, I'd say. As soon as we get these parchments deciphered, we will leave her. I like the paladin enough, but the elf seems to look at me as if she wants to kill me one moment, then as if she pities me the next."

Jude nodded. "I don't know about the pitying, but she surely holds you in some kind of contempt. Perhaps we should return the gold and head back. She does not seem to like you wearing that cloak much, maybe she plans to punish you or something like that."

Lance shook his head stubbornly. "And where do you suppose I would get the translation from, the wandering elf travelers that seek to decipher their own sacred guarded language for a fool human?" Lance asked sarcastically.

Jude narrowed his eyes angrily. "There is no need to take that tone with me Lance, save it for the tavern wenches. I am just saying you might rethink the importance of the translation. If we are dead, there is no point in them," Jude said trailing off.

The pair rode on in silence. Lance seemed to be weighing his words. Jude spoke up again. "Besides, if need be I would ride all the way into Ladathon if you liked. Hell, I would ride next to you into Kingsford City."

Lance gaped at Jude. Ladathon was hundreds, no thousands, perhaps tens of thousands of miles to the south. It was south of Tyrine, the kingdom just south of Beykla. The fact that Jude even mentioned Kingsford City amazed Lance. Jude disliked large cities. He didn't even like Central City, and you could fit over a hundred Central Cities in Kingsford, or so it is said. Lance paused and then swallowed hard before speaking.

"Thank you, my friend. But let us just go to this Vale and then head home for a while. I am sure Davohn is worried about me, though I suspect they will know you are missing too. That should put his mind at a little ease."

Jude nodded his head in agreement when he felt his horse step lightly under him. There was a loud pop of something breaking. Jude quickly moved his horse to the right and peered down.

Lance stopped his horse and scanned the ground also. "What did you step on?"

Jude leaned over the side of his saddle, staring at a large bleached white bone. It was slightly pitted from exposure to the elements, and seemed brittle enough to have a fair level of age to it. "It looks like a bone of some kind, and an old one I would say by how easy it snapped under my horse."

"A bone?" Lance asked. "Good, I was worried that you may have injured your horse."

Jude didn't respond. He dismounted carefully and checked his horse's feet. Jude tapped the animal on the front leg, and it raised it, letting Jude look at the under side as if he were going to clean its feet. "No, the horse is okay," Jude said as he picked the bone up from the ground and held it in his hand. It was shaped like an upper arm bone of a human, but it was twice as thick. It was too small to be a femur and too large to be any other kind of bone.

Lance motioned his horse around to Jude's side. "What kind of bone is it?" Lance asked.

"It's not human, at least I don't think it is," Jude said, as he examined the bleached white bone.

"It's orc," came a honeyed voice from behind them.

Jude whipped around quickly and Lance glared at the elf who sat imposing on her horse, looking down at the two humans as if they were children she was supervising.

Alexis smiled at their frustration as she sat on her horse a few paces away. "We are reaching the Quigen. Best to be mindful of where your horse steps for the next ten miles or so. Those bones could cause a horse to come up lame if they wedge themselves into their hooves," Alexis said before she trotted her horse off to catch back up to the paladin.

Lance frowned. Quigen? That seemed familiar to him from his days as a boy in school.

Jude tossed the bone onto the ground with a disgusted look on his face and turned to Lance as he swung his heavy leg over the saddle. "The Quigen was the greatest battle of the orc wars. The elves were weak and fleeing north back to the Vale. The orc horde was right on their heels. They were numbered over a thousand score, while the elves were maybe five thousand in number. They had their famed legionnaires, but even their skilled blades were no match against so many foes. King Theobold dispatched his entire northern army from the Dawson stronghold to meet the orcs head on and give the elves some time to retreat. They met here," Jude said motioning around them. "The Beyklans were only fifteen thousand strong, outnumbered nearly four to one. But the army, led by General Laricin West, charged on, knowing they were surely to die. I am not sure how many weeks the battle lasted, but some say a season came and went while Laricin and his men fought to the last. The orcs were not defeated but it was known as, 'The Breaking.' After the battle, the orc leaders were crushed and the horde was broken. The remaining clans fought amongst themselves for who would lead for the remainder of the war, keeping themselves from becoming organized again. The elves focused their remaining armies and scattered the orc clans across the plains. Too weak to hunt them all down, the elves left the orcs for the plains. Most of the tribes moved south, but a few remained."

Lance looked at Jude as if seeing him for the first time, his emerald eyes staring in astonishment. "How do you know all this?"

"It was part of your history lessons in school. Had you paid attention as a child, you might have remembered better than me," Jude answered, resting both of his large gloved hands on the horn of his saddle.

"I seem to remember a certain swordsman getting paddled for trying to kiss Sally Mae in the back of the class," Lance retorted.

Jude frowned. "How do you remember that? We were not in the same grade. I am older than you, you would have still been learning your alphabet back then."

Lance smiled a knowing smile. "The whole town knew about that, and other events you and Sally Mae partook in."

Jude felt his face flush. Sally Mae was the most beautiful girl in school. Why she ever was interested in a big lummox like himself, he wasn't sure, but he wasn't about to look a gift horse in the mouth. Jude soon became lost in the memory of beautiful Sally. He recalled slipping back by the Congarn's orchard with Sally during the fall festival and kissing her all day long. How he loved to gently touch his lips to hers. They were so . . .

"Hello, Jude?" Lance asked with an amused look on his face. "Did I drudge up some old memories?"

Jude ignored him. For Leska's sake, what else did everyone in the town know? He might not want to show his face there again for the mere fact that everyone seemed to know some embarrassing stories of his that he thought were private. Of course, it didn't matter now. If anyone tried to embarrass him about his past, he would pop them in the mouth. Fat lips usually spoke softer, at least that is what his father always used to say. Regaining some composure he answered Lance. "Nothing big, just thinking about being a kid again."

Lance nodded thoughtfully, though he was barely out of his childhood as it was. He had many fond memories of years past.

Glancing around himself at the vast flat area that the elf called

496

the Quigen, Lance felt an eerie calm wash over him. He tried to envision the huge battle that raged over the land, but he could not. Armies of that magnitude were beyond his visual comprehension. "The ground must have rumbled as they charged," he said, half under his breath.

Jude nodded in agreement. "It is said that so much blood was spilled on the earth during the months that battle took place, that the grass died and the ground was stained red for years afterward."

Lance took it all in awe. He tried to imagine what it was like to have been there at the battle. The taste of fear and the smell of death. The screams of men and orcs alike as they were cut down. The bravery that the men had in the face of insurmountable odds as they fell to the last man. Lance felt a great sense of loss as he gazed out across the battlefield, and a greater sense of pity for the last man that was standing. To die alone with his comrades—no, his brothers—laying dead around him; a terrible fate.

It took the better part of the day to cross Quigen. Apollisian stopped briefly when they seemed to be in the middle of it and said a prayer for the men that sacrificed their lives there. To Lance's surprise, even the elf seemed to feel a sense of loss. It was late in the evening when they stopped to camp. Apollisian made sure they were out of the Quigen before stopping. It was a typical autumn night on the plains, dark, windy and cold. They set off again at first light.

The following day Apollisian seemed to glance behind them a lot and frown frequently. Lance would turn and look, but he saw nothing except the never ending grassland horizon. He asked Jude about it, but the swordsman could proffer no ideas as to why the paladin might be looking behind him. He didn't think they were being followed, surely the dwarves were all but defeated. Jude decided to keep an eye to the south, just in case. If something was bothering the paladin, Jude figured it was worth taking notice of.

*   *   *

He trudged on into the cold night and then into the morning. The obvious shift in the temperature didn't seem to affect him at all. In fact, he couldn't even detect that there was temperature. He was neither hot nor cold, ever. And as strange as that was, he became

497

quite skilled at summoning that globe of complete blackness that surrounded him during the day, and found he could move in it just as easily as he could with sunlight. He couldn't see the terrain in front of him, but it was as if he sensed it. All these new revelations were bizarre developments for the death knight. He was beginning to wonder about his new powers and how they were applied to him. It had been weeks since he had risen from the dead, and he had yet to eat a scrap of food, sleep a wink, or become tired. He knew there were no spells that could provide such comfort; even magic had limits. Trinidy guessed that it must have something to do with Dicermadon's power, but exactly what or how didn't seem to bother him. It was foolish to take the unexplained for fact and it was a fool that followed the unexplained blindly. He would piece it out eventually, though often enough he had trouble clearing his thoughts. Whenever he would try to concentrate on something, that magical pull at the back of his mind that drove him forever north, seemed to pop up and disrupt him.

Trinidy marched into a clear flat area. He could hear thousands of voices at the edge of his mind, calling out to him. He stopped and glanced around. As far as he could see, the ground was flat, from horizon to horizon. Trinidy couldn't see anyone or anything. It was as if the voices beckoned from the recesses of his mind, yet projected from the earth around him. He could not understand what they were saying, only that they were saying something. Standing motionless in the glaring sun, protected by his globe of darkness, he stopped. The magical pull was still there, he could still feel it, but it was much weaker. Then it happened. Trinidy raised his hands to the heavens and began chanting. He did not know what the words were that he spoke, only that they sounded purely angelic to him. He witnessed great tendrils of deep black erupt from his outstretched hands and shoot out across the plains. The great tendrils thrashed about, plunging into the earth and out again, creating an ever expanding spider web of impenetrable blackness. The webs shot out as far and as fast as he could see, and in a breath they had extended past the horizon, like great porpoises somersaulting in and out of the sea, until they were suddenly gone. When the tendrils subsided, Trinidy felt tainted and foul. The magic that washed over him was different than any magic he had ever wielded. Before, when he cast the will of his god, he felt cleansed, pure. But now he felt infected, and soiled, and worse, he liked it. The raw sensation of the taint seemed to make him lust for it again. Trinidy fought back the urge to loose the magic that was somehow inside of him.

As the death knight struggled against the magic, the ground erupted in front of him. Hundreds of thousands of clawed skeletal hands exploded from the ground, tearing and pulling entire skeletons to the surface. Large pieces of dirt hung from their dark gray skulls and their eyeless sockets emitted a shadowy cobalt glow that bore into the death knight. Trinidy felt as if he should be frightened, as if he should draw his sword and smite the damnations of good, but he did not. The skeletons seemed to thank him in an unseen way, as if he answered their prayers by raising them up from the earth that had claimed them.

In minutes the skeletons stood motionless in front of him as thousands more rose up every second. They were not threatening, and Trinidy could sense every last one of them as if they were extensions of his mind. It was as if Trinidy watched the events unfold from a prison cell. He knew what was happening, or at least had a good idea, but he was powerless to stop it. The sensation of wielding the necromancies was too great. The skeletons slowly and tediously dug themselves out of their earthen tombs with their bony claw-like fingers. In a few minutes, the soldiers of the skeletal army stood before their new master awaiting his commands. Like an addict pleasing his addiction, Trinidy marched north, with an army of skeletons that trailed the stench of death far as the eye could see. Their bony frames clicked and clacked as they walked clumsily, some carrying swords and axes that were rusted to near uselessness. He would answer this call to the north, silence it, and then address the fact that he may not have been raised by his god. When he was finished with this so-called wrong that needed to be righted, someone was going to pay.

*   *   *

Myson opened his eyes. Pain ripped through his naked body from the intense cold as he lay sprawled on his back. He choked and gagged on the sulfuric air that swirled and wafted around him. Sitting up, the legionnaire looked around himself. He sat on cold bare gray rock that seemed to expand forever into the horizon. Bright vapors of yellow billowing clouds that seemed to be filled with a black moisture violently shifted in the deep purple skyline. Huge beasts sailed past in the distance that lacked any fur or feathers, made up of mere skin and bone. The air was cold and stinging, but Myson adjusted quickly, hugging his naked body from the horrible cold.

The legionnaire gingerly tiptoed over the sharp gray rocks to the edge of the small rise that stood before him. He stepped around small wide centipede-like creatures that seemed to try to maneuver themselves under his feet. Reaching the rise, he looked over. Hundreds of small goblin-looking creatures seemed to be scampering his way. They were about three feet tall and had dark blue skin. Some had horns protruding from their elbows and knees, while others had horns shooting from their heads. Some of their horns were on the side and some in front, like a unicorn. But all the horns were twisted wickedly and were jet black. The beasts had bright yellow eyes that seemed to shine like a glittering gold coin in pale fire light. They all wore wicked smiles that bared hundreds of tiny needle-like teeth. Giggling and cackling, they ran at unnatural speeds toward him, hurtling large rocks at small ravines as they closed in like a pack of wolves coming for the kill. Myson turned and ran. He felt his bare feet being cut and sliced as he sprinted across the cold barren slate. Running back down the slope, running for his life, his stinging eyes frantically searched for a cave, or some form of shelter. He could not fight the beasts at once, but if he could force them to come on him one at a time, he might be able to do something. Exactly what he could do, he wasn't sure, but anything was better than being cut down and slaughtered. The legionnaire had seen every kind of forest denizen the realms had to offer, and he knew nothing of these beasts that pursued him. They moved at unnatural speed and it seemed that no two were exactly alike. Yet that changed nothing, he had to find some form of shelter or wherever he was would be his final resting place.

Myson ran as fast as he could, ignoring the hundreds of small bloody cuts that he had endured from running and scampering across the razor-sharp slate. He did not know where he was, and he knew of nothing like the land he was in. Myson ran through causeways that led in between huge rocks that seemed to leap out at him as he ran by, making large cuts in his arms and legs. Though the wounds were not deep, they stung and burned in the cold sulfuric air, bleeding profusely, and left a trail of thin blood across the rocky floor. Myson paused, glancing over his shoulder. He could hear the hideous laughter and giggling of the wicked beasts who pursued him. His chest heaved as he tried to suck in great gulps of air, but he choked and shook his head as he breathed in a toxic breath. The legionnaire turned and scampered up a small cliff face to his left. His hands and knees scraped the unnatural sharp rocks, dripping blood down the cliff's dull gray features. He could hear the disappointed protests of the little beasts under him as they tried in vain to climb the cliff face. Their thick claws dug and clawed at the rocky wall but they could not climb it. Myson placed his bloody hands on the top of the small cliff and hauled his naked body up. He turned and peered back down. His long blonde symas, made dirty by the charred black ash of the rocky slate that he had climbed, bounced around his head as he stood triumphantly over the hundreds of wicked beasts that bellowed below.

"You will find a legionnaire is no easy prey, foul beasts. Despite your speed, you are too stupid to catch me," Myson shouted down, shaking his bloody fist at them. The little beasts fought and climbed over each other as a single drop of blood from his hand landed on the cold rocks below. They bit and clawed at each other, trying to lick up the globule of his blood.

"A wise huntress does not pursue her prey, she lets her prey come to her." Myson whirled, fists tight against his side, to lash out at any enemy. What he saw startled him. Choking on his words he stepped backwards involuntarily. Before him stood the most beautiful woman he had ever seen in his life. She was a full foot taller than him with long straight black hair. Her eyes were the brightest blue and seemed to light the air in an azure hue around her face. The blue orbs bore into him, making his mind wander to lustful areas of thought he had never dreamed before. Her skin was the palest white, like a perfectly carved alabaster statue in a king's court. She was completely naked. Her large plump breasts seemed to be in perfect proportion with one another and an auburn erect nipple crowned each one. She was well muscled from her narrow shoulders to her thick shapely legs, though her beauty stopped there, and was overshadowed by a sinister aura about her. She had two small dark black horns that protruded from under her sleek thin hair, and her two fang teeth on her upper jaw protruded from the top lip of a

501

seductive smile. She had two large red bat wings with small black claws at their crowns that were neatly tucked behind her.

Myson swallowed hard and glanced back down at the beasts below. To his surprise they had vanished. All that remained were the claw marks in the stone where the droplet of his blood had landed. Turning back to face the strange woman who stood before him, he steadied his footing. "What manner of creature are you, and where in the realms am I?" Myson asked through clenched teeth, trying to ignore his nakedness in the presence of the female.

The woman merely chuckled and flipped her hair with a delicate finger that was tipped with a long black claw. She shifted her weight and folded her arms under her firm breasts. She smiled seductively. Her oversized fang teeth danced around her mouth as she spoke. "I am nothing you have seen before, and all that you will see for eternity. As for where in the realms you are, the answer is simple; you are not."

Myson stepped toward her threateningly. He had no weapons, but she was only a woman. As strange as her appearance was, how powerful could an unarmed woman be? Shaking his finger at her, Myson roared, "Do not answer me in riddles, woman. There is a powerful necromancer threatening my Vale, and I'll not stand idly by while it ravages the land. Now, either give me some answers or step aside, so that I might return from only Leska knows where, and smite the beast."

The woman chuckled, though her face scrunched in distaste when he mentioned Leska.

"You amuse me, elf, but I warn you, do not mention that bitch Leska again in my presence, or I will abandon you to your own devices. I doubt you will survive long here in the abyss."

The abyss. The woman's words seemed to echo in his ears. He feebly looked around at the dark yellow sky, the bubbling black clouds of soot, and the unimaginable demons that chased him with unnatural speed, and felt the cold. The horrible cold. Why else would he be naked after fighting the necromancer, but how did he get here? If he was dead, why was he not with Leska in her garden? The woman seemed to understand the blank look of doubt that planted itself starkly on his face.

"You are dead, elf. You were slain by a beast that is neither alive nor dead. I am sure you are the first of many. Fortunately for

502

you, I am here to take you to my lair, though you will work off your debt to me," she said with a seductive smile, biting her lower lip.

Myson felt bile in his throat at the repeated insults of his goddess. "I'll go nowhere with you, wench. You dare mock the Earth Mother? No naked slut is going . . ."

Myson was cut off with a lightning fast punch to his jaw. The demon struck so fast he could hardly see the blow coming. Her delicate fist hit him like a wrought iron sledge, driving his jaw back into his skull. His eyes popped with the resounding crunch of his jaw and he felt the frigid rocky slate rise up, striking him in the back. The cold stone floor of the abyss sliced into his bare back. Bright flashes of light exploded in his mind from the force of the blow. Looking up from his back, Myson gazed dizzily at the naked woman standing before him. Her stern face stared down at him from between her perfect breasts.

"I have powers that you cannot begin to fathom, elf. You may come with me until I grow tired of playing with you, then you will beg to stay."

Myson rubbed his throbbing jaw and sat up. He had overcome the vulnerable feeling caused by his nakedness. He noticed the she devil's eyes roaming over his body, making more than a momentary pause, and licking her lips. Then she reached for his lower midsection.

"Now follow me, fool. The slate is not safe, even for me," the woman said as she turned her back and glanced about the skies. "We must hurry. The arch demon is about."

"Arch demon?" Myson asked hesitantly. "The plains are barren for miles. Wouldn't we see anything long before it approached us?" the elf asked, glancing around. He did not like entertaining the idea of following the wench, but his options seemed more than limited at the moment.

The woman turned and faced him. To the elf's surprise, her eyes were filled with worry.

"Things are not as you are used to, elf. Another detail to recall, fool, is that you are not alive. You are long dead. You are not here as a man. Your body is not really here, it is a creation of this plane," she said as she led him along a narrow walkway atop the barren slate.

"What do you mean?" Myson asked as he grasped her hand,

being led along the cold hard rocks. He recoiled at the cold of her touch, but she kept a firm hold, pulling him along.

Without looking back, she answered him. "You cannot be killed here. No, there are far worse things than death."

Myson ran with her, ignoring the searing pain in his feet from the jagged rocks.

"Strange, I imagined more people in the abyss. Where are the damned?"

Pulling him around the corner of a large slate boulder, she pressed him close, wrapping him in her enormous bat wings. She pulled him in, pressing his body close to hers. He could feel her cold breasts press against his bare chest, but the cool clammy touch of her skin washed away any sense of the reality of being so close to someone so beautiful. As she whispered to him, her acrid breath wafted over his face, making him scrunch his nose in disgust. "The lake is a good distance away. You appeared in the spawning ground. After demons and the like are done with the new arrivals, they discard their twisted and mangled bodies and toss them in the lake."

Myson cringed. The thought of being tossed into the lake did not appeal to him. Perhaps it was a dream. Maybe he would wake and be next to the campfire with Eulic. The wicked lustful gaze of the woman in front of him drew the legionnaire back to the bitter cold reality of where he was.

A booming voice echoed across the barren landscape. "And how many souls have you tossed into the lake, Delania?"

The woman spread her bat wings away from the man and raised her arms in defense of her face. Myson squinted his eyes at the bright spectacle that stood before him. A large man-like beast with great bat wings outstretched, wielding a blue fiery sword in one hand and a snake-like whip in the other. The end of the whip was forked and dripped molten rock. He wore a single loin cloth made of a thick, dark, scaled hide that covered his dark crimson skin, which was ablaze with small flames that flickered across his body. He had a thick jawed head atop his fifteen foot frame, and two great ribbed goat horns that curved back over his head. He had thick black claws protruding from his scaled toes and a large black horn that jutted from his knees. His eyes were bright yellow and had an amber aura that extended horizontally past the demon's face. His large canine maw dripped acidic drool that burned and singed the stone floor. The beast's body emitted cold that made the frigid air of the abyss pale in comparison.

Delania stepped back from Myson and the great beast defensively. She glanced over at Myson with sorrowful eyes and then back at the arch demon with hate. The demon roared with laughter and tossed his head backwards as his massive body heaved with each chuckle. The bright flames that danced across its body flared up, causing Myson to shield his eyes from the brilliance. Delania clenched her fists and scowled at the arch demon. "Was it not enough that you have yet again ruined my chances at a pet? Must you also tell the fool my name?" the she demon snarled. "If he ever speaks to someone from the outside . . ."

"You will have to worry about being summoned. You are weak compared to me, Delania. Do not tempt me into punishing you further for trying to take a spawned," the arch demon warned.

"Pet?" Myson repeated incredulously. "I'll be no one's pet," he said, ignoring the blisters rising up on his soft skin from the incredible cold of the abyss.

Delania shot him a sideways glance and the arch demon roared even louder with laughter. "I love the ignorance of the newly spawned. Of course you would have been her pet, you were well on your way. You would have leapt head first into the lake of the damned had she merely mentioned it. Tell me, did you have any lustful thoughts when you looked into her big blue eyes?"

Myson's look of shock answered the question for the arch demon. "Of course you did. Few mortal souls can resist the look of a succubus."

Myson shot his head back to Delania with a new regard for her. He stepped back warily, looking around for a place to run.

She turned to face him and her expression softened. "I was trying to rescue you, really. You could have at least found some comforts in my arms. Here in the abyss, you will find nothing but endless torment," Delania pleaded.

The arch demon chuckled. "I doubt you would know what to do with him if you had taken him to your little alcove. I am sure you are the only virgin succubus in all of the abyss."

"I wouldn't be if you had not made your sick existence revolve around keeping me so," Delania sneered as she shook her tiny fist at the face of the imposing demon. Her pale face scowled with anger.

Myson slowly stepped back to the edge of the rocky slate they were standing on. Looking below where the little demons had been, he lowered his foot to climb down.

The arch demon shot out the molten whip with a flick of his thick wrists. The searing whip's tail lashed out and wrapped itself around Myson's neck with a loud crack. The powerful arch demon jerked the helpless elf through the air, and with a single stroke, he cleaved the elf's head from his body with his flaming sword. The elf's body bounced and twitched across the cold gray slate, while the demon's massive clawed hand caught the elf's head in the air. He turned the head in his hand until it was facing him.

Myson's eyes were stark wide with terror. The arch demon loved this part. The elf was struggling not only with the fact that his head had just become severed from his body, but with the fact that he was not dead. Myson could still smell the demon's acrid breath and he could feel the overwhelming pain in his neck from the wound.

"You cannot die here," the arch demon growled. "You are already dead. You will spend your eternity here as your head. Think not that I do not know, nor recognize, a Darayal Legionnaire when I see one, and fear not for your friend," the demon said as he hoisted up Eulic's severed head with his other hand. "He is quite safe." With a toss the arch demon hurled the two heads through the thick smoky air of the abyss, and over a deep dark chasm.

Delania scowled at the arch demon. "May the great lord smite your wickedness!" she screamed with her fists and arms tight against her sides.

The arch demon merely smiled and stepped closer to her. His bright yellow eyes washed over her nakedness and basked in the sight of her lustfully. He lashed out his whip with a loud crack, but it merely passed right through where Delania had been standing.

She reappeared instantly. "I am not yours to be taken, Bykalicus!" she yelled defiantly and vanished. The arch demon roared in anger. How dare the bitch say his name aloud. The arch demon turned to sense if any planar creatures were scrying in. If they learned of his name, he would have to answer to more of the pitiful mortals. Bykalicus knew in time he would feast on their souls, but he hated few things more than serving the plots of foolish men. *That whore succubus would pay for that,* the arch demon thought, but he had other matters to attend to. Soon, the death knight Trinidy would be sending many more elves to him. The arch demon knew he needed to gather some of his henchmen to collect their heads. There was much to be done.

Myson felt incredible pain as his head bounced off hard jagged rocks, coming to rest at the bottom of a deep ravine. He could see the back of Eulic's head. His long brown symas hung loosely, matted with dried blood. He started to speak, but was cut short when he saw them coming. Those strange centipede-looking insect-like creatures he saw before scurried toward them, their hundred of legs were moving in rapid succession that seemed to create a ripple effect from the rear of the creature to the front. Their tiny chitin legs click-clacked over the slate rock as they swarmed near. The backs of the creatures were made of many tiny armored plates. Each plate had a single horn atop of it with the tip pointed forward. It was then Myson began to understand the horror of an eternity in the abyss. He could hear Eulic screaming. Whether it was in pain or despair, he wasn't sure, until he saw one of the creatures erupt from the back of the legionnaire's head, and then burrow back in. Myson screamed inside his head but he dared not scream aloud, in case the creatures might hear him. But to his horror, the tiny creatures bounded on him. He could feel each of their tiny razor-like teeth, ripping into the flesh of his face. The elf suffered from each of the hundred tiny legs crawling under his skin, with their backwards horns ripping flesh as they burrowed. He wanted to scream, and his mind commanded the arms he no longer had to claw and dig at the tiny little beasts, but all he could do was endure the hellish torment. Endure it for eternity.

*   *   *

Lance awoke from the cold night and wearily rubbed the sleep from his eyes. Yawning and stretching he sat up and pulled his bedroll tight against himself. He could still see his breath in the late autumn morning, but to his delight, his companions had prepared a fire and were cooking some soup, or so it smelled, for breakfast. Dressing quickly, Lance rushed to the fire and sat down, rubbing his hands together as he tried to warm himself. Apollisian was polishing his armor and Jude seemed to be trying to do the same, though his thin chain mail paled in comparison to the grand plate the paladin wore. Lance didn't see the elf anywhere, but as he glanced around, he was startled by the fact he could see a tree line in the far distance ahead. The trees were tall and narrow, but they were trees. Lance had thought they would never get out of the godforsaken plains, with their blowing dust and howling winds. Wiping the edge of his leather water skin with his shirt, he took a swig. The water was extremely cold, but since he was sitting so close to fire, he doubted the chill would reach his bones. The sun was not quite up yet, but the eastern sky was afire with bright yellows and pinks and a few splashes of orange here and there. There were a few light scattered clouds that hung in the west, colored dark by the eastern dawn.

Jude glanced up at Lance as he polished his armor and sword. "Good morning, my friend," Jude called out to Lance when he spied him sitting next to the fire with his sleeping roll still tightly wound around him. Apollisian glanced Lance's way and offered a brief smile, then diligently returned to his work.

Lance pulled the bedroll tighter around himself and scooted a little closer to the warm fire. "I guess it is, my friend, since we can see the trees. I am more than eager to be out of these damnable plains."

Jude smiled and stirred the wooden spoon in the bubbling cauldron. "I made some soup. It has a bit of plains rabbit, if you don't mind the gamy taste to it, and a few vegetables that Overmoon rounded up before she left, but it ain't half bad," Jude said without looking up from the stew pot before abandoning it to sharpen his great sword. The rough two-handed blade sat long ways across his lap.

Lance frowned. "Where did she go? Hunting perhaps? I am sure there must be a lot of larger game in the forest."

Jude shook his head and answered without looking up. "No, she went to fetch some of her people. I guess since we are not elven, we are only allowed in at certain times, or something to that effect."

Lance shrugged and took anther swig from his water skin. Apollisian frowned, looking up from his polishing. "I do not think that is entirely it," he said hesitantly.

Jude looked at the paladin sideways in between strokes of the whetstone. "What do you mean?" Lance also turned from the fire and looked interestedly at the paladin.

Apollisian frowned and shook his head. Why was being a paladin so difficult sometimes? He just could not sit idly by when he suspected that the elf was up to no good. Despite his personal feelings for her, right was right, and wrong was wrong. Not telling this pair of what he suspected was surely wrong to him. "I suspect she thinks you are some kind of enemy to her people, Lance," he said slowly. "I had to practically restrain her from attacking you during the battle at Central City. You see, the cloak you wear is called a Cadacka. It is an elven ceremonial robe of mourning given by an elven family member to another when a loved one dies. They wear it until they have decided that their period of mourning is over. It is forbidden by elven law for any non-elven to even see a Cadacka, let alone wear one."

Lance jumped to his feet. "You mean, she is taking me to the elven city to try me for some crime I knew nothing about?"

Apollisian tried to speak but Lance cut him off. "This cloak was given to me by my mother!" Lance shouted as he gripped the fringe of the black cloak with silver cuffs and strange runes.

"Calm down, Lance," Apollisian said coolly. "I will prevent that from happening, though the fact that you wear elven property will be addressed, worst case scenario you will have to give it back."

"Give it back? Give it back?" Lance asked incredulously.

Jude just hung his head low and shook it from side to side. He knew Lance was more protective of that cloak than he was of his own life sometimes.

The cold didn't seem to bother Lance as he stood up in the gentle breeze of the plains. "My mother gave me this. She is passed. It is all that I have of her memory. I will not relinquish it, short of it being pried from my cold dead hands!"

"That can be arranged, human," came a voice from the top of the small northern rise. Lance, Jude, and Apollisian whipped their heads up and saw four elven riders atop the purest white horses. Their manes were cut short, save for six inches or so, and were topped with bright green ribbons. The horses were covered in thin sleek elven chain mail and their legs were covered in long thick hair that extended past their hooves. The horses wore green bridles that were enveloped with jewels and bits of silver and gold, making the four riders quite a spectacle. Alexis sat atop one of the steeds, wearing a bright green robe that blew in the breeze, exposing a finely crafted suit of chain armor that hugged her figure well. Her long blonde hair was braided back in a single braid that danced in the wind. Her beauty made Apollisian's jaw drop slightly, but the sternness of her gaze sobered him just as quickly. The other three riders wore cloaks of various patterns, but all were colored in shades of green and brown with bright vibrant runes that danced along the fringes, similar to the robe that Lance wore. Jude touched his hand on the hilt of his sword and Lance touched his mind on the thoughts of some dweamors.

Apollisian, sensing the boiling emotions, raised his hands and called out. "Halt! This nonsense is unnecessary!" His armor and polish clanged to the grass plains as he rose up.

"Do not interfere, Apollisian!" Alexis shouted. "This is above you."

"Above me?" he screamed, drawing his sword and tossing the scabbard to the ground. Jude drew his sword also and Lance began the makings of a spell.

It all happened in a flash. Lance barely saw the flows coming. They shot out from around the middle elf and wrapped him in six green shimmering rings. The rings were made of pure magical energy. They did not hurt, though they prevented him from moving or speaking. All he could do was watch helplessly as the rings revolved around him spinning. They didn't seem to have a beginning or an end, but they were spinning. He could clearly see that.

"Lance, what is wrong?" Jude asked nervously while he widened his stance and swayed back and forth, awaiting the moment to strike. "Lance?" Suddenly Lance watched a single flow of energy come from the elf from the right and surround Jude, just as it had him, though the green ring was thinner and it rotated much more slowly. Lance thought he could see a section of it, like where the beginning and end met. Anger ripped through the young mage, though he could do nothing. He was as helpless as a babe. Lance needed to move his arms to cast the necromancies he had learned from the Necromidus, but he didn't need to move to cast any of his own spells, although the minor dweamors seemed fruitless right now.

Jude stepped forward. The large swordsman didn't see anything, and he was suddenly held fast and could not move or speak. He could still hear and see but he could do little else. Jude could not see what held him, though he was certain it was the same thing that held Lance.

"Stand down, Apollisian," the middle elf said calmly. "There is a reason we brought three wizards with us this morning."

Apollisian looked at Alexis angrily. She avoided his eye contact. He turned his attention from her and regarded the three mages that sat before him. "I will not stand down. This is unjust. I demand that you release them this instant."

"I am afraid that cannot be, my good paladin. They are under arrest for crimes against the elven nation. I have the warrant issued by the king, if you wish to see it. However, I am ordered not to overlook your standings with the Vale, despite how much it may disgust me. It seems our king holds you in favor, as does his foolish daughter," the elf said as he cast a sidelong glance at Alexis. She ignored the gaze and stared down at Apollisian pleadingly. The paladin glared at her and stepped toward the elves. They seemed unaffected by Apollisian's show of force.

"We are instructed to offer you to travel along to ensure their just treatment and their just trial, if you wish. In fact, the king said you may even lobby on their behalf if you so desire, but we are enforcing the law, Apollisian. You may not agree with it, but Stephanis does recognize all forms of law. He is . . ."

The elf was cut off by the paladin's harsh words. "Do not lecture me on my god, elf. I am well aware of what he honors. It is too bad your misfit posse here has no idea of justice."

The elves glared their narrow eyes at the paladin, though he met their angry stares with a gaze of cold death. "I will indeed oversee your treatment of the boy and his friend, and so Stephanis help me, the moment you out-step your laws, you will surely see the wrath of justice unfold."

"You dare threaten us?" one elf called out, turning his mount to face the paladin. The white steed jerked his head in response to the yanking of its reins.

The middle elf waved his hand in dismissal. "Stand down, Malwinar. He may say as he wishes. It hinders our journey not."

The other two elves did not say another word, but they watched Apollisian as he donned his armor and mounted his Vendaigehn steed with virulent glares. Mounting up, he followed the elves as they led Jude and Lance, shielded by magic, north into the deep forest of the Minok Vale.

Lance struggled against his bonds, but he could not budge them physically nor mentally. The rings were twice as thick as the one that was wove around Jude. Lance watched the section that seemed to connect the band around Jude as it slowly circled him. Staring down at weaves that bound him, he searched for a similar section, but the rings were too thick and swirled around him at great speeds. The magical energy seemed to shift and turn within itself, making it impossible for him to see the cross section, but Lance figured if there was one on Jude, there would be one on him.

Lance wondered if the bands around him also stopped him from casting. Obviously he couldn't use any of the spells from the Necromidus, but he could cast some of his own. They took no verbal chants or gestures. Lance narrowed his eyes and focused on the elf that held the weaves around him. Lance watched in delight as shimmering white weaves erupted from him and encircled the elf's head. The elf turned and glared at him in disbelief just as the weaves set into him. Lance immediately started casting another.

The elf started to warn the others that Lance had been casting, but when he opened his mouth, he merely belched loudly. The other two elves gave him a disgusted look and moved their horses away.

"Good gracious, Garlibane," Malwinar said as he cocked to the side in his saddle and regarded the high mage suspiciously. Alexis gave the high mage a worried look, and Apollisian immediately glanced at Lance, narrowing his eyes.

The high mage tried to give another sound of warning, yet a deeper louder belch than before erupted from his mouth. The other two mages deepened their frowns. "What has come over you, Garlibane?"

Lance focused his thoughts and sent the silvery weaves of shiny flows into the girth of the saddle. He had used this particular dweamor on his father's axe. When Davohn hoisted the implement high into the air, it would cause the axe to repel from his grasp. Lance hoped it worked half as well with the saddle's girth strap as it had with Davohn's axe. The fine weaves settled on the strap just under the horse's belly. If he could disrupt the mage's concentration, perhaps this binding spell would weaken, allowing him to escape.

The high mage did not respond and he started to raise a finger to point at Lance when the girth of his saddle seemed to erupt from the horse. The fine leather saddle shifted under the rider's weight and the high mage spilled onto the ground. He hit with a hollow thud and yet another belch erupted from his gurgling throat.

The two other mages looked at the high mage in confusion. Alexis started to dismount when she saw the paladin glancing at Lance, shaking his head from side to side slowly.

"The Abyss Walker is casting!" Alexis screamed as she drew her bow and reached back for one of the white ash arrows with the green fletching that protruded from her quiver. Notching an arrow, she pulled her powerful bow back easily and leveled it at Lance.

"NO!" Apollisian screamed, leaping from his steed, catching Alexis in the shoulders. He wrapped his armored arms around her. The elf's arrow flew high and wide as they fell to the ground with a thud. Her bow landed a few feet from her, and her arrows spilled out onto the ground behind her. Apollisian grabbed Alexis by her wrists and held her to the ground.

The mages whirled their horses quickly. "He is a sorcerer as well!" Malwinar screamed as he immediately shot out magical weaves around Lance. The face of the elf contorted with pain as he struggled to form a shield between Lance and his abilities. "I need help!" Malwinar shouted. "He is powerful."

The other mage formed a similar weave around Lance, but not as strong. Lance watched as the blue weaves enveloped him, making some kind of crude wall. Then they seemed to sink into his body. Suddenly he only felt his ability to cast, but could not summon its use, much like his arms and legs. He felt as if he would be able to move them easily, but the magical rings surrounding him prevented him from doing it. He could feel the energy from each source, though he detected each was different. Fear ripped through Lance as he contemplated his helplessness. Who was this Abyss Walker? These fool elves had the wrong guy. He was nothing of the sort. He was merely an orphan from Bureland. Hopefully the paladin would help him clear himself.

"Get off me! You orc loving buffoon!" Alexis screamed.

"How dare you label me so," Apollisian said with a grimace. "And I'll not let you up until you promise not to harm either of the prisoners before the Vale's courts try them. You forget, I am a paladin of justice, and I'll not rest until it has been served."

"You forget your station, human," Malwinar said venomously as he fought to keep his skittish horse under control. "You are but a privileged guest. She is Alexis Alexandria Overmoon, high elf of Minok Vale, daughter of King Christopher Calamon Overmoon, and daughter heir to the throne of Minok. I suggest you either unhand her immediately or find yourself in chains next to the criminals. After all, privileges can surely be revoked."

Apollisian glared at the elf mage, then softened his look when he peered down at Alexis. She was staring at him with a face of scorn but he detected more embarrassment. How could he have been such a fool? She was not with him on the trail anymore. She was an elven noble. Her father had warned him of that. Shaking his head and pulling her up, he started to apologize, but she cut him off. Her words dripped venom and spite.

"If you ever place a hand on me again, Apollisian Bargoe of Westvon, regardless of what good you think you might be performing, you will find that hand roasting on the picket of some witch doctor. Do I make myself clear?"

Apollisian did not miss the formality in which she referred to him. Her face held scorn but her eyes were soft and full of remorse, yet also seemed to harbor a great deal of fear. No doubt, afraid of the boy and his swordsman. Apollisian didn't understand why anyone was afraid of him, regardless of whatever supposed power he possessed. Right now he was not evil, and he was not dangerous, though their treatment of him might surely set him on such a path. The paladin started to help Alexis pick up her arrows, when she batted his hand away.

"I will retrieve my own belongings, paladin," Alexis sneered.

Malwinar re-secured the loose items on his horse from the incident and aided Garlibane in trying to dispel the dweamor that prevented him from speaking except by belching.

Apollisian mounted his Vendaigehn steed, and patted the stallion's neck. The horse was well trained and seemed to understand how to keep him in the saddle if his weight shifted. It was rare that a horse actually tried to keep the rider on its back, as opposed to helping him fall from it.

Lance focused his eyes on the crude barrier which seemed to be blocking him from using the magical energy that seemed to be innate inside him. He could see the magical energy swirling around inside the milky blue barrier. It was not well made, in fact it seemed very unstable. If he pushed a little there . . . Suddenly the barrier shattered and he felt the flood of energy as it filled him.

"He is free! He is free! He has broken the shield!" Malwinar screamed as he began casting again. Alexis started for her bow and then slowly lowered her arm when she saw Apollisian tensing to pounce again. She did not mean what she had said. Well not entirely, but she would have to make good on her threat in the presence of Garlibane, the high mage. As much as she was furious with the paladin at the moment she would not harm him willingly. She just hoped they could contain the Abyss Walker before the human's ignorance at what they dealt with killed them all.

Lance started to weave another dweamor to set upon the first mage. It seemed incredibly effective in neutralizing the man. He had thought someone of his power would have been able to break his weave easily, but he could clearly see it, snuggly wrapped around the man's head. But before Lance could finish the weave, Malwinar shot out a wave of green sparkling dots. It was no weave he had ever seen. It was, in a way, beautiful. Suddenly Lance felt his mind faltering and his eyes closing. The last thing he heard before he fell asleep was the triumphant voice of Malwinar. "That ought to hold him until we arrive in the Vale and receive our welcome." *Some welcome,* Lance thought. *No welcome I had ever heard of before. Maybe a prisoner's welcome, if there ever was such a thing.* With the last thought, he drifted into a deep sleep.

A prisoner. What do you think of when you hear that title? Most men think of a man in a jail cell, or dressed in gray rags working the fires of some castle, or kept as a slave. Few men think of themselves, or others they may see, as such. In truth, I say a prison is never a building of stone walls, or barred windows. If you searched, you might find that a few of the so-called prisoners that dwelled there were actually more free than you or I.

Is a man who is not a prisoner, free? The answer is all in perspective. My mother was forced from Merioulus and had to live a mortal's life on this plane of existence. To the gods that banished her, it was supposed to be not only a prison, but a death sentence. And the latter proved true, but she was as free as you or I as we walk the land. The truth is no one is physically free. A man must obey the laws of the land, or he will be arrested. The local magistrate must arrest law breakers, or he will lose his job, or be arrested also. The king who makes the laws must govern his kingdom. The vagrants that walk the streets cannot go into many of the establishments they walk among.

Freedom. No one is truly free physically. True freedom comes from within. It is strange that the few mortals who begin to understand this revelation have been imprisoned most of their natural lives, save for the few wise men that may discover this on their own. It took me years of persecution and imprisonment to understand the true meaning of freedom. What is sad is that the men who think they enjoy the most freedoms are most likely the most imprisoned.

—Lancalion Levendis Lampara—

Fifteen
Trials of Innocence

"We cannot afford to debate the issue," Elder Eucladower argued before the elven council as he sat in his grand polished oak chair with hundreds of carvings depicting trees and birds of the forest. The old elf gripped his long golden pipe with his clenched teeth. "The passings clearly state, and I quote: 'He who walks with wrath, shall stride into the Vale as a guest wearing the Cadacka, though he knows not why he mourns. If the children of the forest do nothing, they will surely perish.' It is obvious the boy is the Abyss Walker. He was wearing a Cadacka for Leska's sake!" The room muttered silently at Eucladower's uncharacteristic curse. "We must try him!" he pleaded to the king.

King Overmoon sat on his throne in the great elven hall. He held his weary head up with his hand. He had been hearing both sides of the debate every day since Garlibane, Apollisian, Alexis, and the other two mages returned from fetching the humans. The room was more of a chapel than a hall. It was over three hundred feet long, one hundred fifty feet wide, and its ornate carved ceiling of gold and silver rested some two hundred feet over the polished marble floor. At the far end was King Overmoon's golden throne, set upon a small dais depicting the greatness of Leska, and the names of every Minok king before him. Every twenty feet along the walls of the hall, majestic wooden beams erupted from opulently carved wooden bases depicting unicorns and other majestic creatures of the forest. Every third beam held a shining brass sconce whose flame flickered and danced, sending ripples of small shadows across the great room.

The king shook his head slowly and exhaled leisurely before speaking. "We have been over this, Elder Eucladower. I fear his power as much as the rest, but our hands are tied. What can we charge him with, short of possession of a Cadacka? He claims his mother gave him the cloak. However remote that possibility is, we cannot disprove it."

Garlibane sneered. "He cast a dweamor on me, my king, that was so strong I had to wait for the weaves to dissolve, rather than dispel them. He wields both types of arcane powers. He is a wizard and a sorcerer. That is unheard of! No one in the history of our world, man or elf, has done such a thing. He was carrying the Necromidus, and he carries an elven copy of the prophecy. That alone satisfies a second passing. Need I recite it again?"

"Watch your tongue, Garlibane. I am no maiden that frequents your bed. I am your king!" King Overmoon growled as he slammed both of his hands down on the polished oak table. The heavy slap of his palm against wood silenced the chamber and echoed across the room. " 'A babe, half not of this earth, and half damned by the gods themselves, feared by the children of the forest, will carry his own proclamation naming him for who he is not, but for whom he will become,' " the king recited wholeheartedly. "I am aware of every passing, mage, but in your wisdom, can you tell me how the boy is half of this earth, and half damned by the gods?"

Garlibane looked down and bowed deeply. "I am sorry, my king, I have overstepped my bounds. May your graciousness forgive me, and by Leska's light I am humbled by your words."

King Overmoon eyed the high mage suspiciously.

"My lord . . ." Elder Humas interrupted. "Is it necessary for every passage to be confirmed in order to convict the boy? They were written before our grandfathers' grandfathers. Surely the context of their words is lost in our pages. We cannot place the burden of absolute proof on our shoulders alone."

King Overmoon arched an eyebrow, but did not interrupt Elder Humas.

"I mean, surely there are things in which they speak that we do not understand," Elder Humas stated flatly.

King Overmoon nodded his head slowly, adjusting the jewel-encrusted golden crown that rested there. Today the crown of Minok seemed heavier than it had in a long while. The king glanced at Apollisian. The paladin sat disapprovingly as he witnessed the debate. His finely crafted armor glistened in the pale lamplight of the hall, but his eyes shined with fury and contempt. The king had listened to his argument to free the boy the first two days. Elder Bartoke, Elder Varmintan, and Apollisian had all argued on the boy's behalf. Elder Humas, Elder Darmond, Elder Eucladower, and High Mage Garlibane argued against the boy. As king, he was supposed to be impartial to debates of the council, but in truth, he felt the boy possessed no threat. He surely should be guided, or at least held as a respected guest, but executed, no.

"We will recess until tomorrow. I will hear your final arguments for the execution of the boy then," King Overmoon said as he slowly rose from his throne.

"But, my king," Eucladower protested. "The sun has not set on the day, surely . . ." the elder trailed off as King Overmoon shot him an angry glare.

"I am tired, Elder Eucladower. The boy is shielded and held. He is not a threat. I will retire to my chambers for the evening. I shall not be disturbed."

Everyone in the room stood as the king moved from the table and strode out of the hall. No one spoke until the heavy door at the far end of the great room boomed shut.

Garlibane grabbed the paladin by the heavy plates that covered his arm, and turned the paladin to face him. Apollisian towered over the smaller elf, but Garlibane seemed to match his presence with intensity and hate. "Surely, fool human, the king will hear our cause and see the true wisdom of it, unlike your foolish plight. You are not elven. You do not belong . . ."

Apollisian cut him off, as he easily jerked his arm away from the smaller elf. "It is forbidden by Minok law to speak of the dissension of the hall during the three days the king hears each side," Apollisian said as he turned his back and walked toward the door.

Garlibane growled in contempt. "You dare lecture me on the laws of my people, human? I will speak . . ."

Eucladower yelled above the high mage. "Garlibane! Is it not bad enough that the human must teach you our ways, but must you further insult your own intelligence as to argue with him about it? Let us retire with some dignity. We will address the issue tomorrow. Now, disperse," the elder said as he waved his hand in dismissal.

Garlibane sneered, but said nothing else as he strode from the chamber muttering under his breath about teaching the fool human not to interfere where he did not belong.

*   *   *

Lance awoke in a dimly lit room with no furnishings save for a silver and pewter chamber pot that stood in the corner. There was a small glass bulb that was affixed to the ceiling. The bulb had a bright yellow weave that was simple in creation, yet Lance had never thought to create such a weave. If he could twist it differently, he could make something more practical. Lance tried to reach his inner power but he hit a murky white wall instead. This time the wall was three times as thick and consisted of a clearer white, with little swirls of energy. This one would be much more difficult to break, so he rolled onto his back and studied the roof of his room. There was a door just a few feet away, but he didn't bother trying it until the effects of the spell wore off completely. He still felt a little groggy. The ceiling was old, but well maintained, though it and the wall's olive drab color did little for Lance's mood. His head ached from the magical sleep, so he decided to lounge awhile before trying to stand.

Lance occasionally pushed at the barrier that prevented him from reaching his power, but the barrier seemed to twist at his probing. It was not like he could actually see the barrier, it was more like something he imagined in his head. Yet, he knew it was no imagination. Pushing again, he forced his thoughts around the entire wall, and learned that it was not a wall at all, but an encompassing sphere.

After a few hours of pushing and searching against the barrier, Lance decided to try to stand. His knees wobbled at first, but in minutes he needed only to lean against the wall. He felt queasy, but his head was clearer and his balance better. Taking small steps he walked his bare feet across the dirt floor to the large wooden door. It was not ornate, and lacked any lock or latch. The hinges seemed to be on the outside of the door and he could determine which way it opened. Sitting down in front of the wooden door, Lance hugged himself to keep warm. He was not cold, but the room was anything but warm. Staring down at the gray rags he wore, he immediately missed the cloak his mother had left him. The elves had mentioned something about that. Regardless of what they thought, the robe was his. His mother gave it to him with her bare hands. They would not take it from him. As soon as he escaped from here. *Escape,* the word echoed hopelessness in his mind. He was useless against the elves' magic. He was too weak and too inexperienced to rival them. His only hope lay with Jude, or the paladin, but the paladin seemed cowed by the elves and Jude was probably just as stuck right now as he was. Letting his head fall back against the hard stone wall, Lance closed his eyes. He would think of something, he just needed a little time, and at the moment time was all he seemed in abundance of.

*　*　*

Jude growled inside as he recalled being tossed into this cell. The elves had the audacity to call him a guest, when he was locked in a room with no furnishings, save for a silver and pewter chamber pot and a glowing bulb at the top of the ceiling. The walls were a sickly green color and the old wooden door seemed the only thing he had seen that did not have some sort of carvings on it since he arrived in this forsaken city. Those damnable elves took everything he owned and said he would get it back in time. In time for what? In how much time? He had been here for two days now, trying to get full on small portions of meat and a few nuts they stuffed under the door. Didn't the scrawny pointed-eared hellions know he was not as small as them? He needed meat, and a lot of it. Some ale would hit the spot right now too, but he was sure the fancy little beasts had none of that.

Jude gave up pounding the door that had no hinges, latches or knobs. It just seemed as if the door was magically held in place, and after making that discovery he decided he hated magic a little more than before. He had warned that fool Lance about coming here. In fact he had warned the prissy man—no, child—about ever leaving Bureland. He could be snug in his big warm bed back home chasing a few rogues that had settled in the hills, or some thief that had eluded the local magistrate. Instead, he let Lance talk him into a fool journey. But his father always had asked him, who was the bigger fool? The fool, or the one who followed him? Jude now was feeling very much like a fool. His muscles and strength were useless here, and he hated to feel useless more than anything. Feeling a fool was bad, but his father had taught him that it was a good thing now, for it reminded a man to be humble. Well he didn't much feel like being humble at the moment. Jude ran through his head how he was going to repay the elf, Overmoon, or whatever her name was. Apollisian seemed to call her that, but here the elves called her Alexis something or other. He would call her bent-over-his-knee-and-paddled if he ever saw her again. As for that paladin, he would see the man with a bloody lip, or have his church notified of this, but Jude was not much of the institution-notifying type. He quickly tossed that idea out of his head, and went back to thinking of pummeling the man. As for Lance, he imagined a hundred things to say and do to that fool for getting him locked in this hellhole. Jude hoped the pretty boy was getting no better treatment than he. Yet knowing that hoodwink wizard wannabe, Jude was sure he was up to his scheming and making out like a fat rat somehow.

With a heavy sigh, Jude sat down on the dirt floor of his room and leaned against the wall. Only time would tell how this misadventure was going to go, and it seemed at the moment he had an abundance of that.

*　　*　　*

Stieny crawled through the crawl space between the ceiling and the roof of the great meeting hall of Central City. The crawl space was made of thick wooden planks that were surprisingly free of dust and other debris. He wore only a thin cloak and some small clothes, fearing any extra weight of any kind might cause him to fall through or make some of the wooden shafts creak. Either would be bad. Not only had the little halfling received a poor reception here in Central City, but many of the crazed folk seemed to think him a dwarf and went stark mad, screaming in the streets. He had been arrested twice and he was just now beginning to break the law. That had to be a first.

He had since learned that it was most unlikely that a dragon had the ability to capture his soul in gem, but it was a big chance to take. So the little thief elected to go ahead and fetch the dragon's information if he could. Stieny had learned that this Lance had been here in Central City, but left to the east with a paladin and an elf—strange companions for a dragon like Darrion-Quieness to be interested in, but that was the dragon's business, not his. All Stieny wanted to do was complete the quest, get his soul back, if the dragon ever really possessed it, and get the heck out of town. Heck, out of the country would be nice. There was a lot of money to be made here in Central City and it seemed for some strange reason there was no guild in town. Stieny had never seen a city this size that did not have a thieves guild. The people were wealthy in the higher class area. They wore silks, and often had full coin purses of satin dangling from their belts. Their belts! Never had Stieny seen a city of this size where that happened. Why, given a good afternoon he could make more money than he had in his lifetime. Ah, but now he was on a mission. He needed to find as much information regarding this Lance fellow as possible. He would send word to the dragon and be done with him. He believed dragons were noble creatures. Even if this one seemed evil, he felt it would honor their bargain, and of course, their bargain did not specifically entail that he personally deliver the message.

Stieny deftly crept further along the crawl space between the ceiling and the roof. He had passed many rooms searching for this supposed meeting about the mage, and Stieny had even passed a room where a nobleman was getting along quite well with his maid, so to speak. Had Stieny not been so disgusted with the look of naked human bodies, he might have stayed and enjoyed some of the show, but human females were, well, too stretched out. Rumors around the magistrate were that he and his swordsman, whatever the swordsman's name was, were wanted for a murder in their room a few weeks back. Stieny hadn't heard much more than that. The guards did not want to speak to a halfling, and he had difficulty sneaking about since there were few others than humans in this town. He hated Beykla. Of all the kingdoms in the realms, they were the most intolerant of other races. Nothing like Aboe, where Stieny had been born. Aboe was a coastal kingdom that was made up of a giant peninsula at the southern area of the continent. The land was mostly mountainous near the coast, and its borders kept it, for the most part, unconquerable. Beykla had never been conquered in its history either as far as Stieny could recall, but who would want to have the stinking humans' land anyways?

"Like I said, we have received notification from the elves that they have captured the two murderers," Stieny heard a man say.

The halfling paused and slowed his breathing and tried to get comfortable on the wooden ceiling planks as the voices continued.

"By their description it had to be Lance and the swordsman, Jude. Who else would dare travel to their lands? The pair was seen leaving with the paladin and an elf, though no word was sent whether either of the other two arrived with them. I say it is them," the voice continued.

Stieny strained to listen further as another voice chimed in. "What did the elves say they intend to do with the pair?"

"The letter was brief, but they stated that they were holding the mage for reasons that were their own. But they were willing to send us the swordsman for a one hundred gold crown fee."

"A high price for murder, but I suspect the swordsman will fetch twice that in revenues fighting in the arena. Make the deal. Tell them to send him through the portal at our mage tower in Kalliman castle. If they do not wish to do that, we can dispatch a group of soldiers to meet with them in the Serrin Plains and take custody of him there," the second voice said.

"As you command, my king."

King! Yipes! Stieny thought to himself. What had he gotten into? This low power mage the dragon wanted him to follow was wanted by a king! That was all Stieny needed to hear. He would hire a linkboy to deliver the message to the mountains, give a vague description of where the dragon could be found, and of course, mention that it was a colleague of his, searching for a bounty; but first he needed to make a few coins to pay the man. A trip into the mountains was not going to be cheap.

Climbing back down from the crawl space, Stieny daydreamed about making a few extra coins for himself, and leaving this forsaken country. The trip back south was going to be a long one.

*   *   *

The great elven hall sat quiet. The elders had assembled before King Overmoon at the grand glossy oak table. The table was as ornate as the rest of the room, leaving little if any space, with hundreds of carvings and depictions of elven achievements. The king had heard the second day of arguments against the human. He was now convinced that the boy was indeed the prophesied Abyss

524

Walker, or at least he would become him. The problem the king deliberated over was how to deal with him now. The deafening silence was broken by the gnarled voice of the high mage, Garlibane. "Surely we cannot keep him here among our people, my lord. When will he grow into the power to overwhelm us? We cannot have the liability among us. The risk is too great. He must be executed."

The others frowned at Garlibane, but even the elders who did not believe they had the right to execute the boy based on events he was yet to create agreed he could not be kept in the Vale; it was just not safe.

"Give him to my charge, your highness," Apollisian said as he stood up from the table. His darker mirrored reflection danced across the oak slab and his creaking armor echoed across the stark chamber.

"Surely you must jest?" Eucladower said as he pointed a raised palm at the paladin. "We respect your position and your valor, Apollisian Bargoe of Westvon, but we cannot place the entire future of the Minok Vale in the hands of . . ." Elder Eucladower trailed off and looked away. His hand slowly lowered to the table.

"In the hands of a human," Apollisian said with a sneer.

"That is surely not what I meant to say," Eucladower replied as he wiggled in his seat, trying to ease the icy glare from the paladin.

"Enough!" the king announced. "The bickering will end now! Apollisian is one of us, or he would not be at this table. The banter of his race will cease! He is above the normal behavior of his race, that I must say, you elders have mimicked well."

The elders mumbled amongst themselves, but they dared not interrupt the king. King Overmoon was as lenient as any elven king in speaking out of turn, but he was deep in anger when he felt someone stepped beyond their station.

"It is agreed that something must be done. I have heard the arguments of each side, and in part I agree with each. I will make my decision in one hour," the king said as he stood from the table, as did the elders and Apollisian. The king turned and his long green velvet robe fluttered as he strode out of the chambers.

Unlike days past, there was no bickering between the two sides. The elders, Eucladower and crew, had succeeded in convincing the king that the boy was a threat. But they had not convinced

525

him that he should be executed. Apollisian sat alone in the flickering torch light of the chambers after everyone had departed. He sat against the wall with his knees up, and his elbows rested on them. His brilliant plate mail shimmered under the wavers of the torch. His head hung low with his chin to his chest and his long blonde hair streaked down, covering his face. He ignored the sound of the great door closing. He was in no danger here, and he did not feel like speaking to anyone. He was preparing himself to draw steel in defense of the boy. If they ordered him executed, he would give his life, if need be, trying to protect him, and he knew drawing steel against the elves would surely result in his death.

King Overmoon sat in his chair in the lounge room behind the great hall. The room was small, but ornate as any other room in the Vale. It had a lounging sofa that was covered in dark brown velvet and stuffed with goose down. He had one arm resting on the back of the brown lounging chair and his feet were propped up on a small wooden footstool as he sipped warm wine from a golden cup that was encrusted with emerald and topaz jewels.

"You see, Garlibane, he is no ordinary human. He weeps for those who are wronged, and he weeps for himself. He knows he is in a lose-lose situation and he is undoubtedly preparing himself for his death."

Garlibane turned to the king and frowned. "Why would he be preparing for his own death? He is not the one on trial. In fact, with the favor your majesty holds for him, I would doubt he should fear for his life if he was on trial."

King Overmoon chuckled and shook his head as he leaned forward and refilled his empty chalice. "He prepares for death, because he knows when he draws steel against us, we will kill him."

Garlibane turned from the small peeping hole in the wall and faced the king. His hands were tight behind his back, tucked in the bright yellow cord that kept his robe closed. "Why in Leska's name would he draw steel against us? We surely are not his foes," Garlibane asked in confusion. The high mage stepped to the king and picked up the other jewel-encrusted chalice and filled it.

The king chuckled again at the high mage's lack of wisdom. It was true what he learned. Priests had the wisdom. Wizards merely had intelligence. "You see, my good mage, Apollisian does not fight enemies that you and I might think of. His foes are those that make others suffer injustice, such as he sees us."

"Us?" Garlibane asked incredulously. "What injustice are we causing?"

"We are trying a man over the deeds he has not yet performed. That is why I cannot make my decision lightly. You see, if I sentence the boy to death, I am also sentencing one of the greatest and noble humans ever to walk the earth to death also."

Garlibane nodded as his face lit up in understanding. The high mage turned and looked back out the peephole. "It seems you are not the only one that holds the paladin in such high regards," Garlibane said with an arched eyebrow.

The king frowned, placing his chalice on the small wooden table that was at the end of the sofa, and stood up. "Whatever do you mean?" he asked as he walked to the peeping hole next to Garlibane.

The figure that came in shuffled on padded slippers. Apollisian noticed out of the corner of his eye that the slippers were a silky red. They paused in front of him. It was then he smelled her. She wore the strong scent of morning flowers, and fresh soap seemed to drift from her presence, clouding his mind. He raised his head and peered deep into the worried face of Alexis. Tears streaked down his chiseled face, sticking strands of his golden hair to his cheeks. She stared down at him with worry and pity. Alexis had never seen so much emotion from the paladin. She doubted he cried for himself, but for the welfare of the boy. Pulling her robe tight behind her, she lowered herself next to him on the floor of the great hall. Apollisian merely lowered his head again. He was now sure he loved her, and she would hate him for doing what he had to do. Had to do? Did he? His heart screamed for justice, to help those who could not help themselves, but who was helping him? He was giving up more than just his life. He was giving up on love. He quickly chastised himself for thinking such thoughts. Stephanis had filled him with more love and privileges, since taking up the sword in his name. How could he be so selfish to turn his back on his god now? He was a fool to think he and Alexis had any future anyway. She was an elf, he was human. Their union was forbidden by both races, more forbidden by hers. Plus she was no ordinary elf that could forsake her race. She was the daughter of a king. Daugh-

527

ter heir to the Vale. She had responsibilities that took precedence over her personal wants and needs, much like he did. Plus, from the way she reacted to him in the plains, she did not likely return his feelings, at least not at the level he felt. But did elves even love as men do? So many uncertainties. Too big a risk, too selfish of a risk. Even after coming to the conclusion that he and she would never be, the tears did not seem to stop flowing.

Alexis placed a warm hand on the plate armor that covered Apollisian's shoulder. It was so hard and so cold, much like his heart must be. She could tell by the tears that the man must feel immense remorse and sadness, which she had already learned by traveling with him, but to what level did he feel it now? Were the tears shed on behalf of the boy? She doubted it, but she could not be sure. With the short lives of humans, did they really love as strongly as elves did? She doubted it. She was sure she had grown to love Apollisian on their journeys. He fought and argued with such passion. He risked his life at every turn to try to enforce justice and what he felt was right. He would spit on no man, and if spit upon, he would ask the man for an apology before moving on. Never in all the realms of her kingdom, of her world, had she met a man with those qualities. They were strange, these humans. They lived hectic erratic lives, yet one might find a jewel that would rise so far above all others of any race, only to die so young. They seemed to pack a lifetime of wisdom and knowledge into the time it took her to grow enough before she was allowed to leave the Vale by herself. Yet the human race could produce a man such as Apollisian, but could also create such a vile creature that he would appear as a demon in the body of a boy. She had heard tales of men who raped and killed children, ate other men for food, and even rose to become powerful allies and slaves of the denizens from the dark planes, yet before her now sat the most noble creature she had ever met. He reminded her of a unicorn, in the body of a man. The shoulder plate she had been touching shuddered under her. Alexis scooted closer and lay her forehead on the cold unyielding steel.

"I am sorry for things I have done," she said quietly. "Though I had no choice."

Apollisian nodded his head solemnly. "I too, am sorry for things I have done." *And things I have yet to do.* "But we cannot dwell on what is already done. Those things cannot be changed. We must instead look to what can be changed, and what has to be done," he said grimly.

Alexis lifted her head and was startled to meet the paladin's steel blue-eyed gaze. She could peer into his soul it seemed. Her dark russet eyes locked with his cerulean stare. Did he feel the same as she? She could almost see it in his sea of blue. Or was it reality's pressure to duty that stared back at her? She was sure he thought of her as a friend, sometimes as a spoiled brat, but she wondered if he ever viewed her as an equal.

Apollisian gazed back into her almond eyes. How he could become lost in them. Those russet orbs told a thousand tales and sung a thousand songs of love and devotion to him, but was it real, or simply a figment of his imagination? Did his heart create what he thought he was seeing, merely because he wanted to see it more than anything else he ever wanted? He quickly found himself leaning toward her ever so slowly. Thoughts erupted into his mind like a tidal wave of emotions. What was he doing? He was in the great hall of the elven king of Minok, about to try to kiss the daughter heir to his throne—something that was outlawed by her race. What madness had befallen him? But wait. She seemed to lean forward. Was it his imagination? He stared at her full lips. How he longed to feel their warm embrace on his. He leaned closer, as did she. Apollisian could feel her warm breath against his cheeks. The scent of her drove him wild. They were inches apart. His steel blue eyes remained locked on hers, while her auburn orbs danced across his face with uncertainty.

"Alexis." The sound of her name being called from the distance seemed to echo in her ears. The voice was familiar to her, it warmed her heart in a different way than the current raging inferno. "Alexis!" came the voice, louder and more impatient than before.

She jerked her head around and immediately her face flushed into a sea of red. Her father came striding out of his personal chambers with the high mage, Garlibane. She glanced back and realized that Apollisian was already to his feet, smoothing his pants, and looking quite ridiculous doing so, since his legs were not covered with breeches, but rigid armored plates. She chuckled at his uneasiness and stood up, pulling her cloak tighter around herself. "Yes Father?" she asked and placed an indignant smile on her face, completely contrasting the stark horror that seemed frozen on the paladin's.

The king and the high mage strode over to the pair slowly. Garlibane followed a few steps behind. He was no fool and he saw the confrontation coming, knowing it was going to be more than heated. "You may take your leave, Apollisian," the king said with a forced smile.

Apollisian bowed deeply. "My thanks, your highness."

"You too, Garlibane. I will catch up with you later," the king said without taking his angry gaze from Alexis. She matched his angry stare and placed her hands on her hips.

The high mage frowned. He had wanted to see the little brat get the chastising she deserved, but he dared not defy King Overmoon. "As you command, my liege," Garlibane replied and quickly followed the paladin out of the great chamber.

Garlibane closed both doors to the great chamber and turned to see Apollisian quickly walking down the hall. "You do our nation a great favor, paladin," Garlibane said wryly. Apollisian stopped walking, but did not reply or turn around as the high mage finished. "Go ahead and court the girl. Doing so without the king's permission, beside the fact you are a stinking human, will solve the old elf's dilemma for him," the high mage said with a haughty sneer.

Apollisian wanted to turn and argue with the mage. He knew the elf lacked much wisdom and did not think it would be difficult to slip him up in a verbal tirade, but he feared his emotions. He had lost control in the chamber. Had the king not intervened, he was sure he would have given in to passion and kissed Alexis.

"But who could blame you, paladin? She is beautiful, is she not? Her long hair, her wonderful eyes . . . the way her hips sway when she walks. I mean you are only human," Garlibane taunted.

Shaking his head, Apollisian walked from the chambers. The damned mage was trying to taunt him into a fight. But the elf was right, why shouldn't he want her? It was natural, to an extent, barring the interracial issue. But he was not like other men, he was a paladin, a champion of justice. He was wed to his sword and the way of his god. If he allowed himself to love another being more than any other, he opened the door for emotion to cloud his judgment. Could he allow her to die in order to preserve justice? Even now, he knew the answer to that question was no. No matter what would come of it, he would no sooner allow her to be harmed than he would cast aside his god and denounce him. Now he realized that if he were to choose between his god and her safety, he would have an intense struggle. He could not allow that to occur. Stephanis came first over all mortals. His will, his ideas, were greater than any one life, even his own, even . . . hers.

*   *   *

"What in Leska's name do you think you are doing?" King Overmoon asked, shaking an angry finger in Alexis's face.

"I was trying to comfort the friend to the elves. My friend. *Your* friend. He seemed sad to me. I wonder what struggle is going on in his head, and I wonder what is the cause of it?" she asked accusingly.

Her father shook his head. "I have not given him permission to court you, Alexis. It is forbidden. He is a human, he is . . ."

Alexis cut him off. "I am not being courted by anyone!" she yelled, her fists clenched at her sides. "Has he bought me any trinkets? Composed any ballads in the honor of my name? Has he ever belayed an interest in me to you, or any one member of our family?" Before the king could answer her, she quipped in, "No! He has not. And if he did, father, what is wrong with him? He is the noblest man I have ever met, human or elven." She stressed *elven* harshly.

The king opened his mouth and tried to respond, but only empty air escaped his lips as she continued.

"He is a man that you trusted my life with enough to send me out amongst the humans, amongst their vile wickedness, amongst their wars. For what? So he could be chastised and made second rate before my eyes, before our brethren? If he stands so high in your eyes, then place him up on the pedestal he so rightly deserves, or so help me Father . . ."

"Enough!" King Overmoon shouted. He was not going to take anymore of the verbal tirade from his daughter. "You were in the best care you could have been in, and learned the real ways of the humans, and the ways of Stephanis. None knows justice like Apollisian's order, and none of them knows it as he. He is a beacon of light when there is nothing but darkness, but he is not elven."

531

"You're right, Father," Alexis said with a much quieter tone than before. "He is not elven, and for that reason alone, he has risen to such greatness."

King Overmoon felt the sting in his eyes of unshed tears. He embraced his daughter and held her head close to his chest. "My poor Alexis . . ." he said as she began to weep. "The man will grow old and die before your very eyes. His body will fail him, while his mind and heart will still love strong. The elven bond of love lasts a lifetime for us. As does the mourning of loves lost. If you begin to love this man, in a few short decades you will wear a black Cadacka, and probably never remove it. Few ever do. Not only that, daughter, but the man is wed to his god, and his sword. It would be nearly impossible for him to give those things up. He could easier turn his back on Stephanis than he could stop being who he is," the king said in a near whisper.

Tears streaked down Alexis's face. "Then let me don my Cadacka now, Father. It is too late, I already love him."

King Overmoon wept as fiercely as his daughter did in the cold empty hall. He knew the pain of losing a loved one. He could not imagine that without the joy of the memories to placate the loss.

Alexis pulled away and looked up at the tear-streaked face of her father. "I ask you as my father, not as my king, do I have your permission to wed Apollisian Bargoe of Westvon, if he will have me?"

King Overmoon's soul wailed. His poor daughter could not begin to fathom what she asked, what pain she would subject herself to. But in truth, there was not a man alive, save for the paladin, that was close to good enough for his precious Alexis. "You know not the extent of which you ask, daughter. But if your heart wishes, I consent," the king said sadly.

Alexis looked up at her father with joy and admiration, but the bells of alarm sounded and the screams of the elves outside the hall took away her endowment. There was something that was terribly wrong.

The king hurried to his chambers. "Go to the safe house, Alexis. I will see to the disturbance," the king said as his heart raced. The alarm bells had not been sounded since the orc wars. What could have possibly happened for them to be sounded again?

Alexis rushed out of the chamber, and turned to see if her father was watching her go. Satisfied he was not, she hurried to one of her many private rooms. She needed to fetch her bow, and find Apollisian. If there was going to be danger, she would much rather face it with him.

*　　*　　*

Apollisian marched down the long corridors when he heard the alarm bells sound. He wasn't sure exactly what they meant, but the screams and shouts from outside quickly told him trouble. Drawing his short sword, he quickly rushed outside. The scene that greeted him was something from nightmares. Thousands of skeletal monstrosities attacked and fought with the elven villagers. There were too many for the watchmen to fight. Dead and slain elven children littered the ground, as did women and unarmed civilians.

Apollisian roared into a fury. He set into the skeletons, cutting a path to the center. Their yellow and bleach white bones were difficult to cut with his sword, but he fought on anyway, easily evading their clumsy attacks. He could see great balls of fire coming from the heavens, striking trees and buildings as great pieces of stone and debris erupted from the shattered structures and littered the ground.

Apollisian heard a shriek around the side of the great hall. Turning and making his way there, he saw Alexis surrounded by a pile of broken and shattered enemies, swinging with her unstrung bow. She was surrounded, and it seemed for every skeleton she smashed, three more took their place. It was as if the entire city was alive with bleach white enemies. Seeing her in danger, Apollisian outstretched his arm. Grabbing his holy symbol tightly in his clenched fist, he chanted in a thick deep voice that seemed to echo unnaturally loud.

"By the hand of Stephanis, disperse fetid undead, and enjoy the afterlife you were so evilly ripped away from."

When he finished, a wave of an unseen force, like a ripple in reality, shot out from him in all directions. Skeletons by the hundreds seemed to explode in a shower of bone debris.

Alexis stared wide-eyed as her attackers exploded in front of her. Her face was hit by stinging fragments from the skeletal foes.

She looked to her left and saw Apollisian running to her. The sight of the man in his shining armor and flowing cape was majestic as he ran to her with his face full of worry and compassion.

"Are you all right?" he asked between labored breaths.

The sight of him in front of her at last caused Alexis to momentarily forget about the horde of skeletal enemies that surrounded her. She forgot about the lives lost, and the lives that would be lost in this battle; she forgot about the confusion of how the attacks arrived, and how they would be defended. She only knew that standing beside her man, her friend, her champion, she could defeat all evil that rose against them. In a single moment without hesitation, without fear of the unknown, she reached up and grabbed Apollisian by the sides of his face. His warm skin seemed ablaze under her touch, as she pulled his face down to hers. She reveled in the puzzled look in his blue eyes and his pleasant shock as she kissed him. The kiss lasted a fraction of a second, but to her it extended from the beginning of her existence to the present day. She did love him. She was sure of it, and if they died today in this battle, she would have at least told him. "I love you," she whispered. Without waiting for a reply, she pushed his face away and drew her short sword. She did not need a reply from him. Her heart did not rest on whether he returned her love, though she desperately wanted him to. She was content in knowing that she loved him and no matter how he felt, he would not hurt her, or take advantage of her. He was a pure man.

Apollisian stared in shock. She must have been overcome by the moment. And what did she say afterwards? He must have been confused by the battle. But what if he was not? In Stephanis' name, he would rather face ten thousand more of these skeletons, wearing only his birthday suit and wielding a wet stocking, than face the battle between his god and her, because he did not know who would win.

"We need to make our way to the mage tower," Alexis said as she strung her white ash bow finally and tightened her green cloak. "It is likely that whatever is controlling these things will strike there."

Apollisian gave her a sideways glance. "Overmoon, you do not believe that the boy has summoned these apparitions to fight for him?" he asked.

Alexis shrugged her shoulders and started off toward the mass of skeletal monsters that lay ahead. "How else would you explain them?" she asked. "And my name is Alexis Alexandria."

Apollisian took a deep breath and gripped his sword tighter, following after her. Why had she revealed her real name as if he didn't know it? She told it to him as though she wanted him to call her by it. Her first and second name were only allowed to be spoken by others of her race. Apollisian pushed the thoughts out of his head, including the image of her warm smile. It seemed he was to do battle again today, only this time with steel, not against oppressing elven elders.

*   *   *

Trinidy marched into the thick trees. He could sense that pull ever so close. Finally he would be finished with this quest. But as he neared and entered deeper into the forest, he could hear hundreds—no, thousands—of those mocking drums. Thump-thump, thump-thump. Everywhere they mocked him, taunted him; their very being seemed to insult him to the core. Suddenly the forest was alive in front of him. Elves scurried away like roaches under bright torchlight. Some ran to challenge him, while others seemed to challenge his skeletal army. *An entire city of evil elves,* he thought to himself. How he would enjoy cutting these denizens down. He longed to feel their soft flesh screaming and squirming under his blade.

Attack. He silently commanded the skeletons with a thought. And like an army of ants that were set against a foe that had disturbed their hill, the skeletons rushed into the elven ranks. They moved like rigid clockwork in perfect unison. The ghastly soldiers did not bump into one another, they did not falter or lose morale, they did not fear or grow angry. The skeletons moved and fought as pieces of a game, being wielded and commanded by their master. Everywhere Trinidy looked, he could see elves cutting his army of bones into rubble, but for every ten skeletons that fell, so did an elf. The death knight didn't pause to count, or do the numbers in his head to see if he was winning the battle. The battle was irrelevant. The true fight was yet to come. He would find this wrong he was to right; he could sense it close by. The feelings were incredibly strong here.

535

Trinidy reached out his rusted, corroded, gauntlet-covered hand toward the source of the pull that had led him north for so long. He focused his thoughts on the hunger, and on that which called to him. His rotted and decaying eyes scanned the immaculately carved elven buildings. As they moved from one side to the other, excited black spiders and scorpions spilled out from the corners of their rotted sockets, until those shriveled eyes rested on a small squat structure that seemed to be built into the hill, with no windows that he could see. It was there. His enemy that he needed to kill was close, as was the completion of his quest.

*　　*　　*

"What in Leska's name are they doing sounding the bells?" Garlibane asked Malwinar between breaths as he rushed down the polished wooden floor of the north corridor. The young elven mage shrugged his narrow shoulders and slowed before coming to a thick wooden door.

Garlibane stepped in front of the young elf and knocked on the door. "Isham-dorrie," he said, cutting a small flow of magical energy that he had used to lock the door to anyone but himself. Hastily, Garlibane pushed the heavy door open and rushed inside. The room was large and held hundreds of strange artifacts and decorations. There was no furniture that could be seen, but wands, staffs, and other such equipment littered the walls like tombstones in graveyards.

Garlibane grabbed a staff from the wall and tossed it to Malwinar. The young elf awkwardly caught the gnarled wooden staff with both hands, holding it out in front of himself with awe. "Leska's nook?" the young mage asked, his voice dripping with uncertainty. "Shouldn't we see what the problem is, Cranetium?"

Garlibane paused from rummaging through an old chest, pulling out small wands and other items. The ancient title, Cranetium, was once used in all settings of wizardry in the Vales, but now it held only a ceremonial position. The fact that Malwinar referred to him by his official title gave him pause, though it was only momentarily. He stuck his head back into the deep wooden chest and began to draw out more items. He pulled his upper torso from the chest and tossed the awestruck mage a string of pearls on a leather

536

thong necklace. Malwinar flinched as the pearls landed with a hundred simultaneous sounds of the tiny beads hitting the floor. Malwinar's eyes widened at the sight of the pearl necklace.

"The pearls of Matoon?" he asked with more uncertainty than he did when he caught the staff.

"We are not here for a quiz on the titles of our arcane vault. You do know how to use each, do you not?" Garlibane asked with a muffled voice from digging out more relics.

"Y-yes, but shouldn't I sign them out, or leave one . . ." Malwinar stammered.

Garlibane jerked up from the chest. "Damn you, fool elf! Do you think we have the luxury of standing about? The alarms have sounded! Get your hide outside and help with whatever is the matter! If it is some cruel prank, it is better to be prepared!"

Two more elves rushed into the room. They were dressed in their mage robes and one was bleeding from a deep gash on his right arm. Malwinar turned and regarded them before leaping back when he saw the blood. "Whatever is the matter?" Malwinar asked.

"A legion of undead!" one of the elves panted, on his hands and knees. "The Abyss Walker must have called them down on us!"

Malwinar set a determined look on his face, slipped the pearls over his head, and gripped the wooden staff so tight his knuckles turned white. Striding out the door, he became nothing but a memory to Garlibane.

"What do you mean undead?" Garlibane asked in disbelief. "The Abyss Walker is nothing more than a foolish boy. He could not possibly know how to summon undead, let alone a legion of them."

"It is true, Cranetium," the other elf piped in. "We rushed here to get some tools to battle them. We did not prepare any battle spells today," the second elf said as the first shook his head in agreement.

"As did none of the mages, I suspect. Where are the others?" Garlibane asked as he hastily closed the lid to the chest. It slammed shut with a loud thump as dust wafted into the air.

"We are the only ones who managed to get by. The skeletons number in the tens of thousands, maybe more. They are led by an undead knight that summons balls of fire from the air, and surrounds himself in a globe of impenetrable darkness at will. The order is fighting the apparition in front of the jail, where the Abyss Walker is being held. The undead knight must be trying to free him."

Garlibane felt his face flushing red with anger. His vision became tunneled as white hot rage surged into him. "I warned those damned fools he would bring the death of us all! The passings said if we do nothing, we would die; now we have done nothing, and we will surely perish," the high mage said as he slipped on a thick red robe and placed several gold rings about his fingers.

"What are you to do, Cranetium?" the mage asked, placing on the black leather gloves Garlibane handed him. "The king said that no one could harm the boy until he decided what to do about him."

Garlibane shouldered past the young mage. "I am not going to harm him, but mark my words, I'll not let us perish by the king's foolish indecisiveness. If he can summon legions of undead to free himself, then I will send him to a place more deserving of his talents and his attention."

The young mage started after Garlibane into the polished wooden hallway, clutching the deep wound in his arm. "What are you to do, Cranetium?"

Garlibane stormed down the corridor and did not turn as he answered with a taut jaw. "If the Leska-be-damned boy is powerful enough to break my shield, then I'll send him to the only place in the realms where there are mages and sorcerers with the talent to hold him."

"Where is that, Cranetium?" the young mage asked.

Garlibane did not respond as he marched purposefully down the corridor.

*   *   *

Dicermadon paused as he neared Leska's garden. He could sense hundreds of elaborately woven traps, wards, and glyphs set about the entrance to her lair. She would be the strongest there. Dicermadon knew he still would have no difficulty crushing the Earth Mother, wherever she hid, but if she had time enough to band with the other elemental gods . . . Dicermadon turned back and started toward his room. He would need to gather his supporters and deal with her in that fashion. Once united, the elemental gods were not a group to be trifled with.

As the god king walked back down the glittering streets of Merioulus, he saw every god and avatar standing in front of their domiciles. They no doubt knew of the Earth Mother's treacheries and she was surely spreading her filthy lies about the abyss. How that fool wench discovered his plot was beyond him, but that changed nothing. The boy was more dangerous than anything that had ever existed, he knew that now. Dicermadon needed the death knight to slay the boy, giving Bykalicus, lord of the night, control over his soul. Getting caught in a trap by the elemental gods would not help his plight. Killing the boy was more important than anything. More important than his own existence. Though he would fight to remain in power, if need be, he would sacrifice himself to ensure the boy's demise. But avoiding that outcome was his top priority.

Flunt, Surshy, and Whisten rushed into Leska's garden. She stood on an altar to herself in full plate armor that was brilliantly covered in emerald and bronze. The plant life seemed alive and ready to do battle and she stood among hundreds of magically created wards, glyphs and traps. She turned to regard the others and nearly wept in delight. She started to warn them, when they informed her that Dicermadon had turned back. She fell into Whisten's arms.

"Oh brother, he has meddled with demons. What are we to do?" Leska asked with uncertainty after straightening herself and sitting on a marble bench in her garden. She dispelled her armor and the bright polished mail dissipated in a flash and fizzled into nothingness, replaced by her dark green shift that barely covered her breasts and hips.

Flunt's fiery eyes burned in anger at the attack on Leska. "He is to be disposed," he said with a blazing, cackling voice.

Whisten nodded with Flunt's dire words, as did the water face of Surshy.

"Then it has begun," Leska said solemnly. "The heavens are broken once more."

*　　*　　*

Trinidy forced his way toward the small hill. His legions of skeletons battled the elves back, but his army had stalled in the face of many elven wizards, sorcerers, and a few priests. They hammered at him with a barrage of spells. Most of the weaves and dweamors slid off of him without much effort. Trinidy guessed that he had a resistance to their spells. Sometimes a blue bolt of energy might hit him in the chest with a bright flash and a shower of sparks, but he was managing to force his way forward, despite their attempts to stop him. Nothing would stop him now. He was so close. Trinidy felt the pull; the drive called him to the hill. It was so close. The insects that crawled about his face became more excited, scampering from his eyeless sockets and around his head. Another and another elf fell, as Trinidy paid little heed to whether it was wizard or warrior, male or female; all he focused on was the hill. He could feel the hate building inside, bubbling to a head. The energy welled to the surface, pushing, pushing to escape. The feeling was exhilarating. The imagination of the death of this creature filled him with such ecstatic harmony that he could hardly imagine what he would feel in moments when his desire became reality. Who could stand against him? These elves were helpless against his power.

Trinidy reached the wooden door that held what he sought. He reached for the door, then felt nothing. The intense pleasurable sensations vanished. Whatever he had been seeking was gone. There was no pull, no command, nothing. Rage ripped through the death knight and he turned and faced the elves. The elves had hidden what he sought. They had tried to keep him from his salvation, and now they had moved it. They would pay! He would kill every last man, woman, and child here. Just as he began to summon another white hot fireball, the rage vanished. It was replaced by a feint pull to the west. It was not strong, but it called to him. Trinidy recognized it. The prize would not elude him this time. The death knight took his first step to the west. His first step to redemption. Nothing would stop him now.

*   *   *

Lance strained his ears to the distant sounds of battle that seemed to permeate the thick walls of his room. After looking around at the few furnishings and the mediocre bed, not to mention the fact that he could not leave and was shielded from using either type of his magical abilities, he decided that it was most definitely a prison cell. He had labored and forced his will against the barrier that held him, but the white milky wall did not have any seams, or bend to his prying. Lance marveled at the spell that held him, even if it left him helpless. He could not actually see the wall, it was as if he just sensed it was there; like he knew it was white, and the consistency of it, yet he had never experienced it before. It was much similar to the first one that they had placed on him, though he burst through that one easily; this one was much better constructed. Lance wished he could have tutored under this Garlibane. He was sure he would learn great amounts of knowledge.

Sighing, Lance leaned against the cold hard wall and slowly lowered himself to a squatting position. Pulling his knees into his chest, he hugged his legs and placed his chin on his forearms. The sounds of battle were getting closer. Lance figured it was some sort of elven exercise. He doubted the dwarves had any squabbles with the elves and if they did, how many hundreds of years would it take for them to tunnel under here? The thought of the murderous dwarves here made him shudder. He had never encountered the little folk before, but if he never came across them again in his lifetime, he would consider himself lucky.

Suddenly the heavy door to his cell burst open. Lance jumped to his feet and backed away to the far corner. He had no magical ability and no weapon. If the dwarves were attacking, he would have no way to defend himself. He wished Jude were with him. His friend was quite an accomplished hand fighter. Straining his eyes through the bright light that poured into the room from the open door, Lance saw two small short silhouettes. His heart started to race. It was the dwarves! They had come to kill him. Tightening his fists, he leaned forward and tensed his muscles. The bastard bearded folk were not going to take him without a fight, regardless of how feeble the fight may be.

The voice that came from the two shadows was soft and honeyed, nothing like the dwarven voices he had heard before. To his relief, two elves stepped into the chamber.

"Stand down, boy," came the elven voice. Elves' voices were soft and honeyed, almost sounding like a woman's. "We have come to help you."

Lance narrowed his eyes. "Yea right. You idiots think I am some kind of a . . ." Lance was cut off by absolute silence. He grabbed his neck with both hands as he tried to talk. He could feel the vibrations coming from his throat, but no sound. In fact he could not hear any sound from anywhere. Suddenly those blue rings appeared around him again that held him in place, keeping him from moving. He didn't see the weaves as they came at him this time, but he could clearly see them around him. There were only four, unlike the six from last time, and they were not as thick as before, and did not spin as fast, but he could see the section that held them together. His mind raced. If he could focus his mind and break these rings, he might be able to escape. Lance felt the wall that shielded him from casting with flows weaken, and his mind strained. He watched each ring as it spun, its sparkling green swirls that dipped and rose inside of each ring seemed to slow. He reached out with something. Lance wasn't sure what, but he waited, then in a flash wedged the energy into the section. The ring shook and popped into a glittery nothingness.

"He is escaping!" Malwinar screamed nervously while Garlibane moved his arms and hands around as he chanted slowly.

The high mage did not respond. He remained focused on the intricate spell. Suddenly a bright orange light appeared in front of the two elves, just as the second ring shattered into a flash of green shimmering nothingness.

The orange dot of shimmering light that hovered off of the ground in front of the two elves stretched and quivered until it was a long horizontal line that was about waist high.

Lance struggled to break the rings faster. He figured the wall was weakened by Garlibane's fool attempts at casting multiple spells at the same time. Lance was sure he had memorized the weaves that made the shield. If he could get free in time . . .

The third ring shattered as the horizontal line in front of him grew until it was a tall shimmering doorway. Lance could see an alleyway that led to a city street covered in hundreds of shiny rounded stones. Rain was pouring down and the alley was dark, or he would have seen more.

Focus on the rings, Lance thought to himself. He was vaguely aware of the woman wearing a bright red robe with long flowing red hair, who was frowning as she approached the portal.

542

"Quickly shove him through!" Garlibane said through gritted teeth. Sweat beaded on his forehead as he spoke. "Hurry, before one of the damned women shoves a wedge into the gate, then we are all in for some headaches!"

Malwinar grabbed Lance by the collar, just as he shattered the final ring. The elf wizard shrieked as Lance reached out and snatched the Cadacka from his hands. Malwinar tried to force the larger human through the portal, but Lance fought viciously, punching the smaller elf several times in the face with his fist. Blood poured from the elf's nose and mouth.

"Help me!" Malwinar shrieked as he tried in vain to shove Lance through the gate.

Garlibane narrowed his eyes and whispered as he took a deep breath. He was too small to physically move the larger human into the portal, and he could not allow the boy to escape; the entire Vale's safety depended on it.

"Leska, forgive me," Garlibane said as he wove a thick thread of air. In moments he created a large wall of pure air, and by shoving his hands out in front of him, he forced both Malwinar and Lance into the portal.

Lance hit the wet bricked alley hard. He rolled with the powerful force that had knocked him through the air and came to his feet quickly. Malwinar tumbled head over feet, skidding to a stop before he scrambled on his hands and knees in the pouring rain, reaching out in vain at the rapidly diminishing portal. The elf shoved his hand into the bright orange light, futilely trying to grab something and haul himself back in. As the shimmering orange light of the gate popped into nothingness, it severed the elf's hand that was reaching into it.

Lance was not prepared for the howling shriek that echoed throughout the dark, rainy alley. He hugged the robe that his mother had given him, ignoring the cold rain that soaked him, unaware of the strange woman wearing a bright red robe behind him.

Malwinar rolled on the ground clutching the wrist that had once held his hand. The terrified elf wailed and shrieked, begging for mercy from the gods. Blood poured from the wound and mixed with the rain, making the alley floor turn to a soft red.

Lance started to run down the alley when he felt thick strands of energy whipping around him. Before he could counter them, he found himself once again held by a bright green magical ring. Frustration overtook the young mage at how a spell so simple seemed to frequently ensnare him. Lance watched as three women walked past him. The hard pouring rain seemed to fall around them, but not a single drop hit their crimson robes. It was almost as if an invisible barrier shielded them from the rain. The women wore bright red cloaks that had arcane symbols covering them entirely, and one woman stopped to eye him suspiciously. She was almost as tall as Lance and her long red hair was braided and pulled up in a bun on the top of her head. She had bright green eyes that seemed very intelligent, but her unyielding face was as cold as ice. She paused a moment and then stared into Lance's emerald orbs intently.

"Mother . . ." one of the other women who was dressed in red started to say. They were kneeling down around the quivering Malwinar. Lance could barely see them from behind the stone-faced woman who stood before him, but he dared not take his eyes from her. She held his gaze like a medusa.

"This one is injured. I think he will require extensive healing," the woman called out as they held the shrieking Malwinar to the ground.

The woman standing in front of Lance smiled, and did not take her eyes from his. "You know what to do. Healing costs gold. We do not waste gold on men."

Lance watched in stark horror as the two women casually pulled daggers from their belts and plunged them into Malwinar. The elf struggled for a few seconds, then went limp.

"It is done, Mother," the other two red-clad women said in unison.

The woman with the long red braided hair standing in front of Lance kept her wicked ice-cold smile. "Good. This one will make a fine slave."

"And woe to the world the day the son of mercy was set upon the mothers without children. They edified to him what it meant to hate, and then in turn, he edified the world."
—Ancient prophecy record kept in the great library of Kingsford City—
—author is unknown—

Glossary

Adoria—(a-door-ee-ah) Kingdom just west of Beykla. It is engaged in a bloody civil war against its eastern half, Andoria.

Alexis Alexandria Overmoon—(a-lex-us / al-ecks-zan-dree-uh / over moon) Daughter heir of King Christopher Calamon Overmoon, high lord of the Minok Vale. She travels with Apollisian Bargoe, the paladin of justice, trying to learn the ways of Stephanis to aid her when she becomes queen.

Amerix Alistair Stormhammer—(am-er-icks / ali-stair / storm ham-er) Dwarven general of Clan Stoneheart, formerly of Clan Stormhammer. His clan was wiped out when he was very young by dark dwarves and a white dragon. Amerix fled with a few survivors from his clan and was welcomed into Clan Stoneheart, where he excelled in the art of war.

Andoria—(an-door-ee-ah) Formerly eastern Adoria; this kingdom's brief history began when it declared its independence from Adoria. It waged an eight-month war with Adoria, but was eventually reconquered.

Apollisian Bargoe—(a-paul-issi-in / bar-go) Paladin of justice who was sent from his order in Westvon keep to oversee the negotiations between the humans and the dwarves from Clan Stoneheart in an attempt to derail a conflict, and was caught in the middle of the war.

Aten—(a-ten) Queendom to the far west that is run solely by women. Males of any race are considered inferior and are immediately made into slaves, or killed at birth. Only a few choice males are kept alive for reproduction purposes only. The women of Aten are adept sorceresses and keep a rigid society of back stabbing and political maneuvering.

Beovi—(bee-o-vi) A subterranean fish that lives in the deepest freshwater caverns of the under mountains. They are a delicacy to dwarves, dark dwarves, dark elves, and other subterranean races. These fish can grow to unlimited size, depending on the lake or river in which they live.

Beykla—(bay-kla) Human kingdom on the northeastern corner of

Terrigan. The kingdom is wealthy, militarily powerful, and well patrolled. It has never, in its long history, been conquered.

Blue Dragon Inn—Inn in Central City that is nearest to the Dawson River and the Dawson River bridge, where Lance, Kaisha, Ryshander, and Apollisian battled the dwarven horde, until the king arrived with re-enforcements.

Bordeck—(bor-dek) Dwarven torture device that is made of iron. The device is shaped like a mask with many spikes laid on the inside of the mask. It is placed on the victim while a thick iron bar is fastened to two long screws on each side. The bar is then cranked upwards under the chin until it forces the lower jaw into the victim's upper jaw slowly, causing the teeth to pop and shatter, crushing the jaw, and eventually causing death.

Breedikai—(bree-da-kii) Original gods, or gods that were created. They have no soul and most dwell in Merioulus.

Brohe-tah—(bro-ta) Orc word equivalent to comrade. The orcs use this word in reference to another that he or she likes as a friend. Though the orcish language does not have a single word for friend, it has over a dozen for enemy.

Brother of the Sword—Term given by the Darayal Legionnaire to their legionnaires in training.

Bureland—(bur-land) A small hamlet in the southern part of Beykla where Lance spent most of his childhood and early adult life with his adoptive father, Davohn.

Bykalicus—(bye-kal-eh-kus) Powerful arch demon that controls much of the Abyss.

Cadacka—(ka-doc-uh) Black ceremonial robe worn by elves when they have lost a loved one and are mourning. Most elves never remove the cloak once it is donned.

Calours—(ka-loo-ers) Non-sedimentary rocks found in the under mountain. Subterranean races, mostly species of dwarves, heat them to cook meat on.

Central City—City just south of Dawson Stronghold that is in the center of the Beyklan nation.

Cerebron—(sare-eeb-ren) Human boy that Apollisian saved from the dwarven onslaught at the Torrent Manor.

Christopher Calamon Overmoon—(kris-to-fur / kal-a-mon / o-ver-moon) High king of the Minok Vale.

Colonel Mortan Ganover—First lieutenant of Duke Dolin Blackhawk, and acting mayor when the duke is gone. Was widely considered responsible for the slaughter at Central City by the dwarves, due to his failure to act on the paladin Apollisian's recommendations.

Commander Fehzban Algor Stoneheart—(fez-ben / al-gore) Commander and loyal follower of General Amerix Stormhammer. Was tried and convicted of treason after the Torrent Manor and the Central City campaigns.

Commander Kestish—(kest-ish) Commander of and loyal follower of General Amerix Stormhammer. Commander Kestish vanished after the battle of Central City, and is believed dead.

Congarn's Orchard—(kon-garn) Large orchard by Bureland where Lance would often steal apples and pears as a child.

Council of Wise—Consists of ten elders that sit on the governing seat at Minok Vale, though not all ten are usually present at meetings, there must be at least six to hold a vote.

Cranetium—(krane-tee-um) Official title given to an elven high mage. The title means little to other elves, save for the wizards and sorcerers of their Vales.

Dalton Thornfist—(doll-ton) Dwarven king who died from an illness and left the clan to a young Tharxton Stoneheart.

Darayal Legion—(dar-ray-all) One hundred of the finest elite elven rangers who patrol the Minok Vale in pairs. They are skilled swordsmen that wield a weapon in each hand during battle. They are as feared as they are awed.

Darious Theobold—(dare-ee-us / they-bold) Eleven-year-old son of King Thortan Theobold.

Dark Dwarves—Dwarves who live solely in the under mountain. They have pupil-less eyes that have adapted over time to seeing solely in the dark by detecting heat patterns. They hate bright light as it is painful for them, and have turned to wicked and evil ways as a society.

Darrion-Quieness—(dare-ee-on / kwee-eh-ness) Great white dragon. Oldest of all white dragons and most powerful. His lair is in the mountains of Nalir, but he roams all over the realms. He often leads lesser races against their enemies, and takes the majority of the treasure after the victory. His last major campaign was in aid of a clan of dark dwarves against the dwarven Clan Stormhammer.

Davohn Ecnal—(da-von) Adoptive father of Lance. He is a woodcutter who made his home in Bureland and found the boy when Lance was only six years old. He raised him as his son until Lance left when he was seventeen.

Dawson River—Largest river that runs in Terrigan. It stretches from the Sea of Balfour, north of Beykla, all the way through the southern kingdom of Aboe.

Dawson Stronghold—Capital of Beykla, located at the northern mouth of the Dawson River.

DeNaucght—(day-nok-tuh) Ritual performed by goodly priests to raise a dead person back to life.

Dicermadon—(die-sir-ma-don) God of gods, Dicermadon plots with demons to kill the son of a goddess, drawing the wrath of the gods whom he governs.

Dolgo Seeds—(dole-go) A tasty mountain nut found on the steepest slopes of the highest mountains. Considered a delicacy by all dwarves and mountain people, including Kai-Harkians.

Dorcastig—(door-cast-ig) Tall muscled priest of Rha-Cordan. Follows under high priest, Resin Darkhand. One of the priests that participated in the DeNaucght.

Dregan City—(dree-gan) Home of Clan Stormhammer before it was wiped out by the dark dwarves and a white dragon.

Drunda—(drun-duh) The god the orcs follow. It is not known if he actually exists, or even if he is male.

Duke Dolan Blackhawk—(doe-lin) Duke and general of the Beyklan central army. Was relieved of his position as duke by King Theobold after the dwarven battle in Central City.

Durion—(dur-ee-in) Dwarven mountain god.

Ecnal—(eck-null) Surname given to all orphans of Beykla before they were nearly all killed by unknown assassins.

Edgar Sorenson—(ed-ger / sor-in-son) Powerful cleric of Surshy, advisor and close friend to King Theobold.

Elder Bartoke—(bar-toke) Elder of the Minok Vale, member of the Council of the Wise, and keeper of the sealed passings.

Elder Darmond—(dar-mond) Elder of the Minok Vale, member of the Council of the Wise, and keeper of the sealed passings.

Elder Humas—(hue-mass) Elder of the Minok Vale, member of the Council of the Wise, and keeper of the sealed passings.

Elder Varmintan—(var-mint-ton) Elder of the Minok Vale, member of the Council of the Wise, and keeper of the sealed passings.

Erik Stromson—(strom-son) General of the Beyklan western army and hero of the orc wars.

Eucladower Strongbow—(you-kla-dow-er) Oldest elder of the Minok Council of the Wise and keeper of the sealed passings.

Eulic Overmoon—(yew-lick) Darayal Legionnaire and cousin to Alexis Overmoon.

Fifvel—(fife-vul) Barkeeper and owner of the Blue Dragon Inn in Central City.

Flunt—God of fire, and one of the four elemental gods.

Freedom Festival—Holiday celebrated in Beykla to commemorate the end of the twenty-year-long orc wars.

Garlibane—(gar-lee-bane) High mage and elder of the Council of the Wise in Minok.

Glaszric—(ga-laz-er-ick) Half-orc bouncer at the Blue Dragon Inn in Central City.

Grascon the Nimble—(grass-con) Wererat thief that Lance double-crossed back in Bureland. The thief bears a horrible scar from his nose to his ear that he received from an encounter that stemmed from him leaving the thieves guild in Central City.

Grinder—Main passageways in the sewers under Central City that are used by the wererat thieves guild.

Gweits—(ga-weets) Tiny insect-like demons that dwell on the rocky floor of the Abyss. They feed on flesh, and burrow under their victim's skin with their horrific claws and hooks.

Heart of the Rock—A gemstone mounted on a gold ring that is said to have magical properties that can prevent the wearer from being harmed by any dragon's breath.

Hector De Scoran—(heck-tor / day-skore-an) Evil warrior wizard that is king of Nalir. Believes that Lance was prophesied to destroy his kingdom, and will stop at nothing until the boy is dead.

Illilander Tree—(ill-lee-land-er) Largest trees in the realms. Over five hundred feet tall.

Inn of Aldon—The only inn that is in the hamlet of Bureland, where Lance grew up.

Jahallawa Extract—(ja-hall-uh-wah) Sap from the Jahallawa plant which is extremely toxic if injected into the body. Leaves the victim paralyzed for hours, and it can take weeks for the victim to fully recover.

Jude—(jewd) Mercenary swordsman from Bureland. He sold his services to fight brigands, polecats, and other minor enemies of Bureland. He is also Lance's only friend.

Kai-Harkia—(kay-hark-ee-uh) Mountain kingdom northwest of Beykla. Its people are dark skinned, dark haired, heavy chested, nomad swordsmen. They seldom form static villages, though some such villages do exist.

Kaisha—(kay-sha) Wererat thief guild member from Central City.

Kalen Al-Kalidius—(kay-lin / al-kal-id-ee-us) Grey elf, ex-stepson of King Overmoon of the Minok Vale. Kalen has turned to the shadow and hungers for power, hoping to take over the throne of Nalir when Hector dies.

Kalistirsts—(kal-eh-stirsts) Underground mole people with no eyes that live in the under mountain.

Kalliman Castle—(kall-eh-man) Castle and home of King Thortan Theobold.

Kalliman Theobold—(kall-eh-man) Deceased king of Beykla, father of current king, Thortan Theobold.

Kar—Orc war party; excursion leader.

Kellacun—(kell-eh-kun) Wererat assassin that worked for the guild in Central City before it was destroyed. Now she works for Kalen in an attempt to kill Lance.

Kingsford City—Largest city on the continent of Terrigan, and capital of Ladathon.

Korrin Hentridge—(core-in / hint-ridge) Twelve-year-old son of Master David Hentridge.

Kreegan Malone—(Kree-gun) Acting duke of Central City when Dolin Blackhawk is away.

Ladathon—(lad-uh-thon) Southern country, south of Tyrine, where mysterious animals live in thick jungles. Kingsford City, the largest city in the world, is its capital.

Lancalion Levendis Lampara—Birth name of Lance Ecnal.

Lance Ecnal—Adopted son of Davohn Ecnal. Lance's birth name is Lancalion Levendis Lampara. His natural mother was Panoleen, the goddess of mercy. Lance is prophesied to bring plague and death on the world, though he sees himself as nothing more than an orphan trying to discover his past.

Leska—(les-kuh) The Earth Mother goddess. She rules over all living things, including plants and animals. She is one of the four elemental gods.

Lostos—(low-stoes) Name for the underground complex of the severed heart thieves guild of wererats in Central City.

Lukerey—(lou-kear-ee) God of luck and mischief.

Malwinar—(mal-win-are) Elven mage apprentice of Garlibane.

Master David Hentridge—(hint-ridge) Leader of small mercenaries guild that is disguised as a farm, just south of Central City. King Theobold uses them to hunt and kill orcs that he does not want the public to know exist; keeping the public unaware of the actual number of the green skinned beasts that still live in his kingdom.

Matoon—(muh-toon) Aquatic elf city in the Sea of Balfour.

Merioulus—(mare-ee-oh-you-lus) City of the gods. Set on a form of the Astral plane.

Midagord Milence Stormhammer—Amerix Stormhammer's deceased father.

Minok Vale—(my-nock) Name of the elven sovereignty that is set in Beykla.

Miranhka—(mere-aunk-uh) Wererat thief who managed to survive the dwarven assault on Central City and escape.

Morilla—(more-ill-uh) Town seamstress in Bureland. She was a good friend of Davohn and Lance.

Motivas—(moe-ta-vis) Southern-most city in Beykla. City is built on a large brick foundation that is rumored to be ruins of an ancient civilization.

Mountain Heart—Home city of Clan Stoneheart, located in the Pyberian Mountains.

Myson Strongbow—(mice-in) Darayal Legionnaire who faced Trinidy, the death knight. Myson was the first death in what was later to be named the dead war.

Nalir—(nall-er) Evil southern empire that is made primarily of swamps and quagmires. It is a militarily powerful nation that worships most of the evil gods, primarily Rha-Cordan.

Navlashier—(nav-luh-sheer) Elven city in Vidora.

Necromidus—(neck-rom-eh-dus) A collection of the first four tiers of necromancy spells.

Optis Midigan—(op-tis / mid-eh-gun) Young servant of Hector De Scoran and follower of Soran Songstream.

Orantal Proudarrow—(or-an-tall) Commander of the Darayal Legion and protector of the Minok Vale, friend of Elder Eucladower.

Panoleen—(pan-oh-leen) Goddess of mercy who was banished from the heavens.

Pav-co—(pahv-coe) Fat wererat guild leader in Central City.

Plains of Vendaiga—(vin-day-guh) A large grassland in southern Aten that is home of the Vendaigehn steeds, the fastest horses in Terrigan.

Pockweln—(pahk-welln) Right-hand supporter of Resin Darkhand, high priest of Rha-Cordan.

Pyberian Mountains—(pie-beer-ee-an) Mountain range in the northwest corner of Beykla, near Andoria.

Quigen—(kwi-jin) Elven word for sacrifice. Most widely known as the name of the great battlefield where General Laricin scattered the orcish horde by fighting until every man fell in the Serrin Plains.

Raynard Cliffs—(ray-nard) Large group of cliffs that extend along the entire north border of Nalir.

Resin Darkhand—(rez-in) High priest of Nalir, worshipper of Rha-Cordan and advisor to Hector De Scoran.

Rha-Cordan—(rah-kor-dan) God of death and dying. Not inherently evil; he reins over the placement of souls when they enter the afterlife, though he has been known to be incredibly vengeful to those who prolong their lives through magical means.

Ryshander—(rye-shan-der) Wererat thief that left Central City with Kaisha after the dwarves destroyed their guild.

Sea of Balfour—(bal-four) Sea north of Beykla. Ancient lore tells of the sea once being dry ground and home to an ancient kingdom known as Balfour.

Serrin Plains—(sare-in) Dangerous expansive grassland just south of Minok Vale where most of the evil races that live in Beykla dwell.

Sespie Twinner—(ses-pee / twin-er) Young woman from Bureland who had been practicing medicine with Morilla, who developed her healing ability by helping injured soldiers during the orc wars.

Severed Heart—Unofficial name of the wererat thieves guild that lives in the sewers of Central City.

Sir Oswald Thorrin—(thor-in) Captain of the king's royal guard in Beykla.

Slargcar—(sa-larg-car) Orc tribe chief of tribe Glargcar.

Soran Songstream—(sore-in) High sage, and practicing wizard in the kingdom of Nalir.

Stahlsman—(stalls-man) City guard that works at the north gate of Central City.

Stephanis—(stuh-fawn-is) God of justice.

Stieny Gittledorph—(stie-knee / get-tull-dorf) Halfling thief who became mixed up with the dragon Darrion-Quieness.

Surelda Al-Kalidius—(sir-el-da / al-kuh-lid-ee-us) Ex-wife of King Overmoon and mother of Kalen Al-Kalidius.

Surshy—(sir-she) Goddess of water. One of the four elemental gods.

Symas—(sim-uhs) Bead-like ornaments hung from the ends of the braids of a hairstyle called Varmin, the chosen hairstyle that is worn by the Darayal Legionnaires. Symas are given for meritorious acts of bravery and range from leather, as the lowest reward, to gold, as the greatest.

Tamra Hentridge—Daughter of Master David Hentridge.

Terrace Folly—(ter-is / fall-ee) Small hamlet southeast of Central City.

Terrigan—(ter-eh-gun) Name of the continent where all known civilization exists.

Tharxton Stoneheart—(tharx-ton) Young king of Clan Stoneheart and political rival of Amerix Alistair Stormhammer.

Therrig Alistair Delastan—(ther-ig / al-eh-stair / del-eh-stan) One of the surviving members of Clan Stormhammer.

Torrent Manor—Small keep northwest of Central city that was built specifically for enforcing the trade embargo and taxation on the dwarves who dwelled in the Pyberian Mountains.

Travits—(trav-itz) Wererat thief and guild member of the severed heart guild in Central City.

Trinidy—(trin-eh-dee) Dead paladin of Dicermadon who was raised from the dead by evil priests of Rha-Cordan.

Tyrine—(tie-reen) Kingdom southwest of Beykla.

Valga—(val-guh) Vlargcar's mother who was slain after she fled the ruthless orc village to protect her son from the rest of the tribe. The tribe believed since Vlargcar was abnormally large and his eyes were blue instead of yellow, she must have been consorting with evil gods.

Varmin—(var-men) Long braided hairstyle worn by Darayal Legionnaires.

Vendaigehn—(vin-day-gun) Type of horse from the plains of Vendaiga. The steeds are marked with white spots on their flanks, and are taller than most horses, with longer, thinner legs. Legend says that Vendaigehn steeds are the offspring of a Pegasus and a unicorn, though that has never been proven.

Victor De Vulge—(day-vul-juh) Squire of Apollisian Bargoe.

Vidora—(vie-door-uh) Wild, uncivilized kingdom southwest of Tyrine that is mostly inhabited by elves.

Vlargcar—(va-larg-car) Orc whelp saved by Amerix when he and his mother were ordered to be killed by their tribe.

Vrescan Alistair Delastan—Therrig's father, who was killed fighting side by side with Midagord Stormhammer in defense of Dregan City.

Westvon Keep—(west-van) Large keep and hamlet to Beykla's far east on the banks of the Dawson River.

Whisten—(wiss-ton) God of air, and one of the four elemental gods.

Yahna—(ya-nuh) City in the heavens where souls dwell that are blessed by their gods.